My horse was still anxiously dancing about when th
standing next to the windlass that raised and lowered the gate. The two men with Henry, both
veteran foot archers who had been helping him train the states' soldiers, immediately began
enthusiastically cranking. The rusty chains rattled and the huge gate in the city wall slowly rose.
Behind us I could hear the sound of many horses stamping their feet and much talking and
shouted orders.

As soon as the gate was high enough for Commander Courtenay to ride under it, he raised
his bow over his head, kicked his horse in the ribs and shouted "FORWARD." As he did, he
pointed his bow at the moat bridge in front of the gate and the densely packed camp of the
Greek-led army that began only a hundred paces or so beyond the drawbridge.

I was right behind him as he galloped towards them.

The Alchemist's Revenge

A medieval Novel

Chapter One

Things had gotten confused when the cold weather and a handful of English archers caused the Orthodox Christian army to fail in its initial effort to invade the Latin Empire and replace its Constantinople-based empress with one of their own kings. The surviving Orthodox Christian soldiers, mostly Greeks, had returned to the Greek coast whereupon their Venetian allies somehow managed to put together a fleet of transports and carry part of the Orthodox army eastward along the coast to the port city of Adrianople.

The Venetian sea-lift put the Orthodox soldiers carried by the Venetian transports much nearer to Constantinople than the soldiers it was forced to leave behind. The men carried by the Venetian transports were, in one sense, the fortunate ones in that they only had to march the rest of the way to the great capitol city of the Latin Empire.

On the other hand, the Venetian-carried Greeks and their mercenaries were unfortunate in that they were incessantly attacked by companies of English horse archers as they moved north toward Constantinople. The English hung on their flanks like packs of wolves and used the superior range of their longbows to whittle down their numbers and prevent them from leaving the main column to forage amongst the nearby villages.

The Venetian-carried Greeks arrived outside of Constantinople's walls in the summer of 1219 hungry and somewhat fewer in number. Even so, they were optimistic because they knew they would sooner or later be joined by the rest of the Greek-led army. They would then attack and overwhelm the city's defenders by the sheer weight of their numbers. Their priests assured them that victory was certain.

Indeed, victory was so sure to occur as a result of their army's great numbers that both the would-be new emperor, currently the king of the Greek state of Epirus, and exiled Patriarch of the Orthodox Church had begun making plans for their grand entrances into the city.

The return of Constantinople to Greek control was certain because the rest of the huge Orthodox army was slowly but surely marching to join the early arrivals. When they arrived, they would help the early arrivals finish off the Empress's small army and replace her crusader-French gobbling nobles and Latin-gobbling priests with Greek-gobbling nobles and the Patriarch's Greek-gobbling priests.

The men of the Greek army who had to march all the way to Constantinople finally reached Adrianople in the summer of 1219. They rested for a couple of days whilst gathering some of the food supplies they would need in the days ahead, and then they began marching north on the old Roman road to join those who had been carried to Adrianople by the Venetians. They too assumed they would be able to obtain the rest of the food supplies they would need by foraging for it along the way. And they too were mistaken and arrived outside Constantinople's formidable walls hungry and fewer in number because of a few hundred English wolves.

Despite its losses and desertions, the overall size of the Orthodox army that finally arrived in front of Constantinople's great city wall was huge, well over a hundred thousand men. Constantinople, in contrast, was defended by about seven thousand men of whom approximately three thousand were highly trained English archers equipped with the latest and most modern weapons, namely longbows and bladed pikes with long handles.

Even though the Orthodox army was still huge, it was also significantly smaller and its men somewhat less enthusiastic than when it had first been formed. The reduction of its size and enthusiasm had occurred as a result of constant small attacks by a few hundred horse-riding English archers and a costly defeat they had inflicted on the Orthodox army in the early spring right after the army had been formed.

The Orthodox army's earlier defeat occurred when the entire Greek-led army tried to cross the mountains in order to march directly to Constantinople, the capitol city of the Latin Empire.

An inexperienced Greek commander, almost certainly chosen for the position mostly because he was the brother of the Greek king who would be the new emperor, had made a serious mistake by ordering his men to march to Constantinople on the road through the mountains. It was a mistake because the weather was still much too cold in the mountains and a few hundred horse-riding archers from Cornwall's free Company of Archers had gotten there first and held the narrow Roman-built stone bridges that spanned the raging torrents of the water that ran off the mountains.

Had men of the Orthodox army been able to cross through the freezing weather on the mountain without stopping, they would have already reached Constantinople's formidable walls and begun besieging the city. Instead, they failed; they had been forced to turn back after suffering horribly from the cold and the arrows being pushed out of the archers' longbows.

Even so, and unfortunately for Constantinople's Empress and the men of the Cornwall-based Company of Archers, a good part of the mostly Greek army, at least three men out of every four, had been able to withdraw from the mountains without being killed or becoming so frost-bitten that they could not continue. The survivors had returned to the coast whereupon some of them were carried down the coast to the port city of Adrianople by a hastily assembled Venetian fleet.

Once landed at Adrianople, the Greek soldiers carried by the Venetians, only about a third of the huge army due to the lack of sufficient Venetian transports, had begun marching overland on the old Roman road that ran between Adrianople and Constantinople. The other two-thirds of the army's survivors marched down the coastal road to Adrianople, and then, after they had reached it and rested for a few days, began the long march north to Constantinople. It was the summer of the year 1219 and the days were long and hot.

The stated purpose of the Orthodox army's invasion, according to the Greek-gobbling Patriarch of the Orthodox Church, was to "throw the heretics and their Latin-gobbling priests out of our great capitol city and restore the Byzantine Empire with an emperor chosen by God."

In other words, if the Greek army succeeded, the Patriarch's Greek-gobbling priests would once again be able to tell the people what God wanted them to do and collect their tithes, and the new emperor's Greek-gobbling lords would see to it that they did it and collect their taxes.

Most of the people in Constantinople, of course, did not really give a shite who won the coming war. They were stuck with tithes and taxes no matter who won, and just wanted to be left alone to get on with their lives.

On the other hand, most of the city's residents were Greek-gobblers and looked to the Patriarch of the Orthodox Church and his priests to tell them how God wanted them to behave. As a result, other things being equal, most of the residents of the Latin Empire's great capitol city almost certainly would have preferred that the Greeks win so they could pay their tithes to the Greek-gobbling priests of the Patriarch instead of to the Latin-gobbling priests of the Pope in Rome. The Latin priests, after all, did not make the sign of the cross properly and even their own parishioners could not understand them when they prayed. There was also the very real possibility that God did not understand Latin as well as he understood Greek.

The problem for the mostly Greek-gobbling army and the would-be emperor and the Patriarch, of course, was that other things were not equal. That was because the Latin Empire's Empress and her Latin-gobbling priests and her crusader French-gobbling lords had held the great city and the vassal states of the Latin Empire, over which she supposedly ruled, ever since the crusaders of Fourth Crusade took the city some fifteen years earlier.

It hardly mattered to the people of the city and its vassal states who ruled them. As a result, a goodly number of the city's Orthodox-praying citizens had accepted the Empress's coins and began working full-time to strengthen the city's walls and defences against the on-coming invaders.

In addition to the full-time workers who were paid for their work on the walls, everyone in the city was required to work without pay to strengthen the city's defences on three required mornings each week. The city's residents did not know it at the time, but when the Greek-led Orthodox army arrived every one of the Empress's subjects would be required to work for free every morning.

Whether those who worked without pay supported the Empress was not the question— they were encouraged to work by the reality that the Empress's personal guards, the loyalty-sworn Vikings and Rus known as the Varangian axe-men, who also acted as the city's night watch, would take their heads if they did not. Losing one's head happened when a man was found in the city during the hours everyone was supposed to be working to strengthen the city's great walls and other defences.

Indeed, some of the Orthodox believers even signed on to fight for the Empress—which was more than many of the princes and kings of the Empress's vassal states did. They, some of the Latin Empire's kings and princes that is, had long ago decided to wait to see who was likely to win before they committed themselves and brought their men in to help defend the city.

Cornwall's free company known as The Company of Archers was among the Empress's few reliable supporters. Its commander, George Courtenay, and his captains knew in their hearts that God favoured the French-born Empress—because he had showered her with so many sources of coins that she could use to pay them for their services. Besides that, she had spent quite some time in England where George had actually met her on several occasions and his father, the Company's former commander, had apparently gotten to know her quite well.

As firm believers in God, particularly in matters related to the gathering of coins from people God had blessed with them, the archers could do no less than accept the substantial amount of coins offered by the Empress if they would help protect her and the wealthy refugees fleeing the war if they would carry them to safety. And, of course, the archers also did their best to get even more coins from the Empress's enemies—by taking their galleys and transports as prizes and selling the weapons and armour they were able to strip off the enemy dead.

Most of the revenues the Company of Archers earned from helping to defend the Empress and her great capitol city, however, came from the tolls the Company's galleys collected in the Empress's name from the numerous boats of every type and nation that plied the great waterway that passed in front of Constantinople's walls. The tolls were so substantial and continuous as to make it worthwhile for the Company to take on the risk of helping the Empress defend her Empire from the many kings and princes who coveted it.

The Company's takings from the Empress's many enemies, on the other hand, were decidedly mixed. At first its takings were quite large. For example, the archers' galleys carrying the Empress's coins to Rome to pay for the papal prayers, which had been needed so God would recognize the widowed Empress as her son's regent, were attacked twice by Venetian fleets.

Venice's attacks on the Company's galleys occurred because Venice's king fancied the position for himself and, accordingly, did not want God to agree that the Empress should be the empire's ruler until her son came of age. Also, of course, the attacks occurred because it was a large amount of coins and the Venetian captains wanted them for themselves.

In any event, as a result of the Venetian attacks, the archers took a substantial number of valuable Venetian war galleys as prizes and, equally important, were able to negotiate a lower price with the Pope for God's approval of the Empress. The archers, of course, kept the rest of prayer coins in the reasonable belief that the Pope had not required all the coins they had brought from the Empress because God wanted the Company to have them.

After that initial burst of coin gathering, however, the Company's takings from the Empress's enemies were nowhere near as great as its commander, George Courtenay, and his captains had hoped. The Company's number two and the commander of its horse archers,

Richard Ryder, for example, had taken a huge haul of weapons and armour off the Greek army when he and his horse archers stopped the Greeks in the bitter cold at a bridge on the old Roman road that ran through the mountains.

Unfortunately, Richard's men were forced to throw the weapons and armour they captured into the cold and raging maintain stream the bridge crossed because they had no way to carry them when they hurriedly fell back to an even better blocking position at a bridge higher up on the other side of the mountain's summit.

In one sense, the archers' rapid withdrawal without the captured weapons was very much the great success Richard had intended it to be when he realized the effect the terrible cold was having on his enemies—because the rapid retreat of the archers had encouraged the Greeks and their allies to continue marching even deeper into the mountains, whereupon the archers stopped them again at another bridge.

It was there in the mountains that many of the Orthodox soldiers froze to death before their commander finally understood that Richard and his men were deliberately retreating to draw his army deeper into the mountains. At that point, he ordered his army's survivors to withdraw so they could live to fight another day.

The withdrawal was somewhat of a financial success for the Company in that Richard and his archers captured some of the weapons and armour the army's Greek-led soldiers lost when they froze to death or left behind when they fled back down the mountain in an effort to escape the cold.

Where Richard and his horse archers had failed miserably was in *not* letting the cold completely destroy the Greek army when they could have done so. Their failure was the result of a mistake made by Richard that only he knew about—he had talked too much after he had gotten to know a Greek soldier who had been trying to negotiate a passage over the mountains for the Orthodox army.

As a result of Richard's loose lips, the Greek soldier whose life he had tried to save came to understand that Richard was attempting to draw out the negotiations in order to delay the Orthodox army until the cold weather destroyed it. The Greek was an astute and loyal soldier; he had explained to *his* commander what the archers were doing in time for most of the Greeks and their fellow believers to withdraw.

There had been some takings from the Empress's other enemies as well. The archer-rowed galleys of the Company of Archers that had been sent out from Constantinople to harass the Orthodox ports, for example, had picked off a couple of the slave-rowed Venetian galleys which were escorting the Venetian transports which had carried part of the somewhat reduced Orthodox army to Adrianople.

Unfortunately, the Company's galleys had been forced to ignore the Venetian ships and cogs carrying the Orthodox army. They ignored them because the Venetian transports had already been loaded with Greek soldiers for transport by sea to a port closer to Constantinople.

In essence, as a result of the soldiers they were carrying, the Venetian transports had become too dangerous for the galleys of the English company to try to take. The potential rewards from taking transports loaded with soldiers as prizes were just not worth the casualties that would be expected from the fighting that it would require.

Similarly, after the Greeks disembarked at Adrianople and began marching to Constantinople, the Venetian transports still could not be taken without serious English casualties because they remained clustered together in Adrianople's harbour with a substantial number of Greek soldiers remaining on board to guard them. In the end, the Company's galleys gave up waiting for the Venetian fleet to come out; they sailed and rowed their way back to Constantinople so the archers in their crews could be used to reinforce the city's defenders.

Surprisingly, the Latin lord at Adrianople had welcomed the Greek soldiers when they arrived on Venetian transports—he had turned against the Empress in return for promises of a kingly title recognized by the Orthodox Patriarch and the promises of Venice's and France's protection when the Byzantine Empire was re-established. *He also required, and was given, French-owned estates in France and England in case the Empress won and he had to run.*

News that the Venetians had carried some of the Orthodox army to Adrianople, and the rest of the Greek-led army was marching there, reached Constantinople via the Company's returning galleys. It resulted in the Company's horse archers being hastily recalled from where they had been vainly waiting in the mountains for the Orthodox army to re-appear when the weather got warmer. They immediately returned to Constantinople for supplies and to drop off their wounded and poxed.

The horse archers rested in the city for a few days, and then Richard Ryder, the Company's deputy commander and the man whose good nature and loose lips had allowed the Greek army to escape from the mountains, once again led them out of the city to harass the Orthodox army, this time as it marched towards Constantinople from Adrianople.

Chapter Two

The Orthodox army begins to arrive.

I had a great revelation jump into my head early one evening while we were awaiting the imminent arrival of the first soldiers of the Greek-led army. It arrived, the revelation that is, whilst I was drinking a bowl of ale and thinking about whom else might be a threat to the Empress and the coins she was paying my company to help keep her on the throne of the Latin Empire. *I was also, at the time, trying to distract myself from thinking about women, particularly, the young widow I hoped would be coming to my room for a "visit" later that evening.*

What I realized as I sat there with my bowl of ale was that the Company of Archers which I had the honour to lead, and the Latin Church led by the Pope, were quite similar. And they were similar when a man thought about them and compared them—the Church competed with the Moslems and the Orthodox Church led by the Patriarch to collect coins from people in need of someone to tell them what God wanted them to do; the Company competed with the Venetians and others to collect coins from merchants and passengers in need of someone to safely carry their bodies, cargos, and money orders from Christian ports to wherever they wanted them to be taken.

The problem, of course, was that there were only so many coins in the world—and we all wanted them and were willing to fight for them in one way or another.

Just the thought that my company was very much like the Pope's church and the devious and untrustworthy Venetians was enough to give me a pain behind my eyes. As you might imagine, I quickly called for another bowl of ale and settled in for an evening of drinking and thinking about my company and its future. Truth be told, I hoped it would distract me from thinking about women all the time—something, to my great surprise, I had been doing more and more frequently since I received word of the pox taking poor Becky.

I had a bowl of ale lifted halfway to my mouth a few minutes later when the door opened and Elizabeth slipped into the room.

"Drinking again, are you?"

She was beginning to sound like a wife.

"And a good hoy to you too, Elizabeth. Would you care for a bowl?"

******

The pounding on my door the next morning woke me from a sound sleep. The space next to me on the bed was empty and the familiar light of early morning was filtering into the room from the cracks around the window shutters. Elizabeth was gone so it was unlikely to be her mother.

"Commander," ... "Are you awake commander?" ... "A courier has just ridden in from Lieutenant Commander Ryder with urgent news."

I recognized the voice. It was my senior aide himself, Major Captain Michael Oremus, and he sounded out of breath. Something important must have happened to cause him to get up while it was still dark and ride here to tell me about it instead of sending a messenger.

"Come in Michael. The door is not barred." *Damn, I must have overslept.* I invited him in as I rolled over and put my feet on the stone floor. It was cold and I needed to pee.

"A courier has come in from Richard Ryder, Commander. He says the van of the Greek Army is now moving faster for some reason and is likely to reach the city in the next day or two. He said he had one more horse company's supply wagon to relocate, and then he would be riding in ahead of the Greeks."

"Thank you, Michael. I will be along shortly. Please return to the Commandery and tell everyone it will be a normal day for everyone since it will be at least two or three days before the Greeks can arrive with enough men to give us much trouble." *Unless, of course, they sweep right in on an attack and the city rises behind us.*

"Oh yes. On the way out would you please find Elspeth, the Empress's maid, and ask her to find my father and ask him to meet me in the Citadel's eating hall. I am going there to break my fast there instead of immediately riding to the Commandery. With a little luck, of course, my father will already be there himself."

What I did not explain to Michael was that I was going to the eating hall so that I would be seen breaking my fast as I had not a care in the world. It was important, I had decided, that word get around that the news of the imminent arrival of the Greek army did not distress me; it would hearten the Empress's supporters and confuse her enemies.

"Also, please tell the captain of my guard company that I will be breaking my fast in the Citadel's eating hall, and that he and the men can come in and eat there instead of waiting until we get to the Commandery."

Michael knuckled his forehead and left. I began whistling one of the Company's jolly tunes under my breath and getting ready for the day; meaning I put on my rusty chain shirt and my wrist knives, and then slipped my hooded archer's tunic over them. *The tunic did not hide the fact that I was wearing chain, but it certainly hid my wrist knives.*

To my great surprise, I felt excited and wide awake. The waiting was almost over. I also noticed that the day was already quite warm. It would be another scorcher

****** *Commander George Courtenay*

My recently un-retired father was sitting at the sitting at the Citadel's long wooden table breaking his fast. His back was to me but I recognized his long white hair and hooded archer's tunic immediately. The men sitting around him were a motley crew of the court's courtiers, ambassadors, and visiting lords who had wandered in for the free food. They were sitting with him because they saw an opportunity to talk with someone who might know what was going to happen next and how soon it might occur.

The men sitting across from him looked up expectantly as I approached.

"A good hoy to all," I said happily as I walked up to my father rubbing my hands together gleefully. He had seen the men sitting across from him look up and turned to see what or who had grabbed their attention. So did just about everyone else in the room. The buzz of talking in the hall died away almost completely by the time I reached him. The man sitting next to him scooted over to make room for me to sit.

"There is good news today," I said rather enthusiastically, and a little louder than necessary, as I slid my leg over the wooden bench and prepared to sit down next to my father. I said it knowing that within an hour or two whatever I said would sweep across the city by word of mouth.

"I just got word from Richard that the Greek army is finally approaching. They are all strung out as a result of the beating they took in the mountains, but at least some of them are coming, thank God!

"Our men will certainly be pleased. They were beginning to worry that Richard and his horse archers had scared them off such that they would not share any prize money for taking the Greeks' armour and swords off them."

What I said, of course, was a lie intended to mislead the people of the city and the Latin lords who were still undecided as to who to support. Our men were not stupid; used armour and weapons rarely brought much in the way of prize money to an archer with only one or two stripes on his tunic.

"The Greeks are here?" one of the men asked as if he could not believe what he had just heard. He was well-dressed, but I could not place him.

"Aye, Your Lordship, and it is about time. My lads are getting anxious to see them off. And so am I for that matter—the sooner we finish them off, the sooner we can sell their armour and weapons and get back to our families. It will take time, of course, but the outcome is certain."

One of men sitting at the table was not convinced. It was the French ambassador, a rather sour-faced fellow and newly arrived.

"So you say, English Commander, so you say. But I am told that there are a great number of soldiers in the Greek army, well over one hundred thousand of them is the number I heard—so it looks to me as though the Empress's forces are hopelessly outnumbered and the Greeks will either starve out the city or come over the walls and kill or take for a slave every man who was foolish enough to stand against them."

Of which you will not be one, George thought to himself as he faked a look of astonishment and replied.

"Nonsense, Ambassador, sheer nonsense. Your fears are groundless. You are safe. The Greek army is not even here yet and they have already lost a third of their army to a few hundred or so Englishmen who rode out to challenge them in the mountains. Badly led, badly equipped, and badly learnt to fight is what the Greeks are, eh? In other words, the Greek army is an inconvenience, not a problem."

Everything I said was somewhat true, of course. What I did not say was that the Greeks would now only outnumber us by at least forty or fifty to one and most of their losses in the mountains had been due to the cold weather.

Chapter Three

Hearts and minds.

My personal guard was an entire company of horse archers, all sixteen of them. Thomas Fiennes was their captain. They were newly arrived from England and had been ordered to stay close to me whenever I was out of the Citadel. I did not really want them or need them, but it was not worth arguing about since the Empress herself had ordered them to be with me whenever I was out in public. That was after I had been captured and injured by the former Venetian ambassador and a couple of the Empress's traitorous Latin lords whilst riding alone in the city.

I did for them myself with my hidden wrist knives, the Venetian ambassador and the traitors that is, when I got myself free and made my escape. And my father did his part after the Empress's axe-men found me bloodied and staggering down the street by taking off the head of the barber who had started to bleed me to help me recover from my wounds. It further endeared him to me.

Being captured and desperately fighting to break free was an experience I would not want anyone to have to repeat, although I did appreciate the Empress's daughter, Elizabeth, for moving me into her room to help me recover.

She did so, moved me that is, because my room was unsuitable for use as recovery room for a wounded man. It was a mess because the barber whose head my dear father had cut off had bled a lot of blood. Great puddles of it is what Elizabeth told me when I finally woke up. She and her mother had never seen such a sight and had apparently been quite excited by it.

Truth be told, and even though I claimed and acted as though they were an unnecessary bother, I was glad to have Captain Fiennes and his horse archers with me when I was out and about, at least some of them. Constantinople was a damn dangerous city for an Englishman. It was almost as bad as the outskirts of London up around Saint Peter's Abbey where the lepers and cutpurses still congregate to this very day.

******

Richard Ryder rode in today with his apprentice sergeant and four of his horse archers just as the sun was high overhead on its daily voyage around the world. It was a hot mid-summer day.

It was the second time Richard had ridden in since the Venetian transports carried part of the Greek army to Adrianople. The first time was when I was taken prisoner and Richard had been hurriedly summoned back to assume command of the Company. He had waited until I got back on my feet, and then rode back out to re-join his horse archers in the mountains that separated the Latin Empire from the Greek states.

I heard the noise and commotion as Richard and his men rode into the Commandery's bailey and walked out to see what was causing it. It was a nice early morning despite the relentless summer sun. More than a little warm, perhaps, but nice. There were a number of cats stretched out enjoying the sun or scratching in the dirt for a place to shite. The city was full of them.

Richard and the six men with him were leading their saddled remounts and looked ragged, filthy, and saddle sore—and quite satisfied with themselves and in fine good cheer. They were clearly pleased to be back in the big city with all its delights.

"Hoy Richard. It is good to see you safely returned,"

I shouted out my welcome as I walked briskly up to Richard with my hand outstretched and a big smile on my face—and I truly meant it. Richard was a good friend from our days together as the first students in my Uncle Thomas's school for boys at Restormel Castle.

"Hoy George. It is good to see you too. You heard the Greeks were almost here, did you?" he asked as he swung down from his horse and we gave each other the handshakes and great manly hugs and backslappings that are a tradition of the Company when its captains and commanders meet after a long separation or a successful battle.

"Aye. That I did. Both of your messengers got through. What is the latest? How soon do you think the first of the Greeks will get here?" I was full of questions.

"Their advance party is only about a hundred or so mounted men. They could arrive in a few hours unless they turn back, which is what I expect they will do unless they are poorly led, which is also a possibility from what I have seen so far.

"We bumped into them south of the little village by the river, the one with the mill. They are fairly well mounted, but riding with no spare horses. My lads and I pulled a "wounded bird" on them and culled a half dozen or so of their thrusters when they took the bait and chased after us, so they may have turned back.

"It matters not, however, as the main column of the Greeks carried by the Venetians are on foot and not likely to start arriving here in force for several days at the very earliest, perhaps even longer."

"And the rest of your horse companies? Any news of them?"

"Hanging like wolves all along the flanks of the Greek column to whittle it down and delay them. Of that you can be sure. But here is the thing, George—the size of the main Greek column is too small, only thirty or forty thousand men by my estimate, and not many horsemen. I know for sure they lost a lot of men and horses in the mountains, but not that many.

"What I think is that the Greeks marching towards us are probably only the men the Venetians carried to Adrianople. The main body of the Greek army is either walking down the coastal road to Adrianople, or the Venetian transports have sailed back to carry another load. Maybe both. Either way, the main strength of the Greek army is probably just setting out from Adrianople about now. It will be several weeks, at least, before they arrive."

"Well, that is certainly good news if it turns out to be true. It means the Greeks are going to miss a good part of the campaigning season and will have less time to prepare an attack the city before returning to their farms to bring in the harvest."

"Aye, it is. It also means the Greeks will be strung out and easier for our horse archers to get at." *I appreciated that Richard said "our" horse archers instead of "my" horse archers; he is a company man through and through.*

"Richard," I responded after I thought about what he had said. "Do you have any idea why the men carried by the Venetians did not wait in Adrianople so the Greeks could march on us all together at the same time? Or why they were in such a big hurry to get some of their men here that they used the Venetian transports instead of marching?"

"No. But you are right. That is a bit strange. I would have thought that they would have all marched together and arrived at the same time. It must mean something that some of them are hurrying to get here before the others. It could be that they are over-confident for some reason, or perhaps they just want to get started on their siege preparations." *It turned out to be something else entirely, but we did not know it at the time.*

"Aye, that could be it. They may be wanting to get started so they can take the city in time to get their men back to their farms to bring in this year's harvest—but somehow I think it must be more than that. But what?"

Then, after a pause while we both pondered about the various possibilities, I added more.

"Ah well; we will know soon enough, I suspect. And if the Greeks succeed, it certainly will not be your fault, Richard. Stopping them in the mountains so the cold would take some of them was brilliant."

Actually, it only started out to be a brilliant move. He ended up letting many of them get away, and he and I both know it even if the men do not and never will.

****** *George Courtenay*
Richard and I walked into the Commandery together and talked as he and his men enjoyed a hastily prepared meal of flatbread, burnt meat strips, cheese, and morning ale. They had been riding almost constantly since yesterday afternoon and were famished and thirsty, but full of talk as to how they led the Greek riders to chase after them and almost catch them.

It had been a classic wounded bird of the type used by both our horsemen and galleys. Richard and his outnumbered men had pretended to be fearful and easy to catch such that the Greeks were enticed to gallop after them. The chase continued with the Greeks continuing to almost catch them until the Greek riders were strung out on tired and faltering horses, at which point Richard and his men had switched to the fresh horses they were leading and turned back to roll up the Greeks by putting arrows into their horses and backs.

While Richard and I ate, runners were sent out to all of the Company's available lieutenant commanders and major captains inviting them to join us. They soon arrived and so did Eric, the commander of the Empress's axe-carrying Rus and Viking guards.

Eric's men were called Varangians. They were the Empress's personal guards and served as the city's night watch. More importantly, they were ferocious fighters and the only men we could depend on as allies in the fighting that was sure to come with the Greeks and their mercenaries. At least that was what we thought at the time.

Our conversation continued for hours and covered everything from the recruitment of more auxiliaries to serve in our galley companies and the use of the state forces that had come in to help defend the city, to what must be said about our chances for success and victory—that everyone must be extremely optimistic about our prospects at all times in order to encourage the lords and armies of the Empress's vassal states to stay loyal to her, and to encourage the city's people not to decide against her and attack us from behind.

Indeed, the city's people were more important than the Latin lords—because most of them were Greek gobblers and relied on the Orthodox Church to tell them how to lead their lives and sell them indulgences. We understood that both the Company and the Empress would be in serious trouble if her vassal states rose against her and her subjects living in the city attacked us from the rear whilst we were fighting on the city wall against the Greek army. It was, unfortunately, a very real possibility.

The sun was going down by the time the meeting finished and Richard and I walked out into the Commandery's bailey together. A number of things had become clear. One of them was that we should make an effort to take some high-ranking prisoners to question. We particularly needed to know why the Greek commander used the Venetians to carry part of his army to Adrianople instead of having them all march there, and why he had immediately sent a few riders to Constantinople ahead of the army. And why did the Venetians do it? Something was up; but what?

"Oh, Richard, wait. I forgot something that could be important. Tomorrow morning I want you to ride over to the Citadel to break your fast with me and have a meeting with Aron, the company's alchemist."

"The alchemist fellow who is trying to make gold for us out of lead? What about him?"

"Do not say a word to anyone or mention a word about it tomorrow when you are at the Citadel, but Aron, that is his name, may have developed a weapon we can use against the Greeks. You need to know more about it in case something happens to me.

"So come to the Citadel's eating hall about a half hour after the sun arrives tomorrow morning. We will break our fasts together and let the courtiers and spies see our optimism about fighting the Greeks. And we particularly want the Empress's servants to overhear our optimism since everything they hear and see will quickly spread through the city when they talk to their friends and visit the market.

"And be sure to bring your apprentice sergeant with you so he can listen and be learnt. Mine will be there too. We will visit the alchemist's workshop in the stables immediately after we break our fasts."

******

Richard and I met in the Citadel's hall the next morning just as we had arranged. Usually I sat at the far end of the long table with my guards sitting around me so that none of the Empress's courtiers could get close enough to bother me with their inane observations and stupid questions. This time was different. I motioned for Richard sit across from me amongst a crowd of courtiers at the higher end of the table.

I had, of course, already heard about Richard's men slaughtering the front part of the Greek column on the mountain road and the fate of their weapons and armour. And the men sitting around us and the people in the city had almost certainly heard rumours about what had happened. What I wanted to do that morning was encourage the Empress's supporters and those who were undecided, and discourage her potential enemies so they would not decide to rise against her.

"So tell me what happened in the mountains, Richard. You had six companies of English archers carrying pikes and swords in addition to their longbows. What caused you and your men to let some of the Greek army get away with their weapons and armour?"

"The fighting was easy. The Greek column massed in front of us and we shot them down left and right with our arrows until they ran.

"The Greeks in the rear, however, were able to get away because we could not climb over the pile of bodies in front of us fast enough to chase them. It was a huge pile and it was hard to climb over it to get at the others because some of the Greeks in the pile were still alive and moving about.

"In the end all we got was the weapons and armour of the men in the pile—and then, damn it all, we had to leave most of it behind in the river so we could go further up the mountain and get ready to stop them once again where it was even colder.

"It worked as it always does when we go against the Greeks. We stopped them once again with even more Greek casualties, many because of the cold, and then the whole Greek army turned and ran for the coast leaving as many as thirty thousand of their dead and wounded behind. We took the weapons and armour off the second lot. It is generally inferior and certainly nothing we would use ourselves, but I suppose it will fetch a decent price when we sell it.

"Now the Greek king and the Patriarch are once again spending their men to their deaths with the Venetians helping to transport them. The result will be the same, of course, the only difference being that now we will be grinding the Greeks down slowly instead of taking them all at once.

"At the moment, my horsemen are hanging on to the Greek columns like wolves surrounding a flock of Greek sheep. But their friends keep grabbing the weapons of the Greeks we kill and wound and running away with them before we can get to them. It is making my men angry that the Greeks have no stomach for fighting; my men want to get on with taking their weapons and armour so they can go home and sell them."

"Aye, you are right, Richard. There is no doubt about it; we need to let the Greeks and their supporters assemble all together in one place so we can eliminate the whole flock of them and capture all their weapons. You might want to explain that to your horsemen—that they should pull back and let the main body of Greeks get through to the city. Then they can move back in and cut them off so we can take them all."

Then I pretended that a thought had just crossed my mind.

"You know what? I am bored sitting around here all the time waiting for the Greeks to show up. I think I will ride out and explain things to the Company's horse archers and see for myself what is happening. Perhaps I can try out my new longbow. It is your turn to stay here for a while. You can explain things to the lads who are here."

The wide-eyed men sitting around us were hanging on our every word and taking it all in. So were the servants who were bringing the food and re-filling the bowls. What Richard and I hoped, of course, was that the listeners would be gullible enough to believe what we were telling each other and spread the news that it was not wise to take up arms against the Empress.

One thing was certain—the Empress's vassals and her subjects living in her capitol city had best remain loyal to the Empress for their own sakes; the Varangians were telling the truth about killing everyone who came against her and so were we. The real question, of course, was whether we would last long enough to do it.

And the only other thing that was certain was that it was going to be one hell of a fight because we were so badly outnumbered.

******

Aron, the Company's alchemist lieutenant, and James Howard, the sergeant assigned to assist him, were waiting for us when we arrived to see the demonstration they had been ordered to provide. It was held in the far back corner of the wall that surrounded the Citadel's little-used rear bailey, and it started with a flock of sheep.

No one except Richard and me and our apprentices were there when Thea, the stable master's young daughter, and Aron's betrothed, used a switch pulled off a tree to drive a flock of sheep into the corner. Some sheaves of cut grass had already been brought to the corner where the bailey's walls came together and had been scattered about in great clumps next to the wall. The sheep immediately began eating the grass and stopped trying to get away.

We stood there looking at each other, a bit amused and perplexed, as Aron smiled at us and James disappeared around the corner of the nearby building. Sheep?

A few moments later a heavily-loaded four wheel wagon with no sides clattered around the corner of the Citadel and came into sight. It was pulled by James and three of the Empress's hostlers. We could tell it was heavily loaded because the men were straining to pull it across the bailey's cobblestones.

At first glance the flat-bed wagon seemed to be loaded with a cargo of large and heavy sacks. But then it soon became obvious that the sacks were stacked up to surround something in the wagon, apparently so it could not be seen.

Aron noted our curiosity.

"Those are sacks filled with dirt and stones. They will protect us from the ribald if it comes apart when the lightning escapes."

Aron made the explanation before anyone even had a chance to ask about the wagon and its strange cargo. There was more than a little pride in his voice when he did.

A ribald? Now I knew what the sacks on the wagon were concealing—one of Aron's ribalds, the long gold-making tubes into which he stuffs with rocks to keep the lightning inside so it would hit the lead he puts in the tube and turn it into gold.

Richard had been told the ribalds were used for making gold, and had seen one before he rode off to harass the Greeks, but he and our apprentice sergeants had never seen one actually used to make gold with man-made lightning. I certainly had, and I instinctively began backing away from it until I saw that the candle Aron was holding was not lit. Richard saw my move and raised his eyebrows in a question.

None of the others had seen my concern, or, if they did, they did not understand the danger. They were curious and promptly walked forward for a better look. Richard and I followed them, but only after I saw it was safe to do so.

What we could see when we gathered around the cart was not much—the open end of the ribald where the lightning power and rocks were put in was the only part not covered by the sacks of dirt and stones. I knew what I was looking at because I had seen it before.

This time, Aron told us, he was using a hollowed-out oak log to hold the powder. It was about six feet long and so heavily wrapped with a galley's mooring line that the wood could not be seen. Its open end was pointed at the sheep.

"Is he really going to make gold?" Richard asked out loud, but to no one in particular. The tone of his voice suggested that he did not believe it.

"I think he has something else in mind," I answered. *And you my fine friend are going to be astonished.*

Chapter Four

The new weapon.

We gathered around and watched in fascination as Aron and James Howard started preparing the gold-making log that Aron called a "ribald" since no one ever knew exactly what it would do when he put fire to it.

Aron began by taking handfuls of dark grey powder out of a leather bucket and using his bare hand to push it down into the hollow log to make room for more handfuls. Then he used a rounded pole to push it all the way down to the very end. The pole looked like one of our oars with the paddle cut off. It probably was.

After the lightning powder was pushed in, Aron and James Howard began stuffing many handfuls of small rocks into the end of the log. Every so often Aron stuck the pole into the end of the log and used it to push the rocks tight against the powder. He seemed to know what he was doing. We were obviously watching an expert at work.

"Normally I would have put a piece of gold-making lead in before the rocks, but not this time," Aron offered as he got down on his knees and began putting handfuls of the lightning power on a piece of linen he had laid on the ground.

Aron used his hands to shape the powder on the linen into a narrow line about two feet long. And then, to my surprise, when he was finished he rolled up the piece of linen to make a short rope with the lightning powder in the middle of it.

"This is something new, a fire rope," he explained. "It will make it safer and easier to make the lightning because I can roll the rope in advance and then run to safety after I put a flame to it." *None of us understood a word of what he was saying, of course, but we nodded out heads as if we did.*

When Aron finished making the fire rope, he reached through a gap in the dirt bags and mooring line wrapped around the log, and then stuffed one end of into a hole he had drilled in the log.

"Now I am putting one end of the fire rope into a hole I gouged into the log where the lightning powder is located.

We could not see how Aron was stuffing the fire rope into the log because only his arm fit through the opening between the dirt bags, but he told us all about it as he worked. It must have been important because it took him some time to get it right. A handful of lightning powder dripped out of the open end of the short fire rope as he worked to get the other end into the log.

Finally he nodded to himself and withdrew his hand.

"We are almost ready," he said as he pulled his hand out of the hole between the sacks and rubbed his hands together to dust them off.

"Everyone please go stand over there by the building. Thea, you get behind the building so I cannot see you." He pointed as he gave his orders.

We walked back towards the Citadel; Thea lifted her skirts and ran.

"Further back, Commander, please go further back. You too, James; there is no need for you to risk yourself if things go wrong."

******

Our little group of watchers walked about a hundred paces away from wagon and stopped. Aron waited until we were gathered there. Then he walked towards the corner of the Citadel where Thea had run. He picked up a candle lantern that was already lit, said something to Thea who had poked her head around the corner that caused her to hurriedly withdraw, and walked back to the wagon.

We watched as Aron used the lantern to light a candle. Then, shielding the flame with his hand so it would not blow out, he walked briskly over to the wagon.

Aron shifted the candle to his left hand, murmured something and made the sign of the cross, and then he held the candle to the end of the fire rope.   Suddenly, he spun around, dropped the candle on the ground, and ran desperately towards us. As he did, the fire rope caught fire and began hissing and popping and burning faster and making more smoke than I would have thought possible from burning a linen scrap.

Then the hissing and burning seemed to stop. Nothing had happened.

Aron had stopped running when he reached us, and turned around to look. The smoke from the burning rope was drifting away.

We waited and watched. Nothing. After about one hundred heart beats, Aron started to walk back to the wagon. There was a look of great disappointment on his face. Richard and I looked at each other. Richard shrugged.

Suddenly, without any warning, there was a great clap of thunder and a flash of lightning reached almost from the end of the wagon to the sheep. Both the ground and the air shook and a huge cloud of black smoke appeared in front of the wagon as if by magic. Foul-smelling moke was everywhere and so thick between the wagon and the sheep that we could not see them at first.

My ears seemed to be hurt and for a brief moment I could see that Richard was wide-eyed and gobbling something that I could not hear. Even so, for some reason, I could understand the words his mouth was making.

"Holy God! Did you see that? What happened?"

There was the strange smell of rotten eggs in the air as we all instinctively ran to the wagon and the cloud of black smoke that covered it. The wagon had rolled some distance backwards on its wheels, and its cargo was all askew with some of the bags of dirt having greatly shifted. Some of them had burst open. The hollow log was gone; the lightning had burst the mooring line hold it together and torn the log into pieces, some big, some small.

"Look. Look! My God."

It was Richard's apprentice and he was pointing at the sheep as he ran towards the wagon.

They were almost all down on the ground dead or dying, and a good number of them had literally been torn apart. There were great amounts of sheep body parts and blood splattered up against the bailey wall, and we could see fresh chip marks all over the wall as if masons had been at work with their hammers.

"Oh my God," someone said.

"We will be eating mutton for weeks," someone said with a happy sound to his voice.

Chapter Five

The long night.

There was unrest and rioters were in the streets the day after Aron's ribald killed the sheep. It was a Sunday and that night only the Latin Quarter of the city was quiet. A few hours earlier the city's Orthodox priests, every single one of them, told the Orthodox faithful at their various Sunday services that the Patriarch had intervened to unite the armies of the Epirus and Nicean kings, and that the restoration of the Byzantine Empire was imminent with the King of Epirus as the emperor chosen by God.

That was merely repeating old news. It was what the priests said next that caused the trouble and rioting—that God had spoken to the Patriarch and told him that he wanted his people to rise up against the heathen Latins once again just as their grandfathers had done, and that God said that every person who did not participate in ridding the city of the Empress and her Latin gobbling priests would burn forever in the fires of purgatory. Rising up against the Empress and her supporters was, the priests told their parishioners, what God wanted them to do.

One of the many rumours that had already begun spreading through the city was that the head of the Orthodox Church had offered enough coins and concessions so that Venice had stopped being neutral and Genoa had changed sides. Those two sea-going states were now, it was said, actively siding with the King of Epirus, one of the many men who claimed to be the rightful heir to the Byzantine Empire with Constantinople once again its rightful capitol and the Patriarch of the Orthodox church once again residing in the city.

It was a believable rumour as Venice was already known to have helped carry the Greek army towards Constantinople and had always been the Latin state most defiant of the Pope. And it certainly was an indication that the world was changing rapidly—it was Venice, as everyone knew, that had actively supported the crusaders some years ago when they captured Constantinople and established the Latin Empire with its Latin gobbling priests replacing the Byzantine Empire and its Greek gobbling priests.

The crusaders had succeeded against the Greeks and replaced the Byzantine Empire with the Latin Empire—with a leader of the crusaders as the emperor and others of the crusaders as its princes and nobles. The Greek-gobbling Orthodox Patriarch had abandoned his palatial residence and fled for his life, and many of his priests had been replaced in their churches with Latin-gobbling priests who answered to the Pope.

According to Eric, the trouble had started that morning when the city's Orthodox priests, every one of them according to Eric, told their flocks of worshippers during their morning services that the Empress was a heretic who should be either killed or overthrown so she could be replaced by a Greek-gobbling emperor approved by God.

More importantly, the priests said God had spoken to the Patriarch and told him that he wanted his people to rise up against the Empress and her devil-worshipping Latins once again. God, the priests told their congregations, wanted the Empress replaced by the King of Epirus.

Whatever the cause, the immediate result of the Orthodox priests delivering the Patriarch's "message from God" was scattered looting and the rapid spreading of all sorts of rumours on every street corner and in the markets. We knew it would be much worse that night when the sun finished passing overhead and darkness fell.

My decision to ride out to see the on-coming Greek army for myself was immediately placed on hold, both because of the troubles and because the Empress summoned her advisors, including me, my father, Richard, Eric, her hand-wringing chancellor, and Archbishop Colonna to an emergency meeting. It was mercifully brief, probably because the insufferable Latin archbishop arrived after it ended.

The questions the Empress put to us when we were assembled in her private chamber was "what should we do? And what will happen tomorrow? Will the people of the city turn out to work on the walls?"

Richard and I immediately understood that we would have to send our men into the city to help Eric and his Varangian axe-men maintain order. But neither of us said a word. I just looked over at Eric and nodded. He understood and nodded back.

The answers and suggestions raised by the Empress's questions ranged all over the place from doing nothing and waiting to see what happens to killing them all. The Empress just listened for about thirty minutes. In the end, it was the Empress herself who made the decision and gave the orders.

"Deploy your men as you think best to protect the city, particularly the Latin Quarter and the markets and churches wherever loyal refugees might gather. Also the public baths and the city's underground water reservoir. Eric, I want you to bring me the Orthodox bishops in chains, but leave the priests alone so they can continue to supervise their parishioners on the work gangs.

"First and foremost, however, you and your men are to put down the rioting tonight and for so long thereafter as it continues—and leave the bodies of the rioters in the streets where they fall to encourage the others to go home.

"Oh yes. And turn out the people and their priests in the morning to work on the walls. Immediately cut down anyone who refuses to work, even the priests."

She was a harder woman than many knew; like a mother bear protecting her cubs.

******

Richard, Eric, and I met together as soon as the Empress's blessedly short meeting ended. We were in full accord with the Empress's orders and turned to the task of carrying them out with enthusiasm and determination. Of course we were with her; it was a matter of principle, the principle being that we had a lucrative coin-earning contract with her. Besides, we would lose our privileges and a major source of the Company's coins if she was overthrown by the Greeks.

My senior aide, Major Captain Michael Oremus, and our apprentices listened intently as Eric suggested, and Richard and I immediately agreed, that the archers would guard each of the city's four markets and each of the city's churches and synagogues, as well as the entrances to the Latin Quarter and several other areas where Eric thought refugees might gather such as the city baths and the water reservoir.   He would provide one of his Varangian guards and a translator for each of our galley companies.

It was also decided that the men of the Company's galley companies not detached to serve in the city would continue to guard the city walls and the Commandery, supervise the people working to strengthen the walls, and be our reserves.

The Latin Quarter would function as a general refuge with a few of the Empress's guards patrolling the quarter's streets even though it was expected to remain quiet. Refugees and their Latin-gobbling priests and merchants would be allowed in and Orthodox rioters would be kept out.

Eric was grim-faced as he said he and all the rest of his axe-men would patrol the Latin Quarter and the streets of the other quarters just as they did every night.

"Every available man, including me, will be patrolling the streets of the city tonight. I fear it will not be enough. The priests' calls and the heat will bring the trouble-makers out into the streets for sure. Wherever possible we will send those who are trying to flee from the troublemakers to either the Latin Quarter for my men to guard or to their churches and markets for your men to guard, whichever are closer."

Things moved quickly after the meeting. Messengers were soon rushing in every direction and some of Eric's men were immediately dispatched to collect the city's Orthodox bishops and their priestly assistants, and bring them in for questioning. According to Eric, the head bishop was called the Metropolitan and he had gone to ground in Patriarch's palace where he now lived.

"The other bishops my men and I can quietly catch and bring in. The Metropolitan we cannot capture without fighting our way into the Patriarch's residence. It is not worth it."

Eric did not go with his men to collect the bishops. He rode with Richard and me to the twenty-seven walled enclosures that totally filled the space between the city's outer and inner defensive walls all the way across the peninsula on which Constantinople sat—and, in so-doing, formed a line of fortified enclosures that totally separated the city of Constantinople at the end of the peninsula from any invader who attempted to reach the city by land.

The archers from one of the Company's galleys were camped in each enclosure and charged with guarding the section of the city's outer defensive wall that was their enclosure's northern wall. *The other three walls of each enclosure being the city's inner defensive wall and the somewhat lower interior walls that ran from the inner wall to the outer wall and, in so doing, divided all the land between the city's outer and inner walls into fortified enclosures.*

Thirty or so of Eric's axe-men jogged along behind us as we galloped from one galley's fortified enclosure to the next. We stopped only a minute or so at each company to give its captain his instructions and for Eric to assign one of his Varangian axe-men to be the captain's guide.

As you might imagine, we accepted Eric's suggestions as to where each of the galley companies was to be placed. Of course we accepted them; he knew the city and its potential trouble spots far better than we ever would.

Less than an hour later the Company's archers and their auxiliaries, guided by Eric's axe-men, began flooding into the city carrying their longbows, pikes, and extra arrows. They had very simple orders—protect their assigned market, church, or public facility where people seeking refuge were likely to assemble, cut down everyone who was looting or part of a street mob, and in the morning turn everyone out to work on strengthening the city's walls no later than thirty minutes after the sun arrived on its daily trip around the world.

It sounded simple. But it would not be an easy assignment to carry out once the sun finished passing overhead and darkness covered the city. That was particularly true since it would be a night when the moon would be very small and we only had a few hours to get everything organized.

In other words, we were facing a situation in our rear that we should have prepared for many weeks ago.

Chapter Six

Unrest in the city.

Every galley captain realized that time was of the essence and quick-marched his archers and auxiliaries to their assigned positions—and everywhere the people of the city saw and heard the archers coming and scurried to get out of their way. It was a powerful message to the people of the city.

****** *Captain Jack White of Galley 29*

My men were practicing with their longbows and I was napping in my tent when my number two, Harry Evans, rushed in shouting that the Commander and some riders were coming this way and coming fast. They were, he shouted, just now coming through the narrow entrance in the wall between our enclosure and the enclosure to our north with a great mob of men running behind them.

Harry seemed quite excited. He was not normally very excitable, so I immediately understood that something important might be occurring and rushed out of the tent to greet our visitors.

It was Commander Courtenay himself with a number of riders and men coming one at a time through the narrow wall opening behind him. The running men looked to be some of the city's axe-carrying guardsmen, the ones we had been told were our good friends.

The Commander did not dismount; he merely pointed at one of the axe-men who was on foot and began giving me my orders. The axe-men were carrying shields and battle axes and had obviously been running hard to keep up with the horses.

"Jack, you are to take your company at the double to one of the city's markets and guard it. That man will lead you there and find a translator for you from amongst the merchants. You and your company are to protect the market and everyone sheltering in it against possible looters and rioters. You and your men are to stay there until you are ordered to return. It might be several days or even longer. Leave a steady sergeant and a couple of men here as lookouts on the wall and to guard your company's tents and supplies.

"Every morning you are to send everyone out to work on the walls thirty minutes after the sun returns in the morning. Take your pikes and swords and all the arrows you can carry."

As was expected of me when receiving such a direct order, I immediately repeated it back so George would know I understood it.

"Aye Commander. My men and I are to follow the axe-man to a market and guard it and the people sheltering in it against looters. We are to take our weapons and all the arrows we can carry, and we are to send the people of the city out to work on the walls no later than thirty minutes after the sun comes back each morning. We are to stay there until we are ordered to return which might be several days. A steady sergeant and a couple of men are to remain here as lookouts and guards."

"Exactly so; you have a good memory. And good luck to you, Jack."

And with that the Commander ducked his head low and leaned down so he and his party could ride one at a time through the narrow opening in the nearby interior wall. He was heading towards Dan Tenn's company which was camped in the next enclosure over from mine.

The Commander and his followers were able to pass directly through to Dan's camp because we had left a single very narrow opening in each of the new interior walls, and then covered them over with bridges of loose boards so our men could walk out all along the top of the new interior walls and shoot their arrows down at anyone who got into the enclosures that resulted when the new interior walls went up.

The narrow openings in the new interior walls were as close as possible to the city's much higher inner defensive wall so an archer standing on the much higher city wall would have an easy target of any enemy who tried to use the opening to get out of the enclosure and into the one next to it. Moreover, each such opening was so narrow that only one rider or foot soldier could go through it at a time to get into the next enclosure—and would be at the mercy of archers standing on the nearby city wall when he did.

Because of the narrowness of the openings, each new interior wall was given two temporary wooden plank bridges for the archers stationed on the wall to use. One went over the narrow opening in the wall, the other, a much longer wooden plank, ran from the interior wall, over the moat, and on to the top of the city's inner defensive wall.

In other words, a man could walk from the top of the city's outer defensive wall all the way to the city's inner defensive wall without ever setting foot on the ground. It turned every enclosure into a "killing ground" for the archers on the walls around each enclosure if an attacker was ever able to break into it—which was exactly the purpose of the interior walls.

Harry and I instantly understood that time was of the essence and that we needed to get our men to the market as fast as possible. That was clear from both the Commander's orders and the clipped and anxious way he gave them.

"COMPANY, ATTENTION, I barked in my loudest captain's voice. FORM UP IN A COLUMN OF THREES WITH PIKES, SWORDS, AND SHIELDS AND EVERY MAN CARRYING FOUR FULL QUIVERS."

I roared out my orders even as the Commander began wheeling his horse around and began heading for the opening in the wall to visit Dan Tenn and his men in the enclosure next to ours. I did not have to order the men to carry their longbows and extra bowstrings; that was understood.

Our camp erupted into chaos as the sergeants repeated my order and everyone ran to get their weapons and extra quivers. It was very exciting.

We were formed up and on our way in less time than it would take for one of our galley's sailors to dance a jig.

There were only two ways for us to get out of the enclosure. One was to use the single narrow opening in each interior wall and go from enclosure to enclosure until the enclosure was reached that had the only road that was open into the city.

The enclosure with the road through it had the only bridge still standing that went over the moat in front of the city's outer defensive wall. And then, after coming in over the outer moat and passing through the gate in the city's outer wall, the road continued for several miles all the way to the moat bridge and gate that took the road into the city through the city's inner defensive wall.

That one road was now the only road into the city—all the other roads were closed by having their bridges over the moats in front of the city's outer and inner walls torn down and their gates blocked with great piles of rocks and dirt. It would be easier to break through, or climb over, the city's outer and inner defensive walls themselves than try to break through the wall gates on the landward side of the city.

The only other way into the city on its landward side, the one my company and our wall workers always used, was to climb up the long and rickety wooden ladders that stretched from the ground in each enclosure to the top of the city's inner defensive wall. There were two such ladders in our enclosure and they were quite long because they had to cross over the moat that ran along the front of the city's inner wall and reach all the way up to the top of the wall.

What it meant, of course, was that a man like me could get into the city by climbing up a ladder to the top of the city wall and then walking down the stone steps on the other side. It always gave me a bit of a chill when I went into the city to visit the Commandery or drink because the ladders were quite rickety and I could look down and see the foul waters of the moat below me. Coming back when I was tipsy was even worse. It was well known that a man in another company fell off a ladder and drowned.

In any event, the men of my company and the other companies used the ladders constantly because they were the only way we could get out of our enclosures without spending a lot of time going through enough of the narrow openings and enclosures to reach the one road into the city that was still open.

As a result of the moats and gate blockages, the Greek invaders would have to use similar ladders to get over the city's inner defensive wall and into the city itself—unless, of course, they were willing to stand in line to go through the narrow openings whilst our archers were pushing arrows at them from the top of the inner defensive wall which was only a short distance away. More importantly, they would only be able to do one or the other if they were able get through the city's outer defensive wall and into the enclosures where we were camped.

It would not be easy for the Greeks even if they successfully breached the outer wall and got into one of our enclosures—they would have to bring their own ladders and be able to climb up them to get into the adjoining enclosure or into the city. And they would have to do so despite our arrows coming down on them from close range and the pike men waiting to poke them with their pike points and chop them down with their pike blades when they got near the top of whatever walls they were trying to climb over.

Moreover, to even get to the city's inner defensive wall and erect their ladders, the Greek soldiers would not only have to fight their way over or through the city's outer defensive wall, they would also have to run the length of the enclosure whilst our men were pushing arrows at them from the newly constructed interior walls on either side of them.

It was as fine a set of killing grounds as we had ever established. The only questions, at least so far as my men and I were concerned, was whether we would run out of arrows before the Greeks ran out of men for us to shoot down—and if the Greeks and their supporters had the bottom to keep coming and taking terrible casualties long enough for that to occur.

It did not turn out that way, of course, but that was what we were thinking at the time.

We got into the city by scrambling up the ladders from our camp to the top of the city's inner defensive wall and then climbing down the stairs on the other side of the wall. It was something we were used to doing and it did not take long before we were on the ground in the city, and once again formed up and ready to march.

It was a very warm day and we could feel the heat from the street stones through our open-toed sandals. As you might imagine, the men were already hot and sweating profusely by the time Captain White gave the word and we set out to follow the axe-man to wherever he was leading us.

Our marching drum was beating loudly as we marched and sweated our way through the city's streets. No one had a clue as to where exactly we were being led, not even the captain.

All we knew was that we were marching in the hot sun and what the captain briefly told us when we first assembled—that we would be spending a night or two protecting a market and some refugees from rioters. I myself was hopefully the rioters would come so I would have a chance to distinguish myself. I suspect many of the men felt the same way.

It took us quite some time to reach the market we were assigned to protect. It was, or so it seemed by the time we got there, some distance away on the other side of the city. We initially moved at a quick march, but the captain soon slowed the drum to a normal marching pace because of the heat. It was not so bad when we were marching in the shade of the buildings that lined the city's narrow streets, but it was damn hot and uncomfortable when we had to march in the sun.

Not many people were on the streets, probably because of the heat more than anything else. At first the people we saw along the way were friendly, and we even got a few waves and smiles. That changed after a while. Sergeant Thomas said it was because we left the quarter where the Empress and the city's good people lived with their Latin priests. I did not know what he meant, and I did not want to reveal my ignorance by asking him.

There was a noticeable difference in the responses of the people we met as we got deeper and deeper into the city—the initial smiles were replaced by scowls and several times angry young men shouted and made insulting gestures at us.

We ignored the hostile young men, but not entirely; the captain told several sergeants that, even though we would not be stopping, if someone threw something at us, they were to try to put an arrow into him. Fortunately, or perhaps unfortunately, nothing actually happened. It meant that once again I had no opportunity to distinguish myself.

Our beards and tunics were dripping with sweat and we were extremely thirsty by the time we reached the market. It was the middle of a very hot afternoon without a cloud in the sky.

The captain and I immediately began walking around the outside of the market and posting guards at each of its entrances. It, the market, was partially walled and quite large with many narrow roofed aisles running between roofed stalls.   There were cats and merchants everywhere, but very few customers, probably because of the heat. We walked in the shade wherever possible.

Merchants, at least I think they were merchants, came up to us as soon as we arrived and began pointing and gobbling away at us with big smiles. At first, we had no idea what they were saying and shrugged. That changed quickly when more merchants arrived. Some of them could gobble crusader French even though the market was located in one of the Orthodox quarters and did not serve the port.

"My friends and I are happy the Empress sent you here to protect us. We only want peace, but some of the bad young people in this quarter are looking for trouble. Where are you from?"

We quickly became the new best friends of many of the merchants, especially when the captain opened his coin pouch and began buying food and drink for the men.

Chapter Seven

A long night.

It was a long hot night. The troubles started as soon as the sun was finishing the day and darkness began to fall. The tension in the air continued to grow as it got darker and a bit cooler, and so did the number of people in the market and the unrest in the streets that surrounded it. It was better than standing in the sun, but still damn hot.

Entire families with their children and whatever of their possessions they could carry began arriving to seek a place where they would be safe. Others came to do their normal shopping in the evening when the air was not so hot.

Flickering candles and candle lanterns appeared in almost every merchant's stall as if by magic. Except for a few candles we could see in wall openings above the street and a couple of cooking fires, it was totally dark in the streets around the market.

The market became increasingly crowded with refugees and did not close at its normal time. To the contrary, it got more and more crowded as the evening progressed. The smell of smoke was in the air and we could increasingly hear shouting and noise coming from the city outside the market. Many of the merchants and their helpers were armed and visibly displayed their weapons. A surprising number of them had wood-chopping axes laid out for all to see.

Many of the merchants, or so we were told by a merchant who said he was a Jew, were Orthodox-praying Greek gobblers. To a man, however, the Greek merchants went out of their way to profess great love and undying admiration for someone called the Empress "even though I am a traditional Christian, of course."

We did not have a clue as to who they were talking about and merely nodded our agreement. Our translator was nowhere to be found; it was the Jew who stayed near us and told us what the others said.

Most of the market's merchants either stayed all night to guard their stalls or left their helpers to guard them so they could go home to guard their families. Other of the merchants brought their families to the market so they could guard them both. They all seemed quite conflicted and uncertain as to how best to save their goods and protect their families.

The only exceptions were some of the sellers of gold, silver, and jewellery; they disappeared and took their goods with them. It was almost like magic; one moment they were all there and the next moment they were all gone. It seems they had contracted for one of our galleys and had suddenly decided to go on board with their families and wares.

Those of the merchants who knew how to gobble with us seemed compelled to seek out the captain. They did so both to complain about one thing or another, or to try to find out what he could tell them about the on-coming war with the Greek army. They seemed quite surprised when Jack said he knew nothing about the Greek army or when it might appear, and even more surprised when he told them it did not really matter when the Greeks showed up.

"It matters not. We be archers and anyone who attacks an archer gets killed most terrible. That is how it always has been. There are no exceptions. It is in the Company's contract on which we all made our marks."

Some of the individual merchants employed additional guards and so did the merchant organizations of several sections of the market, the linen merchants and butchers in particular.

The guards were, for the most part, however, even more useless than the merchants' helpers. That was particularly true of the club-carrying men from the protection gangs of the nearby Orthodox churches. They apparently had been collecting money to "protect" the merchants in the market for some years, but they suddenly disappeared just before sun went down when the priests sent messengers calling them to come and help protect the churches instead. At least that is what the merchants told us as they were leaving.

I knew about the "disappearing guards" because the merchants were irate about their sudden departure and came to me and the captain to complain. They wanted us to send messengers to the churches demanding that they return to do what they had been paid to do. As you might imagine, we told them "that galley has sailed" and did nothing.

And, as we were later told by our axe-man translator who had suddenly reappeared, most of the disappearing guards had gone off to join the rioters and looters as their priests said God required.

****** *Chosen man Wat Bargee*

We had a hot march to a partially walled market on the other side of the city. Once we got there, however, it was easy duty whilst the sun was shining and for a few hours afterwards. My mates and I were assigned to guard one of the entrances to the market. As a result, we mostly sat around in the shade and yarned.

It was too hot by half, but quite enjoyable to be able to sit around instead of working. I put new feathers on one of my arrows whilst we yarned and told each other stories and lies about what we had seen and heard. And it got even better when my best mate, Billy Hansen, took a piece of cheese from his pouch and began breaking little pieces of it off and throwing them to the cats. We laughed when the cats snarled and hissed at each other as they tried to be the first to chase after them and pounce on them.

And, as you might imagine, old Jerry Prevo who mumbled prayers out loud all the time did his usual; he got a copper coin off each of us and sneaked away for a couple of hours, and then staggered back filled with wine and carrying a full skin which he promptly shared. Sergeant Taylor pretended he did not see him go and then did his usual by drinking more than his share of the wine. It was a nice red with a good taste.

All the while as we watched and talked, families carrying little children and whatever they could carry continued to stream into the market and settle themselves wherever they could find an open space on which to squat. They seemed wary as they came past us and some of them gobbled at us as they did.

We could not understand what they were saying, of course, so we just pointed to where they were to go and made shooing motions. It seemed to work.

Everything changed about two hours after it got dark. Smoke began drifting into the market and we could hear shouting and other noises in the distance. Suddenly, a whole mob of people carrying their children and all kinds of other possessions began running down the street towards the market entrance where we were posted.

No one said a word, but we all got our feet and began checking our bows to make sure they were properly strung. I pulled out an arrow and nocked it, and so did a couple of my mates.

The relief on the people's faces when they reached us was clear. We could see it by the flickering light of the two candle lanterns Lieutenant Evans had brought us just before it got dark. The new arrivals looked frightened and uncertain, but seemed quite pleased when we waved them on into the market and pointed towards where they were to go to settle themselves.

Sergeant Taylor got increasingly anxious, particularly when a man with blood on his head staggered past us carrying a child. Twice he said the same thing.

"String'um lads and get ready, the buggers look to be coming."

It was an unnecessary order. Not only was my bow strung, I had an arrowed nocked and so did all of my mates by then.

Our basic problem was simple. The light from the candle lanterns lit us and identified the entrance to the market for anyone coming towards us; it also attracted entire companies of flying bugs. We, on the other hand, could not see who was approaching until they were right on top of us.

"Sergeant, maybe we should carry one or both of those lanterns down the street a ways and hang it up somewhere to backlight any buggers who come down it. Then we could push our arrows at them before they reach us."

I made the suggestion and it changed my life.

"Well then, Wat, that is what you should do."

He said it sarcastically just as Lieutenant Evans and a couple of men appeared out of the darkness.

"Do what, Sergeant Taylor?"

The sergeant told him.

"Do you think you could do it, Wat?" Lieutenant Evans asked. He looked at me closely as he did.

"Oh aye lieutenant, I could do it if a couple of men with swords and shields could come with me to guard my back if there be close-up fighting whilst I be finding a place to hang them."

******

A few minutes later I was carrying two candle lanterns and walking warily out of the market towards the darkened street that opened into the market. In other words, I was walking towards the noise of the looting and rioting because I had talked too much. Two of my mates were with me, Andy Salt and Long John Ander's son from Shrewsbury. They were carrying swords and galley shields in addition to their long bows and quivers.

We did not have to go too far to reach the buildings along the street on the far side of the little open area in front of the market entrance. Even so, I got so scared I almost pissed on myself when I suddenly realized we had walked up to within a few feet of a group of people who standing against the wall of the building nearest to the market entrance. It was the best place to hang the lanterns because they would backlight anyone coming out of the darkened street and moving towards the market.

After my initial fright, and when I held up both lanterns even higher, I could see the vague outlines of a man and woman. They were both carrying something, probably a child and their bedding, and standing silent and unmoving against the building. On the whole, as I realized after I got over my initial fright at seeing them, they seemed to be even more frightened by us walking towards them than we were of finding them silently standing so near to us.

I held up the lanterns so they could better see my face and motioned with a nod of my head towards the market. At the same time I quietly said "you can go." They immediately began hurrying towards the market so maybe they could understand the crusader French gobbled by me and my mates.

The whole idea of having to fight in the dark was scary as hell. I always knew it would be better to stand off and use our longbows to shoot down anyone who might want to kill us; now I knew it for sure.

My problem was that I was damn near blind because I was carrying two lit candle lanterns Lieutenant Evans had "borrowed" from a couple of merchants. The light of the lanterns made it easy for me to see where I was putting my feet down, but hard for me to see ahead. At the same time, the light from the lanterns made it as easy as eating a chicken pie for everyone up ahead with a weapon to see me coming.

Knowing that everyone could see me, and I could not see them, made me quite uncomfortable, I can tell you that. So I began holding the lanterns as high and as far out in front of me as possible in an effort to see further ahead. It helped, but not much.

Andy and John walked on either side of me. They were carrying swords and shields, and had them at the ready. Andy was carrying two swords, his own in its sheath and mine in his hand. Not that I planned to take the sword from Andy and use it if anyone came at us out of the dark, that was for damn sure. To the contrary, I had already decided to drop the lanterns and run back to the market like the devil himself was chasing me if anything happened—and I damn near did just that when I first saw the people huddled against the wall.

We walked slowly and listened carefully as we crossed over the open space between the market and the nearest building whose dim outline we could see in the moonlight. It was dark that we could not see anything and so silent that you could have heard a feather drop. Several times people must have seen the light from the lanterns I was carrying, or heard us coming, because we could hear when the sound of their approaching footsteps stopped or began backing up.

It actually did not take very long to reach the building across from the market entrance. It just seemed that way because we were going so fearful-like. But we made it; and then we were stopped because the first door we reached was barred—we could not get inside to hang the lanterns high enough so they could not be reached and blown out.

At first, no one came when I rapped on the door with the handle of my belt knife. But I kept it up because the shuttered wall opening about eight feet above the door looked like the best place to hang one of the lanterns.

Finally a voice shouted down from above us. But we could not understand a word of what he said. It was probably either "who are you" or "go away." Maybe it was both.

"Run back and get one of the Greek gobbling merchants to come tell the man up there that all we want to do is hang a couple of lanterns to help light the street—and that if he does not open the door we will batter it in and kill everyone. I mean it so bring an axe when you come back."

I gave the order to Andy because he only had one stripe whereas John had two and did not have to do what I told him.

Chapter Eight

We place our lanterns.

Whilst John and I waited impatiently for Andy to return, we could hear shouts and other noises in the distance. We were also periodically startled when we saw the dim shapes of people coming past us on their way to seek shelter in the market. What was worrisome was that they inevitably saw us due to the light from the candle lanterns we were holding before we saw them. In other words, we would have been shite out of luck if they had been carrying weapons and wanted to take us down.

The people who came upon us did not know who we might be and inevitably took no chances—some of them warily came past us by walking on the other side of the dark and narrow street, others turned down a narrow side alley with the idea of going around us to another entrance. The rest either froze and did not move until someone else had safely gotten past us, or they turned around and went back the way they had come.

In the distance, as we stood there, the noise of shouting voices was growing louder and seemed to be coming closer. It might have been my imagination, but I thought there was also more smoke and noise in the air.

Somehow, and it is hard to explain, waiting in the dark was both comforting and worrisome. What was worrisome was that someone could see the lanterns and come out of the dark and attack me; what was comforting was that I could put the lanterns down and take a few steps into the dark and not be seen. And that was exactly what I did; I put them down and stepped away from them. I was so scared I was shaking and there was no getting around it.

Andy finally came back with one of our auxiliaries and an axe with a short wooden handle. He had not been gone long, but to John and I it seemed forever. In the lantern light I could see the auxiliary was seriously worried and became even more afraid when I made a "give me" motion and he handed me the axe he had been carrying. I felt the same way; I myself was not exactly in the mood to break into one of the Company's marching songs.

"One of the merchants told this man what you wanted him to say. I think he understands," Andy said.

"I damn well hope so," I muttered as I took the axe and instinctively hefted it to get a sense of its weight. Then I handed it to Andy to hold.

A few moments later I once again pounded on the door with the handle of my personal knife. This time I did it louder and harder. If at all possible, I wanted to get into the upper room without having to destroy the door. That way we could close and bar it behind us.

There was no answer. But I knew someone was in there so I kept pounding and pounding. I was determined because it was by far the best place to hang the lanterns. But to do so we needed to get to the wall opening in a room above door, and the lanterns had to be low enough to backlight anyone on the street and high enough so no one could reach them to blow them out or knock them down.

Finally the same man's voice spoke out to us from above. I could not see him, but he was almost certainly standing in wall opening above the street, exactly where I wanted to place the lanterns. The man's initial message was clear even though I could not understand the words— go away.

This time, at least, we could answer. The auxiliary and the unknown man began gobbling away at each other. After a while they stopped. The sounds of the rioting were getting louder and louder and seemed to coming towards us. Men and women began periodically running past us, refugees for sure. We could hear their footsteps and see their dim outlines.

"He is coming down to take the bar off the door," the auxiliary finally said. "I told him we were peaceful and would guard him, but that if he did not open it, we would break it down." *At least that was what I thought the auxiliary said; he was hard to understand.*

A few moments later, with me holding one of the candle lanterns in one hand and my sword in the other, and John Long doing the same with his sword and the other lantern, there were the sounds of the door's bar being removed. It opened a crack a few seconds later. I could see it in the lantern light.

I instantly stepped forward and put my foot in the door so it could not be closed, and at the same time pushed hard using the hilt of the sword I was clutching. There was initial resistance, but then none. Whoever was holding it must have stepped aside; it swung open and hit the nearby wall with a bang.

A moment later I was inside and could see the man by the light of my high-held lantern. And I could see him even better when Andy came in behind me with the other lantern. He was bearded, fairly young, very anxious, and carrying a young child in his arms. It was as if he thought that holding the child would protect him from being attacked for fear of injuring the child. He backed away and kept the child between us as I hurriedly entered with John and Andy right behind me.

It was actually quite a smart thing for the man to do, holding the child that is, as it announced his intention to be peaceful. It might well have saved him if we had been forced to batter down the door.

I led the way as the four of us crowded further on into the little street-level room. The man who let us in backed into a corner still holding the child. In the lantern light I could see that it was some kind of a workshop with a loom, several spindles and a sack filled with some kind of material. The black-bearded auxiliary started to come in behind us—and then whirled around and ran off into the darkness. There was no way we could have stopped him.

"Goddammit. The bugger has run," shouted John unnecessarily.

There was a moment of confusion, but then I headed for the ladder at the far end of the little room. The family obviously used it to climb up to the room or rooms above their workshop. It was almost certainly the family's sleeping room above their workshop, the room that had the wall opening that looked out onto the street and the entrance to the market.

I began climbing the ladder. It was well made, not rickety at all, just steep. That was when I discovered how damn difficult it is to climb a steep ladder with a lighted candle lantern in one hand and a sword in the other.

"Hold this," I snarled at John as I stepped down and handed him the lantern. Then I went up the ladder slowly, one step at a time, while still holding my sword—which required me to lean hard against the ladder and periodically let go with my left hand in order to quickly grasp the side of the ladder again, but slightly higher, in order to go up another step.

There was nothing but a hole in the ceiling above me through which the end of the ladder protruded. Beyond the hole was total darkness.

I was more than a little anxious at what might happen when my head came up through the hole. And then, to top it off, as I climbed I realized that I was sweating profusely, and I somehow became aware of a big drop of sweat on the tip of my nose. It almost caused me to fall when I, for some reason I never will understand, I tried to wipe it off by twisting my head so as to rub my nose on my shoulder. It almost overbalanced me.

My effort to climb the ladder did not go well. I had the impression there were people in the darkened room above us, but I could not see into the room and time was passing. Even worse, as I climbed towards the hole I realized my sword would be totally useless if someone decided to chop down on me as I came through the opening.

There was no question about what I needed—I needed to see so I could protect myself by staying away from whoever was in the dark room. Carrying a sword that I could not use to fight them off made no sense. So down the ladder I came in order to exchange my sword for the lantern John was holding. Going down with a sword was somewhat easier than going up, but not much.

"Take this and give me one of the goddamn lanterns," I said to John as I held out my sword to him. I was anxious and it showed.

With the lantern in hand, I once again made a one-handed climb up the ladder. This time I did so while holding the lantern as high as possible above me. The man who had opened the door had not yet said a single word. He just sat silently against the wall whispering to the child in his arms and gently smoothing her hair. At least I think it was a girl; I could not tell for sure in the dim light.

I took a deep breath to steady myself and slowly and carefully raised the flickering candle lantern up into the room through the wall opening. I kept my head off to one side and under the ceiling as much as possible.

Nothing happened so I moved up another step. And then another. Finally, I took a deep breath and, holding the lantern as high as I could get it, slowly raised my head into the room— and exhaled with a profound sense of relief.

Sitting in the corner was a terrified woman with her arms around a couple of children. An older woman with white hair was huddled next to her. They were afraid of me and no threat at all. I was greatly relieved. There was no one else in the room.

"Hoy," I said softly with a little smile and a nod of my head. "I am a friend."

And then I spoke again more loudly, but still with somewhat of a smile in my voice as I climbed the rest of the way up the ladder and stepped into the room. It was obviously the room where the family slept, watched the activity in the street from the opening in the wall, and talked out of the wall opening to their similarly situated neighbours. The wooden shutters of the wall opening were partially open so they could see and listen.

"Hoy, Missus, we mean you no harm."

I said it gently as I held the lantern high and made a soothing motion with my free hand that they should stay where they were sitting. I wanted to see what was happening in the street so I headed to the wall opening as I motioned for the women and children to stay seated. The wooden floor planks creaked as I walked and there was noise and shouting coming up from the street below us.

"Bar the damn door," I shouted down to John and Andy as soon as I reached the opening and looked down at the street and the open area between me and the market.

"We already have," came the response.

Even though I could not see them, the street was obviously full of people shouting and talking. They were mostly men's voices, and they were almost certainly not refugees seeking shelter.

Against the light from the lanterns at the entrance to the market I could make out the vague outlines of a large number of people. They were slowly, and somewhat tentatively, moving along the street below me and heading towards the market.

I immediately placed the lantern I was carrying on the sill of the wall opening. It did not add much light to the street and there was no response from the men who were gathered and talking excitedly on the street below me. More importantly, it was too high above the street to backlight the mob for the archers at the market entrance.

"Bring up the other lantern and hurry," I went to the ladder opening and gave my order in a whisper loud enough that John and Andy could hear me. "And keep that damn door barred whatever you do. The street is full of men and they sound dangerous."

Less than a minute later Andy came up the ladder and handed me the second lantern.

I placed the second lantern on the sill of the wall opening next to the one already there. It provided additional light, but nowhere near enough; the lanterns were too high off the ground to backlight the men standing below us. Damn.

"Quick. Take one of the lanterns and go back downstairs and see if you can find a line or something we can use to lower the lanterns down closer to the street."

Andy understood the seriousness of the situation. He grabbed one of the lanterns and rushed back to the ladder.

Suddenly there were great screams and shouts and the sound of running feet on the street below. I knew exactly what it meant—my mates at the entrance to the market had finally seen the approaching rioters and begun pushing arrows at them. Hopefully they were close-packed, the rioters that is; it is hard to be accurate when you are pushing arrows at men you can barely see.

I shouted more orders at Andy as he started down the ladder. There was no longer any need to whisper.

"And tell John to send the man and his child up now and to run for the ladder if they start to break in. We can pull it up behind us and shoot arrows down at the buggers."

We are safe up here unless they start a fire and try to burn us out, I decided. Then I had another thought—it would be better to pull the ladder up now and pretend no one was here.

******

Things had quieted down outside by the time Andy climbed back up the ladder. He was carrying something that, in the dim lantern light, looked like a large ball of string. John came up right behind him. The man who opened the door had come up with the child before they did. He was now sitting on the floor in the corner with his arms around his family.

"It was all I could find," Andy said as he handed the ball to me and moved back to the opening to pull up the ladder.

The ball had a sticky feel to it. One sniff with my nose and I knew exactly what I was holding—recently spun wool. Of course I did; me mum used to spin wool to feed us after my father fell off the barge he was poling and drowned himself by not being able to breath. That was before the pox took her, my two sisters disappeared, and I went for an archer.

"It should work," I said with more assurance in my voice than I felt as I got to work unrolling the ball. It took me a few minutes in the dim light to get enough of the spun wool unrolled, and then a few more to be sure it would be strong enough to lift one of the lanterns.

My plan was quite simple. I was going to tie a wool line to each of the lanterns and lower it down so it would be closer to the street and better backlight the rioters for the archers in the market. And then I was going to tie it off to something in the room so we three archers could run back to the market and join in the pushing whenever rioters came.

It was a fine plan and simple as all good plans must be. Unfortunately, somewhere along the line I realized that it would not work because of the family. They could, and probably would, haul up the lanterns or cut their lines as soon as we ran back to the market. Or the rioters might reach up from wagon beds and knock the lanterns down with sticks, or break in the door and cut them down.

There was no alternative; we would have to stay the night and defend the lanterns. But first we had to hang them, the lanterns that is, not the family.

******

We worked feverishly to hang the lanterns. We brought one of them into the upper room so we could use its light to see what we were doing whilst the ball of woollen yarn was being unrolled. Andy cut a piece of line off what was unrolled and John tied one end to the lantern while Andy was unrolling and cutting another line for the other lantern.

But where should we tie the other end in order that the lantern would hang above the street? We were flummoxed. There was nothing to which the end of line could be tied. I even briefly considered turning one of our longbows sideways across the window opening and tying the lantern lines to its middle. The weight of the lanterns would hold it in place.

"Not with my bow," said John emphatically. "Use your own."

It was clear that I would have a revolt on my hands if I tried to use anyone else's bow except my own to anchor the lanterns. And worse, a rioter on the street might use the branch of a tree or stand on a wagon to pull the lanterns down and the bow along with them. Losing his bow was one of the most terrible things an archer could do. It would cost me my stripes for sure, and I might never get them back.

The only alternative was for the three of us to stay in the room and dangle the lanterns down while holding on to the lines so they could be quickly pulled up if anyone tried to get at them. So that is what we did. Well, almost.

Chapter Nine

The long night.

John carefully let out line and lowered his lantern lower and lower, until shed light on the men on the street below us and was just out of their reach even if they jumped. I leaned out of the opening and watched as it slowly went down. Then I lowered the second lantern, the one I was holding, and did the same thing. John and I stood at the opening and watched intently. We were ready to instantly pull them up.

The lanterns certainly had an impact. We could see that the partially lit street was full of men carrying clubs and knives. A few of them had swords and spears, but not many. There were even a few women. They all looked up. But, to our great surprise, they were not alarmed. Several of them pointed and cheered.

"My God," John said softly so only I could hear. "The bastards think we are helping them by lighting them up for our lads to see."

But were they only rioters, or were they something else? Perhaps it was my imagination because I could only see dim shapes, but the mob below us appeared to be somewhat organized with orders being shouted at them by a couple of men who appeared to be wearing priest's robes. And then, of all things, I had a terrible urge to pee.

There was no time to look for the family's piss pot.

"I have to pee," I announced to no one in particular as I handed my lantern line to Andy.

Andy took my place at the wall opening and looked down while I moved a couple of steps to the right and pissed against the wall of the room. I was feeling much better when I took the line back from Andy and resumed my place.

It did not take long before our fellow archers at the market entrance reacted to being able to see the gathering rioters. We did not see or hear the archers begin pushing out their arrows, but we certainly knew when it started and had a close view of the results.

One moment everything was relatively quiet below us; the next there were screams, curses, and confusion. Andy pushed into the window openings so all three of us could look down and watch. We rarely saw the blur of the arrows as they landed in the mob gathered below us, but we certainly heard the thuds and the cries of surprise and distress as they hit.

And then it happened—there was a loudly shouted order and the mob below us began running out of the street and towards the market entrance with great shouts and cheers. There were hundreds of them.

Some of the mob went down to the arrows coming out of the market, but within seconds the shouting mob had reached the market and began pouring into it. They got in even though archers at the entrance had taken a fearsome toll—in the dim light we could see shapes lying on the street and in the open area in front of the market that were clearly dead and wounded rioters.

"Quick, we have to help them."

John had shouted as soon as the storm of arrows began biting into the crowd below us. There was barely room for two of us at the opening and John and I were already there.

We both handed our lantern lines to Andy who was standing behind us, our bows came off our shoulders, and we stood on either side of the opening and began trying to pick off the moving shapes below us that we could see outlined in the dim light. It would have helped if we had more light to see the men below us and something to stand on so we could better look downward out of the opening. But we did not.

"Damn. My string broke. Step in," John suddenly shouted after we had each pushed out four or five arrows. His bowstring had frayed or broken. He stepped back so Andy could take his place whilst he quickly took a spare out from under his cap and began restringing his longbow.

Taking John's place did not happen instantly because Andy could not hold the lantern lines and push out arrows at the same time. He temporarily solved the problem, and caused the lanterns to jump up and down and bang together, by wrapping the lines around his leg and holding the ends in his teeth so the lines would not unravel.

We were late to the fight and the wall opening was narrow. In the end, I stood on one side of the opening and pushed arrows at the late arrivals who were following the rioters' thrusters into the market whilst Andy, and then John once again, stood on the other side of the opening tried to take those they could see on the street below us.

I am not sure when the people below us began to realize that arrows were coming out of wall opening above the lanterns, but they finally did—about the time they began running away down the street.

A few of the wounded and their helpers moved tightly up against the wall directly under us in hopes we would not be able to get clean shots at them. It did not work—I stepped back to give John enough room to get his bow all the way out of the wall opening and shoot straight down at them.

Whilst John was leaning well out the opening to push at the men directly below us, I counted my arrows. It did not take long. There were only two in my quiver. A moment later John pulled in his head. "I am all out, and the buggers are at the door with an axe," he shouted.

Andy handed the lantern lines back to John and moved into the wall opening to take John's place. He similarly leaned out of the opening so he could shoot straight down at those at the door. I looked around to reassure myself that we had long ago pulled up the ladder and there was no other way anyone could get up to us.

"Christ, you are right," Andy said as he leaned out and pushed an arrow straight down—and damn near fell out of the opening as he did. There was a particularly loud scream and the sound of pounding on the door below us abruptly stopped.

******

We had no idea how long it was before we only had two arrows left between the three of us. I nocked one, John the other. Andy was standing at the ladder hole in the ceiling with his sword. At that point, all we could do was listen to the battle sounds coming from the market and watch in the dim candle light as looters hurried away with their arms full of goods from the market and wounded rioters periodically staggered or were carried out of the market's entrance in an effort to get away from the fighting.

First one, and then the other, of the candles burned out as we stood at the wall opening and watched. The heavy pounding on the door to the street began once again not too long afterwards. It sounded as though someone was chopping on it with an axe and it was splintering and coming apart.

It was the older of the two women in the room who saved us. I was still trying to decide whether to use my last arrow when she rushed to the opening with the room's piss pot and emptied it on to the street below. We had been shown it after I had hurriedly pissed on the wall, and we had all used it by then, including a very smelly and soupy shite by Andy. It was full to the brim.

The chopping instantly stopped and was replaced by obvious curses and cries of rage in a gobble we could not understand, probably Greek. The old woman leaned out of the opening and screamed down at them. Someone shouted something and she screamed an answer back. Then there was silence.

"I know not what she said to them," John said with a wry smile in his voice. "But I surely wish she had said it earlier."

Chapter Ten

What should we do?

"We need food, water, candles, and more arrows if we are to stay here any longer." I said it out loud without meaning for anyone except me to hear my words.

It had already been a long night, and we knew it was far from being over.

We had watched as rioters attacked and overran the entrance to the market and the company's lanterns went out. Then, after we had used up almost all of our arrows, we had watched helplessly and silently as looters with their arms full carried things out of the market. We know that happened because they had passed under our lanterns and hurried down the street to wherever they were going.

At some point as the night progressed, the company must have launched a successful counter-attack, for we listened to sounds of fighting and then watched from the wall opening as the vague outlines of a steady stream of men, some wounded and others with their arms full of loot, came running past us in the dim light of the lanterns we had hanging above the street. And we cheered and danced around when the candle lanterns appeared once again at the entrance to the market. A short time later our lanterns flickered one after another and went out.

We needed all kinds of supplies. The question was whether to try to get them in the dark or wait for morning. Dark sounded better to me because a man could hide in it.

It was the dangerous condition of the hovel's door to the street that decided me as to what had to be done. I could tell by running my hands over it that it was almost finished. Rioters seeing its condition in the morning light would likely try to get in, and they would almost certainly be successful if they did.

We had our swords, of course, but what we needed most were arrows so we could shoot down at anyone trying to get in through the door, and from the hole in the ceiling if they were able to in. If we did not get more arrows, and more candles, we would have no light to shed on the street and no arrows to protect us from intruders; we might end up having to run and the only way out was through the door and into the street. Some food and water would be useful as well.

We listened and tried to watch as Wat slipped out of the battered door and made a run for the market. I was at the door to the street to cover him and Andy was at the wall opening. As far as we could tell, there was no one in the street when Wat made his move. He had a sword in one hand and Andy's shield in the other in case he bumped into someone in the dark.

I temporarily stepped out of the door behind Wat with an arrow nocked and our last remaining arrow in my quiver. Andy was above me and had none. Fortunately, no one was waiting in the darkness. I quickly stepped back inside and barred the door once I was sure Wat was off and running with a sword in one hand and a shield in the other.

Andy remained upstairs with the family and Wat's longbow. We had considered having Andy come down to the door with us but, finally, after we talked it over, we decided against it. It would have been hard enough for two of us to climb the ladder and escape if the rioters were waiting for the door to open and charged in when it did; three would have made things even more difficult.

I heard Wat calling out whilst I was putting the bar back on the door and Andy heard him from the wall opening.

"Ahoy in the market, it is me, Wat Bargee from Tilbury. Captain White's Galley Twenty-Seven. I be coming in."

"Hoy the market" … "Archer coming in" …. "Archer coming in" … "Archer coming in."

We heard Wat start shouting his hoys as soon as he cleared the street and never stopped shouting until he reached the market. It only took a few seconds.

There was an answer from the market early on but we could not make it out.

******

"My God, Wat, you be alive! We thought you were dead when your lanterns went out. And the other men? How be they?"

It was Captain White himself who greeted me, and then questioned me closely by the flickering light of a candle. He had a cut on his arm that was wrapped in a linen rag to stop the blood from leaking out. There were a number of archers visible in the flickering light of a dozen or more candles, many more than when we had left a few hours later. The captain looked haggard and tired. A wound and no sleep will do that to you every time.

Captain White began giving orders to the company's first sergeant as soon as I finished making my report.

"Tom, send five of our best men and a Greek-gobbler with Sergeant Bargee. He is in command of the outpost and they are to do whatever he tells them to do.

"They are to carry enough food, candles, and water for twelve men for three days plus all the arrows they can carry.

"Do you want to send the family in to us, Wat, or do you want to keep them with you?"

"The family can come in, Captain, but I would like to keep the old woman. Damn convincing she sounded. I think she told them they were breaking down the wrong door after she dumped the shit pot on them.

"But begging your pardon, Captain. I cannot use more men where I am. They would be better used hanging lanterns from the wall opening across the street or the next door down from it, or both. And they would need a steady man to sergeant them at each place. That way we could cover each other's doors from the wall openings above the street."

Captain White did not say a word at first, he just gave me a long and hard look in the flickering lantern light. And then he nodded his head.

"How many men and steady sergeants do you think you would need to hold that street and keep it lighted, Wat? And think a bit before you answer; you are a sergeant now with another stripe."

******

It was still dark when I headed back to re-join John and Andy. Seven men came with me, three men for each of two additional window openings on the street and an unhappy merchant who was full of fear and could gobble Greek. Every man including me was carrying a heavy load of food, water, and arrows. I was tired and so were they; it had been a long and difficult day—and the real war had not even started.

It took some doing but we finally got into the rooms across the street where more lanterns might be helpful. Having the fearful merchant gobble for us helped greatly, and so did the old women when she shouted across to her neighbours that we had protected her family and shared our food with them. At least that is what the merchant told us she said.

We worked feverishly, and by the time the sun came up, we had our lanterns ready to hang and archers in the room across from us and in the room above the next door further down the street. We also took the two long wooden poles from the weaver's loom and used them to brace up the badly damaged door so it would be harder to push in. Then we climbed up through the hole in the ceiling and pulled up the ladder behind us. The lads across the way had done the same. I know because I went across the street and checked on them before I climbed the ladder.

I had quickly explained to Captain White what we had done and made sure the men across the street with the other lanterns were ready to do the same before I re-joined John and Andy. We kept in contact the same way the people living on the street had done—by leaning out of the wall openings and shouting to each other.

Everything was quiet once the sun arrived. The street was empty except for the bodies of a dozen or so dead rioters, although one of them might be alive since once I thought I saw his leg twitch. After a while some women came and tried to search the bodies for loot. They ran off when I shouted out the wall opening at them and pointed an arrow in their direction.

We rested and slept all day except when one of the archers from across the way slipped out to retrieve whatever arrows he could find. An archer with an arrow nocked stood on either side of every wall opening to protect him whilst he picked up the arrows he could find and pulled them out the bodies. As soon he was finished, he searched the bodies for any coins or other loot he might find. There was not much, just a couple of pouches with a few coppers in them. The looters and rioters were clearly not rich men.

It was not until it first began to grow dark on our second night in the upper room that all hell broke loose. It was still light and we were just beginning to hang out our lanterns when it did.

****** *Chosen Man John Long picks up the tale.*

It started with a shout from Ralph Fisher, a fisherman's son from Herne Bay. He was on lookout duty in the wall opening on the other side of the street and had a better view up the street away from the market.

"Hoy the archers. A force of men be coming down the street. There looks to be hundreds of the buggers. A priest carrying a cross with a tilted spar be leading them."

"No pushing until I give the order," Wat shouted. He had rushed to the opening to see what he could see.

And then Wat leaned even farther out the opening to look down the street and said it again, and then some, for the men in the wall openings on the other side of the street.

"No pushing until I give the order. Put a man on either side of the opening with the third ready to step in fast if a string breaks. And everyone be damn sure to stay out of sight until I give the word. Then push long to pen them into the street."

Wat did not have to tell everyone to pull up the ladders to the upper rooms in case the rioters broke into the rooms below them. He had already told them that several times during the night, and gotten confirmation each time that every ladder was up. He also told them about the effect of pouring the shite-filled piss pot on the rioters trying to break-in, and ordered them to be prepared to use theirs the same way.

A great column of men almost immediately appeared in the lantern light. They were coming slowly and, as sure as God made old bread get green spots, they were being led by a priest carrying an Orthodox cross. We knew it was an Orthodox cross because it had three crossbeams and one was drooping as if Jesus had been lop-sided when the Romans nailed him to it.

Chapter Eleven

The Greek army arrives.

Richard had been wrong about the Greek army not arriving for a couple of days. The Greek horsemen he and his men had bloodied had not turned back. They were seen Monday at about midday when they came down the Adrianople road—and stopped close enough to the outer wall to see that the last bridge on the Adrianople road, the one over the moat in front of the city's outer wall, had been destroyed.

After a bit of sitting on their horses whilst the men at the head of the column talked, they all began banging their swords on their shields and rode along the road that ran along in front of the wall. They were calling attention to themselves. It was a strange thing for them to do.

Our men, at least those that had not poured into the city on the previous day to put down the riots, hurriedly manned the outer wall and watched as the Greek horsemen rode past to go further on down the wall. They had had no orders to push arrows at riders who were merely passing by and, as a result, did not do so.

It was my fault they did not push at them; I should have ordered the archers to take any Greek soldier who came too close. It was a mistake I quickly corrected.

******

"Why are they here ahead of the main army and why are they calling attention to themselves like that?" I wondered out loud to Henry and Richard.

"I can understand a scouting party arriving in force, but calling attention to themselves in such a way does not make any sense. They seem to be looking for a fight. Or could it be something else?"

Richard and I were at the Commandery prior riding into the city to visit our men who had been deployed yesterday to put down the rioters. Henry would remain behind to command archers on the wall.

"Well at least we got the word about their arrival," Henry said with a smile.

We certainly had. A steady stream of messengers had arrived at the Commandery because whoever was commanding each enclosure as the Greek horsemen rode past had dutifully sent a messenger to report their sighting and the riders' strange behaviour, and asked for instructions.

Moreover, every one of the galley captains whose men had not been sent into the city to put down the possible rioters reported that they had called out their men and manned the outer wall. They had not been sure who the riders might be, or what they should do, so they had not started pushing out their arrows even though their longbows had enough range to be able to reach the road from certain places along the wall.

"Well, there is only one way to find out what the Greeks are up to," I said. "The men and horses of the horse company riding with me as my guards are fresh and bored out of their minds. So I am going to ride out with them and try to find out. You stay here and command the city's defences."

Richard grumbled and said something about his being the one who should go because he was in command of the horse archers. I smiled and ignored him.

****** *Commander George Courtenay*

We rode out of the city's one remaining landward gate two hours later. It was a damnable hot and muggy day that did not even have the hint of breeze. There were eighteen of us in all; the sixteen men of the horse company assigned as my guards plus me and my apprentice, Nicholas Greenway.

Thomas Fiennes was the captain of the horse company. As was our custom, every man was riding his second best horse and leading his best. That way every rider's best horse was kept as fresh as possible for when it was needed most. Moreover, both horses were saddled so that, if necessary, the changeover could be made on the fly without slowing down.

We expected to be out for only one or two days at the most. Accordingly, and somewhat unusually for a company of horse archers, we brought only two company supply horses with us. Moreover, the supply horses were also saddled in addition to being loaded with extra arrows and grain for making bread and feeding the horses.

It was Richard's suggestion that led to our putting saddles on the supply horses so they too could be used as spare mounts; he thought the horses he and his fellow horse archers had been provided might need to be suddenly replaced as they were not nearly as strong and dependable as those he and his horse archers had left behind in England. They certainly were not all amblers.

Before we saddled up, I paraded the men and explained that we were going out to take prisoners to question, not to inflict casualties on the Greeks.

"So go for their horses and their riders' legs at all times, and do everything you can to take a prisoner and keep him alive. No mercies until a prisoner talks; we need to question as many prisoners as we can get our hands on."

We would probably try to use, I told the men, the old "wounded bird" ploy since it is relatively easy to shoot an arrow into a rider's horse or legs from behind if he is trying to escape from you. It was a ploy the horse archers understood because they had practiced it constantly and had periodically used it whilst they were in England.

In this case, it meant encouraging the Greek riders, who were likely to initially outnumber us by quite a margin, to continue chasing after us until their horses were tired and most of them had given up and turned back. Once we outnumbered those who were still pursuing us, we would mount our relatively fresh spare horses and double back to pick off those who had made the mistake of continuing to chase us.

It worked for Richard so it might work again; I hoped so.

******

"There they are, Commander. Moving past old farm house up ahead where the wall curves."

And so they were. I promptly gave the orders the men expected to hear.

"String your bows and watch for my hand signals. Horse holders are to go back to the second crossroads in our rear, the one we crossed about five or six miles back, and wait there. We will try to provoke the Greeks into chasing us in that direction. Everyone is to be ready to change horses on the fly and follow me either north or towards the open gate. Stay close and watch for my signal."

The men understood and nodded their agreement and understanding. They were all experienced horse archers and had heard similar orders many times, both during real battles on the approaches to Cornwall and when they were practicing.

Fourteen of us moved out and rode towards the Greek cavalry; four men including a steady sergeant took the company's remounts and began riding back to where they were to wait. Hopefully the Greeks and their horses were tired after spending the day riding along outer wall and none of the Greeks were bowmen. It was a lot to hope for. Well, we would know soon enough.

Those were my thoughts as I walked my horse towards the Greek horsemen with Thomas Fiennes riding on one side of me and Nicholas, my apprentice sergeant, riding on the other. Old Sam Smith, the company's senior sergeant and most experienced man, rode next to Nicholas. The company's horn blower, a young one-striper, rode right behind us. We rode slowly to keep our horses as fresh as possible and give the men leading our remounts enough time to get in position.

The Greek cavalry were three or four miles ahead of us and moving on the road that ran along the outside of the outer wall. We slowly caught up with them by riding directly toward them over the farmland and instead of along the curving road that fronted the city's moated wall. Our horses were relatively fresh and, if it was at all possible, we intended to keep them that way for as long as possible.

Suddenly the Greeks pulled up their horses and stopped. They had seen us.

We continued with our horses moving at a walk towards the distant Greek horsemen until, at my signal, and still walking our horses, we prematurely spread out into a line abreast as if we were preparing to launch a charge and engage the Greeks.

The Greeks had spent the day riding up and down along the city wall behaving as if they were looking a fight. Now we seemed to be offering them what they wanted. And best of all, from their point of view, they outnumbered us by a substantial margin.

Even though they were still more than a mile away, the Greeks suddenly wheeled around and came for us at a gallop. They had accepted our challenge. The Greek horsemen were riding hard and waving their swords over their heads when I, or so I hoped it would appear, realized my mistake in challenging them. I waved my hand in a circle over my head and pulled my horse around—and pointed back in the direction from whence we had come.

Thomas's horn blower, riding immediately behind us, instantly tooted a blast to draw the men's attention to my signal. His noise was expected but not needed; everyone had been watching for my signal and the order had been anticipated. The men wheeled their horses around and began following me as I led our retreat.

We were, or so we hoped it appeared to the Greeks, scared because we were outnumbered. As a result, we were running for safety—with the Greek cavalry riding hard in pursuit because they saw a good chance of catching up with us and cutting us down from behind.

Of course they were chasing us. It was well-known that it is much safer and easier to cut down a frightened and fleeing enemy whose back is to you than it is to face someone charging at you with a sword in his hand.

******

At first we moved away from the galloping Greeks at a fairly leisurely pace. The Greeks, after all, had more than a mile to catch up before they could reach us. We also pretended to flog our horses in a futile effort to get more speed out of them.

Unfortunately, our so it appeared, our desperate efforts to get away did not seem to work, perhaps because the reins and whips we appeared to be using so generously never actually touched our horses and the heels of our sandals never touched their flanks. It was a deception the horse archers constantly practiced.

The ground was dry and our horses' hooves were kicking up dust as we thundered down the road along the wall whilst giving the impression we were desperately trying to escape. Behind us the Greek riders were adding to the trail of dust our horses' hooves kicked up such that our pursers were riding in a cloud of dust that at times made it difficult for us to see the Greeks who were bringing up the rear.

It was the middle of a hot day and there was no wind. The dust hung over the road like a great cloud. Archers and auxiliaries were manning the wall and gaping at us as we galloped past them on our apparently weak and tired horses. Our prospects of outrunning our pursuers looked desperate, or so we hoped.

We were still well ahead of the Greeks after the first mile or so, but the gap continued to close as they galloped hard in an effort to catch us. Our horses were in good shape; theirs had been ridden all day. By the third or fourth mile, Greek riders began dropping out of the chase with blown horses and the rest were increasingly beginning to stretch out behind us in groups of twos and threes. The Greek thrusters were now close behind our designated stragglers and closing in on them.

Slowly but surely a handful of Greek thrusters caught up with us. The closest of them were a dozen or so Greek riders strung out behind a well-mounted fool who was lashing his horse with his reins and waving his sword in the air. The sword waver and his followers were close on our heels and, for several miles, only a few lengths behind and on the verge of catching up with our laggards.

What we were doing was offering the Greeks one of the company's classic "wounded bird" manoeuvers wherein we pretended to be distressed and fleeing in order to draw our pursuers after us because we were an "easy catch." Our initial purpose was to string our pursuers out further and further behind us by constantly being almost caught by those of them who rode the hardest.

So far it seemed to be working. Thomas Fiennes and I were riding at the front of our little company of fleeing Englishmen so we would be in the lead when we changed horses and turned to engage the Greeks; Thomas's lieutenant and his senior sergeant, Sam Smith, were riding as the rearmost stragglers to make sure the Greek riders never actually caught up with one of the company's men.

After we had ridden a few miles we began catching up to our relatively fresh remounts and riding alongside of them. Looking back over my shoulder I could see the Greeks strung out behind us for some distance. By now only a few thrusters were keeping up with us and still trying to get to our "stragglers," Sergeant Smith and the Lieutenant Milton. I reckoned that it was time for things to change.

"Change horses," I signalled by waving my hand over my head and pointing, first to the various horse archers and then to the remounts which were now slowly galloping just ahead of us at the same speed.

Our first casualty came when the archers began changing horses. One of my guards, I did not know who it was, somehow lost his grip as he tried to transfer over to the empty saddle of his remount, and went tumbling head over heels. The rest of us mounted our new horses successfully and wheeled them about whilst taking our bows off our shoulders and nocking arrows.

Chapter Twelve
Prisoners are taken and things become clearer.

The horse holder leading my replacement horse watched like a hawk as I came alongside my remount, leaned over to grab both sides of its leather saddle, and swing aboard. Changing horses and pushing out arrows from a longbow whilst galloping were amongst the most important things the Company's horse archers constantly practiced. It was literally, for the rider, the difference between living and dying; and often, for the Company, how well its horsemen did made the difference between winning and losing a battle or war.

Thomas's men were good at changing horses on the fly, and had been practicing and training their new horses whenever possible whilst they waited to accompany me to wherever I might be going next. I, however, had not changed horses whilst galloping for some years. As a result, Thomas and the sergeant in charge of the company's horse holders had been concerned at what might happen. And so was I, for that matter—it had been a long time since I last served as a horse archer and had to move from one galloping horse to another.

But it went well and I shouted my appreciation as I veered off on my fresh mount and got ready to gallop back towards our pursuers. Almost immediately another man moved in and changed to one of the three replacement horses galloping on the other side of the sergeant.

All around me horse archers were coming alongside their remounts, changing from one saddle to the other on the fly, and unslinging their bows and nocking arrows as they turned back towards our recent pursuers. It is hard to describe, or even understand, but at that moment I was as excited and elated as I ever had been in my entire life.

I pulled my horse around as soon as the others were ready and we started back towards our fallen archer and the on-coming Greek riders and their exhausted horses.

Within seconds Thomas and most of his men were in a line abreast on either side of me and we were closing fast with the first of our one-time pursuers with our arrows nocked and ready to push. It was about then, after we had changed on to our fresh horses, that most of the nearest of the Greeks, their most determined thrusters, finally began to realize what was happening, and also began turning back.

My new horse was one of the company's strongest, a six-year old brown with chopped bollocks. Later I learnt he had been assigned to me because he had been the steadiest of the company's mounts when the horse archers practiced changing horses on the fly. Thomas had assigned him to me because he had been afraid I might fall off my horse and somehow embarrass his company by getting myself hurt or killed. It was the best he could do.

Our move to change horses whilst at a gallop had absolutely confounded those of the pursuing Greeks who were close enough to see it happen. One of their thrusters was so determined that he kept coming and never did turn back. He was easily avoided and his horse, a big black, went down with several arrows in its side. We did not stop for the rider who went somersaulting out of his saddle; we would attend to him later.

Thomas's entire company galloped side by side back along the route of its false retreat. They soon began reaching and shooting down the individual Greek riders who were strung out for several miles along the path of their initial pursuit.

Each of the Greeks they reached, in turn, sooner or later realized what it meant when he saw a pack of archers galloping towards him with their bows drawn and arrows nocked. They inevitably responded by desperately pulling their tired horses around and trying to escape by riding back in the direction from whence they had come.

Turning around and trying to run for safety was the usual response of a man when he suddenly discovers that he is badly outnumbered by men who are coming to kill him. It did not work for the Greeks because of their tired horses and because they were strung out all along the line of their initial pursuit.

Their fate was sealed. We fell upon each of them as a pack of wolves might fall on an individual deer or two—and then continued on to the next man or small group.

We wanted prisoners so we continued chasing our recent pursuers and shooting arrows into their horses, and into their riders' arses and legs, until we had ridden the entire length of the Greek cavalry column and totally destroyed it. It was great sport. Even so, more than a dozen of the Greek riders were able to escape by breaking away from the main route of the fleeing Greeks and heading off by themselves in a different direction.

By the time we finished off the last of those we could catch, we had prisoners, my horse and I were breathing hard and sweating profusely, and I had a pain in my side and my legs were shaking. That and being terribly thirsty was my condition by the time I had used up almost all the arrows in my two quivers and watched as the last Greek horse went down and broke one of its rider's legs by rolling over him. The rider was a particularly good catch as all we would have to do to get him to talk was pull on his leg whilst offering to bring a barber to help him as soon as told us all we wanted to know.

It took the rest of the afternoon to gather up the prisoners and put down the wounded horses. We had lost one man killed and two slightly injured, all of which occurred when their horses went down for one reason or another. The Greeks lost seventeen killed and thirty-three captured. Many of prisoners had either been wounded, or had been hurt in some fashion when their horses went down, or both. Nineteen had escaped.

Our return with our prisoners was a triumphal march along the road that ran in front of the city's other wall. The cheering and waving archers and auxiliaries manning the wall had seen the Greeks' pursue us and been dismayed, and then watched in stunned disbelief as we came storming back on our fresh horses and rolled them up one after another.

The Greek with the broken leg missed it all. He had been draped over the front of a horse ridden by one of Thomas's archers and slept all the way.

******

We questioned the Greek prisoners under the shade from a line of trees running along a farmer's field near the one remaining road into the city. Translators hastily summoned from the city assisted us. It took all the rest of the day and the early part of the darkness that followed. Then, to the absolute astonishment of the Greeks, we rode off with their weapons and left them to fend for themselves.

What we had learned was that the Greek riders were all ambitious young noblemen and gentry who owned their own horses and had volunteered because they were seeking preferment from their king. A few were greybeards with military experience, but most of them were arrogant young fops with little or no experience and fine weapons they had never before used.

In any event, they became much less arrogant after a brief period of pleading ignorance—which quickly ended when I carried out my promise to cut off a finger off every time a man refused to talk to me or told me something that turned out to be a lie. One finger, and the resulting howling and sobbing of an arrogant young nobleman, was all it took.

To my surprise, the answers we received to our many questions were both consistent and somewhat hard to believe. They did, however, give me an idea. Accordingly, my guards and I rode into the city in the darkness, not to fall exhausted into our beds, but rather to visit the dungeons in the Empress's Citadel where the city's three Orthodox bishops were being held.

So far as I knew, no one had yet questioned them. That was about to change.

The Orthodox bishops were, I was told by the Empress's gaoler, arrogant and demanding. I briefly considered using a bit of finger chopping to warm up their memories and encourage them to call off the rioting. But I settled instead on a totally different approach—I would befriend them and tell them stories, stories that might even be true for all I knew, though I doubted it.

"I am George of Cornwall," I said through the Empress's interpreter as the three black-gowned greybeards sitting on the floor of their damp and dank little cell rose to their feet as the door was unbarred and we entered it. The Empress's gaoler held up a candle lantern so I could see them. The room was foul from several days of use.

"I got here as soon as I could. It is disgraceful, just disgraceful, what the Venetians and French have caused to be done to you and the other good men of the Orthodox Church. The King of Epirus should be ashamed of himself for betraying the Patriarch and making an agreement to give those treacherous Latins so many of your churches and your great cathedral with all its important relics and icons. I will explain this to the Empress the next time I see her and try to get you freed."

I was not sure what the three bishops expected me to say, but that was obviously not it. The eyes of the three men opened wide in surprise at my words. So did the mouth of one of them. His breath was most foul.

"What are you talking about? Who are you?" One of them finally demanded as he squinted to look at me. He had a great beard and was wearing a funny-looking hat with pointed corners.

"I am George Courtenay, Commander of Cornwall's free Company of Archers, the company whose galleys carried the Patriarch to safety those long years ago when the crusaders took the city. I know all about the betrayal of the Patriarch and your church because of the Venetian galleys we took several weeks ago and the Greek prisoners we just captured.

"But first," I ordered the turnkey who had come in to their cell with us, "bring these fine men some wine and food. And empty their shite pot. How dare you treat such important men this way?"

My translator, a white-haired old scrivener from the market, translated for me as I turned my wrath on the turnkey. *Later, of course, I begged the gaoler's pardon and slipped him a coin with my finger at my lips—and then had him transferred so he could be replaced by a Greek-gobbling archer.*

"You said the Patriarch and the Church have been betrayed," one of them asked. "What do you mean?"

I acted as if I was surprised at the question.

"Do you really not know? Theodore, the King of Epirus thinks his army is so powerful that he will win without the help of the Orthodox Church. He sees the Patriarch and your church as rivals for the people's coins and affections. So he wants to weaken the church and, above all else, keep the Patriarch from returning to the city. That is why he made a contract with the Venetians and the French to let their merchants return to the city and give them some of your churches for their priests, including letting a Venetian archbishop appointed by the Pope take over your great cathedral.

"Theodore of Epirus, the man you would have as emperor, thinks he will easily overwhelm the city with his great army and, as a result, does not need your church's help to do it. That is why he told the Empress's guards about your rising and deliberately held his army back—because he wanted to weaken the Patriarch by having the Empress's men cut down the Patriarch's supporters before his army arrived."

The bishops were clearly appalled at what they heard, but needed more convincing. So I laid on more lies.

"Do you truly not understand?" I asked, and then continued without waiting for an answer.

"The Patriarch was gulled into calling for your parishioners to rise. In fact, King Theodore does not want to share power with the Patriarch or anyone else when he becomes emperor. So he gulled the Patriarch into ordering your church's faithful to rise against the Empress. He did so knowing the Patriarch's strongest supporters would be cut down and the Orthodox merchants and priests reduced so there would be room for the Venetians and the French.

"It was many chests of coins the Venetians and French gave to King Theodore for the right of their merchants and money lenders to return to the city, and for the priests and bishops they will be bringing with them to take over your cathedral and many of your churches.

"I know that for a fact because I heard it with my own ears from the captains of the Venetian and French galleys we captured when the Venetians and French were carrying Theodore's army to Adrianople. And even you must admit that it was Venetian transports that carried Theodore's army down the coast. Do you really believe that the Venetians and French are helping King Theodore out of the goodness in their hearts?"

"It cannot be true," protested one of the bishops. He was aghast at the implications of what he was hearing.

"Of course it is true. Why do you think Theodore kept his army away after promising the Patriarch that his army would attack on the day your supporters rose? It was so your uprising would fail and the Patriarch's strongest supporters and some of the Orthodox merchants would be killed.

"Theodore sees the Patriarch as a threat to his power and wants to destroy the Church's strongest supporters. What better way to weaken the church and discredit it than have you call for an uprising and then warning the Empress's guards that it was coming so they would be ready to kill off the Patriarch's supporters, eh?"

******

We talked for a while, and then I called it a day and bid them farewell. In the lantern light as I walked with them to a hastily summoned horse cart, the three Orthodox bishops were gobbling intently to each other in Greek. They were still doing so and waving their hands all about as their cart clattered away over the cobblestones.

A strong guard of archers and axe-carriers went with the bishops. They would see them safely to the city's great Orthodox Cathedral with its massive dome and the grand residence where the current Patriarch's predecessor lived until he fled the crusaders years ago on a chartered Company galley.

I was tired but satisfied with myself as I bowed to the bishops and their horse cart clattered away surrounded by its guards. What I had told the bishops was in every way a believable story, and I was proud of myself for making it up on such short notice. And best of all, it was supported by the absence of the Greek army, the smoke in the air, the bodies of the rioters in the streets, and the red glow in the sky from the fires in the Orthodox quarter.

What pleased me most, however, was that I was able to mislead the bishops about the French even though they were not involved, at least not so far I knew. As my father always says, an Englishman can never go wrong by confusing the French and helping them make new enemies.

****** *George Courtenay*

What we had actually learned from the Greek horsemen and the Orthodox bishops was a more than a little different from what I had told the bishops, and had been somewhat of a surprise, a least to me—the Greek army had expected to march over the mountain in time to launch a major attack on the outer wall *yesterday*. And that was the night when the city's mostly Greek residents were supposed to rise in revolt in our rear.

The Greeks had assumed that a Sunday attack on the city would cause the Empress's forces to rush to man the outer wall and, in doing so, leave the city unguarded so their supporters could rise up that night and take it.

Unfortunately for the Greeks, their army's inexperienced commander, who had been given the post primarily because he was the brother of the would-be emperor, had delayed in getting word to the city's Orthodox priests that his army's arrival would be delayed due to its inability to cross the mountains. And then he made things worse by not even sending his cavalry in time to make a demonstration in front of the city walls before the Patriarch's call for an uprising was announced in the Orthodox churches.

As a result of following the orders they had received from the Patriarch, the city's Orthodox priests had called for the revolt to begin on the Sunday specified by the Patriarch even though none of the Greek army was had arrived to attack the outer wall.

The hundred or so of Greek riders were all the Greek commander could provide. They had been sent ahead to attack the outer wall in lieu of an attack by the whole army—but they arrived a day late and, when they did, they were not even able reach the wall because all but one of the bridges over the moat had been destroyed and the one remaining bridge had been raised.

Strangely enough, the Greek strategy had worked as intended. Almost all of the city's *available* defenders had indeed rushed to the city's outer wall to defend it when the Greek cavalry appeared. Even so, and only because the Greek cavalry had arrived a day late, most of the city's defenders did not rush to the wall—they were *not* available because they had already been sent into the city to help put down the riots.

****** *The Empress and William Courtenay*

"But why did George let them go? He should have killed them or sold them for slaves, both the Greek cavalrymen he took as prisoners and the bishops as well."

The Empress was irate when she learnt what my son had done with his prisoners and the bishops—he had freed them. I disagreed and told her as much.

"Letting the prisoners and bishops go was the right thing for my son to do," I said.

"Right thing to do?" she asked incredulously. "Freeing men so they can once again try to kill me and my family and take the throne?"

"Of course it was the right thing to do. Some of the prisoners George and his men freed will find their way back to the Greek army and the story will come out. The word will spread that they were once again defeated by a handful of English archers.

"Defeats in earlier battles, and the bad prophecies and warnings of the blind fortune tellers you sent out to scare the Greek soldiers, those are the kinds of things that cause mass desertions and fighting men to hold back when an attack is ordered.

"And it is the same for the bishops and the Metropolitan who answers to the Patriarch and leads the bishops and priests here in the city. They will be hesitant to order another rising if they think King Theodore might give some of their churches to the Venetians and prevent the Patriarch returning, and particularly if they think you will not.

"So stop your fretting about my son's decisions. I did not come out of retirement and sail all the way from England and Cyprus just to listen to you blather, eh? So come to bed and make yourself useful.

Chapter Thirteen

Mopping up the rioters.

No one paid attention to the six lanterns that were hanging down to light the street below us. It was not possible to see what was happening in the darkness at the other end of the street, but I could tell the street was filling up because in the dim light of the lanterns I could see the men assembling below me become more and more packed together.

The sound of the talking and shouting below us grew louder and louder as more and more of men assembled below us. Some of them seemed to be talking overly loud as men often do when they are nervous. If they had been proper soldiers their captains and sergeants would have long ago banged them on the side of their heads and told them to shut their mouths.

We waited nervously in the darkness of the upper rooms as the rioters once again filled the street below us. I was waiting for the men at the market entrance to begin launching their arrows. Surely they could see the mob forming up below me.

But what if Captain White was waiting for me to go first? I finally decided not to delay any longer. The men in the street were just too juicy a target to wait until someone told me what to do.

"ARCHERS ATTENTION." … "ARCHERS ARE TO GO LONG," I shouted out of the wall opening in my loudest voice. "ARCHERS, NOCK YOUR ARROWS" … "PUSH LONG" … "PUSH LONG." And with that I stood on one side of the opening and began pushing out arrows as fast as I could. John stood on the other side and began doing the same.

Across the narrow street at the other two wall openings I could hear the sergeants in the openings on the other side of the street instantly begin repeating my order, and, for a brief moment until it was drowned out by loud shouting and screaming, the familiar sound of archers' bowstrings hitting their leather wrist protectors.

My order had been expected and the arrows from my little band began flying out of the wall opening where we stood as fast as we could get them off. The mob on the street below me instantly dissolved into chaos with much shouting and screaming and with everyone running every which way in an effort to save themselves.

The chaos and confusion was to be expected; most of the men on the street did not know what was happening or, if they did, where the arrows were coming from.

A few moments later we began hearing the distinctive whoosh of a flight of incoming arrows. An unknown number of archers at the market's entrance had joined in with my little band of men who were standing at wall openings and pushing arrows into the mob below us every few seconds.

It was the first time I had ever given an order and had it repeated back to me. It was very thrilling. I decided then and there that I liked being a sergeant so I could tell my mates what to do.

******

The arrows kept coming and the screaming and movement in the street below us went on as long as they did. At some point, when I stopped looking down the street and reached to pluck an arrow from the pile at my feet, I realized that Andy had taken John's place on the side of the opening facing the market.

Our ability to see what was happening got worse and worse very quickly. Somehow during all the excitement at least half of our candle lanterns had gone out for one reason or another.

Finally, when I realized there was only one more arrow on the floor in front of me, I leaned out of the wall opening and called a halt.

"CEASE PUSHING." .. "EVERYONE SAVE AT LEAST TWO ARROWS."

I felt more than a bit foolish as I watched the street by the light of the remaining lanterns. Not much of the street was visible, but that part of the street right under the lanterns was covered with bodies, and a good number of them were moving. That was no surprise. For every man killed immediately by an arrow, three or four are only wounded and are still able to move enough to stagger away by themselves or with the help of their mates.

Before we started I had ordered everyone to save at least two arrows for an emergency. And now, dammit, I had only one arrow left for myself. All I could do was hope the lads in the wall openings across the street had done what I said they should do instead of what I did—and it would be even better if they never found out that I only stopped pushing out arrows when I had only one left.

The archers at the market entrance continued pushing arrows for a while longer, but then they too stopped.

Below us we could hear the familiar sobs and pleas for help from the wounded who had been abandoned on the battlefield when their mates ran. I had heard such sounds before, but not as loud and terrible as this. Or perhaps it just seemed that way because I was so close and the one who started it.

"Wat, what should we do about John?"

The question surprised me.

"What? Where is he?"

******

Captain White and a big party of archers showed up right after my men and I moved out into the street to begin picking up the arrows on the street and pulling and pushing them out of the dead and wounded Greeks. Some of them would be instantly usable and the points and shafts of many of the others could be reworked. As you might imagine, I quickly grabbed a couple that looked as though they were still useful and put them in my quiver.

We were not the first men into the street. Andy had gone out before Captain White arrived to search the dead and badly wounded Greeks and lift their purses. He offered to take the risk of doing so with the two of us splitting most of the takings.

Andy's takings turned out not to be very much. The men in the other wall opening obeyed my orders and stood ready with arrows nocked in case Andy was challenged. It was understood that the men at each wall opening would each get one share for being ready with five for Andy taking the risk and five for me being the sergeant who gave permission.

John Long's death took some explaining to Captain White and Lieutenant Evans, but not much.

"He must have been leaning out of the opening to push an arrow when he got hit by one of our incoming arrows, Captain. It took him in the side of his head so he never felt a thing, thank God."

"Shite happens, Wat. John was a good archer and we will miss him. But his time was up and there was nothing you or anyone else could have done to prevent it, so get over it."

"Yes, Captain," I replied. What else could I say, eh? Besides, I agreed with him.

Captain White had no more than arrived when the first of many weeping and distraught women, and a number of old men and boys, showed up to search among the dead and wounded for their friends and family members. Some of them looked familiar so perhaps they were the would-be looters who had also been here yesterday.

The dead and wounded rioters were a sad sight, for sure, but they had gotten what they deserved for trying to attack us. We watched the searchers like hawks with the intention of culling any who appeared to be looting instead of trying to find or help those who were down, not that it mattered because we had already been at the dead and dying ourselves and there was nothing much left for anyone to find.

******

Andy and I wrapped John in some bed linen from the market and lowered him down through the hole in the ceiling into the arms of Sergeant Taylor, who promptly surprised us all by tearing up when he carried John out to the handcart someone had found. I was not exactly unmoved myself, but managed to hide it.

After John was gently laid in the cart, some of the archers gathered around the cart and pulled off their knitted caps as the captain muttered a brief prayer and explained what would happen next.

"We will put him with the others until we can bury them all nice and proper in a churchyard with all the right words. In the meantime the rioting and looting in the city is not over. We will have to bide here for a while in case the looters come again."

Afterwards, Captain White walked over to me, paused for a moment, and then said something that sent my spirits soaring.

"You and your men did good work, Wat. Lieutenant Evans and I will not forget it. We will try to get more arrows and supplies to you and your men as soon as possible."

I started to tell the captain that we had already picked up quite a few arrows because of those pushed out by the archers at the market entrance, but then I decided not to bother him by mentioning it.

Chapter Fourteen

George whittles them down.

We could see the dust cloud raised by the approaching Greek army from where we were standing on the top of the wall in front of Enclosure Seventeen. Richard had ridden in yesterday evening with the news that the Greek army brought to Adrianople by the Venetians would probably begin arriving in force the next day. He was right. It was a scorching hot day

All of the Company's senior men were standing with me on the wall along with our apprentices and Eric, the commander of the Empress's guards. Also on hand were the commanders of the armies of two of the Empire's vassal states. We were all tired and red-eyed from staying up all night as a result of the heavy fighting that had occurred throughout the night in several parts of the city.

We had broken our fasts together at the Commandery that morning so we could tell each other what we knew about the state of the riots and the condition of our men. And, because he had just ridden in from a day of scouting, we listened carefully to what Richard had to say about what he had seen whilst watching the Greek army.

After we finished eating flatbreads, cheese, and duck eggs, and washing them down with bowls of surprisingly poor morning ale, we rode out together to examine the current state of the city's defences.

Our inspection tour stopped for a few moments at Enclosure Seventeen. It was where the road from Adrianople entered the city wall through what was called the "Southern Gate." The Southern Gate was one of the gates that neither the Greek army nor anyone else would be able to use for some time.

It was no longer usable. Not only had the bridge over the moat in front of the Southern Gate been pulled down, but the gate itself had been blocked with so much rubble and dirt piled up against it that it would probably be easier for the Greeks to break through the wall or try to climb over it than try to force their way through the gate.

Everyone was optimistic and we spent a good deal of time assuring one another that the Greeks did not know the Southern Gate was blocked and were, as a result, likely to waste time and men trying to take it. *Or so we initially hoped.*

I shared my lieutenants' hopes, but considered them overly optimistic. That was because much of the work to block the Southern Gate and remove its bridge had been done by the city's mostly-Greek citizens during their mandatory work mornings. As a result, the Greek spies in the city were almost certain to know about its blockage and the similar blockings of many of the city's other landward gates.

In fact, all the landward gates in the city's outer wall had been blocked but one, the *Farmers' Gate,* which was the gate nearest the river estuary that flowed alongside one side of the city. Indeed, I was counting on the Greeks knowing the Farmers' Gate was still open and all the others blocked—because we wanted them to make a major effort to break into the city at the Farmers' Gate where we and our allies in the states' forces were prepared to give them an especially warm welcome.

******

My lieutenants and I spent the entire day reviewing the city's defences and what moves we would make under various circumstances. Whilst we were doing so, the rest of the Venetian-carried Greeks finally began arriving in force and setting up the tents of their siege camp all along the outer defensive wall on the landward side of the city. They had somehow acquired a surprisingly large number of horses, wagons, and camp followers for an army that had travelled part of the way by sea.

After talking it over, my lieutenants and I agreed that our condition was not altogether bleak despite the previous two nights of rioting in the city, and last night's intense fighting at several of the churches and markets in the Orthodox quarters.

Indeed, some things were quite encouraging. For instance, the Latin Quarter of the city, according to Eric whose axe-men had been deployed there, had been quiet both nights. The Latins in the city's population were sticking with the Empress, not that they had much choice if they wanted to avoid once again being massacred by the Greeks who constituted a majority of the city's people.

Similarly encouraging, according to Harold Lewes, the Company's toll collections which our galleys were collecting, were continuing and there was no sign of any sea-borne threat on the city's three seaward sides. Harold assured us that our galleys were on alert and safe, and immediately available to carry the Empress and our men to safety in the unlikely event the Greeks were able to break through our defences and get into the city.

"In the meantime, we are continuing to collect large amounts of coins from the Empress's subjects and others who want to book passages on our transports and flee before the Greeks attack."

"It helps," Harold went on to say with a big smile and a nod towards my father, "that the Empress ordered that no one else was to be allowed to carry passengers from the city whilst it was under the threat of an attack."

What would happen that night when darkness fell was the big question. And although no announcement had yet been made, it was obvious to everyone that the Company's foot archers would only temporarily be able to be help the Empress's guards keep the peace in the city. Once the Greek army arrived, most of them would have to man the walls to help fight off the Greeks.

****** *Horse Archer Captain Alan Strong*

My company was down to eleven men because we lost another two men the day before yesterday, one killed and one badly wounded. Of the eleven of us, eight were standing with me on a hillside overlooking the Greek army passing along the Adrianople road in front of us in great clouds of dust, and the two I could most spare were at our battle camp guarding the supply wagon and tending Mark Bell, our wounded man.

We did not know for sure if the Greeks had reached the city yet because we were more than a day's ride from it, but it seemed likely as their army had been passing in front of us almost continuously since yesterday morning.

At the moment the nine of us were in a stand of trees quietly watching some men who had walked away from the main Greek column on the road that was a mile or so south us. There were forty or fifty of them, and they looked as though they were going off to forage for food and women in the little cluster of houses that were in and around a stand of trees three or four miles north of the main road.

There was no reason to risk our necks unnecessarily, so we were standing next to our horses whilst we waited for the Greeks to get *closer* to the little village—and *further away* from the road on which the Greek army was slowly marching towards Constantinople.

My company had been down to only me and seven somewhat able-bodied men when we finally came off the mountain with Commander Ryder, but we picked up two newbies newly arrived from Cornwall and still green with seasickness and five men from Edmund Down's company, the poor sod.

Unfortunately for Edmund, his company had been disbanded when he and eight of his men lost some of their toes to the cold pox on the mountain. Turned black with a pox from the cold, their toes did, and began to smell and hurt most terrible. So did a couple of the toes of one of my men, for that matter, Ewan Spitalfield for one, him that was a tailor before he went for an archer.

I am not sure what happened to Ewan. No one knew where he was when the lads and I went to visit him at the hospital which had been set up next to the Commandery. They remembered him at the hospital but had not seen him for several days. Ewan was not the type to run so he was probably sent somewhere on limited duty just as Edmund had been.

In addition to losing some of his men with poxed feet, Edmund also lost one man who fell in the river whilst pushing out arrows and was never seen again. He, Edmund that is, ended up with soft duty for his troubles. He was now hobbling about on a stick and drinking wine every night whilst sitting on his arse atop one of the gates into the city. Indeed, whilst we was out here sweating our arses off in the hot sun, he was probably sitting up there in the shade with a bowl of wine and looking at the arriving Greeks.

I had tried to count the Greeks what was marching past us on their way to the city, but finally stopped when someone said something and I forgot my count. But there was certainly a shite pot full of them, and that was a fact. They stretched along the road to Constantinople as far as the eye could see.

On the other hand, to my surprise, the Greeks did not seem to have as many horse carts as I would have expected or much in the way of cavalry, camp following women, or sutlers. As I recall from years back, the armies of both Cornell and the rebel barons had many more of all of them when they came against us in Cornwall.

What I learnt later, as everyone now knows, was what we were seeing was only a part of the Greek army, and that even more of the bastards were coming in behind this lot. This bunch had come part of the way by sea which is why they did not have so many of an army's usual wagons, cavalry, sutlers, and camp followers.

******

We watched quietly whilst the men who had peeled off from the column got closer and closer to the little village. I waited to give my battle orders until the foragers were far enough away from the main column so a relief force, if one was available and came out of the men marching on the road, would not be able to get to us in time to save them.

There was a little stream running near us. All of us, horses and men, had drunk our fill when we reached it about an hour earlier.

"Time for one last drink of water, lads. Get it now because only God knows when there will be time for another."

Finally, about ten minutes later, I decided that the forage party had gotten far enough away from the road. I had waited longer than usual because of our sad experience a couple of days ago—when we lost a couple of lads due to the unexpected appearance of some Genoese crossbowmen. One of my men was killed and the other, with a bolt still in his leg, was in our battle camp being tended by our camp guards.

"Mount up, lads, and string your bows. And may Jesus and the saints bless us one and all.

After I got myself settled in my saddle I made an effort to reassure my men.

"We should be all right," I said so they all could hear me. "Yonder forage party looks to be too far from the road to run back to the column before we hit them, and there are no cavalry in sight who might ride out in time to drive us off and save them.

"But there is no sense taking unnecessary chances—so we will do the usual and pull up some ways off from the foragers, and push our arrows into them from there until they break and run. And the horse holders are to go around to the north three or four miles and wait there for us in case something unexpected comes up and we have to run for it and need fresh horses."

And, with that settled, and the men clearly pleased with my caution, I made the sign of the cross, scratched the lice in the hair around my dingle to settle them, swung myself up on my horse, and handed the reins of my spare horse to one of the company's two remaining horse holders.

Then I put my heels in my horse's ribs and off we went. She was a mare, my riding horse was. It was the first time I had ever ridden one in all my years in the company. Even worse, she was not a natural-born ambler and my arse was getting sore.

The lads followed me with my lieutenant, Alfred Black, riding on one side of me and the company's first sergeant, Paul from Croydon, riding on the other. We rode at a slow trot and curved around as if we were not going for the foraging party. It was damn hot and we began sweating profusely as soon as we came out of the shade provided by the trees, at least I did.

My plan was simple and I could tell from watching their faces that my men agreed with it— we would try to appear to be non-threatening members of the Greek army until it was too late for the foragers to escape or for anyone to come out of the column to rescue them. Accordingly, we trotted peacefully, not towards the foragers, but towards the head of the column as if we were new horsemen coming in to join the army or returning scouts coming in to report what we had seen.

Not until we were directly between the foraging party and the great mass of men and wagons moving along the road did we change direction and head directly towards the foragers. And even when we did move towards them, it was only at a leisurely pace, a slow and easy canter.

My hope was that the foragers would think we had come out from the column to help them, or perhaps to get to the little village and forage in it before they did. With a little luck, everyone marching in the cloud of dust that hung over the column would think the same, particularly since the foragers outnumbered us. If they did, the alarm would not be sounded until it was too late to save the foragers or, even better, it would not be sounded at all.

Our plan seemed to work, at least at first.

******

We slowed down and rode at a relaxed trot in the boiling sun until we were between the foragers and the men marching in the cloud of dust that hung over the seemingly endless Greek column. No one came out of the column to challenge us, at least initially. It was as if we did not exist.

That no one came out to challenge us was somewhat surprising since we and our brother companies had been constantly raiding the column ever since it marched out of Adrianople. We had done so by riding along it, just out of range of an arrow from a regular bow, and using our longbows to push our arrows into the men and horses walking along the road or shitting or cutting grass or eating on either side of it.

Our attacks inevitably caused delays and confusion amongst the Greeks and discouraged them from sending out foraging parties. They also caused us to run through our supply of arrows rather quickly since they were virtually impossible to retrieve. That was why we had been surprised when we saw this one—so much so that my first thought upon seeing it was that the Greeks might be baiting a trap. More likely, however, it was going out because the men in the foraging party were low on supplies and getting hungry.

The Greeks had responded to their mostly unanswered losses by putting together files of crossbowmen from amongst their Genoese mercenaries and spacing them out along road to act as rapid reaction forces. That was how they were able to kill one of my men and put a bolt into the leg of Geoffrey Cook, the son of Thomas Cook, one of the Company's original archers.

It was the need to retrieve our arrows after we used them that caused my eyes to light up when I saw the foraging party head off from the main column. We were not short of arrows, but it was still early days and we had already opened the third of the five arrow bales in our supply wagon.

Richard's orders had been quite direct and we had all heard them. Priority was to be given to keeping the Greeks from getting food to feed their army. That meant killing their cart-pulling horses, attacking their foragers, and, wherever possible, wounding the Greeks instead of killing them—since wounded men would help eat up their supplies and dead men would not.

In other words, killing or wounding Greek foragers and retrieving the arrows we used on them was a pangloss, the best of all possible worlds so far as me and my lads were concerned.

******

At first the foragers merely stopped and watched us as we rode towards them. Then, as we approached them, they hurriedly gathered together and raised a shield wall facing us with the large infantry shields they were carrying. They obviously had planned ahead and had a good captain.

"Alfred, take your men and ride over there towards that big tree and spread out; Paul, you take yours the other way and do the same. Tell your men to take any pushes they think they can make. No wasting of arrows."

The men moved out and arrows began to fly moment later. The Greeks responded to having a couple of their men hit by spreading around in a half circle to face us whilst they crouched behind their shields. We saw no crossbows but there appeared to be a few men amongst them carrying regular bows.

"Do not get too close, lads. They have archers amongst them. Try to take out the archers first."

And then, less than a minute later, after taking a long look at the distant road to make sure it was safe, I added another order.

"Spread out and circle all the way around them, but stay awake in case we have to leave in a hurry, but for God's sake watch where you place your pushes; do not hit one of us who is on the other side of the Greeks."

At first, placing our men all the way around them did the trick. In an effort to protect themselves, the foragers formed a complete circle facing outward with the shields each man carried—and in so doing left the backs of the men facing outward available to the archers on the other side of them.

. The result was inevitable; several more of the foragers were hit as me and the lads moved around whilst we looked for a clean push.

The remaining able-bodied foragers, forty of so, must have had a particularly capable captain, for they soon responded by doing something totally unexpected; they began forming very tight little circles of five or six men each with their overlapping shields facing outward and one or two wounded men in the middle.

Setting themselves up in such a way was a smart thing for them to do because made them virtually unreachable with our arrows. It also left unprotected those of their wounded who were not able to stand with them. We, of course, did not push at those who were seriously wounded because we wanted to leave them alive to help eat up the Greeks' food.

Fortunately, standing in tight little circles also made their bows unusable. We had a standoff and time was on their side—sooner or later help was likely to come from the main column or darkness would arrive and they would be able to slip away to safety.

Sergeant Black was the one who broke things apart. He did so by moving himself and his three men back and out of the way, and then he motioned for the Greeks to run for safety though the opening he created. And some of the fools did; they threw their shields and weapons down, abandoned the wounded men they were shielding, and ran for the distant road. Perhaps they thought they were being offered a chance to escape. If that was what they thought, they were wrong.

"Mount up, but wait," I shouted as loudly as I could. "Let them run."

We waited on our horses until the disorganized runners were clear of those who remained standing firm in three tight little circles. It was every would-be escaper running separately for himself, and it was a fatal mistake for many of those who ran.

"Now lads, ride them down. Wound them if you can. And be sure to pick up your arrows."

The next few minutes were hectic. The fleeing Greeks had run in every direction, but mostly towards the cloud of dust hanging over the column on the road to Constantinople. We responded by splitting up with every archer galloping after one of the runners.

A few of the Greek runners got away whilst we were chasing the others and picking up arrows. In several cases they got away because it took more time than it should to retrieve our arrows because they had to be pulled out of, or pushed through, a wounded man who began jumping about as we did. The problem was that the wounded Greek runners usually had to be knocked on the head to put them to sleep before we could get the arrow out of them.

After we retrieved all the arrows we could quickly find, including pulling them out of the dead and wounded, we reassembled and rode towards the little village. As we did, we watched as the Greeks who had stayed together began slowly walking back towards the dust-covered road to Constantinople.

The escapers stayed close together all the way back to the road, always ready to instantly form the tight little circles of infantry shields that are so effective against archers, and so rarely used. They had escaped, yes, by abandoning, at least temporarily, their dead and wounded. But they had not brought back any food or water with them. Hopefully, they would come back later to bring in their wounded so they would have to feed them.

The sun was unbelievably hot as we finally headed towards the little village and the shade of the trees around it. My men and horses desperately needed water and a bit of a rest, and so did I.

Chapter Fifteen

Preparations and uncertainties.

The main body of the Greek-led army raised by the Orthodox Patriarch finally reached the walls of Constantinople in the blistering heat of mid-summer. It arrived weeks after it was expected, and long after the popular uprising that was supposed to occur at the same time and support its attack. The horse archers' constant attacks all along the way had delayed and confused the army's leaders and reduced its strength through casualties and desertions.

Despite the archers' initial successes, the Greek-led army that finally arrived was intact and still huge and powerful. On the other hand, it was also untrained, poorly led, and woefully short of supplies. Surprisingly, those were not significant problems, at least not according to the Orthodox priests who had accompanied the army. To the contrary, they assured the army's soldiers that victory was assured because God would make up the shortfalls.

Things were no better for the Greeks in the city even though they constituted the great majority of the city's population. For various reasons, the city's Orthodox priests and their parishioners had become confused and uncertain as to what they should do next. Encouraging their confusion and uncertainty was that the news had spread that their would-be emperor was being assisted by the Venetians and French in return for promises of great benefits, many of which would be at the expense of the local Greeks and their priests and churches.

The possibility of the Venetians returning to Constantinople caused a great deal of anger in the city's population. The Greek-gobbling priests and their parishioners hated and feared the Venetians because they remembered their unacceptable behaviour that had led to the "massacre of the Latins" during their grandfathers' time and the Venetians' participation, fifteen years earlier in 1204, when they helped the crusaders of the Fourth Crusade take Constantinople and replace the Byzantine Empire with the Latin Empire.

In contrast, they did not hate the Latin Empire's Empress, they just disliked her despite her efforts to keep the Venetians out in order to protect them, mostly because she prayed with the help of Latin-gobbling priests and looked to the Pope to tell her what God wanted her to do instead of the Patriarch. But at least she and the emperor before her had left her Orthodox subjects and their churches alone.

In essence, the thought George had planted in the minds of the Orthodox bishops about the Venetians helping Theodore in exchange for being allowed to return to Constantinople and re-take some of their old churches had struck home. That King Theodore of Epirus would take some of their churches and give them to the Venetians in exchange for the Venetian's assistance in his becoming the emperor was entirely believable to the Orthodox bishops and their priests. Theodore was, after all, a Greek king.

Similarly, losing some of their churches to the Latin-gobbling priests of the Venetians and the French was also entirely believable to the Orthodox priests and bishops—because they themselves had done the very same thing by taking over the Venetian churches after the "Massacre of the Latins" thirty-seven years earlier in the spring of 1192. Now, or so it seemed, they would have to give them back if the Empress was defeated.

Indeed, it was the massacre of the Latins, many of whom were Venetians, resulting from the previous Patriarch's call that led the vengeance-seeking Venetians to encourage the crusaders of the Fourth Crusade to sack the city.

That sacking, in turn, caused the Patriarch and the then-emperor, a Greek, to flee—and in the chaos and confusion Cornwall's Company of Archers had somehow ended up with the gold and silver coins in the emperor's treasury and many of the Orthodox Church's priceless relics and icons.

Now everyone's role was reversed. The Venetians were attempting to return to Constantinople with the help of the Orthodox Patriarch. They, the Venetians that is, were helping their once-hated enemies.

The Venetians were now helping the Greeks because the emperor installed by crusaders, and now the empress who followed him, had refused to let the Venetians and their Latin-gobbling priests return to their previous dominance in order not to upset their many Orthodox subjects in the city and its empire.

It was all very confusing and everything was uncertain—which meant it was a splendid opportunity for the Company during that inevitable tender moment when coins and power are changing hands and no one has a firm grip on them.

In essence, and despite all the bad blood between the Venetians and the Orthodox Church in the recent past and the generosity of the Empress, the Patriarch had ordered his bishops and priests to support the Orthodox army and the would-be emperor's deal that would allow the Venetian merchants and priests to return so long as the Patriarch was allowed to return to his cathedral and splendid residence.

So what did the city's Orthodox bishops and priests tell their followers that God wanted them do?

It was an easy decision for them to make. They were traditional churchmen. So they carried out their Patriarch's order by dutifully informing their flocks of parishioners that God wanted them to rise against the Empress and her supporters. They were encouraged to do so by the Patriarch's trusted assistants who quietly passed the word to the churchmen that the Venetians would be dealt with once again after the Patriarch and the Church hierarchy were safely back in the city.

All the archers could do in response to everything that was happening in the city was to thank God for the city's Greeks getting the dates wrong so the city did not rise against the Empress on the day the Greek army arrived, and pray for heavy rains that would keep everyone inside instead of rioting in the streets and attacking them in the rear.

****** *Commander George Courtenay.*

Work on improving the city's defences did not stop when the Orthodox army began arriving and setting up its siege camp outside the city's landward outer wall. If anything, it increased with many of the full-time wall workers being re-assigned to help the men and women who had already been hard at work for several months making additional arrows.

Almost all of the archers on limited duty due to their wounds and poxes were assigned to be sergeants over the arrow makers. And, of course, additional bales o arrows continued to pour in from Cyprus, the Company's shipping posts, and the many merchants everywhere with whom we had placed orders. There was no one with whom we were unwilling to deal when it came to getting more arrows for our longbows, even the Moors.

Even my father did his part. He got some of the Company's sailors who were carpenters off Harold and began buying wood in the city's markets and using it to make catapults. He even accepted my suggestion as to where they should be located.

"Initially place them in the enclosure of the states' forces, and spread the word that they have been placed there to protect the states' forces from a Greek attack. That is a reasonable thing to say since that is where the Greeks are most likely to attack because the gate in the outer wall is still usable."

In fact, I was not sure we would need catapults anywhere unless the Greeks settled in for a long siege and began building siege towers. But building and placing them would keep him out of my hair. In any event, they turned out to be quite useful for another reason entirely.

Similarly, the training intensified both for the foot archers and their auxiliaries, and for the state forces that had come in to stand with the Empress. The latter were very mixed in that the princes and kings of three of the more distant states had come in with their armies, such as they were, whereas those of the other four states of the Latin Empire had merely sent token forces with various and sundry excuses whose only common theme was that they needed to stay at home to defend their own lands.

Only the Latin state of Trebizond on the Black Sea was excused from sending its army to help defend Constantinople. It had gotten a pass from both the Empress and the Patriarch because of the fact that it was completely surrounded by the lands of the Islamic state of the Seljuks. In essence, its Christians were uniquely united by the fact that they feared the Moslems who surrounded them even more than they hated each other for making the sign of the cross incorrectly.

The three Latin states which sent only token forces, according to my father, would have new kings on their thrones as soon as the Orthodox army was defeated. He was rather emphatic about the fact that the Empress was seriously pissed at the no-shows and intended to separate them from their thrones and heads as soon as possible. Her intentions were something my father would know being as he had been a particularly close personal friend of the widowed Empress when he had been a young man. More importantly, their friendship had resumed, some said reignited, when he and the Company's other retirees came to Constantinople to help the Company defend it.

What was not mixed was the quality of the state forces. With the exception of the Bulgarians, they had all arrived with very poor weapons and uniformly unready to do anything except eat and foul their campsite. The same was true of their princely commanders and nobles except that they had better swords and very shiny armour.

As a result of the poor quality of the state forces, Henry and my father had vetted them carefully for me, and even sent some of the states' men and camp followers home as hopeless mouths to feed who could not be made useful in any employment.

The rest of the state forces were camped out and being learnt to fight all along the newly enclosed road whose roadway and walls ran for some miles—all the way between the one remaining usable gate in the city's outer defensive wall to the one remaining usable gate in its inner defensive wall.

As you might imagine, the resulting long and narrow enclosure, Constantinople's largest by far, soon became quite foul. On the other hand, it had something very few of the archers had to make up for it—direct access to the delights and markets of the city without having to climb over a moat or wall.

The princely commanders of the state forces fared much better than their men and did not bide with the men they commanded. Each already had an elegant palace in the city's Latin Quarter and, with the exception of the prince who commanded the Bulgarians, was rarely seen except at court—which was a blessing both for their men and for George and his lieutenants as it spared them of their insipid chatter and foolish suggestions. They did, however, according the Empress's daughter, wear fine clothes and bow most elegantly.

On the other hand, there had also been a number of bright spots for the Company. Among them was the arrival of the initial Greek forces *after* the uprising in the city instead of at the same time, the fact that the main force of the Greek army was still a week or two away from arriving, and the success of the horse archers' attacks on the army's stragglers and foragers. Taken together, they greatly encouraged everyone who supported the Empress or was considering it.

The Greek army's unexpectedly late arrival also suggested that its commander would have to quickly launch a massive initial attack as soon as the main body of the army arrived. He would have to do so, it was commonly thought, so his army's men would not starve as a result of not being able to forage in the countryside for food and so they could return to their homes in time to harvest their crops as they had been promised. That was somewhat encouraging because it suggested the Greek army's attacks might begin without adequate preparation.

Another somewhat bright spot for the city's defenders had to do with the leadership of the state forces. After much discussion and several shouting matches in the presence of the Empress, Henry had been assigned to command all of the state forces except the Bulgarians.

Some of the lords who were the state commanders and captains had been pissed off by the decision to let Henry command their soldiers and threatened to leave. But they soon came around when their choices were quietly explained to them by the Empress's new chamberlain—allow your men to be learnt to fight on the walls and in sorties, and do whatever the archer Henry Soldier tells them to do, or the Empress will not let you leave the city alive and you and your family will be replaced as the lords over your lands.

The state commanders, being both experienced statesmen and reasonable men, instantly agreed with that Henry was indeed a fine fellow and should be the one to give orders to their men.

Chapter Sixteen

We launch a sally.

We stood together on the wall and watched as the Orthodox army continued setting up its camp right in front of us in the dust and glaring sun. There were men and women walking around everywhere. It looked like an overturned ant hill and from the walls we could periodically hear snatches of distant voices.

The main part of the would-be emperor's army carried by the Venetians had begun arriving yesterday morning, and now its tents and wagons filled the area beyond the moat in front of the city's outer wall for as far as the eye could see. The huge camp appeared to be totally disorganized and a dark haze of dust and smoke constantly hung over it.

The Greeks also appeared to be unaware of the distance a longbow arrow could carry. Some of them had begun setting up their tents next to the moat that ran in front of the outer wall on which we were standing. It was as if the Greeks thought that having the wall and its moat between us and them would protect them from harm.

"That is a piss pot full of men," said Michael Oremus quietly. "And there are many more to come."

"It is a pity we closed off so many of the wall gates. This would be a good time to make a sally whilst they are so disorganized and defenceless," Richard suggested wryly.

And then he added a suggestion.

"We could send some of our men sallying out of the one gate that was left to be usable. And the others could go over the walls and then over the moat on the ladders they use to get over the city's inner wall and its moat."

Everyone nodded their agreement and smiled a pleased and satisfied smile at Richard's suggestion—because how and when to launch just such a sortie had already been extensively discussed and planned whilst he and his horse archers were off fighting in the mountains. It was one of the reasons why the state forces were camped where they were camped and the moats had been drained and worked on earlier in the summer.

But Richard was certainly right that the disorganized chaos we were looking at was too good of an opportunity to pass up. A few minutes later I began giving orders and messengers began galloping off to deliver them.

Our plan was to fall upon the Greeks and take them by surprise.

The two hundred or so horsemen of the state forces, mainly knights carrying swords and old-fashioned tournament lances, would start the sortie and lead the way. They would come charging out of the city's one remaining usable gate in the outer wall, immediately cross the only remaining moat bridge which was in front of the gate, and gallop all the way through the disorganized Orthodox camp causing as much death and destruction as they could manage. The states' horsemen would be followed out of the gate and over the bridge by all of the states' foot soldiers who would fall upon the Greek encampment and attempt to do the same.

If all went well, the states' riders would spread out and ride through the entire length of the Orthodox camp, and then turn around and make another pass back through the entire length of a different section the camp until they were back at the one remaining usable gate. At some point the riders would meet their foot soldiers, who would then turn around and join the riders to ravage and loot their way back to the gate where the sally began.

What neither the states forces nor our own men had been told, was that when our lookouts on the city's outer wall saw the men of the states' forces charging out of the gate, they would pass a signal along the wall from company to company and all the available foot archers, those stationed in the narrow enclosures that stretched between the city's outer defensive wall and its inner defensive wall, would also attack.

Our men would come over the wall on the long ladders they used to come and go from their enclosures, wade across the moat on the narrow causeway that had been installed in front of each galley company's enclosure when the moat was drained "for repairs and deepening."

The foot archers would advance only as far beyond the moat as they needed to go in order to push their arrows at the men and animals in the Orthodox camp. They would not have to advance far, if at all, because the edge of the Orthodox camp began at the far side of the moat.

Launching a sortie large enough to do substantial damage to the Greek army was doable, but it would not be easy. For one thing, in order to keep our ability to launch such a sortie from being known to the Greek spies, the archers and their auxiliaries had never practiced going over the outer wall on their ladders, nor ever even tried to cross the moat in front of it. They had all, however, much experience using their ladders to get over the inner wall and its moat.

What was important was that the archers did *not* need to use their ladders to cross the foul, black water of the slightly wider outer moat, at least not in the way they used their ladders to cross the moat in front of the city's inner wall in order to enter the city. They would, instead, wade across on the narrow under-water causeway we had built into the moat in front of each enclosure for that very purpose.

Each causeway was several feet under the moat's foul and dark water, and was only wide enough for one man. We had built them by stacking up dirt and rocks when the moat was emptied for deepening.

Only the captain and lieutenant of the galley company in each enclosure knew exactly where his enclosure's causeway was located a few feet under the moat's foul waters—and even they had not been told why they needed to know where it was located, only that they must know and at all times have a rope available that was twice as long as the moat was wide. They would lead their men as they waded over their enclosure's causeway to participate in the attack, and then lead them back when they ran out of arrows.

The forces that had come in from the Empress's vassal states were another matter entirely, particularly in terms of sortieing out to do substantial damage to the Greeks. They would do so by coming directly out of their camp on the road that ran through it.

The road along which they were camped ran from the one still-usable gate and moat-bridge in the city's outer wall to the one remaining usable gate and moat in the city's inner wall. They were the two gates closest to the river estuary called the Golden Horn that flowed with fresh water just outside the city wall.

Work was still going on to finish the new interior walls that would run along both sides of what had already become the only usable road into the city, the road along which the states' forces were camped. When the new walls were finished in the next few days, they would run on both sides of the roadway all the way from the city's great outer defensive wall to its equally formidable inner defensive wall.

In other words, the states' forces, like the galley companies of the archers, would be camped in a walled enclosure of which every inch of ground could be reached by an arrow pushed out of a longbow by an archer standing on one of the walls that surrounded it. That all of the new interior walls had been installed with that in mind was a fact known only to me and a handful of my senior lieutenants.

Soldiers of the state armies were permanently camped in tents and wagons all along both sides of the road with their women, horses, and supplies. As a result, an enemy or traveller or anyone else who came through the gate in the outer wall would immediately find himself in the middle of several thousand soldiers, soldiers who would have to fight if the intruder were an enemy because the new walls that now ran along both sides of the road meant they had no place to run.

In essence, if the soldiers of the Greek-led Orthodox army somehow got through the Farmers Gate, the one still-usable gate in the city's outer wall, they would have to fight their way through the men of the states' armies camped all along both sides of the road to get to the Farmers Gate in the city's inner defensive wall which, hopefully, would be closed and strongly defended behind its moat.

And, even worse for the invaders, they would have to do so while the archers from the galley companies camped in the enclosures on either side of the road were pushing arrows down on them from atop the interior walls that ran all along both sides of the road.

In other words, the roadway between its one remaining gate in its outer defensive wall and the one remaining gate in its inner defensive wall would be death trap if Orthodox army charged into it—which is exactly why my lieutenant commander, Henry Soldier, the Company's master at fighting on land, had insisted that interior walls be built all along both sides of the roadway.

As you might imagine, we intended to do everything possible to lure the Orthodox army into trying to fight its way through the city's one usable gate where they would be particularly vulnerable, as opposed to launching its attacks on the gates which had been rendered unpassable by the removal of their bridges and the piling up of huge amounts of dirt and rubble to block them.

What concerned us was that the Greek spies in the city might have reported that *all* of the city gates in the outer wall had been blocked and the bridges over their moats destroyed. Hopefully, the Orthodox spies knew and reported that food supplies and firewood were still coming into the city through the Farmers Gate, and that meant that its draw bridge was still down.

In any event, in the unlikely event the captains of the huge Greek-led army did not already know the Farmers Gate was still usable, they soon would—when the men of the Empress's vassal states sortied out of it and fell upon their newly established camp.

Of course the enclosure where the states' forces were camped was where we wanted the Greeks to attack. It is always better to have someone other than our archers do as much of the fighting as possible.

******

It was midway through the afternoon by the time we were ready to launch our sally. And it was only after there had been a heated dispute between Henry, Richard and me—we had each claimed the right to lead the riders of the states' forces into the Orthodox camp. There were only a few of our horse archers in the city, my guards and a few who had either stayed behind to act as couriers, and a few of Richard's wounded and poxed from the mountain who had recovered enough to be returned to active duty.

Richard said it was his right as the leader of the Company's horse archers to lead them, and Henry said it was his right to lead them because he was the commander of the state troops; I said that it was mine as the Company's commander. Reason prevailed and the dispute was finally settled in the best tradition of the Company—I won the argument because I had more stripes on my tunic.

Henry and Richard both had important roles and accompanied me to the sally gate. Henry remained there to organize the return of the sally force and lead any rescues; Richard and his apprentice, as soon as I led the sally force out of the gate, were to ride through the enclosures along the outer wall to make sure the archers in each enclosure had gone over the wall to attack the Greeks camped directly in front of them.

******

It took a while for me to lead the available horse archers, twenty-three in all including my apprentice and all sixteen of my personal guards, to the encampment of the states' forces. All the rest of our horse archers were somewhere beyond the Greek encampment harassing the Greek forage parties and raiding the columns and camps of those who were still inward bound from Adrianople.

I led the way to the sally gate with Nicholas Greenway, my apprentice, riding immediately behind me. We rode in a long single file from one enclosure to the next through the narrow openings in the new interior walls until we finally reached the walled roadway where the states' forces were camped. It, the main roadway into the city, ran all the way from the city's outer wall to its inner wall and was jammed full of people, a surprising number of whom were camp-following women and merchants. There were even some women with babies and children. As you might imagine, it smelled most foul and I was glad not to be on foot.

We were watched and cheered, and people rushed to look at us, as we came through the narrow passageway in the final interior wall and began picking our way up the crowded road to the Farmers Gate. A translator provided by Henry rode ahead of us waving his arms about and shouting the same refrain over and over again.

"Make way. Make way. The commander of the Empress's army is coming to lead the attack in person."

The last half mile took even longer than it had taken us to get through the baggage trains and camp followers because the state troops were already being formed up on the road itself.

We reached the states' foot soldiers first, and they were hard to miss even though they wore a wide variety of gowns and tunics—for Henry had given each of them a circle of blue linen to sew on the front and back of whatever clothes they were wearing and a hat of woven straw to help shield them from the sun.

The purpose of both items was to help identify the states' foot soldiers to the archers, and to each other and their own knights. The Company of Archers had provided them in an effort to reduce the friend on friend casualties that were inevitable in the confused and chaotic fighting that was about to begin.

We did not, of course, provide the hats and circles out of the goodness of our hearts. Rather we provided them so the state troops would be more likely to fight more with our enemies and less with each other—so that our archers would not have to fight as much and our losses would be less.

****

My arrival to lead the sally in person seemed to give the state troops and their captains a great deal of satisfaction. There was no surprise in that—my leading the sortie meant, or so the state troops undoubtedly hoped, that they were not going to be sacrificed in some kind of "forlorn hope" assault that was doomed to fail.

And the state troops were partially right. I would not be leading a "forlorn hope;" it was an effort to inflict serious damage on the invaders. I would, in fact, be leading them through the gate, over the moat bridge, and into the Orthodox camp.

What they did not yet know, however, was that after we got a little ways into the Greek camp, I would merely wave them on, and then stop and wait with my little band of horse archers for them to return—for that was what I had to promise my lieutenants I would do in order to get their agreement on my participation.

Chapter Seventeen

The Commander leads the sally.

The Commander's horse and some of the horses of the men riding with him had somehow caught the excitement of the moment despite the stifling heat. They were skittish and prancing about. I was on my horse and next to the Commander. It was my proper place as his apprentice sergeant. There were about twenty of the Company's horse archers just behind us, and then the Bulgarian commander and his knights and those of the other states.

The Bulgarian commander led the largest contingent of knights and would be right behind us when we passed through the gate and over the moat bridge. His name was Ivan something or other. The other states' riders and their foot soldiers were immediately behind the Bulgarians and, at least so far as I could see, they too looked ready to go.

My horse and many of the other horses sensed something was about to happen. They were snorting and anxiously moving about as Commander Courtenay looked over his shoulder at the Bulgarian commander, and raised his eyes in an unspoken question.

The Bulgarian nodded his readiness and similarly raised his hand and shouted words I could not understand to get the attention of his men. The captains and sergeants of the various groups behind him had seen their moves and did the same.

I could hear orders rippling down the close-packed ranks of the riders behind me, and watched as the Bulgarian commander and his knights put on their helmets, pulled their visors down to protect their faces, and drew their swords. It was both a hot and sunny day and time to ride. We were already warm and about to be very warm. I, at least, was not wearing armour as many of the riders behind us were wearing. Hopefully, the Greeks were not ready to receive us.

My horse was still anxiously dancing about when the Commander nodded to Henry Soldier who was standing next to the windlass that raised and lowered the gate. The two men with Henry, both veteran foot archers who had been helping him train the states' soldiers, immediately began enthusiastically cranking. The rusty chains rattled and the huge gate slowly rose. Behind us I could hear the sound of many horses stamping their feet and much talking and shouted orders.

As soon as the gate was high enough for Commander Courtenay to ride under it, he raised his bow over his head, kicked his horse in the ribs and shouted "FORWARD." As he did, he pointed his bow at the moat bridge immediately in front of the gate and the densely packed camp of the Greek-led army that began only a hundred paces or so beyond the bridge.

I was right behind him as he galloped towards them.

****** *George Courtenay*

The thundering rumble of horses' hooves and the battle cries of the riders behind me were loud as we surged through the now-open gate. They remained loud even though the sound of our horses' hooves changed as we clattered over the wooden bridge over the moat. I was guiding my horse with my knees, and by the time I cleared the bridge I had an arrow nocked and my bow drawn.

We swept into the crowded Orthodox camp and my archers began fanning out abreast of me as they had previously been ordered. Nicholas was the man riding nearest to me. He was about ten paces away and to my right.

Surprised and suddenly desperate people immediately began running about in every direction as soon as we came out of the gate. We had to ride this way and that to get around the haphazardly placed and closely packed tents and wagons. Our horses chose the path we rode because our hands were full of our longbows and the arrows nocked in our bowstrings.

Almost instantly I came upon a young man who had paused with a look of surprise on his face as he was in the process of lifting some kind of sack out of the back of a wagon. I had ridden around one side of the wagon and Nicholas the other. The young Greek did not even have time to drop the sack.

It would have been embarrassing to miss at such a short range, and I did not. I pushed an arrow straight into the middle of him and kept going as I quickly reached over my shoulder for an arrow from my quiver and immediately nocked it.

My horse was running as fast as she could and constantly turning and twisting to avoid the closely packed tents and wagons ahead of us. All about me were the sights and sounds of chaos, surprise, and desperation. Shouting and screaming people were suddenly running about in every direction in a desperate effort to escape.

I had already ridden past a number of surprised and panic stricken men and women by the time I finished nocking my second arrow and picking out my next target. He was large, heavily whiskered man who came rushing out of a tent pulling up his Greek trousers. I saw the spurt of blood that came out of his back when the point of my arrow went all the way through him.

A boy wearing no clothes, probably due to the heat and possibly his grandson, was standing behind him. I sometimes still remember him with his hand raised to his mouth in surprise and a look of horror on his face.

All around me the Bulgarian riders were leaning out of their saddles to chop on the Greeks with their swords and the Company's archers were pushing arrows into them. I could not see what was happening behind me, of course, but I somehow knew that the first of the men on foot, the Bulgarians, were already across the bridge.

Nicholas and I were galloping between a cart and the tent next to it when my horse swerved slightly to avoid running into a fleeing woman, but not enough. She went tumbling down as the shoulder of my horse hit her, and I felt the bump as I rode right over her and my horse stepped on her.

I was nocking another arrow a moment later when Nicholas came right up alongside of me in such a way as to change the direction my horse was moving. It was a deliberate move and it annoyed me. My displeasure must have showed for he promptly shouted out an explanation over the noise and chaos.

"It is time to stop and wait for the foot to reach us, Commander. You ordered me to make sure you stopped and waited for them."

******

Nicholas and I pulled up our excited horses and turned aside into a small open area beyond a collapsed tent and an overturned wagon. A dead man lay in the middle of it with a terrible wound to his head, obviously a sword cut from a man with a very strong arm. To my surprise, I was breathing hard and almost out of breath.

Six or seven archers had been riding abreast of us on either side. They pulled up their horses and joined us as the last of the Bulgarians and state riders flooded past. The Bulgarians were brandishing their swords and looked red-faced and excited. There was already blood on the swords of some of them. The rest of my horse archer guards must have been caught up in the excitement and ridden on. All around us were dead, wounded, and terrified Greeks.

Two more archers soon weaved their way through the tents and wagons of the chaos-filled camp to join us, and then another three. They reached us whilst I was standing on my stirrups trying to see what I could see.

What I saw was that the Latin states' foot soldiers, a great shouting and running horde of them, all totally disorganized, had passed over the bridge and were just now beginning to enter the Greek camp. It was easy to understand how the missing archers had lost sight of us in the chaos and not seen us stop.

When the Latin foot entered the camp, they would find some of the Greeks who were still alive trying to hide in their tents and under the wagons, and probably under the tents that were down and everywhere else as well. Most of the still-living Greeks who could run, however, seemed to be running, and some of them were carrying swords and spears they had grabbed up when they realized what was happening. Our about-to-arrive men of the Latin foot would have to deal with them.

We sat together on our horses and watched the massacre of the Greeks as it unfolded all around us. It was as if we were holding a small island of calm amidst a sea of horror.

After a while we rode back to the gate and received a warm welcome from Henry and my father. Four of the horse archers who had sallied out with us were still missing, and one of the returnees had a nasty slice in his leg that needed sewing.

****** *Major Captain Daniel Tenn.*

I was up on the parapet of the city's the outer wall and getting anxious. Sam Ridley was with me. Sam was the four-stripe galley captain of the fifty or so archers standing on the wall with us. The rest of his archers were waiting on the stairs and in the enclosure below us. We were anxious because the signal for the archers to start their attack was overdue.

We were particularly anxious because the city's outer defensive wall curved such that we ourselves could not see the gate through which Commander Courtenay would lead a sortie involving a handful of our archers and all the available soldiers of the Latin states. What we could see, however, were the archers posted further on down the wall in that direction as lookouts.

The lookouts able to see the gate were ordered to energetically wave a linen flag tied to a stick as soon as the commander led the state forces out of the gate. Each subsequent enclosure's lookout, upon seeing the waving flags of the others, was to wave his own flag stick. In that way the signal to attack would pass rapidly down the outer wall so that every galley captain would know it was time for him and his archers to climb down from the outer wall, cross the moat immediately in front of them, and begin pushing out arrows to kill or wound the Greeks in the camp across from them.

We waited impatiently. Finally, there it was—the signal; vigorous flag waving came rolling along the top of the wall towards us like a great wave.

"Follow me, lads; follow me. And remember that a badly wounded Greek is even better than a dead one."

I shouted out my orders as the ladders which had been lying atop the wall were being grabbed up and hurriedly lowered into place. One of the archers assigned to the ladders helped put one over the side and then he and another archer grabbed it to hold it steady.

An instant later Sam swung himself on to the ladder and began to climb down to the narrow piece of land between the city's outer wall and its moat. He went first with his lieutenant, Edwin Draper, and a two stripe archer from Dover named Bill Street following close behind. I followed them.

The lieutenant was carrying a line. When he got to the little strip of land between the wall and the moat, he would hand one end of the line to Bill and then follow Sam as he waded across the moat on a narrow foot causeway that had been installed when the moat had been drained so the rest of it could be dug deeper.

Lieutenant Draper and Bill Street would then hold the line tight over the foot causeway so the seventy-six archers who were to follow Sam into the enemy camp would have something to hold and would know where they could safely put their feet down when they walked across.

Before we started down the ladder, Sam had once again loudly reminded his men that no arrows were to be pushed into the Greek camp by the archers who were on the wall. That was because we did not yet want the Greeks to know the distance arrows pushed out of longbows could reach—we would wait for another time to let them learn about the range of our weapons, such as when their army was formed up in front of us and getting ready for a major assault. At least that was the plan according to Commander Courtenay.

There is nothing more likely to ruin a man's day, and cause him to turn back from an attack, than a shower of arrows raining down on him and his mates when they least expect them.

****** *Daniel Tenn*

I followed Sam, Edwin and Bill down the ladder and my apprentice, Edward Fast as he was called, followed right behind me. A long line of anxious archers and their auxiliaries followed us down file by file. Each archer had his longbow strung and slung over his shoulder along with four quivers of arrows; the auxiliaries were carrying the bladed pikes produced by the Company's smiths at our stronghold on Cyprus.

The Greek camp in front of us did not appear to be on alert and I was not a bit nervous; I was sweating profusely, no doubt because it was already a hot day.

Another ladder was soon in place and the company's archers and auxiliaries began coming down it as well. Every man had his longbow slung over his back with his quivers so his hands would be free to hold on to the ladder whilst he was climbing. It was the auxiliaries carrying each file's pikes who had the trouble. They had never before climbed down a ladder carrying a pike.

"Drop it down, damn you. You can pick it up when you get down the ladder."

A sergeant bellowed out his command when the first of the auxiliaries hesitated at the top of the ladder. The man did not understand and just stood there looking helpless until the sergeant grabbed it out of his hands, shouted "Pike coming down," and dropped it over the wall.

****** *Major Captain Daniel Tenn*

Getting on the ladder and climbing down to the sliver of land between the wall and its moat was difficult but doable. What was even more difficult was staying on my feet whilst holding loosely on to the guide rope and sloshing through the black and foul-smelling waters to get to the other side of the moat.

It was probably my imagination, but I had a sense that the narrow causeway was crumbling under my feet as I walked on it. My apprentice sergeant, Edward Fast was right behind me. Edward was a good lad who could scribe and gobble Latin. He was useful running errands for me. Although I would never admit it, of course, I had come to rely on him.

The water was up to my knees and, in an effort to avoid falling all the way in, I found myself holding on to the line Lieutenant Draper and Bill Street were holding tight between them, walking slowly and taking small steps, and putting my feet down carefully. There were rapidly growing sounds of conflict coming from the encampment in front of me, but I did not dare look up to see what was happening. My fear of slipping off the underwater walkway into the foul waters had temporarily pushed everything else out of my mind.

Ahead of me I heard the grunt of an archer pushing out an arrow and the slap of a bowstring against his leather wrist protector. Sam was already in action. I did not dare look up to see what he was doing, rather I concentrated on walking carefully and allowing to slide through my hand as I walked.

I was walking slowly and somehow instinctively knew that grabbing the line and holding on for dear life was something I would have to do to save myself if the slippery ground under my feet suddenly gave way. And although it might have been my imagination, it felt as though the walkway was literally breaking apart under my feet as I walked on it.

Strangely enough, or perhaps it was not so strange under the circumstances, I felt a profound sense of relief when I finally reached Sam's lieutenant, and had both of my feet firmly on dry ground. Sam was standing near his lieutenant to guard him and to give his archers their orders as they came across the moat. He had already pushed out three or four arrows.

"It felt like it was giving way under my feet," I said to Sam as I unslung my bow and nocked an arrow.

"Aye, I noticed that myself," he said as a wild-eyed man came around one of the nearby tents carrying some kind of spear. He leaped over a body sprawled in front of the tent and started running away when he saw us.

Whose arrow hit the man first, mine or Sam's, or perhaps Edward's, I do not know for sure, but I think it was mine. It did not matter; the poor sod was done for. He gave a great howl and went tumbling with his now-empty hands flailing about. We ignored him as he tried to crawl away. The next time I looked, a few minutes later, he was face down on the ground and not moving.

In less than a minute Sam and I had assembled half a dozen or so archers. It was enough to get started so we began moving slowly, very slowly, a couple of hundred paces into the outskirts of the Greek camp.

Edwin, Sam's lieutenant, would send the rest of the company's archers to join us as fast as they came over the moat. Similar actions were occurring all along the wall as a little over two thousand archers and pike men moved into the Greek encampment from their positions in the narrow enclosures all along the city's outer wall.

It was easy at first. We pushed out arrows at everyone who moved as we moved cautiously into the Greek camp and the rapidly growing cloud of dust that hung over it. Everywhere around us was a great mass of chaos and confusion with panic-stricken horses and shouting and screaming men and women running about hysterically in every direction.

We had caught the Greeks totally by surprise, that much was clear. For the first few moments they did not know which way to run. Getting away from us and the wall seemed to be the safest move.

As a result, those who had set up their tents closest to wall, the people we reached first, mostly ended up running towards the middle of the huge Greek camp—which put them right into the path of the states' horsemen and foot soldiers who had been ordered to cut a wide swath of destruction through the middle third of the camp.

Moreover, once they had swept through the middle third, the men of the states' forces were to turn around and come back to where they started by riding through the far third. The archers coming over the wall and moat were responsible for destroying the closest third. At least, that was the plan before we started.

Each of our men, of course, was only concerned with what was happening immediately around him. In my case, at that moment, it was a great bearded man who came charging out of nowhere swinging an old-fashioned long sword.

He was screaming something, either some kind of battle cry to frighten us or give himself courage, when our arrows hit him. And they hit him too late. He stumbled past one of Sam's archers, and managed to give him a good backhand cut, and even started to go for another archer, before he was jabbed in his side and pressed to the ground by a pike in the hands of one of Sam's auxiliaries.

The wounded archer fell to knees and then steadied himself with one hand on the ground whilst he tried to hold the great cut in his side together with the other and get to his feet. There was a look of surprise and amazement on his face.

Sam immediately ordered the two archers nearest the wounded man to help him get back across the moat.

"And do not leave him until the sailmakers sew him up and he has eaten some flower paste."

More and more archers and pike-carrying auxiliaries came over the moat and caught up with us as Sam and I slowly, very slowly, led more and more of his men into the Greek camp. It was rich in targets so there was no need to charge ahead rapidly.

As we spread out, and slowly advanced whilst constantly pushing out arrows at the Greeks and their wagon-pulling horses, a great and growing cloud of dust began rising over the camp. It was the result of everyone running about and the many stampeding and galloping horses.

Chapter Eighteen

Things start to go wrong.

Sam and I stood inside the Greek camp and watched as the galloping horses of the knights and other riders of the states' force sent people running, at least those who still could, as they swept through the main part of the camp in front of us dealing out death and destruction.

The foot soldiers of the states' forces who had sallied out behind the riders had not yet reached us when, suddenly, people trying to escape from the states' riders started coming out of the dust cloud and running towards us. We no longer had to move forward to find targets—they were flooding towards us on both sides. We had a target rich position.

I had just succeeded in putting an arrow into the side of a stampeding horse pulling a driverless two-wheel cart, when an out-of-breath archer sent by Sam's Lieutenant, Edwin Draper, rushed up to Sam. He brought a disturbing report. I was standing nearby and heard it all despite the noise around us—the underwater causeway in front of his company's enclosure had collapsed after only about half of Sam's men had gotten across. Our wounded man was trapped on this side of the moat and so were we.

According to the out-of-breath messenger, two of Sam's men had been crossing at the time to join us. They had been saved by holding on to the guide rope and being pulled back to the wall. A third man, he said, a long-serving veteran by the name of David Curry, lost his grip and went into the moat. He did not come up.

Sam was more than a little unhappy.

"Shite and damn, David was a good man."

And then, a moment later after he finished pushing out an arrow he had nocked, and given a satisfied nod at the result as his man went tumbling down with a loud scream, Sam told me what I already knew.

"We will have to get back using the causeway in front of Basil Tower's company. Basil is the captain of the company in the enclosure just to the west of mine. He is a London man, but uncommonly steady even if he does talk about money all the time," he added unnecessarily.

"Right. And you best begin moving your men in that direction. Listen to the noise; the fighting seems to be coming this way. It must be the states' foot. They were supposed to follow their riders up the middle, but only God knows where they might be what with all this dust."

******

It was not the states' foot soldiers who arrived first, however. It was the states' knights and other riders. They had ridden all the way through the middle of the Greek camp and had turned around to ride back through another part of it.

According to the orders I had heard Commander Courtenay give them, the states' riders were supposed to circle around to the right and ride back to the gate through that part of the camp that was even further away from the wall than the path they initially took up the middle. Some of them, however, had apparently turned the wrong way and were now coming back through that part of the camp that was closer to the wall—the part of the camp which the archers coming over the wall and moat had occupied.

By the time we heard the riders approaching, we had either put down or scared the hell out of numerous fleeing men and women who were attempting to flee by running through that part of the Greek camp where we stood. We often heard them coming through the dust and closely packed tents before we saw them. Surprising enough, they were coming at us both from our left and from our right. Terribly confused they seemed to be; they knew they needed to run to save themselves, but they did not know in which direction.

My initial thought when I heard the approaching states' riders, and Sam's too, was that the Greeks had somehow been able to mount a counter attack. He hurriedly gathered in the men he could see and positioned them behind an overturned wagon. It was a reasonable thing to do because the states' riders were not supposed to be coming towards us. Edward and I stood and waited with him.

We began to see the states' riders through the dust cloud as they got closer and closer. Worse, we could hear them as they began trying to cut down the foot archers who had come over the wall from the enclosure to Sam's north, Basil Tower's men. When they got close enough, and were just beginning to veer off, we could see for the first time that the men trying to ride us down were our supposed allies from the states' forces.

It was a great and unforgiveable military mistake by knights and other riders who had been led in the wrong direction by their confused captains. Unfortunately, as we later learned, some of the states' riders died for it just as they would have done if they had deliberately attacked us.

There was no surprise in that some of the states' riders had been killed—trying to cut down a disorganized and poorly armed and trained Greek soldier, or one of his camp followers, was one thing; going after a highly trained English archer carrying the most modern weapons in the world was something else and altogether different—and much more likely to be fatal.

It apparently was a fatal mistake in this case, for the survivors amongst the horsemen soon changed direction and veered off. They ended up passing to the north of where we were standing. As they went past us we could see the dim outlines of riders and horses in the heavy cloud of dust that hung over the camp.

We could also hear the growing sounds of strife that suggested the states' foot soldiers were coming closer from the opposite direction. It was time to back up to the moat and get out of harm's way. We had done all the damage we could do to the Greek camp. It was time to pull back, so I told Sam what I wanted his company to do and he began giving the necessary orders.

"Listen up lads," he shouted. "The time has come for us to get back inside the wall. The causeway across the moat to our camp is down so we are going to move along the wall to the west and use the causeway in front of the next enclosure."

A few moments later he began giving his orders.

"Form on me, lads. Over here. Form on me."

His sergeants repeated his order and archers hurried from all around us to form up around Sam in a battle-marching formation with those of the men carrying bladed pikes walking between the longbow-carrying archers. The men were scared and worried as we began withdrawing. There was no question about it in my mind; any Greeks we came upon were doomed.

****** *Major Captain Daniel Tenn*

The Greek encampment was still filled with the sounds of struggle and covered with a great cloud of dust as we closed in together and began moving westward. We knew which way to walk because we were close enough to the wall to be able to catch glimpses of it through the dust.

Several of Sam's men were wounded and being helped by their mates, or perhaps they had merely been overcome by the heat. And one man in an archer's tunic was hanging head down over an archer's shoulder and being carried. I had no idea who he was or how he died. I suddenly staggered and realized I was a bit tipsy from being too hot and extremely thirsty.

We moved closer to the moat and walked along its edge through rapidly clearing dust until we came to an archer standing next to a ladder on the other side of the moat. He was skittish when he first saw us coming and started to climb up the ladder to escape. But he came back down when he saw our archers' tunics. A large number of archers were standing on the wall above him. They began shouting welcomes and questions.

"A hoy to you," Sam loudly croaked so the men on wall could hear him. "I be Captain White of Number Twenty-seven. Where be Captain Tower and your walking causeway through the moat? We need to cross."

"A good hoy to you too, Captain," came the respectful answer from a sergeant on the wall who was looking down at them.

"Captain Tower be going along the moat with Lieutenant Harper and the lads who made it into Greek camp. They be looking for a place to cross the water to get back. Our causeway sank before me and the rest of the lads could be getting across."

"Shite and damnation."

That was all I could think to say at first when I heard the sergeant answer Sam. Finally, I pulled an idea out from behind my eyes.

"A hoy to the highest ranking man up there on the wall. Listen up sharp-like," I shouted up to the men who lined the wall and were peering down at us.

"This is Major Captain Tenn. We have wounded and need a place to cross. Send runners, fast runners, all the way along the wall in both directions asking if any of the companies have a causeway open across the moat. Tell the runners to run fast and to send a man back each time they find one that is usable. And they are to keep going and find them all. We will wait here and rest until we hear from you.

"Oh yes. And tell the runners to ask about the condition of each causeway that is open. We need to know whether or not it can handle a lot of men. Also send a runner, a rider if you have one, to the open gate where the states' forces are camped. They are to request Commander Courtenay, or any Lieutenant Commander they can find, to hurry here as fast as possible.

"Now run, goddammit, run. We have some wounded lads here who need barbering."

"Aye Major Captain, you have wounded and we are to run." It was a battle command and was repeated most proper. My hopes rose.

My high hopes did not last long. After a few minutes I began getting anxious and realized I was desperately thirsty. The dust cloud over the camp was drifting away and the noise level was already distinctly lower. It would only be a matter of time before the Greeks got their shite together and came for us, particularly when they found out we were a small force and realized we were trapped on the wrong side of the moat.

****** *Major Captain Daniel Tenn*

I was wrong. We were not a small force. Whilst we waited for word of which way to walk to find a crossing point, the men of two more companies came westward on the cart path that ran along the moat. They had caught up with us because we had stopped and they were still walking west along the moat looking for a place to cross. I told them to bide with me until we knew which way we should walk to find a crossing.

Commander Courtenay himself and Henry showed up on the wall above us almost at the same time a few minutes later, and then Richard, the lieutenant commander in charge of the horse archers appeared. They had all heard about us being stranded and had been galloping along the top of the wall to see for themselves and organize a rescue. The men and I were pleased to see them; our hopes rose once again.

A few moments later we watched as Henry said something to Commander Courtenay, and then mounted a horse and galloped westerly along the top of the wall with his white hair flying out behind him. The Commander slid off his horse and leaned over the outer ledge of the wall to look at us whilst talking to Richard. A moment later Richard hurried off in the other direction

"We have companies all along the wall who cannot get back across," Commander Courtenay shouted down to me. Then he gave me a fateful order.

"Dan, I want you to stay right where you are and wait until Henry brings in those who are stranded outside the wall further to the west. When they get here, we will cover you from up here on the wall whilst you lead the whole group east along the wall to the sally gate. Your force will get stronger and stronger as you are joined by more and more of the men who are stranded west of you."

His order and attempt to encourage us sounded ominous, so I had to ask.

"Can you see any sign of a Greek force coming this way to engage us, Commander?"

Chapter Nineteen

The long walk.

We sat and rested for a while under the hot sun and watched the nearby Greek camp. The dust cloud over the camp was beginning to settle and people, both men and women, were beginning to appear. They were gathering in small groups to talk, walking about to check on the condition of their possessions, and, of course, to loot the dead and barber the wounded.

In the distance we could see a small band of horsemen walking their horses through the camp. No one came near us. That would come soon enough when the Greek captains realized we were still here and how badly we were outnumbered. I was getting increasingly anxious and so were the men with me. We needed to move if we were to save ourselves—and we were under orders to wait.

The Greek encampment continued to slowly recover whilst we waited the arrival of the men who had gone over the wall further to the west. I was drowsy and almost ready to fall asleep. That lasted until I heard one of our wounded men cry out. An idea had been asleep behind my eyes and the poor sod's groan woke it up.

"Captain," I shouted at Sam as I jumped to my feet. "Take some men into the Greek camp and get some wagons we can pull by hand. We can load our wounded and dead in them. Hurry Sam, there is not a minute to lose before the Greeks come back."

******

A constant stream of dusty and very tired and thirsty archers came hurrying in from the west carrying their dead and wounded. Several of them had commandeered Greek wagons to carry them just as we had done. While we waited, swords, pikes, infantry shields, and fresh quivers of arrows were hurriedly brought down from the wall and attempts were made to throw them over the moat to us. Most of the throws made it across although more than a few ended up splashing into the water, particularly the shields.

Water skins were also brought down and thrown across the moat to us. At the moment, so far as I was concerned, the water was more valuable than the weapons. The men passed the skins from hand to hand and we did not think we would ever get enough. The water in the moat was not drinkable—it was as thick as soup and foul beyond belief.

The captains and lieutenants of the galley companies which had been stranded west of us, seven companies in all, and I hurriedly distributed the available water and weapons to our best advantage and, at the same time, organized our men and wagons on the assumption that we would have to fight our way through to the gate.

My best guess, and it was certainly only a guess, was that I now commanded a force of about four hundred archers and auxiliaries. We were still thirsty beyond belief, but at least we were better armed and more organized. All of my men were good men and well-led; in every case the captains and lieutenants of the galley companies had gone first and were sharing the hardships with the men of their galley companies who had gotten across the moat before their walkway failed.

Finally an out-of-breath Henry Soldier arrived on the wall above us, slid off the horse he had ridden along the top of the city's outer wall, and gasped out the words we were waiting to here.

"The last company is coming in to you now. Leave as soon as its men reach you, and move as fast as you can without leaving anyone behind. Give them water to drink as you move. There is a dust cloud to the south that suggests a sizable force of Greeks is coming this way on the Adrianople road."

Commander Courtenay then shouted out some news that heartened everyone.

"We are assembling a large force of archers, many hundreds of them, to move along the wall in front of you and behind you. They will cover you with a great storm of arrows if there is an attack or blocking force."

He added more good news after a pause whilst he consulted with his lieutenant commanders.

"Another large force of archers will be going down the wall ahead of you to discourage a Greek blocking forces from being established on the moat path in front of you."

****** *George Courtenay.*

The news was not good. Our plan for the archers to cross the moat and then return did not even last long enough for all of our men to get across. And now reports were coming in that a large force of Greeks was rapidly coming up on the Adrianople road. It was undoubtedly the main body of the Greeks the Venetians had carried to Adrianople—and they would almost certainly be pissed off and looking for blood because of the destruction we had caused.

Richard and Henry hurried off to gather in and organize the archers who had not gotten across. I remained where I was in order to command the archers who would move along the wall to provide cover for Dan's increasingly-formidable force that was stranded on the other side of the moat.

All of the auxiliaries outside the wall now had pikes and shields, and some of the archers were now carrying them as well. The archers were not carrying sharpened stakes they could set, so the pikes would be needed if Dan's men were charged by mounted knights and their squires and mounted men-at-arms.

At that point, the most important question was whether or not Dan's men could be reached by the small groups of archers who were still stranded further to the east along the wall. Fortunately, at least so far as I knew, the archers stranded closer to the Farmers Gate were already moving as fast as possible towards that gate and carrying their dead and wounded with them.

It was the stranded men from the far western enclosures nearest the sea who had had the farthest to walk that concerned us the most. They would likely be exhausted by the heat and their earlier efforts in the Greek camp by the time they reached the relative safety of Dan and his men. He would march for the Farmers Gate as soon as they arrived, but he would be able to move no faster than his slowest man.

Then I had a thought.

"Dan, grab up a couple of extra wagons with you in case some of your men are overcome by heat and exhaustion."

I was heartened by his response; he had already done so. Dan was a good commander and we all knew it; and he had just proved it again.

******

"That is the last of them," Henry said as he once again slid off his horse and handed his reins to Nicholas.

Moments later we heard Dan shout a command and his entire force set off down the moat road. They were not yet being chased and were marching relatively fast under a hot sun. I was not sure how long they would be able to keep up their current pace despite the brief rest most of them had taken and the water skins that had been thrown across to them.

It was a reasonable concern—the last arrivals had already quick-marched four or five thirsty miles in the hot sun and dust whilst pulling a cart loaded with their dead and wounded. There was no time for them to rest. They would have to carry the water skins we threw to them and drink as they marched.

Dan and his captains were marching with a line of their pike men across the front of the column and bending back around its side. Many of the pikes were now being carried by veteran archers. They would know best how to kneel and set the butts of their pikes if the column was charged by mounted knights. The auxiliaries who previously carried the pikes were now helping to pull the carts.

I began rapidly walking along the top of the wall to keep pace with Dan and his men who were now marching on the moat road below me. So did a large and growing force of archers with grimly determined looks on their face. They apparently felt guilty about not having gotten across the moat to suffer with their mates.

An idea began coming together behind my eyes as I walked.

******

"George," someone shouted from the men marching ahead of me on the wall. "Look off to the east."

It was my father. He was walking with the archers who were about a two hundred paces ahead of me where the wall curved. I had been so intent on the archers marching below me, and the dust cloud rapidly approaching on the Adrianople Road, that I had not seen him arrive.

A few moments later I was able to see around the bend in the wall. My heart skipped a beat when I saw what had caused the shouted warning—a large company of horsemen, as many as a hundred and perhaps more, were coming up the road between our archers and the Farmers Gate towards Sam and his men. The riders were definitely not ours.

It was quite surprising. We had not known the Greeks had so many horsemen. Then it suddenly dawned on me as what might have happened—the knights and other horsemen accompanying the main body of the Greek army carried to Adrianople by the Venetians must have been detached from the main Greek column and ridden through the dust cloud to cut off our retreating men.

My mouth had no sooner gaped open in surprise at seeing the horsemen when, quite suddenly a ripple seemed to pass through their ranks. They began to scatter in all directions a moment later. There was no surprise in that—the archers walking along the top of the wall ahead of us had obviously begun pushing arrows at the Greek riders in an effort to move them off the road so Sam's men could continue marching towards the distant gate.

Our arrows turned out to be particularly effective against the horsemen. That was understandable—it was much too hot to be wearing armour and the horses and men were easy targets because they were bunched up and so close to the archers on the wall above them.

******

The Greek horsemen who had their horses under control abandoned their dead and wounded mates and galloped away from moat-front cart path in order to escape from the archers pushing arrows at them from atop the wall. Even at this distance we could hear the screams of the wounded horses. Some of their riders were motionless on the road and others were moving about.

It was a chaotic scene. Wounded and out of control horses, some with riders still on board, ran in every direction, including up the road towards us. Several of them had blindly dashed into the moat with their riders and were thrashing about. One of the riders who had come unhorsed was trying to climb out of the moat.

As we watched, some of the unhorsed riders who had been moving on the roadway about went down as additional arrows reached out to them from the archers on the nearby wall. So did the man who had been trying to climb out of the moat.

Dan and his men did not know about the Greek force coming in behind them in the rapidly approaching dust cloud. So they would undoubtedly stop to gather up the available arrows and finish off the rest of the Greek casualties when they reached them—unless they were ordered otherwise.

"Dan," I shouted. "You are at least five miles short of the gate and there are wounded Greek horsemen on the road ahead of you and a big force of Greeks coming in fast that may reach you before you get to the gate. You need to increase your rear guard and move even faster if you can.

"We need as many of the wounded Greek horsemen as possible for questioning. So pass the word to your men to throw them in your wagons as you pass them. But do *not* stop for even a moment to retrieve any of the Greek wounded or pick up arrows. Just grab up whatever you can as you go past."

As I gave my orders, I was watching both the surviving Greek riders work their way through the camp towards the approaching column, and also the column itself. More of the riders seemed to have survived than I would have expected since they were almost certainly not wearing armour because of the heat. Or perhaps there were more of them than I initially thought.

At that moment the surviving Greek riders were riding through a devastated camp that was beginning to come back to life. They were clearly headed for the rapidly approaching dust cloud. More horsemen and a large force of rapidly moving men on foot could now be seen coming through the dust. It looked like the main column of the Greeks who travelled by sea to Adrianople was arriving.

It did not take someone who could read and scribe to see that the men leading the Greeks' main column were going to cut off Dan and his men before they reached the safety of the open gate. The men marching at the front of the column had probably begun moving fast as soon as word reached them with the news that the camp of the early arrivals was under attack.

Chapter Twenty

Preparations are made.

We watched with bated breaths, and prepared our bows, as the pursuing Greeks got closer and closer to Dan's slow-moving and outnumbered band of exhausted archers. He and some of his able-bodied men might still be able to escape by running if they abandoned the wagons carrying the dead and wounded archers. But that was unthinkable. Wounded men were never abandoned. It was in the Company's contract and the contract's requirements were always followed.

George began giving orders and men began running and galloping off in all directions. He sent Nicholas galloping back along the top of the wall to see if there were any more archers or stragglers coming to join Dan and his men.

****** *Major Captain Daniel Tenn*

We picked up three wounded Greek riders as we hurried through the site of the recent fighting on the moat road. They were unceremoniously thrown into one of the wagons we were pulling that was already carrying some of our wounded and the bodies of four dead archers.

The latest word shouted down to me from Commander Courtenay was grim—a large force of Greeks was going to catch up with us before we reached the gate. There was no doubt about it. I looked back and saw for myself that he was right; we would not make the gate.

"Hoy, Dan," the Commander shouted. "The road gets a bit closer to the wall up ahead. It would be a good place to stop and form up your defences. We can give you and your lads more cover from there."

We were walking fast as we shouted across the moat to each other—me with my men on the road that ran along next to it and the Commander with the archers who did not get across the moat on the top of the wall on the other side. A moment later the Commander shouted more information across to me.

"We are collecting ladders from the company enclosures. Some of them may be long enough to go all the way across the moat."

It sounded encouraging, but I knew something that most of my men, and perhaps the Commander, did not—we had already tried to use the ladders in the enclosures to cross the outer moat and failed; the outer moat was much wider than the inner moat—the ladders the companies used to get in and out of their enclosures would almost certainly not be long enough. But it was worth a try.

"Hoy, Commander. The ladders may not be long enough. If they are not, we will defend ourselves until something can be negotiated. In the meantime, please throw more water skins and shields over to us. Additional pikes and arrows would be useful as well."

There was a brief pause before the Commander responded.

"Hoy, Dan. I understand your message. More water skins and weapons are being collected. They will be thrown over to you as soon as you and the lads stop up ahead. We will try to open negotiations."

I hoped he understood what I meant about something being "negotiated." More weapons and water may not be enough to save us. We may be forced to surrender.

******

George and his lieutenants talked as they walked, and he was soon issuing order after order as they hurried along the top of the wall. They had to walk fast to keep up with Dan who was marching along on the road below them with his men in a desperate effort to reach the one bridge over the moat that was still up.

As the Company's leaders walked rapidly and periodically jogged in order to stay abreast of the fast moving marchers below them, archers began running past them carrying shields, pikes, and water skins. Others ran past them with the ladders that would be needed to bring the shields and skins down to the foot of the wall so they could be thrown across. The top of the wall became a beehive of activity.

It was a hot summer day with sun beating down mercilessly. Everyone was puffing and sweating. No one stopped when one of the archers ahead of them suddenly fell down on the path that ran along the top of the wall and went to sleep. They just stepped over him and kept going. A few seconds later one of his mates pulled him to one side so a galloper's horse would be less likely to step on him.

"Ropes, by God. We might be able to tie ropes around our lads' waists and pull them across if the ladders are not long enough," suggested Richard hopefully.

"How about another "all hands" sortie from the states' troops, Henry?" George asked. "Could they launch a sufficiently strong sortie soon enough to save them?"

"Probably not," Henry replied. "Most of the captains and many of their men went into the city to celebrate getting back alive from today's sortie. But I will go and see. If it is possible, I will lead it myself."

Then George had another thought.

"Major Captain Oremus, I want you to take a horse and gallop to where our galleys are pulled ashore. Send a fast-moving wagon to us with all the lines and line-throwing sticks you can quickly gather. Then row out to the galleys holding our coin chests and bring back a wagon with at least twelve chests of coins from the toll collections—if all else fails we may be able to ransom Dan and his men. And get some lines and line-throwing sticks from them as well. And hurry."

George's father was listening and smiled when Michael repeated the order so that George would know he understood it and would immediately comply. George was a good commander. It pleased his father immensely.

****** *Major Captain Daniel Tenn*

More shields, water, and pikes were already being thrown across the moat when we reached our defensive position and halted. It was the best available place for us to stop, and not very good at all because there were no natural barriers to slow down an enemy charge.

In addition, the men were exhausted and thirsty. Half a dozen or so had already collapsed from the heat and gone to sleep, and many more, including me, were on the verge. Those who did had been quickly thrown into one of the wagons so our desperate, and now failing, attempt to run for safety could continue. No one had been left behind, at least not so far as I knew.

I took a big swig of water from the skin Edward had fetched for me and began giving more orders.

"That is the way to do it, Captain, swing their horse-shafts aside and bring the wagons tight up against each other so there are no gaps between them. Good. Good.

"Fred, have your men take some water to the men in the wagons, and try to find something to cover them from the sun."

The men around me were exhausted. Many of them were sitting or lying down on their backs to rest and catch their breath, and every inch of shade under the wagons was taken. Others were guzzling water from the skins that had been thrown across the moat to us or were picking up the shields and pikes that had been thrown across with the skins. Their captains were gathered around me getting their assignments.

At least a dozen archers had come down the ladders that were now leaning against the city wall on the other side of the moat. They were throwing more of everything over the moat to us as fast as it could be carried down the ladders or dropped down to them.

A couple of ladders had been tipped into the moat to see if they would reach all the way across its foul waters. They did not. They reached almost all the way across, but almost was not good enough. And everyone was too busy to waste time pulling them out.

More and more archers were appearing on above us on the wall and shouting encouragements. The distance they would get on their arrows from being up that high was impressive. But would the storm of arrows they pushed out be enough to stop the many thousands of Greeks who had arrived and seemed to be forming up to charge us? Probably not.

"Over there, Charlie. Move your men over a little more. Good. Make sure their shields leave enough room for the pikes."

From the looks of things, we had about ten minutes to get ready; then we were likely to be hit and hit hard. That was when an idea began swirling around behind my eyes. Somehow I knew I had seen something important; I just did not know what it was.

Chapter Twenty-one

Fighting along the moat road.

Our defences were centered on the four wagons that had been carrying our wounded men and prisoners. They were parked nose-to-arse on the road with their noses facing the distant gate we had been trying to reach. Parked in such a way meant their sides were facing towards the devastated camp of the early arrivals that was now being rapidly filled by the main body of the Venetian-carried Greeks. The rest of the Greek army, the men who would have to walk all the way, were still somewhere on the old Roman road that ran towards the city.

The four captured wagons were the centre of a quickly established horseshoe-shaped defensive wall, with the men carrying shields and pikes forming the rest of the horseshoe-shaped defensive line, both of whose ends curved around until they reached all the way to the moat. In other words, every one of my hastily assembled company of stranded archers would either be pushing out his arrows from behind the shield wall or whilst standing in the wagons or behind them.

After briefly thinking about it and getting the opinion of a couple of galley captains, I decided to leave our most seriously wounded men and the three prisoners in the wagon beds. That way they would be less likely to be trampled or slaughtered when the Greeks broke through our horseshoe-shaped defence line.

The butts of all of our long-handled pikes were set in small holes hastily dug with the archers' personal knives. That was so the pikes would not slip or give way when a Greek horse or foot soldier ran himself on to their points. In essence, all a man had to do was sit or stand at his position and hold his pike's point high enough so it would stick into the belly of a charging horse or man who ran into it and impaled themselves. A pike's point, of course, could also be jabbed into an attacker or its blade brought down hard on his head or shoulders. It was a formidable modern weapon.

Those of our wounded and heat-stricken men who were strong enough to point a pike were given pikes to hold. We sat them in the shade under the wagon beds and told them to hold their pikes up to impale anyone who charged the wagons. Similarly equipped archers and auxiliaries sat amongst them and in the beds of wagons with the dead and wounded. In other words, our defensive line bristled with pikes from one end of its horseshoe shape to the other.

Every second man in the shield line that extended out from the wagons was crouched down behind a shield holding a pike; the man next to him was crouched behind a shield and holding a short stabbing sword to finish off anyone who was able to get through the arrow storm and past a pike point. The pike and sword carriers all "took a knee" and crouched down so the archers standing behind them could push their arrows straight into anyone who was running at them.

It was a formidable defence even though we were relatively few in numbers, and most of us were exhausted. Moreover, behind the pikes, and on the wall above them, were almost two thousand of the world's best archers. In essence, the Greeks might break through our line of pikes and overrun us by the sheer weight of their numbers. But, if the past was any guide, the first of the Greeks lucky enough to get through the arrow storm would have very short and exciting lives when they reached our pikes and swords. So would we when the rest of the Greeks reached us.

What was frustrating to me was that I still had the thought behind my eyes that I had seen, and perhaps even commented on, something important that might save us—but I still could not put my finger on what it was. Strangely enough, I felt quite calm.

****** *Commander George Courtenay*

I was standing with both of my hands on top of the wall looking down at the great mass of men in the arriving Greek army and the little band of stranded archers immediately below me on the other side of the moat. It was quite a depressing sight, and very noisy and dusty.

Archers with their arrows ready and their bows strung were packed all along the top of the wall on either side of me. Others were using hurriedly brought in ladders to climb down to the narrow strip of land, only a few paces wide in some places, between the city wall and the moat which guarded it. They would push out their arrows from there. Even more archers were available, but they literally had no place to stand that would provide them with enough room to use their bows.

In front of us, for almost as far as the eye could see, was a good part of the Orthodox army the Venetians had carried to Adrianople. Its men were packed closely together as if they were fish in a sack. Knightly banners and crosses carried by priests were sticking up into the air everywhere.

Except for the men trying to work their way through the crowd to get to the front, it was as if the Greeks were all waiting for someone to tell them what to do. A great cloud of dust hung over them from their constantly moving about. There were a few clusters of horsemen in the mass, mostly gathered around the banners.

At the front of the Greeks, and closest to the wagons and shield wall were almost certainly the religious zealots who, egged on by their priests and in search of martyrdom, had pushed their way to the front in order to lead the attack.

As the Greek army waited for the order to attack to be given, and without knowing they were doing it, those in the rear trying to press their way forward in order to impress their lords and priests, or perhaps just to get a better look, were crowding up against the men in the front ranks—and pushing them closer and closer to our seriously outnumbered band of stranded mates who were huddled behind their wagons and pikes.

It was about then that I noticed something else and decided it was important—large numbers of Greek soldiers were drinking from the foul moat and others of them, many others, were pushing their way towards it. They must have been both desperately thirsty as a result of an entire day spent marching in the dust and totally unaware as to the foul soup that festered in front the city's wall.

That they were half-mad with thirst was likely the case since the last available water on the road from Adrianople was a small stream that came out of the mountains and crossed the road. It was just before the road entered the peninsula on which the city stood at the very end, about a day's march away from the city.

As I watched, I realized that the men of the Greek army were making much more of an effort to get to the moat and its water than to Dan and his beleaguered men. The whole Greek army seemed to be moving towards it.

"Richard, look over there—the Greeks are spreading out and going for the moat water despite it being so foul. We need to move some of the archers we have here, those with no room to push, down there to get those Greeks as well."

"By God, you are right. They must be desperate." … "Hoy, Jack, Bob, follow me and bring your archers. Hurry."

Richard and his men had barely reached the mob of men rushing to the edge of the moat for water when the Greek mass moved even closer to Dan and his men. They were close enough for our arrows to reach and those who were closest to our shield line seemed to be readying themselves to charge.

"ARCHERS," I roared. "NOCK ARROWS" …. "PICK YOUR MAN" … "PUSH" …. "PUSH" … "EVENS GO LONG" … "PUSH … "PUSH."

The sergeants repeated the order over and over again and, as was expected, continued doing so for long as did I.

In the course of the next five minutes the sky above our trapped archers was constantly filled with arrows. They fell upon the Greeks like great sheets of rain.

Almost one hundred thousand well-aimed arrows had been grabbed out of their quivers by the best archers in the world and pushed into the nearby, unarmoured and closely bunched soldiers of the Greek army—and then the archers grabbed up arrows from the bales that had been opened and pushed out another hundred thousand.

Great clouds of dust began to be kicked up as men and horses tried to run every which way, and the noise of the screaming and shouting was so loud that it was hard to think. And we mostly did not even try. Every archer from the Company's commander to its newest one-striper was at work.

One might have thought the Greeks would have hurriedly pulled back out of range. It did not happen. Many were still in range as our arrow supply began to run low—because the poor sods were so tightly packed together that they could see nothing and did not know which way to run—and most of them could not have successfully withdrawn even if they wanted to because they were so jammed together and had lost all sense of direction in the chaos and dust.

The fighting was not entirely one-sided. The arrival of the arrows was as if an order to "charge" had been given by the Greek commanders. Many thousands of the Greeks responded to the sudden arrival of the arrows by surging forward against the four hundred or so archers and auxiliaries huddled behind the wagons they had been pulling.

Sam's men and the archers on the wall shot them down by the hundreds, and then Dan's shield-carrying pike men and sword men cut down even more of them when those who escaped the initial onslaught of arrows reached their defensive line. But there were too many of them, and they broke through Dan's shield wall on the left by the sheer weight of their numbers.

It was a scene of absolute chaos which became hand to hand fighting at such very close quarters that the archers above the struggling men could not always get clear pushes.

****** *Major Captain Daniel Tenn*

A great deluge of arrows suddenly came from the archers on the wall and began falling on the Greeks in front of us. It was as if a signal had been given—a great mob of men from the front ranks of the Greek army began charging towards us brandishing their swords and spears, with many of them falling as the arrows took them. It all happened at virtually the same moment.

"Here they come, lads. Take the thrusters. Take the thrusters."

And that is what we did. At first it worked. It was hard to miss, and any arrow that did miss inevitably hit someone in the mob behind its intended target. Many of the Greeks were carrying only spears, the rest were wielding swords of various sizes and shapes, and they were all screaming and shouting as they came out of the dust cloud and ran towards us.

Entire ranks of them fell either dead or wounded or tripped and were climbed over by the wild-eyed men behind them. The moving and screaming pile of bodies in front of us grew and grew. Those few of the Greeks who somehow got over or past their fallen friends were hit by arrows or stopped by our pikes and swords.

For a few moments I thought we would be able to hold them off. Then everything changed. I was looking elsewhere and never did see the great mass of Greeks as they pushed back the left side of our shield wall and broke into the archers grouped behind it.

It happened right after I put an arrow into the chest of a bearded and wild-eyed man trying to bull his way past one of our pike men. He was broad in the beam, had big yellow teeth, and was only a few feet away. It was one of the easiest shots I had ever made, and the last.

I never saw the archer who was pushed back into me and knocked me down. What I did see was a sword coming down to chop into my leg as I went down. It was as if its blade was moving very, very slowly. Then I saw a foot moving slowly to step on my stomach and a spear coming down. Strangely enough, I never felt a thing.

Chapter Twenty-two

The butcher's bill.

As more and more of Dan's men went down it became easier and easier to hit the Greeks crowded in amongst the archers who were still on their feet. They attracted the attention of all the archers and many went down with four or five arrows in them. And those Greeks who went down were not replaced as it became more and more difficult for the rapidly declining number of Greeks who were still willing fight to climb over the growing and wreathing pile of bodies in front of our men.

Suddenly, most of the Greeks inside of what was left of Dan's perimeter were either dead or running, and those who were wounded were trying to stagger away. The wounded Greeks did not get far, and neither did most of the runners nor those who were still alive at the bottom of the great piles of Greek casualties. They were either shot down or suffocated from not being able to breath.

Unfortunately, the Greeks who had broken through the shield wall ran away too late to do much good for Dan and his men. From where we stood on the wall above them, it appeared that almost all of Dan's men were either dead or wounded.

Surprisingly, the men who had been in and under the wagons fared best of all, even the archers who had stood in the wagon beds and pushed their arrows straight into the Greeks who were only a few feet away. We on the wall above them, however, did not know this until some hours after the last arrow flew.

It was about then that I realized how we might bring Dan and his men to safety across the moat. It had been right in front of us all the time—ever since we had seen the ladder that did not reach all the way across the moat.

******

"Push one of the wagons into the moat," I shouted down to Dan's men after I had quieted the men around me so that I could be heard.

I shouted my order down to the men below us who were moving around to offer help to their wounded mates. At first they were all so shocked and paralyzed by what they had been through, and what they had seen and experienced, that there was no response.

"Hoy down there. You there, the sergeant in the wagon. Yes you. Unload the men from your wagon and push it into the moat. We are going to run ladders to and from that wagon and get you and the lads out of there."

The sergeant did not understand the order, at least not at first, but he had heard an order and it somehow encouraged him. A wounded apprentice sergeant bleeding from a wound to his head also heard it and understood it. He struggled to his feet to wave his acknowledgement.

It did not take long before an understanding of what I wanted spread among the men below us. They suddenly realized they might yet be saved and began frantically working, at least those who still could. So did the archers on the wall.

Ladders suddenly began arriving from every direction. They were quickly passed down to the archers who only a few minutes earlier had been pushing out arrows from the narrow strip of land between the city wall and the moat in front of it.

What was left of Dan's men did the right thing by hurrying to build what I hoped would be an escape route. The Greeks who successfully fled from our arrows had retreated deep into the recently ravaged camp of the early arrivals; they would be back sooner or later and much more ready to fight.

The Greeks' initial attack against our stranded archers had been totally disorganized and unplanned. It had failed because their commanders ignored the thirst of their men and had neither organized nor directed the attack. Indeed, they almost certainly had never bothered to tak the time before they arrived to train their men to make one.

Unfortunately, the Greeks' lack of command and control looked to be changing. From where we were standing on the wall we could see that some of the Greeks seemed to be reforming under the banners of their princes and lords. It suggested that the next time the Greeks attacked they would be much more organized and, therefore, even more dangerous. We needed to hurry.

There were so many dead and wounded men in the area between the wagons and the moat that they had to be dragged out of the way before a wagon could be emptied of its dead and wounded archers and pushed into the moat. We watched from the wall and shouted encouragements as the wagon was pulled to the moat and pushed in. It settled to the bottom almost immediately with only the driver's bench above the water. But that was enough to know where it was.

We immediately began laying ladders across the moat to the sunken wagon. A volunteer from among the men at the foot of the wall immediately began carrying a ladder across and laying it from the sunken wagon to the far shore where a number of anxious archers were waiting to hold it in place. It was a sign of our stranded men's desperation that several of the men holding the ladders were wounded and dripping blood.

It was dangerous work for the volunteer. The wagon suddenly lurched as it settled under the first man's weight, and almost dumped him off the ladder and into the water to drown. The look on his face was one of sheer terror. I suddenly understood why.

"Swimmers?" I shouted. "Does anyone know how to swim?"

No one responded except Nicholas Greenway, my apprentice. That was not surprising. Boys and men were rarely learnt to swim. Even sailors refused to learn because they thought it better to die quickly rather than slowly if their galley or transport went down. Indeed, it was widely believed in England that immersing one's body in water, even bathing, weakened a man.

"I can," said Richard who had rushed back from where he had led the attack on the moat drinkers. And so can Peter Cartwright, my apprentice when he gets back."

"Me too," said my father as he moved towards one of the ladders to climb down from the wall. "And so can your brother, John."

We had all been learnt to swim in the River Fowey by my Uncle Thomas who had insisted on my father and every boy in his school knowing how. It had already saved me more than once, the last time being when I rode a falling galley mast into the sea during a fight with the French off the mouth of the Seine.

I could not, I instantly decided, stand by idle whilst my father and my number two and good friend faced the likelihood of swimming in the foul moat, or being in the middle of it and defenceless when the Greeks launched another attack. Some of my men knew I could swim, and all of them surely would when the tale of the moat was told around our campfires in the years ahead.

What would the men ever think of me if I stood by whilst archers died because too few swimmers came forward, especially if the few who did included my father and my number two but not me? I had no choice.

"Take command up here," I snapped at Henry who had just returned and had started to tell me about the condition and casualties of the state armies which had returned from their great sally into the Greek camp.

"John," I said to my newly arrived younger brother who had been assigned to my father as his apprentice, "you are to stay with Henry Soldier to carry his messages and run whatever errands he gives you." *He was too young and would just get in the way.*

I promptly shucked off my quivers and sandals, and then pulled my tunic over my head to take off my wrist knives and chain shirt. For a moment I was as naked as a wild bird until I pulled my tunic back on. I probably should have left it off because it is hard to swim whilst wearing a tunic; but for some reason I did not.

Within a moment I was following Richard down a ladder set against the city wall. My father was already moving towards a nearby ladder and taking off his tunic and chain shirt and knives as he did.

"Set up more ladders against the wall and send more down," I snapped to Henry as I began moving down the ladder. "And send down the strongest men you can find to carry up the wounded. Attach lines to them in case they fall.

"And take off your damn chain and knives before you go out," I shouted over to my father and down to Richard.

I almost smiled; I was enjoying this for some strange reason, probably because I thought it would impress the men.

******

My father and Richard were still taking off their tunics and chain shirts when I grabbed and shook one of the two ladders that ran from the edge of the wall to the mostly submerged wagon. Then I grabbed and shook the second. It seemed to be the steadier of the two so I decided to use it.

As I started inching my way out towards the wagon, the ramparts above me were crowded with watching archers. I could hear Henry shouting out orders about getting more ladders and something about strong men and swimmers. I was a couple of feet above the moat's black water as I slowly inched my way out to the wagon on the ladder.

My knees immediately started to pain me as I put them down on the steps of the ladder and began crawling across it in an effort to reach the wagon. The brave, but terrified, archer on the wagon was trying to hold the ladder steady to help me. The water below me smelled most foul. Hopefully, the ladder would not tip to one side and dump me into it.

I made it across and stepped gingerly down into the bed of wagon. The water came up almost to my waist.

"Pass me another ladder," I shouted to the men on shore next to the wall. A few moments later I was working to place the second ladder more securely on the wagon.

******

My father and Richard soon came across and joined me, and we hurriedly began running more ladders from the shore to the wagon and from the wagon to the other side of the moat. The brave archer who could not swim was most helpful. He was a two-striper named Albert Albert's son from a village I had never heard of, probably because it was near Leicester, just on the other side of the city common where the boys of Leicester play.

When we were about half way through placing enough ladders side by side and on top of each other to make a rickety bridge, I thanked Albert for his service and told him to climb back over the new ladders to the wall. Albert Albert's son was a two-striper who, although he did not know it yet, would soon be wearing a third.

My father stood in the wagon and did his best to hold the ladder bridge steady whilst Richard and I climbed over to the other side of the moat to take command of the men stranded there. Dan Tenn, I had already been told by one of the surviving galley captains, was dead of being cut and stabbed too many times.

****

Richard and I fed the stranded men on to the rickety ladder bridge as fast as possible. Those who were wounded, but who were still able to crawl, were fed into the line of would-be escapers as fast as we could get a line around their waists so they could be hauled ashore if they fell into the water. The others were told to crawl whilst holding on to the line that had been run across the ladders. When they got to the other side they would be helped or carried up the wall ladders by the strong men Henry sent down to the foot of the wall for that purpose.

Whilst we doing that, two additional wagons were rolled into the moat and Richard and my father left me to help the men get across, and began working to install an additional ladder bridge across to one of them. The other wagon tipped over on its side and sank too far to be useful.

Crawling across the ladders was taking far too much time because every man had to carefully put a knee securely on the narrow edge of a ladder step before he could move his hands and then get other knee ahead to the next sharp edge. I knew that from experience; my knees had immediately gotten so painfully sore that at one point I did not think I would be able to continue.

Things went slowly, and only a few men had escaped over to the city wall, until Henry and some men began dropping down some wooden boards which were quickly laid over the sharp edges of the ladder steps. That enabled the men to crawl much faster across from one side of the moat to the other.

Where Henry got the planks I did not know, but they joined those that one the trapped galley captains had wisely begun ripping from the bed of the remaining wagon as soon as he understood what we were trying to do and why.

Moving the wagons, the loss of so many men, and the escape of others left us with fewer and fewer defenders from amongst Dan's men. There was no way a second Greek attack could be stopped. We had to hurry.

******

About half of the trapped men had scrambled across our makeshift bridges to safety by the time we began turning our attention to the men who were seriously wounded. They would have to either be carried across or thrown in the water with a line tied around them so they could be pulled ashore on the other side. *Which is what we probably should have done for everyone instead of wasting so much time building the two ladder-bridges.*

Twice men had somehow fallen into the water amidst great shouts of alarm from everyone watching. Both times the man involved had managed to tighten his grip on one of the guide lines we had strung over the bridges and pull himself to safety. The third time, however, the ladder lurched and the archer somehow lost his grip on the line even though it had been sliding through his hand as he crawled. He disappeared into the moat with a great splash.

Unfortunately, it happened whilst I was standing near what remained of the last wagon with a line in my hand. My father and I were about to tie it around the waist, under the shoulders actually, of the last of the archers who had been terribly wounded with a sword slice that had taken off part of his arm.

Someone's tunic belt had been tied around what was left of it to stop more of the poor sod's blood from leaking out. He would be pulled across through the water and probably not even know it because he was sleeping. *It was not likely he would survive, but others had survived such wounds and we were honour-bound by the Company's contract to do our best to help him until he died.*

I did something stupid when I heard the splash and the many resulting cries of alarm; I grabbed the line that was about to go about the wounded archer, moved my left arm in a circle around the line a couple of times so it would not slip off, and jumped in to try to rescue the man in the water. If I could grab him and hold on to the line, we could both be pulled ashore on the wall side of the moat.

The drowning archer was not hard to find because the moat was not too deep and I jumped right on top of him. He felt my legs hit him and instinctively grabbed them in his desperation—and he pulled me under with him when he did.

He had a desperate grip on me and was flailing all about. It was almost as if he was trying to climb up over me in an effort to get out of the water. After a moment of panic I managed to get my head out of the water so I could breathe and, at the same time, grab a handful of his tunic.

"Pull the rope in," I managed to gasp before I went under again.

If there is one thing an archer serving on a galley knows, it is how to respond to an order to pull on a line. A moment later I was being pulled rapidly through the water with my desperate cargo. For an instant he let go of me, but them desperately grabbed me by the legs and once again tried to climb over me to get out of the water. I never let go of his tunic belt.

Within seconds we reached the side of the moat next to the wall and were pulled ashore to great hoorays and many cries of congratulations and pleasure. My God but the water tasted terrible.

Chapter Twenty-three

Rescues and a surprising idea.

Henry called down to me while I was sitting on my arse trying to catch my breath after being pulled to the edge of the moat and being hauled ashore. My face felt red and burning, but my wet clothes felt cool and good in the burning hot sun.

I had been looking at the almost-drowned archer who had fallen into the moat when Henry called down to me. He, the almost-drowned archer, had been asleep when his mates first pulled him up on to the bank of the moat, and was still asleep when held him up by his legs and bounced his head on the ground so the water would run out of him.

Holding the sleeping archer up by his legs had worked. Water had run out of his mouth, and he had barfed as well. Now he was coughing and sputtering whilst they pounded on his back to get him going again. He was also bleeding badly from his wound.

The last of our trapped men, two very battered looking galley captains, were crossing the two ladder bridges by the time the wounded archer woke up and began barfing again. The men who had been too wounded to crawl over the moat had already been pulled across through the water with lines tied around their waists. The last of them had just been hoisted up to the top of the wall.

Dan and our other dead had been hastily buried, if you can call it that, by having some dirt thrown on them with a couple of shovels that had been thrown across to the two captains who had been the last archers to leave. We would return to retrieve their bodies and bury them with the proper church words after the war.

There was no time to do more; a sizable Greek force was in the process of returning to recover their casualties and make another go at our trapped men, and this one somehow gave the impression of being more capable. Its men were now milling about at a distance that their captains thought was outside the range of our arrows. I was tempted to show the Greeks the error of their ways, but decided against it in the hope that doing nothing would cause them to move too close during a more critical time in the days ahead.

"Can you climb up here, George?" Henry shouted down to me. "There is something important you need to know. I will come down there and tell you if you are not ready to climb."

I sort of waved my hand to acknowledge him, and then held it out for one of the men who were standing around looking at me to pull me up on to my feet.

Behind me I heard someone give an order as I lurched toward one of the ladders that were up against the city wall. For some reason, I was very tired. It was probably the heat.

"Stay close behind him, Bob; catch him if he falls."

****** *Commander George Courtenay*

I made it to the top of the ladder without looking down to scare myself, rolled over the top of the battlement's outer wall between two archer slits, and fell on to the little stone road that ran along the top of the wall all the way around the city.

Henry bent his knees and squatted down next to me. His information was very interesting, and I quickly understood why he had not shouted it down to me.

"Ivan Skavinsky, the prince who commands the Bulgarians, thinks his men and the other state forces would be willing to do another large-scale sally if they knew there would be coins in it for them—and we have the coins we were going to use to Ransom Dan and his men."

"Henry, what are you suggesting? I am not sure I understand."

"I am suggesting we send the state forces out on another sally as early as the first thing tomorrow morning. It is the last thing in the world the Greeks would expect us to do after today. If they go out soon enough we would likely catch the Greeks before they have time to get organized."

"Are you sure? Do you really think another sally would work if we launched it so soon?"

"I think it might, and it would probably help us by killing some Greeks even if the states' men are defeated.

"Ivan's men and the other state forces had a relatively easy time of it this morning. Their confidence is high at the moment, so he thinks they would go again, particularly if they were offered a big incentive to do so. The thing to remember is that every Greek they end up killing or taking out of the fight is one less for our lads to have to worry about.

"Besides, it is always better to let someone else to do the fighting and dying than our lads, eh? What counts is that every Greek the states' men kill means one less for our lads to have to fight."

What Henry said made sense.

"Well, it makes sense when you put it that way. And you are almost certainly right that the Greeks will not be expecting another large-scale attack so soon. You and Ivan have obviously given it some thought. How do you suggest we go about it?"

"Ivan knows our galleys are collecting the toll coins. He thinks we should offer a silver coin for every man who goes out in the sally and returns with a Greek sword and ten copper coins for every Greek spear he brings back. That way they would only be paid if they bring back weapons they have taken from the Greeks. For himself; if he encourages the sally and leads it, Ivan wants the Empress to award him some disputed land.

"Offering every man in the states' armies what amounts to prize money for bringing in Greek weapons and prisoners, and then letting them keep the weapons, which is what Ivan suggests, is probably the only way we will ever be able to get the states' men to actually fight the Greeks. As it is, I do not think we dare not trust them to defend any part of the wall by themselves. And, like I said, every Greek they kill or wound means one less for our lads to face."

I thought about it behind my eyes for about a minute, and then made a decision.

"Ivan is probably right. Some of the states' forces men are likely to be keen to get the coins on offer both for weapons and for useful prisoners such as lords and bishops. And you are right that it is probably the only way we will be able to use the states' men in a fight."

Actually, I lied. What I did not tell Henry was that a sally was not the only way we could use the states' forces to fight the Greeks instead of using our archers. I had another plan already underway that Henry did not know about yet—and it might work even better if everyone thought the state forces had been weakened and discouraged by taking casualties during another sally.

"Alright," I finally said. "Why not, eh? We will give it a try unless it looks like a forlorn hope. I will make the final decision in the morning when we see what faces them outside the gate. But do you really think the state forces can be ready to sally out as early as tomorrow morning? Can you and Ivan get it set up by then?"

I was full of questions, and totally exhausted, as I was helped to climb aboard a horse after watching my father crawl over the ladder and get back to the wall.

****** *William, the Company's retired Commander*

Man after man came past me as I stood in the wagon bed with the water up to my knees and helped them get on the ladder bridge stretching towards the wall. It was so tiring that I had to lean up against the wagon seat at times to catch my breath. To my surprise, my son, John, George's much younger brother by way of Helen, had come out when I was not looking and was doing the same on the other wagon.

I ended up being the last man to return to the wall. Before I did, I climbed up on to the driver's seat of the sunken wagon. Then I shouted loudly towards the Greeks to get their attention. They had stopped just out of what they thought was the range of our arrows. When I thought I had it, I made the sign of the horns at them and lifted my wet tunic and pissed at them whilst I did.

The archers on the wall behind me cheered. It was like old times and I felt young again when I lifted my hand to acknowledge them.

But then something bad happened as I crawled off the ladder bridge and reached the wall. My chest began to hurt so fierce that I had to be carried up to the top of the wall and then carried in a wagon to the Citadel for barbering. John rode with me and held my hand.

And who would have thought that getting wet with foul water would cause a pox that made a man's chest hurt and made it hard for him to walk?

****** *Commander George Courtenay.*

Henry immediately galloped to the camp of the states' forces to meet with Prince Ivan. They would spread the word about the sally and the coins that would be paid for weapons and prisoners. Richard went with him. It was then that I knew for sure that Henry thought the sally was important—because it was well known that he absolutely hated to ride aboard a horse and usually refused to do so. He said it always made his arse sore and rubbed it red.

I waited and watched until I saw my father get safely across the moat. Then I rode back to the Commandery with Nicholas to await the return of Michael Oremus and the coin chests he had been sent to fetch from the galley where they were stored. The chests were, of course, kept safely in the hold of a well-crewed galley in case we needed to make a fast getaway.

Michael had been accompanied by the entire strength of one of the galley companies to help him guard the coins. The company's men were fresh and ready to go because it was one of the two companies that had remained behind to guard the gate whilst the others were off on their successful but ill-fated sally across the moat.

It was early in the afternoon of a very hot and tiring day. At first, whilst I was riding back to the Commandery in the sun, my clothes had steam rising from them, but now they were dry.

Eric appeared while I was waiting at the Commandery for the coins to arrive. He reported the city had been relatively quiet during the night. The die-hard Orthodox supporters of the Patriarch had switched their efforts to daytime attacks on people coming and going from the markets and the Latin churches. Some of the Empress's own servants had been attacked.

******

Wagons carrying the coins, two of them, arrived at the Commandery about two hours before sundown. We immediately set off for the gate in the city's inner wall that opened on to the road that ran through the states' encampment. Henry and Prince Ivan had both said they thought it was important for the men to actually see the coins.

Once again a translator rode ahead and repeated his cries in both crusader French and Greek.

"Make way for the coins to pay for the captured weapons" … "Make way for the Empress's Commander" … "Make way for the coins to pay for the captured weapons." … "Make way….

Our arrival in the states' encampment caused great excitement. It began as soon as we passed through the gate and entered the camp. That was no surprise since the coins and the terms had already been announced throughout the camp, as had the fact that they would soon be arriving for all to see and would be waiting at the sally gate tomorrow to immediately pay the returning salliers for the weapons and prisoners they brought in.

What was also interesting was that Henry now had the gate through the city's inner wall being guarded by an entire galley company of archers. They were letting people into the camp of states' forces, but allowing no one to leave it no matter how much they pleaded. There were also pairs of archers walking all along the top of the interior walls that penned in the states encampment and turned it into one long and narrow enclosure running for three or four miles all the way along the roadway from the gate in the outer city wall to the inner wall.

It did not take a longbow craftsman to understand why so many archers were at the gate and on the walls—Henry and Prince Ivan were trying to keep word of tomorrow's sally from reaching the Greek army via its spies in the city.

Chapter Twenty-four

Good news and bad news.

"The excitement of the states' men is understandable," Henry said by way of greeting as I dismounted near the gate and the coin-carrying wagons came to a halt behind me. He had seen me waving to the people in the states' camp and heard the cheering.

"Most of them are in the village levies and have never had a silver coin of their own in their entire lives. Ivan has announced that his men and all the others may keep any coins they receive for the weapons they bring in, and do not have to turn them over to their lords. And, get this, George, he said they can also keep the weapons and do whatever they want with them.

"Keeping both the weapons and the prize money is unheard of, and the men seem to believe him, probably because they want it to be true. As a result, the response of the states' forces has been very encouraging. It looks to me that tomorrow's sally is going to be stronger and much more aggressive than the one that went out this morning."

I told him I agreed, at least about the enthusiasm of the men of the states' forces. And I really did; it had taken an unexpectedly long time to bring the coins to the gate because of the enthusiastic response we received as we rode through the states' camp with the coin chests.

And then Henry chuckled and leaned closer, and whispered in my ear.

"Prince Ivan told his men that the latest Greek arrivals brought wagons full of swords and spears for the men who are already here, and that they are on the other side of the Greek camp where he told them the Greek commander has his headquarters.

"Some of his knights are so anxious for coins they can use to buy land of their own that they plan to take wagons with them to carry back the weapons they intend to capture. He says the men of the other states' forces are equally enthusiastic."

I was surprised at what he told me and said as much.

"Ivan and the other princes are actually agreeable to letting their men keep the coins instead of demanding a share? And they are also going to let them keep the captured weapons as well? That surprises me."

I made the comment with a question in my voice. And Henry had an answer.

"I do not know about the kings and princes of the Empire's other states, but Prince Ivan is more interested in getting his hands on some disputed lands that a couple of other states are also claiming."

Then he smiled and added something that sounded more believable.

"Besides, he thinks he will soon get the coins by increasing everyone's taxes and selling some of the disputed lands to his knights so they can be lords over the lands and serve as buffers between his state and the others.

"He undoubtedly sees it as a win-win opportunity for everybody, and so do I." Henry said it quite adamantly and waved his hands about to help make his point.

Henry smiled a very smug and knowing smile as he explained what Prince Ivan had told him about the facts of life in the Empire, the reality of its various kings and princes' ambitions, and the great risks the rulers of its various states were willing to have their men to undertake to achieve the rulers' goals.

"But what makes Ivan think he will get the disputed lands?" I asked Henry when he finished.

"Because I promised him that *you* and the Company would see that he got them if he contributed more to the Empress's victory than any of her other princes."

"Of course we will." It was all I could think to say.

I was completely done in and said as much.

"It has been a long day and I am too exhausted to continue. I am going back to the Citadel for a good night's sleep and, hopefully, to find a new tunic. I smell like the damn moat, which is no surprise since I went swimming in it.

"I used to think Brereton's moat was the blackest and foulest in the world, from when I visited Chester with Uncle Thomas years ago to buy some ambler mares. But Constantinople's foul moat has Brereton's beat by a county mile and then some."

Henry wrinkled his nose and agreed that a new tunic was a good idea—and that from a man who never bathed and never even took off his tunic until it was threadbare or a woman insisted.

******

It was whilst I was just finishing my talk with Henry that I first heard about my father. A messenger came from the Citadel informing me that my father was seriously poxed and the Empress's personal physician had been summoned. The messenger knew nothing else.

"I will be back before dawn and make the final decision then," I said as I swung aboard my horse and pointed at Nicholas.

"Nicholas, you are to place the coin wagons where I showed you and make sure the coins are heavily guarded all night long. Then return to the stables and get a good night's sleep. Just make sure I am awake an hour before sunrise so we can ride back here before dawn."

With that, I dug my heels into my horse's side and started down the road with my horse guards following along behind me. We rode at the fastest gait possible, which was mostly not very fast at all because so many people were on the road and in the city streets. I did my best; I rode straight to the Citadel as fast as I could.

******

"Oh George, I am so worried. I do not want to lose him again."

A tearful Empress greeted me with those chilling words and a brief hug when I rushed into the Citadel. She had gotten word of my imminent arrival and been waiting for me at the bottom of the steps. We hurried up the steps together.

My father was in the smaller room next to the Empress's reception room. Her bedroom with its several entrance doors was immediately behind her reception room. The windowless room that was Empire's treasury was behind her bedroom which had the only door by which the treasury could be entered. There was a door into her bedroom from the room where my father was being examined.

"I put him there so I could be close to him in case he needed me," she explained as she gestured towards the room where he was being treated.

We started to enter my father's room, but stopped immediately when one of the physicians in attendance held up the flat of one of his hands to warn us not to come in. He did so without even looking at us. We immediately stopped in the doorway.

I could see my father lying on his bed with his eyes closed. He was covered by a piece of linen and clearly had no clothes on under it. He was not moving and appeared to be either asleep or dead. The room was very warm from the heat of the day despite the wooden shutters on its two small wall openings being open. They would, of course, be closed at night when the air became dangerous.

The physician was a tall and gaunt man wearing a robe with all sorts of symbols and signs embroidered on it. He kept his eyes on my father as he spoke.

"The foul smell that causes the chest pox is still in the room from his body and clothes, so it is too dangerous for you to enter. My assistant and I have bathed him and cut his hair to remove as much as possible of the dangerous smells clinging to it, and I have given him a potion to help him sleep. There is no need to bleed him, and I do not recommend it for such a pox. Potions mixed by an expert and lots of sleep are always much better for the chest pox."

"What did you say caused it?" I asked because I was not sure that I had heard the physician correctly. His crusader French was not the best.

"The foul smells of the moat water he stood in are almost certainly what caused the sudden onset of the painful pox inside his chest and arm. It happens when men breathe such smells for too long. Mostly it strikes older men with great pains in their chests and arms and shortness of breath.

"You are younger, but, even so, if you were near enough to smell your father after he was wet with moat water, you should change your clothes and rub the smell off your body with wet rags. And you should trim off as much of your hair as possible as the smell is known to linger there."

A cold chill gripped me and made my arms prickle. *My God! I was in the moat for hours and went all the way under. Everyone can smell it on me. Even Henry commented on it.*

******

The physician started to tell me that he would come to my room and tell me more about my father's condition in a few minutes. I hardly heard him, I had already turned around and was rushing down the Citadel's long hallway towards my sleeping room at the other end of the hall.

As I did, I began calling for clean water and rags, "and a tunic, any tunic." Then something suddenly struck me as I was jogging towards my room; did the Empress just say *lose him again*?

There was one of the Empress's servants standing at the top of the stairs. It was his duty station where he waited to be given orders. As I hurried past him, I ordered him to run and get me a bowl of water and some rags. Immediately after I got into my room I began pulling my tunic over my head and once again shouted for water and rags.

It was already dark but I had had no trouble finding my way to my room because the hall candles were lit, as were both of the candles in my room.

Elizabeth must have heard me shouting and seen that I had left the door open, for she came in without knocking a few moments after the water and rags arrived. She gaped at me when she saw me standing there holding a wet rag and wearing nothing except my wrist knives.

"Get out, you damn fool," I shouted at her. "Do you want to catch the chest and arm pox like my father? Save yourself; go to your room and light candles to kill the smell?"

Elizabeth's jaw dropped open and she put her hands to her mouth in shocked surprise. A moment later she spun around and rushed out of the room.

I know, I know. Women rarely catch it. But I was tired and needed a good night's sleep.

By the light of the hallway candles I saw Nicholas hurrying down the hall towards my room as Elizabeth went flying out the door and passed him going in the other direction. Nicholas looked serious and worried about something. I did not give him a chance to tell me what was on his mind.

"Nicholas," I shouted. "The Empress's physician says the smell of foul moat water can cause the painful chest pox that kills men if they smell it too strongly for too long. That means you and I are both at risk, and so are all the men who waded through the moat water to get back from the attack.

"So here is what I want you to do—you are to immediately go to the stables and stand in one of the horse troughs to wash your legs until the smell of the moat is gone. Then, to be sure, I want you to throw away your tunic if the moat-smell is on it.

"But on your way back to the stables, I want you to tell the captain of my guards that he is to ride along the wall telling each galley company's captain that he and every one of his men who got wet with moat water must throw away their tunics if their tunics smell; and they are to use rags and good water wash off the smell of the moat off their bodies.

"Also tell the captain of the guards to send his lieutenant and a wagon to our galleys to raid their slop chests for new tunics. He is to take a new tunic to every man who walked in the moat water. He will need at least four hundred."

Nicholas eyes widened in alarm at the terrible news, and he left at a run without telling me why he had come from the stables to see me. And, with that, I blew out the candles, gave a good scratch around my bollocks, and climbed on to my bed to sleep naked in the heat.

And then I cursed and put both my feet back on the floor—I had to wait for the physician.

******

The physician showed up a few minutes later. He was a Greek. That surprised me even though Greek physicians are well known to be the best. We were, after all, fighting with a Greek army and the Greek-gobbling people of the city had risen against us. But if the Empress trusted him, then so would I.

His name was Andreas something or other and he came straight to the point.

"I cannot stay long because I must return to your father. My diagnosis has not changed. He is suffering from the painful, and often fatal, chest and arm pox caused by particularly foul smells. I understand he spent hours wading in the waters of the outer moat so his sad condition is no surprise.

"On the other hand, there is reason to be hopeful. His death is not certain because I may have gotten my potions into him in time. They are very rare and expensive, but they offset the effects of the foul smells if they are administered soon enough. I used all I had because the Empress said I was to spare no expense."

I thanked him for his efforts, and then started to ask him if other smells such as those a man makes when he eats bad cheese can cause the chest pox. But then I decided against it. He was a physician so his fee was undoubtedly already too high.

Chapter Twenty-five

To sally or not to sally; that was the question.

There were no pains in my chest or arm the next morning when Nicholas rapped on my door to wake me. It was about an hour and a half before the first light of dawn. I immediately inquired about my father and was pleased to learn that he was still alive after a quiet night and would likely survive if he did not suffer a relapse. The family luck was still holding and I felt much better because I had gotten a good night's sleep.

Nicholas, as had become our custom, had stopped at the Citadel's kitchen to pick up bread and cheese that we could eat as we rode off to wherever we were bound. This time we ate as we rode to meet Henry at the gate from which the states' forces would almost certainly launch their second sally in as many days.

The early morning darkness was pleasantly cool and we talked as we rode. I asked about the distribution of the tunics, and then, after I nodded my appreciation at what I had been told, inquired as to if he had heard anything at the stables about the Alchemist and his work on the ribalds. That is when I finally heard the sad news about the alchemist's betrothed and her mother—there would be no wedding; the girl and her mother had been killed by rioters yesterday as they walked home from the market.

"Aron is absolutely distraught, Commander. "He is overbalanced with more anger and despair than I have ever seen in a man. James Howard fears for him and so do I."

******

Our ride to the sally gate though the city's quiet streets in the moonlight took us to the one remaining usable gate in the inner defensive wall on the landward side of the city. We passed through the gate and immediately entered another world; the totally awakened camp of the state's forces. There was much more activity than usual for this time of day. Cooking fires were being lit and people were moving about everywhere in the moonlit darkness.

Such a high level of activity so early on this particular day was not a surprise. It was likely the state's forces would be launching a sally in an hour or two, or so they thought and hoped.

Indeed, I had already decided to allow the sally *if* it seemed likely to succeed—and perhaps even if it did not.

My decision would depend on the readiness of the Greek army outside the gate or, perhaps it would be more accurate to say, the lack of its readiness. I probably would not allow the sally, no matter how much the states' forces wanted to sally out and fight for the Greek weapons, if the companies of the Greek army had gotten the word and were waiting with such an overwhelming force that success of the states' men would be a forlorn hope.

It would be a difficult decision if the Greek army was ready and waiting. It was one thing to send men into a battle in which they had a chance to live through it with a chance to enjoy the prestige and loot of a victory; it was something else to send them to their certain deaths.

On the other hand, Henry was right; the states' forces would take some of the Greeks with them even if they were annihilated—and that would reduce the number of Greek soldiers trying to kill my archers and our auxiliaries in the days ahead.

How best to use the states' forces, and whether or not to commit them to a sally, was a decision I would make in a few minutes, when dawn's early light arrived when I could see what was happening outside the sally gate.

******

It was still dark when I climbed the stone steps to reach the top the wall where it stood over the city gate. Prince Ivan, Henry, and almost all of my lieutenant Commanders were already there and waiting. Only my father was missing from those who were expected to be there.

Word of my father's affliction had spread through the ranks and I received the expected quiet good wishes and muttered encouragements. My lieutenants received a very brief report from me in return.

"He has a chest pain pox from spending too much time standing in the moat's waters. But the Empress's personal physician is attending him and he looks likely to make a full recovery."

Astute readers will no doubt note that I was now saying standing too long in the moat's foul waters instead of smelling them. The men would be manning the wall near the moat in the days ahead and I did not want to spook them about being near its foul smell any more than I had already done by ordering some of them to wash wherever the moat water had touched them and burn the tunics that had gotten wet.

We talked whilst we waited. Henry was both anxious and in great good cheer despite not getting much of a night's sleep under one of the heavily guarded coin wagons. He took me aside and chuckled as he whispered to me that Prince Ivan was almost smart enough to be an English moneylender. The prince, Henry explained with more chuckles, had spread the word among his men and the other states' forces that the newly arrived Greek column had brought five wagon loads of additional swords and spears for the men who were already here.

According to Henry, Prince Ivan had whispered to his men that the commander of the Greek army had the wagons carrying the weapons parked near his tent on the other side of the camp. In other words, Henry whispered with more than a little delight in his voice, if the men of the states' armies want the weapons and the coins they would fetch, they would have to fight their way through the entire Greek camp to reach them.

And that, Henry said with another chuckle, was exactly what some of the states' forces were apparently going to try to do.

"Do the wagons full of weapons actually exist?" I asked.

"Probably not. But it is a very good story and the states' men seem to want to believe it is true. It gives them an excuse for fighting their way all the way through the Greek camp to get to them. And then, at the very least, they will have to fight their way all the way back to save themselves."

According to Henry, Prince Ivan said his knights and some of the others were so excited about the possibility of getting enough prize coins to buy lands of their own to lord over that some of them had taken extraordinary steps to insure their success. They were bringing wagons with them so they could carry back enough captured weapons to be forever rich and landed.

How they would get their wagons all the way through the closely packed tents and wagons of the Greek camp, and then all the way back, he did not know.

Henry also confessed that he had heard disquieting rumours that there would be an effort to gull us out of the coins we had promised to pay for captured weapons.

Some of the states' men, Henry said, apparently intend to carry two weapons out the gate so they can return with them and claim one was captured. Others were reported to be planning to hand their weapon to a mate, return without it, and then split the coins their mate collected for showing it. Neither action would have any risk since it was proclaimed that anyone who returned with captured weapons would both be paid and could keep them.

Even the camp wives were getting involved. Some of them were trying to borrow weapons belonging to the men who were not going out for one reason or another—with the idea of carrying them out in the sally so they could hand them to their men so they could be claimed as captured weapons when their men returned.

As a result of hearing the rumours and schemes, Henry and Prince Ivan wanted the sally temporarily delayed so they would have enough time walk through the sally force to make sure no one was carrying more than one weapon into the Greek camp. As they did, Henry said, they would pass the word that women would not be allowed on the sally and any unwounded man who returned without his weapon would be severely punished.

He and the prince, Henry assured me, would start walking through the salliers as soon as the sun arrived so I could see enough to give the order for the sally to proceed—"assuming you give it, of course."

What none of us realized at the time was that something else would be the main source of false weapons claims—and there was nothing we could do about them except smile and pay.

******

The early light of dawn came up a few minutes later and we saw what there was for us to see. In front of us, and starting just outside the city wall, was the huge and tightly-packed Greek camp. Everywhere it seemed to come right up to the edge of the moat, even in front of the sally gate bridge.

The Greek campers apparently still thought the moat would protect them, especially after yesterday's sally almost ended in a massacre of the archers. Or perhaps those now camping near the gate on the other side of the moat were new arrivals and not aware of what had happened to those who had been camping there yesterday when we launched our first sally.

In the end, it did not matter *who* the campers were or *why* they were camping within the range of our arrows and near the sally gate; they were there, and that meant some of them would likely die for their mistake.

On the other hand, coming off their march and going straight into an attack on the trapped archers without first setting up their camp and getting organized had apparently confused and scattered the Greek soldiers. Many of them had appeared to still be wandering around seeking their lords and mates when the sun went down.

But had their commanders learned of the states forces' coming sally and spent the night pulling their companies together to oppose them? That was the question on everyone's mind as we waited in the moonlit darkness on the wall above the gate tower that stood over the road in which the state forces were forming up for their second sally in as many days.

We were waiting for the sun to arrive so we could see whether or not the greatly enlarged Greek army was prepared and waiting for our sally. Not that it would have made much difference, mind you; I had long ago decided to send out the sally. The argument that every enemy soldier killed or wounded meant one less for the archers to have to fight was very persuasive.

Finally, the sun arrived on its daily trip around the world and we could see the enemy encampment.

"Yes," Exclaimed Henry as he pounded his fist into his hand.

In front of us the close-packed camp of the Orthodox army seemed to stretch all the way to the horizon. Its tents and wagons and men sleeping rough were everywhere and seemed to take up every inch of available space.

What was significant was that there was *not* a single Greek force in sight that was arrayed for battle. To the contrary, everything appeared to be peaceful and totally disorganized. It was as if everyone had just flopped down on the ground wherever they happened to be standing when darkness fell.

In any event, the camp was just beginning to wake up with people coming out of their tents and from under their wagons to find water and to piss and shite wherever they could find an open space. Indeed, many of those who had been sleeping rough began picking up their packs and seemed to be setting off to find their mates and captains.

At first there was no dust hanging over the Greek camp. What we saw was the beginning of another clear and hot summer sky that was marred only by the smoke of a few cooking fires, those which had already been started while it was still dark.

That, of course, would change as more cooking fires were lit and the men and their camp followers and animals started moving about. And it would really change, particularly for the Greeks nearest to the gate, if I allowed the sally to go forwards and thousands of states' soldiers suddenly rushed out of the gate and fell upon them.

Behind us on the roadway was a totally different scene; it was bustling with noise and activity. The two hundred or so knights and horsemen of the states' armies were lined up on the road nearest to the gate just as they had been yesterday. They and their wagons would lead the charge.

Immediately behind the riders, the roadway was packed with the five thousand or so foot soldiers of the states' forces, almost all of them untrained and poorly equipped village levies. They had been brought in by their kings and princes to help defend the city.

The states' foot had several wagons in amongst them as well. Indeed, the road was packed with the states' foot all the way to where the road curved around and the men on it disappeared from view due to the interior wall that ran along. How many men were beyond the curve? I did not have a clue.

It might have been my imagination, but there seemed to me to be more horsemen and more foot soldiers waiting to charge out the gate than were present in yesterday's sally. They also somehow seemed more eager, or perhaps that was just my imagination telling me that I was seeing what I wanted to see.

They really wanted to go out and fight? Well, that certainly worked for me.

"Yes, they can go. Raise the gate as soon as you are ready."

With those words I announced my decision. I made it in the hope that another sally by the states' forces would cause enemy losses and desertions that would, in turn, end up reducing the casualties suffered by my archers.

Henry and Prince Ivan dashed down the stone stairs to the roadway as soon as I announced that the sally could proceed. They and several of their sergeants began walking through the ranks of the salliers in an effort to make sure no one received coins by carrying more than one weapon out the gate, and then returning with the second weapon claiming it had been captured from the Greeks.

Coins we were willing to pay for weapons; but we wanted the coins to be paid for the weapons they actually took from the Greeks, not for weapons they temporarily borrowed from their friends. *We thought the warnings and inspection would be sufficient to eliminate fraudulent claims; we were wrong, very wrong.*

The gate holding back the sally would be raised as soon as Henry and Prince Ivan finished their last-minute weapons inspection. They estimated it would take them less than thirty minutes. All along the roadway men were already trying to move forward to get closer to the sally gate. Their enthusiasm about once again fighting their way into the Greek camp surprised everyone including me.

Chapter Twenty-six

The second sally.

It was a stirring scene. I looked down from atop the gate tower and watched as Henry walked swiftly to gate and Prince Ivan swung himself aboard his horse which was at the very front of the column, lowered his helmet visor, and then drew his sword and held it high over his head. Henry must have shouted something to the two archers manning the windlass that was used to roll up the rusty chains that raised the gate—because the gate slowly began rising even before he reached them.

The slow upward movement of the gate coupled with Prince Ivan simultaneous boarding his horse and drawing his sword had a noticeable effect on the long column of men waiting for him to lead them into the Greek encampment.

Not everyone waiting to sally could see Prince Ivan as he made his final preparations for fighting, but those who could see him immediately dropped their helmet visors and drew their swords; and the men behind them who saw them do that, in turn, dropped their visors and drew their swords. It was as if a great wave of last second preparations washed down the column of men.

At the same time, the level of noise caused by men talking overly loud in an effort to keep up their courage changed. It suddenly became so quiet that we could make out individual voices.

Going into harm's way seems to do that to a man for some reason.

******

At some point, as the gate was going up, I realized that a red-faced and puffing Henry had come up the stone stairs to join me and Nicholas on the wall above the gate.

A few moments later we looked down and watched as Prince Ivan came charging through the gate below us waving his sword over his head. He rode over the moat bridge at a hard gallop and charged straight ahead into the unsuspecting Greek camp. The states' riders were right behind him.

From where we were standing we could clearly see the surprise that the sudden appearance of the prince and his riders caused amongst the Greek campers nearest to the sally gate. They stopped whatever they were doing for the briefest of moments and gaped in absolute disbelief—and then most of them ran for their lives, and a few for their weapons. There was much more of the former so far as I could see.

Dust rose from the galloping horses' hooves and the sun caused the swords of the riders to flash as they reached out to cut down the fleeing men and women. We could hear their screams over all the shouting and the thundering noise of the horses' hooves. Several times I saw riders lean far out of their saddles to pick up something on the ground. They were almost certainly picking up weapons.

And it was not all one-sided, even in the first few seconds when the Greeks soldiers and their camp followers were totally surprised. We saw a lone rider slashing about with his sword as he rode into a large group of fleeing Greeks, both men and women, and then watched as his horse suddenly stumbled to its knees and went down. The rider came flying out of his saddle and landed on the ground ahead of his horse.

The fleeing people kept running and we did not see the fallen rider get up. What was more than somewhat surprising, at least to the archers watching from the wall, was that none of the other riders stopped to help the man who had been unhorsed. Either he was a friendless and hated man or his mates were too excited and did not see him go down.

And to my surprise, and Henry's too, not all of the riders followed the prince and the handful of knights riding with him. Some individuals and small groups of riders immediately began going off in different directions. It was as if every man had his own ideas as to where he might find weapons to capture.

A moment later we looked down from the wall and watched as the last of the hard-charging riders were followed by an absolute horde of men on foot shouting their battle cries and waving their spears. These were the men we were counting on to sack the Greek encampment.

What was strange was that men on foot moved so slowly and quietly as they came forward on the road that ran through their camp. They were almost shuffling until they reached the gate. But then they burst out of the gate running and shouting. I would have thought they all would have started running at the same time.

We began to hear the plaintive screams and cries of the wounded and other nearby Greeks who were still alive once the states' men on foot moved further into the Greek camp. The dust was drifting towards us which made it difficult to see. Some of the states' foot could be seen poking into tents and wagons looking for weapons. In the distance we could hear shouting and the unmistakable scream of a horse, which suddenly stopped.

It was going to be a long, hot, and dusty day, especially for the Greeks.

******

A wounded and helmetless knight on horseback, or perhaps he was still a squire since he appeared to be so young, was the first man to return for coins. His sword was sheathed and he was holding tight to a couple of spears with one hand and trying to hold a nasty gash in his side closed with the other.

We watched from the wall above the gate as he passed under us and rode directly to the coin wagon on the south side of the gate and gestured towards the sword and held out one of the spears. We could not hear him from where we were standing, but he was obviously asking for a silver coin for the sword and ten coppers for the second spear.

Henry, to my surprise, started cursing and began moving to the stairs. He obviously intended to walk down and confront the man for some reason. I decided to follow him down since the fighting had raised such a cloud of dust that all I could see was the nearest small area of the Greek camp with its dead bodies scattered all about and some of the states' foot soldiers searching amongst the tents and wagons for weapons. There were also a few wounded men and women staggering around looking for help.

We reached the coin wagon on the south side of the gate in time to listen to part of the friendly exchange in crusader French between my brother John and the young rider.

"But I brought in a sword and a spear. I am to be paid one silver coin for the sword and ten coppers for the captured spear, yes?"

"Those are the prices we pay, Sir Knight," my young brother said apologetically. "But you are a rider and every rider went out with a sword or axe. Not a single rider carried a spear. Only the foot of the states' levies carried them."

"Ah well, you may be right," the young man admitted with a smile. "My wound is painful, it must be confusing me. Give me the coins for the two spears," he said as he grimaced and held out his hand.

"That is nowhere near enough," the wounded young man said with a sigh a few seconds later as he pouched his coppers.

A moment later, to everyone's surprise, he threw the spears down even though he was entitled to keep them, pulled his horse's head around, and started to go back out to get more Greek weapons.

"Hold, Sir Knight," I called out as I walked towards him. "There are some sailmakers from the archers' galleys in that tent over there. They can sew you up with stitches most fine before you go out again. And I have a question for you before you go—is your father a noble?"

"No. But he will be if I can bring in enough coins to buy some land or the king recognizes me for being brave. This horse is all my father had enough coins to buy, that is why I must go out again after I get sewed."

"What is your name?"

"My name is Guy."

"Are you a knight or squire?"

"I am neither," the young man aid with a little laugh as he shook his head and replied, and winced slightly as he did.

"My name is Guy. Just Guy. That is why I am riding alone instead of with the knights. My father is a hostler which is how I came to ride a horse. He thought it would help me get ahead if I was a rider, and he was right."

"Ah, well then, Guy the rider, please come visit me after this is all over. I may have some opportunities for you. Ask for Commander George at the Citadel."

The cheerful young man smiled his thanks and nodded his head in agreement. Then he put his heels to his horse and rode towards the waiting sailmakers.

"Now there is a likely lad," said Henry with approval in his voice. "I wonder if he really is a commoner such that we could recruit him?"

We never saw Guy again. I have sometimes wondered about his fate and why Henry changed his mind about him.

Chapter Twenty-seven

Unexpected problems.

The number of returnees grew and grew as the day progressed. And they surprised us by bringing unexpected problems. We had mistakenly thought we knew what to expect from this sally because the same men had sallied the day before. We were wrong. There were differences that caused problems, and we were not ready for them, perhaps because we had been too busy yesterday trying to save the stranded archers.

A steady stream of men bringing Greek weapons began coming along with a few unambitious men with naught but the spears they had carried out. What grew even faster, and quickly became a problem, was the large number of camp followers, street women, thieves, and Orthodox priests who surrounded the coin wagons and accosted the returnees as they came through the gate. There were an amazing number of them and they all seemed to be reaching their hands out to the returning soldiers for the coins the states' men were being paid for the weapons they captured.

"I do not remember so many people waiting at the gate yesterday," Henry Soldier said when Commander Courtenay growled about them. "It is something new. It must be the coins the men are being paid."

"I do not care *why* they are here," the Commander replied. "They are slowing down the coin paying. So get rid of them. Tell the captain of the archers at the gate to move those people back at least five hundred paces beyond the sailmakers' tents."

Eric arrived with some of his Varangians just as the archers stationed at the gate were beginning to herd the camp followers further down the roadway. The camp followers were unhappy about it and loudly resisting, particularly the women. Eric strode towards them and roared at the camp followers in a strange tongue while waving his axe at them. Their protests and pleadings instantly stopped and they began moving back.

"What did you tell them?" Commander Courtenay asked Eric when he re-joined us on the wall.

"I told them to move back and stop bothering the returnees or they would lose their heads. The problem is that most of the camp followers and many of the priests are from the villages and do not understand that I really mean it; this is the first time many of them have ever been away from home.

"The street women and thieves, on the other hand, are from the city. They knew I meant it and would have taken them first. It was them hurrying to move back that caused the others to follow."

Commander Courtenay was surprised and said as much. So the Varangian captain explained.

"The village levies are mostly Greek and Orthodox. That is because the crusader lords kept the Greek-gobbling Byzantine villagers to work the fields when they replaced the Byzantine lords. They are mostly Greeks just like our attackers and the majority of the Empress's subjects in the city.

"This is probably the first time many of them have ever been out of their villages or earn coins. There is a good chance that many of the states' foot soldiers and their priests do not even know who they are fighting or why.

"I will assign some of my Varangians to stay with you to translate. They can do it because we have been in Constantinople guarding whoever is the emperor since before my grandfather's time. Many of my men are like me. Their families have lived here for generations and they can gobble Greek better than they can crusader French."

Within minutes George and Henry had Varangian translators assigned to them and so did the coin wagons, the sailmakers sewing up the wounded, and the archers at the gate.

Despite the newly arrived translators and Eric's threats, there was jostling and complaints as the archers from the galley company guarding the gate herded the unhappy camp followers further and further down the road. Their displeasure meant nothing so long as they were well away from coin wagons and the growing line of men waiting for their coins.

******

The archers on the city's outer wall watched as the number of returning sortiers slowly grew from periodic ones and twos to a steady stream that got larger and larger throughout the day. Our need for translators to tell them what to do and where to go was not the only problem. The men coming in with weapons and wounds brought more and more unexpected problems with them as the day wore on.

One of unexpected problems was the number of wounded men coming in by themselves or with the help of their mates. There had been wounded yesterday, but not many, and they had somehow been sorted out. Today there were more wounded coming in, apparently because the men were more willing to fight with the Greeks who were carrying weapons.

At the same time, there appeared to be fewer of their mates coming in with them to care for them. The problem had been solved by quickly sending to our galleys for some of our sail makers and their needles and thread; *we* would sew them up if their mates were staying out to fight for weapons.

The wounded were soon being taken to hastily erected tents where our galleys' sail makers, hurriedly brought in from the galleys in our moorage, were standing by for the inevitable sewing and barbering that followed every battle. Those most painfully wounded were give flower paste from our galley stores; mercies were left to their friends.

Another problem was that the returnees were almost all were hungry and thirsty. Hunger could always wait. It was something the villagers were used to enduring; it was thirst that became a problem.

Yesterday the thirsty men returned directly to their tents after they had rampaged through the Greek camp and, when they got there, were able to enjoy whatever was their regular source of water.

Today the states' men were staying out longer and coming back thirstier. But today, because we were paying out coins, they could not return to their tents for food and water until they were paid. To prevent fraudulent claims, men who went past the archers holding back the crowd were not allowed to return carrying weapons they could claim entitled them to coins. So they all had to wait in the hot sun until it was their turn to show their captured weapons and be paid.

Another problem was the men who died whilst they were being sewed and barbered and the dead men brought in by their mates who then turned around and went out searching for weapons. Yesterday there had been fewer of them and their mates had taken charge of their bodies. Today those of the states' dead who were not immediately claimed were carried some distance down the wall by the auxiliaries attached to the archer company at the gate, and laid out there for their mates and the camp followers to find.

"Not to worry. Tomorrow we will gobble the church words and bury those who are not claimed," Commander Courtenay announced.

Prince Ivan and his lieutenants and personal guards, all knights, were among the early returnees. They came in right after the wounded young hostler. It was clear that the prince had copied yesterday's action by Commander Courtenay—he had led his men out of the gate and into the Greek camp, and then moved aside in order to make a safe and early return "so my men can get all the coins."

******

We were looking out of the archer slits of the wall above the gate and could hear the distant sounds of fighting, but we could not see much what was happening because of the great clouds of dust. The sounds continued to move further and further away until the middle of the very hot afternoon.

At first only a few of the returnees brought in weapons for coins, and what they brought was mostly just a spear or two. According to my new translator, they were the men who had gone out so they could say they had done so—and then quickly returned so they could stay alive a bit longer. He spit towards them as he described them.

"It is a good sign that so few of the states' men have come in early," Henry Soldier suggested hopefully as he stood with his hands up to shield his eyes from the sun. He was doing what we had all been doing all day long—futilely attempting to look into the dust cloud hanging over the Greek camp to see what was happening. "It means those who want coins are still out there fighting to get them."

After a brief pause he added unnecessarily, "We can hear them even if we cannot see them."

Commander Courtenay was apparently not so sure. He just grunted to acknowledge that he had heard, not that he agreed or disagreed. But he said nothing and just continued to stand on the wall above the gate and watch both the Greek camp and the roadway below with its coin wagons on either side of it and the large group of camp followers who were now waiting anxiously five or six hundred paces beyond the coin wagons. A line of archers and Varangians kept them there.

****** *Galley Captain Steven Harper*

My men and I had been at the gate all day. The number of returnees began increasing after the sun passed overhead and increased dramatically by mid-afternoon. More and more of the returnees were carrying captured weapons, and a few had priests and nobles as prisoners for which they were paid a silver coin for priests and knights and a gold coin for bishops and nobles. It was a prize money scheme for weapons and prisoners that was working unexpectedly well. My lads and I were more than a bit jealous that we had not been sent out with them.

The lines of desperately thirsty states' men in front of the coin wagons began to grow. I could see that Commander Courtney was worrying because he and his lieutenants were looking out from the top of the wall above the gate and pointing. So I climbed the stairs to see for myself.

What I saw was more and more of the states' men walking and riding through the sacked camp towards the gate. They looked tired and were coming from all corners of the Greek camp. It was quite a scene—and, for the first time, the sounds of battle were coming closer.

There were already long lines of anxious men waiting with their captured weapons at each coin wagon. It was obvious there would soon be many more.

I was still standing up there when I heard Lieutenant Commander Henry Soldier speculate that seeing more and more of the states' men withdrawing to return to the sally gate might have emboldened the surviving Greeks. Commander Courtenay allowed as how he was probably right. If it did, he said, it might give us a new problem—the Greeks returning to their sacked camp as the states' men fell back might turn into a counter attack.

There was increasing chaos and confusion at the gate by mid-afternoon as more and more of the states' men returned and the sound of the fighting drew closer. In addition to the fact that we were running out of copper coins, the returning men did not know water was waiting for them. As a result, some of them had gone past the gate and walked to the nearby estuary to drink the fresh water coming out of the rivers that fed it. If they did not hurry, the arrival of the returning Greeks might well cut them off.

It was well past high noon when the Commander announced a decision and began giving us new orders. I was there when he did.

"Henry, we need to get more archers up here on the wall and also out by the moat to cover the withdrawal of the last of the states' men. Summon the nearby galley companies to gather here at the gate as soon as possible. We may need to lead some of them out to establish a defensive line to hold off the Greeks whilst the States' forces return.

"Captain Harper," he said to me. "Lead your company across the moat and form them up seven-deep about a hundred paces beyond."

I, of course, immediately repeated the order and ran down the stairs to comply.

****** *Commander Courtenay*

Despite the dangers of a possible counter attack engulfing the states' men remaining the Greek camp, the stories of the men who had already returned and the large number of Greek weapons they were carrying seemed to suggest that the states' forces had scored a great victory. If it was true, it meant that five thousand or so of them had destroyed most of the Greek camp which had had about thirty thousand Greek soldiers in it along with many thousands of camp followers and sutlers.

Sudden attacks on unsuspecting and disorganized enemies will do that every time if the attackers are aggressive enough. And the prize coins had apparently made the states' men much more aggressive than they had been yesterday.

On the other hand, not all the Venetian-carried Greeks in the camp had been killed or despite initially being taken totally by surprise. Far from it; many of them had undoubtedly been alerted by the noise and the arrival of fleeing people in time to snatch up their arms and either retreat with their possessions or use them to fight back.

The noise and dust of the fighting coming closer suggested the Greeks were rallying and beginning to push the remaining state forces back as more and more of them withdrew. It would almost certainly *not* be an orderly withdrawal, and that, no doubt, would embolden those among the Greeks who were willing to fight.

****** *Lieutenant Commander Henry Soldier*

Things really picked up about an hour before sunset. A great and totally disorganized mass of returning states' men could be seen approaching out of the dust. Even so, the distant dust cloud hanging in the distance over the far end of the Greek camp suggested that some of the states' men were still fighting the Greeks for their weapons, but perhaps that was just wishful thinking.

Of all things, it was water the returnees began wanted more than coins. The archers had almost lost control that afternoon as the new arrivals began riding past the coins wagons to get water and then tried to return with weapons to get coins. Many succeeded such that some of the weapons we paid may have come from the camp instead of the Greeks.

Orders had been quickly given and water was hurriedly fetched from the nearby estuary by camp followers who were paid one copper for every skin they brought to the line of waiting men. Some ran back and forth to the water three or four times that afternoon and early evening. It ended up being a great coin earner for the women of the camp—and in the process it totally depleted our supply of copper coins long before the coins for the last captured spear could be paid.

At the same time, those of the returnees who were waiting with captured weapons were pointedly told that if they rode past the coin wagons and into their camp for water they risked not being paid—they would not be allowed to return to collect the coins because it would look as if they were bringing weapons from the camp instead of from the Greeks.

No sooner had the water problem had been solved than another arose.

"Archers are disciplined and were willing to quietly line up for their prize monies; this lot is not." Someone remarked.

Commander Courtenay was concerned.

"Henry, the coin lines are getting too long. They are almost out the gate and soon will be if we do not do something to speed things up.

"We need to get down there and open new lines before the men waiting in line start thinking that they might not be paid. God only knows what might happen then; they may turn on each other and us."

And that was exactly what the Commander and I did. The line was starting to stretch out through the gate by the time they set up three more weapons paying lines and began passing out coins. The tension that had been growing immediately disappeared when the lines suddenly shortened, particularly when those waiting in line could see the men in front of them being paid.

And then another problem arose—we suddenly realized that we were running out of copper coins. We had not brought enough even though we did not know it at the time. And the water carriers walking up and down the lines made the coin problem worse because they were being paid an immediate copper for each water skin they brought to the lines of waiting men.

The result was that we ran out of coppers; we had gold and silver coins, but not enough coppers.

Michael Oremus and young George, the commander's son, were sent galloping off to get more coins. While they were gone the Varangians walked up and down the line asking men to club together with their mates for immediate payment in silver or gold.

Offering gold and silver, instead of coppers, had to be done because there was a shortage of copper coins. We had offered ten for a spear and the usual rate was forty coppers for one silver and twenty silvers for one gold bezant. We had silvers for the swords and prisoners, but not enough coppers for the men who had only brought in a few spears.

"Hoy to any man with four spears, go over to that man and get a silver coin."

But then the problem was that some men had five or six or only two or three. What should a man do if he had more or fewer than four captured spears?

It was an unknown man in the line who suggested a fix for the problem—the men began to join with their mates to turn in four and share the silver coin. They would exchange the silver coin for forty coppers and split them later. The idea was a good one and the Varangian translators began walking up and down the coin lines touting it.

"There are more than enough silver coins. If you do not want to wait for the coppers that are coming, you can join your captured spears with those of your mates' and share the silver coins that are being paid."

There was a sudden burst of activity all along the coin lines. Some of the men were too thirsty to wait and began negotiating with the men around them. But at least there was no anger. Those who did not have mates they could trust knew they would be paid and were used to waiting.

Chapter Twenty-eight

Sallies and ribalds.

More and more galley companies double-timed into the gate area as sundown approached. Some of their archers were placed along the wall above the sally gate and others on the tiny sliver of land between the moat and wall. Henry himself marched two more companies out over the drawbridge and stood with them in the Company's traditional seven-deep formation with the road running between them. I allowed him to do so because I knew he would watch like a hawk to make sure they did not get cut off.

The number of returnees coming past Henry's two companies, and the company of Captain Harper which was already out there, initially rose as the first signs of dusk appeared, and then tailed off as darkness began to fall. The noise of battle soon became quieter and closer, and ended entirely when it became dark. Even so, States' riders and foot continued to straggle in with captured weapons for several hours, guided perhaps by the candle lanterns placed on the wall above the gate. By then Henry and the three companies had crossed back over the moat bridge and were once again safely behind the city wall.

Enemy horse and foot could be seen in the distance as night fell, but they never approached. Henry led the three galley companies back over the moat bridge without their ever pushing out an arrow.

One of the two galley companies which had stayed on the wall side of the moat, however, continued to stay there in the dark. Its men remained in place all night to welcome any returnees from the states' forces who might have somehow made their way out of the sacked camp. There were only a handful of them.

****** *Major Captain Michael Oremus*

"Only one of the wagons returned with a load of weapons," Henry commented the next morning when we were breaking our fast at the Commandery. "But I have no idea what happened to the others, or how many of the states' riders and foot made it back. Quite a few if the amount of coins we paid out is any indication."

"How does Prince Ivan think his men did? And how many men does he claim to have lost?" someone asked.

"I am not sure he knows or cares," was Henry's sarcastic reply. He delivered it with a mouthful of bread and a waving of his bowl of morning ale.

"Well, his men are very good at making sallies that inflict damage," Commander Courtenay replied. "How soon do you think we should let them make another and earn more coins?"

And then, before anyone had a chance to answer his first question, the Commander asked a question that surprised us all.

"And how long do you think it would take our archers to quickly move the states' forces out of their encampment and into the city if they left everything behind?"

My God! Does he think we cannot hold the outer wall when the rest of the Greek army gets here?

****** *Commander George Courtenay*

Things went quite well immediately after the second sally. Elizabeth resumed visiting me that very night and I was glad to see her and get to know her again. Actually, that was not exactly true; it was dark so I did not actually see her. But I certainly heard and felt her as we joined together to celebrate the great victory of the states' forces.

But was it a meaningful victory? I thought so, but I certainly was not sure. It certainly was not decisive since the main body of the Orthodox army had not yet even arrived. No matter, Elizabeth and I celebrated it privately by drinking too much wine and getting to know each other again, and so did the entire city, celebrate this is, via the Empress proclaiming a non-working day of thanksgiving.

The best news, however, was that my father continued to recover from the chest and arm pox. He was already walking around like a horse chomping at the bit in his efforts to get back to active duty in the Company. The Empress was clearly delighted with his progress.

But now what? The Empress's spies were saying that the great mass of the Greek army would arrive in a few days. These were the men whose commander had marched them up the mountain, and then back down again. Now they were marching to Constantinople.

One thing was certain, even though I did not announce it. I had already decided to let the states' forces sally once again for coins in exchange for captured weapons and prisoners. They did not know it, of course, but they would probably be let loose on the very day the main body of the Greek army arrived. Hopefully, that would be before the Greek commander had a chance to get his men organized to fight them off.

It was a decision I did not announce. To the contrary, I told no one and pretended to be unsure and indecisive whenever the possibility was mentioned. The Empress was not the only one who had spies in both the Citadel and in the city.

****** *Commander Courtenay*

"He is overbalanced and working with an absolute frenzy, Commander. It has been that way ever since Thea and her mother were killed. It is as if he is possessed by demons and devils behind his eyes."

That was how James Howard, the sergeant assigned to assist Aron, described the Company's alchemist. There was a great deal of sympathy and concern in his voice.

"How so, James? What is he doing?" I asked my question as we walked towards the Citadel's stable where Aron and James lived and worked

"He has been mixing powders and hollowing out logs constantly ever since he was told about the girl and her mother. I am not sure he has even eaten or slept ever since he heard the news.

We walked into the stall where Aron usually worked and then the one next to it where he slept. He was in neither of them.

"He must be in the horse-training yard behind the stable," James suggested.

And that is where we found him when we walked out into the bright sunlight. We watched quietly as he and two of the Citadel's servants attempted to lift a huge stone off a wagon on to a partially built platform of stones. They obviously were attempting to make it taller for some reason.

Nothing was said. We just stood there and watched silently until the stone was finally wrestled into place.

"Hoy, Aron. What are you doing?" the Commander asked when they finished. *My God, he looks terrible. James was right; he does look overbalanced. He probably has not eaten or slept since Thea was killed.*

"Hoy, Commander. I did not expect to see you today, did I?"

"I was greatly sorrowed to hear of your great loss, Aron. I will say a prayer for her the next time I am in a church."

"It was God's will so it could not be helped, could it, Commander? So now I must take the revenge God wants me to take."

"And what might that be, Lieutenant?" *Uh oh; that sounds like trouble.*

"Why to destroy the Orthodox churches, of course," was his answer. "That is what God demands. And rightly so—their priests sent men out to kill Thea and now God wants them punished."

Aron was red-eyed and trembling as he announced God's decree. I had a most sympathetic look on my face and in my voice as I tried to re-direct him into a more useful revenge.

"You are absolutely right that God wants you to punish whoever sent men out to kill Thea. Of that there can be no doubt. And you have made your mark on the Company's roll which means every archer is honour-bound help you get your revenge. But God knows that it was the Patriarch and the Orthodox princes and their men who are most responsible for Thea's death, not the priests.

"The priests merely passed the word they were ordered to pass. They are innocents. It is the men who gave the order, the Patriarch and the Orthodox king, that God wants punished along with the men who have taken up arms and joined with them.

"So you are absolutely right that God wants you to have your revenge, but he wants you to take it where it belongs most of all—on the Patriarch and the Orthodox king, and on their great army which is about to arrive and attack us.

"I know that is what God wants you to do because, as you know, I can talk to God because I can gobble and chant in church-talk and have been ordained as a priest as a result."

Aron thought about what I said for a moment, and then nodded his head in agreement.

Did I really talk to God and know those things? Of course not. But it was a good story and I told it to try to re-focus the poor sod on revenging his lass by hurting our most dangerous enemies, the ones at the city's gates. Besides, the Orthodox priests were not going anywhere unless, of course, they bought very expensive passages from us and fled. After the war we would deal with those who were not smart enough to flee when they had the chance.

Chapter Twenty-nine

Ribalds and prisoners.

After Aron agreed to redirect his efforts, the Commander asked James Howard to walk back to the Citadel with him and me, Nicholas Greenway, the Commander's apprentice. They talked as they walked. I, of course, merely listened.

"Watch him like a hawk, James, and stay with him at all times. Do not let him take a ribald or anything else anywhere near an Orthodox church. Tie him up if necessary and come to me immediately if you think he is going to try something. On the other hand, we need as many ribalds as he can make in the next week or two and we want him to recover from the sad thoughts behind his eyes and continue in the Company.

Then the Commander got deadly serious.

"How many ribalds do you think Aron can provide to us in the next couple of weeks?"

"We already have six with lightning powder in them and there is no shortage of logs to be hollowed out and strong galley lines to prevent them coming apart, Commander. I am not sure, Commander, how many more we can make in the next two weeks. Two or three, at least, perhaps more. It will depend on the amount of lightning powder available."

"Does he need more men to help him with the work?"

"A couple of carpenters to help carve out more logs would be useful."

The Commander did not say anything for a while. He just kept walking. Then he stopped and began giving me orders.

"Nicholas, go to the strand where our galleys are pulled ashore and give Lieutenant Commander Lewes my best regards, and ask him if he can spare five galley carpenters and the tools they will need to help hollow out logs under the direction of Aron and James. Wait there until all the men are collected, and then bring them to James and Aron at the stables."

Then he handed James his pouch of coins.

"Take these coins, James. I want you to use them to buy more of whatever Aron needs to make more of his lightning-making powders. We need as many ribalds as he can make in the next ten days.

"Come to me immediately whenever there is a problem and for any additional coins or men you need. And come to the Citadel tomorrow afternoon and tell me how many ribalds you think Aron can complete in ten days, and also how many you think he can make if he has twenty days."

The Commander had obviously seen or heard something that had given him an idea. I wondered what it could be. Now, of course, I know.

****** *Commander Courtenay*

After visiting Aron and talking with James, I briefly visited the prisoners taken by the states' forces during their second sally. They were being held in a foul and damp dungeon room under the Commandery. There were not all that many, but a couple of them had prospects. One was a real catch, a bishop who had fetched his delighted captor a gold bezant. There were also two wounded knights from Epirus.

Most of the rest of the prisoners were Orthodox priests. The states' men had taken them because they thought the priests might be bishops because their black clerical gowns were different from those with which they were familiar. They had also brought in three Greek soldiers who had swords or pikes in their possession such that the states' village levies who captured them thought they might be knights.

The mistakes that had caused some of the prisoners to be brought in were understandable—the inexperienced and untraveled men of the levies had never seen a bishop up close and, at least so far as they knew, ordinary soldiers only carried spears.

Overall, the captured men were not much of a haul for so much fighting and weapons capture, but they would have to do for what I had in mind for them—exchanging them for any of the archers and states' men who had been captured in the recent fighting—and sending a misleading message with them.

My plan for the imprisoned bishops and the captured men involved the use of one of the city's Orthodox priests who could gobble crusader French, and Adam Gravesend. Adam was one of the archers assigned to our shipping post at Athens' port of Piraeus. He had been there at our shipping post ever since it was established.

Some years ago Adam had gotten a local Greek girl in a family way and ended up marrying her. Now he had six children and was available because was one of the many archers who had been temporarily summoned to serve at Constantinople. He was also one of the few archers who could gobble Greek.

Adam was one of the Company's reliable old sweats, a grey-haired and somewhat overweight two-stripe archer who had been married to his very religious Greek wife for many years. As a result, according to his post's captain, he had learned to gobble Greek fluently and regularly accompanied his wife and their children to an Orthodox church.

I interviewed Adam and three other Greek-gobbling archers at the Commandery, and decided he was the best of the lot for what I had in mind. I spent the entire next day with Adam helping him understand what I wanted him to do and what he should say to the prisoners—and then changed all of the prisoners' guards and appointed him as the "lieutenant" in command of the new guards.

Adam was quickly given the symbols of his temporarily higher rank so he would look the part.

"You there, Lieutenant," I called out to one of Michael Oremus's men. "Strip off your tunic and give to this man." ... "Yes, right now. You too, Adam. Give him yours" ...

"Now you take his tunic, Lieutenant," I told the somewhat confused and totally naked man, "with my thanks, and either draw a new tunic from your galley's slop chest or sew your rank on Adam's." ... "And here is a direct order for you—do not say a word about exchanging tunics to anyone except your galley captain and Commander Oremus, and only if they ask."

Adam did not know it, of course, but he would be getting a new stripe and promoted to sergeant if he carried out his assignment. I am sure from the keenness of his responses that he hoped to gain from his unexpected opportunity to distinguish himself.

****** *Archer Adam Gravesend*

A long line of newly appointed guards followed me into the foul cell the three captured bishops were sharing. They were carrying three candle lanterns, a table, beds, shite pots, and food. I myself carried a wine skin and bowls and smiled at the prisoners as I did.

The bishops, to say the least, seemed pleased at the obvious improvement of their fortunes and their ability to see each other for the first time. I stood aloof and waited until everything was in place. Then I ordered the archers out of the cell.

As soon as they were gone I rushed to the oldest bishop and knelt in front of him.

"Forgive me and bless me, Bishop. I came as soon as I could," I said it in Greek. The bishops, of course, were astonished.

"My name is Adam Gravesend. I am the lieutenant of the company assigned to guard the city's moat bridges and wall gates. My wife in Athens is a believer and I attend church with her every day when I am there. That is why I am only a lieutenant with no hopes of advancement or ever getting the prize money I need to become a merchant. I have been ordered to take command of your guards because I can gobble Greek."

The three bishops, as you might imagine, were elated to see me and the many good things I brought them. I was quickly forgiven in the name of God for all my sins and blessed quite copiously.

We talked as they ate and drank, with me doing most of the talking because they were too busy tucking into their food and drink to do much more than ask brief questions and listen.

They munched, swigged, pissed, and listened as I explained that my drunken captain had added guarding them to all of my regular duties which mostly involved supervising the archers and sailors who watched over the moat bridges and wall gates.

"Unlike the other companies, we have sailors in our company because the cranks and lines that are used to raise and lower the wall gates and moat bridges constantly need repairs to get them to open and close properly.

"It is terrible for me to be here in the bridge and gate company because it means there is no chance for advancement and I have six children to feed and a wife who always spends more than I earn. I have even thought of leaving the Company and becoming a merchant, but that, of course, is impossible because I have no hope of saving enough coins to buy a place in the market.

"Anything," I lamented, "I would do anything if I could afford to leave the Company and safely live in Athens with my wife and children."

I looked at them keenly as I said it. Then I told them how and where I spent my time in Constantinople when I was not on duty.

Chapter Thirty

Prisoner exchanges and fish.

We contacted the captains of the Greek army in the traditional way—we opened the gate and one of the city's black-robed Orthodox priests walked out of it along with a horn blower tooting loudly to draw the Greeks' attention. Adam went out with the priest, and so did Michael Oremus. My son, Michael's apprentice, did not go with them.

The three men waited for some time amidst the partially restored devastation. Finally, after a long pause caused because the camp dwellers had begun fleeing as soon as the gate began going up, a similarly clothed Orthodox priest from the invaders' camp hurried forward to meet with him.

First, the two priests greeted each other with what appeared to be the formalities and fashions of all first meetings between two Orthodox priests. Afterwards they immediately started talking about the possibility of a prisoner exchange. Adam, as he had been instructed, listened carefully.

"I am Father Innocent from Saint Gregory's Church in Constantinople," said the priest who had accompanied Adam. Then he explained why he had come out of the city with two of the Empress's soldiers, the captain in command of the city's only usable gates on its landward side and his lieutenant who had the additional duty of being in charge of the men guarding the prisoners in the Citadel.

"The Empress's men have captured some of your army's men including a bishop, a number of priests, and a couple of knights. And your army has captured some of the Empress's men. I have been ordered to inform you that the Empress, in her great benevolence as a true Christian, is willing to exchange prisoners right here in front of the only gate that has not been permanently blocked.

"So tell me Father, how many English archers and soldiers of the Latin states do your masters hold that they are able to exchange?"

As might be expected, the Greek priest did not have any idea how many prisoners the Orthodox army held. But he instantly agreed that the idea of an exchange that would obtain the release of one of the Patriarch's bishops and a number of his brother priests was a good idea. The two priests agreed to meet again the next day at the same time.

The prisoners were exchanged about a week later—after the more distinguished amongst them had spent a five or six days in the cells next to the city's three Orthodox bishops, and often with no one standing nearby to overhear them.

******

The main body of the Greek army began arriving a few days after the exchange. It was a huge army of men and they were accompanied by numerous horses, wagons and camp followers. They just kept coming and coming until they had filled up a good part of the narrow peninsula and all the available space outside Constantinople's outer wall.

Our men watched them arrive and grew uneasy. It was the largest number army of men any of us had ever seen—and they had come to Constantinople to either kill us or make us run.

Similar to those who had come before them, the new arrivals assumed the moat that protected the city against them would also protect them against the city's defenders. Accordingly, to the astonishment of the watching archers, the new arrivals pitched their tents and parked their wagons all the way up to the moat just as the late and unlamented early arrivals had done.

"Some people never learn," Henry said with wonder in his voice and a disbelieving shake of his head. He smiled as he said it.

"Henry is right, Commander. We should hit them again with another sally as soon as possible," said Richard Ryder, the Commander's number two.

The men standing with the Commander on the wall above the gate all nodded their agreement when he turned and looked at them with a questioning look on his face.

"You are right, Henry, and I agree. It is just too good of an opportunity to pass up. What do you suggest? Offer coins to the states' forces once again for the weapons and high-ranking prisoners they bring in?"

"Aye, we cannot go wrong using the states' forces to reduce the number of the bastards we have to fight."

And after a brief pause, Henry added "and there surely are a lot of them."

******

The same group of men were assembled on the wall above the gate and once again were looking out at the Greek encampment when the sun came up over the horizon the next morning. Eric, the captain of the Empress's guards was also with them and so was Prince Ivan, the commander of the Bulgarians, the largest contingent of the various forces that had come in from the Empress's vassal states. Prince Ivan had led the second sally; he had obviously decided to only watch this one.

"Any idea as to how many men are going out this time?" someone asked the prince. I think it was the Michael Oremus, the major captain who was the Commander's principal assistant.

It was a good question. Unlike the previous two sallies, the column of salliers did not extend far enough back to even reach the curve in the road. We could see them all. There were no wagons in sight. It would be a significantly less powerful sally than its two predecessors.

"This time about one hundred of my horsemen and another eighty from the other states, and perhaps thirty-five hundred foot," Prince Ivan answered.

And then, after a long moment of looking at the men packed into the roadway below us waiting for the gate to be raised, Prince Ivan added another thought as he used his chin to point at the column of foot soldiers waiting immediately behind the riders.

"They are all that are available of the six thousand or so men who went out on the first sally. They are the best of them though, the thrusters who are willing to fight for more coins. The others have mostly been killed, wounded, or are staying camp because they are too afraid to go out again. Some, of course, have deserted to go home with their coins."

After a pause, he added.

"Mostly the men who are not sallying today are missing because they are afraid or deserted." Then he hastily added, "with exception of my personal guard of knights and nobles; I ordered them not to go out this time because I cannot afford to lose them."

Commander Courtenay nodded his understanding and replied.

"Well, this is the states' men's third sally this week. At least we all have some experience under our belts and are better prepared to see that they get paid, watered, and sewed up when they return. What astonishes me is that the Greek commander does not have at least some of his men standing ready to fight us off. Surely he must know about our first two sallies?"

The talking amongst the watchers was stopped by the creaking sound of the huge wall gate as it began to rise. Below them the loud talking was fading away, the men with helmets were dropping their visors, and every man was taking a firmer grip on his weapons.

A moment later the states' riders ducked their heads and poured through gate, and galloped over the moat bridge and into the Greek camp waving their swords over their heads. What was left of the states' foot came running out of the gate right behind them.

The salliers began trickling back about an hour later. This time we were organized with the coins, sail makers, and water carriers waiting when they returned. There were no long lines of desperately thirsty men. And an entire company of archers from a nearby enclosure kept the camp followers, priests, and other coin-seekers well away from the returnees.

It had been another successful raid in terms of both weapons and prisoners. And this time some of the salliers led in captured wagons pulled by captured horses, seven of them in all. Several of the wagons had valuable armour and weapons in them. Their owners had not had time to unpack them.

******

Surprisingly enough, until the two days *after* the arrival of the main body of the Greek army, the road through the Greek camp had remained open. No one in the Greek army had thought to order it closed. As a result, food supplies of meat, early-harvested grains, and firewood had continued to be brought in to feed the city and build its reserves. So did similar supplies arriving on barges coming down the rivers into the Golden Horn and transports coming out of both the Black Sea and the Mediterranean.

And, of course, there were always the fish. They were the most important food for many of the poorer people of the city. And they continued to be caught by the local people who stood shoulder to shoulder every day all along the miles of shoreline that ran next to the city's walls. The city's people had fished along the shoreline to feed themselves and supply the city's markets since time began.

The fish catches of the local people were substantial. And little wonder; the number of fish constantly making their way along the shoreline where the city protruded out into the water was astonishing. Fish could be seen and caught everywhere along the miles and miles of city wall, even during a siege. That was significant because so long as there was enough firewood with which to cook the fish, the city was not likely to ever be brought to its knees by running out of food, even if both the land and water approaches to the city were totally cut off.

Moreover, if push came to shove and a siege lasted many years such that there were not any more wooden houses in the city that could be torn down and burned for cooking, the defenders and the city people could eat the fish raw.

Indeed, I had been told by no less than Eric, the commander of the Empress's guards, that some of Constantinople's people who cannot afford to buy firewood regularly eat raw fish. That, of course, is not likely to be a true story since it is well known that eating too much raw fish can cause fish scales to begin covering certain important parts of your body.

In any event, the implications of the huge supply of readily available fish were significant—it meant a siege to starve the city into submission would never work. And that, in turn, meant an army attacking the city would either have to launch a great assault and fight its way into the city, as the crusaders had done some years earlier, or it would have to get into the city by gulling or bribing some of the city's defenders as the crusaders had also done.

Chapter Thirty-one

Whittling them down.

What was left of Number Nine Company picked its way through the thick stand of trees until Lieutenant Baker raised his hand. That stopped the nine tired archers, and one terrified prisoner tied to a horse, that were strung out in a line behind him. The lieutenant, and each of the archers, was leading at least one saddled horse, the relatively fresh "remount" that every horse archer always kept close at hand in case he needed to run for safety or catch a fleeing foe.

"This will do for our new camp," Lieutenant Baker announced as he looked around and nodded his head to agree with himself. "We can see the cart path and village from here, and we can run either up the hill or through the trees over there if any of the Greeks are unlucky enough to find us again.

"Sergeant, post a good man as a lookout at the edge of the trees over there beyond the big rock. That is the way the Greeks will likely come if they try to sneak up on us."

Lieutenant Baker was in command because Number Nine Company's captain had been killed in a skirmish some days earlier on the Adrianople road. Afterwards, when the Greek army finished passing in front of them, the lieutenant had led what was left of the company from its initial "rest and recovery" camp along the Adrianople road to what was intended to be their company's permanent base camp for the duration of the Greek siege.

Each of the horse archer companies serving in the Latin Empire had a hidden base camp that, for their safety's sake, no one else knew about. From their base camps, the companies rode out to pick off the Greek army's stragglers and chop up its foraging parties. They would then periodically return to their hidden camps for rest and resupply.

Number Nine Company's initial base camp had been in the hills just beyond the long peninsula that poked out into the sea with the great city of Constantinople at its very end. Lieutenant Baker had led the men of his company into their ready and waiting first base camp after the company finished harassing the Greek army as it marched past it on the road from Adrianople.

Lieutenant Baker and his men had begun hitting the stragglers and foraging parties of the Greek-led army camped outside Constantinople's walls immediately thereafter. And they had continued doing so right up until their first camp had been stumbled upon by the Greeks. That is why they had temporarily relocated to their backup camp and spent the past several days looking for a new one.

The company's basic assignment was actually quite simple; it was to inflict as many casualties as possible on the Greek army and prevent its foraging parties from bringing in food and other supplies for the Greek soldiers. Hopefully the Greek soldiers who were not killed outright would be weakened and demoralized by their wounds and lack of food and begin deserting.

In other words, the men of Lieutenant Baker's company were to act like a pack of a dozen or so of roving English wolves which had come across a great flock of Greek sheep. The problem, of course, was that the sheep had weapons and some of them knew how to use them. The company's captain had discovered that the hard way when a Greek soldier got him in the stomach with a spear. A mercy put him out of his agony.

Since Lieutenant Baker had taken over command of Number Nine, two of the company's archers had been wounded, one fatally and the other seriously enough that he had been evacuated on one of the Company galleys that constantly moved up and down the rivers that drained into the Golden Horn estuary which flowed along one side of the Constantinople city wall.

The casualty ratios had not been favourable to the Greeks. To the contrary, the archers of Number Nine Company had made the Greeks pay dearly for the men the company had lost; they had over and over again stood off and used their longbows to inflict a large number of casualties on the Greeks marching past them on the old Roman road to Constantinople. They had also either turned back or destroyed a number of Greek foraging parties.

The Greeks had responded to the way Number Nine Company and the other horse archer companies operating against them by reducing the number of foraging parties and greatly increasing the number of armed men who accompanied each of them. This had not occurred because of a decision by their absent commander, but rather instinctively by the individual Greek soldiers—they had come to understand what would happen to them if they went out alone or in small groups, so they stopped doing so.

Unfortunately for the archers of Number Nine Company, their initial base camp on one of the hills overlooking the peninsula had been blundered into and destroyed by such a large force of Greek foragers two days earlier. That was why they had been looking for a new campsite, but only after they finished off the foragers who had stumbled upon their old one.

Lieutenant Baker's badly outnumbered, but well-trained, horse archers had done exactly what they had been learnt to do when the equally surprised Greek foragers came upon them—they had hurriedly mounted their always-saddled horses and ridden away to regroup. The riders of the foraging party, seeing them flee, had chased after them.

Several times the Greek riders "almost caught" the company's stragglers and, as a result, continued pursuing them for some distance in hopes of an easy victory and the acclaim of their commanders. That, of course, was a mistake, and it cost the Greeks dearly.

The enthusiasm of the Greek riders for chasing the Englishmen changed dramatically when Lieutenant Baker shouted an order and the archers suddenly switched over to the fresh horses they had been leading—and began charging in a line abreast back towards the Greeks whose exhausted horses had become strung out in ones and twos all along the route of their failed chase.

It was the English archers' old and reliable "wounded bird" ploy, the tactic the Company' greybeards had learned from the Saracens years earlier when the Company was first formed and went crusading with King Richard. And it worked once again as the archers of Number Nine Company turned back on their fresh horses and began systematically shooting the Greek riders off their exhausted horses as they came upon them one or two at a time.

The archers continued riding on their fresh horses all the way back to where the main party of foragers was resting after looting the company's camp. They then pulled up their horses some distance from the Greek foot and began shooting them down until they ran out of arrows. Afterwards, they set about collecting as many of their arrows as they could find and selecting a prisoner to be sent down the river to Constantinople for questioning.

In fact, the fate and failure of the Greek foraging party had been sealed as soon as its men stumbled upon the company's base camp. It would almost certainly have been no different even if the riders amongst the foragers had *not* chased after the archers in hopes of an easy victory—for if the Greek riders had *not* chased after them, the archers would almost certainly have immediately ridden back to surround the Greeks and pick them off one by one using the superior range of their longbows.

There was one last thing to be done.

"Eddie, you and Joe are to take the prisoner to the river and wait for one of our galleys. Tell its captain what we have seen and done since our last report and bring back all the arrows you can carry and some grain we can grind for bread. Do not take any unnecessary chances; you know the drill, eh?"

There was no doubt about what the soldiers of the Greek army were discovering, if they did not already know; going after a company of longbow-carrying English horse archers was like slapping a hungry bear on its arse to get its attention.

******

"Will you live long or will you die soon? Your future told by the blind woman from Delphi who sees everything and is never wrong. Only a penny or a piece of bread and it will be returned to you if you do not believe the fate she sees for you or accept the way she says you can avoid it."

The man called out the offer as the great army passed in front of the wagon in which he and the woman lived, but only infrequently when she had no custom. Normally there was a line of anxious soldiers waiting to learn their fate and how to avoid it.

 Those who paid were quietly assured of her powers.

"It is true as God is my witness; she can see a man's future even though her eyes are blank. All you need is to let her hold your hand and give her one small copper coin or a piece of bread—which she will return to you if you are not satisfied."

It was a great story told by the blind woman's protector and wagon driver—and each and every word in it was selected to convey a specific fact about the man who was anxiously wait to have his fate told to him.

The blind woman who would soon tell the soldier about his future sat nearby quietly listening to what was being said. A moment later a small coin changed hands and yet another very concerned young soldier was introduced to the blind woman by her assistant.

"Here is a man come to learn his future, dear lady. Will you hold his hand and tell him what his future holds? He is anxious to know so he can make his plans."

"Give me your hand. Hmm. Oh. Yes. You have red hair and are wearing a tunic and you are only carrying a spear since you have no sword or helmet or chain shirt. And you have two of your mates with you and a scar on your face. Oh no," she said a moment with a tone of despair and a sad shake of her head.

The woman croaked out every word quite sincerely. Then she leaned forward and quietly gave him the bad news so the others would not hear it.

"My boy, I am sorry to have to tell you this, but the life line on your hand is short, very short. And the spear you are carrying will not help you and neither will your homemade shield. It seems the angel of death knows your name and the arrow that has your name on it is already nearby.

"Your only hope is to leave the road as soon as it gets dark and walk straight back to your hovel. When you get there you must stay inside until the next full moon begins to wane. Do that and your red hair will stay on your head long enough to turn grey. If you do not leave immediately, you will soon die a most painful death with an arrow in your stomach. And the same will happen to you if you ever tell anyone I told you how to avoid your fate."

And with that she sighed and waved the white-faced and shaking lad away with a gentle and resigned flick of her hand.

It was quite surprising how many men were convinced by the blind woman's knowledge of their future and immediately deserted. On the other hand, her story would have been quite different if the words in her assistant's introduction had told her the client was a suspicious priest or a noble. If he had been a priest, for example, he would have been told that he would live well and prosper if he prayed to Jesus every day and was always loyal to his bishop and the Patriarch. It worked every time.

How did she do it? Every single word her helper said with his introduction meant something specific. For example, the word "dear" if he addressed her as "dear lady" or "dear one" meant she would be talking to a common soldier; the word "lady" meant he was carrying a spear whereas "one" meant he was carrying a sword. Other words in the introduction told her such things as the colour of his hair or his rank.

It had taken a while to learn what each of the words in her assistant's introduction meant, but she had learned them. And then the coins rolled in and she scared the soldiers who talked to her into running.

The woman and her assistant ate well as a result of the coins she fetched; the bread was fed to the horse that pulled their wagon.

Chapter Thirty-two

Two weeks later.

Commander Courtenay and his key lieutenants gathered at the Commandery on the eve of what was shaping up to be a great and decisive battle. Three weeks had passed since two back-to-back sallies had ripped apart the Greek army's early arrivals, the men who had been carried part of the way by the Venetian transports, and it had been almost two weeks since the third sally by the states' men had welcomed the newly arrived main body of the Greek army.

The third sally by the states' forces had occurred when the main body of the invaders first reached the city walls. The new arrivals had fought back and the states' men had suffered for it in addition to earning a considerable amount of coins.

Henry's current best guess was that there were now only about twenty-five hundred able-bodied states' soldiers left in their camp inside the walled roadway into the city—and an ever-growing number of camp followers who had been attracted to the coins the states' men earned. They, as all camp followers inevitably do, wanted the new-found men in their lives to sally out again to earn more coins.

Equally important, a week had passed since a prisoner exchange had brought back a handful of captured archers and a dozen or so of the states' forces—and, in exchange, resulted in the archers freeing a number of captured Greeks, including a captured bishop and a couple of knights. If all went as planned, the newly released Greeks would carry false and misleading information back to their fellow invaders.

It had been time well spent with every archer's day filled with training and practice on matters such as who and how the companies were to respond if the enemy broke through the wall somewhere, or if the galleys in the harbour were attacked and in need of help at the same time the wall was being attacked.

One thing, however, had been quite disappointing. I had had high hopes for the false information and offers of assistance we tried to plant by releasing the prisoners, but so far it was not having its intended effect—no effort had been made to contact Adam, the archer who had claimed to be the captain of the gate guards and had offered to open the Farmers' gates for one hundred pounds of silver coins. *That was a lot of silver, of course, but he might not have been believed if he had only asked for a small amount.*

The three sallies, the fighting in the mountains, the constant attacks by the independent companies of horse archers, and the desertions caused by the warnings of the blind prophets sent out to "see" the future of individual Greek soldiers, had combined to whittle down the Orthodox army. Even so, it still numbered well over one hundred thousand men plus another fifty thousand of so of camp followers and sutlers. It was little wonder that when the wind blew towards the sea we could smell the Greek camp from where we stood on the city wall.

Holding Constantinople's walls against the invaders were over three thousand archers from Cornwall's Company of Archers and their nine hundred locally recruited auxiliaries, the twenty-five hundred or so men remaining from the Latin states loyal to the Empress, and about four hundred of the Empress's personal guards.

In addition to the archers manning Constantinople's walls, what was left of two hundred of the Company's horse archers were harassing the invaders' flanks from battle camps secreted in the hills beyond the peninsula and foraging parties and forty-two of the Company's sea-going war galleys were here with their crews of archers and sailors.

Many of the Company's galleys were pulled ashore and others were anchored nearby because their archers were now on the city walls. But others were still crewed and actively defending the water approaches to the city and carrying away its refugees. In essence, the Company was "all in" in an effort to continuing getting some of the Latin Empire's great and growing riches.

Unlike the archers who knew they were in Constantinople to earn coins and promotions, many of the lower ranking invaders still had no idea why their lords had brought them to Constantinople. They also had inferior weapons and little or no training in how to use them.

What the Greek soldiers did know was that they were living and increasingly hungry in their army's huge, crowded, and increasingly foul camp—and that it was damn dangerous to go out foraging for food or get too near to the city's walls.

According to the Empress's spies, the Greek commander and his retinue had finally arrived. If so, he probably could not help but be aware of the size and state of his army. What he would do, however, was totally unknown. Anything was possible.

****** *Commander George Courtenay*

The reports of my lieutenants were mostly encouraging. The Company had been doing more than just preparing to fight the Greeks for the past several months. Our galleys and transports had also been earning a considerable amount of coins by carrying away refugees who could afford to flee the coming siege and its dangers and hardships. They were mostly the city's priests, merchants, and money lenders along with almost all of the city's idle gentry and the Empress's courtiers.

It was easy money for us—the refugees did the rowing on each outward bound voyage with each galley's full crew of sailors working its sails and a token number of archers on board to help to defend it.

Each galley then turned around and returned to Constantinople from wherever it had unloaded its passengers using paid volunteers to do the rowing. The rowers would join our defence force as auxiliaries when they reached Constantinople.

So far, we had only lost one galley despite the most popular refugee destination being Athens' port of Piraeus where a good part the Venetian fleet was based. And the only loss we knew about was a galley full of refugees that was apparently taken north of Cyprus by a fleet of Moorish pirates.

Venice had not been a problem for the past few months despite the fact that the Venetians hated the Company due to our past victories and support for the Empress. According to what our refugee-carrying captains had been told at Piraeus, the Venetians had been ordered by the Patriarch not to interfere with our refugee-carrying operations because so many of the refugees we were carrying out of Constantinople were Orthodox Greeks.

The Venetians, as you might expect, obeyed the Patriarch because their goal was much bigger than merely taking a few of the Company's galleys and transports as prizes—it was to in all ways replace the Company at Constantinople and, additionally and even more important to them, return to its previous domination of the city's markets and money lending. This, the Venetians assumed, would occur when the Orthodox-praying King of Epirus replaced the Latin-praying Empress on the throne.

Similarly continuing to prosper was our collection of the Empress's tolls for allowing transports and galleys to pass through the Sea of Marmara whilst coming to or from the Golden Horn, the Dardenelles, and the Bospherus. If anything, the city's increased importation of food to build up its siege supplies had caused a minor uptick of sea traffic in the local waters and, thus, of the tolls we had been collecting and keeping in exchange for helping to defend the city.

That fine state of affairs, the collection of the Empress's toll coins that is, had not slowed in the past few days even though our galleys and transports had almost entirely stopped sailing with archers on board.

Similarly, the galleys that had been rotating as toll collectors at the Dardanelles and Bosphorus entrances to the Sea of Marmara had been summoned back to the city. This was done so their archers could reinforce those who were already defending the walls.

Indeed, some of our galley and transports were still carrying refugees and collecting the Empress's tolls—but without any archers on board at all. They were sailing without them.

Sailing without archers on board had worked successfully in the past because they *might* be on board. Besides, the Company was well known for routinely pretending its transports were unarmed in order to lure pirates into coming alongside and grappling them—so our men could dash out of the deck castles and cargo holds where they had been hiding to throw their own grapples, shoot down the pirates with their arrows, and take their attackers' galleys as prizes.

What we hoped, of course, was that the war for the Empress's throne would be over and the archers back on board our galleys and transports by the time the Venetians and Moors discovered they had been gulled.

The reports coming in from the horse archers harassing the Greeks were also encouraging, albeit always late in arriving. Each week two archers from each horse company would ride northeast from their company's hidden supply camp to the nearest river that emptied into the so-called "Golden Horn" estuary that ran along the city wall on one side of Constantinople.

When the two archers reached the river, they would hail one of the Company's three fully crewed galleys that we had constantly moving up and down the river. When the archers made contact with a galley they would report on what their company had seen and done since their company's last report, and sometimes they would bring prisoners to be taken to Constantinople for questioning or wounded archers who needed barbering. In turn, the galley would give them any new orders that might have been issued and provide them with supplies such as sacks of bread-making grain and bales of arrows.

The reports from the horse companies operating furthest to the south indicated that they were keeping the road from Adrianople totally cut. Deserters and others moving south away from Constantinople were not stopped or harassed in any way; supplies and reinforcements moving north to join the Orthodox army, on the other hand, were subject to constant attacks and destruction.

Similar reports came in from the horse companies operating from their hidden bases closer to Greek encampment on the peninsula on which Constantinople was located. They claimed to be keeping the Greeks penned into their camp and preventing foraging parties from foraging unless they were extremely large and looking for a fight.

Even more important, however, was the information we continued to receive from the prisoners the horse archers were taking about the intentions of the Greek commanders—they had promised their men they would be able to go home in time to bring in the crops they had planted in the spring.

The promises of the Orthodox commanders to their men were truly important so far as we were concerned. They strongly suggested that the Greek army would attempt a massive assault instead of a prolonged siege similar to that of the crusaders that preceded their final assault. That was what we had always expected would be the case, but it was useful to our plans to have it confirmed.

Similarly suggesting a massive assault instead of a long siege were the behaviour of the Greek foragers and the statements of the prisoners taken by the horse archers. In addition to foraging for food as one might expect, the Greek foragers seemed to be particularly focussed on finding tall trees that could be cut down and used to make wall-scaling ladders, not shorter trees that might be used to build siege towers and catapults. The prisoners confirmed that it was only very tall ladders and long wooden foot bridges that were being built in the Greek camp.

Richard was particularly anxious for the Greek's big assault to begin because his horse archers were themselves being whittled down during their constant harassing attacks. Every horse company had lost men killed and wounded. Some of them were down to half strength or less. Even worse, there had been no reports from several of his companies for some weeks.

Although he never mentioned them directly, I understood Richard's concerns about his men and shared them. If the Greek army broke into the city, we could hastily load the surviving foot archers into our waiting galleys and make a run for it—but when we did, we would be leaving his horse archers behind. And that was something Richard and I could *not* and would *not* do.

Amongst the many problems of withdrawing the horse archers if the city fell was that each company's battle camp was separate and secret so that it could not be betrayed by an archer from another horse company if he was taken prisoner. Only Richard had been present when the horse archers' many different camps were initially located. In any event, the hidden camps of the independently operating horse companies would have been relocated if they had been discovered.

Accordingly, the only thing we could do if it looked like Constantinople was going to fall was have our three galleys patrolling the river send the horse company messengers who hailed them back to their camps to retrieve their mates. And then, when and if the men arrived, take them down the river and on to Cyprus.

Collecting the horse archers was likely to take weeks because it would take that long for the men of the last surviving company to contact a galley on the river and be withdrawn. Worse, we were likely to wait overly long because we would never know when the last of the independent companies had come in if some of them had been totally destroyed.

And that was only the beginning—because the Company galleys which waited to rescue them would then have to come down the river and fight their way through the Venetians and their allies whose galleys, if the city was lost, would undoubtedly be controlling the river, the estuary, and the Marmara Sea's exits and entrances.

In essence, rescuing the horse archers was not impossible even though it would be a nightmare of difficulties and very close to a forlorn hope. But it was the only thing we could do if the city fell.

In other words, victory was our only real option and we all knew it.

Chapter Thirty-three

We are well and truly surprised.

It was a balmy night and quite pleasant even though it had gotten cloudy late in the previous afternoon and it looked and smelled like there would soon be rain. Our men had been on high alert for several days. It meant that each galley company's sentries were tripled and all of its archers slept on their company's assigned stretch of the outer wall with their weapons close at hand and their bales of extra arrows open and ready.

My lieutenants and I had begun quietly walking along the top of the outer wall as soon the sun finished passing overhead. Initially, during the first hour or so of darkness, the men were sleeping and snoring everywhere, usually with their heads on one of their quivers and always on their backs. They were sleeping that way because, as every soldier knows, sleeping on one's side on stone often gives a man pains in his hip.

Similarly, sleeping on one's stomach can put a foul taste in one's mouth if he is sleeping too close to his company's latrine or where birds and mice have been shitting whilst they searched for food. It also can put a crick in one's neck from turning it too far. There was no doubt about it for a soldier sleeping rough—being flat on your arse with your head on a quiver was the only way to go.

Things began to change after a couple of hours or so of darkness. We began hearing muffled voices and strange noises coming from both sides of the nearby moat. But they did not sound like the normal noises one would expect from an army's encampment. To the contrary, the noises sounded like squeaking wagon wheels and periodic loud thumps as if something large and heavy had crashed to the ground.

Messengers soon began pouring in to report what we already knew—voices giving orders and, most surprising of all, strange noises were being heard everywhere along the city's outer wall on *both* sides of the moat. The Greeks were up to something for sure.

Our response was inevitable. All along the wall anxious archers and auxiliaries were shaken awake and orders whispered to them to be ready to move out with their weapons on a moment's notice.

Simultaneously, I sent warning messages to Richard and Harold at the harbour where our galleys were tied up and pulled on to the strand, and to Henry at the gate next to the states' forces encampment. Similar notices were sent to the commander of the Empress's Varangian guards, and to my father who had recovered enough from his chest pox to be able to take command of the Citadel's defences.

Indeed, the only people we did not bother to wake up and inform were the states' forces. We did not wake them because there was nothing for them to do since, according to Henry who had been working to train the states' forces, we could not trust them to defend even the smallest stretch of the wall.

The archers on the gate in front of the states' forces, however, were awakened and my senior aide, Michael Oremus, was sent to take command of them so they would be good hands now that Henry was needed on the wall. Henry was the Company's most experienced ground commander; I wanted him with me to help direct the defence of the wall if the Greeks were going to attack. He came immediately.

My son, also named George, accompanied Michael to the gate as his apprentice and scribe even though he was much too young to be on active duty with the Company, let alone in a real fight. George did not know it, of course, but two carefully selected chosen men, both long-serving veterans, followed him everywhere he went. They were to do whatever it took to keep him safe and out of trouble "including throwing him screaming and kicking over your shoulder and carrying him away."

Two hours later, in the middle of the night, I changed my mind about not using what was left of the states' forces. I sent a message to Michael and Prince Ivan suggesting they form them up at dawn for a possible coin-earning sortie that might start as early as an hour or two later.

What I did not tell anyone, not even Henry who had joined me by then, was that I only intended to send the states' men out on a sally if the Greek army launched an all-out attack such that the Greeks left their encampment undefended and easily sacked—because the sally of the states' forces might cause some of the Greeks to abandon their attack in order to save their camp.

Something was happening. That much was certain. But we had absolutely no idea what it might be. All we could do was assume that the noises we heard all along the wall *on both sides of the moat* meant an imminent attack was possible and get ready to repel it. Or, of course, the Greeks might just be jerking our dingles.

We spent the rest of the night assuring each other that we were ready for anything whilst constantly worrying about what was about to happen.

*****

We finally saw what had kept us awake all night when the sun appeared in the morning. It was the entire Orthodox army and it was breathtakingly huge, by far the biggest force of men any of us had ever seen. And it was formed up in a surprising place—two or three miles away on the *far* side of the Greek encampment instead of close to the wall that it apparently intended to attack.

Its men were massed several miles or so beyond the moat and the Greek encampment in about mob-like formations that looked to each have about five or six thousand men—and there many such formations, we could see at least a dozen from where we stood. They stretched all along the wall in front of us until they disappeared from sight where the wall curved.

"But why are they so far away?" Henry asked no one in particular as he shook his head. "Surely they do not intend to march someplace else after putting all those foot bridges over the moat? And where would they go?"

What Henry was saying was particularly worrying. It just did not make much sense for the Greek army to be formed up so far away. What made a lot of sense, on the other hand, was what had caused the noise that kept us awake all night—the numerous newly installed narrow wooden foot bridges that had been ingeniously thrown across the moat in the dark.

What was ingenious about them was the way they had been delivered. In the darkness of the night, each of the footbridges had been carried *upright* in the bed of a wagon to the edge of the moat, and then pushed over to so that its other end landed on the other side of the moat.

What was surprising was that the men who had pulled the wagons into place and toppled their footbridges over to cover the moat had done so, and then run off leaving the wagons unattended at the edge of the moat. Why had they done that?

And what were Greeks waiting for now that the bridges were in place? These were the questions behind everyone's eyes and much talked about by the waiting archers. One would have thought the Greeks would have immediately attacked as soon as there was enough light for them to see what they were doing. But they did not. Why were they waiting?

We were confused and uncertain. Could it be that the Greek commanders were knowledgeable enough to wait for the rain that looked to be coming this way to begin falling so our bowstrings would be affected? And how did they know in advance that there would be rain? We did not have a clue.

The delay of the Greek attack suggested that the Greek commander was either exceedingly stupid or very lucky or very smart. In any event, we all worried because the Greek assault had not started even though there were now at least a hundred narrow foot bridges across the moat. Why were they waiting?

"Henry, you go to the left and make sure each company has enough pikes and that our best archers and best pike men are in front of every wagon bridge; Nicholas, you go to the right and do the same. Pass along my order to the captains about getting their archers and pike men in front of the wagon bridges. Then continue on to the gate and look around, then come back and report. The gate is easiest way for the Greeks to get in and these foot bridges might be an elaborate feint to draw our attention away from it. "

They both knew exactly what I wanted them to do about the pikes, and so would the captains—having our best men on the pikes meant taking them from the auxiliaries and assigning them to our steadiest archers.

******

Our increased readiness had actually begun two days earlier when one of the Empress's spies came in from the Greek camp and reported that the long awaited major assault on the city's outer wall would begin as soon as the weather was right and the Greeks had collected enough wagons. We did not know what "the weather was right' meant or why they needed more wagons, but we certainly understood "major assault."

The Greek army, or so it now seemed, was either waiting for tonight's darkness so they could cross the moat with their ladders on their newly installed foot bridges without being seen, or they were waiting for a storm to wet our bowstrings. Or could it be that the Greeks were waiting for word that the Venetians had launched an attack on the harbour? No one could think of another reason.

It was the possibility that the Greek army had been waiting for a rain storm that particularly worried me and my lieutenants—there was the distinct smell of rain in the air.

Although the Greek commander was probably not experienced enough to know about it, or, based on what we had seen so far, smart enough to take advantage of it, rain greatly reduced an archer's ability to push out his arrows by wetting his bowstring. And while it was true that every archer was required to carry at least four bowstrings with him at all times, one on his bow and at least two more under his knitted cap and one in his coin pouch, it was equally true that bowstrings get wet quickly and lose their effectiveness when it is raining.

****** *Archer Harry Driver.*

"It will not be long now." That is what one of my mates, Guy Falmer, said he heard the Commander say. It happened a few minutes earlier when Guy was standing near the Commander on the narrow pathway that ran all along the top of the city's outer wall.

Guy was near the Commander because, at the time, they were both pissing over the wall at one of the places on the wall where the men of our company are supposed to piss and shite.

According Guy, the Commander also said "It was a good idea for the Greeks to use their wagons like that; we will have to remember it."

What the Commander was talking about were the abandoned wagons we could see down below us in the early light of a cloudy Thursday morning. The Greeks had quietly pushed them up to the edge of the moat in the darkness, and then the long and upright wooden plank each wagon had carried was somehow toppled over so as to fall across the moat and create a footbridge.

We knew from the word that had been passed from man to man along the wall that there were many such "wagon footbridges," and that they were spread out for miles all along the wall on either side of where Guy and I were sitting with our backs against the wall.

What was even more surprising and worrisome to me and my mates was that the wagons what brought them were still there. Footbridges we could understand. They meant the Greeks intended to come across them and attack us. But the wagons?

Last night my mates and I had known something was happening in the dark because we had heard what we now knew was the sound of the bridges' wooden planks hitting the ground below the wall on our side of the moat. We had all heard them because our entire company had spent the night on the wall anxiously waiting on high alert.

And we were fairly sure we knew how the moat bridges had been installed because we could see one of the Greeks' wagons that had carried them off to our left. The long and narrow wooden plank it had been carrying was still upright and pointing towards the sky. What we did not know was why that particular plank had not been toppled over to bridge the moat the way all the other wagons had done with the long wooden planks they had been carrying.

One of my mates, David May, a long-serving one-striper like me, said that whilst he was visiting the company shite hole earlier he had heard someone say that Alan Gaddie, one of the archers in the company next to ours, was telling everyone that he whilst he was taking a shite he had a heard a lieutenant explain why some of bridges were still on the wagons instead of being pushed over to fall across the moat.

According to Alan, the lieutenant was telling someone that the bridges had not been completed because the wagons carrying them had had trouble getting through the Greek camp. As a result, some of the wagons reached the moat too late for the men who pulled them to the edge of the moat to finish the job.

What had happened, according to the lieutenant, was that the sun had arrived before the Greeks could finish getting the wagons up to the edge of the moat. They were afraid of being picked off by the archers when the sun arrived so they, being Greeks without proper bottoms, had run away to save themselves.

It sounded reasonable. On the other hand, we were never sure about believing what Alan said since he was well known to talk constantly and be a teller of tall tales who was willing to keep talking so long as anyone was paying attention. Last year, for instance, he told us that when he was a lad in the village he had seen a pig that had been born without any front legs because its mother had eaten too many green apples.

I listened to David tell me what Alan said the lieutenant said without saying a word of my own in reply. In fact, I was too worried behind my eyes to talk. So far as I was concerned, it did not really matter how the bridges had been installed, or why a particular wooden plank had not been toppled over to put another foot bridge in place; the reality we now faced was that the Greek army had numerous foot bridges by which it could bring its men and their scaling ladders across the moat and attack us. And then what would happen?

But where are the Greek soldiers who are to use the bridges and why are they not here for us to fight? The waiting was worrying me and making me think of all the bad things that might happen. And I could tell that it was getting to the rest of the lads as well.

****** *Commander George Courtenay*

Seeing the foot bridges in place all along the wall and the huge size of the Greek army formed up and waiting to attack was worrying my men. They were talking too loudly and being overly friendly with each other because they were afraid of what might be about to happen to them, and also because they did not know why the Greeks were waiting to launch their attack.

They were not the only ones. Neither my lieutenants nor I could understand why the Greeks were waiting to launch their attack. What we suspected and feared was that they were waiting because it looked like rain was coming which would greatly reduce the effectiveness of our longbows.

On the other hand, we thought it possible they were waiting for darkness to fall once again so they could cross over to the wall with their ladders without us being able to see well enough to push arrows at them. And somewhere along the line we came to understand why the wagons had been left in place—to mark the location of each bridge so the attackers could find it.

It was not until sometime later that we learned that the real reason the Greek army had not immediately launched its attack was because its commander had just awakened and had not yet finished breaking his fast. It would not have been proper princely behaviour, his courtiers had advised him, to get up early to order an attack.

And then when he did wake up and break his fast, he got nervous and decided to wait in order to consult his astrologers and the priest who was his personal confessor. They told him to wait until he got word that the Venetians had begun attacking us by sea.

In any event, after an hour or so of anxiously waiting for the Greek army to begin moving and the attack to begin, I became aware that an idea had popped into the empty space behind my eyes.

"Bring me a line," I shouted, "and a man who knows the knots our sailors use when they make a sling to pull a landsman aboard a transport from a dinghy."

A few minutes later I found myself being trussed up with a line under my arms and bollocks secured with sailors' knots so tight they probably would have to be cut to get me loose. Immediately thereafter I was slowly lowered down to the narrow patch of land that lay between the wall and the moat. One of the newly installed Greek foot bridges was only a few paces away from where my feet touched the ground.

Archers were crowding the wall above me and peering down to watch as I inspected the bridge, and then bent down and tried to pick up and move its end. It took some effort to pick it up and move it because it was so heavy and I still had the rope tied to tight around me.

I was finally able to lift it by spitting on my hands to get a good grip, and then grunting and suddenly pulling it up. And then, with such a great deal of difficulty that I was afraid my dingle would be strained, I managed to pull the narrow footbridge around sideways so that its end fell into the foul water with a great splash.

"Haul me up," I shouted as the men on the wall above me cheered.

I had just come over the outer wall and begun issuing orders when I felt the first drops of rain. And that was when the Greek army began moving forward into its camp and towards us—with many of its men carrying what were almost certainly long ladders.

"Belay those orders," I said to the men who were gathered around me trying to untie the knots, "and sound the order for the men to repel boarders.

"And cut the damn line off me."

Chapter Thirty-four

Here they come.

The Greek army began moving through their camp with their long ladders almost at the same time as it began to rain. First one and then another of the big groups of men in the distance began streaming towards us. The rain was only a few drops at first, but we knew it would be on us soon. But how hard would it rain and for how long? That was the all-important question. It takes time to change a bowstring, and every archer has only four or five, and they lose their strength when wet.

"Here they come," one of the archers further down the wall shouted excitedly. Mostly, however, the men just muttered curses under their breaths and got themselves ready to fight. We had had enough time to prepare, so there were now thirty or forty archers standing shoulder to shoulder on the wall above every one of the wagon bridges—nowhere near enough since it looked as though a thousand or more Greek soldiers and dozens of ladders were heading towards each of them.

The order to repel boarders meant the archers were free to push out arrows anytime they had a target. But I was not taking any chances. I made damn sure they knew they were to do so.

"ARCHERS TO START PUSHING AS SOON AS THEY ARE IN RANGE. PASS IT ON," I shouted the order as loudly as I could while the men gathered around me were still trying to cut me free from the lines that bound me.

All around me the sergeants and captains repeated the order loudly and it was then repeated over and over again as it quickly travelled down the wall in both directions.

At the same time, the signal men of each company did their duty by quickly tying red rags to the ends of their bows and waving them frantically over their heads in a totally unneeded effort to let the archers and auxiliaries up and down the wall know that they should stand to their arms.

"The buggers started too soon," Henry muttered to no one in particular. "They should have waited until our bowstrings were wet."

I could tell from the way he said it that he thought we were about to be in serious trouble. I certainly did.

"Henry, take one of the horses in the enclosure and gallop through the enclosure openings to Prince Ivan and the states' men. Tell them to sally immediately for double the usual coins, and then come back along the wall giving whatever orders you think are necessary."

My recently un-retired lieutenant commander repeated his orders whilst he was running down the stone steps to get to his waiting horse. There were horses up on the wall he could have boarded faster, but I knew he would make much better time going through the narrow openings in the interior walls since everyone was now up on the wall.

A minute later I gave my apprentice sergeant, Nicholas Greenway, the very same orders. Why? Because it was always wise to send at least two messengers when a battle message was of vital importance. And the one I was sending certainly was important.

What I hoped, of course, was that a sally by the states' men into the Greek camp when the Greek army was nearby would encourage some of them to hurriedly return to defend their tents and women. It was not likely, but it was all I could think to do.

And then it struck that I had made a mistake by waiting too long—I should have ordered the states' men to sally while the Greeks were still waiting in their formations.

****** *Commander George Courtenay*

My men and I watched in fascination as the huge mass of the Greek army surged forward and began streaming through their encampment towards us. The rain was still only scattered drops and all around me the archers were holding their bows close to their tunics in an effort to keep their strings dry. They were good men, but would a few good men be enough against so many?

As the Greeks coming through their camp got closer we could see that many of them were indeed carrying long ladders. They clearly intended to cross the moat on the new installed footbridges and scale the wall using the long ladders.

There were many tens of thousands of screaming and shouting men running towards us and, at first, there were none of the usual stragglers or runners when an army moves forward in an attack, at least none that we could see. It was as if each man had been given a sense of safety and certain victory by having so many of his mates packed around him.

Perhaps, the thought came to me as I watched them, it was for the Patriarch and their priests were running with them to make sure they knew that God was watching them and would protect them. Whatever the reason, the Greek movement through their camp to get to the wall was quite impressive both for its size and for the distance it would have to cover. It looked like a tide of men sweeping into through a tidal flat that was full of tents, wagons, and cheering camp followers..

It also appeared to be a well thought out attack in the sense that the Greeks carrying the ladders knew where to run because they could see the wagons from which the bridges had been pushed. *They had been left as markers.* I was sure of it. That was worrisome. It meant someone over there was not entirely incompetent.

The first of the arrows from the men around me began being pushed towards the Greeks coming towards the wagon bridges just before they came into range. A moment later the Greek thrusters weaving their way through the camps tents and wagons were clearly reachable and our arrows began filling the sky like the great flock of birds I had once seen when I was a lad.

More and more Greeks began to go down as they came hurrying towards the moat. But there were so many of them charging towards us that those who fell or turned aside were the equivalent of a few drops in a bowl of ale.

All around me I could hear the grunts as they archers pushed out arrow after arrow at the Greeks charging towards us. It became instantly apparent that the Greeks were organized according to the ladders they were carrying and the bridges they were trying to cross.

In essence, each of the long ladders was acting as a unifying force in the sense that six or seven unarmed men were helping to carry each of the ladders with the sixty or seventy Greek soldiers who had been assigned to climb it running along close behind it. The men assigned to carry and climb each ladder were, in a sense, a ladder company, and there seemed to be at least a dozen of them coming through their camp towards each of the newly installed footbridges. At least that was what it looked like from where I was standing.

As they got closer we could see that the Greeks running behind the ladder carriers were carrying various weapons. Some were running towards us with swords in their hands, but most of them, to my surprise, were carrying spears and shields. We could also see priests trotting alongside the ladder carriers and encouraging them as the ladders weaved their way towards us through the tents, wagons, and camp followers of the attackers' closely packed encampment.

I was not the only one surprised to see the Greeks carrying spears and shields. An out-of-breath Henry had just returned from ordering the states' forces to launch a sally and noticed them a well.

"It is going to be interesting to watch those buggers try to climb a long ladder with a shield in one hand and a spear in the other."

There was no question about what the Greeks were trying to do. They were attacking on a broad front in an all-out attack to get over the city's outer defensive wall and take out most of the city's defenders before we could fall back to the inner defensive wall.

There was soon so much noise and shouting from the approaching Greeks that I could barely think about what else I might do to get the men ready to receive them. Even so, several things became instantly obvious. For one, most of the attacking Greeks were going to get through our arrow storm and reach the moat with their ladders. For another, there seemed to be quite a number of ladders heading for each of the wagon bridges.

We had every available archer on the wall. The problem was that their pushing of arrows into the Greeks below us would not be occurring as rapidly as it normally would have been because our bowstrings were getting wet and would have to be constantly changed—until we ran out of them.

Our reality was quickly becoming clear. No matter how good a half-company of thirty or forty archers might be, and that is what we had in front of each of the wagon bridges along with ten or fifteen auxiliaries, there was no possible way they could stop many hundreds of attackers, especially if they all came up their ladders at the same time. We would be overrun.

And there were so many Greeks coming at us that the possibility we would run out of arrows as well as bowstrings came out of nowhere and suddenly became a concern behind my eyes. We had bales and bales of arrows laid out all along the top of the outer wall. But did we have enough if the bowstrings lasted?

"Concentrate your arrows on the men around the wagons and pick your man. Do not push unless you are sure of a hit."

Sergeants heard the order and began repeating it. It quickly spread along the wall from sergeant to sergeant. The rate of pushing fell around me, but only very briefly. And the Greeks who fell were mostly those who were closest to the wagons and the moat. It was then that the rain began in earnest and the men began changing their bowstrings.

******

Things went well for the Greeks until they reached the wagons next to the moat which marked the location of each footbridge. Then everything became confused and things began to fall apart for them.

It turned out to be quite difficult for five or six excited men to carry a long scaling ladder across a wet and slippery slab of wood that was only a couple of feet wide. What made it almost impossible was that thirty of forty of the world's finest archers were standing on the wall above them, and they were, quite rightly, particularly concentrating their arrows on the Greeks who were trying to come across on the narrow foot bridge.

What I could see from where I was standing turned out to be a good example of what was happening all along the city's outer wall.

I looked down from the wall where I was standing and watched as the first of the ladder carriers reached the moat below me and began trying to carry their ladder across a wagon bridge that was about one hundred paces west of where I was standing.

The man at the very front of the ladder was trying to feel his way slowly and cautiously across the narrow bridge on the wet wood; the men behind him, however, were pushing in their desperation to quickly get over the bridge and next to the wall so they could set their ladder and run away to safety.

It did not work for them. The first man started to go down on one knee and his foot slipped—so the first of the arrows intended for him took the second man in the chest and they both fell into the water whilst still desperately trying to hold on to the ladder. That overbalanced the other men holding on to the ladder and a couple of them also fell in the water. The only survivors ended up being the last two men who were still standing on land and the ladder-climbers for that ladder who were massed immediately behind them.

The clouds opened and rain became to come down as the place of the fallen ladder was taken by another ladder from amongst the many ladders waiting nearby to come across despite the casualties being put on them by the archers.

Less than a minute later the second ladder followed the first into the water and the number of arrows biting into the men waiting to across the narrow bridge slackened noticeably as the archers began hastily restringing their longbows with dry bowstrings.

Although I did not know it, similar events were occurring all up and down the moat. The result were a great masses of Greek men, often a thousand or more, waiting to cross at almost every wagon bridge *one at a time* while archers on the wall above them placed their arrows where they would do the most good. Greek casualties began piling up and some of the Greeks began pulling back.

And, because I did not yet know that the Greeks' attempt to use the bridges were having the same problems everywhere along the wall, I damn near panicked and did not know what to do when, one right after another, two messengers arrived. The first was a messenger arrived from Eric saying that the city was rising against the Empress in our rear. He wanted me to send archers to reinforce his men.

My response was negative.

"We are under attack. Try to hold the Latin Quarter and fall back on the Citadel if necessary. We will come as soon as we can but it may be many hours."

The second message was from Richard with news that was much more alarming—a Venetian fleet had been sighted approaching the harbour where our galleys were anchored and pulled ashore without their archers on board to defend them.

It was raining few minutes later and already a third ladder, and then a fourth had failed to get across. But then our arrows stopped being delivered because all of our bowstrings were wet and the Greeks fifth attempt to get a ladder across the moat was successful.

A few moment later, as a sixth ladder was coming across, two more messengers from Richard came in one right after the other. Both reported the arrival of a large number of Venetian galleys and that heavy fighting was about to begin at the harbour—and Richard said he and Harold desperately needed reinforcements, and quickly.

That was when I finally realized something important and gave what appeared to be, at that moment, the necessary orders.

"All Evens to the harbour. Double time." … "All Evens to the harbour. Double time."

Of course I sent reinforcements to the harbour and not to the city. The Company could survive and continue to collect the tolls even if the city was destroyed; it would not survive if we lost all our galleys and could not get away.

Chapter Thirty-five

Trouble beckons.

Captain Smith shouted his order loudly so it could be heard above the noise of the fighting going on all along the wall on either side of us.

"COMPANY ATTENTION," the captain roared. "Evens, one minute to get yourselves ready and then follow Lieutenant Eden with your quivers full. Evens with pikes, swords, and shields are to carry them."

My mates and I knew exactly what the order meant—it meant the men in our company who were "Evens" were about to double-time to the harbour to reinforce the archers and sailors who were already there. And we all knew exactly where we were going, and why. We knew because we had already heard the same order and made practice runs all the way to the harbour four times in the past couple of weeks. In any event, we quickly gathered up our weapons and unused arrows, formed up in a column of twos, and off we went with Lieutenant Evans leading the way.

There was a lot of talking as we were forming up. Every one of us was very excited—and damn pleased to be ordered away from the Greek buggers who were trying to get across the moat so they could get at us. A couple of men had been hit early on by crossbow bolts and carried away to the hospital galley at the harbour. One was dead for sure, a Welshman named Jones who was one of our best archers. But now, at least, we were safe because the Greeks' crossbows were no long useful due to the rain fouling their strings—just like our longbows.

I was an "even" and had to go wherever Lieutenant Eden led us because every man who made his mark on the Company's roll was given a permanent number that was his forever. I was number 5018 which meant 5017 men had made their marks on the Company's roll before I made mine. My mate, Albert, said that made me an "even" because my Company number ended in eight.

Albert may have been right; but it did not matter. The sergeant said I was an even and had to follow Lieutenant Eden. That was fine with me, especially since it meant I could say goodbye to crossbow bolts and them buggers what was trying to climb up the wall on ladders and kill us.

Less than a minute later the lieutenant waved his hand in a circle over his head and shouted "FORWARD" as he pointed, Sergeant Everly swore at us and began calling the step, and we were off and moving at the double. It happened just as we had been practicing.

We were not the only ones on the move. Already the men who were "Evens" from the company to the north of us were hurrying along the top of the wall towards us with their funny-looking lieutenant leading them, the one who had one eye looking someplace else whilst the other looked at you. They would follow us all the way to the harbour and, as sure as God made green apples, they would try to run fast in order to get past us to make us look bad.

Marching at the double in the rain got old in a hurry. Even so, I was glad we had been ordered to the harbour, and so was everyone else. Of course we were—our bowstrings were wet and the damn Greeks were once again trying to get some of their ladders across their little walkway in the moat below us. I must have hit half a dozen or more of the bastards myself before my last bowstring got stretched too far from the rain.

My mates and I were worried because most of us, including me, would only have our longbows to use as weapons when we got to the harbour—and they were temporarily useless because we were out of dry bowstrings. We did not know whether we would be issued pikes or swords and shields when we got there, but we surely hoped so.

We were not at all sure it would happen, us being issuing more weapons that is; we never had been issued any when we marched there when we were practicing, probably because we had never practiced when it was raining and our bowstrings were wet.

Some of the men were talking as we double-timed along the top of the wall instead of saving their breath. They said we would be issued our galley's short swords and shields when we got there, whilst others claimed we were just going back to board our galleys and that we would soon be rowing for Cyprus because there were too many Greeks to fight.

Leaving the fighting behind and sailing for Cyprus sounded like a fine idea to me, but somehow I doubted we would be going back, at least not yet. I did not say anything, though; it is too hard to talk and breathe at the same time after you have been double-timing for a while.

My best mates, Albert and Guy, were not with me. They were "Odds" and had to stay behind to help Captain Smith fight off the Greek buggers what was trying to take the wall.

Someone said Commander Courtenay himself was watching us when we started out, but the last thing I saw as we started jogging towards the harbour was the top of a ladder peeking over the wall and Captain Smith going after it with a pike.

******

As we double-timed in the warm rain to the harbour, we every so often came past the "Odds" archers of the other galley companies who were continuing to man the wall in front of each foot bridge. Several times we were able to gobble with them when we were held up for a moment or two by auxiliaries and archers moving rocks and stones that could be dropped on the ladder climbers. They shouted out to us the latest news and rumours traveling along the wall as they were passed from one man to the next.

Some of the men we came upon were getting ready to fight with the ladder-climbing Greeks coming across the moat, and some lucky buggers were just standing around doing nothing. One thing was certain—every man who spoke with us complained in one way or another that his longbow was useless due to the rain. Mostly the lads just held up their bows and shook their heads in disgust as we came past them.

What we also heard from the men we jogged past, and those we met coming in the other direction, on the other hand, was both very encouraging and very discouraging, *if* any of it was actually true instead of just being more of the many tall tales that were being passed along the wall by men who enjoyed making up stories.

The good word we both heard and saw was that some of the Greek foot bridges had broken or fallen in the moat instead of providing a way to cross it, and also that some of the bridges had been abandoned in the face of our mates' arrows; the bad word was that the Greeks were now across the footbridges in a number of places and trying to climb their ladders to get to us. There was also an unverified report that some of the Greeks had been able to climb up their ladders and fight their way on to the wall in several places further to the north towards where the states' men were camped.

As my "Evens" mates and I were hurrying in one direction towards the harbour, archers who were "Odds" were also double-timing the other way, coming towards us. We were passing in the rain because our captains were moving their men from where there were no functioning bridges and fighting to where the Greeks had gotten ladders across the moat and were trying to climb them, at least that was what they told us as we went past them. Sometimes the men coming from where there had been no fighting still had dry strings under their caps and in their pouches.

By the time we reached the place where the wall turned and began to run along close to the shoreline of the sea, the rain was really pouring down hard. All my mates and I knew for sure at that point was that *none* of the Greeks had reached the top of the wall along the parts we had just run past on our way to our galleys. Not yet, at least.

Chapter Thirty-six

The Venetians are coming.

"Hoy the deck. Captain Spencer, there be a shite pot full of Venetian galleys in the strait and they be coming fast."

I immediately gave the order "Cast off and get underway" in response to the lookout's warning report of the on-coming Venetian fleet. It turned my coin-collecting galley into an absolute frenzy of activity.

The men of my crew were mostly sailors and volunteers from the city since all of our archers were on the wall. But they understood what was at stake—their lives and freedom if the Venetians caught us and the lives and freedom of their mates at the Company's harbour if we did not get the word to them in time for them to get ready to fight.

Our alert horn blower immediately began tooting and everyone in the crew rushed to their assigned places—the rowers to their seats on the rowing decks and the sailors to raise the sails. The rowing drum began a beat that got faster and faster as we picked up speed, and my sailors began raising every sail they could crowd on to both our galley's main mast and its smaller forward mast.

We pushed off from the transport whose tolls we had been collecting and were underway and picking up speed in less than a minute. I had rushed up the mast to see the Venetians for myself, shouting orders to get underway as I did, and was back at my place on the roof of the stern castle a few moments later as our oars began to bite into the water and we surged forward. A few minutes later I moved forward to the roof of the forward deck castle. I did so as soon as I was sure there was no immediate threat coming up behind us.

It was literally a matter of life and death that we got underway quickly as soon as possible after the alarm was raised. Our mates at the galley harbour would need time to get ready to fight off the Venetians—and we wanted them to be ready because *we* would be going ashore and joining them in the Company's battle ranks as soon as we arrived.

My rowers pulled with a will. Many of them were sailors who had made their marks on the Company's roll. They understood why we had to reach our under-crewed galleys to sound the alarm before the Venetians reached the harbour where the Company's galleys were anchored and pulled ashore. They also understood that we had to get there enough ahead of the Venetians so that our mates back at the harbour would have enough time to get to their weapons and be ready to fight to save them.

My crew had no slackers even though my lieutenant and I were the only archers on board now that every archer in our regular crew was serving on the walls. Every man was an experienced rower, and every man was pulling with a will as we surged away from the Moorish transport that had stopped to pay its tolls. I called for a runner to bring me my bow just in case. One never knew when an opportunity might come along.

Commander Lewes had warned us about the possibility of a Venetian sally coming through the Dardanelles, and we had deliberately been given a substantial number of extra rowers so we could get to the city before the Venetians did and sound the alarm. As a result, every oar on my galley had two men pulling it and there were more men squatting in the aisle between the benches ready to take their place when they needed to go for a drink of water or take a brief rest.

We quickly left the slave-rowed Venetians so far behind that they could not be seen without climbing to the top of our main mast.

Only one thing was certain so far as I was concerned—there was no way the slave-rowed Venetians could catch us once we were underway and ahead of them. What was uncertain was whether we would get to Constantinople in time for our mates to get themselves properly ready to fight to save the Company's galleys.

******

I did not know how far the Venetians were behind us as we rowed for Constantinople. All I knew for sure after the first few hours was that they were no longer in sight. There was little wonder in that—despite the heat, and then the rain storm which we entered, we had pulled hard all the way and made very good time.

The crews of the other sails we passed, both coming and going, rushed to their decks and gaped as we went flying past them. Some of them waved and tried to hail us. They probably never had seen a galley moving so fast in these waters. The more experienced of them probably knew something was up.

Indeed, our need for speed was so great that both Lieutenant Williams and myself, and the sailing sergeant too, took a turn at the oars. We rowed so the men would understand the importance of getting to the harbour as soon as possible to sound the alarm. My painful blisters were a small price to pay for encouraging the men to keep putting everything they had into their rowing.

It was pouring rain and the one lookout we had aloft was waving the "enemy in sight" flag even though we could not actually see them. We were still rowing hard, as we came flying into the little harbour in front of the city wall. It was the harbour where some of our galleys were beached and the rest were anchored with only minimal crews on board.

I was standing on the roof of the forward castle shouting the rudder instructions to the rudder men on the steering oar as we entered the harbour. Bill Meadows, my sailing sergeant, who normally would have giving the rudder orders, was in the bow nervously sergeanting the three strong-armed sailors who had been assigned to throw the tow lines ashore.

Normally we would have thrown just one line ashore. Not today. We needed to get all the way ashore and fast. Hopefully there would be men on the shore waiting to place rollers under our bow and help pull us out of the water. That, at least, was the plan.

As soon as the tow lines were thrown, Sailing Sergeant Meadows and some of his men would jump into the surf and begin pulling on the lines to keep the galley's bow pointed towards where we want it to go when it slid up on to the strand. Others of them would run for the rounded rollers waiting nearby and begin placing them under the hull so the galley could roll over them and be quickly pulled all the way out of the water.

Hopefully some of the men on shore would join in to help pull us up on to the strand alongside galleys that were already there. That was the plan, but we could not count on them.

Everything was as ready as it could be for our galley to come up on to the strand and keep on going on the rollers until it was all the way out of the water. The rowers, once their oars were no longer in the water would first run to the stern to weigh it down and, in so doing, lift the bow up so we could get further ashore before we touched.

Once the galley touched the strand and stopped moving forward, the entire crew, including me, would run forward and jump into the surf and onto the strand to lighten the galley and help pull it further forward until it was all the way out of the water.

In all my years with the Company it was the fastest I had ever been moving when my galley entered a harbour. As a result, Sergeant Matthews was nervous and we were moving much too fast as we approached the place on the strand where we were supposed to pull our galley out of the water.

Men who were already on the strand had stopped doing what they were doing to watch. We could see by their tunics that they were mostly Company sailors. Someone must have said something for a moment later they all began running towards us to help pull us ashore.

A second or so later I gave the orders to change our speed.

"ROWERS STAND BY TO BACK OARS" ... "BACK OARS." ... "PULL" ... "PULL." ...

There was a great scraping noise and much shouting from my crew as the bow of our galley reached the strand and began sliding up on to it. The sudden slowing as the galleys hull first touched bottom almost threw me off my feet.

A few moments later more than a hundred shouting men, including me and all the sailors and rowers, even the rudder men, made a mad dash for the stern bow, and stayed there until the galley stopped moving forward. Then, with much shouting we all ran to the bow jumped down into the surf and on to the strand and began pulling on the lines that had been cast ashore as soon as the galley stopped moving forward. Men on the strand were already picking up and pulling on the thrown tow lines to help pull us further ashore.

I had been satisfied with myself and breathed a great sigh of relief as I jumped down on to the strand, and twisted my ankle as I did. My galley had sounded the alarm and come ashore acceptably close to our assigned position. We might lose the coming battle with the Venetians, but as I grabbed the tow line to help pull I felt as though I had done all I could to prevent the loss.

Captain Spencer was wrong about having done all he could to prevent a Venetian victory. But no one knew it at the time.

****** *Lieutenant Commander Harold Lewes.*

The Venetians must have scheduled their sea attack on our idled galleys to occur on the same day as the Orthodox army assaulted the outer wall and the city rose. They were all almost certainly planned to occur at the same time because it meant the archers of the galleys who were manning the walls would be pinned down and unable to come to their galleys' rescue. What neither they nor we had anticipated was that it might rain on that day.

It was about then that we began to understand the reason the Greeks had placed their bridges in the night, and then delayed their attacks—they knew the Venetian galleys would need many hours of daylight to get clear of the Dardanelles strait and row all the way to Constantinople. It was the benefits the Greeks and Venetians hoped to gain from attacking at the same time, not the rain, that explained why the Greek army had waited until early in the afternoon to launch its attack against the wall.

Richard Ryder was with me at the harbour. He was in command of the sailor men who would fight on land if the Venetians tried to attack the galleys we had pulled ashore. He had been training them to do so every day for more than three weeks, ever since every available archer was summoned to man the walls.

It was Richard's idea to pull all of our floating galleys ashore at the last moment so they would be easier to defend against an attack by sea—and a damn fine idea it was.

Our toll-collecting captains and their crews had been on high alert at the entrance to the Dardanelles strait for several weeks, ever since word had been received that the Orthodox Army was on the move. Their galleys had been from amongst our fastest and they had also been sent out with extra rowers so there would be at least two rowers available to pull on every oar with a good number of spare rowers as well.

We first knew the Venetians were actually coming when one of the lookouts on the mast of Galley 43, our toll-collecting galley at the mouth of the Dardanelles, sighted them coming through the narrow strait alerted his captain. The captain of the galley, one of our fastest, a good man by the name of Mark Spencer, had quickly gotten his galley under way and rowed hard in order to bring us a timely warning.

Captain Spencer had not stopped to count the Venetians sails coming through the Dardanelles, and rightly so, but he thought there were at least twenty of them. He had a head start and his crew rowed hard. They were able to give us a good twenty minutes of advance warning before the first of the Venetians reached us. That was almost enough time for us to finish putting into effect our plan to fight the Venetians on land, instead of at sea, if and when their fleet of war galley attacked in force.

Our main problem, the reason we decided to pull all our galleys ashore, was that almost all of their archers were fighting on the walls; our main advantage was that a Venetian attack had been expected and we had had almost a month to make the various preparations needed to give them a very unfriendly welcome.

One of our early preparations was to pull some of our galleys, those with the deepest drafts, all the way up on to the strand so we could fight on land to keep them from being destroyed or taken as prizes. The galleys with the shallowest drafts, on the other hand, were emptied as much as possible and placed in a row across the harbour entrance so they would appear to be in a defensive line.

We anchored the shallow draft galleys in a row after we did everything possible to lighten them so they would be easier to pull out of the water. Then we attached long tow lines to their bows so their anchor lines could be chopped and they could be quickly pulled ashore without having to wait for rowers to go on board. We also had rollers, rounded logs with their bark stripped off by our sailors, ready to be placed under their hulls so the lightened galleys could be brought well up on to the strand.

Our hope was that the Venetians would get reports from their spies that there were a dozen Company galleys at anchor in a defensive line that closed off most of the mouth of the little harbour that had been assigned to us, and perhaps twice that many of our galleys pulled up on the strand with some of the Company's poxed and wounded men on board for barbering, but without their crews.

In other words, what we hoped was that, if and when the Venetians came to join the battle for the city, they would arrive expecting to have to fight a sea battle with our galleys blocking the harbour entrance—and be surprised to find that they would have to fight on land if they wanted to take or destroy them whilst their crews were fighting on the city's walls. What we also hoped was that deciding what to do next would delay the Venetians from coming ashore to attack us long enough for reinforcements to arrive from where the galleys' archers were stationed along the wall.

Forcing the Venetians to come ashore to fight us was not the only thing we could think to do to get ready, but it was amongst the most important

Lieutenant Commander Harold Lewes

The very first thing I did upon seeing the high-speed approach of our toll-collecting galley waving its "enemy in sight" flag was order everyone to turn out to help pull ashore the galleys anchored in the harbour. I also send immediately sent a galloper with a warning message to Commander Courtenay on the wall.

And then, a few minutes later, as soon as Richard and I heard Captain Spencer's breathless report and knew we were badly outnumbered and in for a real fight, we sent three messengers, one right after the other, two galloping and one running, to the Commander asking for all the help he could send to us from the archers fighting on the walls.

We sent three messengers, instead of the usual one and a backup, in order to emphasize the seriousness of the situation.

My sailors had all been trained to fight at sea using swords and shields. It was required of all our sailors. And Richard had spent the better part of the previous month putting even more learning on them about how to move about and fight on land with their mates by their sides.

Man for man, because they had been trained to fight alongside the archers, our sailors had always been better fighters than the Moorish pirates and, perhaps, as good or better the Venetian soldiers and sailors who manned their galleys and sometimes helped their slaves and convicts with the rowing.

Now, of course, the sailors at the harbour were even better fighters as a result of Richard's efforts. But they were still not real fighting men and we were about to be badly outnumbered if the Venetians actually came ashore, which seemed likely.

The Venetians, on the other hand, would be fighting on land where they had absolutely no fighting experience or training. Even so, they were likely to outnumber us and might well overwhelm us by their sheer force of numbers and take or destroy our galleys. It was something we were determined to prevent.

There was also no question about our need for more men to help defend our galleys if Captain Spencer was right about the size of the Venetian fleet. Twenty galleys full of Venetians were just too many for our sailors to hold off without reinforcements.

We had to have them, the reinforcements that is, or we risked losing most of our galleys, and perhaps the entire Company. There was no doubt about it, we would be in deep shite if some or all of the archers who had been detached from their galleys to help defend the city were not quickly returned to us.

It took us more than twenty minutes to get ready for the Venetians despite all of our preparations and practices. As a result, the last two of the galleys that had been anchored across the front of the harbour were still being hurriedly pulled up on to the strand when the first Venetian galleys cautiously made their way through the harbour entrance. It was raining when they did.

The two Venetians came in a bit too cautiously, actually. That may or may not have been a good sign. It probably meant their captains were aware of fighting abilities of English archers as a result of the losses their fleet had taken lately. Their spies had almost certainly reported that their archers were helping guard the walls. But spies were often wrong and the Venetian captains were taking no chances.

If the Venetian captains had known for sure that we only had a single file of seven archer sergeants at the harbour helping to teach the sailors to fight on land, they probably would have behaved differently and come straight at us. Unfortunately, the fact that we were short of archers was something they would know soon enough if we did not get reinforcements before they attacked.

Indeed, had the Venetian thrusters dashed forward they might well have been able to take the last two or three of our galleys, those that were still being pulled up on to the strand. But they did not. They were flummoxed and overbalanced by *not* finding our galleys in the harbour where they had been told to expect them and fight them.

I understood exactly how the Venetian captains must have felt—I had the same experience years ago when we swept into the harbour at Tunis and found the forewarned Tunisian fleet had been pulled ashore and was being guarded by an army of soldiers.

Bringing their galleys ashore worked for the Tunisians by forcing us to blockade the harbour for days, and then leave with a relatively minor ransom instead of immediately sailing away with prizes.

What we hoped was that having our galleys pulled up on to the strand, and having their sailors in a battle formation and ready to fight, would delay the Venetians until reinforcements could begin reaching us from the men on the city's walls; what we had not taken into account was the possibility that attacks on the wall and on our galleys would be coordinated so they occurred at the same time, or that the bowstrings of the archers we were counting on as reinforcements would be wet and usable.

Chapter Thirty-seven
The tide of battle turns—but which way?

There was chaos and desperation all around me on the wall as the last of my archers' longbows ceased to be able to push out arrows and half of all of the available men began running through the pouring rain to join the battle at the harbour.

The men had to be sent to the harbour. It was a decision I did not regret. We needed to save our galleys so we could escape on them if we were defeated on the walls. But sending half of all the available men meant there would only be fifteen or twenty archers and auxiliaries in front of each Greek footbridge. That might have been enough if the archers could use their longbows. But they could not because of the rain.

Making things even worse was the fact that the spirits of the archers on the wall were low. Many of the men who remained felt abandoned without weapons even though their captains had stayed with them, and Henry and I constantly moved up and down the wall to show our men that we were still on the wall with them.

Our problem was not that our numbers were few, but that the rain had caused our men to be woefully under-armed and unable to defend themselves. A few of the archers were now carrying the pikes that had been issued to their auxiliaries, but most of them had no other weapons at all except for their personal knives and the piles of large stones that could be dropped on anyone trying to climb a ladder.

Truth be told, dropping rocks on attackers was a sad and unexpected comedown for men who had rightly considered themselves to be the best trained and best armed fighting men in the world—and the only ones who were Marines ready to fight both on land and at sea.

Looking back, I could see that weeks ago I should have ordered the men to bring their short swords and shields to the wall as well as their longbows and all the pikes that had been aboard each of our galleys. But I did not. And now we were about to pay heavily for my not considering the possibility of rain until it was too late to prepare for it.

In any event, all of our longbows had been rendered ineffective by the rain by the time the archers with even numbers began running for the harbour. The men with odd numbers who remained and I pressed ourselves up against the stones of the archer slits so the men of the galley companies who were "Evens" could come running past us on their way to the harbour.

Henry watched them go. And then he suddenly turned to me and said something that so surprised me that my jaw dropped and I slapped my own face in disgust and dismay when, a few moments later, I understood what he meant.

"Richard and Harold's men at the harbour do not need pikes because the Venetians will not be charging them with horses. Besides, they can use their longbows."

"No, they cannot use their bows; not with this rain."

"Yes, they can. The sails Richard set up to keep the men from having to stand in their ranks in the sun will also keep the archers' bowstrings out of the rain. Using tents is what your father did years ago right here in Constantinople when the Byzantines took some of our men for ransom."

"My God, Henry; you are right." *And I just sent the men with half of the pikes that had been on the wall to the harbour.*

At Henry's suggestion, I had an order passed down the wall from man to man—I ordered each captain to send four of his remaining men running back to the harbour to bring back all the pikes they could carry, even those that the "Evens" had just carried to the harbour. Immediately thereafter, Henry and I each once again ran in opposite directions along the wall to make sure the order was being carried out

And then, whilst both the "Evens" and the pike fetchers were gone so that the strength of the wall's defenders was at its weakest, encouraging news began to come in even though the Greeks had begun pouring over their footbridges unopposed such that it seemed to everyone that all was about be lost.

Everyone's spirits rose a bit when word was passed from man to man along the wall that some of the Greek footbridges, perhaps as many as half, had failed for one reason or another and were unusable.

"They cannot cross the bridge at enclosure eighteen. They are just standing in front of bridge looking at it." … "They are only crossing on one bridge at thirteen." … "They be just standing there."

Those were the word-of-mouth reports coming along the wall that turned out to be true. Some of the footbridges had apparently broken when they were toppled off the wagons. Others appeared to have fallen short when the wagons carrying them failed to get close enough to the moat before they toppled them over. And some bridges appeared to be usable but the Greeks assigned to them had run away as a result of taking fearsome casualties before the archers' bowstrings became unusable.

Unfortunately, saying that as many as half the Greeks' footbridges were unusable was also the same as saying half of their many foot bridges were intact. And they were intact and were either already being crossed in the rain by the surviving Greek ladder carriers, or soon would be when the Greeks realized we were no longer capable of pushing arrows at them.

Our situation was difficult and we all knew it—there were a lot of usable footbridges across the moat, an average of perhaps two or three in front of every enclosure, and many hundreds of Greek soldiers waiting to cross at each of them and begin climbing the wall.

I began moving along the wall to once again consider our prospects. Was it time to pull the archers out of the city and try to make a run for it?

As I moved along the wall I discovered something important and, without being aware of it at the time, my hysteria and panic passed and I totally calmed down. Indeed, my spirits rose and I shouted a joyful "Yes!" when I saw Captain Smith of Number Nineteen Galley use one of our long-handled bladed pikes to push a ladder off the wall with its Greek climbers still on it.

Indeed, I literally skipped for glee and clapped my hands when I saw how effective the bladed hooks on our long-handled pikes could be used to push over a scaling ladder that was leaning up against the wall. And every company had at least a few of them left even though I had just sent half the pikes to the harbour when I sent half the men there with their weapons.

But then I asked myself if there were pikes in front of every usable footbridge over the moat—and I did not know. It was time for another run along the wall.

******

I met Henry coming the other way as I moved along the wall. He had gone all the way down to the gate, and was coming back along the wall to see what was happening. He immediately reported that he had seen the same thing I had seen—Greeks crossing on the footbridges but unable to climb the wall on their ladders both because our men kept pushing them over with their pikes and dropping rocks on them, and because their ladders were too short.

Henry and I hurriedly conferred, and enthusiastically agreed, that the long-handled bladed pikes made by our company's smiths had found a new use at which they excelled. Then he and I began running along the top of the wall in opposite directions to move men and pikes from in front of the unusable bridges to reinforce the men in front of the usable bridges where the Greeks were now crossing or soon would cross.

Once again, Henry ran along the top of the wall back towards the wall gate; I ran towards the harbour with Nicholas pounding along behind me with a pike I had taken from a company that seemed to have more pikes than it needed and thrust into his hands.

Several things were certain—the archers on wall knew Henry and I had not deserted them, and my feet and legs were getting sore. I decided that if I got out this alive, I was going to find a better pair of sandals as soon as possible.

Richard, Michael, Eric, and my father were not on the wall with us. Michael was still at the gate organizing the return of the states' soldiers from the coin-earning sortie that was underway; Richard was at the harbour to lead the sailors and the "Evens" against the Venetians; Eric was in the city with the Empress's Varangian guards defending the Latin Quarter; and my father was commanding the citadel's defences in order to keep the Empress happy and him and my younger brother occupied and out of trouble.

The Empress, her daughter, Elizabeth, and her son, Robert, the boy Emperor, were, or so I suspected, hysterical with fear and shouting at their servants and lackeys. Or perhaps my father and Eric had not yet informed them how serious the situation had become and they were still calm. I never did find out.

****** *Henry Soldier returns to the gate.*

What I found as I made my way back towards the gate was that we were continuing to keep the Greeks from reaching the top of the wall despite the rain. Along the way I periodically ordered men and pikes to move to new positions opposite the Greek bridges that appeared to be usable.

I was not surprised that no Greeks had yet made it on to the wall—it is hard to climb a long ladder if you have never done so before, particularly when it is wet and you are carrying a weapon in one hand and the men above you are dropping big rocks on you and trying to push the ladder over so that you fall on to the rocks or into the water below you.

The situation at the gate, however, had greatly worsened during my brief absence. In a word, the states' men who had sallied out in response to the offer of double coins had been mauled by the Greeks who had abandoned their useless bridges and returned to their camp carrying their weapons. The states' men had taken heavy losses and come away with relatively few weapons they could exchange for coins. They were clearly disheartened.

And, to make matters worse, Prince Ivan had suddenly disappeared. Apparently he had run because he was afraid his men and those of the other states, particularly their nobles and knights, would turn on him for sending them out on the failed sortie. According to Michael, the prince was last seen riding into the city's Latin Quarter with his personal guards.

Michael and I agreed: It was likely the end of the states' forces as an effective fighting force, though it is well known that a hot meal, a bowl of ale, and a good night's sleep sometimes works surprising wonders on a defeated soldier, especially if he is young and inexperienced.

Later, and much to my surprise, George seemed quite interested and almost pleased when I re-joined him on the wall and told him about the sad shape of the states' men and Prince Ivan's sudden departure. At the time, of course, I did not know how George intended to use what was left of the states' men, or what the surprising outcome of the plan he was hatching would be.

Chapter Thirty-eight

Confusion at the harbour.

Confusion reigned everywhere on the decks of the first two Venetian galleys as they slowly and cautiously rowed into the empty harbour for a look. Both the sea-poxed Greek soldiers who had been recently added to their crews and their regular crewmen were on deck and as ready to fight as they could be, but there was no one to fight.

All they could do was stand in the pouring rain was watch as the last two of the Company's galleys were each hauled up on the strand by several hundred men pulling on tow ropes. The Venetians had obviously received bad information from the Patriarch's spies.

What the Venetians saw as their galleys slowly approached the shore were thirty or forty of the Company's war galleys pulled up on to the strand, and two more galleys in the final stages of being pulled ashore by a large number of men pulling on tow ropes. They also saw what appeared to be a line of tents on each side of the galleys. Other than that and the men pulling on the ropes, the strand appeared totally empty.

"How many men do you see, Antonio?" the Venetian captain asked his lieutenant. They were standing on the roof of their galley's forward castle. Unlike the sailors and soldiers crowding the deck below them, the two Venetians were wearing foul weather rain clothes and were fairly dry.

"Four hundred would be my guess, Captain. Perhaps a few more, but not too many more. And they do not seem to be carrying weapons. They look like unarmed sailors."

"That is what I think also. It would seem the Greek report that there were lightly crewed English galleys in the harbour was wrong, but that only the English sailors were at the harbour to defend their galleys was correct."

"Ah, look there. We are about to have visitors."

What the Venetian captain was referring to was a small group of men wearing brown hooded tunics who had walked casually down to the water's edge and were watching them as they approached. To the Venetian's surprise, one of them raised his hand in greeting. The captain lifted his hand in return and gave an order.

"Tell Giuseppe to move in a little closer. Perhaps we can hail them. They may realize they are outnumbered and want to surrender."

The lieutenant hastened to shout an order to the overseer of the galley's slave rowers. They both knew it was too good an opportunity to pass up. The prize money and fame would be tremendous if they could take the galleys on the strand as prizes before the rest of the fleet reached the harbour. And they needed to hurry—because prize money was shared with every other galley in sight and already a third galley was coming into the harbour behind them.

******

The thinking of the men who had walked down to the shoreline to look at the Venetians was not about surrender, very much to the contrary. It was Richard himself who had led the little band of archers down to look at the Venetian galleys and lifted his hand to greet the Venetian galley.

"We might as well give them a welcome," he said as he picked up his unstrung bow and motioned for his men to follow him. "And bring your longbows."

There were only nine of them—Richard, the seven archer sergeants who had been helping Richard improve the sailors' abilities to fight, and one of the wounded men, a lieutenant who had recovered enough to be able to climb walk about. Every one of them was carrying his unstrung longbow and four dry bowstrings.

"Their captain is probably the man on forward castle roof with the hood up on his foul weather tunic. He lifted his hand to acknowledge mine and then said something to the man next to him who leaned over the railing to give an order. Everyone is to mark him for their first target."

******

The shade tents the Venetians saw as they rowed closer were Richard's doing. He knew from bitter experience that nothing saps a man's strength faster than working or fighting under a blazing hot sun.

Accordingly, he had taken no chances that the sailors and archers guarding the galleys would be weakened by the hot sun that usually fell upon Constantinople in the middle of the summer—he had taken the spare sails out of our crewless galleys and hung them over upright wooden poles to provide shade in which he and his men could stand whilst waiting for enemy attackers to advance. The poles were available from the galleys because they had been bought with the intention of using them to make pike handles.

Erecting the shade tents had been easy since there were plenty of men available to do the necessary work, and more than enough spare sails with so many galleys pulled ashore. And because he did not know where the Venetians would land their men in order to attack us, Richard had the Company's sailors set up a line of open-sided "shade tents" on each side of the thirty or so Company galleys which had already been pulled ashore or soon would be.

There were only two lines of tents because the nearby city wall towering over the little strip of land between the city and the harbour meant there was no room for the Venetians to form up their attackers on the city side of the galleys, and the nearby water meant there was no room for them to form them up on sea side.

In other words, if the Venetians and their allies came ashore to fight, they would have to land their men and come at the galleys' defenders from one side of the strand or the other, or both. Those were the only places where there would be enough space for the Venetians to gather a force strong enough to launch an effective attack. And when and if the Venetians did attack, they would find Richard and his men waiting out of the sun or rain and as ready as possible to defend themselves and their galleys.

Richard's decision to set up the two lines of shade tents had suddenly became very important when the rain began to fall and the Venetians arrived—because tents that would protect the Company's men from waiting hour after hour in the hot sun would also protect them and the bowstrings of their longbows if it started to rain. The basic problem with Richard's plan for defending the galleys, of course, was that the defenders he had immediately available only included a small handful of archers, just nine of them including himself and his apprentice sergeant.

Using the shade tents to protect the nine available longbows from the rain would help, of course, but the few arrows they would push out would not likely be sufficient to stop the attack or even greatly weaken it. There was no doubt about it, he thought bitterly, either reinforcements arrived or the Company was likely to lose most of its galleys.

Strangely enough, the use of a line of open-sided tents made from galley sails to protect the galley defenders' from the weather was not a new idea. Richard had been learnt about using them when he attended the Company's school for apprentice sergeants and Angelovian priests at Restormel Castle—where he had heard many times about the Company using such tents from the very men who had successfully used their galleys' spare sails as open-sided shade tents many years earlier during a somewhat similar scorchingly hot summer campaign. It had been during another war and the Company's shade tents had been erected near where the Orthodox army was now camped.

George's father had been the Company's commander at the time and the use of shade tents to keep his men combat-ready in the hot sun had been his idea. At the time, the Company was outside the walls fighting against the Byzantine defenders holding the walls; now it was inside the walls fighting to hold the walls against attackers trying to restore Byzantine rule. Such was the lot of an English free company trying to earn its coins in an ever-changing world.

Interestingly enough, for those who care about such things, both George and Richard had attended the Company's school at Restormel Castle and had been schoolmates, and both had learned about the tents and to gobble and scribe Latin and both had been ordained as Angelovian priests with the school's properly bought papal dispensations so that its students could lead normal lives and know women if they served on active duty in the Company.

Similarly, both had been accepted as being fit to make their marks on the Company's roll and serve in the Company rather than being rejected as inadequate and shunted off to grub for coins in priests' positions somewhere far from Cornwall. Their abilities and their preference for women instead of young boys probably had a lot to do with their being allowed to join the Company.

******

The rain was slowing, but still coming down, as the Venetian galley with the ambitious captain slowly made its way towards the shoreline where a small band of men seemed to be waiting to gobble with them. Everyone on the galley's deck could see the little band of nine or ten men waiting at the shoreline and realized their galley was slowly making its way towards them. They were watched intently. It was first time many of them had ever seen an Englishman up close.

Aboard the Venetian, the captain was so anxious to get a surrender before any more of his fellow Venetians arrived to share the prize money, that he did not consider the possibility that he would not be able to talk about it with the waiting men because he spoke only the Venetian version of Italian and the Englishman spoke only the dialect of crusader French that was becoming known as English. It turned out not to be a problem.

Richard walked his little group of archers all the way up the shoreline where the sand was still wet. He gave them their orders as he did.

"Get your spare bowstrings ready for quick changes. We will let them get closer before we string. And when we do push, everyone is to go for the men on the forward castle roof until they are down."

A smiling Venetian raised his hand in return. He was smiling because the English galleys on the strand would be worth a fortune in prize money even if he had to share it. The deck of his galley was absolutely packed with men. They were silent because there was a sailor in the galley's bow casting a depth stone and constantly calling out the results of his casts.

Richard smiled back at the approaching Venetian, waved his hand most friendly in acknowledgement, and began giving orders to his men. He could see the Venetian captain clearly now. He was rather portly man with a dark beard and wearing a fine tunic over what was almost certainly a chain shirt.

The bow of the Venetian galley was less than a hundred paces off the shoreline and coming in slowly with only two oars rowing on each side when Richard gave new orders and raised his hand in a friendly greeting towards the men on the galley's roof.

"The men on the roof may be wearing chain so use your heavies," he said with a smile as he nodded benignly towards the Venetian captain.

"Get ready to string your bows when I give the word, but wait to pluck a heavy from your quivers until you hear me give the order. We will let them row in a little closer, all the way in if possible. And when you do string, do it leisurely and do not reach for an arrow or nock one. We do not want to alarm them, do we?"

Richard gave the order to string a few moments later. The Venetian galley was now only fifty or so paces from the shore.

"Be casual and string now, lads. Everyone string and do your best to keep them close to you so they stay dry, but do *not* pull any arrows out of your quivers until I give the word."

Richard waited and gave the order when the bow of Venetian galley was almost to the shoreline, and its hull was about to touch bottom.

"NOW LADS, GET THE BASTARDS."

Nine veteran English archers pulled arrows from their quivers and began pushing them into the men standing on the roof of the approaching galley's forward castle, and they began doing so before anyone on the galley realized what was happening. Each of them repeated the process every four or five seconds until they needed to take a few seconds to change to dry bowstrings. The nine men kept changing bowstrings and pushing out arrows until their quivers were empty.

Chaos, screams, and shouts began as soon as the first arrows hit home, although it is doubtful that the captain and his lieutenant and sailing sergeant ever knew it, the captain especially. He was still thinking about the prize money and smiling when the first of at least five iron-tipped arrows passed through his chain shirt and took him deep in his chest.

The lieutenant and sailing sergeant lasted but a few heartbeats longer before they too took multiple arrows and went down. The archers were all long-serving veterans. It would have been embarrassing if any of the arrows had *not* hit their targets at such a short distance.

Surprise and dismay were clearly visible on the faces of the hundred or so men standing on the galley's deck with their swords and spears. Even better, there was no one in command of the galley to give its rudder men orders to turn around or its slaves to stop rowing. As a result, its rowers just kept slowly rowing and brought the screaming and shouting men on its crowded deck closer and closer to the hard-eyed archers who were standing at the water's edge pouring arrows into them at close range. The galley kept coming until its hull began grinding over the shallow bottom and slowly began turning sidewise.

Arrows did not stop being pushed into the Venetian galley until the last of the archers ran out of bowstrings and arrows. By then the galley had turned sideways to the waterline and those of the men on its deck who were still not hit were lying below its railing amongst their dead and wounded mates in order not to be seen by the archers standing a few feet away on the shore.

"Well, they are not likely to forget that for a couple of days, are they?" said one of the sergeants with a great deal of satisfaction and excitement in his voice.

A few minutes later Richard and his jovial band of sergeants had turned and were briskly walking in the warm rain on their way back to the galleys. It was whilst walking back to their galleys that the implications of what had just happened dawned on one of the other sergeants. He too, like the others, had been able to keep changing bowstrings until he had run through all the arrows in his quivers. Now he was out of arrows and all of his bowstrings were wet and useless.

"Our lads coming to reinforce us will have wet strings as well, I expect?"

The sergeant addressed his question to Richard, but his warning was clear.

"My God, you are right." Richard said softly a moment later when he fully understood. "The bowstrings of the archers on the wall will be wet just as ours have become. How can they reinforce us if they have nothing with which to fight?"

A moment later he shouted and broke into a run towards the nearest of the galleys.

"Everyone to the galleys. Hurry men, run. The archers coming to reinforce us will have wet strings too. We need to get the swords and pikes out of the galleys and into the tents for them to use, and fast. And search everywhere for dry bowstrings. Paul, you check the wounded."

Richard and the archers were soon so desperately busy retrieving weapons from their galleys that they did not pay much attention when the oars of the wounded galley began beating the water as it moved away from the shoreline and two other Venetian galleys came alongside to assist it. Indeed, they barely looked up as the three Venetian galleys moved towards the harbour entrance to report the situation to their rapidly approaching fellow Venetians.

Chapter Thirty-nine

Confusion on the strand.

Swords and shields were still being pulled out of our empty galleys and hurriedly carried to the shade tents when a long line of Venetian galleys began entering the harbour. Their decks were crowded with men. It was about then that the first of the archers sent from each galley company to fetch swords and shields for their mates began to arrive.

A few minutes later, one after another, the Venetian galleys nosed into the shore and began unloading the Venetian sailors and soldiers they had been carrying. They were landing them about two thousand paces west of the nearest Company galley on the strand.

Normally it would not have been a good place for the Venetian captains to land their men because almost every bit of it could be reached by arrows pushed out by archers on the nearby city wall. Indeed, the harbour had been selected by Harold as the place to bring the Company's galleys ashore for that very reason. But now it was raining and the archers' bows had become useless because of their wet bowstrings.

So was the Venetian commander a very smart and decisive man who had moved quickly to seize the unexpected advantage the rain had handed him, or was he just stupid about military matters and lucky that it was raining? It was an important question that everyone was too busy to ask. Besides, at this point it really did not matter *why* the Venetians had arrived at that particular time. They were coming ashore and it was raining.

Even worse for Richard and his men, the Venetians were wading ashore from their galleys and appeared to be forming up for an attack in the open area on the west side of where many of the Company's galleys had been pulled up on to the sandy strand.

The Venetians decision to land to the west of the Company's galleys was unfortunate for the archers because that was the side which had the gate in the city wall which opened on to the harbour. It meant the archers' reinforcements, if any came from the men stationed on the wall, would have to march along the top of the wall past the harbour, and then use the next gate which was some distance further to the east along the wall to get out on to the strand. And then they would have to run *back* along the narrow strip of the strand between the city wall and the water to get to where the galleys had been pulled ashore.

The Venetians were still coming ashore when everyone got a big surprise. The gate, which the city's Varangian guards had closed and barred as soon as the Venetians began landing nearby, suddenly opened—and the first of what turned out to be the "Evens" coming to reinforce Richard and his men began pouring out. They were about forty men from the galley company assigned to the enclosure closest the harbour

It was hard to tell who was the most surprised at seeing the other, the "Evens" who were coming from the enclosure nearest to the harbour, or the Venetians who had waded ashore from the first of at least twenty Venetian galleys that were coming in to unload their men.

******* *Archer Stanley Jack's son of Galley Thirty-nine*

All of us "Evens" from our galley's company began double-timing to the galley harbour as soon as the word was passed down the wall and reached our captain, Captain Ford. Lieutenant Jones, the Welshman who thought he was the best archer in the entire damn Company, immediately formed us up and led us in a column of twos along the top of the wall. We were in a hurry to get to the harbour and moving at the double.

I was in the middle of the column, about ten men back, with Roger Small next to me. Roger was from London and sometimes quite full of himself because he thought it made him better than the rest of us because his father had worked as a money changer. We were carrying our longbows even though all our strings were wet and totally useless.

Lieutenant Jones led us along the top of the wall for quite some time until we came to some stone steps and ran down them to the ground inside the wall on the city side. The stairs were slippery from the rain and someone behind me went down with a great deal of swearing all around him, and knocked the man in front of him off the stairs.

It was lucky the man who slipped did not do so at the top of the stairs. If he had, the poor sod in front of him probably would have broken his arm or something. As it was, he just picked himself and stood there swearing at the man who pushed him off the steps until a snarling sergeant told him to "shut your goddamn mouth and get back in the ranks."

There were some of them Varangian fellows trying to stay out of the rain near the gate at the bottom of the steps. Lieutenant Jones ignored them. He headed straight towards the gate so it must have been the gate we were supposed to use to get out to our galleys where they had been pulled ashore. The gate was closed, but the Varangians just stood there and looked surprised when the lieutenant lifted the bar and pushed it far enough open such that we could get out.

We followed Lieutenant Jones and went trotting out on to the strand. And then the lieutenant stopped and we all stopped behind him in a jumble. The rain had slacked off somewhat but it was still coming down.

"Holy shite," Roger said next to me. That was when I saw all the strange-looking men with swords and shields who were coming off the galleys nosed into the shore in front of us and walking on the strand towards us. Our own galleys were pulled up on dry land off to our left with a line of Company men in front of them. They were standing under what looked to be some kind of galley sails that had been raised to keep them out of the rain.

"Go back men. Back through the gate," Lieutenant Jones shouted as he turned around. We turned too—and saw the gate closing behind us with the men at the rear of our little column stepping backwards through it in time not to be trapped out on the strand along with the rest of us. We were well and truly up shite river.

"Over here. Run for it," a voice shouted in the distance. It came from the line of men formed up over by the stranded galleys.

We ran.

****** *Lieutenant Commander Richard Ryder*

There were moments of great anxiety on the strand about thirty or forty minutes after our arrows had seen off the first Venetian galley. They started when a fleet of twenty or so Venetian galleys began entering the harbour and landing men along the shoreline to our west.

It was hard to know for sure how many armed men they intended to put ashore, but it looked as though it would be several thousand. They appeared to be mostly Venetian sailors, not Greek soldiers, and were almost certainly coming to try to take the Company galleys we had pulled shore.

And the new arrivals had already had an unexpected effect as the first of them walked up on to the strand. Everyone, both our men and the Venetians, had been surprised when more than a dozen men wearing archers' tunics, apparently the first of our reinforcements, had suddenly come bursting out of the city gate and been briefly trapped between the wall and the first of the Venetian arrivals when the gate closed behind them. Fortunately, they were able to run across the strand to us before the Venetians could get themselves organized to go after them.

Lieutenant Jones of Galley 39 was the lieutenant who led the archers who ran safely to us. He said he and his men were the first of the archers, all of the company's "Evens," who had been sent to help us even though their bows were mostly useless due to the rain.

"We are supposed to get our galley's swords and shields and join you," the somewhat out of breath lieutenant said with a big smile as he saluted by banging his head with his knuckles and officially reported for duty.

As you might imagine, my men and I were overjoyed to see the new arrivals, and even more so to hear that the "Evens" men of the other companies would soon be joining us. And we were ready for them; we had already stripped the weapons, and everything else that might be useful in a fight, out of the Company galleys that had been pulled ashore. As a result, there were quite a large number of short swords and galley shields immediately available or anyone who showed up to join us.

Much more importantly, however, was that whilst rummaging through the galleys we had come across some dry bowstrings and the makings of more in some of the galleys' stores chests. And we had also picked up several dozen bowstrings from the bows and pouches of the wounded and poxed archers sheltering and being barbered in two of our galleys.

Lieutenant Jones and his men, and most of the men of the Evens of the next two companies that had come in behind them, had been given one of the dry strings for their bows. They were all desperately working to string them and test them as the Venetians continued to land their men. The archers who came in after we ran out of dry bowstrings were issued swords and shields.

****** *Lieutenant Commander Richard Ryder*

Enough additional archer "Evens" had arrived by the time the Venetians finished coming ashore and began gathering in the rain to attack us, that more than a hundred archers with dry bowstrings were waiting under the tents on the west side of our empty galleys. They were busy adjusting their new bowstrings and inspecting their arrows to make sure none had gotten warped as a result of being wet. They were yarning as they worked and everywhere the men's spirits began to rise. Mine certainly did.

Standing just behind the archers, and also under the shade tents, were almost four hundred of the Company's sailors armed with swords and an ever-increasing number of exhausted sword-carrying and pike-carrying archers—the out-of-breath "Evens" who, after double-timing along the top of the wall from wherever their company had been fighting, had run across the strand from the closest gate to the east of the harbour to join us. The new arrivals all had their bows and wet bowstrings in addition to their hurriedly issued short swords and galley shields.

It was an anxiety-provoking situation for all of my men despite our greatly improved morale. They were watching Venetian galleys as they unloaded soldiers and sailors to the west of us and exhausted archers with wet bowstrings and newly issued swords were coming along the strand from the east to reinforce us. No one knew which force would end up being the strongest.

We were not initially sure who the men were who were being landed, only that they were coming off Venetian galleys and were almost certainly about to attack us. They could be Greek soldiers instead of Venetian sailors. Whoever they might be, however, and we all thought they were mostly Venetians from the looks of their tunics, they were coming ashore in the rain on the western side of the strand.

The galley-landed arrivals had it easy. All they had to do was wade ashore through the surf. Our "Evens," on the other hand, had already double-timed for some miles along the top of the wall when they reached the harbour and could look down at our galleys below them on the strand. Then they had to keep going along the wall to reach a gate in the wall further to our east so they could get down the strand and hurry back to join us.

The "Evens" could not use the harbour's regular gate because, as Lieutenant Jones and his men had discovered, it opened out on to the western part of the harbour's strand where our enemies were landing. As a result, they had to run about a mile or more further along the wall to the next gate, exit there, and then run back to the galleys which had been pulled ashore in the middle of the harbour's strand.

When they finally reached our galleys, the exhausted "Evens" were stopped momentarily at the line of empty shade tents immediately east of our galleys. There they were told to quickly pick up whatever weapons Harold and his sergeants pointed to, and then to thread their way in the rain through our empty galleys to join our defensive line sheltering from the rain under the shade tents lined up to the west of them. "And run, goddammit, run."

Our "Evens" were still arriving and being fed into our defensive line as fast as possible. If they all got here and were in place before the Venetians attacked, the battle would occur with approximately the same amount of men on both sides—and that was very encouraging because most of my men were "Marines" trained to fight both on land and sea. The Venetians, on the other hand, were a sea-people without a land army.

In other words, the situation was becoming more and more encouraging. Indeed, now that we had some useful archers, it was possible that we could score a big win if our attackers were mostly Venetian galley crews instead of experienced Greek soldiers wearing armour. I even began thinking about how, at some point, we might suddenly run down to the shoreline and take some of the Venetian galleys as prizes.

But then things got complicated just as the Venetian captains moving their men into place to attack us. The Commander's apprentice, Nicholas Greenway, came out of nowhere and rushed up to me with new orders from George that countermanded his original orders.

We were, Nicholas said, to immediately send all the pikes back to the men defending the outer wall. According to young Nicholas, the pikes with their long handles and hooked blades were especially effective against men climbing ladders. We were also no longer required to send any of our swords and shields. It was the pikes the men on the wall needed most.

Mass confusion was the result of George's newest order. There was little wonder in that— it was the third weapons order to arrive in less than an hour and once again changed everything.

Some of the men who had come in earlier had already left carrying the swords and shields they were ordered to fetch from their galleys. The later arriving archers from further down the wall, however, arrived to find the swords and shields they had been sent to fetch had already been removed from their galleys and were now being issued to the "Evens" of other companies.

As you might imagine, the men sent to bring back their galley's swords and shields were upset and arguing that their mates fighting the Greeks on the wall would be unarmed and defeated if they did not return quickly with the weapons and shields they had been sent to fetch from their galleys. And they were even more upset when they were ordered not to immediately return to their companies to fight alongside of their mates as their captains had ordered them to do, but rather to seek shelter from the rain under the shade tents and get ready to fight the Venetians.

Compounding the confusion, those of the late-arriving sword fetchers who were still at the harbour were more than a little surprised when some of those same mates of theirs, their galley company's Evens, began showing up expecting to use the very same swords at the harbour to fight the Venetians. And making it even more confusing, many those of the original sword fetchers who were "Evens" had been intercepted on their way back by their galley's lieutenants and ordered to return to the harbour with their swords and shields.

And now, to top it off, the Commander's apprentice sergeant and a third body of men had come from the companies on the wall seeking all of the available pikes.

Tempers were flaring and uncertainty ruled. It was a disorganized and unruly mess, and the Venetians were beginning to form up and about to attack us.

Chapter Forty

Getting ready for the fight.

Richard understood the situation as soon as George's apprentice explained the ever-changing circumstances and revelations that had led to the ever-changing orders. He and Harold immediately started to sort things out. They did not get very far.

There was a lot of shouting and pointing as the newly-landed Venetians began walking in groups of about a hundred across the strand towards the line of sheltering archers. Even as they did, exhausted "Evens" from the more distant enclosures along the wall were still coming out of the gate to the east of the Company's galleys and running across the strand to pick up weapons and join the Company's defensive line.

Only a few of the pike carriers had departed with the pikes they had been sent to fetch when Richard over-ruled George's order and ordered the pikes and the archers carrying them to remain "until we see this lot off."

The Venetians were about to attack, Richard thought, both to help the Greeks and because they knew this was a chance to destroy or greatly weaken the Company, their greatest single competitor. Accordingly, he had ordered the archers and weapons to stay with the Company's galleys as soon as he realized the Venetians attack was imminent.

Richard's reasoning was simple and similar to George's—losing so many of the Company's galleys to the attacking Venetians would be disaster that could destroy the Company, a disaster that might be avoided by having the pikes and their carriers in the battle lines defending the galleys.

In contrast, losing the battle on the outer wall would merely be a great embarrassment since the Company's survivors could then either retreat to defend the inner wall or return to the harbour to launch the empty galleys and row away from the city altogether to fight again another day.

In any event, it was Richard's decision to make and he made it—he ordered everyone and all the weapons to stay and fight at the harbour instead of hurrying back to help George and the mates fight on the walls.

Nicholas was sent hurrying back to George to report his decision.

"Tell him we will come as soon as possible."

****** *Lieutenant Paul Jones of Galley 39*

My men and I were spread out along the front of a two-men-deep battle line of sword and pike carriers from the "Evens" of galleys 71, 9, and 32. We had our longbows and were part of a loose line of archers. A few minutes earlier my men and I had each been issued one dry bowstring.

Immediately behind us were two lines of sailors and archers with swords and shields in a tight-knit battle formation. Some of them had only just arrived and were trying to catch their breaths after double-timing all the way along the wall from the other side of the city. We were all under the sails and out of the rain.

All of a sudden the men around me were getting to their feet and pointing. Little wonder. Some of the Venetian companies had begun moving towards us, and the others seemed to be picking up their weapons and getting ready to follow them. They were the same bunch that had scared the shite out of me earlier when my men and I came through the city gate and walked out on to the strand.

The men behind us were still carrying their longbows, but did not have them strung because all of their strings were still wet. Similarly sheltering with us under the sails, and strung out all along the line on either side of us, were some of the archers from other galley companies. They had arrived right after we did and had also been given dry strings. Altogether there were about a hundred of us with bowstrings capable of pushing out arrows.

We, the archers with dry bowstrings that is, were sitting in front of the two lines of sword and pike carriers with our arrows laid out and ready. Initially, we would sit on our arses and use both feet to hold our bows and use both arms to draw them. At least that was the plan.

Shooting arrows whilst sitting was not very accurate, but it would have given additional distance to our arrows. On the other hand, accuracy was not that important so long as we could put an arrow into a close-packed mob of men and be fairly certain it would hit someone. When the Venetians got close enough we would scramble to our feet so we could push out our arrows faster and with much more accuracy.

Standing immediately behind us shoulder to shoulder, and also being sheltered from the rain by the sails hanging above us, were two lines of sailors and archers carrying swords and shields. Amongst them were a number of men with some of the Company's long-handled pikes with hooked blades.

The pikes were carried by the men in the third line such that a pike would be sticking out from between every two or three of the men who were carrying swords and shields. But that ratio was not certain due to the lack of pikes and the last minute arrival of more "Evens" carrying their newly issued swords and shields. In any event, and what was important, using what amounted to only three lines of defenders allowed everyone to remain under the shelter of the sails and out of the rain.

Commander Ryder came down the line a second time when some of the Venetians began moving forward and again reminded everyone that those of the men with swords and pikes were to move forward and take up positions in front of the men with functioning longbows just before the Venetians reached us.

In other words, we archers were to stay in place and the others were to step past us and out into the rain. That way they would have a bit of momentum, and also would be less likely to being trapped and unable to defend themselves by having a sail pulled down on top of them. We archers, on the other hand, would remain under the sails in order to keep our bowstrings dry so we could continue to push out our arrows. It sounded like a reasonable plan.

It did not exactly happen that way, as everyone now knows, but those were the orders at the time and I did my best to see that my men followed them. Not since the Company fought near here many years ago had anyone in the Company waited under sails for a battle to begin. And that, as I heard it, was when the sails were used to keep the Company's men out the sun whilst waiting for the fighting to begin outside this very same city.

According to Commander Ryder, who made it point to continue walking up and down along the line and explain what was happening to us, our attackers were Venetian galley crews who had come ashore to try to take our galleys. They had come, he told us, to destroy our Company so the Venetians could earn more coins for themselves by carrying the passengers and cargos we were now carrying.

What the Commander told us was probably true and explained why we had been ordered here to help defend our galleys. Indeed, the Venetians galley crews were well-known to me and my men. We had constantly seen them in the taverns of the ports we visited, and also when they were loading passengers and cargos in those ports—passengers and cargos that *we* could have carried and earning coins that *we* could have earned.

Knowing we were facing the crews of Venetian galleys was somewhat encouraging, however. That was because we *knew* the Venetians for what they were—armed sailors who were only good at taking unarmed transports, guarding the Venetian merchants who sailed with them, and using slaves to do their rowing.

We also knew that almost all of the Venetians had no experience or training whatsoever when it came to fighting on land or actually using their weapons. In other words, they were not like us, Marines trained to fight both on land and at sea. Indeed, so far as we were concerned, the only similarity between them and us was that they bought their indulgences from Latin-gobbling priests just as we did and used the same taverns and street women.

Usually just the appearance of the Venetians' galleys, the launching of a few crossbow bolts to prove they were serious, and the swords they were waving about over their heads, was enough to cause a rival transport company's unarmed sailors to surrender if they could not escape by sailing or rowing away. And that, according to Commander Ryder, was what the Venetians were trying to do—make us fearful and flee.

"They think we are no better than poxed French sailors, do they?" the Commander roared. "Well, by God they are about to be learnt a lesson they will never forget, eh lads?"

We cheered.

Commander Ryder was right; Venetian sailors thinking they could make us fearful so we would flee was insulting and there was no half way about it. Venetians? Can you believe it? They must be either daft or stupid. In any event, it made us angry and more determined than ever to come to grips with them. I could see it and feel it as I once again checked out my men. With a few exceptions, very few, they were ready to fight.

In any event, some kind of signal most have been given by the Venetian commander because a few minutes later groups of eighty to one hundred men each, probably the men who had arrived together on a specific Venetian galley, began casually walking across the strand towards us in the warm rain.

Almost immediately, Commander Ryder and his apprentice moved out in front of the archers to stand in the rain and watch the approaching Venetians. They all seemed to be carrying swords and many of them were carrying small and rounded galley shields similar to ours. Some of the poor sods were wearing helmets, but very few.

As the first group of Venetians approached the first of the piles of rocks that had been set out to mark the beginning of our arrows' "killing ground," the Commander turned around and loudly gave us an order as he walked back to join the archers standing under the sails. The sergeants, of course, immediately repeated the order all along the line.

"Archers with dry strings on your feet." ... "Wait for it." ... "Hold your pushing." ... "Do not push until the signal is given."

Someone handed the Commander a bow as soon as he was out of the rain and had turned to watch the Venetians walking towards us.

The first group of Venetians continued casually walking and talking until they were about two hundred paces from us. Then they stopped. By then several more of the Venetian groups had casually crossed into our killing ground and were walking up to join the first group. They were obviously coming to form up at what their commander intended to be the start line for their attack.

Some of the other Venetian groups were walking across the strand towards us and some had not even gotten started, when Commander Ryder gave the order. He did so after six or seven groups of enemy soldier had walked past the piles of rocks that marked the beginning of the killing ground we could reach with our arrows and three or four more groups were about to do so. By then it was clear, at least to me, that there were several thousand of Venetians in all and they would be forming a start line where the first group had stopped.

The Venetians' move towards us through the rain was, at first, quite confusing because it was so casual. It was also a great mistake on their part because, being mostly sailors, they were wearing neither armour nor chain—and because we had somehow found dry bowstrings for about a hundred of our best archers. Mostly it was a mistake, however, because they had walked into our killing ground to form up.

About half of the Venetian companies were inside our killing ground, and the rest were still walking casually towards it, when Commander Ryder gave the order and the sergeants began repeating it.

"Pick your man" ... "Push" ... "Pick your man." .. "Push" ... Pick your man. ..."

Our archers' arrows began reaching out to the Venetians who were close enough to be hit. The Venetians in our killing ground immediately began faltering as our archers pushed out their arrows. And most of the men walking to join them stopped and began backing up. We were not the handful of poorly armed sailors they had been told to expect.

We could hear the Venetians closest to us as they began to scream and go down. There was little wonder in that—a hundred of the Company's archers could put over a thousand well-aimed arrows into an enemy force in less than a minute. And that was what we did.

Chapter Forty-one

Galley 39's men move forward.

Our massive and continuing flight of arrows seemed to catch the Venetians by surprise. They were still in the early stages of gathering to form up for their attack when our arrows suddenly began falling on them. Whoever was leading the Venetians had obviously not appreciated the distance a Company archer could get with his "longs" when his arm was fresh and both of his feet were planted solidly on the ground.

Some of the Venetians responded to the unexpected arrival of death and destruction by breaking and running back the way they had come. Others just stopped in confusion and waited until they and their mates had taken a few more arrows. A few, however, started to run towards us—and then, as our arrows began to take the thrusters, thought better of it and turned around to try to run to safety. Some of them succeeded.

****** *Lieutenant Commander Richard Ryder*

The Venetians quickly retreated leaving several hundred of their men dead and wounded on the field. Others were hit and were able to keep running with our arrows in them.

For a brief moment, I thought about ordering a charge and attempting to roll the Venetians up. I decided not to do so after I saw the Venetian groups who had not been engaged forming up into new battle lines and most of the fleeing Venetians moving to join them instead of moving towards their galleys. I gave a prudent order instead.

"Retrieve your arrows and watch your arses when you do. And leave your bows behind so the strings do not get wet."

Of course I warned the men to be careful. It was well-known that wounded men often play dead and then suddenly come alive and try to fight off anyone who tries to pull an arrow out of them.

****** *Lieutenant Paul Jones*

Most of the surviving Venetians began moving into some sort of formation whilst we were amongst their dead and wounded retrieving our arrows. This time they began forming up well out of range and seemed to be acting with more order and organization. Some of the men who had run back toward their galleys seemed to be walking back to join them. And then, miracle of miracles, the rain stopped.

Commander Ryder did not wait more than a minute after we returned with the arrows before ordering me to take advantage of the end of the rain. He came over to me, and then called and motioned for the two lieutenants whose "Evens" also had dry bowstrings to join us. When they did, he used a nod of his head to point at the Venetians.

"I want you three to take your archers with dry bowstrings out there and do as much damage as you can to the Venetians whilst they are forming up and whilst they are marching towards us.

"But do not under any circumstances let your men be cut off or picked off. Fall back as needed to keep your men safe if the Venetians come after you. And immediately have your men stow their bowstrings in their pouches and return here on the double if it starts to rain again. Take at least two quivers each."

Then Commander Ryder said something that pleased me immensely.

"Lieutenant Jones will be in command. He knows how to run to safety when the need arises. Good luck. Jones?"

"Aye, Commander. Thank you. I am to take the archers with dry bowstrings out there to do damage to the enemy, make sure they do not cut us off, and return immediately with our bowstrings in our pouches if it starts to rain."

And that is exactly what we did.

I twirled my pointing finger over my head to assemble my men around me, told them what we were going to do, and gave them to the count of thirty to get their quivers. The other two lieutenants ran back to their men and did the same. A few moments later we were walking briskly towards the Venetians to do what we had been ordered to do.

The rain had stopped but the sand on the strand was still firmed up for walking by being wet. I motioned for the men to spread out as we moved towards the waiting Venetians. They were gathering about half a mile down the strand. We could see what seemed to be a steady trickle of shield-carrying men walking up from where their galleys were nosed into shore and waiting.

"Tread cautiously, lads, cautiously. We will stay in contact as long as possible. But be ready to run like hell if they start chasing us; no taking of foolish chances, eh?"

Ordering them to take no foolish chances was exactly what the men wanted to hear me say, and I meant it.

I briefly thought about my wife on Cyprus as I gave my orders. I knew she would be very pleased when she heard I was selected to lead the archers out to harass the Venetians. She was always after me to do something to get recognized. She wanted me promoted so we would have enough coins to build a bigger hovel far away from the insufferable captain's wife who lived next to us.

My men followed behind me as I led them out from under the rain sails amidst various cries and shouts wishing us well from the men who would remain behind.

****** *Archer Stanley Jack's son of Galley Thirty-nine*

Lieutenant Jones seemed quite pleased as he gathered us around and told us what we were to do. I particularly liked the part about running like hell in order to avoid being cut off. Jones was not so bad as a lieutenant, just too damn keen on volunteering us because he wanted to be promoted.

We followed the lieutenant as he walked briskly towards where the Venetians were gathering. There surely were a lot of them. Several of my mates stopped for a moment to piss and I stopped with them. Afterwards we ran to catch up.

The Venetians began pointing at us and moving around a bit as we got closer and closer. After a while, to our surprise, a small group came out and began walking towards us. They obviously wanted to talk.

Lieutenant Jones was having none of it. He motioned for everyone to spread out and keep going, and gave an order that the sergeants repeated so that we all heard it.

"Move up into position off to the left, lads, and start pushing as soon as you can reach them. Just do not push at this lot whilst I be gobbling with them. Stanley, you and James come with me and be ready for anything. Keep an arrow nocked and ready at all times."

What could James and I do but follow him. So we did.

We followed Lieutenant Jones as he walked towards the four men who had come out of the Venetian formation and were walking directly toward us. One of them was wearing a priest's robe and another had fine clothes and a helmet. The man with the fine clothes had his sword in its scabbard. The other two, however, were carrying their swords bared. They looked like tough veterans. James and I had arrows nocked.

"Hoy," Lieutenant Jones gobbled at the four Venetians when they got about fifty paces from us. "What do you want?"

"Hoy," the man with the fine clothes answered rather arrogantly as the distance continued to close between us. "I am Jacobo Tiepolo, a captain of Venice, and we want you English to pull back into the city to avoid any more unnecessary deaths on either side. We have no quarrel with you."

The Venetian gobbled his words in bad crusader French. That was no surprise. Venetians, being a seafaring people, were all merchants of one kind or another and most merchants could gobble crusader French in those days.

"And let you and your sailors take our galleys? Are you daft?" Lieutenant Jones replied incredulously. "You must not know much about Englishmen or the Company of Archers. Is this your first visit to Constantinople and the Holy Land?"

That was as far as things got—because the arrows of our mates began to fly as Lieutenant Jones was gobbling his reply. The Venetians looked back over their shoulders in surprise as shouts and screams erupted from their men. So did the lieutenant.

Lieutenant Jones looked beyond the Venetians for a moment as screams and shouts erupted from the assembled Venetians. He never did see the sword that one of the Venetians suddenly swung that almost took off his head. I certainly did and so, I later learned, did all the Company men lined up under the sails.

My response was instinctive. I pushed my bow out and put my nocked arrow straight into the swordsman's side. And it was a good thing I did because his blade had already changed direction and was moving towards me. It missed when my arrow drove him back.

The Venetian gave a great "whoosh" when my arrow hit him and went down backwards to sit on his arse and elbows still holding his sword. James and I were already running for our lives by the time he hit the ground. So were the three other Venetians, the difference being that they were running in the opposite direction.

****** *Lieutenant Commander Ryder*

We could clearly see our men when they began pushing out arrows and the fighting that erupted almost immediately amongst the handful of men wearing archers' tunics who had gone forward to meet with some of the Venetians. It was clear that at least one of our men was down and that everyone who had been at the meeting had run off and left him on the ground. There was uncertainty and much talking in our ranks, with some of the men stepping forward to point and gawk.

"Silence in the ranks. Get those men back into our lines," I shouted.

"Harold, you stay here in command. I think it might be Lieutenant Jones who went down. I am going out to take command of the archers and try to find out what happened. Keep everyone here on high alert. I will send for reinforcements if I need them."

I did not wait for an answer. I immediately began trotting across the strand to join up with the archers who were busy pushing arrows into the Venetian mob. Paul was right behind me. We had gotten about half way to them when the entire body of Venetians began moving forward towards our galleys. The archers responded by moving backwards at the same speed whilst continuing to push out their arrows. And then the arrows stopped.

"Fall back." ... "Fall back." I could hear the sergeants shouting. For a second I was surprised and angered. And then I realized what had happened—they had used up all their arrows.

What I did not immediately see, but later learned, was that the Venetian army was already in the process of falling apart. The Venetians who were moving forward to attack us were fewer and fewer. They were leaving behind more and more able-bodied men in addition to their many dead and wounded. Some of the able-bodied men were staying to aid the many Venetian wounded; but many were hanging back because they had had enough. Fighting at sea for prizes was one thing; fighting on land against archers was something else.

I had barely reached the first of the archers, and had already pushed out a couple of arrows of my own, when I heard drums beating out the marching step and turned to see the men who had been sheltering under the tents marching toward us and putting their feet down to the beat of a galley drum. Harold was coming even though I had told him to stay put.

At first I was angry that he had not obeyed my orders. But then I understood. Harold had seen what I had not—that the Venetian army in ront of us was falling apart.

Suddenly, right in front of my eyes, the Venetian army dissolved like butter thrown into hot soup. One moment they were moving towards us, the next they were throwing away their weapons and running for their galleys.

Chapter Forty-two

A temporary victory.

"Hoy the Commander," a voice shouted up to me from Galley Seventeen's enclosure. "Hoy, Commander. There is a messenger come from Commander Ryder. He says it is important. Should we allow him to go up to you?"

"Send him up," I replied, and then turned my attention back to the opportunity at hand.

The rain had stopped a few minutes earlier. At the time the messenger arrived, I was standing on the narrow roadway atop of the city's outer wall with all the available men of Galley Seventeen and its captain.

Scaling ladders were up against the wall under us and more were being manhandled into place. We were waiting for the Greeks at the foot of the wall to begin climbing their ladders since it is always best to push over scaling ladders when men are on them. They were almost ready to raise their ladders and start climbing, and so were we.

And it was about then that I realized something significant—there was no chance the Greeks gathering below us would ever be able to climb to the top of the wall. It would never happen; the ladders they were about to raise were not long enough.

The ladders were high enough to reach the top of the wall if they were stood up straight against it. But ladders could not stand straight against a wall if a man was to climb them; they had to lean.

Someone spying for the Greeks had measured the wall and sent a message as to how high the wall stood. So the Greeks had wasted several weeks making ladders without taking into account that a ladder *also* had to be long enough to lean against the wall if it was to be climbed. Many of their ladders had turned out to be too short and we had enough pikes to push over those that were long enough.

Being assaulted by Greeks carrying short ladders had been a common occurrence along the wall all during their attack. And those ladders which were tall enough were easily pushed over with our long-handled pikes. The day looked to be ours even though the Greeks were still trying to climb their ladders.

After I ordered the messenger to be sent up, I turned my attention to the men standing about me. "Wait just a moment," I said with a grin. "More of the damn fools are coming across the footbridge. We might as well get them too."

The men standing around me smiled back and nodded their heads enthusiastically. As well they might. It always better to kill an enemy before he has a chance to kill you.

We were waiting because the Greeks below us were in the process of bringing more ladders and men across the footbridge below us. Why they were still trying after the others on either side of them had failed escaped me, but we could not go wrong by inflicting by dropping a few rocks on this lot as well. And that is what we did.

Galley Seventeen's men stood back and watched as their captain, Dan Daniels, and I periodically took quick looks over the outer edge of the wall and then placed our little piles of marker stones to show the rock droppers where the Greek ladders were coming up.

Dan and I were not taking any chances; it had stopped raining and there was always the chance that one of the enemy crossbowmen had found a string that was not wet. Of course, we were not taking chances; Dan and I had both been schooled at the Company's school at Restormel Castle and been regaled there by my Uncle Thomas's stories about crusading with murderous old King Richard, him what managed to get himself killed by a boy with a crossbow. That was after he abandoned his men and scampered for home.

I took one last quick look, and rearranged a couple of marker stones.

"Alright lads. Get ready. We will go on a count of three."

All along the wall on either side of me the men of galley seventeen began picking up the heavy stones and rocks that were stacked up on the parapet all along the wall next to the archers' slits and placing them on the top of the wall next to a marker stone. Some were so large it was all a man could do to lift them high enough to reach the outer edge of the parapet wall and push them over.

"Get ready. Here we go."

I gave the word a minute or so later when I could see that there were rocks and stones in place next to each of the markers and the Greeks were starting to climb their ladders. "One .. two ... three ... PUSH."

Over the side the rocks and stones went with many of the men moving along the parapet to push off three or four that had already been balanced on top of the parapet wall.

The Greeks below us did not see them coming until it was too late. There were the crashing sounds of rocks hitting the rocky ground between the wall and the moat, the distinctive sound a rock makes when it lands on a man instead of the ground, and many screams and shouts and splashes.

We, of course, could not restrain ourselves despite the possibility of a crossbow bolt; we immediately looked over the side of the wall to see what we had accomplished.

The big rock I had struggled to lift and so carefully placed had apparently bounced off the wall and missed the bridge I had hoped to destroy. It was still standing. But many of the men who had crossed over to the wall on it were down, including some who had been knocked into the moat and disappeared after thrashing about in its foul waters for a few seconds.

There was no doubt about it; having a rock dropped on your head from a great height can definitely ruin your day.

****** *George Courtenay*

Our meal was a festive occasion that night. We were drinking bowls of wine and eating burnt meat strips by the light of candles, and telling each other what we had done and seen. Everyone was there including my father who reported he had had a celebratory bowl of wine with the Empress who was much cheered by the day's successes.

Eric of the Varangians was also present. He and his men had successfully held the Latin Quarter against the Orthodox rising. They had done so by leaving the people and merchants in the two Greek quarters and their markets to their fates.

"The rain was sent by God," Eric was convinced. "Many of the looters stayed inside because of it and not many fires were lit. There was only one effort to get into the Latin Quarter and attack the Citadel and it was easily driven away."

Everyone was laughing and cheering each other's stories, and cautioning each other about not knowing what the Greeks and Venetians would do next. Some of the more cheerful amongst us thought the Greeks would give up and go home so that we would soon be able to resume our normal coin-earning operations.

"It is possible they will leave, but all we can do is wait and see, eh?" That is what I said. But I did not believe it possible, not in the least; I expected them to try treachery or a long siege, or both.

We also talked about the Venetians. They had scrambled aboard their galleys and sailed away. Richard had not pursued them when they ran for their galleys, and rightly so. He had, instead, begun double-timing the archers under his command to come to help us fight off the Greek attack.

It turned out that Richard and the reinforcements he was rushing to us were not needed, but we certainly did not know it at the time. There was no question about it, and we all knew it and said as much—he had done the right thing in hurrying to reinforce us instead of chasing the Venetians.

The Venetians and where they were, and what they might do next, and what we should do, were still being discussed when one of the Commandery's servants came in and whispered something into Nicholas's ear. He got up and followed the man out of the hall.

A few minutes later Nicholas returned and came straight to me.

"There is someone waiting outside you need to talk to immediately, Commander," he said as he bent over and spoke very quietly in my ear so that I was the only who could hear.

Nicholas did not say who it was or what it was about, and I did not ask; if he thought it important, it probably was. Everyone stopped talking and watched as Nicholas spoke to me, and I got up to follow him outside.

Standing outside near the door was Adam from Gravesend, the Greek-gobbling make-believe lieutenant who had guarded the bishops and the prisoners we had exchanged. The Greeks had made contact with Adam at the tavern he had just happened to mention that he frequented almost every night when his day was done. That was right after he implied that "for enough coins" even the city's gates could be opened.

Adam had been at the tavern with some of his mates when the alewife had whispered to him that someone wanted to talk with him outside "on a matter of great importance." Adam put down his bowl, gave a great belch to clear his head, and had walked out the door. When he got outside, a nondescript man motioned him to go around the corner.

"Over here," a voice said from the dark alley next to the tavern. "Be you Adam from Gravesend, the lieutenant of the guards?"

"Oh aye, that I am."

According to Adam, the man waiting for him was a priest whose face he could not see in the dark, at least Adam thought he was a priest. And he could gobble crusader French.

The Greek king, the priest told Adam, were very interested in making him a very rich man if he would help them open the gates in the wall so they could get in and *stop* the unnecessary fighting.

"He wanted to know if I was still interested in becoming very rich, and if I could really nobble the gates and drawbridges on the Farmers Road so they could get in without a fight."

"I answered as you told me I should."

"Oh I can open them anytime I want," I told him. "That is for sure. It is, after all, my company what guards the gates and me what sets the guards.

"And I know which of the lads would be willing to help me for enough coins. And for enough coins to pay his debts, the captain will give all the others leave to go into the city and get drunk to celebrate someone's birthday.

"But there is no chance in the world that I will arrange it unless there are enough coins in it for me and my mates."

I was elated at the news, although I found it most interesting that they had apparently sent a priest to negotiate with Adam, someone who could gobble crusader French—and also that the priest had immediately agreed to the large number of gold and silver coins Adam said he had to have in order to get him and his mates to open the wall gates early next Saturday morning before the sun arrived.

"Tell me about the priest," I said when he finished telling his tale.

"Oh, I am not sure he really was a priest, but I certainly got that impression. He said he had been sent to talk to me because he had been learnt to gobble crusader French."

"What kind of an accent did he have?"

"Well Commander, I am not sure. But it was not Greek. I know that because my wife is Greek and we are with her family and at church frequently. It was more like the accents of the Latin priests and merchants here in Constantinople."

"That is very interesting, Adam, very interesting indeed. And you are sure he was not Greek?"

"Oh aye, Commander, he was not a Greek for sure. And he did not even try to bargain with me, did he? That is why I think he was a priest. A merchant would have tried me to get to do it for less."

"I told him exactly what you said I should say—that it would be best to first break the moat bridge's windlass so the bridge could not be raised until it was replaced, and then a couple of days later open the outer gate half an hour or so before the first light of day.

"Nobbling the bridge first would let us spread a rumour that the Greeks would be attacking as soon as they found out. Then some of the states' forces would surely be afraid and leave, and then there would be few of them to stop you from getting to the inner gate.

"That way, if I was ever caught, I could claim the inner gate broke such that my mates and I were not able to shut it in time when the Greek army pushed its way in behind those who were fleeing.

"The priest said he thought it was a good plan and offered to pay me one hundred pounds of silver coins to do it. I did what you said and told him that I needed much more, at least double, because some of my mates would also have to be paid to help or look the other way.

"He immediately agreed to two hundred without even trying to bargain. I am to get the first half of the coins tomorrow night when I come back to the tavern for another visit. I told him I would collect the chests with a horse cart and bring some of my mates to help guard them."

Did you tell him the gate would be guarded?"

"Oh yes. I said exactly what you told me to say. I warned him that he would need to have a very strong force Greek soldiers assembled in front of the inner gate and ready to pour into the city and fight because there would be some guards the inner gate.

"My mates and I will open the gates and put the bridges down by nobbling the windlasses that hoist them," I told him. "But that is all we will do. It is up to you and your friends to do the fighting once you are through the gate. We will want to be long gone and in hiding before the fighting starts.

"And then I told him what you suggested—that for another hundred pounds of silver coins, for a total of three hundred, my mates and I would start a rumour that night that the archers had been paid to open the outer gate and leave the city; and that they needed to get themselves inside the inner wall that very night to save themselves.

"Some will panic and leave for sure. Then your men would be able to go straight to the inner gate without having to fight so hard to get through the camp."

The priest agreed that an early nobbling of the drawbridge and spreading a rumour that the archers were leaving was a good idea and worth another hundred.

"I also told him I had to have the coins there in time for us to carry away before I would nobble the gates so the Greeks could push them open, and that I needed at least three days to arrange everything and find a place to hide myself and my share of the coins until the new emperor was in place and it was safe for me to come out and spend them."

"Did he ask you where you intend to hide yourself and the coins?"

"Aye, he did. As you suggested, I told him my wife's sister had a widow friend who lived here and I would hide with her until the streets were safe."

"You did well, Adam, you did well," I said jovially as I clapped him on the back and shook the hand of the man whose temporary promotion to sergeant had just become permanent.

******

Adam and I spent some time talking things over, and then agreed that he would come to the Commandery tomorrow night after dark to make a plan for getting the first half of the coins safely away. We wanted, of course, to get them without the Greeks knowing that both they and the second batch were destined for the Company's chests at Restormel Castle.

There was much to do to get ready for Adam's betrayal of the city and the Company, but I decided tomorrow morning would be soon enough. It had been a long day and I was ready for another bowl of ale and some of Elizabeth's comforts. Besides, I needed to think about who needed to be let in on the secret, and what lies I should tell to everyone else.

Chapter Forty-three

Preparing for the betrayal.

Only Richard and Henry knew about my plan. And their eyes opened wide when the three of us met the next morning and they first heard about what I had decided we needed to do. The alchemist and James Howard almost certainly also knew most of what I had in mind without me ever having to tell them. It was, after all, something they had suggested to me. Everyone else, however, would only know the bits and pieces of what they needed to know in order to carry out their part of the plan.

Earlier, before meeting with Richard and Henry, I had gathered half of my company of guards, eight horse archers in all, around me and ordered them assist Aron and James and guard them. Their company's lieutenant, Lieutenant Sharp, would be their commander.

Lieutenant Sharp and his men had been sombre and quiet as they heard me tell them that they were being detached effective immediately to assist and guard Aron and James—and that what they would be doing was important, very important, and could be dangerous.

"You are to immediately do whatever the Aron the Alchemist or Sergeant Howard tells you to do and *never* ask them any questions or anything you see or hear with anyone. No exceptions. Consider anything they ask of you to be a direct order from me that is to be obeyed instantly no matter how small or insignificant *you* think it might be.

"Also, and without ever telling Aron or mentioning it to anyone else, I want you to guard Aron closely as his life may in danger in the days ahead from a murderer or poisoner. So keep your weapons and wits about you at all time and never let him out of your sight. Even when he is sleeping, several of you must be awake and watching over him with your weapons ready at all times.

"There are several other things you need to know and should keep behind your eyes at all times and, once again, do it without talking to anyone about them. One is that Aron has made his mark on the Company's roll and holds the rank of lieutenant.

"Another is that keeping him alive is important to the Company and that Aron has no fighting ability or weapons training whatsoever. In other words, he is unlikely to be able to defend himself if he is attacked. Please keep that in mind when you are guarding him or if you see someone trying to get close to him. And that includes women and priests, especially Orthodox priests.

"The third is that the girl he was to marry in a few weeks was killed by the rioters in the city a few days ago. As a result, Aron may have become temporarily overbalanced and try to kill himself, or hurt some of the Orthodox people in the city. You must not let him do it."

The men all saw how seriousness I was about their new assignment. They did not know why they were to help Aron and guard him, but they would do so or die trying. I could see it in their eyes.

******

A hot day followed the day of the fighting in the rain and the Greek camp was quiet. After speaking with Aron's new guards, and taking them to meet him, I rode to the Commandery to meet with Richard and Henry to tell them about the plan. Afterwards, I met with all my lieutenants to go over Company's butcher's bill from the previous day's fighting. That was what we were doing when a runner arrived with a message for Harold from Eric.

According to Eric, the captain of a Syrian transport had watched a fleet of Venetian galleys take one of our galleys on the Aegean Sea side of the Dardanelles. There had been no fighting; our galley had surrendered immediately.

Harold thought the galley was Number Twenty-two, Captain Cartwright's. It was one of our older galleys with a deeper draft and Cartwright had come up through the ranks as a sailor, which is why that particular galley was one of those chosen to keep sailing instead of being pulled ashore.

Twenty-two had sailed from Constantinople bound for Cyprus several weeks earlier with a crew of nine Company sailors and its refugee passengers doing the rowing. Apparently it had been taken on its return voyage with no archers on board.

Harold was not sure who was on board other than Captain Cartwright and his sailors, but he suspected the rowing was being done by volunteers who had been paid to help bring it back to Constantinople so that it could pick up more refugees. Paid or not, they were all the Company's responsibility and under our protection, both the passengers and the crew.

If it was Cartwright's, the captured galley was one of those which we had been sending out without archers so that its regular crew of archers could be employed to help defend the walls.

And the news got worse. According to the merchants, we had also lost another transport and its crew. One of the Company's transports, a big two-masted cog, had been taken by the Venetians yesterday afternoon as it came through the Dardanelles with no archers on board. It too had surrendered without a fight.

There were also rumours, almost certain to be true, that we had lost a toll-collecting galley returning with coins from the entrance to the Bosporus. It was overdue to return and almost certainly had been taken by the fleet of twenty-three Venetian galleys that had earlier landed their men in a failed effort to take or destroy the Company galleys which had been pulled ashore. It also had no archers on board.

Our losses at sea were significant. At the very least, the Venetians now had twenty or thirty of our sailors as hostages along with cargos, money orders, and as many as two or three hundred of our passengers and volunteers. To say that we would be doing whatever we could to get them back and then exacting a terrible vengeance would be comparable to saying birds fly and the Pope is a Christian.

We were not, however, surprised by our losses. To the contrary, they were to be expected—the Venetian galleys which had hurried out of the harbour leaving their dead and wounded behind now controlled the Marmara Sea, the inland sea between the Bosporus straits and the Dardanelle straits.

The Venetians' presence in the waters off Constantinople was an unfortunate fact of life. It meant the Company would continue to lose transports and galleys until we re-floated our galleys, boarded our archers, and either destroyed the Venetians or drove them off. Until we did, we would almost certainly lose more of our galleys and transports—because all of our captains sailing toward Constantinople had no way of knowing that we had lost control of the straits and the waters in front of the city.

Our conundrum was that if we boarded our archers to fight the Venetians at sea, we might very well lose the undefended city to a land attack whilst we were gone. But then again, the Empress could safely hole up in the Citadel until we returned. Hmm.

****** *George Courtenay*

Henry was furious with me and there was no mistaking it. He was shouting and so angry I was afraid he would fall down and go to sleep and have a sagging face and weak arm when he woke up. I did not blame him and told him as much, and also warned him of the risk. It did not seem to help.

What got Henry so riled up was that I decided to pose as one of the archers Adam had recruited and accompany him to the tavern when he went to get the coins for opening the wall gates to the Orthodox army. I wanted to listen to what was gobbled and see if I could learn anything about the Greek plans.

I think I decided to do it, go with Adam that is, when Adam mentioned me that the priest who met him and offered to pay him handsomely to open the gates had gobbled at him in crusader French. I found that very strange since the Greeks knew that Adam gobbled Greek, had a Greek wife, lived with her family, and attended Orthodox Church prayer services with her.

The more I thought about it, the more it set me to wondering if someone else might have been in the dungeon with the captured Orthodox priests and bishops, and what they had heard and who they had told. Was it possible there was more than one active plot underway against the Empress? There were, after all, many others in addition to the Greeks who might want to encourage her to flee.

Chapter Forty-four

Who are they and what do they really want?

It was dark when I went with Adam to the tavern the next night to collect the first half of the coins. Two of the best swordsmen in the Company were sworn to secrecy and came along with us, a sergeant and a lieutenant. All three of us wore old and battered tunics with the two stripes of a chosen man. We looked like what we really were—three of the Company's tough old sweats.

Elizabeth had helped me prepare myself for the meeting in my room in the citadel by gathering my hair and tying it in a knot behind my head with a piece of leather string in the manner used by many of our sailors. She was more excited than I was even though I refused to say why I was disguising myself or what I intended to do.

After she finished, she watched as I put on a shabby old tunic with the two stripes of a chosen man over my chain shirt, made sure my two wrist knives were ready, and warned her once again to say not a word to anyone. When she finished I gave her a brief kiss, murmured thank you, and promised to return in a few hours with the hope of finding her in my bed. Then I hurried out of the room, walked briskly through the citadel and out the gate into the dark with the hood of my tunic pulled up.

No one recognized me in the dim candlelight of the Citadel or in the moonlight when I stepped out into the bailey, at least not so far as I could tell. Neither did the Varangians at the Citadel gate. They barely looked at me since I was outbound and thus no threat.

Nicholas, Adam, and the two swordsmen were waiting for me in the darkness beyond the Citadel's gate. They had a two-wheeled handcart with them and each was carrying a sheathed short sword and had a galley shield hung over his back instead of quivers.

Adam was wearing his lieutenant's tunic; the others had all already changed into the old tunics Nicholas had found in the slop chest of one of the galleys. Nicholas was also wearing a chosen man's tunic even though he was not supposed to be going with us. They had changed into their temporary new clothes in the dark a few minutes earlier, Adam assured me, so that no one would see them doing it. Their original tunics with their proper ranks were in the cart.

I could tell from the way the two swordsmen moved and their alertness that they were excited. They did not know why they had been quietly been ordered to arm themselves and report to Adam that afternoon, but the presence of my apprentice sergeant, the air of great secrecy, and my arrival wearing a chosen man's tunic and my hair fixed like a sailor's, had convinced them that they were involved in something important even though they had no idea what it might be.

When Nicholas handed me the galley shield and sword I would carry, I could see in the dim moonlight that he had also put on an old tunic and was similarly armed and disguised himself. No doubt he was hoping that I would change my mind and he would be allowed to come with us. I did.

******

We pulled the handcart through the streets to the tavern in the quiet darkness. It was in the Latin Quarter so it was safe for us to do so, particularly since there were five of us and we were heavily armed. I spoke to the men in a low voice as we walked.

"Everyone is to address me as "Pierre," never as "Commander." It is an important Company secret that I am with you and so is everything we do and see tonight. Tell not a word or even a hint to anyone about what you hear or see tonight until this war is over."

People were on the streets going about their normal business and the voices we heard were not excited. Our pulling of the handcart seemed somehow to reassure the people we came upon even though they mostly heard us since the light was so poor. Having a handful of men accompanying a handcart clattering through the city's dark streets at night when it was cooler seemed like a reasonable thing to do.

The tavern where we were going to visit was called The Black Swan. It was in a poorer part of the Latin Quarter so there few candles and lanterns being carried by people in the street or flickering in the hovels along it. Even so, we could see the dim outlines of people in the moonlight as we passed them, and we could heard them talking around us and in the wall openings above us. We passed a number of small fires with women huddled around them cooking their family's bread and soup in the street. They had their children with them.

It had been a hot day, but the sun had been down for several hours and it was actually quite comfortable to walk in coolness of the night. The city even smelled better since the recent rain had washed away the piles of shite that inevitably accumulate each day in the streets and alleys of such a closely packed city. Several times we heard the scurrying sound of one of the city's many feral cats, and once we heard sounds of a couple of angry cats growling at each other and a short-lived cat fight.

Everything was so normal that it was hard to believe that only one day earlier we were fighting for our lives and our Company's future was in doubt. In fact, the entire city seemed quiet for the first time in several weeks. At least it seemed that way to me. Yesterday's defeat of the Greek and Venetian attacks must have taken some of the fire out of the protesters' bellies. I certainly hoped that was the case.

The tavern where Adam and his mates were to meet the Greeks' representative was in the Latin Quarter and on a street corner as was common in those days. The black swan painted over its door could not be clearly seen in the moonlight, but I had ridden past it several times and remembered it.

The wooden shutters of the tavern's street-level wall openings were thrown open and we could see and hear that the "Swan" was packed with boisterous people as we approached it. Seeing and hearing them after passing through the quiet streets was an unexpected event.

When we reached the end of the street we could see the outline of the Black Swan's door opening from the two candle lanterns hanging from the tavern's low ceiling. We walked past the window openings, ducked our heads and entered through the narrow doorway.

I was not taking any chances. Nicholas stayed with the cart; the two swordsmen came in with me and Adam. I murmured orders to them as we did.

"Stay calm, lads, and keep your swords sheathed unless we need them. Be casual as if we only stopped in for a bowl. But stay alert for a surprise attack."

There was no door that had to be opened for us to enter the tavern, just a hole in the wall through which a man could walk. A portable door would be brought in from the alley when the tavern needed to be closed or it was too cold outside such that a fire was needed in its fireplace. The Black Swan was, in other words, very much like all the other taverns that might be found in such a neighbourhood. From the looks and smell of the place, its dirt floor had soaked up many a spilled drink over the years.

The tavern seemed particularly boisterous and crowded that night, so crowded in fact that we immediately understood that there would be no chance of finding a place to sit. The Black Swan's being crowded was not surprising, however; the danger and rioting of the last few weeks, and the presence of refugees from the other quarters, had undoubtedly kept many people sitting in their hovels with their doors barred. That night was likely the first in some days that some people felt safe enough to venture out after dark.

Adam led us in and, because he had been coming in every night for some weeks, was immediately recognized by one of the tavern girls who was delivering bowls of ale to the men sitting at one on the tables. No one else paid any attention to us.

"There was someone asking about you earlier, Luv; a nob for sure. He seemed most anxious to see you. He gave me a piece of a copper and said to tell you if you came in that he would be back shortly."

Whoever it was that we were meeting must have been outside waiting and watched us enter. We had not even time for our bowls to arrive before a young street boy slipped into the tavern and approached Adam. He tugged on the sleeve of Adam's tunic to get his attention.

"Be your name Adam?"

"Aye, that it be."

"A man outside gave me a copper to tell you to meet him where he met you the first time."

****

Adam went out the tavern door first and sighted the Greek's representative before I did. He was standing a few paces down the street at the entrance to the alley that ran alongside the tavern.

I was going out the door behind Adam and saw his reaction when he spotted the man standing off to the side of us. I knew exactly what it meant and turned to see the unknown bribemaster for myself.

When I got closer I could see in the moonlight that the man we had come to meet had grey in his neatly trimmed beard and was wearing nice clothes, but carrying no weapon, at least not so far as I could see. He was definitely not a working man or a sailor. The barmaid was right; he was a nob for sure. He was middle-aged and carried himself with the sureness of a successful man used to getting his way.

The man made a somewhat arrogant little "follow me" motion with his hand and head, and promptly turned and walked into the darkened alley next to the tavern. He clearly did not want to be seen. We cautiously followed him; this is where we would be attacked if this was a trap. Adam would have to come back later and pay for the bowls of ale we had ordered.

Nicholas had seen us come out of the tavern and started forward to join us. I motioned for him to stay where he was and continue guarding the cart. He drew his sword as soon as he saw me draw mine.

******

Adam's would-be co-conspirator disappeared around the corner into the alley that ran along the other side of the tavern. Adam drew his sword as he walked, and followed him into the alley without hesitation. We were right behind Adam with our swords drawn and our shields held at the ready in case it was an ambush. My heart was pounding.

The alley smelled liked piss despite the recent rain. No doubt it was where the tavern drinkers and the locals living nearby came to relieve themselves. It was even darker than the moonlit street. I could barely make out the shape of the man once he walked into it.

It bothered me to follow the unknown man into the dark alley, both because I was wearing open-toed sandals, and because I did not know what to expect. But I drew my sword, hefted my shield too make sure I had a good grip on it, and followed them in. As I did, I nodded my approval at our two swordsmen. In the moonlight I could see that they had drawn their blades when Adam did without being told.

Nicholas stayed with the handcart. He was holding his sword by his side so it could not be seen in the moonlight.

"Can you and your friends really open both gates for the Greeks?" the dim figure asked Adam in crusader French.

"Aye. Nothing has changed. We can do it, but only if you have the coins and they are as agreed, and the second half of the coins are waiting for us at the inner gate thirty minutes before early light on Saturday and all of the coins are there. Today's coins buy you the nobbling of both of the moat bridges and the opening of the outer gate at dawn. The inner gate stays shut until we have the second half of the coins safely away.

"Also, and here is another idea for you, for enough additional coins, say another hundred pounds of silvers, me and my mates will also make an effort the night before you enter the city to cause an evacuation of some of the states' forces on the roadway. If we do that, your men will face fewer of them and will be able to reach the inner gate faster."

"And how could you accomplish that?"

"By telling some of the truth—around sundown on the coming Friday night we will walk through the states' camp and spread the word to everyone that the archers are pulling back to the inner wall because an attack is coming and the outer wall's drawbridge and its gate have been nobbled and cannot be immediately repaired.

"The nobbling of the drawbridges and the outer gate will be done a day or two earlier so that everyone will believe what we are telling them is true. Some of them will surely panic and run when they hear the archers are pulling back. Indeed, the people desperately fleeing with their possessions out of the states' camp Friday evening and early Saturday morning is how you will know we have already finished doing most of what we were paid to do.

"But as I warned you the first time we met, the inner gate will *not* be nobbled to prevent it from being closed until we have the second half of the coins in our hands and are safely away. And, as I also warned you earlier, there will be archers camped near the inner gate and charged with guarding it, perhaps several companies of them. Your men will have to fight them when they come through the gate and enter the city.

"The archers are not likely to be pushovers who will turn and run when they see your men coming. They will fight. I hope you know that. It means your best men will have to come through the inner gate in great numbers and be ready to fight. My mates and I will make it possible for your men to get through the two gates; but we will not fight for you. That you must do for yourselves."

I could not see the briber's response because the alley was so dark, but I heard it.

"We understand that you and your friends are only getting the Greeks through the gates and that they will have to fight.

"So rest assured that the other half of the coins to pay for doing that will be waiting where we agreed. And so will all the additional coins for frightening the states' men into running. It is a good idea and quite helpful.

Suddenly it hit me. He had just referred to the Greeks are *they*? I listened carefully as the briber continued to gobble. Something did not make sense but I was not sure what it was.

"I have the first half of coins here with me," the unknown man said with a gesture towards the dark alley. They are in there against the alley wall in three chests. Did you bring a cart to carry them?"

"Aye, that we did," Adam answered.

"Well then, I will leave you to carry them off and I expect to see you again in five days, just before dawn Saturday morning in the alley three hundred paces or so south of the inner gate. The coins will be waiting there for you to inspect, but they will only be released to you after my friends and I know the inner gate is open."

"Aye. That is agreeable," Adam said cautiously. And then he issued his own warnings just as he had been instructed.

"But please remember that my mates and I will be bringing a lantern to inspect the second payment of coins and a hand cart to carry them. We will only proceed to nobble the inner gate if all the coins are there shipshape and proper and my mates and I are safe.

"I hope you believe what I am telling you, because I will run back to signal the men waiting to nobble the gate to proceed *only* if we find every coin and our safety to be as you and I have agreed.

"Also please remember that we will have men watching *both* your payment of the coins to us and the secret place where we will be taking them—and they will know how to quickly un-nobble the gate if the coins do not safely arrive at our secret place. So please keep that in mind. No tricks, eh?"

"Of course not," the man said indignantly and rather threateningly. "But that applies to you as well. You need to remember that *we* will be sending someone with you to make sure the gate is truly nobbled before we release the coins to you," the man warned.

"Aye. That is what we agreed," Adam said. "And I will bring an archer's tunic for him to slip on so he does not draw attention."

"So be it," said the increasingly nervous briber as he began moving to leave. "I will be there with the second batch of coins an hour before dawn in the alley south of the inner gate."

"Wait," Adam said a bit too anxiously. "Where can I reach you if there is a problem?"

"You cannot. My friends and I will know if there is a problem and will do whatever has to be done."

Aron's asking what he should do in the event of an unexpected problem was only the first of the two important questions I told Adam he must ask. There was another question that was even more important than the first.

We walked out of the alley with the man until he reached the street and the moonlight revealed him once again. And then, before the man could disappear, Adam asked the second question.

"Would you bless me and say a prayer for our success, father?"

"How do you know I am a priest? Did you have someone follow me after we first met? The anger in the man's voice was clear.

"Of course, I did not follow you. But you talk like a priest and walk like a priest so I thought you must be one. And I want your blessing and for you to swear in the name of Jesus that my mates and I will be protected if we stay in the city with our coins."

The priest, for that was what he was, reluctantly agreed. He murmured a few words at Alan and crossed himself automatically as he did—and from the way he crossed himself I knew he was a Latin.

But whose priest was he? And why was he doing this to help the Greeks? My thinking was running fast behind my eyes and going nowhere.

Chapter Forty-five

Preparations are made.

The long days that followed passed quickly, and so did the short nights with Elizabeth which were quite enjoyable. There was much to prepare and only a few days to get everything done. It was the best of times.

Thankfully, and of overwhelming importance, the sun returned and our bowstrings dried and became usable. We were once again a fully equipped fighting force of almost three thousand archers. It was by far the biggest force of the Company's men ever assembled in one place. In other words, most of our eggs had been placed in one nest and we were about to *try* to begin hatching them by gulling the Greeks into doing something stupid.

One of our most important preparations began immediately—organising the last minute movement of our archers and their bales of additional arrows to where they would be most useful during the crucial first few hours after the Greeks came through the outer gate early Saturday morning. What made it difficult was that our men could not be moved until darkness fell without the Greeks seeing them move and being forewarned.

Making sure the archers were quietly moved into their new fighting positions in the dark of the Friday night preceding the Greek attack became Henry's responsibility, and he relished his role once he understood the plan and how we were trying to gull the Greek army into entering the enclosed roadway that was now occupied by the states' forces—and trapping them there for our archers to kill.

Henry spent an entire day personally showing every company commander where his company's men and all of its arrow bales were to be initially placed on one of the two interior walls that ran on either side of the road where the states' forces were camped. He himself would command the galley companies assigned to positions on the interior wall running along the east side of the road.

Richard would be Henry's counterpart to the west. He would command of both the galley companies on the interior wall running along the west side of the road and the men who remained on watch along the outer city's adjacent and higher and stronger outer wall.

I would be in overall command and in direct command of the ribalds, the two wall gates, and the galley company that would begin moving through the camp prior to the sun going down Friday night to sound the alarm. It would then pass through the inner gate and join the two companies that would already be there to help them defend it. My senior aide, Michael Oremus, would be my number two at the inner gate and remain there at all times.

The "secret" explanation our galley captains were given was that the position they were being shown was their company's assigned position if the states' forces mutinied—which was feared because of their recent losses. The captains were ordered to keep the possibility of a mutiny secret, even from their own men. The captains of the galley companies nearest to the inner gate were additionally shown a second position further from the inner gate, but not told why they might be required to temporarily move there on very short notice.

Because each company would have to find its initial position in the dark if the states' forces mutinied in the middle of the night, as was expected, each captain was required to take three of his company's men, including a steady sergeant, and post them until further notice at his company's "mutiny" position. They would remain there as "place holders" to mark his company's initial position and help him and his men find it in the dark.

Each captain was told that if the call came to take up their new positions to put down mutineers, the order would be passed from man to man along the wall as "all companies to quietly take up position number five." The captains of the companies closest to the inner gate were also told that a subsequent order coming along the wall to "move to position nine" required them to double-time their men to their company's secondary position. Those moving to their secondary position were also told to leave their arrow bales and supplies behind as they would soon be ordered to return to their initial positon.

When the initial order to move arrived, every company was then to immediately pick up its arrow bales and full water skins *and very quietly* double time along the top of the wall from their old positions to their new positions. No talking was to be allowed and only the seven men of the company's most dependable file were to be left to man their company's original position on the city's outer wall.

The seven archers who remained behind were there in case the company's regular position on the wall and its adjacent camp needed to be defended whilst most of its men were gone. Wherever possible, each of the seven was to be armed with one of the Company's bladed pikes in addition to their longbows. Henry was charged with making sure they had them.

Two nights later the captain, lieutenant, and first sergeant of every galley company on the wall was required to prove he knew exactly where to lead his company's men in the event the states' forces mutinied—the three men, without the men of their company, were required to double time along the wall and find their company's assigned position and its place holders in the dark.

Even my father did his part, although he neither liked my order nor understood it—he and his crew of carpenters began taking apart the catapults they had painstakingly built and lined up on either side of the Farmers Gate in the outer wall, and moving them to similar positions inside the city's inner wall.

****** *Commander George Courtenay*

I spent most of the days following the meeting at the Black Swan making sure Aron's ribalds were ready to be used. He had completed eleven of them and was working on number twelve. All but two involved hardwood logs he and his helpers had carefully hollowed out to hold the lightning powder and rocks, and then wrapped tightly with ropes to prevent them from coming apart when the lightning occurred.

What Aron and his helpers had not finished doing was getting them to where they were needed—on to wagons that the men assigned to them could pull along the top the inner defensive wall. The ribalds needed to be placed on wagons that were atop the wall so they could be pulled into positions overlooking the wall gate that the men of the Greek army thought Adam and his fellow traitors would be opening for them.

Unlike horses which could be blindfolded and led up the narrow stone stairs that stood near the gate and ran up to the top of the wall, it turned out to be no small task to get a wagon up on to the city's inner wall in a location from which our men could drag it along the wall to its assigned place above the gate.

The problem was solved by bringing in Harold and a hundred or so of the Company's sailors from the harbour. I naively assumed they would know how to set up and use pulleys and tackles to hoist the wagons and ribalds up on to the wall so we could move them into place the night before the Greeks' dawn attack. I was wrong. Hoisting wagons and ribalds, I learned, was not the same as hoisting sails.

Harold and his sailors ended up getting their job completed the old-fashioned way—the wheels were taken off the wagons and everything was carried up the nearest stairs by a great mob of sailors, and then reassembled; the ribalds were then carried up the stairs and placed on the wagons by a large number of sweating and swearing sailor men using a net the sailors made of many ropes to hold them from bumping on the stone steps.

At the same time, whilst all that was going on, others of the sailors carried up the rocks that would be packed in the tubes and around them to contain the wood fragments if the tubes came apart despite the lines that were wrapped around them to hold them together.

And, of course, there were the inevitable mistakes that had to be corrected. The biggest of which was a ribald that was carefully placed and prepared only to discover that the opening was pointing in the wrong direction and the wagon on which the ribald was mounted could not be turned around because the roadway on top of the wall was too narrow.

Everything was done several miles from inner gate so that the Greek spies in the city would not associate the wagons with the gate. I personally walked along the top of the wall with Harold to make sure the sailors would be able to pull the wagons from their initial locations on top of the wall to their positions above the gate and on either side of it.

The sailors needed three full days to get the wagons up on to the wall and loaded with the ribalds to Aron's satisfaction. It was interesting to listen to the sailors as they worked. It was likely that never before have so many foul oaths and profane words been heard in one place, probably because the sailors did not know why they were doing it and thought it was useless busywork whose only purpose was to keep them occupied and out of trouble.

It probably would have been even worse if they had known they would be staying to help pull the wagons to their assigned places on the inner wall. On the other hand there was tavern at the bottom of the steps the sailors had to use so they happy to be working where they were working even though they had to walk back to the harbour at night to eat and sleep.

Somewhere along the way I decided that placing a couple of the ribalds over the gate in the outer wall might be helpful as well—with their open ends pointing toward the states' forces encampment instead of the Greek camp. So Harold and I walked to the outer gate to see if it might be possible to pull them there. We determined that it was if some of the stones in the wall were dug out moved. Accordingly, moving two of them to the outer gate was added to the plan.

Chapter Forty-six

Battle preparations.

Adam continued to lead the process of gulling the Greeks. In the middle of Friday afternoon he led what was left of my guard of horse archers in a march through the entire states' forces enclosure from the outer gate to the inner gate. With them were an entire galley company of foot archers and their Greek-gobbling auxiliaries. I rode wearing a chosen man's tunic once again.

Our constantly repeated message was a simple warning.

"Get out. Leave immediately to get inside the city's inner wall. Run for your lives. Hurry. The gate in the outer wall has been nobbled and the Greeks will be here in force before the sun comes up in the morning.

"The archers are falling back to the city's interior wall because they know they cannot hold the outer wall now that the gate is broken. That is why they have been moving their catapults back for the last several days.

"You must relocate immediately to the square just south of the central market. There is a place to camp and food and water there. Hurry. Run. Save yourselves before it is too late."

******

Chaos, confusion, anger, and tearful hysteria reigned as we spread out into a skirmish line and moved through the states forces encampment sounding the warning that "the Greeks are coming." The result was pandemonium. Tents were quickly struck and desperate men and women began gathering up their possessions. Panic-stricken people and their carts and wagons were soon hurrying up the road towards the inner gate.

Within minutes a steady stream of distressed and sweating states' soldiers and their camp followers and sutlers began pouring into the city through the gate in the inner wall. The Greek spies would report that Adam and his mates had kept their word; they were doing what they had been bribed to do.

Only a handful of guards and a single company horse archers remained on the ground at the outer gate. Everyone else was on the wall watching the states' force abandon their camp. It was very hot in the merciless late afternoon sun so the horse archers dismounted and their horses were kept tight against the wall to stay in its shade. The men in the galley companies on the wall above them sought shade wherever they could find it and argued over the choicest spots.

My guard of horse archers and I turned to ride back to the outer gate after we had gotten about halfway through the camp of the states' forces. The foot archers from the galley, the men many of us were beginning to refer to as Marines, continued towards the inner gate spreading the word. They would take up new positions on the other side of the inner gate along with the Marines from three other galley companies.

We were not the only ones making changes. The Greek encampment in front of the wall had been a beehive of activity all day long despite the heat. It was clear to everyone that something big was about to happen.

Indeed, several warnings to that effect came from the Citadel late Friday afternoon. Both Eric and my father had ridden separately to the Commandery to tell me the Empress's spies had reported that the Greeks were preparing for a major attack as early as the next morning.

Eric and my father also reported that the city had been restless all day with several flare-ups of looting that the Empress's guards had been hard-pressed to put down. And they were both particularly concerned because the states' forces appeared to be abandoning their camp along the roadway between the gates and retreating into the city.

"The city is alive with rumours," Eric said to me.

"Yes, I know the states' forces are leaving their camp in a panic and moving into the city. I cannot say that I blame them. They heard a rumour that the archers were pulling back because the drawbridge over the outer moat cannot be lifted and the gate in the outer wall cannot be fully closed.

"Unfortunately, the rumour is true. Both the bridge and the gate of the outer wall have been nobbled, and so has the drawbridge over the inner moat. It was probably an inside job when the states' forces were passing through the gate on a sally and we were not watching."

My saying that the gate in the outer wall and both of the moat bridges had been nobbled and could not be repaired appeared to shock them both.

"Our men are working to repair the gate in the outer wall as we speak. If we cannot repair it, I will almost certainly have to begin moving some of my archers tonight to fill whatever defensive gaps are left in the inner wall by the departure of the states' men."

"What about the moat?" my father asked. "Can you raise the moat bridge or tear it down in order to keep the Greeks away from the gate?"

"Unfortunately the windlass used to raise the bridge was also badly damaged."

"Are you sure you can keep the Greeks out of the city?" Eric asked anxiously. "Or is it time for me to take the Empress and her family to safety out of the city? The chain across the Golden Horn is keeping the Venetians out of the rivers. We could get the family out on one the Company galleys you have in the rivers."

"Oh, I do not think it necessary for the Empress and her family to run," I replied, "at least, not yet. Although you are right to be concerned; we may have to retreat to the inner wall if we have to send so many archers to replace the states' forces that we do not have enough archers to hold the outer wall."

It was all lies, of course, both about the gate and the bridge over the moat being irretrievably nobbled, and also about the need to send archers to replace the states' forces who had been panicked by the situation into fleeing. But they were useful lies because they explained why our archers would be moving to new positions as soon as it got dark.

I did not tell them the real reason the archers were moving to new positions because I had begun to get suspicious of Eric—and I did not know why.

******

I stood with Nicholas at an archer slit above the outer gate whilst we waited for total darkness to fall on Friday. It seemed to take forever. When it finally did arrive, I stood in the moonlight and gave the "quietly take up position number five" order. It was immediately passed along the wall from man to man such that it quickly reached every captain. The galley companies on the wall picked up their arrow bales and water skins and began hurrying to their mutiny positions overlooking the states forces' camp.

Many people had abandoned the states' camp, but there were still a surprising number of people in it when darkness fell. Whether they would still be there when the Greeks arrived in a few hours was a good question. An even better question was whether any of them would resist and, thus, how long it would take the Greek army to reach the inner gate.

I had made one last effort to save them about an hour before sundown.

"Nicholas, please find Captain Fiennes and ask him to lead his men on another swing through the states' camp even though it is dark. Give him my compliments and tell him that I would like him to ride through the camp all the way to inner gate, and then ride back here whilst once again repeating the order to leave.

"I will wait for him here. Oh yes, and please tell Captain Fiennes his men that they are to suggest to everyone they meet that only traitors will be remaining behind to greet the Greeks—and they will be dealt with most severely by the Empress's guards *before* the Greeks arrive. Maybe that will get them to move." *I knew that many of the remainers did not gobble the crusader French that some people are now calling English. But some of them did and they would tell the others.*

Henry and Richard were not with me when, about two hours later, I gave the order for the galley companies on the wall to begin moving quietly along the top of the wall to their mutiny positions. Henry was on the interior wall near the inner gate awaiting the arrival of the galley company whose archers would be on that wall and closest to the gate; Richard was across the way in a similar location on the interior wall on the other side of the road.

All the companies were soon moving along the wall to their new positions. They came past me one after another. As soon as they arrived at their assigned position, Richard and Henry would move up the wall to the next position to wait for the next company to arrive. In that way they would insure that each of the companies was in its proper place, and also work their way back along the wall until they ended up atop the gate through which the Greeks would pour in a few hours when *we* threw it open.

I would not be with them—as soon as the outer gate was up and secured, I intended to mount a horse and gallop to the inner gate to take command there.

The moonlight was too weak for me to actually see the Greek army in the camp on the other side of the moat. But I could periodically hear noises in the distance as the Greek army tried to assemble in the moonlit darkness.

But would they actually try to rush into the states' encampment through the nobbled gate and move towards the inner gate in force?

Chapter Forty-seven

Chaos and treachery.

It was the middle of a clear Friday night with a partial moon when Henry, Richard, and I shook hands, wished each other good luck, and went off to carry out our respective assignments. Henry and Richard went off to once again make sure the archers who had moved on to the interior walls were properly placed, and I went down the stone stairs with a couple of burly archers to crank the gate up far enough such that a man could walk under it without hitting his head.

Nicholas and a couple of sailors who were good at tying knots followed me down the stairs. The three of them would crawl on their bellies under the gate as soon as it was high enough and tie ropes to the drawbridge over the moat so it could be raised up without using the windlass that was inside the wall next to the gate—by men pulling on the ropes from atop the wall.

Somewhat similarly, as soon as I shouted up to the men on the wall that the gate had been raised high enough, they would tie it in its raised position with rope lines. Then my helpers and I would remove the chain and crank handle. Once that was done, the gate could be lowered by cutting the lines that were holding it up—but it would not be able to be raised back up once the lines were cut and it was lowered.

My plan, or perhaps I should say my hope, was that a large part of the Greek army would rush through the raised outer gate into states' camp, and then run several miles through it to get to the inner gate which they expected to find open—and there they would be forced to stop because it would not be open.

Once the Greeks were inside the states' camp, the draw bridge over the outer moat would be pulled up using the lines Nicholas and his sailors attached, and the gate in the outer wall would be closed by cutting the lines that were holding it up. The gate would then drop to the ground and be closed with no way to open it.

If either of those two things happened the invaders would be unable to get back to their own camp—they would be trapped inside the states' camp with archers all along the walls that surrounded them.

To make sure that the Greeks did not get back to their camp, there would be more than a thousand archers on each side of the long narrow roadway. They were heavily concentrated near the gate in the city's inner defensive wall. That was where the Greeks would mass whilst waiting for the inner gate to be opened by Adam and the archers posing as his fellow traitors.

It was a fine plan since every inch of the states' encampment could be reached from atop one of the walls that surrounded it. My two lieutenant commanders and I had spent several days wondering how long our plan would last after the first Greek soldier came through the outer gate and entered the encampment of the states' forces.

"About ten minutes," was Henry's cynical estimate.

****** *Commander George Courtenay*

The archers assigned to the section of the outer wall which included the gate were waiting on the parapet behind me as I cautiously made my way down the stone steps in the moonlit darkness. The sailors with them were in the process of throwing the bridge-lifting ropes down to Nicholas and his sailors, and getting other ropes ready to tie the gate in place as soon as it was raised.

There was no shortage of ropes on the wall for the sailors to toss and tie. Harold had sent several wagon loads of them to us from the stores of the galleys that had been pulled ashore. Usually the ropes were used to raise and lower sails and anchors. Using them to hoist wagons to the top of the wall may have been difficult for our sailors, but not tying knots that would not slip. Knots were something every sailor knew how to tie.

A few moments later I was standing next to the gate and watching in the faint moonlight as the gate was partially raised and Nicholas and his knot-tying sailors slipped out under it to tie ropes to the drawbridge over the moat. The gate was soon cranked up far enough so the Greeks could get in. A few minutes later Nicholas and his sailors ran back through the gate and headed up the stairs to the top of the wall. They had tied overly long ropes to the draw bridge that could be gathered in and used to pull it up.

"I do not think anyone saw us," Nicholas said. "And we pulled the extra length of the lines off to the side so they would not appear to be running from the bridge up to the top of the wall. It ought to work—unless one of the Greeks looks closely when he is crossing the bridge and stops to cut them."

A moment later the captain of the galley company on the wall above me shouted down that the gate had been secured by the sailors so that it could not be lowered except by cutting the lines. As soon as he did, the two archers who had cranked the windlass to raise it removed the crank handle and did whatever had to be done to remove the chain which was normally used to raise and lower the gate.

Our plan to trap the Greeks was simple—after they had finished passing through the open gate in the outer wall, the archers on the wall above the gate would pull the draw bridge up and the gate in the outer wall would be dropped by cutting the lines that were holding it up.

The Greeks would then be trapped inside the enclosed roadway. At that point, the archers on the walls around the states' camp would begin pushing arrows into them. The archers on the wall overlooking the gate would also guard the stone stairs leading up to the top of the wall to prevent the Greeks from climbing the stairs next to the gate in an attempt to escape.

It was a fine plan. The only question was whether it would work. I felt like a fisherman who could see a fish coming towards his lure and wondered if it would bite.

******

My eight remaining personal guards were mounted and waiting for me on the roadway with my horse. I swung myself into the saddle, and then we waited and listened until we could hear the windlass chain being dragged up the stone stairs to the wall above the gate. The chain being removed meant that the windlass could not be used to lift the gate after we cut the lines to drop it back into place.

Once the gate was so nobbled, the only alternatives for the Greeks to get back out through the gate would be to dig a hole under it or pry it up far enough that men could wiggle under it. Alternately, of course, the Greeks could install another chain or fight their way up the stairs and get enough men with ropes on the wall above them to pull the gate up by brute force.

Neither possibility was likely. To the contrary, each would take time to organize, and neither would be possible so long as there were archers with arrows and dry bowstrings on the wall above and around the gate and a determined band of men armed with pikes holding the top of the stairs.

In any event, our raising of the gate meant the Greek army could now pass through the outer wall whenever its commanders decided to do so—which looked to be soon, and probably no later than dawn's early light since they already could be heard assembling in the darkness on the other side of the moat.

One thing that was totally uncertain was how many of the Greek soldiers would actually come into the states' encampment and move through it to the gate in the inner wall that they expected to find similarly opened. Another uncertainty was whether anyone who was still in the states' encampment would try to fight back and, in so doing, delay or prevent the Greek soldiers from reaching the inner gate.

Those were amongst the many thoughts and questions that were behind my eyes as my guards and I kicked our horses in their sides to get them going and we began riding up the road toward the inner gate. The Greeks were coming; anyone still in the states' camp after all of the warnings we had given them was just shite out of luck.

****** *George Courtenay*

There were not many people on the road as we rode towards the inner gate in the moonlight. Those who were going to run had already done so. But not everyone had gone; in the moonlight we could see tents and wagons scattered on either side of the roadway, but there were nowhere near as many as there had been previously. The remainers were either incredibly stupid and misinformed, or they were supporters of the invading Greeks and had decided to wait to welcome them.

Up ahead we could see a couple of candle lanterns marking the gate at the entrance to the inner wall. It was partially open and the lanterns backlit a horse-drawn wagon on its way toward the city. The wagon's driver and a few walkers were the only people we had seen on the road, perhaps because the gate was not normally open during the hours of darkness.

A few moments later, Captain Fiennes barked an order and one of my guards galloped forward to announce our imminent arrival. The captain and the rest of his men stayed with me. They did not know it yet, but they would soon be reunited with their mates who had been guarding and assisting Aron.

We passed through the inner gate a few minutes later. Major Captain Michael Oremus and the captains of the three galley companies at the gate hurried forward to greet me and get any last minute orders. Also waiting at the gate for my arrival was Adam Gravesend and the two swordsmen who had accompanied us when we picked up the first half of the bribe-coins.

The noise of our arrival awakened many of the archers of the three galley companies guarding the gate. There had been nothing for them to do so they had been sleeping as all good fighting men do when they have an opportunity. In the moonlight we could see them as they began sitting up and getting to their feet to piss and see what all the commotion was about

"The Greeks will be coming soon and the interior walls are being manned," I announced loudly as I dismounted in the faint light of the moon and the lanterns.

"Standby to raise the drawbridge and close the gate on an instant's notice. All archers are to immediately take up their defensive positions on the wall. The wagons with the ribalds are to be immediately pulled into position over the gate."

"And the two wagons assigned to the wall over the outer gate, Commander?" Michael asked.

"Aye, Major Captain. Them too. Thank you for reminding me. Please get them on their way."

And with the use of Michael's rank I effectively announced that we were in a battle mode and all orders were to be repeated back to make sure they had been properly understood.

"Aye Commander. We are to take up our defensive positions and standby to raise the drawbridge and close the gate. The wagons carrying the ribalds are to proceed immediately to their assigned positions both here and at the outer gate."

What I did not do, and should have done, was order the drawbridge raised and the gate closed. I did not give that order because there appeared to no immediate need and a few more of the states' forces or their camp followers and sutlers might decide to leave. Also, and more importantly, I wanted the priest who was bribing us to be able to see that it was open so he would think his scheme was working and release the second half of the bribery coins to us without a fight.

"Adam, it is time to collect the second half of the bribery coins and take, if we can, the bribery priest. Did you bring a tunic for me?"

"Aye, Commander, and also a lantern so we can see the coins and a hand cart to carry the coin chests."

Chapter Forty-eight

We are betrayed.

Adam led the way as we walked in the darkness toward the alley where the second half of the bribe was to be paid. Captain Fiennes and five of my personal guards dismounted and were quickly armed with swords and shields so they could accompany us. The ten of us set out to collect the coins immediately thereafter. We pulled a small four-wheeled wagon we could use to carry the coins away.

Our destination was deeper into the city than I remembered. Or perhaps it just seemed that way because we were all so anxious. As you might imagine, our swords were drawn as the little wagon we were pulling announced our passage by clattering over the cobblestones of the silent street. There was little wonder in our anxiety—it was dark, we were being noisy in one of the city's Orthodox quarters, and we had long ago walked past the two archers manning the last of the Company's sentry posts.

The street was silent and surprisingly empty. Usually there were people sleeping in the street. It did not feel right. The hair on my arms began to prickle.

"Over here," a nervous voice said quietly in the dark.

As we got closer, I could see that it was the same man from whom we had collected the first half of the coins. At least that is who I thought it was. It was hard to know for sure in the dim moonlight.

"Do you have the rest of the coins for us?" Adam immediately demanded. He sounded anxious and that was no surprise. I certainly was.

"Yes Lieutenant, the chests are stacked up in the alley. The coins are all there for you and your men to count."

"Good. Please have your men bring them out so we can see them. And tell them to hurry. We need to act whilst it is still dark so no one can see us when we nobble the inner drawbridge and gate. The outer drawbridge and the outer gate have already been done."

Adam told his lies very convincingly. He was very sincere.

"My men are gone," the priest said. He sounded very tense. "So you will have to go into the alley and get the chests yourself if you wish to open them and count them. Whilst you are doing that, I will go to the wall to make sure the bridge and gate are both open and will stay that way."

No men guarding the chests and he is going to leave us with them whilst he goes to see that the gate has been nobbled? Something is wrong.

"Suit yourself," Adam replied as the priest hurried off to see for himself that the gate was open. "But hurry. Dawn is approaching."

Something was wrong. I could sense it as the priest hurried away in what I suddenly realized was the wrong direction. There was absolute quiet and stillness all around us. Suddenly I heard a sound I had heard before—and it was coming towards us.

"Run Lads. Back to the gate. It is a trap."

I turned and ran as if the devil himself was snapping at my arse. The others followed. It was every man for himself and God save the hindmost. I was the first man away and led for a while as we ran through the dark streets just as the first light of dawn began to appear.

******

"Stand to arms. Close the gate; raise the bridge," I gasped out my warning and orders twice a few minutes later as I pounded down the street towards the open gate and the candle lanterns that stood on each side of the wall opening to light it. *My God; I should have closed them earlier. I was greatly worried.*

There were shouts in the distance behind me and four or five of my men, the fastest runners, had already passed me. Once I heard the distinctive sound of someone behind me slip and fall with a curse.

Several things seemed to be clear. One was that the priest and his followers, whoever they might be, had no intention of paying Adam the rest of the coins. Another was that they intended to take control of the inner gate by force.

What was totally unclear was why they were doing it and who was involved. Was it to close the gate in the face of the Greeks, or to keep it open for them, or to block it so the Greeks could not enter the city if the gate could not be closed? And what about the coins that were not paid? I had not a clue about any of it.

As you might imagine, I was not thinking of such things at that moment. What I was doing was running for my life and so were the men with me. All we knew for sure was that a very large number of people from the city were chasing us. They were almost certainly coming to try to take the gate.

"Run you fools," I gasped out as loud as I could as I passed the two gape-mouthed archer lookouts. They were still standing there in the moonlight even though four or five archers of the coin party had already run past them.

"Raise the bridge; close the gate," I gasped out as I entered the open space next to the gate and approached the stairs next to it.

Without breaking my stride, I scooted up the stone stairs to the top of the wall taking them three steps at a time. All around me, both on the ground and on the wall, sergeants were beginning to shout and men were fetching their weapons.

The wall above and around the gate was crowded with men and wagons carrying ribalds. Even so I easily found a place to stand right at the top of the stairs between two wagons. Dawn's early light was just arriving.

******

It was very noisy and there was a lot of confusion around me as I stood at the top of the stairs with both hands on my knees trying to catch my breath. In the moonlight I could see that Captain Fiennes was still with me. All I knew was that I had made it back to the wall safely and was standing at the top of the stairs between two of Aron's ribald wagons. Nicholas and some of the others showed up next to me moments later.

My arrival, my frantically shouted orders, and my mad dash up the stairs to the get to the top of the wall, all combined to cause consternation amongst the rank and file archers who had been standing and sleeping on the ground near the gate. Some of them began moving toward the stairs that led up to the top of the wall. They all did a few moments later when the spear and club carrying thrusters from the mob suddenly began flooding into the open area in front of the gate.

The area around the base of stairs suddenly became full of panic-stricken archers shouting and pushing as they tried to follow me up the stairs to safety. Why so many of them were down there instead of up on the parapet in their defensive positions I did not know.

What I did know was that there was a great and disorganized crowd of pushing and shoving archers gathered around the bottom of the stone stair steps and trying to climb them to escape the mob that now surrounded them. Several times men fell off the steps and landed on the desperate men below them.

"Raise the bridge and drop the gate. Everyone get up on the wall. Stand by to repel boarders. Bring the windlass handle," I shouted as some of the men at the foot of the stairs turned to face the mob and arrows began to fly.

My voice was lost in the noise and I knew it.

******

The shouting and angry mob of men which had pursued us toward the gate was huge and totally disorganized. It was not an army of soldiers.

In the early light of dawn I could see there were thousands of them, all men, and more coming. They quickly and completely filled the open area in front of the gate while there were still archers trying to climb the stairs to get to safety. I could not be sure because it was still somewhat dark, but it looked to me as if a few of them were carrying swords and spears, but many of them were carrying clubs or were unarmed.

What I saw in the dim early light had the makings of a disaster. The huge mob surged into the open area around the gate before the bridge could be cranked up and the gate could be cranked down. The mob instantly overwhelmed and pulled down the archers who had rushed to work the windlasses along with those who were the last to reach the bottom of the steps in an effort to escape.

A few of our men had enough sense to run out the gate and over the bridge to get away, others ran for the stairs and did not make it. They were pulled off lower steps of the stairs and disappeared into the angry and shouting crowd.

The mob had totally surprised us by their sudden arrival in our rear. That much was certain. But they, in turn, had been surprised to find more than two hundred heavily armed archers guarding the gate instead of the usual handful of Varangians from the city's night watch.

It was still somewhat dark and the visibility provided by the moon and the sun's early light was not the best, but it was hard for an experienced archer to miss when his targets were packed together in front of him and only a few feet away. Arrows began to fly almost immediately and the tide rapidly turned against the poorly armed arrivals.

In less than a minute, those of the mob who still could were trying to flee in every direction including out the gate. A few minutes later the light of day arrived to find the bridge up, the gate down, and several hundred dead and wounded men in the open area around the gate including some of ours.

"Stop killing the prisoners. We need to question them first."

I shouted the order when I realized the enraged archers were killing the wounded men. Pulling arrows out of a wounded enemy was one thing; killing him before he could be questioned was neither acceptable nor wise.

******

We had barely seen off the mob and managed to get to the windlasses for the drawbridge and the gate before the first of the Greeks began arriving. We had reached the windlasses and finished cranking them just as dawn's early light appeared. The Greek thrusters on horseback began to reach the gate about thirty minutes later. They arrived too late; we had already raised the bridge and closed the gate.

"My God, that was close. If that mob had shown up thirty minutes later we would have been in deep shite. How many men did we lose?"

The questions poured out of me as I stood above the gate and watched as the number of sword waving Greek cavalrymen in front of the closed gate grew and grew. They had obviously ducked their heads to get under the partially raised gate in the outer wall and galloped up the road thinking the bridge over the inner moat would be down and the inner gate open.

We just watched and waited atop the wall as the Greek riders milled about in confusion. Apparently no one had told them what to do if the gate was not open. Or, perhaps, they were waiting for it to open as they had been promised. Everyone was under the strictest of orders to stay out of sight and not push at them.

After a few minutes, the Greek foot began arriving and the mass of men in front of the moat grew and grew until, almost an hour later, they stretched back down the roadway almost as far as the eye could see. There were many thousands of them. It may not have been the entire Greek army, but it certainly looked like it from where I was standing.

Our men, in contrast, were sitting side by side on their arses out of sight behind the parapet's outer wall and archer slits with their backs up against the wall and, in many cases, their legs under one of the ribald-carrying wagons. They were waiting for the word to be given for them to jump up and begin pushing out their arrows. Three men were assigned to each archer slit and archers would be shoulder to shoulder in the open areas between the archer slits.

Keeping the men out of sight was a wise precaution as the Greeks were known to have crossbowmen amongst them. Besides, it gave the impression that the gate was unguarded as they had been promised.

All the Greeks could see, or so my lieutenants and I hoped, was that the gate closed, the drawbridge was raised in front of them, and a line of wagons was parked along the top of the unguarded wall above the gate.

The Greeks were just standing there in front of me filling the roadway. They were apparently waiting for the bridge to come down and the gate to open. It would be a long wait and, hopefully, eternity and the fires of hell for many of them.

Our enemies were not the only ones watching. People had appeared in the wall openings of the hovels on the streets and lanes behind us. A few had even come out into the street and were hurrying off to their market stalls or to do their family's daily shopping.

******

We, in turn, waited and waited for word about the outer gate had been closed to be passed down the interior wall from man to man. It did not come quickly—and that was actually encouraging because it meant the Greek army was still coming through the outer gate.

Whilst we waited, I watched the Greeks and Michael Oremus took Adam and a couple of other translators and went down to question the prisoners.

It did not take them long to find out who had attacked us—they were men from the protection-selling gangs of the Greek-gobbling priests whose churches were concentrated in the Greek Quarter. There were even two Orthodox priests, one of whom had an arrow in his chest and was in great agony. He had no chance of surviving and needed a mercy.

Michael's initial report stunned me. Why had Eric and the Empress's chancellor, who also functioned as her spymaster, not known they were coming and warned us?

Something did not make sense. There was much I needed to know.

"Tell Sergeant Rutherford to set the priests aside and particularly try to keep them alive, Michael. We will want to question them and the others when there is more time. Give no mercies until we do."

Then, once again, I raised my head for a quick look at the Greeks who were packing into the roadway in front of the gate. It was, as always, a very quick look. Of course it was a very quick look. I had heard all about old King Richard and how a mere boy had taken him with a child's crossbow.

After another quick look, I began giving orders for the sheltering of our handful of wounded against the wall so there was no line of sight between them and the wagons on the wall above them. A couple of sailmakers were already hard at work trying to sew them up and feeding them flower paste to kill their pain. Michael and his apprentice sergeant, my young son, were soon busy making sure my orders were carried out.

The dead and wounded members of the mobsters that attacked us, on the other hand, had been left where they fell with a handful of furious archers guarding over them. The archers were doing so from where they were standing with their wounded mates.

Some of the sixty or so prisoners on the ground in front of the gate were in agony from having arrows in them or having the arrows pulled out so they could be used again. As a result there were periodic scuffles when an archer pulled out an arrow and constant moans and agonized screams and babbling from the wounded prisoners. On the other hand, at least, none of them were trying to get away.

The prisoners had been warned as to what would happen if they tried to run. Several of them had apparently decided to see if we meant what we said. They were now amongst the dead and the rest of them had gotten the message. We would decide what to do with those who were still living after we finished questioning them.

Chapter Forty-nine

Final Preparations and the alchemist's revenge.

We waited atop the city's inner wall and carefully watched the Greek army as it gathered below us. It continued to grow larger and larger for what seemed like hours. And all the time I and everyone else was getting more and more anxious. Finally, the words we had hoped to hear came down the wall from archer to archer.

"The outer wall gate has been closed. Pass it on."

I was ready and did not hesitate for a second when the word reached me. I loudly sent my response back along both the interior walls.

"Blue companies begin pushing. Red companies, ribald men, and everyone else move to your second positions. Pass it on."

All of the companies on the walls near the inner gate had been designated as "Red Companies" and given secondary positions on the interior walls along the roadway to which their men were to temporarily run when the order was given. Henry and Richard would be waiting for them there and assign them to temporary new positions. The men did not know why they were running to new positions, but they soon would. Henry and Richard would know where to place them and when to send them back.

My order was immediately passed from man to man along the parapet both to the left and to the right. It caused the men atop the wall to explode into a great burst of activity with every sergeant shouting to repeat my order. Even the sailors who had pulled the wagons into position ran.

It was as if a hive of bees had been suddenly overturned.

****

The Greeks who filled the roadway in front of the moat bridge were able to see the activity as men began running along the top of the wall. There were now many thousands of Greek soldiers in front of the gate and there was much pointing and shouting. If anything, the Greeks were encouraged to see the archers and sailors running along the top of the wall to move away from the area around the gate. The tightly-packed Greeks even surged forward slightly in anticipation of the gate opening. So be it. The time had come.

I gave my first order.

"Lower the draw bridge and clear the parapet."

A great cheer went up from the Greek army as the drawbridge began to come down. I was standing close enough to it that I could hear the rattle of its chains as it did. The Greeks surged forward towards the gate and the last few of our men on the parapet above them ran. Our men were running for their lives even though neither they nor the Greeks knew it at the time.

I made my way along the wagons towards where Aron and James Howard were waiting. Actually, I met them as they were making their way from wagon to wagon doing a last minute check.

"Are you ready, Aron?"

"Aye Commander, I am. The fire ropes and ribalds are ready on every wagon."

"The Greeks are here in force, Lieutenant, so please proceed to take your revenge. Not you, James. You are no longer needed here. You are to leave with the others. Get yourself to safety."

Aron wanted more.

"And you too, Commander. There is naught for you to do here. So please go down the stairs with James and get behind the wall so you will be protected in case the lightning escapes or the ribaldis come apart. I will start putting a flame to their fire ropes as soon as I see you safe."

Aron demanded it of me with assurance of an expert who knew what he was talking about and would brook no interference. He looked very tired, but there was fire in his eyes and determination in his voice.

I nodded my acceptance of Aron's reasonable request and ran for the stairs by the gate, and then went down them two at a time when I reached them. James and Michael Oremus were right behind me. We were all very excited.

We ran down the stairs to the ground and turned left to run north along the wall. We would, I decided, take shelter next to the wall with the Company's wounded. Those of our men who had been killed by the mob were laid out beyond them.

"Get back against the wall with the wounded," I shouted to one of the archers who saw us running towards him and started walking out to greet us. He stopped and looked confused.

"Get back to the wounded and stand with your back against the wall. Hurry damn you," I shouted as I reached him. He turned as we rushed past and followed us.

****

We had barely reached the wall and were still catching our breaths when Aron made the first lightning. I was kneeling to speak to a wounded archer when, quite suddenly, there was a great clap of thunder that made everyone jump with surprise and the earth shake.

Almost immediately there was another great thunder clap and another one right after that, and they kept coming until I lost count. Finally, there was a long pause such that we thought the lightning storm might have ended, and then there was another.

My ears were ringing as if I had been boxed hard on both of them. But I had the good sense to shout "wait" to James who had started to move back toward the stairs. *He of all people should have known better.* After a very long pause, there was yet another great thundering lightning strike.

By then the air next to the wall had become filled with the strange-smelling smoke caused by the lightning. Everyone was coughing and our eyes began crying from the smoke even though we were not sad. Our wounded men and the sailors and archers tending them were dumbstruck.

After several minutes of cowering amongst our wounded and trying to reassure my men by saying "it is a new weapon and it is ours," I finally decided it was safe to move.

In the distance, as my hearing returned, I became aware of cries and screams coming from the wounded members of the mob who had been left lying in the open area in front of the gate when their fellow mobsters retreated.

I paid them no attention. The wounded prisoners were of no interest to me except as a source of information. I was not what Uncle Thomas called a hypocrite; I did not wish them anything but bad luck and short painful lives, particularly after having just spent time with the dead and broken archers they had attacked and gratuitously killed and wounded.

"Follow me," I said to Michael and James. "It is time to see what happened to the Greek army."

I had high hopes and was very excited as my hearing returned and I started to walk briskly back to the steps. I had only taken a few steps when I was suddenly very thankful we had moved the wounded archers out of the open area on the city side of the gate—because big pieces of some of the ribald wagons had been pushed backwards off the wall by the lightning and landed on top of the wounded prisoners.

"That is a not a good outcome," was my thought, as I climbed the stairs to get back up to the top of the wall—we would have to buy more wagons.

We ignored what was left of the wounded prisoners as we bounded up the stairs. Their injuries and troubles did not interest me in the least; I was anxious to see what had happened to the Greeks who had arrived expecting to find the inner gate open, and had instead discovered flying rocks and the man-made thunder and lightning of Aron's ribalds.

******

The sights and sounds that greeted us at the top of the stairs were beyond belief—for almost as far as the eye could see, the roadway beyond the wall was covered here and there with the bodies of dead and wounded men. They had fallen wherever the ribald stones had been carried by the lightning. There were also a number of dazed survivors wandering around trying to help the wounded and a number of bodies in the moat itself.

Dead and wounded horses were on both sides of what was left of the bridge, probably because the riders had arrived first and had come over the bridge to be closer to the gate when it opened. The terrible screams of the wounded horses' as they staggered about and tried to rise and run was so horrible that, for a moment, I tried to block it out by putting my hands over my ears. I felt much more sympathy for them than their riders.

What we mostly saw, however, were the backs and arses of the surviving Greeks as they ran. They were obviously falling back as fast as possible in an effort to get away from the possibility of more rocks and lightning strikes.

It was a great mistake on the part of the fleeing Greeks and it delighted me so immensely that I laughed and pointed.

What was so funny was that they were running from the one part of the states' enclosure where there were no archers or defenders on the walls to that part of the enclosure where our archers were on the walls in force. Moreover, if the fleeing Greeks somehow got past the archers' arrows they would reach the now-closed outer gate where there were more archers and the two ribalds that had been pulled along the top of the wall and positioned above the gate.

It was, of course, a good thing for us that the Greeks were terrified and running away—for we had had neither archers nor any more ribalds at this end of the roadway. The only two ribalds we had left were in place over the now-closed outer gate.

On the other hand, a number of things were abundantly clear to me and everyone with me, even if the Greeks did not know about them. One was that the survivors of the lightning and stones, and particularly the knights and nobles on horseback who had initially massed before the gate in the expectation that it would soon be opened, had suffered such great casualties that they were not likely to return in force in the near future.

The second thing that was clear was that the Greek soldiers who survived the ribalds' stones were now running to where they would be subjected to a constant storm of arrows and death. The third was that the fleeing Greeks were going to find it somewhere between difficult and impossible to escape now that the outer gate was closed and the interior walls along the roadway were manned by thousands of archers.

What we did not know for sure was how much of the Greek army we had caught in our trap. Was it enough to defeat them and end the war or not? We had not a clue.

Only one thing was certain, at least from our perspective, that it was a good thing the Greeks had turned back from continuing to move against the inner gate. That was because the gate and wall near it were temporarily undefended, and the battlements over the gate were so covered with the wreckage of many of the ribald-carrying wagons that it might have been impossible for the returning archers to find a place where they could stand to push out their arrows.

A few of the wagons atop the wall appeared to be somewhat intact, but most of them and their ribalds appeared to be beyond repair. In several places the wall itself been damaged, the worst being an archer slit just north of the gate which had somehow lost the stones that protected one of its sides.

"Where are you James? And where is Aron? He needs to run to the gate in the outer wall so can start the lightning when the Greeks gather in front of the gate to escape."

"Aron is gone, Commander. One of the ribalds got him. What is left of him is over by where the last of the ribald wagons was parked."

"Oh shite. Are you sure it is him?"

"Aye, Commander. I have been afraid something like this would happen ever since Thea was killed. It appears the poor sod did not even try to take shelter after he put fire to the last ribald."

Chapter Fifty

A few minutes later.

"Nicholas and I are going to the outer gate, Commander Oremus. Sergeant Howard is coming with me to put lightning and stones on the Greeks from the two ribalds on the outer wall. You and your apprentice are to stay here and remain in command of the city's inner wall. Throw the wreckage of the wagons and ribalds over the wall if that is what it takes to clear enough space for the archers. Just be careful it does not land on our own dead and wounded.

"I will send some of the "Reds" on the southern roadway wall back to help you as soon as possible. But you are only to send your apprentice to summon the Red Companies that were sent to the northern wall if you actually need them to fight off an attack."

With those parting words, and after listening carefully while Michael repeated them back to me, Nicholas, James, and I set off for the gate in the outer wall.

We heard the moans and cries of the wounded Greeks soldiers in the enclosure below us as we walked briskly along the city's deserted inner wall for a couple of minutes. We continued until we came to the newly installed, and lower, interior wall that stretched along the southern side of the roadway all the way out to the outer wall. It took but a moment to climb down a short wooden ladder to get aboard the lower interior wall and begin jogging along the top of it towards the city's outer wall visible in the distance a few miles ahead.

The only Greeks we saw and heard at first were either dead or seriously wounded. Those of the Greek soldiers who could run away from the ribalds' devastation had already done so. They did not yet realize that there was nowhere safe for them to go.

Some of the Greek wounded on the ground near the wall called out to us when they saw our heads bouncing up and down as we ran along the top of it. We ignored them and soon began sweating because we were moving fast in the heat. The early morning coolness had already begun to turn warm. Already the gulls and other birds had begun to arrive to pick at the dead. It was going to be another scorching hot day for sure.

It did not take long before we began seeing able-bodied Greeks and reached the first of our archers. They were shouting encouragements to each other and competing to pick off the

Greeks who were trying to seek shelter amongst the tents and wagons the states' forces had abandoned when they fled.

The archers we encountered paid us little heed as we hurried past them—just a brief nod or two or a knuckled forehead salute. Then they returned to nocking their arrows and seeking more targets for them.

Our men were in rare good spirits and shouting encouragements to each other. Being able to kill or wound an enemy who is not able to fight back effectively will do that for a soldier every time, especially if he had just been scared out of his wits by seeing so many of them.

At first, each time I came to a "Red" galley captain, I ordered him to send his lieutenant and his "Evens" to reinforce Michael at the gate, and help him "clear away the wreckage from the ribalds and hold the wall." Our conversations, when we had them, were brief, to the point, and very similar.

"Yes, what that loud thunder did to the Orthodox army was a great surprise. No, your "Evens" are not to return to their old positions; they are to report to Commander Oremus at the gate and do whatever he requires."

******

Nicholas, James, and I continued to jog along the top of the interior wall until I finally got tired and had to slow down to a walk. We began to see more and more live Greeks as we got closer and closer to the outer gate.

Many of the Greeks we saw were pretending to be dead to avoid attracting an arrow. Those who were moving appeared to be frantically running back and forth trying to find a way to escape, and rightly so since captured soldiers were usually killed or sold as slaves.

Those who were still trying to escape were mostly in the middle of the enclosure. They were there in an effort to stay as far away as possible from the archers on the walls, and most of them were still on their feet were moving towards the gate in the outer wall through which they had entered.

Heading back to the gate in the outer wall was logical direction for the surviving Greeks to run—they were desperately trying to get back to their camp and best way to get there, so far as they knew, was to go back the way they came. There were also a number of dead and wounded Greeks on the ground, but none who looked able-bodied. They had either run or were pretending to be dead or wounded in order to not attract an archer's attention.

We saw a few riderless horses peacefully grazing amongst the remains of the states' forces camp, but what we did not see was any Greeks on horseback or anyone who looked like a captain or sergeant trying to rally his men.

It was increasingly clear that the Greek lords and knights had either fallen or abandoned their men. Probably some of both since the Greek riders who reached the inner gate first and were closest to the ribalds when Aron delivered his revenge. And, of course, some of the riders may have dismounted when they realized that being on horseback made them and their horses splendid targets for the archers on the walls—which had been carefully built along both sides of the roadway with exactly that in mind.

What we did not see, at least not at first, were any of the states' forces and their camp followers who had remained in their camp instead of running away when they had the chance.

At first we thought that the Greeks might have slaughtered them all. But then a few of what appeared to be remainers began coming into view and we realized we might have jogged right past others of them without knowing they were there.

We had not seen the remainers at first because they were huddled tight up against the wall and we had not stopped to look down over the side to see if anyone was down there.

The presence of the remainers tight up against the wall was quite understandable—those of them who had not been cut down by the Greek riders galloping through their semi-deserted camp had run when they realized what was happening. And running away from the road had inevitably taken them towards the nearby walls where the archers had arrived hours earlier in the darkness.

The problem the surviving remainers had then encountered, of course, was that the some of the archers on the wall had not realized they were friendlies and had targeted them along with the invading Greek soldiers. It was similarly difficult to know for sure about the dead and wounded men we saw as we hurried towards the outer gate because most of the attackers and remainers dressed similarly. All we knew for sure was that there were a tremendous number of men on the ground.

******

We met Richard as we came around a curve and could once again see the city huge outer wall in the distance. He was standing atop the interior wall and in the process of moving some of his archers closer to the outer gate where there were more of the surviving invaders.

According to Richard, those of the surviving invaders who were able to reach the gate were well and truly screwed. They had escaped the ribalds' lightning and stones, and had somehow managed to retreat through the archers' storm of arrows, only to find the outer gate had been closed and the walls around it were teeming with archers.

As a result, Richard told us with a great deal of enthusiasm in his voice, the surviving invaders were either playing dead or were leaderless and running about in a desperate search for a place to hide from the arrows being constantly pushed by our men at anything that moved. I agreed and said I had reached the same conclusion.

The wisest of the surviving invaders, when they realized the gate was closed and there was no chance of escape, had begun falling down and pretending to be dead. Others had raised their hands in an effort to surrender. Nowhere, Richard reported, was there any resistance. We had not seen any either.

I had been hurrying to the outer gate with the intention of trying to destroy more of the invaders with lightning strikes and stones from the two ribalds wagons which had been pulled along the top to the wall and positioned above the outer gate. They, the ribalds' wagons that is, were now clearly visible from where we were standing.

After I finished telling Richard what I intended to do, and why I had ordered some his Reds to return to the inner gate, I started walking toward the remaining ribald wagons once again. But then I changed my mind and came to a stop after I had taken only five or six steps.

It had finally dawned on me that the Greek army was totally defeated and Aron was gone. It meant we could use the Greeks we took as prisoners to trade for the men taken by the Venetians and in any negotiations we had with the Greek commanders. Perhaps even more important for the future of Company, it also meant we did not need to use the remaining ribalds; we could keep them and use them to learn more about using the lightning to throw stones at our enemies in the years ahead.

"Stop pushing. Accept surrenders," I shouted. "Pass the word."

Richard looked up in surprise at my sudden change of heart. Then he smiled and nodded his agreement.

"Do you have anyone nearby who can gobble Greek?" I asked Richard as I turned around and walked back to re-join him.

Chapter Fifty-one
The aftermath.

It took most of the rest of that long, hot day for my lieutenants and I to organize the surrender of the defeated Orthodox soldiers. Our first move was to stop pushing arrows at them and send some of our Greek-gobbling auxiliaries along the wall calling on the Greek soldiers and their mercenaries to lay down their arms and surrender. We offered them better terms than they could have reasonably expected.

"All those who surrender immediately will be treated well and eventually ransomed and released; those who do not surrender immediately will be killed or sold to the Moors for slaves."

It took a while for the message to reach everyone. But it did and the Greek survivors gratefully surrendered, and rightly so since they were surrounded by archers on the walls around them and had no hope of escape. Almost all of the Greeks quickly threw down their arms and hurried to where we initially ordered them to assemble—to the road that ran through the middle of the states' camp.

Our second move was to walk in the hot sun among the prisoners, and separate them into groups and count them. It was harder than one would have expected to get to the prisoners since there was, at first, no way for us to climb down from the interior walls.

It took time, but it was an easily solved problem. Men were sent running to the outer wall to bring ladders from our ill-fated sally down the steps next to the gate, and then bring them through the enclosure to where the archers were waiting to descend on both sides of the enclosure.

Whilst we waited for the ladders to arrive we gathered the captains and sergeants from the nearby galley companies and gave the necessary orders and explanations.

The orders they were given were quite simple—every prisoner who had entered the enclosure of the states' forces on horseback, or whose clothes suggested he might be able to pay a ransom, was to be moved south to a position on the road next to the gate in the inner wall; all who might be Orthodox priests were to be moved north to the gate in the outer wall.

Everyone else, meaning the Orthodox army's great mass of rank and file foot soldiers, was to be gathered in the middle of the enclosure.

A message was sent to my father tasking him to send wagons to gather up the wounded prisoners and bring them into the shade along the walls for barbering by their fellow Greeks. He was also to arrange for the watering of our prisoners. Their food would have to come from their commanders and camp followers.

Letting them live was one thing; spending our coins to feed them was a step too far.

****** *Commander George Courtenay.*

The Orthodox army's common soldiers were the first to be counted and questioned. I took charge of them with Adam as my interpreter whilst Richard went off to question the prisoners from the city, the men who had attacked us in the rear just before the Orthodox army attacked.

Amongst the many things I asked Richard to try to discover was who sent them and why the first half of the coins was paid, but not the second. And what happened to the second half of the coins? Did they even exist and, if they did, how could we get out hands on them?

For my part, I particularly wanted to know if all the Orthodox army's fighting men had participated in the early morning attack, and also what, if anything, the Greek soldiers had been told before the attack. Most of all, however, I wanted to know who was left in the Greek camp. In other words, did we catch enough of their effective soldiers to end the fighting?

Translators who could gobble Greek were rounded up and our apprentice sergeants were put to work asking questions and periodically sending someone off with an escort of archers to join the priests and nobles who were being held elsewhere.

Late that afternoon, whilst we were still counting, separating, and questioning the prisoners, the Empress and my father arrived with a great guard of the Empress's Varangians. Richard opened the inner gate so she could ride into the roadway and he proudly accompanied her. It was a triumphal procession complete with a beating drum and a horn blower to announce her arrival.

The Empress was obviously savouring her victory even though she was clearly appalled when she saw the wretched condition of the wounded prisoners and the mangled bodies and body parts of the dead and badly wounded Greeks lying in front of the gate. It was a hot day and already some of the dead Greeks were beginning to swell and smell and attract seagulls and other birds. She arrived savouring her victory and ended up leaving abruptly in a state of distress with my father holding her arm to steady her.

By the end of the day we knew we had captured almost forty thousand men, and had killed and wounded more than ten thousand. It was my initial impression that the prisoners had been totally cowed by the noise of the ribalds, but that most of the dead and wounded had fallen to arrows pushed out of our longbows.

It also appeared to me that, for all practical purposes, the Orthodox army had ceased to exist as a fighting force. I certainly hoped so, and so did my men. As the soldiers' song the men often sang around our campfires at night said so true—"I want to go home, oh how I want to go home"

***** *Lieutenant Commander Richard Ryder*

My apprentice sergeant, Paul Cartwright, and I returned to the inner gate to question the men from the city who had attacked the inner gate just prior to the arrival of the Orthodox army. We took one of the auxiliaries with us to translate.

We started with the Greek-gobbling Orthodox priests. One was mortally wounded and asleep, but the other quickly became quite forthcoming, particularly after a bit of persuasion involving an offer of some pain-killing flower paste for his mortally wounded friend. What he told us absolutely astonished me.

According to the priest, it was the Empress's own guards, the Varangians, who had organized the bribery effort to open the *outer* gate to the Orthodox army and arranged for the necessary coins to be paid to the archer they thought was a turncoat.

He believed the story to be true, he said, because he had heard the "Metropolitan Andreas," the leader of the Orthodox Church in and around Constantinople, tell the priest's bishop what the Church's spies had learned about the Varangians' plan.

What was also stunning was that the captured priest also claimed to have heard the Metropolitan tell his bishop why the Varangians did it—because they assumed that sooner or later someone would be bribed to open the city's gates at a time and place when they and the other defenders, meaning the Company's archers and the states' forces, were not fully prepared to fight them off.

The Varangians did the bribing themselves, according to the priest, in the belief that knowing when and where the attack would occur made it likely that the attack would fail. It would also allow the Varangians to be fully prepared to move the Empress to safety in the event the defenders could not hold the city despite knowing the time and place of the attack.

In essence, the priest told us the Varangians took the lead in organizing the bribery to open the *outer* gate so they and their allies would know exactly when and where the attack would come. And even more importantly, so the attack would come when and where the Empress's supporters, meaning the archers, were most likely to defeat them.

We, of course, could hardly fault the Varangians since we had effectively solicited the bribes and accepted them for exactly the same reasons. The Orthodox priests and their "Metropolitan" apparently did not know this.

Where the Varangian's plan almost went wrong, according to the priest, was when the Metropolitan heard of the Varangians' plan. He decided that his city's faithful should be mobilized to make sure that the entrance of the Orthodox army did *not* fail as the Varangian's commander intended.

If what the priests told us was true, the Metropolitan himself was deeply involved in all aspects of the effort to get the inner gate opened so the Orthodox soldiers coming through the outer gate could continue on and get through the inner gate as well.

The Metropolitan's efforts, they said, had two parts. The first was to bribe the Latin priest whom the Varangians had used to bribe Adam to open the outer gate so that the priest would additionally bribe Adam to open the inner gate.

Secondly, according to the Orthodox priest, the Metropolitan did not trust the Latin priest to keep his word to additionally bribe Adam to open the inner gate, so he had *also* ordered the Orthodox Church's protection gangs to prevent the inner gate from being closed when the Orthodox army made its appearance.

A certain Konstantinos was charged by the Metropolitan with preventing the inner gate from being closed when the Orthodox army arrived.

Konstantinos was just the man for the job, the priest explained, being as he was the leader of the Orthodox Church's protection gangs in the city. As such, he was the only man in the city who could gather up a force of men on such short notice that the Empress's spies would not be able to learn about it in time to warn her so she could stop it.

We were in process of trying to verify the priest's astounding stories when who should appear but the Empress accompanied by her son and daughter, George's father, and a large number of her Varangian guards and courtiers. She wanted to see her victory so I, of course, stopped questioning the prisoners from the city and accompanied her and her retinue to the scene of her forces' triumph.

Unfortunately, she became a bit overbalanced by what she saw and decided to leave with George's father solicitously holding her elbow to steady her. That was fine by me; we had work to do and there were only a few hours left before darkness fell.

****** *Commander George Courtenay*

It was late in the evening by the time Richard and I, and our various lieutenants, finally sat down at the Commandery table to compare notes and discuss what we should do next.

Ours was not the victory supper and celebration one might have expected. To the contrary, it quickly became quite subdued when Richard told us that it was Eric and his Varangians who had bribed the outer gate open, and about the attempts of the attempts of the Orthodox Church's Metropolitan to both bribe open and force open the inner gate so the Greek army could enter the city.

We broke up earlier in order to get some rest. It had been a long and exhausting day and the prisoner counting and initial questioning was just beginning.

Our reality was that we faced a huge immediate problem because we had so many prisoners. Should we fatten up and sell our prisoners as slaves the way Uncle Thomas said the first Caesar did to enrich himself, or would the Company being known as a slaver be counterproductive in the long run?

It was an interesting question, but I quickly put the thought out of my mind and told everyone to forget it; it was contrary to the Company's policies about slaves and would piss off my father and Uncle Thomas for sure.

The decision I announced as I got up to leave the table was firm and somewhat of a compromise.

"We will not sell them and we will not spend a penny to feed and barber them."

Chapter Fifty-two

The war is over and we turn our
thoughts to profiting from it.

My lieutenants and I spent the night of the battle sleeping on the battlefield and on the wall with our men. The next morning we put some of the prisoners to work gathering their dead and loading what was left of them into the horse-drawn wagons we had used the day before to gather up the Greek wounded.

Our initial thought had been to dump the dead Greeks outside the gate in the outer wall for their own army to bury. But we reconsidered and changed our minds the next morning. What we saw that changed our minds was that there were too many dead Greeks and that what was left of their army was packing up to leave or had already left. So we had some of the prisoners dig a big hole and tossed them in.

What we also did on the morning after the fighting was send the wounded Greeks out beyond the moat to be cared for by their own people. We repaired the drawbridge, carried them out to the other side of the moat in wagons, and set them down in long rows of moaning and distressed men. Then we withdrew. Within minutes soldiers and camp followers could be seen passing amongst them.

"More likely to rifle through their clothes for something they can steal."

That was what I heard one of our grizzled sergeants say as we stood above the gate later that morning and watched the activity around the Greek wounded. The Greeks were out of luck if that was what they were doing—our lads had already cleaned them out.

****** *George Courtenay*

Much of time on the day after the battle had been spent closely questioning the captured nobles to find out who they were so we could decide how much ransom each of them might yield. Suffering such great losses and more than a day without food and water had definitely softened them up for our questioning. I and my helpers kept copious notes as we asked each of them about himself *and* the others.

Some of the riders proudly claimed to have lands and wealth and others to be the sons of rich merchants or land-owning gentry and franklins, but many were quite cagey—they each claimed to be able to afford only a small ransom, and then pointed to others as being much richer when we asked who they thought could pay more. They did so in an effort to distract us into looking for coins elsewhere instead of from themselves.

Later that afternoon I decided it was time to see just how gullible the two Orthodox priests at the inner gate might be now that Richard had softened them up. I passed the word for Adam to join me at outer gate and he arrived all out of breath about twenty minutes later. He would be, I informed him, my translator.

My preparations consisted of sending Nicholas and Adam to the largest market in the Latin Quarter to buy elegant clothes for me and a civilian tunic for Adam such as one of the city's scribes and translators might wear.

I was hungry so I rode to the Commandery for something to eat while they went shopping. They returned with an elegant embroidered tunic, a dandy's hat with a feather in it, and a fine sword and scabbard suitable for an ambassador. This time I decided to tie my hair into a sailor's knot and be an ambassador instead of one of Adam's fellow traitors.

Adam and I donned our new clothes and walked with Nicholas to where the two priests and the other survivors from the city mob were being held under the watchful eyes of half a dozen archers. They were sitting on the ground talking and eyed us intently as we approached.

One of the priests got to his feet, the other, the mortally wounded one with an arrow in his chest, was mostly asleep. He just lay on the ground and groaned every so often. The priest who stood had no idea who I was or what I wanted, but he knew instinctively from my dress and bearing that my arrival was somehow significant.

Despite some of the wounded men dying during the night, there were almost sixty men from the city's Orthodox protection gangs who had survived yesterday's attack including eight or nine who had been severely wounded. Most of the wounded men still had our arrows in them and were in great pain. Their screams and sobs were clearly distressing their unwounded mates.

Nicholas walked ahead of me and waved away the archers standing guard so they could not listen to what I had to say. Several of the older guards had looked startled when I arrived and eyed me rather keenly as they walked away. I suspect they may have recognized me.

"Who amongst you can gobble French or the crusader French some are now call English?" I called out to the prisoners. "Is there anyone who can gobble Varangian or Rus?"

I asked my questions loudly so all the prisoners could hear me, even those of the wounded who were not sleeping. Adam immediately repeated what I said in Greek. No one raised his hand.

Good. No one was likely to challenge me if I lied about my identity in order to tell lies for the priest to hear that would mislead his masters when we released him.

My effort to feed the priest information that would help mislead his masters was understandable; lies and deceptions were part and parcel of how important financial business was done in the civilized world the days following the Fourth Crusade. The old days when a man's word was his bond were gone.

There had been no response to my questions so I decided it was safe to claim to be the Ambassador of the Kievan Rus to the Empress's court, a position it was reasonable for me to pretend to hold for several reasons, not the least of which was that neither the position nor the Kievan Rus state still existed.

"Greeting fellow brothers in Christ," I announced in crusader French with Adam translating what I said into Greek. The prisoners were all listening intently. I pretended to be speaking to all of them. In fact, what I had to say was aimed at the able-bodied priest even though I did not look at him as I gobbled.

"I am Andrey of the Kievan Rus. Until today I was my country's ambassador to the Latin Empire. As you know, my and I people are Orthodox Christians and supporters of our beloved Patriarch. That is why I stopped for a few moments to talk to you even though I am on my way to the harbour to sail for home.

 "As you may have heard, I have been expelled by the Empress and must immediately leave begin my long trip home. But I heard of your capture whilst doing God's work and wanted to tell you what I have learned whilst at the Empress's court."

"The gate in the interior wall was supposed to be open for your army to enter peacefully. But it was not opened—because the French and Venetian ambassadors heard about the plan and informed the Empress in time for her to send her guards to fight you off and keep it closed.

"Unfortunately, I only this morning learned about the French and Venetian betrayal of our dear Patriarch. The French and Venetians betrayed our Holy Father when they realized that the Greek army could not win a war against the Empress's English archers.

"What the French and Venetians hoped to get from betraying our dear and most holy Patriarch was more merchant and money-lending stalls in the city's markets, and control of more of the city's churches.

"Having said that, I believe you still have a chance to keep your churches. That is because the Empress trusts the French and Venetians even less than she trusts you, her Greek-gobbling subjects.

"So it is up to you, my dear brothers in Christ, to decide whether or not to ransom yourselves and your churches by paying the Empress and the English archers for the losses you have caused them. If you do, I believe the Empress will let bygones be bygones and you will be able to continue to hold your churches; if you do not, the Venetians and French will almost certainly compensate her for her losses and take your churches and sell you to the Moors for slaves."

******

My story blaming the French and Venetians for the prisoners' troubles was well received. So was my suggestion that paying a ransom would be a viable path to their freedom, particularly since it was the common people in their parishes who would inevitably end up paying the ransom coins, not the priests and the men of each church's protection gang.

As a result of the favourable reception my lies received from the captured priest and the men of the churches' protection gangs, I decided to also visit the priests who had accompanied the Greek army and repeat a slightly different version of them—and that is what I did a few hours later. It was my first visit to them and I did so whilst once again posing as the departing Orthodox ambassador.

Of course I repeated my lies; an Englishman can hardly go wrong by convincing others to pay ransom coins to his company and causing trouble and confusion for the French and Venetians.

******

All in all, I was quite satisfied with myself by the time I changed back to my regular clothes and rode back to the Citadel Sunday night to spend my first night there in almost a week. I had planted the seeds for the Greeks and the priests of the Orthodox Church to become distrustful and angry with the Venetians and French.

But would the seeds grow? And would Elizabeth come for a visit that night? I was not sure, but I was strangely pleased and excited by both prospects.

Before I rode back to the Citadel, however, and after much thought and another discussion with my lieutenants, I scribed and sent a message to the commander of the Greek army about his captured men and the barbering of his wounded.

My message was carried by two prisoners from the Greek army, a priest and poor noble with no coins with which to pay a ransom. The two men were released late in the afternoon of the day after the battle to carry my message to the Greek commander about the care and feeding of his captured men.

The released prisoners were accompanied by hastily summoned three Greek food merchants from the city. The Greek army's "commander" was available to receive the message because he had avoided being killed or captured by remaining behind in his tent when he sent his men off to fight.

The message I scribed to the would-be emperor's brother informed him that I had taken the liberty of informing his captured subjects that he and his brother had agreed to ransom and feed them and to see to it that their wounded friends and family members were properly barbered.

We had done so, I scribed, because we were concerned that the men we captured would otherwise rise up against his kingly brother, and because we wanted to re-establish friendly relations with the king. A new friendship was something, I scribed, which might be possible now that he and his kingly brother knew they had "been betrayed by the French and Venetians just as we had been." *If that does not make him and his brother view the French and Venetian with suspicion, nothing will.*

We would, I further scribed to the Greek commander, send him our modest ransom requirements when we finished the lengthy task of getting the names and importance, *meaning their ability to pay*, of the nobles, knights, and priests we had captured.

In the meantime, I suggested, he might want to do make arrangements with the merchants for his men's food and water as soon as possible "since your men seem to be getting hungrier and angrier with you and your king as every hour passes."

In addition, I also scribed, "as I am sure you understand, all of the archers and others being held as prisoners by his army and the Venetians must be immediately released before the release of our prisoners can begin."

I was particularly pleased with myself when I re-read the message and made my mark on it—because before I sent it I had reached an agreement with the merchants for the Company's local shipping post to be immediately paid one coin out of every three the merchants received for the prisoners' food.

The merchants were honourable men in the best fashion of the Greek nobility and the moneylenders of London. They readily agreed to cheat the Orthodox army and pass the savings on to us. It would be a profitable end to a just war.

Epilogue

I was off to meet with my father privately in his room at the Citadel to discuss some family matters. The Company had re-floated its galleys and used them to clear the Venetians out of the Marmara Sea. My father and I needed to talk before I sailed for Venice and launched a surprise attack to take our well-deserved revenge on the Venetians.

Sweeping into Venice's harbour and attacking the city and its shipping was a matter of honour and ha to be done. It was also required by the Company' contract as a revenge for the men on the Company's roll who had lost their live or been wounded because of the Venetians. Besides, it was also an opportunity that might yield additional chests of coins and result in fewer Venetian transports competing with ours to carry passengers and cargos.

In any event, a major fight with the Venetians had become inevitable when Venice's transports carried the Orthodox army to fight us and its galleys directly attacked us at the harbour. In essence, our move against Venice would be a payback for the Venetians' assistance to the Greek army and their attacks on the Company's galleys and transports during the fighting that had ended several weeks ago.

The fact that the Venetians had sailed off whilst still holding some of the Company's men captive merely encouraged us even more, particular since the Venetians had refused to release or ransom them.

Hopefully, and with a little luck, an attack on Venice and its harbour would be as profitable as the recent war and motivate the Venetians to release our men. And even if it did not turn out that way, there would be a great deal of satisfaction in making the effort. In essence, they started the war and we would finish it.

In any event, it was too good of a coin-making opportunity for the Company to pass up, particularly since now most of our galleys and men were all together in one place and fired up by our recent victories.

My father knew all this and had asked me to visit him before I sailed. He did so, I assumed, because he intended to try to convince me that my younger brother and my even younger son were not ready to go on such a dangerous voyage. He wanted, I was sure, that they be sent to Cyprus for more seasoning as apprentices under new captains.

What he really hoped to accomplish, I knew, was that not all of the family eggs be put in one basket. I agreed and was pleased to be able to tell him so—I had already decided to announce that the two boys would not be going to Venice with us before he had a chance to ask.

It turned out that I was wrong; the boys were not the reason he wanted to talk with me.

******

I heard laughter and exuberant men's voices coming from my father's room as I walked alone down the corridor towards it. The door was cracked open.

The laughter and good will in the room was so great and real that it somehow lifted my already high spirits even higher as I walked up to the door.

"Hoy to all, may I come in?" I inquired with a cheerful sound in my voice as I rapped my knuckles on the wooden door frame, and entered unbidden.

A moment later my mouth gaped open in shocked surprise when I stepped into the room and realized who was sitting there drinking with my father—three of the Company's greatest enemies: the commander of the Varangians who had bribed Adam to open the gates to the Greek army, Ivan the Bulgarian who had refused to sally to help relieve the pressure on us when the Greeks were assaulting the wall, and the Metropolitan of Constantinople who had bribed Adam to open the inner gate and then sent the Orthodox Church's protection gangs to attack us to make sure the inner gate was open.

"Come in, George, come in. You know Eric and Ivan, of course. But please meet our friend Father Andreas, the Metropolitan of Constantinople."

I merely nodded towards the Metropolitan with a stony face. Making peace with Ivan and Eric was one thing; the Metropolitan, however, was going too far.

"You have strange drinking friends, father. I am surprised," I said harshly.

Truer words were never spoken. I was shocked and glaring at his visitors as I said it. And then, to make it worse, they all started laughing.

"Hoy, my boy, and good day to you too. And please come in and take a stool. We have much to talk about."

My father said it all with a merry twinkle in his eye as if what I was about to hear was something minor. But I immediately knew it was important.

"The thing is, George, that the four of us were more deeply involved in your recent moves and countermoves against the Patriarch's army than you know."

He made the announcement as he stood up, grabbed a large jar and began pouring wine into a bowl, which he promptly handed to me with a gesture towards an empty wooden stool.

I took it and sat with a stony face whilst he topped off the bowls of the other men and his own.

"You did not tell anyone about your plan to trap the Greek army in the states' enclosure, and rightly so. But it was plain to see that was your plan. And the spies of the Empress, the Varangians, and the Orthodox Church all confirmed it by telling us the various different stories you were spreading to different people. We, fortunately, were the only ones with all the information and able to figure it out. It was brilliant, by the way. I am truly proud of you.

"The thing is this—we wanted to help you since all four of us wanted the Company to be successful and the Empress to be unharmed and stay in power. I, of course, because of my deep affection for the Empress; Eric because he needed to know exactly when the Greeks would attack because he was sworn to protect her and needed to know when to be ready to evacuate her.

"Somewhat similarly, Ivan absented himself and took his men from the state's enclosure because he wanted the Greeks to think they could enter it and rush to inner gate unopposed so your men could kill them. He did so because he wants one of his sons to marry Elizabeth to get her late husband's estates in France in case the Greeks come back and he has to run." *Marry Elizabeth?*

I was astonished as you might imagine.

"Excuse me, father, all that may be true, but we would not have won if we had not beaten off the Greek mob that attacked us in the rear." I looked hard at the Metropolitan as I spoke.

"But you did beat them off, George—because they attacked too soon, eh?"

"Well, yes. We were lucky."

"And why did they attack prematurely, George? I can tell you why—because the Metropolitan told them when to attack just as he somehow forgot to tell them, the first time the city rose, that the arrival of the Greek army would be delayed."

"But that does not make any sense."

"Oh but it certainly does, George, it certainly does. Let me ask you this: If you were Andreas here, and serving as the Metropolitan over all the Orthodox churches in the Empress's empire, you would have to appear to be loyal to the Patriarch by calling out your faithful and your protection gangs to help fight his enemies, would you not?"

"Well yes. I suppose."

"But if you were my friend Andreas, would you really want the rising of the people or the protection gangs to be successful in helping the Greek army enter the city—if it meant the Patriarch would return to take your place as the city's most important churchman, especially if you liked living in the Church's fine palace in Constantinople with many servants and getting all the coins from the Orthodox churches in and around the city?"

"Well no."

My father just grinned at me and nodded. "Neither did Andreas," he said.

-End of the book-

"Are you sure, really sure?"

"Yes, I ran the DNA tests myself and there is no doubt about it. There are three from the family in Cornwall directly in the paternal line where they should not be. Two are from early in the thirteenth century and one very recent one from the twentieth."

"From the twentieth century? My God. Should we tell Her Majesty?"

The Venetian Gambit

Chapter One

Today's enemies; tomorrow's friends.

It was the summer of 1219 in Constantinople and the Latin Empire's war with the invading Greeks and Venetians had just come to a somewhat satisfactory conclusion. As a result, a few days later, the commander of the Cornwall-based Company of Archers, George Courtenay, was sitting with his lieutenants at the long wooden table in the main hall of Company's recently acquired Commandry.

The Empress of the Latin Empire had given the walled fortress-like Commandry to the Company to use as it headquarters during the recent war. It was in the city's Latin Quarter, the section of the city where most of residents attended church services performed by Latin-speaking priests. The Company's leaders intended to garrison the Commandry and keep it permanently in case the Greeks and their allies came back and the Company needed it once again.

More specifically, the Commandry was located near the imposing inner defensive wall on the landward side of the world's greatest city. The city itself was located on a peninsula that jutted out into the Marmara Sea such that on three sides the city's walls were right up against the water. It was the landward side of the city that was the most vulnerable and the only side that had both an inner and an outer defensive wall. They were strong; so high and thick that a cart path ran along the top of them.

The men were gathered around the table to talk about something of great importance—what their company, the Company of Archers, a free company from Cornwall, should do in the immediate future with their galleys and men now that the Empress's war with the Greeks and Venetians was over. It had successfully ended with the defeat of the Greek army and its total collapse.

As a result of her victory, in which the Company had played a significant role, the Empress was still on the throne as her son's regent. That was important so far as the assembled men were concerned—it meant the Empress's various toll-collecting and defence agreements with the Company of Archers remained intact.

George Courtenay and all of the Company's lieutenant commanders were present except for Yoram Damascus and George's Uncle Thomas. Yoram commanded the multi-walled fortress the Company had built and was continually strengthening on the island of Cyprus just off the coast of the Holy Land. It was the hub of all of the Company's operations east of Gibraltar and the home of its galley repair yard and six of its weapons-making smiths and their assistants. It was also the home of the Company's efforts to make man-made lightning and the "ribaldis" from which the lightning could sometimes be made to throw rocks at the Company's enemies.

The formidable fortress was located immediately next to the city walls of Cyprus's bustling port city of Limassol. Large stores of grain and firewood, a deep well inside its innermost bailey, and a large flock of chickens in one section of its outer bailey provided the fortress's defenders with a two-year, or longer, supply of the food and water they would need whilst they waited for a relief force to reach them. A short and narrow walled road somewhat safely connected the fortress to the much weaker defensive walls of the city.

Yoram and a handful of the Company's archers had spent the recent war hunkered down behind the fortress's imposing curtain walls. They had done so in order to hold it for the Company despite the temporary absence of most of its garrison to serve in Constantinople. George's Uncle Thomas had similarly remained with a few men in Cornwall's Restormel Castle, the site of the Company's archer-training grounds and its scribing and summing school for the likely lads that were destined to lead the Company in the years ahead.

Similar small numbers of the Company's men had hunkered down to hold the Company's shipping posts at the various ports where the Company provided shipping services and at the Company-controlled castles of Okehampton, Launceston, and Exeter's Rougemont, the fortresses that guarded the approaches to Cornwall.

Everyone at the table was in high spirits despite the heat of the day causing them to sweat profusely and have great thirsts. The sun came through the openings in the walls of the Commandry and lit the little pieces of dust floating in the air, and the wine flowed freely. The men had gotten so used to the poor visibility in the dark and damp Commandry, and the foul battlefield and human smells that hung in the air around them, that they no longer noticed them.

Distant voices in the bailey and the city beyond it could be heard through the Commandry's unshuttered wall openings and open doors. The fighting had ended only a few days earlier, but already life in the great capital city of the Latin Empire was proceeding as if nothing much had happened during the past few weeks. The only other activity in the room involved a couple of the city's many cats. They were prowling and growling under the table as they searched for scraps and discarded bones. It was an altogether peaceful and relaxed scene.

The Company's Commander and his lieutenants were a cheerful lot as they laughed, drank, and made fun of each other as only men that have for long years been brothers in arms can do—and they certainly had every reason to celebrate; they had, they happily reminded each other, out-fought the forces of the Orthodox Patriarch and his would-be new emperor, the Greek king of Epirus. More specifically, they had, and there was absolutely no doubt about it, done most of the fighting that had won the war to keep the Empress on the throne. Moreover, they had done so despite being badly outnumbered.

It was a significant victory. It meant the Greeks' Byzantine Empire would not be resurrected to replace the Latin Empire and once again rule over the various states around Constantinople, not this time at least.

The victory was particularly good news for the Cornwall-based Company of Archers and gave the men sitting at the table a great deal of satisfaction, and rightly so—it meant the coins their Company had begun earning by helping to protect the Empress's regency and her walled capital city would continue to flow into the Company's coin chests in its Cyprus stronghold off the coast of the Holy Land and into the even more numerous chests in the windowless treasury room above Restormel Castle's great hall.

Restormel Castle, as everyone now knows, was the great stone castle in Cornwall where the family of the Company's commander traditionally lived, the Company's school for young boys was located, and its new recruits received their initial training as archers. Even some of the Company's retirees had chosen to live year-round in the nearby villages for some unfathomable reason or another.

George Courtenay, the Company's relatively new commander, was sitting at the Commandry's long table in Constantinople's scorching summer heat only because of the recent war. Traditionally the Company's commander spent the summer half of the year in Cornwall and the winter half at its great citadel on Cyprus, whilst stopping to visit the Company's various shipping posts as he sailed back and forth between the Company's two great strongholds.

Being able to be where the weather was relatively good was one of the perks of wearing the seven stripes of the Company's commander on the front and back of his hooded Company tunic. The downside, of course, was that he had to do a lot of travelling in dangerous waters and was expected to be wherever the Company's men were fighting.

What was not at all satisfactory to the men sitting at the table, most of whom were wearing the five or six stripes of major captains and lieutenant commanders, was that the Company had suffered a substantial number of dead and wounded men in the recent fighting.

As a result, George and his lieutenants had spent the past few days dealing with a large number of war-related problems—making sure their wounded men were properly barbered, deciding what to pay their men in prize money and how soon to pay them, and deciding what to do with their many Greek prisoners. What they had *not* yet resolved were the all-important questions as to what the men of the Company should do next now that the war was over, and how they should replace the men that had been lost.

All of the men at the table were Company veterans and their talk was animated with much arm waving and table pounding. Even so, a consensus was quickly reached on everything except what to do in the days ahead *after* the Company's many war-related uncertainties and concerns were resolved.

The question as to what the men, galleys, and refugee-carrying transports should do now that they were no longer needed to carry away refugees and help defend the Latin Empress and her great capital city was both understandable and significant. George had summoned almost all of the Company's archers and war galleys, over three thousand men and thirty-six seagoing galleys, to help defend the city and the Empress's expensively purchased God-given right to rule it as her young son's regent.

Indeed, the need for men to help defend the city and the Empress that ruled it had been so great that some of the older boys attending the Company's school at Restormel Castle had been ordained early as Angelovian priests and sent out as apprentice sergeants to run errands for the Company's mostly illiterate captains and to help them by running errands for them and doing their reading, scribing, and summing.

Even the Company's retirees had been asked to return to duty—and almost all of them that could had answered the call, even one of the Company's previous commanders, George's father, and two of his honorary uncles who had retired a couple of years earlier as lieutenant commanders, Henry Rower and Harold Lewes.

The cloying stench of the dead and dying Greeks outside the great city's walls still fouled the air and testified to the great victory that had resulted from the Company's efforts. Or, as the recent fighting had been so elegantly described by the Commander's scar-faced honorary uncle, Harold Lewes, who had been brought out of retirement to once again take charge of the Company's galleys and sailors, "we kicked the shite out of them Greek bastards and their Venetian friends."

Harold was not the Commander's real uncle, of course; only his Uncle Thomas was actually his father's brother. Harold was, however, someone who was even more meaningful to George in many ways. Harold and Henry Rower and the seventeen archers that George's father, William, had led away from a Saracen siege in Lebanon's Bekka Valley, and helped carry young George to safety, were his "uncles" because the Commander had grown up among them and accompanied them on many of their campaigns. He had called them "uncle" for as long as he could remember.

Lieutenant commanders Harold Lewes and Henry Rower had not been with the Commander's father and what was left of the Company's men until the archers reached the Syrian port of Latika, and then managed to get their hands on a decrepit war galley and use it to carry them to safety. It was a story George had heard many times.

Harold and Henry had been rowing on the galley as slaves when George's father and his Uncle Thomas bought the galley from its poxed captain with coins they had taken off a murderous bishop. William had freed them and they had promptly joined the Company as its second and third new recruits. The first had been the bishop's clerk, Yoram, now the commander in Cyprus. Those three and the seventeen surviving archers had been George's "uncles" ever since.

Now there were only seven of George's honorary uncles left and only four of them had been among the one hundred and ninety-two archers that had originally gone crusading with King Richard. Crusading and serving in a free company were dangerous ways for a man to earn his bread and coins.

Lieutenant Commander Harold Lewes was strongly in favour of sallying forth in the Company's galleys and using them to quickly re-establish the Company's control over the Sea of Marmara and the narrow straits that lay at either end of it. As soon as that was accomplished, Harold wanted the Company's galleys to sail straight back to Cyprus and do whatever it took to resume the Company's normal operations—the carrying of wealthy refugees to safety from wherever there was fighting between the Christians and the Saracens, and the moving of passengers, cargos, and money orders back and forth among the many ports where the Company had established shipping posts.

Harold Lewes was in favour of such a course of action, the men gathered around the table all understood and appreciated, because he was oriented towards the sea, not because Cyprus was where he, Henry, and William Courtenay, the new Commander's father, had each built imposing three-room retirement villas with stone floors a few years earlier. That was where their wives and gardens waited. Besides, as Harold loudly emphasized while banging his bowl of wine on the table, carrying passengers, cargos, and money orders was a lucrative trade.

So far as George and his other lieutenants were concerned, Harold was right to be concerned about the need for the Company to resume its normal coin-earning voyages and other activities as soon as possible. And he was also right that the first order of business was to rid the Marmara Sea of the Venetians. Clearing the Venetian galleys out of the Marmara was necessary so the Empress's tolls could once again be collected at the entrances to the narrow Bosphorus and Dardanelles straits which were at each end of the relatively small Marmara Sea.

But what should be done after that? Harold Lewes, once again the Company's "first sailor," at least temporarily until he retired again, was certainly right about the need to re-establish the Company's normal coin-earning operations. But were there other things that should be done first? That was the real question in front of them.

It was no secret that the ever-present Moorish pirates as well as other merchants, various free companies, and several maritime states, particularly Venice and Genoa, had quickly stepped in when the Company withdrew most of its most of its men from the Mediterranean and elsewhere in order to concentrate them at Constantinople. That was to be expected. Unfortunately, as a result, it was the Company's competitors and enemies that were now carrying many of the passengers, cargos, and money orders that the Company's galleys and transports would have carried had George not summoned every available man and galley to help defend the Latin Empire's French-born Empress.

That some of the Company's competitors were now earning the coins that would have otherwise gone into the Company's chests did not in any way distress the men seated at the table. To the contrary, every one of them had enthusiastically agreed, and still did, with George's decision to bring almost all of the Company's men, galleys, and transports to Constantinople.

They all understood it was something that had to be done if the Company was to continue receiving the coins that it earned by protecting the Empress and collecting her tolls. They were not fools—they wanted to continue collecting and keeping the tolls *in addition* to continuing to earn coins by charging high prices to carry panic-stricken refugees trying to flee from wherever there was fighting and normal prices to carry regular passengers and cargos from port to port.

Of course they did; having two ways to get their coins was always better than having only one and much better than having none. They held their high ranks in the Company because they understood such things.

But was re-establishing the Company's normal operations the first order of business *after* what was left of the Venetian fleet was thrown out of the Marmara and the Empress's toll-collections were re-started?

Richard Ryder, George's number two and the commander of the Company's horse archers was not at all sure. He and his horse archers were normally stationed at Okehampton, Launceston, and Exeter on the approaches to Cornwall. He was anxious to return and restore the patrols that kept the peace in Cornwall and troublemakers out.

"You may be right, Harold, but it is Cornwall that I am worried about. We have not heard from anyone in England for weeks, so only God knows what is happening in Cornwall now that I and most of my horse archers are here instead of keeping the peace and patrolling the approaches.

"It is worrisome because the crown cannot be trusted, particularly if the rumours are true that William Marshal has been replaced as the boy-king's regent. The crown could become particularly dangerous if whoever is the boy's new regent finds out how much wealth the Company has accumulated at Restormel.

"And there are always greedy priests and land-seeking nobles to be turned away. We need to use a couple of our faster galleys to get me and our horsemen back to Cornwall before winter arrives and the weather in the Channel turns so foul that we dare not sail."

"Aye, both of you are right," was George's response as he lifted his bowl and waved it in agreement before taking a sip.

"But we cannot ignore the Venetians and the French. They are responsible for many of our losses, especially the Venetians. Our men know it as much as we do."

George took a sip from his bowl and then stood up looked at his lieutenants intensely as he continued. The room suddenly went silent. They instinctively knew that a decision had been made.

"The Venetians, in particular, must be made to pay, and pay handsomely, for helping the Greeks come against the Empress and us. The articles of our Company's compact, on which every one of us and all of our men made our marks, require a terrible revenge on anyone who causes an archer to be hurt or killed. And that has surely happened in the past few weeks.

Then George stopped and looked at his lieutenants sitting at the table with him before he emphatically stated the obvious.

"Our men expect vengeance, and rightly so. Besides, if we do it right we should be able to get a fair amount of coins out of it. So the only questions are how soon do we hit the Venetians and where and how do we best hit them?"

George's lieutenants growled their agreement and nodded their heads.

Then he told them his plan. *At least the first part of it.*

****** *George Courtenay*

"Well, what did you decide?" Elizabeth asked as she ran her finger down my chest. She seemed strangely subdued.

"If we can finish getting our galleys ready, we will sortie out tomorrow with all of our galleys and clear the Marmara Sea of Venetians from the Bosphorus to the Dardanelles. Then we will return to Constantinople to drop off our wounded for barbering and to take on water and supplies.

"But there is no need to worry—some of our galleys and men will stay here to collect the tolls and be available in case the Greeks or Venetians are foolish enough to come back and try again. Most of them, however, with me leading them, will immediately sail for Cyprus in case our fortress needs to be relieved."

I was telling Elizabeth a lie, of course, but she talked too much and that was the message I wanted her to spread to the court's gossips. It was the same message our men had been told when they were given advances on their prize monies a few hours earlier. As my lieutenants and I knew they would, the men took their hard-won coins and most of them rushed off to visit the city's taverns and public women to spend them.

There was no doubt in my mind that with both our men and the Empress's courtiers knowing our plans—every pimp, tavern owner, and public woman in Constantinople would soon know we would be sailing for Cyprus. And that meant the new Venetian ambassador and every other Venetian spy in the city would also know. I was counting on it.

"I will miss you," Elizabeth said.

"Not to worry, it will not take long to see them off. I will probably be back by the day after tomorrow or soon thereafter. The only question is whether we will find any Venetian galleys in the waters near the city."

"That is not what I meant," Elizabeth said as she got my attention by grabbing a couple of hairs on my chest and pulling them. "Have you not heard what my mother has arranged for me?"

"Ouch. I guess not. What has she done?"

"I am to marry the oldest son of the Epirus king and move there with him."

"What! How soon?" I was so stunned that I almost shouted as I sat up and stared at her in the dim and flickering light provided by the candle in my room.

"As soon as the Epirus king finishes ransoming back the men you captured. Probably next Sunday according to my mother, maybe even sooner. She wants to hurry and get it over with so I can be married in the cathedral and accompany the king's entourage when he returns to Epirus. *And I want to hurry too; I must.*

"But why the hurry? What happened for God's sake?"

"My mother says King Theodore wants to join our families so she will be an ally if anyone comes against him now that he has been defeated and weakened. She says *he* wants the marriage prayers said next week, but I think she is the one that insisted—probably because I am a widow and his oldest son is much younger than me. She is afraid the king will change his mind." *That is not the only reason for my mother's hurry, but it is certainly all I am going to tell you.*

"Oh." I did not know what to say. So after a few seconds I pulled her down on top of me and said it again. "Oh."

I vaguely remembered Elizabeth slipping out of my bed sometime in the night. In any event, she was gone when I woke up in the middle of the night with such a tremendous need to pee that I barely made it to the ornately-painted clay piss pot in the corner of the room. I was able to find it in the total darkness because it was in the very corner of the room.

My room in the Empress's citadel was pleasantly cool, as it always was first thing in the morning, and I was ravenously hungry when the crowing of the roosters in the citadel's bailey woke me at dawn.

/Centuries later George's piss pot would be prominently displayed in the British Museum as the royal punch bowl used for the mulled wine when the head of the house of Saxe-Coburg

made a winter visit to Windsor to arrange Prince Albert's marriage to Queen Victoria. It was probably part of Elizabeth's dowry and found its way to Windsor as a gift when some Greek prince or princess married into the royal family./

****** *George Courtenay*

After breaking my fast I walked down to the harbour to wave farewell to Major Captain Michael Oremus and give him a few meaningless last minute orders and admonitions. And then I stood on the busy quay and watched as Michael's galley cast off its mooring lines and began its voyage to Cyprus. He was returning there with his galley's archers to reinforce, or attempt to relieve as the case might be, the small Company garrison that was holding our Cyprus stronghold.

The rest of us did not sail later in the day as I had hoped and intended. I reluctantly accepted the need for a further delay because our galleys were not ready. Instead, we spent the day re-floating the last of the galleys that would be going out and re-stocking them with food and water for the voyage and with the weapons and arrows from their stores that had been removed for use when we were fighting on land.

Our sailors did the work necessary to prepare the galleys; most of the archers spent the day recovering from drinking too much the night before. They did so as they practiced archery and sat around telling each other yarns whilst they used goose feathers to re-fletch the arrows that had been damaged when they bounced off the ground or were pulled or cut out of the dead and wounded Greeks and their horses.

As a result of the delay, my lieutenants and I were able to sup together in the Commandry again that night. And once again, as you might imagine, our meal and our men's was cooked goose with fresh flatbreads that we cover with cheese and sausage slices or dipped into a tart vinegar from Italy and olive oil. It was all very tasty, especially when taken with numerous bowls of wine.

And once again our young apprentice sergeants silently listened from where they sat at the end of the table and the cats hissed and slapped at each other as they fought over the bones and other scraps that were thrown on the Commandry's stone floor. It might have been my imagination, but there seemed to be more of them every day, cats that is. We found them quite amusing, especially the little kittens.

My lieutenants got the bad news right after one of the serving girls finished using a wineskin to fill our bowls and was motioned away to give us privacy.

"Well lads, I spoke with the Empress this morning and I have a bit of bad news—it looks as though we will *not* be raiding along the Greek coast after we clean the Venetians out of the Marmara. It seems as though, as some sort of a peace gesture, Theodore, the King of Epirus, is going to marry his oldest son to the Empress's daughter next week before he returns to Epirus. In so doing, it will make the Empress, and thus the Company, one of his allies."

The news that the Greeks we had been fighting so bitterly a few days earlier would now be our friends and allies was a great surprise to everyone, except for my father. He had become quite close to the Empress *once again* and already knew all about it. From the looks of sympathy on their faces, it was not just because yesterday's enemy was about to become a friend; they obviously knew Elizabeth and I had been getting to know each other on a regular basis ever since I had arrived.

They were mostly concerned about the effect of the marriage on the Company.

"What about the rest of the ransom coins we are due from King Theodore for his men?" Richard asked. "Will we get them or not? The remaining prisoners we are holding are getting hungry and weak, especially the wounded. Does the peace agreement mean we are supposed to buy food for them?"

"We are supposed to get the rest of the ransom coins tomorrow, so hold off on using the Company's coins to buy food and barbering for the Greek prisoners," I replied. "Theodore has already been told he can buy food for the men we captured if he wants them to eat."

The men mumbled their agreement so I proceeded to explain what I knew.

"When I met with the Empress, she told me she had informed King Theodore that the prisoners belonged to the Company, not to her, so he would have to pay their ransoms to us and feed them if he wanted them back. So far as I know, the ransom price we agreed with Theodore's chancellor for the return of his men is still in effect. I understand he has some of the coins he needs and is trying to borrow the rest from the city's moneylenders.

"Retired Commander Courtenay," I said as I grinned across the table at my father, "will stay ashore with the Empress when we sortie tomorrow to make sure that both she and the Company stand firm about our receiving the rest of the ransom coins before our prisoners are released. He is the best man for the job as he is rumoured to be quite knowledgeable about her .. ah, thoughts, .. as we all know."

Everyone roared with laughter and pounded their bowls on the table, even my father. We had survived the fighting and life was good.

"Now about tomorrow's sortie," I said.

Chapter Two

Where are the Venetians?

"Cast off the forward lines."

I was daydreaming when the sailing sergeant standing next to me on the roof the forward deck castle of Harold's galley suddenly leaned forward and bellowed out the order to the men standing below us. He shouted so loudly that I jumped and a gull flying overhead suddenly changed its course. It was going to be another very hot summer day.

The sergeant's name on the Company's roll was Arthur Smithson because he was the son of a village smith from somewhere in the north. Arthur did not know it that day, of course, and neither did anyone else, but he would only be setting foot on land a few more times.

Twenty-nine of the Company's galleys followed Harold's galley out into the Marmara Sea. They were fully crewed in order to be at maximum strength in the event of a fight. I may have ranked Harold, but I was on board as his honoured passenger, as was our tradition, not as the galley's captain. And it was a good tradition in this case—because Harold was thought to be the best and most experienced sailor in the Company, and certainly a better sailor man than I would ever be.

There were only twenty-nine Company galleys following us out of the harbour. That was because seven of our galleys, the least seaworthy according to Harold, remained pulled ashore and empty on the strand in front of Constantinople's great wall.

The galleys we were leaving behind would bide there and remain empty because we did not have enough men available to crew them due to the butcher's bill of the recent war. In the interim they would be used as the sleeping quarters of some of our wounded men until we could return and either recover them or destroy them, the galleys that is, so they could not be used against us.

It was a lovely day as I stood on the roof of the forward deck castle as Harold Lewes's galley rowed out of the harbour. Harold was standing next to me along with the galley's sailing sergeant. It was a bit crowded on the little roof as our new apprentices, my Roger Abbot and

Harold's John Soames, were standing behind us. There was not a cloud in the sky and the day was already getting uncomfortably warm. There was a nice breeze.

Every one of the galleys we were going out with were of the type favoured by the Company—seagoing two-deckers with deep and narrow hulls, two masts, oar-hole plugs so they could handle heavy weather if their crews pulled in the oars of their lower tier of rowing benches and ran with the wind, and deck castles fore and aft on which the captain and some of his sergeants and archers could stand. Each galley had a small deck castle forward for the use of whoever was the highest ranking man on board, meaning me on Harold's galley, and a larger castle in the stern near the galley's shite nest for Harold, our apprentices, and Harold's lieutenant and key sergeants.

About a third of our galleys had the protruding underwater rams favoured by the Venetians. They were subject of an ever-continuing dispute amongst our captains and sailors as to whether their slightly slower speed and nose-down tendency caused by the weight of the ram protruding out of the front of galley's hull was worth their slightly slower speed.

The captains whose galleys had rams inevitably defended them; those whose galleys did not claimed the rams to be a hindrance. Harold's galley did not have a ram. Privately he had long ago told me that he did not sail with one because he thought galleys without rams were safer in heavy weather.

Every one of our galleys sailed ready for a fight with the Venetian fleet. There were two archers on almost every oar and every galley was fully loaded with weapons, water, and supplies, but *not* so heavily loaded that piles of meat and live chickens and other livestock were making noise and pooping on our decks to make the decks slippery and get in the way if there was fighting.

Even so, the decks of our galleys were not entirely clear. To the contrary, every deck was crowded with arrow-making supplies of goose feathers, wood that could be carved into arrow shafts, and all the potential arrow points that could be found. Sitting on the deck and rowing benches "arrow making" was a major occupation of the archers on every galley in the days that followed.

We had more than enough arrows to fight the Venetian fleet if we were able to find it. Although the men did not know it yet, it was what we would be doing *afterwards* that made having more arrows a very real necessity. As a result, the captains had been ordered to use their sails whenever possible instead of having their archers row—so the archers could spend their time practicing their archery and making more arrows.

In any event, we were ready for almost anything in the Marmara, including the Venetian fleet if we were able to find it. Whether we would actually be able to find the Venetians in the next few days was not at all certain—they had retreated and disappeared after we had fought off their efforts to destroy the Company's unoccupied galleys, the ones that had been pulled ashore on one of the narrow bits of strand that lay between the sea and the city's walls.

The galleys had been pulled ashore so their crews could fight on Constantinople's walls against the Venetians' Greek allies. If we had not done so, our galleys would have been at anchor without anyone to defend them, thus, vulnerable to being taken by the Venetian fleet or destroyed in a storm. Now, of course, the galleys that remained pulled up on the strand were still empty because we did not have enough men to properly crew them for a fight.

It was likely to be awhile before we did, but we would return for them.

******

So far as the men and everyone else in the city knew, we would only be out searching for the Venetian fleet for a few days but, out of an abundance of caution, were prepared to be gone for ten or twelve days, or even longer if the Venetians ran for it and we had to chase them—at least that was the story that had made its way into the city as our sailors visited the taverns and street women.

The only people in all of Constantinople who knew the truth, that most of our galleys would not be returning any time soon, were the Empress, my father, and Henry Rower. Henry was staying behind to be my father's deputy with Michael Oremus as their number three when and if he returned from Cyprus.

I had thought about telling Elizabeth that I would not be returning immediately, but decided, under the circumstances, to leave that to her mother. The Empress had nodded her head with a sad look of understanding when I pointedly told her that she and my father and his deputy were the only people who knew we were not likely to be back for several months.

My younger brother, John, and my son, George, were *not* sailing with us. They too were staying ashore in Constantinople. That was because, or so I had claimed when I ordered them to remain ashore, we needed to shuffle around all of our Company's apprentices so as to give them new experiences.

As a result of my order, John was staying in Constantinople as my father's apprentice sergeant and George, my thirteen year old son, was staying as the apprentice sergeant of old Henry Harcourt, the old galley rower who had become the Company's expert at fighting on land who had come out of retirement to help us fight the Greeks. Running errands and reading and scribing for my father and Henry was acceptable for the boys; they were both much too young to be put in harm's way if it could be avoided.

Henry Rower was staying behind to hold the Commandry. He was also charged with making sure the two hundred or so of the Company's wounded and poxed men not sailing with us were fed enough flower paste to eliminate their pain and were being properly barbered, watered, and prayed over such that they might survive and return to active duty. They would tend to each other with the assistance of physicians and barbers hired from the city.

Additionally, if the past was any guide, our wounded and poxed men would soon attract a large number of hopeful local widows, runaway girls, and street women. That was because any man who had served honourably and was unable to return to duty was always provided with a place to live and half pay for the rest of his life.

The high priority the Company gave to protecting and barbering its wounded and poxed men, and their ability to attract women to care for them, was a good thing for John and George and all of our apprentices to see and understand. Not acting like kings and abandoning our men when a war was over or they were wounded was a good thing; it made our recruiting easy and discouraged desertions.

Also staying behind in the city were the four hundred or so archers and sailors crewing our four toll-collecting galleys and about two hundred of our temporarily reactivated retirees and some of the men that were permanently stationed at our various shipping posts. The latter would stay at the Commandry and be returned to their various shipping posts and retirement homes as soon as transportation to their posts and homes became available.

Remaining ashore with them were the six archers permanently assigned to our local shipping post and our newly appointed post captain, Edward Frost. Edward did not have an apprentice assigned to help him because he already knew how to scribe and sum as a result of having been a student at my Uncle Thomas's school for boys at Restormel Castle.

My father had answered the call and come out of retirement to join us for the duration of the war. He was left in overall command of our men in Constantinople with Henry Rower as his number two. He, my father that is, would continue to be based in the Empress's citadel so he could stay in close contact with the Empress and lead the defence of her citadel if the city turned against her again or another enemy approached its walls.

It would be up to my father, as the Company's highest ranking man in the city, to decide when things had settled down enough such that he and Henry could return to Cyprus to resume their retirements. When they and the others left, men seconded from the toll-collecting galleys would help guard the local shipping post guard and the coins that were constantly being accumulated there for shipment to Cyprus and Cornwall.

I could tell from talking to my father that he was itching to get back to Cyprus and my stepmother, and it was not because of the lice around his dingle; he was getting bored now that the fighting was over and the Empress needed less and less advice and personal attention. I felt the same way; I was increasingly thinking about my family in Cornwall.

Truth be told, I was glad for an excuse to leave Elizabeth behind.

******

We waved farewell to the surprisingly large number of people that had come to see us off, mostly women despite our men having been in the city for only four or five weeks, and rowed out of the harbour an hour or so after sunrise. The other galleys in the fleet were waiting and followed us out.

The women, or so it seemed to me, thought we would be back in a few days. So did everyone else for that matter. That was encouraging; it suggested that the first of our Venetian gambits had been successful.

My father, Henry, and the Empress had come to see us off. Elizabeth did not. She was either royally pissed because her mother told her I would not be coming back, or, and this was my very foolish hope at the time, so distraught at permanently losing me that her mother would not allow her to come because showing her distress in public might affect her coming marriage.

I nodded to Harold as soon as we cleared the harbour and he immediately turned our fleet to the left for the purpose of sailing north and easterly. In so doing we were sailing straight towards the Bosphorus, one of the two narrow straits near Constantinople that, along with the relatively small Marmara Sea that lay between them, divided the lands and states of what some were now calling Europe from the lands and states on the eastern side of the water.

The weather was good, the skies were clear, and the sea was somewhat calm. Our galleys were spread out in a line across the Marmara; there was little chance of the Venetian fleet not being seen if it was in these waters.

It was already uncomfortably warm despite the early hour. As usual, I immediately became sea-poxed and barfed my breakfast of breakfast ale and buttered bread over the deck railing whilst making sure, of course, that I was standing upwind. I was not the only one afflicted. My new apprentice, however, and somewhat to my initial dismay and embarrassment, did not lose his breakfast until well after we cleared the harbour. Harold, as usual, never did.

Being sea-poxed and getting the Company's fleet underway and out of the harbour kept me quite busy. And that distraction was good because it kept me from thinking about Elizabeth, and the fact that she would soon have a new man in her bed such that I was not likely to ever see her again. Even so, truth be told, I was disappointed that she had not come down to the quay to see me off. What also surprised me was my suddenly realizing that I was somewhat relieved to be sailing off without her.

Our fleets' initial destination was the narrow Bosphorus strait. It was fairly close to Constantinople and opened on its far side into the Black Sea. The other strait, the Dardanelles, was about a day's sailing to the south at the other end of the small inland sea. The Marmara lay between the two long and narrow straits. The far side of the Dardanelles Strait, in turn, opened into the island-dotted Greek Sea that many landsmen and merchants were beginning to call the Aegean for some reason. The much larger Mediterranean Sea was just beyond the Aegean.

The two narrow straits and the relatively small inland sea which lay between them divided the mostly Christian lands of Europe from the mostly heathen lands of the east. The non-heathen exceptions, of course, were the Orthodox state of Nicea, the Christian lands of the Holy Land surrounding Jerusalem, and a princely state of the Latin Empire that lay along the Black Sea.

It was said by many that the two straits and the sea between them were the busiest waters in the world. I certainly believed it from all the sea-going activity I could see and so did Harold and the Company's captains.

Ever since time began, hundreds of years earlier according to the bible, the coins sailors paid as tolls to be able to use those waters were collected by whoever ruled the great city of Constantinople. It sat at the very end of a narrow peninsula of land which poked so far out into the water that people standing on its walls could see everything sailing on it.

As a result of Constantinople's location, the tolls it collected made the city's ruler the richest person in the world—unless, of course, he or she had to turn most of the toll coins over to a religious military order or to a free company such as ours in order to have enough fighting men to hold their throne.

In fact, my men and I were members of both a free company *and* a religious order. Being both had been my priestly Uncle Thomas's idea, and a very good one it was. As a result, Richard, Michael, and I and forty or so other men in the Company, including my son and young brother, had been learnt to speak and scribe Latin when we were boys in Uncle Thomas's school at Cornwall's Restormel Castle.

Richard and I were among the very first four boys to finish being learnt at the Company's school, and the process had not changed much ever since. Basically, our schooling ended and we were ordained as Angelovian priests when Uncle Thomas decided we were strong enough to push arrows out of a longbow, smart enough to put down our feet to the beat of a marching drum, and sufficiently full of Latin and summing to be able to scribe, do sums, and chant the prayers that could only be understood by God and his priests. Four or five boys were usually examined and found sufficiently full of learning each year.

At that point, being able to push out arrows and being found full of scribing and summing and knowing the prayer chants, most of us were allowed to make our marks on the Company's roll and begin our active service as apprentice sergeants doing reading, scribing, and summing for the Company captains to whom we were assigned. And, of course, by being constantly by their sides we learned how to be captains ourselves so we could take their places someday when the time came.

Educating the boys helped the Company because they could scribe messages, contracts, and money orders for the Company's illiterate captains. It also let the Company read the messages and contracts of our competitors and understand what the priests that acted as their clerks, *and were known as "clerics" or "clarks" as a result,* were saying when they spoke to each other in Latin in the belief that no one could understand what they were saying.

Having archers in the Company that were also ordained as priests and could read, scribe, and gobble Latin was useful, according to Uncle Thomas. He said it was comparable to using dice whose edges were shaved or moving a chess piece when one's opponent was not looking.

My uncle knew about such things, and much more, because he had been brought to Bodmin Monastery when he caught the eye of a monk. He ended up being ordained himself. That was before he ran off a few years later to rescue my then-young father from spending his life walking behind a plough and took him for a crusader with King Richard.

Uncle Thomas had actually begun his school and teaching career long before he bought his bishopric from the Pope and could ordain priests. Indeed, he had added his teaching to his archering and praying long before he and my father stopped crusading and began to find new ways for the Company's men to earn their bread and coins. He had begun doing it, according to my father, because he wanted my father and me to be able to scribe, do sums, and be able to gobble Latin in case he fell and could no longer do it for us.

My uncle's being able to ordain us as priests after he bought his bishopric had been an unexpected bonus. It allowed him to add prayer chanting to what the boys were being learnt so he could ordain them as priests in addition to teaching them to scribe in Latin and push arrows out of a longbow.

Indeed, Uncle Thomas considered the Company having its own bishop so important that he had recently begun suggesting that it was time for the Company to buy another bishopric from the Pope for one of his students. He said the Company should do so because it would allow the bringing of archer priests into the Company as apprentice sergeants to continue when he was gone.

The former student he had in mind was presently working as a scribe and Company spy at Windsor for the Pope's ambassador, the papal nuncio. I had already decided to provide the necessary coins for the Pope's prayers as soon as I got back to England.

In any event, Richard and I were among the very first of the school's students that Uncle Thomas had decided were sufficiently full of learning to be ordained and join the Company. Now, many years later, my young son and my much younger brother, John, were among the most recent.

On the other hand, our Company's religious order, the Poor Landless Sailors in the Service of God, was mostly a way for us to justify collecting additional coins from the Company's passengers. The passengers paid them for the Pope's prayers for their survival on the voyages on which the Company carried them.

It was a good earner for us because bringing a pouch with a few of the prayer coins to the Holy Father each year helped to keep him sweet about the Company's transgressions even though we kept most of the coins. Moreover, it was not only a good coin earner for us but it also allowed us to claim that we were on "a mission from God ordered by the Holy Father" if we were captured or needed something from a churchman or a devout Christian merchant or lord.

As you might imagine, my fellow students and I being ordained as priests in a papal order was particularly useful if we needed to get something from a true believer or someone that was worried about angering the Pope, or hoped to get a favourable appointment or something of value from him without having to pay too much for it.

In other words, proclaiming ourselves or the Company to be "on a mission from God" or a "mission from the Pope" and that we were carrying out "God's will" could often be used successfully on almost everyone except the Orthodox believers and the Jews and Moors. And even they were sometimes impressed—it inevitably depended on how the political winds were blowing and their wars were going.

Making such claims frequently worked since it was well known that God frowned on anyone that killed, tortured, or impeded his priests and their servants and slaves. It also helped when we needed something such as a special favour from a Christian prince or noble who wanted to keep the Pope sweet in order to get God's approval for something he wanted to do or a dispensation for something he had already done.

Moreover, ordaining the boys that graduated from the Thomas's school as Angelovian priests also provided employment for the students if they were not up to joining the Company for some reason, such as overly enjoying the company of young boys—they could be sent to London or elsewhere to seek their fortunes as priests or clerics or members of parliament.

In any event, as my lieutenants and I had explained to our men before we boarded our galleys and rowed out of the harbour, the plan for our sortie was quite simple. It was to seek out and either capture or destroy the galleys of the Venetian fleet wherever we found them. Then we would return to Constantinople to take on supplies for a voyage to Cyprus.

It was all a lie, of course, a gambit designed to fool the Venetians. What we had not yet told our men was that after we cleared the Marmara of Venetians we would *not* be returning to Constantinople and we would *not* be sailing for Cyprus. To the contrary, and despite what we had led our men to believe and talk about in Constantinople's taverns and alleys, we would be sailing elsewhere to begin taking our revenge on the Venetians for the losses and suffering they had recently caused us.

Our plan was to have our fleet well on its way to Venice before the local whores and tavern keepers, and thus Venice's ambassador and his spies, realized that we would not be coming back and thought to warn the Venetians that we might be coming for them to exact our revenge. At that point, or so we hoped, it would be too late to warn the Venetians. It was the first of the many gambits in our plan.

Any Venetians we took in the Marmara and afterwards, the galleys that is, not the men, would almost certainly be burned if they were not thought to be good enough to be added to the Company's fleet. That was because we had long ago learnt that any galleys we took and sold as prizes would not bring much in the way of coins and, much worse, would inevitably end up in the hands of one or another of our enemies and sooner or later be used against us. In other words, it was better to burn captured galleys immediately if they were not good enough to be added to our fleet.

We also would treat the sailors and passengers on any Venetian galleys and transports we captured differently from how they and our other competitors would treat them. We took the long view—instead of selling everyone we captured for slaves as the Venetians and our other competitors often did, we would send them ashore as free men to tell the tale. We did it so that other sailors in the years ahead would be encouraged to surrender instead of fight when our galleys came alongside.

On the other hand, because we were often good Christians, pirates such as the Moors were always treated as the bible required when we took a pirate galley—they were tossed over the side so the water would wash away their sins as they sank.

Our immediate intention was to sweep the Marmara Sea clean of Venetian galleys so we could begin once again peacefully collecting the Empress's toll coins. Accordingly, if we reached the entrance to the Bosphorus without finding the Venetians, we would leave two galleys behind to once again begin collecting the tolls that seafarers had to pay to sail on those waters. The rest of us would then turn around and head south through the Marmara to see if we could find the Venetian fleet in the waters to the south of Constantinople.

Once the Venetian interlopers were gone we would continue to keep the toll coins as our payment for continuing to protect the Empress and the city that served as the capital of her great empire. It was very much God's Will that we do so, continuing to collect the coins and keep them that is. We knew it was God's Will, otherwise the Empress would not have known of our trustworthiness and God would not have showered such great riches and powers on the Empress for her to be able to use to pay us to help protect her.

The toll coins the Empress had contracted for the Company to collect and keep explained why I had called in every available archer, including our retirees and Uncle Thomas's older students. I had done so as soon as I learned that a huge Greek army had been summoned by the Patriarch of the Orthodox Church and was going to march on Constantinople and try to replace the Empress and re-establish the Byzantine Empire. The fact that many years earlier the Empress, as a young girl, had been a newly widowed Norman lady at Okehampton Castle and periodically spent time getting to know my father had nothing to do with it.

Indeed, as the Empress herself had reminded me when I reached Constantinople, I had actually met her at Okehampton years earlier when I was still a very young boy, and then again a few years later after I had joined the Company. That was when the Earl of Devon and his supporters from amongst the barons opposed to King John had attempted to invade Cornwall.

Our initial meeting, which I only vaguely remembered, was either when I was with my father when the Company took Okehampton, or when I had accompanied my father on one of his frequent visits to Okehampton to inspect the Company's horse archers that had somehow ended up being headquartered there to guard the approaches to Cornwall.

The Company had taken Okehampton when its former lord, the man that had apparently been newly wed to the lady at the time, attacked a band of the Company's archers led by my father when they were passing by on the old Roman road that ran near the castle. Afterwards, his young widow and subsequent son had remained at Okehampton for a number of years. She and her son finally left when what remained of the men in her family, a couple of cousins, married her off in a second marriage to a minor French noble in exchange for adopting her son and a farm she had inherited in France.

Many years later, and to her and her second husband's immense surprise, her second husband had been named by the Pope to be the Emperor of the Latin Empire. It happened when the old emperor, a crusader that had also started life as a minor French noble, died in Constantinople without an heir, except for a much younger half-sister he had never seen.

He had never seen his half-sister because he had gone crusading and fought his way into the emperorship before she was born. The half-sister turned out to be my father's dear friend, the young widow he had met when my father and his men had responded to her first husband attacking them on the old Roman road near Okehampton by killing him and taking the castle.

It was not exactly clear when the Empress left Okehampton to remarry, but years later her second husband had been appointed as the new Latin Emperor, with his wife then becoming the Empress, because that was the only way God could keep the bloodline of the old emperor on the throne. Much more important, at least so far as the Holy Father was concerned, God's decision to name her second husband as the emperor would keep men that would almost certainly not obey him *off* the throne.

In essence, God had informed the Pope, his only representative on earth, that he wanted the dead emperor's bloodline to continue through one of the sons of his half-sister, the dead emperor's only living relative. It ended up being her second son because her older son, the one born in England, had recently married a girl who did not want to move to Constantinople. He would remain in France as the lord replacing his stepfather.

Having an emperor on the throne that would continue the old emperor's blood forward had been a fine idea, except that it did not work—someone who wanted the throne for himself had waylaid and killed the new emperor even before he reached Constantinople. He had not, however, killed the new emperor's younger son and heir. The boy had already reached Constantinople with his mother, the new Empress by virtue of her marriage and God's Will.

Soon thereafter, the Company had contracted to help the Empress deliver a sufficient weight of gold and silver coins from her empire's treasury to buy enough prayers from the Holy Father such that God decided to recognize her as her young son's regent. The Company had helped her do so in exchange for various benefits including additional concessions for our shipping post and for being allowed to keep some of the coins we carried to Rome for the Pope's prayers.

The Empress had trusted what she always referred to as "The Company" to carry her coins to Rome, instead of sailing away with them, because she knew from her time at Okehampton that the Company always did its best to honour its contracts in order to attract repeat custom. Another reason, of course, was that she had no other choices available.

Our delivering the prayer coins and getting God's blessing for her regency should have been the end of the Empress's troubles. But it was not—despite the fact that God himself had chosen her to be the Regent, the Empress still had a number of mortal enemies who were willing to ignore "God's Will" because they wanted her son's throne.

It was soon after we delivered the prayer coins and God chose the Empress to be her young son's regent that the Patriarch of the Orthodox Church and several of her Empire's traitorous Greek-gobbling kings and princes began raising an army to replace her.

The Patriarch did so in order that he could return to Constantinople and his luxurious palace from which he had been chased years earlier by the crusaders and their Latin-speaking priests that no one could understand. He had been in exile ever since. But then the crusader emperor had died, his replacement had been killed, and the murdered man's wife was on the throne as the Empress and the regent for her son.

A woman on the throne who had *not* been approved by God speaking through the Patriarch? It was an opportunity. Accordingly, the Empire's remaining Greek princes and nobles, some of whom had foolishly been left in control of their states by the crusaders, joined with the Patriarch so that one of them could take the current Empress's place.

The proposed new emperor, being Greek and therefore a member of the Orthodox Church, would, of course, look to the Patriarch to tell him what God wanted him to do. The Empress and her crusader nobles and their heirs would be killed or cast out and the Byzantine Empire restored with the Patriarch once again back in his palatial home and his priests in their churches.

Venice's king, the Doge, promptly agreed to help several of the traitorous Greek princes despite the Doge being told by the Pope that God did not want him to help them. The Doge did so in exchange for the promises of the Greek princes that Venice's merchants and their Latin-gobbling priests would be allowed to *return* to Constantinople and the various states of its great empire.

The Venetians needed permission to return because some years earlier, before the crusaders arrived, they had been massacred and expelled by the fathers of the very same Greek princes and nobles they were now willing to assist.

More specifically, the Venetians agreed to help the Greeks because the Patriarch and the Greek princes promised that *this time* the Venetians and their priests would *not* be massacred and expelled. Also, and probably even more important, the Venetians hoped to put their king, the Doge, on the Empire's throne when the Empress was gone and Greek princes began fighting amongst themselves. The Venetians, prematurely scenting a Greek victory, had already begun encouraging the various Greek claimants to go for each other's throats.

It was when the Patriarch and his various supporters actually began forming their army of Orthodox believers that the Company was able to negotiate a new and even better contract with the Empress—wherein we began collecting and keeping *all* of her empire's toll coins in return for permanently helping to defend her family and the Latin Empire she ruled.

As you might imagine, my lieutenants and I had not felt at all guilty in demanding all of the Empress's shipping tolls as the price of defending her and her realm from the Patriarch and his princes. That was because we would earn them with our blood, and also because the Empress did rather well from the taxes and gifts she received from her allegedly loyal princes and other land-holding nobles—the men who acted as her tax farmers and constantly plotted to take her place.

In any event, and most important of all, she had to agree to our terms because no one else was willing to help her; we were her only chance to hold on to her wealth and power.

****** *An unknown Company captain.*

Our rowers were fresh and it did not take long to reach the entrance to the Bosphorus Strait despite the wind being against us and the day being particularly warm. And it was warm, very warm— my rowers were constantly visiting our galley's scuttled butt, the water cask with its lid pulled off so drinking water could be dipped out with a bowl. The men periodically did so, visited the scuttled butt that is, in order to get a drink and to exchange rumours with their crewmates as to what was happening.

Unfortunately or fortunately, depending on how much one looked forward to fighting with the Venetians, there was nothing to report or learn. All we saw along the way was the usual steady stream of transports of all sizes and types going in both directions. What we did not see was a single Venetian war galley.

In any event, we immediately turned around after we reached the Bosphorus and headed for the Dardanelles Strait at the other end of the little inland sea that lay between the two straits. Before we did, however, two of our galleys were ordered to remain behind to begin collecting the Empress's tolls once again. They would be based in Constantinople for the foreseeable future. My galley, unfortunately, was not one of them.

The wind was now full in our sails. Even so, it took us almost the entire rest of the day to sail the length of the Marmara and reach the entrance to the Dardanelles—and we did so without seeing a trace of the Venetian fleet. The Venetians had sailed for parts unknown.

When we reached the entrance to the Dardanelles, another two of our galleys were left at the mouth of the strait to collect the tolls, and two others, the two believed to be the most seaworthy because they had the deepest hulls, were assigned to carry Richard and his horse archers on the long voyage back to Cornwall. The horse archers were horseless, of course. The horses they had ridden on behalf of the Empress had been left behind, just as they had left their horses in Cornwall behind when they had sailed out from England to join us in Constantinople.

No sooner had we shouted our "fare wells" and "best wishes" to the departing horse archers and the men on the galleys that would be staying behind as toll collectors, than the "all captains" flag was waved from one of Harold's masts to summon the captains of the remaining twenty-four galleys to a meeting on Harold's galley. The day had gotten even warmer and our archer-rowers were sweating profusely despite the cooling effect of sea breezes that constantly swept over us. They were pleased to be able to take a break whilst the captains gathered.

My fellow galley captains and I climbed aboard Harold's galley thinking we were there to get our sailing orders to return to Constantinople or, perhaps, even to continue on to Cyprus. It was not to be.

"I know what you are thinking."

That was what the Commander said to us as soon as we captains were all assembled. As you might imagine, he said it with Harold's crew standing around behind us and straining their ears to listen. Whilst he was speaking, the deck under us constantly moved from side to side and periodically rose and fell. It was moving in response to the sea waves and the wake of a big two-masted transport being pulled out of the nearby narrow strait by sailors rowing its dinghies. There were two more transports right behind it. The Dardanelles strait was always busy.

"You think you are here to get your sailing orders for our return to Constantinople. You are wrong. What we are all going to do next is sail to Rome with a valuable cargo of gold and silver coins from the Empress. She is sending them to the Pope as the contribution she promised to make to the Church if the Holy Father's prayers to God for the success of the recent war were successful.

"But here is the thing, lads; there is a strong possibility that we did not find the Venetian fleet in the Marmara because they heard about the coins from their spies. As a result, the Venetians may have gathered their forces and are waiting for us off Crete. That is where they will try to take the coins off us when we call in there to replenish our water and supplies.

"We cannot take the risk of getting separated and losing the galley carrying the coins to the Venetians. So you can tell your crews that for the sake of keeping the Empress's coins safe, we will be avoiding the waters between here and Crete. Instead, we will follow the Greek coast and call in at Piraeus to take on the water and supplies we will need in order to reach Rome.

"I know Piraeus is slightly out of the way for a voyage to Rome, but it is the sensible thing for us to do because it will not only let us avoid the Venetians waiting off Crete, but it will also let us stay closer to land in case the weather turns bad and we have to run for shore to save the coins.

"But here is the good news you can also share with your men—we are in no hurry to deliver the Empress's coins to the Holy Father, so we will stay at Piraeus for a few days to take on supplies and give the men a well-deserved liberty amongst the Greek women. Then we will continue on to Rome."

Of course, as everyone now knows, what Commander Courtenay told us was not true, both about the Venetians waiting for us off Crete and about our final destination. It was all part of a great gambit to mislead the spies of our enemies as to where we really intended to sail and what we would do when we got there.

It was a wonderful gambit, however, although we did not know it at the time. It meant we would be misleading the Venetians, without hurting ourselves, as we spread the false tale about our destination in the Piraeus taverns and brothels we visited. The exceptions, of course, being the usual painful heads of the drinkers and the inevitable sore dingles and itchy skin if the Piraeus women were poxed.

Best of all, as everyone now knows, the Commander's gambit worked. It also gave our men extra time ashore whilst they spread the lies about the Empress's coins and our destination.

Those of us that survived the weeks that followed certainly approved. We lifted many a bowl to celebrate the Commander's efforts to keep our butcher's bill down and our prize coins up.

Chapter Three

We reach Piraeus.

Piraeus in the year 1219 was, as it is now, the main port of the adjacent and much larger Greek city of Athens. According to what I had been learnt in school, Athens was where, in the olden days, naked men used to compete to run faster than each other, throw spears farther, and tell each other how kings and princes should govern their subjects. It had been a terrible place because those that lost their contests or were wrong about how rulers should behave were forced to drink tree sap so their guts clogged up and they died.

Things were quite different by the time we rowed into Piraeus's harbour. Both Piraeus and Athens had become modern Christian cities with their own city walls, fresh water delivered by aqueducts, and all kinds of markets including a particularly large one in Athens for slaves and other livestock.

Piraeus, because it was the principal seaport for Athens, had a long and busy stone quay and a number of waterfront warehouses. Most of the people in the two cities and the lands around them were Orthodox followers of the Patriarch, our once and future enemy. In other words they were people that gobbled in Greek and made the sign of the cross incorrectly, and in so doing received imperfect messages from God.

The Duke of Athens, the man that ruled in and around both cities, on the other hand, was neither Greek nor Orthodox. He was the son of one of the crusaders that had helped to defeat the Greek-speaking Byzantine Empire some years earlier. His father had helped put one of the crusade's leaders on the throne of a new empire, the Latin Empire, and been given Athens and its port as his reward.

Athens had been one of the states of the old Byzantine Empire. Now it was part of what was called the Latin Empire because its priests and bishops gobbled to each other and chanted their prayers in Latin even though most people could not understand them. God did, however, and that was enough for most of us even if the Greeks did not like it.

God had appreciated the efforts of the Duke's father to remove and replace the Patriarch and the Byzantine Empire, and, as a result, blessed him with the Dukedom of Athens as the vassal of the crusader king who ruled the much larger adjacent state of Thessalonica. The current Duke, as his father's heir, had inherited the title as God intended.

As a result of his crusader-related birth, the current Duke prayed with priests and bishops who spoke Latin. Thus he could get the true word as to what God really wanted him and his subjects to do from the Pope in Rome. That was because, as everyone now knows, God only speaks in Latin, and certainly never in Greek or Moorish or one of the other heathen gobbles.

In any event, as was always the case when we came into Piraeus, we saw many different types and sizes of shipping anchored in the harbour and tied up along its great quay. There were even, to our surprise, two Moorish-rigged transports anchored side by side in the eastern side of the harbour.

As you might imagine, because of the port of Piraeus's many arrivals and departures, it had been one of the first ports in which the Company had established a shipping post. That was more than twenty years ago and it had produced a steady stream of coins for the Company's chests ever since.

******

The weather had been good in the days before we reached Piraeus and we were able to stay together at night by hanging candle lanterns on our masts. There were no problems except for the usual bumps and a broken oar or two when one of our galleys got too close to another in the dark. Accordingly, our galleys were sailing together in one large fleet when we rowed into Piraeus's crowded harbour on a sunny and overly warm Thursday afternoon.

We rowed in fast and ready to fight in case the Venetian fleet was there. It was not. Indeed, there was no Venetian shipping of any kind in the harbour except for a couple of small cogs owned by a couple of the Venetian merchants who had somehow been allowed to return and had stalls in the Athens market.

The sudden and battle-ready arrival of twenty-three of the Company of Archers' war galleys in the harbour caused more than a little commotion and distress on many of the transports that were at anchor in the harbour and tied up along the Piraeus's long stone quay. It also caused havoc and confusion amongst the wharfies and merchants that were on the quay.

Some of the men on the quay and the crews of some of the transports panicked because they thought we might be raiding the city to punish it for its lack of support for the Empress during the recent war. Their behaviour, in turn, caused other men and crews to panic because they thought those who initially got overly excited knew something they did not.

In any event, our sudden arrival caused instant chaos all along the waterfront. Boarding planks were hurriedly thrown down, anchor and mooring lines were cast off and cut, hysterical orders were shouted, and men ran all about. Some of the sailors on the transports in the harbour ran for their dinghies and rowed to shore. Others rushed to raise their sails so they could sail away to safety. There were even a couple of splashes as men jumped in the water in order to swim ashore.

It was the usual panicked response of men that lost their heads because they saw others losing theirs. It happens all the time with undisciplined sailors and soldiers when an enemy suddenly appears or someone shouts "fire" in a tavern or church. And, of course, it was the prudent thing to do since they did not yet know that all we wanted to do was give our men liberties to go ashore and spread misinformation whilst we took on water and supplies.

In fact, the fear amongst the sailors and the wharfies and merchants on the quay was not entirely unreasonable. Both Piraeus and Athens were under the rule of the Duke of Athens. The Duke, despite being a subject of the Empress, and also making the sign of the cross correctly and using Latin-gobbling priests to tell him what God wanted him to do, had made no effort to help the Empress during the recent war. Accordingly, it was quite reasonable for the Duke and his subjects and the visiting sailors to think we might have been arriving on a punitive raid.

There was no great surprise in the Duke's lack of support for the Empress—it was his duty to do nothing because he was, in turn, a vassal of the King of Thessalonica. The King had assumed the Greeks would win and, accordingly, in the best tradition of the heads of state and parliaments to this very day, had gone out of his way to appear neutral whilst doing all he could to help the Greeks because he thought they would win.

In other words, stated another way, the fears of the sailors and landsmen were grounded in reality. They feared we had come to attack the shipping in the harbour, and perhaps the port as well, because the people of Piraeus and Athens knew their lord had betrayed the Empress by not supporting her when the Patriarch's army attacked Constantinople.

Indeed, we might well have launched just such a punitive raid on such traitors, despite the hastily arranged "peace wedding" of the Empress's daughter and eldest son of the King of Epirus. We did not, but only because Thessalonica's ambassador to the Empress's court, realizing the significance of her victory, quickly attempted to make peace on his king's behalf by announcing that Thessalonica would be making a huge contribution of coins to the Empress "to help defray the cost of your magnificent victory."

Whether or not the King would actually make the promised contribution, however, would undoubtedly depend on how the Empress viewed the King and if the payment was sufficient for her to let him keep his head. Were I him, and knowing my father was advising the Empress, I would fear the worst and rush to make the payment.

After all, letting an enemy get away after hurting you, and not having to pay dearly for doing so, was never a good move and always to be avoided—because it would encourage others to do the same. At least that is what Uncle Thomas always told his students, and he would know being as he was so experienced and well-read. Besides, it made good sense.

In any event, so far as our men knew, we were in Piraeus to take on water and supplies for the continuation of our voyage to carry another shipment of the Empress's coins to the Holy Father in Rome. Additionally, and even more important, although my captains and their men did not know it at the time, we were also there as part of a series of Company gambits designed to gull Venice into making serious mistakes by misleading its spies and supporters.

****** *George Courtenay*

Activity in the Piraeus harbour settled back down to normal rather quickly as soon as our lack of hostile intent became obvious. Harold's galley and several others rowed up to the quay and moored. The others dropped their anchors nearby. Merchants and the pimps of the port's public women immediately began coming out of nowhere, almost like a conjurer's magic, to solicit our custom.

Within a few short minutes the captain of our local shipping post, Robert Archer, hurried up to greet us. His young lieutenant, Edward Sparrow, was with him. Edward was a graduate of our Company's school at Restormel Castle and, as a result, could scribe and do sums.

Sparrow had been Edward's nickname at school because he had once been called that by the school's cook when he had been seen pecking at his food. It had been scribed next to his name on the Company's roll when he made his mark because we already had too many Edwards with only numbers after their names.

Our shipping post that served the port of Piraeus and the nearby city of Athens was somewhat unique in that it operated out of two locations. One was in a warehouse near the port's largest quay. The other was just inside the Athens city wall on a narrow lane near the city's huge central market. There was also a small Company-owned retirement compound in Athens where a dozen or so of our older and disabled retirees had chosen to live on half pay.

The shipping post's crew and the Company's retirees were all under the command of Robert Archer, the son of one of the Company's old sweats, Martin Archer. Martin had run away from a farming village in the midlands to join the original Company of Archers and go crusading with King Richard. Years later his only surviving son had been allowed to make his mark on the Company's roll and also joined.

Now Martin was retired in Cornwall and it was his son, Robert, who commanded one of our shipping posts with the four stripes of a captain on the front and back of his tunic. Robert and his family lived in the Company's Athens compound; Edward Sparrow was his lieutenant and he and his family lived in the Company's Piraeus compound.

Unfortunately, Robert Archer was an undependable but well-meaning man who, like his father before him and his sons, was not the brightest candle in the lantern. *They were traits which seemed to run in the family and would, in time, propel their descendants to high places in the kingdom and in its parliament and gentry and gaols.* Accordingly, one of Uncle Thomas's best students, Edward Sparrow, was stationed with Robert with the rank of lieutenant to "help" him do the right things.

"Hoy, Commander," Robert shouted over to me as he walked up to the edge of the quay and looked over to where I was standing on the roof of Harold's forward deck castle. A beaming Edward Sparrow, his lieutenant, was standing next to him.

"Welcome to you. Be you and the lads here to fight the Greeks or just to take on supplies?"

Robert was always very direct, too direct actually, and talked too much. This time, however, his big mouth helped because it gave me a chance to reply in a way that would mislead the Venetians.

"Only to take on supplies, Robert, only to take on water and supplies. Then some of us are bound for Rome with a cargo of the Empress's coins for the Holy Father to thank him for his prayers that resulted in her victory. There are a lot of us here today because we are carrying a lot of coins."

I shouted my reply back from where I was standing on the roof of the forward deck castle. Everywhere men had stopped what they were doing to listen. Robert's loudly shouted question could not have been more useful if I had planted it; now every Venetian spy in the city would think we were carrying a fortune in coins.

What I told Robert was consistent with the lie I had earlier told to the galley captains and their men. It was a believable story since we had done it before, carried some of the Empress's coins to the Pope that is, in order to get the prayers needed so God would recognize the Empress as her young son's regent. It was also part of the gambit the Company was running to mislead the Venetians.

I remained on the roof of the forward deck castle with Harold for quite some time so I could see what was happening in Piraeus's harbour and on its quay. We stood there watching as the initial chaos and confusion faded away and some of our galleys tied up at the quay and others dropped their anchors in the harbour.

Five men of the Company were gathered at the deck railing a few feet below me. They were saying their farewells to their friends in Harold's crew. Three of them were archers who had been sent out from Robert's post to help reinforce us at Constantinople. They were returning to their families, if they had them, and to their regular active duty assignments at our shipping post. The other two were old sweats from the Company's local retirement compound. They had voluntarily come out of retirement to join us in Constantinople as volunteers.

"Hold on there, Lads," I shouted down to them as I jumped down on to the deck. "Wait for me."

A minute or so later, I was shaking the hands of the three archers and wishing them well. A number of men from Harold's crew beamed their approval at my recognition of their mates.

Then I very quietly pulled the two retirees aside and gave them great manly handshakes and salutes—and the good news that they were both being promoted such that their retirement half pay would be substantially increased. It would be doubled, actually, since each additional stripe doubled a man's annual pay and his share of any prize money that was paid.

Perhaps it was the way the men's faces lit up at the news, or it could be that someone was able to hear us and spread the word about the retirees' good fortune. But whatever the source, the men of Harold's crew were absolutely beaming as they gathered around a few minutes later and helped the five men climb up on to the quay. No one said a thing about the sixth man, an older archer from the Company's retirement compound who had gone to Constantinople with them. He had been buried two weeks earlier.

Robert helped by reaching down and pulling the men up on to the quay one after another. He started to jump down on to the deck to report to me after they were all aboard the quay, but stopped when I motioned for him to wait.

"Wait there, Robert, and keep all those men with you," I shouted. "I will be coming ashore in a couple of minutes."

At that moment, for some reason, after all that time at sea I had a sudden urge to stand on dry land as soon as possible. There was no special reason for the intense desire that popped into my head as I stood there on Harold's deck; it was probably just that I was not made out to be a sailor man even though I usually found my sea legs and stopped barfing fairly quickly after each voyage started.

******

"I just gave another stripe to Adam and Tom," I quietly told Robert a minute or so later when Harold and I had climbed up on to the quay to join him. "Please make sure they get their increases when you give them their retirement coins each month."

"Oh aye, I will. I will. You can count on me for that. They are good men for sure. But can I ask what happened and when Big Jack will be coming back? His wife will be asking."

"Big Jack did not make it. He is buried in Constantinople with the other lads that fell."

"My God! What happened? Did we lose the war? I heard we won."

"Yes, we won it. We won it big as a matter of fact. But we lost a lot of good men doing it and Jack was one of them."

After a moment, I added a couple of small lies, but kind ones.

"It will be up to you and Edward to see that Jack's woman is taken care of and gets half of his retirement pay for the rest of her life. And it will be the same number of coins as he was getting before he died since he earned another stripe before he fell.

"She is also due his death benefit of a year's pay since he went down whilst on active duty, and also his share of the prize money even though we are not yet sure how much it will be. You must make sure she gets them both."

"Oh aye, I will, I will. You can count on me."

"And tell her he did not suffer at all. He took an arrow in the eye and died instantly. He never knew what hit him." ... "No. Wait. I think it best that I go with you and his mates to tell her myself how he died." *Otherwise his mates might tell her the truth.*

And that is what I did whilst Harold went off to visit the port captain to pay for our moorage. Immediately after visiting the Port Captain Harold would make arrangements for the delivery of water and supplies from the great gaggle of merchants that followed him and constantly called out their offers.

The enthusiasm of the merchants and their agents was understandable when one considered the amount of supplies our fleet of twenty-three fully crewed galleys would require "to sail to Rome with a stop at Messina, with enough extra food and water on board in case bad weather causes our voyage to last longer."

Chapter Four

Many uncertainties.

My former apprentice sergeant, Nicholas Greenway, received a well-deserved promotion to lieutenant prior to our sailing. He was now the number two on Ian Smith's Galley Forty-One. He was promoted so he could begin getting command experience at sea. My new apprentice sergeant was young Roger Abbot who had come out earlier in the year. Roger was fifteen or sixteen years old and an older classmate of my son, young George, and my younger brother, John. He had come out to Constantinople with my son and Richard's horse archers.

Roger was thought to be from Manchester because of what was left of his accent. His father was supposedly a leather tanner who had died of a pox, but was more likely an abbot in view of Roger's family name and his being brought to Uncle Thomas's school to be learned. He had been six or seven years old at the time and had never heard from his mother or anyone else again.

His family, or lack of it, had not in any way been a problem for Roger. Taking an abandoned or orphaned lad into his school was a common occurrence for my uncle. And it had certainly worked in Roger's case; he was a tall and cheerful lad and had thrived in the school's warm friendships and plentiful food. He stood well over five and half feet tall, perhaps almost six, as I and many of the school's lads were when we finished growing. Roger, like me, had long ago become a son of the Company, and would be until the day he died.

Roger had also long ago lost most of his northern accent and picked up the Company's which had, or so I had been told because I had not noticed it myself, become more and more of a combination of Cornish and London-like crusader French. Much more importantly, Roger had learnt to scribe Latin with a particularly fine hand, did not stay sea-poxed for long when a voyage started. He was also good on a horse according to Richard. If he lived long enough, Roger had a future captaincy and perhaps even a lieutenant commandership, scribed all over him.

In other words, Roger was exactly what my uncle had intended those many years ago when I became his first student after my father and Richard his sixth.

Most of the others of my friends who had been with me at school were gone now, lost over the years to various poxes and vaguely remembered battles and disasters at sea. But the school continued to churn out their replacements and then some; the number of old school boys in the Company had been slowly growing for years.

******

I talked with Robert Archer and Edward Sparrow as we walked from the quay and on to the cobbled-stoned street that fronted the Company's Piraeus compound. Roger Abbot and Robert's apprentice, a tall and skinny lad I had never met before by the name of Samuel Drake, followed dutifully along behind us and listened intently. The returning archers followed dutifully along behind us.

People stared at us briefly and hurried to get out of our way as we walked and talked. Their behaviour was understandable. We did not fully realize it, but we were a ferocious-looking band of veteran fighting men as a result of the longbows, short swords, and galley shields most of us were carrying. Every man was wearing one of the Company's light Egyptian-made hooded tunics with his rank displayed by the number of stripes on its front and back and the little battle dots sewed on above them for each fight in which he had participated. In addition, every man carried a sheathed knife on his belt.

Additionally, although they could not be seen, I myself was also wearing the chain shirt and wrist knives the men of my family traditionally wore under their tunics. The only men *not* walking with longbows and quivers slung over their shoulders and carrying galley shields were Martin and Robert. They only were carrying sheathed swords.

The Company's Piraeus compound, because it was close to the quay where cargos were loaded and unloaded, was where much of the Company's in-coming and out-going cargos were stored until they could be loaded or retrieved. Also stored there were some of the post's coins and a few chests of pain-relieving flower paste, the only thing that the Company routinely bought and sold.

Piraeus was also where most of our passage-selling business was conducted. Edward lived there with his family and four of the archers that were permanently stationed at the shipping post, including one of the three men that had returned with us from Constantinople.

Robert, on the other hand, lived with his wife, his apprentice, and several archers in our shipping post's other much smaller and nicer compound which was in the Latin Quarter of the nearby city of Athens. It was well-located near Athens' great market which was next to the citadel that housed the Duke's night watch. The huge palace of the Greek archbishop and the Cathedral where he delivered God's instructions to the Greek people were nearby. The Duke himself lived in a castle on a nearby hill overlooking the city. From a distance it looked to be quite defensible.

The compound in Athens was where the contracts for most of our cargo shipments were scribed and money orders were sold to merchants and churchmen for the delivery of coins in distant ports. It was also where most, but not all, of the post's coin chests and flower paste chests were stored.

Both types of chests were kept there and at our Piraeus compound so the coins would be available to be paid out if a money order was presented, and the flower paste chests could be delivered if a buyer appeared with the relatively large amount of coins needed to buy a chest. Young Samuel Abbot, Robert's apprentice, did the required scribing and summing in Athens; Lieutenant Sparrow, being a graduate of the Company's school at Restormel, did for himself at Piraeus.

The pain-killing flower paste was the only thing the company routinely sold at all of our shipping posts. It was worth its weight in silver and highly profitable, and we kept it that way by requiring our post captains to do whatever was necessary to protect the Company's exclusive ability to sell it.

The efforts of our post captains to protect our monopoly mainly involved convincing other would-be paste sellers that they had two alternatives since the Company did not engage in murder. One was to stop selling immediately—the other was to be put to sleep by being hit on their heads and then loaded on outbound transports and galleys bound for faraway places. The Company had a great deal of credibility in terms of honouring its promises. As you might imagine, our would-be competitors usually withdrew.

******

We talked about almost everything as we walked the short distance from the quay to the Company's Piraeus post—the recent war and the fighting at Constantinople, our intention to sail for Rome after taking on supplies and giving the men shore leaves, and the condition of the people and merchants living in both cities.

It did not surprise me at all to hear that when the war started the Duke of Athens and his men retreated into the Duke's citadel and his castle for fear of an attack by the city's Greek population, and had not yet come out. Mostly, however, we talked about how Robert and Edward thought the Company's affairs were going in Piraeus and in Athens and what might be done to improve them now that the recent war had ended.

Robert told us his view of the local situation.

"Up until recently we were getting a lot of rich refugees and their families coming in from Constantinople to escape the fighting and the possible sacking of the city. They were mostly Greeks since this is a Greek city. That did not help our ability to earn coins to add to our chest, of course, since they were paying for their passages in Constantinople and landing free here.

"Indeed, up until the last few days our coin chests had been emptying because we have been paying out coins for so many money orders written in Constantinople by people trying to protect their wealth by depositing it with us there and collecting its equivalent here.

"Now that the fighting is over, however, the situation has turned around. People and coins have begun going back to Constantinople now that it is once again safe to live there. As a result, we have begun selling many more passages and money orders than usual and our coin chests are beginning to fill back up."

"And how do the people here see the Empress and those that supported her during the recent fighting?" I asked.

Robert was not sure what answer I wanted to hear so he initially hemmed and hawed. But finally, at my insistence, he told me what he actually thought.

"At first, as you might expect, Commander, there was hostility towards us from the local people. That was because a majority of the people living in Piraeus and Athens are Greeks and almost all of the Greeks are all Orthodox believers who look to the Patriarch to tell them what God wants them to do. We and the Empress, on the other hand, look to the Pope in Rome to tell us what God wants, and we make the sign of the cross differently.

"But there was not as much hostility as Edward and I first feared, and it appears to be almost all gone now that the issue has been decided. Is that not so, Edward?"

"Oh aye, Captain, of course you are right."

Robert beamed at me in response to having his thoughts confirmed. Unfortunately, he did not see Edward who was on the other side of him shake his head; I did. What it meant I did not know.

******

We stopped talking when we turned off the busy street that ran along in front of the quay and entered a narrow and rather foul-smelling side dirt lane which might or might not have stones under the dirt. The gate into the compound that served the Company's harbour trade was only about twenty paces beyond the warehouse building on the corner.

There was a little alley between the warehouse and our post. Two smiling sword-carrying archers with strung longbows and quivers of arrows slung over their shoulders were waiting for us just outside the post's gate to open it and let us enter.

"Hoy lads," I said to the two archers as they knuckled their heads in salute and stood to attention. "It is good to see you and find you alert and ready. How be you on this fine day?"

That is what I said as I smiled at the two archers, returned their salutes by knuckling my own head, and then extended my hand to greet them. I stopped for a moment to listen to their cheerful responses. They were pleased to be recognized. And they were even more pleased, and their smiles widened even more, when they saw the returning archers accompanying us.

One of the waiting archers pushed the gate all the way open to admit us into the compound's little bailey. As he did, I noticed that a very narrow and low door had been cut into the gate since my last visit, and that it had a small eye-level peep hole so that visitors could be identified before the door or the gate were opened. The entry door and its peep hole were new since the last time I visited the post more than a year earlier.

We passed through the open gate and it was immediately slammed shut and barred behind us with two heavy wooden bars. As the gate shut, I turned towards Edward, who lived in compound with his family and two of the archers, with a questioning look on my face.

"Normally we use the little door and leave the gate barred except when wagons and carts are coming or going. And then we all turn out with our weapons in case it might be an effort to gull us into admitting a gang of attackers. But we did not want to inconvenience you by making you bend your head and squeeze through the door."

I nodded and started to say something. The appearance of the battle-ready guards intrigued me. I had noticed Edward put a hand on his sword and give an intense look into the empty dirt lane as we turned off the crowded street and entered it, and then again when we came to the alley next to the warehouse. Robert, however, seemed blithely unconcerned.

Was there a threat that I had not been told about, or was this just for show to let me know that Edward and his men were alert and ready? I started to ask, but stopped when I saw a woman and two small children waiting in front of the post's building to greet us most kindly and usher us into the building.

******

What we saw as we ducked our heads and walked into the entry room of our Piraeus post was what we expected to see. It had three rooms starting with the smallest, an outer room next to the bailey. That was the room where meetings were conducted and payments were made.

The outer room had a heavy wooden door and six narrow wall openings high on the front wall, the street-side wall, to let in light. The wall openings were covered by thick wooden shutters that could be closed at night to keep out the dangerous night airs. Its stone floor was covered by rushes. They looked fresh.

A short wooden ladder lay next to the wall. It was used to climb up to open the shutters during the day to provide light for the room, and then climb up again at night to close them when the sun went down. There was also an unlit candle lantern that could be lit if one needed to better see what was being examined or scribed.

It was a safe and secure room—the wall openings covered by the wooden shutters were too high and too narrow for a man to use and the door could be double-barred to keep out thieves and robbers. The only furniture in the room was a small wooden table and a three-legged stool behind it. There was a scribe's inkpot and some sharpened goose feathers on the table. The candle lantern was on the floor next to it.

A second much larger room lay immediately behind the first. The only way in or out of the second room was through a sturdy entrance door from the first room that could be double barred. The larger room had no other doors because it served as a protected storehouse for our in-coming cargos prior to their retrieval, and for out-going cargos prior to their being loaded on one of our galleys or transports. It was surprising cool, perhaps because of its thick walls and the sun not shining directly into it.

The second room looked to be every bit as secure as the first. It too had very narrow wall openings to provide a bit of light during the day. The openings were high on its walls and, similar to those of the front room, much too narrow for even the skinniest thief or attacker to use to enter the building. The openings also had similar wooden shutters to keep out the dangerous night airs. There were a great mass of bales, crates, and amphorae and tent-like shelters in one corner where the archers lived. There were no rushes on its stone floor.

Three archers, including one of the men returning with us, lived in the larger room to help guard the post's cargos. There was a second much longer ladder already up in the room. It protruded through a hole in the ceiling and had to be climbed to reach the room above it. Several women lived in the room with the archers. They had been quietly waiting together in a far corner of the compound's bailey when we came through the gate to the street.

The returning archer had come through the gate behind me and got the warmest of welcomes from both the women in the bailey and the men. He was soon standing with them waving his hands about as he told his mates and the women about his experiences in Constantinople.

A third room stretched out above much of the first two. It was where Edward and his family lived safely in relative comfort with their bedding and their own piss pot. It also held the wooden chests where some of the post's coins and flower paste were stored. Valuable cargos were hoisted up and stored there.

The room above the first two was even more secure. That was because it could only be reached by the long wooden ladder that could be pulled up into it through a hole in the ceiling. Wall openings with shutters let in light and allowed people in the room to look out into the street and talk to their similarly situated neighbours. It also had a long ladder going up to the roof so the family could sleep up there on a hot night. I briefly climbed both of the long ladders to make my required inspection.

As you might imagine, the entire arrangement was designed to make things difficult for robbers or rioters. After getting past the bailey gate and into the bailey, intruders would first have to either break or gull their way through the building's heavy outer door and then break or gull their way through the heavy interior door into the cargo storehouse where the archers slept.

Once into the storehouse, the invaders would have to find a new ladder to replace the post's regular ladder which would have been pulled up through the hole in the ceiling by Edward Sparrow who lived up there and any of the post's other defenders who had been able to climb up to join him.

The invaders would then have to use the new ladder to climb up to the hole in the ceiling and into the room above—all whilst Edward and his men were chopping down on them with their swords and axes and others of Edward's men were shooting arrows at them through several small "kill holes" that had been cut in the ceilings of the two lower rooms.

But that was not the whole of the post's protections for its people and coins—the upper room also had a second hole in its floor into which the pulled-up ladder could be lowered. The second hole in the floor was covered by a trapdoor and opened into a very small secret room behind the far wall of the second room.

Escaping archers and their families appreciated the safety it provided. They could use the ladder they pulled up into the upper room to climb down into the secret room, and then use it again to climb down into an escape tunnel that ran some distance under the city and came up three streets away in a small chicken coop. Alternately, and certainly second best and not recommended unless there was no other alternative, they could additionally climb up on to the roof and, if need be, try to jump down from there and escape.

All of our shipping posts had somewhat similar defences and escape routes in place or under construction, including the shipping post in Athens where Robert lived with his family and the archers assigned to the post. They were based on a similarly constructed Company shipping post in Rome where rioters and robbers were in abundance because of the riches of the Church's leaders and their constant fighting with the city's leading families and merchants for control of the city's streets and markets.

As you might imagine, many of the archers initially posted to each of our shipping posts tended to be Welsh and Cornish miners who had dug mine tunnels for tin before they made their marks on the Company's roll and went for archers.

Our Rome facility, in turn, had been based on our post in London which was a very dangerous city, both because of its rapacious robbers, merchants and money lenders, that were often one and the same, and because the kings of England and France inevitably both claimed it and periodically fought over it. It was our finding of the hidden entrance into the mine tunnels under one of the Company's holds in Cornwall, Launceston Castle, that had given us the idea in the first place.

Such defences and escapes were neither excessive nor based on our men being unwilling to fight to defend themselves and the Company's chests of coins and paste. To the contrary, we had learned from bitter experience that our shipping posts would sooner or later need them in every port we served.

Our posts' protections and escape routes were inevitably needed because it was inevitably well known that there were valuable coins and flower paste on the premises and only a small handful of men guarding them. In addition, we had jealous rivals that wanted to destroy us. Also, in many ports, our men were considered heretics because they were known to be members of the Latin Church that did not make the sign of the cross properly.

It all added up. As a result, in many ports our shipping posts were the periodic targets of both organized robberies and also of religious and anti-foreigner mobs when the local lords and religious leaders needed scapegoats for some problem they could not solve or explain.

Somewhat similar defences and escape routes were already in place, or were still being built, at every one of our shipping posts. It had to be done to protect our coins and the small band of hopelessly outnumbered men that were stationed at each post. It was one of the many costs the Company had to shoulder in order to earn its coins in the civilized world.

Chapter Five

A confused post captain.

Our arrival at the Company's Piraeus shipping post resulted in a warm greeting from Edward's wife, and also from the two little girls that peered out at us shyly from behind her skirts. Seeing the girls sent a pang of homesickness through me. I smiled at them and suddenly realized that it had been almost two years since I'd seen my daughters and would most likely not see them again for many more months.

Roger, after getting a nod from me that he should carry on, immediately went to the post's records and began scribing a list of the post's recent coin receipts and expenditures. The totals from the various entries would be compared to the amount of coins in the post's chests, and then sent to Cyprus so they could be additionally compared against the arrival and departure reports of our other posts.

Inspecting the records of our shipping posts and sea captains was something every student was taught to do at the Company school at Restormel Castle. It was a task required of each apprentice sergeant when he arrived at one of the Company's shipping posts. Indeed, just knowing that an independent and unscheduled inspection would periodically occur was usually enough to keep our post captains and their scribes honest.

There was little wonder in that our post captains and their men tended to remain honest—stealing from the Company or its men was a hanging or chopping offense and not worth the risk. Even so, although infrequent, it sometimes happened. Equally important, perhaps, was that promotions were slow for those who kept poor records.

Yoram was the lieutenant commander permanently stationed on Cyprus and the man responsible for all of the Company's records and operations east of Gibraltar. He had a cleric he trusted and several apprentice sergeants that spent hours each day comparing the apprentice sergeants' reports with the reports that constantly flowed in from our various captains and shipping posts.

Being a coin and paste inspector was a much sought after assignment for those on the Company's roll who could scribe or sum. That was because the inspectors not only had safe berths, they also received token prize money for any "missing coins and flower paste" discrepancies they uncovered, and serious prize money for any "missing coins and flower paste" that that the Company recovered as a result of their efforts.

On the other hand, taking undue advantage of competitors and the higher gentry on behalf of the Company was acceptable. Indeed, it was encouraged, particularly if it was done quietly and those that were relieved of their coins were people such as churchmen and nobles from whom the Company would be merely taking coins that they had similarly gulled or stolen from others.

What was absolutely forbidden was the unwarranted taking of coins from potential customers or allies. On the other hand, as you might also imagine, it was greatly encouraged if the men being robbed or fleeced were outright enemies of the Company such as the Moors, Venetians, and French.

It was a reasonable way to behave. The Company of Archers was, after all, a free company; we needed coins to pay and feed our men.

For better or worse, the men at our shipping post were overwhelmingly considered to be "Latins." That was because Latin was the language in which their priests prayed and their leader, the Pope, consulted with God. In contrast, the great majority of Athens' merchants and people were Orthodox-believing Greeks whose priests prayed in Greek.

On the other hand, and fortunately for our shipping post, the Orthodox merchants and people had recently gone from being subjects of the Empress who was their hated enemy to being subjects of the Empress who was, at least temporarily, their new ally as a result of her daughter's marriage to a Greek and some rather substantial "gifts" her daughter's new father-in-law hurriedly provided in an effort to save his head and throne.

Both Robert and Edward agreed that the recent improvement in the post's prospects was due to the Empress's recent victory and to the peace-making marriage between the son of the Greek King of Epirus and the Empress's daughter, my friend Elizabeth, the widow whom I had come to know so thoroughly.

It was still uncertain as to whether or not the sudden changes would increase the safety of our men and allow the post to earn more coins. About all that could be said was that they probably would not make things worse. Robert, as always, was optimistic; Edward, however, was cautious and concerned.

I quickly came to understand that the most that could be said about our Athens shipping post was that it was hard to know its future despite the Empress's victory. That was because

Athens was ruled by the Duke of Athens, a Latin. He was the heir of one of the crusaders that had taken Constantinople and been given the dukedom of Athens as his reward.

The Duke was, supposedly, one of the Empress's subjects. He was also one of the Latin lords who had *not* helped her in her recent battle with the Greek army. Accordingly, his future was as uncertain as his control of the city and his Greek subjects.

The Duke's ambassador to the Empress had tried to explain away the Duke's lack of support on the grounds that Athens was part of the state of Thessalonica and that he was a vassal of the King of Thessalonica, another crusader heir. As such, he was required to be a loyal vassal of his King even though he loved the Empress most dearly and had very much wanted to help her. It was Thessalonica's king, not the Duke, according to the Duke's ambassador to the Empress's court, who had treasonously refused to help defend the Empress in the belief that the Greeks would win.

"The Duke," his ambassador claimed, "could do nothing to help her and did nothing to hurt her. He obeyed the law; he is not a traitor."

Knowing as I did the Empress and that my dear father that was advising her, I thought it likely she would sooner or later take the Thessalonican king's head for not supporting her during the war.

On the other hand, there was always the possibility the Empress might accept the rather substantial "peace gift" she received from the Thessalonican king as being sufficient just as she had accepted the son of the Epirus king for her daughter so that she would someday become a queen. It was, therefore, possible that the King might be able to buy off her anger at his treachery, or at least delay it. I rather doubted it. But how would whatever she ultimately decided affect the Company? I had not a clue.

Whether or not the Empress would also take the heads of the Duke and the other Latin nobles that were Thessalonica's vassals was also uncertain, which was probably why the Duke was reported to be hunkered down in his citadel on the north side of the city. I certainly would have been worried and hiding behind my walls if I had been wearing his sandals and the Company's galleys were in the harbour.

There was, of course, no way of knowing how many archers were killed and wounded because Thessalonica and Athens did not come to the aid of the Empress, but there were undoubtedly some. That alone would normally have been more than enough to seal the fates of both men so far as the Company was concerned. What was uncertain was not whether we should take the revenge required by the Company's compact, but when and how.

It was somewhat confusing. But one thing was certain—if the marriage agreement and the ambassador's promise of a substantial gift from Thessalonica's king had not occurred, we almost certainly would have been "provoked" by the presence of the Empress's enemies and, at the very least, would have already seized the shipping in the harbour.

Indeed, and despite the Empress's apparent acceptance of her enemies' peace offerings, if we did not have a much bigger Venetian fish to fry we might have decided to stay and hold the Piraeus Harbour until the Duke or the city paid a serious ransom. It was, the more I thought about it, an interesting idea—but only after we settled things with the Venetians. We could, and almost certainly would, stop at Greek ports on our way back to Constantinople and see how much we could get out of each of them.

Hmm. I wonder how the Pope and the Empress would react if we gave them a decent cut of the proceeds?

****** *Commander Courtenay*

Roger did not remain behind to continue his inspection of the post's records. He came with us when Robert and I bid cheerful farewells to Edward's wife and moved on. If time allowed, Roger would return to the Piraeus records after we finished inspecting our shipping post in Athens and the Company's nearby hospital which sheltered our retired archers and sailors.

The day had become quite warm by the time we began walking on the cobbled roadway between Piraeus and Athens. I could feel the heat of the stones through the leather soles of my sandals. The returning archers walked with us; all except for the veteran archer who had made it all the way home when he reached Piraeus. Edward Sparrow also accompanied us to Athens and so did Robert's apprentice sergeant, Samuel Drake.

As we walked up the crowded road towards Athens and talked, several realizations suddenly jumped into my head—one was that neither the Duke of Athens' war galleys nor any others had come out to challenge us when we first swept into the harbour. The second was that I had seen several Moorish-rigged transports both at anchor and tied up along the quay loading cargo.

Surely the harbour must have some defenders; where were they? Or did the Duke of Athens even have war galleys these days? And if there was no one here to defend the harbour, why were the Moors leaving the Piraeus alone? It was obviously ripe for the picking. Why was it not defended?

"Ah, Robert. What protects the shipping in the harbour and the surrounding waters from being taken by the Moors, or by the Venetians or anyone else for that matter? And when was the last Moorish attack on a transport in these waters?"

"Why that is a fine question, Commander, It really is. I am not sure when it last happened, am I? Not since I arrived, that is for sure."

Robert was well and truly puzzled. He clearly did not know much about what was happening locally. I tried not to let my disappointment show; it was obviously something that had never occurred to him.

"And you, Edward, what do you think?"

"I have heard it said, and believe it to be true, Commander, that many of the merchants of Piraeus and Athens make an annual payment to the Moorish king and are allowed to mark their transports so they will recognized and not be taken by the Moorish pirates. The Moors call it "tribute." I am told it is quite common.

"What is certain, however, is that the Moors are allowed to trade here and also in Thessalonica and in many of the smaller ports along the Greek coast. Their transports are frequently seen coming and going both to deliver cargos and passengers and to pick them up. There are merchants in the Piraeus market who act as agents for the various Moorish states and merchants.

"And, of course, there has always been a constant stream of Moorish shipping calling in here, including a number of large Moorish-rigged three-masted ships. And that does not seem to have changed at all, even though none have called in here during the past few days except for the two in the harbour. The same is true for the Venetians; there are Venetian merchants here and their transports are constantly coming and going.

"On the other hand, now that you mention it, I do not recall any recent visits by Venetian galleys. There were several that made port calls here earlier in the year. But so far as I know not a single one of them has been here since they helped carry the Greek army towards Constantinople.

"What I do know is that they, the Venetian galleys that is, have always behaved themselves in these waters, at least for so long as I have been stationed here. They certainly have not attempted to take any of our cogs and ships, probably because they fear it might be one of our pirate-takers.

"Their good behaviour towards everyone in these waters is understandable for several reasons. One, I think, is that the Duke of Athens and the king in Thessalonica are both Latins, as are the Venetians. The Pope has always been opposed to Latin Christians killing other Latin Christians unless the church approves.

"What is probably more important, however, is that the subjects of the Duke and his king are mostly Greeks who pay their tithes to the Orthodox Patriarch. The Patriarch has obviously become one of Venice's most important allies. He would almost certainly be unhappy if the ability of the Greek merchants to pay their religious tithes was reduced by the Venetians seizing their cargos.

"But having said all that, I am not certain what will happen now that all four of them, the Venetians, the Moors, the local Orthodox Greeks, and the Thessalonican king and his nobles, all effectively supported the losing side. Will they blame each other for losing and each try to do a deal with the Empress such that whatever peace that now exists between them falls apart? I do not know.

"On the other hand, even if they fall out, I think it likely there will be no efforts by the Venetian galley captains to take prizes in the waters off the Greek coast. That is because there are quite a number of Venetian merchants and moneylenders in Athens and the other Greek ports that would be damaged and complain to Venice's ruler.

"Indeed I almost wish the Venetians and Moors would decide to raid here and take prizes in these waters, especially the Venetians. Then the need of the local merchants for the services of our more-dependable archer-crewed galleys and transports would be even greater. It would also burn the Venetians' bridges with the local merchants whereas now the Venetians are our biggest competitors for passengers, money orders, and cargos to the Christian ports."

Then Edward offered an idea that turned out to be significant.

"We have a good customer, a Jew, who is a grain merchant with a stall in the Piraeus Market. He would almost certainly know if there are any other reasons why the Moorish and Venetian galleys have not been active in these waters. Would you like me to ask him?"

****** *Apprentice Sergeant Roger Abbot.*

Our little band walked in silence towards the big gate in the Athens city wall. It was directly ahead of us at the end of the road. People and carts of all kinds were coming and going despite the heat, and there were tent stalls all along the road offering shade and various bowls of things to drink and fruits to eat. The road was quite crowded. We had to be careful where we put our feet down to avoid all the horse and donkey shite.

We walked briskly despite the heat and did not stop to refresh ourselves. I, of course, as was my duty, stayed close to the Commander and listened carefully. It was the first time I had ever been in Athens. It was very exciting. In the distance I could see the columns of old ruins on several of the hills near the walled city.

There were great numbers of cats everywhere but not a dog to be seen. Perhaps the rumours are true that the Greeks eat them, the dogs that is. The people certainly look hungry enough. I started to ask, but decided against it because I am supposed to keep my mouth shut and only listen unless someone speaks to me.

"Edward and I heard about a couple of English slaves two days ago," the captain of the local post suddenly offered To the Commander in an attempt to break the silence. "The Moors brought them in. It is said that they are to be sold in three days at the next auction."

The Commander abruptly stopped walking, turned towards the captain, and raised his eyes in surprise. Openly selling English slaves sounded like a direct challenge to the Company, something that might have started when the Greeks and their supporters thought they were going to win.

"They are sailor men from a Liverpool three-master taken by the Moors off the Holy Land last year," Lieutenant Sparrow added. "One of the merchants came to me about them just two days ago.

"Apparently, there is a new man running the slave market, a local hard man from one of the church protection societies. The old auctioneer disappeared. According to the merchant, the new slave master is one of the gang that recently began selling protection to the merchants in the market, I am not sure if that is true or not, but it sounds reasonable."

Lieutenant Sparrow saw the raised eyebrows and the questioning look on the Commander's face, and began telling him more as we resumed walking.

"Everything changed when the war started going badly for the Greeks. That is when the Duke and his men retreated into the castle and closed its gate. As a result, his guards were no longer patrolling the markets and collecting taxes from the merchants. That is when, some of the Orthodox Church's protection gangs stepped in to replace the Duke's men.

"After a bit of fighting amongst themselves, they began collecting both the protection money from the merchants *and* the Duke's taxes that the merchants are required to pay. That is also when they took over the selling of slaves in the city's slave market.

"What is interesting is that I am fairly sure the Greek merchant who sought me out to tell me about the English slaves did so in order to see how we would respond. According to him, the two sailors are the first Englishmen in many years that have been brought here to be sold.

"What is puzzling is why the merchant sought me out to tell me. It may be that the market's new protectors have increased the protection fees and taxes he and his friends must pay and he hopes we will remove them. Or perhaps the Duke sent him in an effort to get us to do his dirty work so his tax collectors and slavers can return once things settle down.

"Or perhaps the merchant was warning me that we will be next if the new tax collectors are not stopped. I really have no idea why he approached me.

"On the other hand, it is also possible that the new slave master and the market's new protectors do not know how much it will distress us if they sell British slaves and, as a result, do not fully understand the consequences. It is also possible, of course, that they know and are testing us to see how we will react."

Commander Courtenay responded immediately and angrily.

"Testing us and knowing how we feel about English slaves be damned. We need to talk with the new slave master and the captain of the merchants' new protectors to make sure they understand what will happen to them if the Englishmen are not immediately freed."

After a moment of thinking, he made a decision.

"We will visit our Athens post and Jack's widow this afternoon, and go to the slave market first thing in the morning to talk to them.

"When we make our visit, whoever does your post's Greek-gobbling will have to come with us to translate. Who is he and where is he?"

"Old Demetrius does our Greek-gobbling. He has been with us for years, long before I arrived to become the post captain."

"Oh, I think I remember him myself. Is he the old fellow with a beard that hangs down past his dingle? When I visited here years ago as an apprentice sergeant we used to laugh and suggest that he had to hold his beard out of the way in order to pee. Where is he? at the post?"

"Yes, That is Demetrius. He spends the day at our Athens compound in case someone comes in to buy a passage or money order and cannot speak French or crusader French.

"The merchants and many of the men around the Duke of Athens can gobble one or both, of course, but the city's population is almost entirely Greek and most of them cannot understand anything except Greek. Demetrius is even teaching Greek to Edward, eh Edward?"

"Oh aye, that he is, Captain Archer. And I am virtually certain that he is also earning a coin or two spying on us for the Duke's chancellor."

Our post captain was shocked.

"What is that you said, Edward? Demetrius is spying on us? Are you certain? My God, we will have to send him away if it is true."

The Commander listened intently as Edward anxiously responded.

"Oh no, Captain, please do not say anything to Demetrius or send him away. It would be a great mistake, would it not? It may not be true. And even if it is true, we can pretend we do not know he is a spy and use him to pass information to the Duke and his men that we want them to have."

"Eh, what are saying? Why would you want to give Demetrius information if he is a spy?" Robert asked.

Commander Courtenay stepped in and agreed with Lieutenant Sparrow before Lieutenant Sparrow had a chance to answer for himself. The Commander had started walking again, but then he stopped and turned back to speak with a good deal of intensity to the post captain. He pointed his finger at the post's captain and spoke in a low voice so that the rank and file archers walking with us could not hear what he was saying.

"Edward is right, Robert. We can use your translator to mislead the Duke of Athens and his men when we find it useful to do so. So you must *never* let on to Demetrius that you even think he might be a spy.

"Keep in mind that he might *not* be a spy, and that he has been with us a long time and can be useful even if he is. So you are never to do or say anything to Demetrius about being a spy. Just be sure you only let Demetrius learn about things, or overhear things, that you want the Duke or any of our enemies to know, eh?

"And I want you to check with Edward and make sure you both agree before you tell him about what your post and the Company are doing or let him overhear anything that might be important. Do you understand what I am telling you?"

Captain Archer seemed confused, and clearly did *not* understand what he had been told, but he nodded his head in agreement.

"Make sure it never happens," the Commander said to the lieutenant.

Chapter Six

Our post in Athens.

Our post's comfortable little tenement inside Athens' walled city was a well-located two-level hovel sitting inside a small compound on a narrow cobblestoned street near the city's main market. It appeared to be relatively new. Its only drawback was that all the tenements on the street were so close together that there were no alleys or walkways between them where people could piss and dump their shite and garbage. It was not a problem, of course, as long as people walking on the street watched where they stepped.

As we walked through the gate into our post's tiny bailey, we could see the entrance to the city's grand market further on down the street. Beyond that was the city citadel of the Duke of Athens which was also the barracks of the city's night watch. The Duke's castle, where he lived with his family and servants, could be seen on the hill in the distance. It appeared to be a strong fortress that would be hard to take.

The Company's tenement, despite being quite appropriate for a merchant and his family and servants, was significantly less imposing than either the citadel or the castle. It was made entirely of wood with a daub and wattle exterior. And, as was usual for a merchant's residence in a large city, it had two floors and three rooms.

Two of its rooms were at street level, and one room was up above them both and could only be reached by climbing a ladder up to a hole in floor of the upper room. The roof on the upper room was flat so that people could sleep on it at night when it was too warm to be inside. It had the usual slight incline so the water would drain off when it rained.

A large wooden gate opened out into the street from a little bailey that stood in front of the post's building. The gate had the usual short and narrow door cut into it such that someone could enter and leave without opening the gate. Both the door and the gate could be double-barred to keep out robbers and unwanted visitors.

Other somewhat similar buildings sat so close on either side of our shipping post. Their walls were so close to the walls of our post that there was not enough room for even a narrow walkway to run between them. The entire neighbourhood was full of similar structures.

In the past, when times were peaceful, the gate had usually been left open and unguarded during the day, and only closed and barred at night. Ever since the Greek army began gathering, however, according to Robert, both the gate into the bailey and the little door in it had been constantly closed and barred and always guarded. Edward, it seems, had prevailed upon him to do so "just in case."

After passing through the gate we entered a small cobblestoned bailey with enough space for a single horse-drawn wagon and a kitchen with open sides that was covered by some kind of roof to shelter its users from the sun and rain. In other words, it was a conventional merchant's bailey with a fire pit and a sheltered table for the cooking and preparation of food in one of the corners of the bailey, and a low place next to the bailey wall by the street for pissing.

The building itself had a familiar design that was particularly favoured by merchants and as a city residence by wealthy rural landowners. Indeed, we used similar versions of it wherever possible for the Company's other shipping posts. A ladder was used to climb up to the large upper room which sat atop the two lower rooms. The ladder was important because it could be pulled up to separate the shipping post's people and coins in its upper room from thieves and robbers that were able to break or gull their way into the rooms below.

Our Athens compound was quite similar to our Piraeus compound. It differed somewhat in that it was smaller overall and it had the walls of its neighbours' tenements so close against its walls that there was no room for an alley or walkway between them. It was also different in that its similarly one-door cargo storeroom where the archers lived was smaller and its kitchen and pissing spot were in front along the street instead of in a second bailey in the rear.

Robert's wife, Mary, had obviously been alerted that we would be arriving. Her welcome at the tenement's comfortable compound was as warm as the day had already become. I remembered her from my previous visits to Athens and from Limassol where Robert had previously been based as a lieutenant serving on one of our galleys.

Mary smiled warmly and curtsied when Robert re-introduced us. He had forgotten that we had already met several times on Cyprus. As you might imagine, I smiled and bowed towards her and kissed her hand as if she was a great lady. It was a courtesy to the Company wives that was greatly appreciated and always expected.

"Of course, I remember your dear Mary. How are you, Mistress Mary? It is good to see you again. I hope you and your children are enjoying life in Athens. Are you finding it very much different from Cornwall and Cyprus?"

Mary was very pleased with my remembrances and courtesies. After a few meaningless assurances that she enjoyed being in Athens, she invited us to cool ourselves off with the bowls of morning ale and some oranges and other fruits she had provided for us. They were set out on a rough wooden table that stood between the tenement and warehouse building and the hearth of the post's kitchen.

The gate from the little bailey that opened into the street remained open with a determined-looking archer carrying a sword and shield standing by to guard it. Mary motioned for the archer to close it when she saw me looking at him. *Hmm. Robert may not be worried about his safety, but his wife and men certainly are.*

We promptly crowded around the table for something to eat and drink, and then stayed there and talked because the sun was such that the table was in a shaded part of the little bailey. The only exceptions were the post's archers that had just returned from Constantinople; they rushed past the ale and oranges and into the arms of their women and children, and then temporarily disappeared into the overly warm tenement to talk for a few moments in private.

As they did, out of the corner of my eye I saw Edward help the archer close the gate and say something to the sword-carrying archer as he did. The archer immediately grabbed up one of the gate's two wooden bars and dropped it into place, and then hurriedly did the same with the second bar. The little door in the gate was already closed and barred.

Mary's efforts to welcome us were greatly appreciated and I promptly told her as much. It was not until I saw the bowls of wine and ale she had set out on the table that I realized how thirsty I had become. The men with me obviously agreed; within minutes we had drunk enough that we had to pee against the bailey wall and the ground around the table was covered with orange peels.

The oranges were surprisingly sweet and delicious, and many of them were almost round. They were not at all like the bitter oranges I had enjoyed in the past.

"Where did you find these oranges?" someone asked Mary. "They are uncommonly tasty."

******

"Tell me again what you know about the Athens slave market and the men that are now running it? They are new you say; how is that? And what do you know about the Englishmen who are being held there?"

Those were the questions I put to Robert, Edward, and Demetrius later that afternoon. I did so right after I had given the sad news to Jack's widow and explained how she would be cared for and protected by the Company. She had turned up whilst we were visiting the Company's nearby hospital tenement that housed a dozen or so of the Company's disabled and elderly retirees and the women they attracted.

My asking questions about the slavers turned out to be a serious mistake. In doing so I had, I later learned, inadvertently done the very thing I had ordered Robert and Edward not to do—shared information about the Company's intentions and concerns. In this case, it was letting Demetrius know of my interest in the two captured English sailors and the men running the slave market.

"Oh aye, Commander, the men running the slave market and protecting the merchants are new. You are certainly heard right about that," Robert said. Demetrius and Lieutenant Sparrow nodded their heads in agreement.

I thought about immediately walking to the slave market to visit it and, as it turned out, I probably should have done it there and then. But I did not; I decided to wait until the morning and, instead, went to look at the escape tunnel that was in the process of being dug in the post's warehouse.

The tunnel was being extended because the current outlet came up too close to the compound such that the escapees might be seen. The main reason I did not go immediately to the slave market, however, was that I had decided I needed to prepare for my visit in case things went wrong and we were attacked.

"Roger, take one of the local men to show you the way and go back to the harbour. Tell Lieutenant Commander Lewes that you are to return in the morning with the fleet's three best swordsmen. They are to be here no later than thirty minutes after first light and they are to bring galley swords and shields with them in addition to their bows."

With that, Roger took off for the harbour and we walked back to the bailey of our shipping post to eat the meal of chicken, cheese, and bread that Robert's wife had prepared for us. The sun had already gone down so we stood in the relative cool of the night and ate and drank in the moonlight.

Smoke and the smell of food being cooked was heavy in the air as the city's wives began to cook their families' evening meals in their baileys if they were prosperous enough to have them, and on the streets in front of their hovels for those who were not. It was a warm summer evening with the stars and the moon providing enough light such that the two candle lanterns Mistress Mary set out were not needed.

Every so often we could hear the distant voices of people talking in the street on the other side of the bailey wall and from the upper wall openings of the hovels around us. I cannot explain why, but I somehow found it to be quite peaceful and comforting—and began thinking about my own dear family in Cornwall.

Soon after everyone finished eating, the little bailey was full of people sleeping and talking in low voices. They were everywhere except in the low corner by the bailey's wall where everyone went to pee so it would run off through a little hole in the bottom of the wall. So far as I could tell, none of the men tried to slip out to visit the city's taverns and public women.

We were sleeping outside because the rooms inside the post's tenement were much too warm. Robert and his family slept on the gently sloping roof and had graciously invited me to join them. I expressed my thanks for their kind offer and declined.

Sleeping in the bailey was an altogether peaceful scene. One of the post's archers dozed with his back to the short and narrow door built into the closed entrance gate. It was his job to raise the wooden bar on the little door, and then stand guard with an axe or sword in his hand, so that someone could squeeze through it to go out into the street to poop and water his arse.

It was in all ways a normal hot summer night in Athens. I felt safe and comfortable as I stretched out on the string bed that had been brought out for me to use. The last thing I remember hearing before I fell asleep was the murmur of men talking softly and the sound of a brief cat fight somewhere in the distance.

****** *Apprentice Sergeant Samuel Drake*

Captain Archer had already come down from the roof and was talking to the Commander the next morning when my friend and fellow apprentice, Roger Abbot, returned from the harbour. It was soon after sunup and the men and residents of the post were still breaking their nightly fast and preparing for the day when Roger, Lieutenant Commander Lewes, and six heavily armed archers came hurrying through the hastily opened gate.

"Hoy George. I brought six of our very best in case you underestimated your needs."

That was the first thing the burly white-haired lieutenant commander in charge of the Company's fleet said as he walked into the bailey and marched up to the Commander. He said it with a big smile and an overly grand salute. And then, before the Commander had a chance to reply, he asked several questions that sounded important.

"And why do you need the lads I brought you, pray tell? Who are we going to fight and what are we eating this morning to break our fasts? It smells good whatever it is."

"A good hoy to you too, Uncle Harold. I should have known you would come with them."

Commander Courtenay said it with a smile and a pleased laugh as he held out his right hand to the lieutenant commander and took a bite out of what he was holding in his left hand at the same time. It was a flat bread with cheese melted on it. He had picked it up from the bailey table as he walked past to get to the Commander.

"I'll tell you all about what we are going to do after you and the lads have had something to eat and a bowl of morning ale to wash it down."

And with that, the Commander went over to greet and shake the hands of the men Roger had led back to the post. Roger and I followed him. Of course we did; it was our duty. Besides, something was up and we wanted to know what it was. Even old Demetrius went with us. He had appeared earlier than usual, at dawn, in order to accompany us to the market.

Commander Courtenay appeared to be well rested and in a very good mood. He should be, he slept on *my* string bed. A couple of the post's archers carried it out to the bailey from the storeroom where the post's archers and I usually slept, except on the nights such as last night when it was so hot that sleeping on the roof or in the bailey was a better choice despite the bugs and flies.

Rank, I suppose, has its privileges, but the rest of us had to sleep on the bailey's cobblestones and they were damn hard. Actually, it was not all that bad compared to sleeping on a galley with a hundred other men; I slept on my back with my head on my quivers.

What I saw when I got into the food line impressed me. The little band of new arrivals was composed entirely of hard-eyed men, and a more fearsome looking lot as I had ever seen. They were mostly sergeants and chosen men, and they somehow looked as if they were ready for a fight to begin and anxious for it to start. One of them was wearing the stripes and circle of a lieutenant on his tunic.

More significant than their ranks, at least to me, was that each and every one of the new arrivals had a large number of battle dots on their tunics above his rank stripes. In a word, they looked like the most dangerous group of men I had ever seen together in one place. I was thankful we were on the same side.

****** *Lieutenant Thomas Bolton*

We gathered in a corner of the little bailey to listen to the Commander. He surprised us with what he had to say.

"All right, lads. Here it is. Captain Archer here is our post commander. He and his men have received word that a couple of Englishmen, apparently sailors from the crew of an English ship taken by the Moors off Acre, have been brought to Athens to be sold as slaves. If we stand by and let it happen, they will be auctioned off in a couple of days."

There were looks of shocked surprise and disbelief, and one of the new arrivals standing behind me quietly said "no way."

"Aye, Lads. It apparently be true. The word be that two Englishmen from a Liverpool three-master taken by the Moors off Acre are going to be sold at auction the day after tomorrow.

"We just cannot let that happen, even if it means a close-quarters fight inside the market and the spilling of Greek blood. The Company would lose too much respect if we stand aside and let them be sold. That is why I asked Lieutenant Commander Lewes to bring a handful of the Company's best fighting men to join me when I go to visit the slavers this morning.

"And when we get there, I propose we do whatever it takes to free the Englishmen and, if they deserve it, teach the local Greeks and their slavers a lesson about taking English slaves they will never forget.

"Are you with me?"

There were many shouts and cheers of agreement and thumping of chests and swords. The eyes of everyone in the bailey were on us. I, of course, shouted my agreement along with everyone else.

The Commander had more to say after all the noise and commotion died down.

"But here be the thing, lads—the control of the slave market recently changed hands. It used to be run by some of the men of the city's Latin lord. But the fool did not support the Empress and now, because he is rightfully in fear of his life from thinking the Empress might have sent us to kill him, he has retreated into his castle and is hiding in it with his men.

"As a result of him and his men being away, the slave market and the night watch protecting the merchants' stalls have recently been taken over by the one or more of the neighbourhood protection gangs of the city's Orthodox churches. They are apparently all Greeks just like the lot we recently tore apart in Constantinople.

"But here is the problem: We do not know if the new slavers are aware of the Company being opposed to the taking of British slaves and our commitment to freeing them wherever we find them.

"It may be they *do* know and are challenging us. But it is also possible that, being new to the trade, they do *not* know and are willing to free them in order to avoid a fight. So in a few minutes we are going to walk up the street to the slave market and find out which it is going to be.

"If the slavers know about the Company's rule that there be no English slaves and are holding them despite knowing our rule, we will free the two Englishmen even if it means cutting down the slavers and anyone else that stands against us.

"On the other hand, it may be that the slavers are merely unaware of our rule because they are new to the trade. If that be the case, we will explain it to them, and be satisfied with the freeing of the Englishmen, and *not* kill the slavers.

"So here is the thing, lads; we must be ready to put down as many of the Greek slavers as possible on an instant's notice. On the other hand, we will stay peaceful if the Greeks are willing to free them without a fight and agree to take no more. Do you understand?"

There were nods and growls of agreement. And every man instinctively checked and adjusted his weapons.

"Alright. Everyone listen up. We will leave in five minutes. Everyone take one last piss before we march. The market is nearby so there will be no time to do so on the way or after we get there.

"And one last thing. Roger, you and Samuel are not going with us. There are too many men going as it is. And the fighting, if there is any, it is likely to be at close quarters inside the market and require the Company's very best swordsmen. You are both fine lads, but the truth of the matter is that you are not yet anywhere near as good at fighting as Lieutenant Bolton and his men.

"I know you two are willing to stand with us and fight to free the English slaves, and I am sure that I speak for Lieutenant Bolton and his men when I say we all appreciate your willingness to come with us."

The Commander looked at me and the other lads when he said we all appreciated the sprats' willingness to come with us, so we all nodded our heads and murmured out agreement. Agreeing with the Commander was the least we could do after he said we were the very best fighters in the Company and they were nowhere near as good.

"So, Roger, you and Samuel are to stay here and help guard the post until we return. Whilst we are away you are to continue inspecting the post's records and counting its coins. Samuel can help you."

Chapter Seven

We meet with the slavers.

Ten archers and the post's elderly translator walked the short distance from The Company's shipping post to Athens' great market. Nine of us were carrying double-edged galley swords and round galley shields in addition to each man having a strung longbow and two quivers of arrows slung over one or both of his shoulders.

The streets were filled with people and horse carts going about their normal business as we walked down the middle of the street in a column of twos. We had no drum to beat the step and no one called it, but almost immediately Lieutenant Bolton matched his step to mine and the men copied us. The sound of our leather sandals hitting the cobblestones became the beat of our marching drum.

Everyone's swords were sheathed, but ready to be instantly pulled. We were not, after all, looking for a fight, just ready for one if it was forced upon us. As you might imagine, people gave way before us, everyone eyed us with a great deal of curiosity, and several young boys began following us.

My longbow was strung and my quivers were full of arrows and slung over my shoulder, but I was *not* carrying a sword and shield; Edward Sparrow was carrying them for me in addition to carrying his own. I was, however, at least as far as I knew, the only one wearing a chain shirt and carrying wrist knives. They were covered by my tunic and out of sight.

Why was I *not* carrying a sword and shield? Because we were not looking for a fight and I wanted to show everyone that I was coming to talk, not to fight. Besides, not holding a sword in my hand or carrying one in a sheath often let me get closer to an unsuspecting enemy, whereupon I could finish him off faster with my wrist knives. That was particularly true if he was lulled into a false sense of safety by not seeing me with an immediately usable sword or knife hanging on my belt.

Pulling a sword on a man who would then pull his own sword in response was never a good idea as he might turn out to be a better swordsman. It was always better to put someone down quickly with my wrist knives before he could get his sword out of its scabbard to defend himself.

There was, in other words, no need to take any unnecessary chances in the event someone might need to be threatened or killed. It was something my dear father had taught me.

******

It did not take long to reach the nearby great market of Athens and enter it through its main gate. Demetrius walked in front to lead us as we began walking in a single file through the crowded aisles of the market towards the cages holding the slaves.

As you might imagine, we got a lot of stares from the merchants and their early morning customers as we moved briskly through the market in a single file. As you might also imagine, no one tried to stop us or called out to in an effort to draw our attention to themselves and their wares. I walked immediately behind Demetrius with Harold bringing up the rear in case we were attacked from behind. None of our swords were drawn.

We found the foul-smelling cages of the slaves on the far side of one of the market's stone walls. They lined both sides of a narrow cobblestoned market aisle that ran next to the wall. The cages themselves were almost entirely made of upright logs planted in the ground so close together that even a small child could not squeeze through them. Similarly close together logs were laid across the tops of the cages so the slaves could not climb out.

A solid wooden door with a heavy wooden bar to seal the slaves in was the only way in or out of the cages. The wooden bar was far enough from the nearest opening such that it could not be reached by someone who was inside the cage. The cages themselves were foul beyond belief, almost as bad as the slave decks on some of the Moorish galleys we had taken.

The roof logs of some of the cages, but not all of them, were slanted and covered somewhat with mouldy old thatch to keep the sun and rain off slaves until they could be sold. The equally foul open area of the live sheep, cattle, and horses sections of the market began just beyond them. There were great swarms of flies buzzing about and the usual market cats were everywhere. Some of them appeared to be sleeping on top of the slave cages.

Men, women, and children of all ages and colours were jammed into the cages. Some of them were wearing ragged clothes, but many were not wearing anything at all including some of the women and almost all of the children. They had apparently been arriving for the past few days in anticipation of the coming sale.

A few of the slaves stood up and watched us warily without saying a word as we walked past them. Most, however, just sat quietly amongst the filth. And we certainly did not pay attention to them—our eyes were fixed on the large number of men holding swords and clubs that were waiting for us in the open space just beyond the slave pens where the livestock section of the market began. There looked to be a hundred or so of them.

A moment later and there was no doubt about it in my mind; the slavers and their supporters knew we were coming and were waiting for us. We had been betrayed.

On the face of it, we were badly outnumbered. So much so that for a very brief instant I thought about turning my little army around and hurrying away. But I did not do so for several reasons. One was that it would have been the wrong image to convey, one of weakness. More important, however, was that there was no need to run because the narrow aisle between the cages was an excellent fighting position because the cages and the wall would prevent our being attacked on our flanks.

It was also an easy decision because I did not see many swords amongst the mob of men and no shields or bows. Most of them appeared to be street toughs carrying wooden clubs and wearing knives. In any event, we had cages full of slaves on either side of us and there was nothing to do but brazen it out. So that is what I did.

"Stop here whilst I go forward to parley with them," I quietly ordered Lieutenant Bolton who had been walking immediately behind me as we moved through the market. "But bring your men up fast and hard if trouble starts. And for God's sake keep your men in the aisle so they cannot flank us."

Lieutenant Bolton nodded grimly and said "aye, I am to come up fast if there is fighting and keep my men in the aisle." There was a definite look of excitement and a thin smile of anticipation on his face. There was no doubt about it; the lieutenant was hoping for a fight.

With that settled I motioned for Demetrius to come with me and started walking down the aisle towards the waiting men. As I did, I put my hands into the sleeves of my tunic to make sure my wrist knives were ready for immediate use.

I quite deliberately did not walk all the way to the mob; I stopped just short of the end of the narrow market aisle, and then waited quietly with Demetrius standing next to me. A quick glance behind showed me that Lieutenant Bolton and his men had moved forward and were already in position behind me. They were shoulder to shoulder in several lines across the narrow aisle and had not yet drawn their swords. Lieutenant Bolton was in the middle of the first line.

Nothing happened. The slavers men just stared at me and I stared back. After a short wait, I spread my arms wide to show my open hands, cocked my head to the side, and said "well?" to the men standing together in the open area about a hundred paces away. It looked to be the open area into which the cattle and sheep, and horses were brought to be sold.

My move and the invitation it implied seemed to surprise them. They clearly did not understand a word I said, but they did understand my open-handed gesture and the questioning sound of my voice. It triggered some shuffling about in the ranks of the mob and a bit of talking amongst its members. A few moments later a group of five or six men began walking towards me.

I am not sure what made me do it, instinct I guess, but after they had taken only a few steps I held up the flat palm of my left hand towards them in a stop gesture, and then I shook it and my head disapprovingly, and casually said "wait."

The men stopped as I somehow knew they would. Then I shrugged my shoulders and cocked my head to convey my surprise at their need for numbers, and lifted my open hands towards them and their weapons, and then back towards me that had no weapons in sight. It was what I hoped would be seen as a "surely you are not afraid of meeting unarmed me" gesture.

A moment later I raised the pointing finger of my left hand and cocked my head to the side to indicate that only one of them should come forward, and then opened my hands again in a welcoming gesture that pointed to the ground immediately in front of me.

The men that had come forward towards me exchanged a few words amongst themselves, and then one of them came forward to talk whilst the others waited. He was a large heavy-set man with a greying beard and a filthy tunic. As he walked towards me his face took on a look of scowling ferociousness. He was carrying a very large club and had a knife stuck in his belt in front of his bulging belly.

Once again I held up the palm of my hand, and then sort of smiled and grimaced whilst I pointed the open palm of my other hand towards his club. Then I spread my arms and opened my empty hands towards him. I took a couple of soft and friendly steps farther up the aisle towards him as I did. He got my meaning and, without a word being spoken, he turned and handed his club to one of the men behind him.

It was as I had expected he would do; he could hardly do otherwise without indicating to his men that he was afraid of a smiling man whose hands were empty. My gambit had worked.

My on-coming visitor was almost certainly one of the leaders of the slavers, if not their leader himself, and was probably used to being able to intimidate minor merchants and bully his followers with his size and his scowl. At least, that was what I thought and hoped.

Demetrius diffidently moved through the archers and came to my side in response to a gentle "come here" motion from my hand and a smiling order from me. He was so clearly a harmless translator, in addition to likely being the man who had betrayed us, that neither the slaver approaching me nor the members of the men watching us reacted as if they considered him to be a threat.

I immediately smiled towards Demetrius to encourage our traitorous translator and gave him an order. "Please tell this good man that I have brought you to interpret for me because I cannot gobble Greek."

Demetrius immediately began doing so; at least I think that is what he was saying. The big man had stopped just outside the entrance to the aisle, about three or four paces in front of me. He continued giving me what was apparently his best hard look as he listened to whatever Demetrius was gobbling at him.

The big man began talking and pointing as soon as Demetrius finished. Demetrius translated his words as he spoke them.

"Gregori says you are a fool to come where you are not wanted. ... He says you will be very sorry if you do not leave immediately. ... He is telling you to go now whilst you and the men with you are still alive and able to walk away." *Gregori? He knows this man?" Now I knew for sure it was Demetrius who had betrayed us.*

The slaver's threat and warning was delivered loudly enough so the men standing behind him could hear. His men listened intently and several of them nodded their agreement to what the big man was saying with smiles on their faces. They appeared to be pleased that he was threatening me and putting me properly put in my place.

My reply was delivered with a smile on my face and a brief nod of my head to acknowledge that I had heard him. I stepped another couple of paces towards him and spread my arms as if in a warm gesture of peace and friendship as I spoke.

A great flock of flies were buzzing about everywhere and several times I swished my hand to drive them away as I was speaking. Gregori and Demetrius were doing the same. The flies were bothersome.

I did not begin my comments by mentioning that it was a Company rule to free all English slaves. I tacked in another direction as I drew my hands back into the baggy sleeves of my tunic to get them away from the flies and began periodically moving my arms to keep the flies away from my face.

"My name is George Courtenay," I said as I kept my hands inside my sleeves and periodically grimaced and shook my elbows up and down in a vain effort to drive away the pesky flies. "I have been sent by the Patriarch to meet with you and tell you of his wishes. And also to remind you that both the Patriarch and His Holiness, the Pope, have ordered that no Christians be taken or held as slaves.

"You have two English sailors, both Christians, and it is said in the market that you intend to auction them for slaves in a couple of days. My men and I have come to take them and any other Christians you might be holding off your hands so you will no longer have to feed them.

"No harm will come to you and your men if you turn them over to us peacefully. If you do not do so immediately, however, today will be the day you and the men with you will die and go to purgatory to burn forever."

Actually, of course, I was not at all sure that either the Holy Father or the Patriarch had given such an order since both Churches owned so many slaves. But if they had not given it, they should have done and that was good enough. Rome, after all, was many days away and I had no idea what the Patriarch was thinking these days now that we had defeated his army.

In any event, it was a good story and I told it quite earnestly with all the sincerity in my voice that I could muster.

The slaver literally growled and spluttered with rage as he listened to Demetrius repeat my threat. His face got red and fearsome and he said something to Demetrius.

As the slaver was speaking I put my left hand up to my ear and leaned forward with a hopeful and friendly look on my face—and moved even closer so I could better hear what he was saying. It was clear to everyone watching that I was interested in what the man was saying and meant him no harm.

"His name is Gregori. He claims he owns the slaves and he thinks you are mad for asking him to free them without paying for them. He says his friends have come to help him protect the slaves from being stolen." .... "He says that if you do not leave now you will be sorry." ... "He says...."

My hands were holding the handles of both of my wrist knives under my tunic as I interrupted Demetrius.

"Please remind Gregori that my men and I are archers and that we are required by the Pope and the Patriarch to free all Christian slaves, both Latin and Greek, as well as all of our passengers that are taken as slaves and ....."

Demetrius began doing so.

At that point, whilst Demetrius was still translating what I said, Gregori began leaning forward and gobbling belligerently right into my face. He was giving me quite a bollocking and got ever more loud and angry as he did. His breathe smelled awful.

Whether the slave master was actually angry or merely shouting threats at me to impress his men is something that would never be known. As he spoke, he reached out to poke me in the chest with one hand, and then, an instant later, went for the sheathed knife hanging from his belt with the other.

I never did hear a translation of what the slaver was saying as he made his move, but it was the last thing he ever said or did except for falling down with a lot of gurgling and bleeding.

My right hand wrist knife came straight out from under my tunic and took him in the throat up under his chin. At the same moment the knife in my left hand went through his tunic and up to its hilt in his belly, and then, a split second later, I jerked it upward as hard as I could. It happened so fast that the slaver did not have time to finish pulling his knife or even try to pull away.

The slave master gasped, his eyes bulged out, and he sort of gasped and squeaked at the same time as he grabbed at his throat with both hands and stared at me in total disbelief.

He was still on his feet as I held him up and pulled him towards me for a brief moment with my right hand's knife in his throat. I did so while I simultaneously gave another pull to finish ripping the knife in his belly upward.

It was an over-kill for sure, and not at all necessary, but sticking my left hand blade in and then ripping it upward was what I had constantly practiced almost every day of my life ever since my dear father gave me my first set of wrist knives. I did it automatically without even thinking about what I was doing.

Time and the slave master seemed to stand still for the very briefest of moments while everyone was too stunned to speak or move. Then I let go of my knives and gave him a little push as I stepped back deeper into the aisle and watched as the slaver staggered backwards and turned around as he fell, first to his knees and then, a few moments later, as he slowly toppled over on to his side. My knives were still in him and he was still moving about and gurgling as he did.

As I stood there and watched Gregori go down, the gang of weapons-carrying men waiting in front of me, who had clearly seen and heard everything from about twenty paces away, gave great angry shouts and began surging forward waving their swords and clubs. I only saw one man carrying a shield.

Simultaneously surging forward behind me were Lieutenant Bolton and his swordsmen. They were much closer to me than the mob and had already drawn their swords. They moved forward and stepped in front of me with their shields up and their swords at the ready. Edward Sparrow somehow appeared at my side and handed me my sword and shield as they did.

"Get behind me, Edward, and you and Robert watch our rear." I ordered as I grabbed the sword and shield from him. The first of the mob reached Lieutenant Bolton and our front line of swordsmen as I hastily took them.

Harold was by my side and so was one of Lieutenant Bolton's men. Another of the Lieutenant's men stood on the other side of Harold so that we filled the aisle with another line of four.

****** *George Courtenay*

The fighting that resulted was very noisy with much shouting and screaming. It was also extremely bloody and did not last very long. The men in the slaver's mob must have thought there would be some sort of tavern brawl at which they would somehow excel and we would run away because we were intimidated and outnumbered.

It did not happen. We did not run. Instead we stood together and held the opening at the end of the aisle between two slave cages with a line four men across and four men in a second line immediately behind them, and the last two in a third line.

What our being in the aisle with slave cages on both sides of us meant was that only a few of the slavers' poorly armed and untrained toughs could get into the aisle and actually come to grips with the Company's best swordsmen.

The result of the poorly armed slaver's gang having to fight one on one against expert swordsmen was inevitable. It was not long before those of the mob that had made the mistake of being thrusters stopped trying to climb over their fallen friends to get to us and began trying to turn around to escape. Things were clearly not going as they had expected.

I saw it all because I spent most of the short battle standing in the second line with Harold next to me and two of Lieutenant Bolton's swordsmen on either side of us. We ended up mostly watching as the Lieutenant and the little line of men in front of us did most of the fighting and killing.

Indeed, the fighting was over so quickly that it never did reach Robert Archer and Edward Sparrow in our third line. It also did not last long enough for the mob to run around and try to get at us from behind. And it would not have done them any good if they had tried since a couple of men from our second line would have turned around to join Robert and Edward so that we would have had four good fighting men facing them in that direction as well.

Our only serious casualty was one of our swordsmen, a sergeant, who had somehow gotten hit on the side of his head with a club and fell down to sleep. It happened whilst he was stabbing into the mass of men in front of him and his sword got stuck for a moment. I briefly stepped up to take his place while Uncle Harold grabbed the sleeping man's leg and pulled him back to safety so he would not get trampled or stabbed whilst he was down. The fighting was mostly over by then, but not completely. There was more to come.

The slavers that led the charge suffered grievously. More than a dozen of them were dead or seriously wounded less than a minute later when the surviving attackers began trying to pull back and escape by running into the livestock section of the market.

Lieutenant Bolton led the way as we climbed over their dead and dying friends and immediately began chasing after them. We cut down four or five more as easy as if we were harvesting grain. I only gave the order that ended it so we would not get to far from our natural stronghold in the slavers' aisle.

"Enough. Let them run. Fall back to the aisle and take prisoners to question. Take prisoners I say."

I gave the order as I stood leaning over with my hands on my knees trying to catch my breath after running down one of the slaver's gang and chopping him in the side of his neck with my short sword. Then I looked down; I was standing in cow shite amidst a line of cows tethered to logs and tree stumps.

The cows' wide-eyed minders were nowhere to be seen. They had watched the brief battle, and then run for their lives when we pursued the slavers into their midst. Only the cows and a handful of cats and the buzzing flies remained. The cats ignored us.

Chapter Eight

The aftermath.

Demetrius was nowhere to be found and, although we did not know it at the time, would never be seen again. He had obviously betrayed us and decided to run while he still had a chance to escape the Company's vengeance.

"England or Britain," I shouted several times as I trotted down the aisle that ran through the slave pens. "Who is from the islands?" I shouted my question in crusader French, the language many people were beginning to call English.

"Hoy. Over here, your lordship. Me and Tom be from Manchester."

The frantic calls came from two ragged men with long and dirty beards in one of the fly-infested cages. They were desperately shouting and waving their hands between the posts of a cage about half way down the aisle.

"Is anyone else from England or the islands, lads?" I loudly asked the excited men as Robert and I hurried over to them.

Robert immediately tried to pull off the rusty chain that held their cage closed. He was unsuccessful; it was one of the few in the aisle that had some kind of newfangled iron lock that could not be opened without a metal key cut to fit into its grooves.

In the background I could hear Lieutenant Bolton redeploying his men to block both ends of the aisle.

"Who has the key?"

I shouted my question at the two Englishmen even though they were now only a foot or so away and literally dancing up and down with excitement. A half dozen or so of their equally wide-eyed and excited cage-mates were standing right behind them. The noise around me was getting louder and louder, both from the slaves and from the market. Or perhaps I was just paying attention to it for the first time.

The aisle between the slave cages was soon filled with joyous screaming and much shouting as the bars came off the doors to the cages and the slaves came pouring out, many of them at least. Some of the slaves, quite surprisingly, hung back.

Harold knew how to gobble Moorish because he himself had once been a slave pulling an oar on a Moorish galley. He promptly began asking the newly freed Moorish slaves about the keys and soon had an answer—there was only one key and it was hanging in plain sight at the end of the aisle.

One of the archers knew how to use a key. He grabbed it and opened the cage holding the Englishmen, and then he used it to unlock the other two slave cages that had been both locked and barred. At the same time, more and more slaves were coming out of their cages and I could see more and more curious merchants further down the aisle in the market trying to see what was happening. The only slavers in sight were either on the ground or grievously wounded and trying to crawl away. We ignored them.

What everyone saw and heard was a chaotic and noisy scene with the wounded gang members crying out for help and the jubilant slaves loudly talking and shouting as they crowded into the aisle and began moving about in every direction.

Whilst the chaos was growing there were also several very short arguments when our archers saw slaves and men from the market beginning to rifle through the pouches of the dead and wounded gang members and picking up their weapons such as they were. The archers rightly believed the coins belonged to them and that the weapons belonged to the Company as prizes.

On the other hand, no one said a word or lifted a finger when one of the slaves gobbled to one of the wounded slavers in a strange tongue as he stomped his foot over and over again on the slaver's neck until it broke.

Despite the chaos, I immediately and loudly made the traditional Company offer in crusader French to the slaves, and then had Harold repeat it in Moorish and one of the newly freed slaves in Greek. We did so several times.

"You are free to go to wherever you want to go. If you wish to come with us as free men and women, the Company will give you food and a safe place to sleep in exchange for you working for us each day. If you come with us, you may leave us whenever you wish."

We left the aisle of slave cages almost immediately. The two Englishmen and quite a number of the slaves followed us all the back to our Piraeus shipping post with Lieutenant Bolton and his men carrying their bloody swords at the ready and leading the way.   Our sleeping swordsman was shaken awake and staggered along with us with the help of one of his mates.

As you might imagine, people hurried to get out of our way. Everyone else stared with surprise and disbelief as we streamed through the market aisles and began hurriedly walking the short distance back to our shipping post. Edward and a couple of Lieutenant Bolton's hard-bitten swordsmen were carrying young children that had been abandoned in the cages when the older slaves fled without them.

Not all of the slaves came with us. At least a third, and perhaps more, quickly disappeared. Interestingly enough, some of the slaves were, at first, reluctant to leave their cages until they were forced out and some that followed after us seemed to think we were their new owners. It was something we had seen previously, particularly when someone had been born a slave.

Even before we reached our Athens post it was obvious that it would be too small to accommodate everyone. Accordingly, we walked right past it and headed for our Piraeus post and its much larger bailey and warehouse. The only exceptions were the four small children that were being carried by Edward and the swordsmen. They were handed over to Robert's wife and would remain in Athens.

******

"Well, what are we going to do with them?"

Harold asked the question when we finished the counting, and began to clothe and feed, those of the slaves that had followed us back to our shipping post in Piraeus. We had led them all the way to Piraeus because it had a much bigger bailey than our post in Athens. There were eighty-eight of them including the four small children left with Robert's wife.

"I suppose some of them can work for their food by helping us dig longer escape tunnels and the rest can work on strengthening our compound walls. But if the past is any guide, a goodly number of them will leave as soon as they can find a way to get back home."

"Aye, I hope you are right, George, but I think you may be wrong, at least in part. This lot, except for the English sailors, are not like the galley slaves we have freed in the past. Many of them have always been slaves or serfs and most of the rest are Moors that have not a clue as to what to do or where to go."

"Well Uncle, you are one of the few men in the Company that knows how to talk Moorish, so it will be up to you to find those that want to work their way back to their homes as sailors on transports bound for a Moorish port. And best you hurry to make the necessary arrangements because it is likely we will be sailing tomorrow afternoon."

"Can you give me all day tomorrow so I can find out where they want to go and make arrangements with the Moors' agents in the market? We could sail the next morning."

"Oh aye, if you think it important. But be sure to let the merchants that help the slaves know that we will remember and reward their assistance, and especially remind them that the Company has spies in every port and will be back to take their heads if the sailors' berths and other transportations they arrange do not put the freed slaves ashore as free men."

Harold just smiled his agreement at my unnecessary cautioning. Of course he did; he had been a sailor man for many years and dealt with many captains and merchants; he knew exactly what to say to them.

Was the Company foolish to free Christian and other slaves whenever possible instead of selling them as was the common practice? My lieutenants and I did not think so—because it generated many a good contract by endearing us to Christian sailors and to the Christian merchants whose sons often sailed on voyages to buy or sell things. It also was a source of recruits if the slaves were not poxed or too far gone from not eating enough food and being beaten. We knew that for sure—Uncle Harold was one of them and so was Uncle Henry.

****

It was a beautiful moonlit night and all the stars were out. From where we sat on the forecastle roof of Harold's galley we could hear the sounds of singing and talking coming from the nearby waterfront taverns. That was no surprise—they were crowded with several thousand archers and sailors that had gone ashore with liberty coins.

We were sanguine about what we saw and heard. Some of the men would run for sure, but most of the men that were missing when we sailed were more likely to have been too drunk to return in time. If the past was any guide, most of them would sooner or later end up reporting in to our local shipping post and losing a stripe.

My lieutenants and I talked again about the slaves that night as we sat on the stern castle roof of Harold's galley and ate our suppers. We had gone aboard his galley to eat and sleep because the bailey of the Piraeus post was overly crowded with the newly freed slaves. There was no place we could have talked except inside the post's building where it would have been much too warm.

Robert was perplexed.

"It be strange, Commander, it be strange. Except for about twenty Moorish sailors that will be able to make their own way home by joining the crews of the Moorish transports that call in here, almost all the rest of the Moorish slaves want to stay with us, more than forty of them including all the women. They be feared of being taken again for slaves if they board a Moorish transport."

"More than forty? That many? Damnation. Well, Harold, you are the Company's expert on slaves. What do you suggest?"

"This is a Christian land where Moors be having trouble because of how they pray. So I think you should sprinkle water on the ones that stay and tell them they are now Christians. We can put them to work improving our posts in exchange for their food and a safe place to sleep. Even better, put some of them to work building a Company warehouse on the quay where they can live until they wander off."

Robert liked the idea.

"Harold Lewes is right, Commander. Most of the slaves will sooner or later wander off. They always do. A year from now there will not be a dozen left, and we will have a much stronger shipping post for all the work that they do before they leave."

I disagreed after I thought about it for a few moments.

"Aye. I agree about putting them to work for food and protection. It is what we always do with slaves and refugees when they have nowhere to go. But I am not so sure about using them to build a separate warehouse. It would mean another place that would have to be guarded. Better, I think, to either strengthen the two we already have or find someplace bigger and stronger for either one or both of our current tenements."

We spent the next couple of hours listening to sounds coming from the nearby taverns whilst we yarned about the slaves, the company, our families, and the recent fighting at Constantinople. It was a peaceful and comfortable time. After a while, Robert and Edward went home and everyone drifted off to try to get whatever sleep they could with so many drunken men returning from the taverns.

******

Because of the crowding of our shipping posts, I stayed on board Harold's galley that night, slept like a log in my private sleeping space, the forward castle. The next morning I awoke at dawn to poop into the harbour and break my fast with the bread, cheese, and an apple. They were brought to me by Roger whose berth was in the much larger stern castle with Harold and his lieutenant and key sergeants.

It had been my intention to spend the day visiting our Piraeus post to see how Edward Sparrow and his men were doing with the slaves, and then return to see how the resupply of our fleet was proceeding. Whilst I was doing that, Harold would walk into the Athens market with a strong guard of archers to visit with the Moorish merchants to discuss our Moorish slaves. Our plan was to give our men another night of liberty and sail in the morning.

It had the makings of a fine day, but it was not to be. I was just finishing a bowl of morning ale when who should arrive on the quay but Robert Archer, the captain of our shipping post. He was accompanying an unexpected visitor—a Latin bishop riding in a two-horse cart. I knew my visitor was a bishop because he was wearing a fine bishop's robe and a mitre despite the heat, and accompanied by two priests riding in the cart with him and eight sweating guards in livery running along behind it.

The bishop and the two priests were riding in the horse cart whereas Robert, presumably because he was deemed not sufficiently important to ride in the cart with them, was hurrying along behind the cart with the bishop's guards. Keeping Robert out of the cart was a serious mistake; it irked me.

There was room for the horse cart to park on the quay in front of Harold's galley. That was because we had already taken on most of the galley's supplies, all except the deck cargo of live sheep and cattle that were waiting at the end of the quay. They would be loaded in the morning. I watched impassively as the cart came to a halt and the bishop climbed out.

My visitor was clearly trying to impress me, and he certainly did—both as a fool that did not know how to dress properly for warm weather and as a fool who thought I would be impressed by his rank and religious symbols. My mood turned even sourer as they got closer and I saw how hot and tired Robert had become by being forced to run through the streets behind the trotting horses that pulled the cart.

It was a visit from which no good could come. At least that was my initial thought. And I found myself getting angrier and angrier because Robert, a captain in the Company of Archers had not been thought important enough to be invited to ride with the priests. Accordingly, I just stood on the castle roof with a stony face and stared across at the new arrivals without saying a word or making a gesture—and plotted behind my eyes to put the fool in his place.

Our visitors did briefly gain some attention both from the sailors on the galleys moored along the quay and from the wharfies, sightseers, pimps, and the merchants' men further down the quay that were delivering the last of the supplies we had purchased to our other galleys.

Most of the men and women on quay looked at the new arrivals for a few moments, and then returned to whatever they were doing before the bishop and his men arrived—which for many of them was nothing except yarning with each other as they sat on the quay whilst they waited for employment.

Even so, as you might expect, both the Company men on our galleys and the men and women on the quay were curious about our visitors. Some of them continued to stare at them whilst others returned to whatever they were doing and continued to watch the new arrivals out of the corners of their eyes.

None of the watchers said a word. But their curiosity was understandable; many of them had probably never seen a bishop before, especially one foolish enough to wear warm clothes on a hot day.

After a vainly waiting in the sun for a short time for someone to come to welcome him, the bishop dismounted with the assistance of the two priests. One of them climbed down the ladder to the deck before he did in order to help him if he decided to climb down. The other priest stayed on the quay to hold the ladder steady. I just continued standing on the castle roof staring over towards him without moving, even after the bishop climbed out of the cart and stood on the quay.

Finally, Robert called out.

"Commander, the Duke's chancellor is here to talk to you. He is a bishop."

The Duke's chancellor is he? Well that is interesting. I wonder what he wants.

I nodded at Robert without saying a word. And then, after waiting a few moments with a rather cold expression on my face, I cocked my head slightly to indicate my willingness to talk and sort of opened my left hand and swept it lower towards the deck of the galley in such a way as to invite the bishop to come on board.

Robert and the three churchmen just stared at me in surprise. It was definitely not the reception they expected. Had I not just been told he was an important man? I continued to stand on the castle roof without moving or saying a word.

A moment later Harold climbed up the three stairs to the castle roof and joined me. He had heard the commotion and come out to see what might be causing it.

"Please go down to the deck, Lieutenant Commander, and see that the ladder for the bishop is properly held *if* he decides to come on board." I heavily emphasized the word "if."

There were no flies on Harold. He instantly understood what I was doing.

"Aye, Commander. I am to go on deck and make sure the ladder for the bishop is properly held *if* he decides to come on board."

It was an order so he repeated it back to me, and did it rather cheerfully with just the slightest hint of a pleased smile on his face.

Of course Harold was amused; we had known each other even since I was a small boy riding on my father's shoulders. He knew I did not like pompous churchmen and had something in mind. He just did not know what it might be.

Harold and his apprentice promptly jumped down on to the deck and moved towards the boarding ladder leaning up against the quay. Roger followed me down to the deck a few moments later as I casually descended to the deck using the stairs. When we reached the deck we moved to stand in a patch of shade on its sea side, not to the side of the deck next to the quay where the bishop and his party were preparing to climb down.

******

The Duke's Chancellor had obviously expected me to rush to greet him because he was wearing a bishop's robe and had a mitre on his head. I had not and now he obviously had to either come to me or leave. He decided to come to me, but was visibly uneasy about climbing down the ladder to board the galley. That he was willing to do so suggested to me that he had something important to tell me or ask me.

I found his unease to be interesting. Perhaps he was fearful because he had never before climbed on a ladder. Or it might have been that he had heard about the papal nuncio and the bishop from Constantinople that had mysteriously disappeared earlier this year—after trying kill me and then trying to steal the Empress's gold, the gold my galley had subsequently carried to the Pope for the Holy Father's prayers on behalf of the Empress becoming her son's regent.

The bishop, of course, was mistaken to worry about my lack of enthusiasm to receive him. Had I wanted to get him on board so I could take him out to sea to hang him or throw him over the side to join his fellow churchmen from Constantinople, I would have rushed to kiss his ring and welcomed him to come on board to join me. It was, after all, always better to get things like that done without a struggle, at least that is what my father and Uncle Thomas always said.

In any event, the bishop finally took a deep breath to steady himself, handed his mitre and crosier to the priest who had remained on the quay, hitched up his ornate embroidered robe, and stepped on to the ladder. I got the impression it was the first time in his life that he had ever set foot on one. The two priests held the ladder steady. As an additional precaution, Harold's apprentice had his foot up against it at the bottom to help the priest keep it from slipping when the deck moved.

Harold and I just stood together impassively on the other side of the deck and watched. Roger stood with us to listen and learn.

I still had no idea why the bishop had come to visit me, only that it was obviously important enough that he was willing to climb down an unsteady ladder in order to speak with me.

After a moment's hesitation, the bishop finally started down the ladder to bring me whatever message or threat he was carrying. He was a particularly bulky man and it took him a while because he went down one slow step at a time with his hands tightly holding on for dear life. He did, however, make it to the galley's deck without falling off the ladder or breaking it.

The priest on the quay hurried down behind him, handed his staff to him, and helped him put his mitre back on his heavily bearded head.

I just stood on the other side of the deck and waited without moving or saying a word even after the bishop reached the deck and wiped the sweat off his face. Finally, after the second priest had joined him, he gave up waiting for me to come across the deck to greet him, and walked across the deck to where I was standing.

"I am Bishop Francois, chancellor of his Excellency, Duke Antoine of Athens."

That was how the bishop rather arrogantly identified himself in Parisian French after walking across the deck to where I was waiting and holding out his ring for me to kiss.

I said nothing and did nothing. I just stared at him impassively and made no move of any kind.

"Are you not a Christian?" he finally asked as he extended his hand and literally shook his ring at me.

My reply in Latin stunned him.

"And are you such an uneducated churl that you do not even know our church's hierarchy of ranks or how they are displayed?"

I asked my insulting question scornfully in Latin with a sharp cutting edge to my voice, pointed to the stripes on my tunic, and then continued before he could respond.

"Do you not know what these seven stripes mean? Obviously not, which means you are an improperly educated lout who bought his position without being qualified for it. I am sure the Holy Father will be disappointed when I mention your inappropriate behaviour to him when I meet with him in Rome next month."

It was definitely not the response he expected. The poor man was so shocked and taken aback at my words that I almost felt sorry for him. His mouth dropped open and he gaped at me in dismay with eyes that almost bugged out of his head.

"You," I said as I shook my pointing finger in his face and with as disdainful a sound to my voice as I could muster, "are merely a minor bishop serving as the clerk of a minor lord. Whereas I, on the other hand, am the commander of a papal order and rank above an archbishop. If I thought your disrespect was based on anything but ignorance, I would have you immediately burnt or hung as an enemy of the Church."

To say that my words surprised and distressed the poor sod and his two priestly assistants would be an understatement. He was so taken aback and astonished that I thought for a moment he might fall down on the deck and go to sleep. The faces of two priests that had followed him down the ladder turned white and one of them actually began trembling. This was definitely not the reception the bishop and his men were used to receiving.

"Now tell me why you have come to visit me and made such a fool of yourself," I ordered rather harshly with a touch of arrogance.

Did I know that the commanders of papal orders, especially minor ones such as ours, ranked bishops in the church's scheme of things? No. But they should and that was good enough since this lout did not know either. I decided to ask my Uncle Thomas next time I saw him.

******

Bishop Francoise stammered and started to say he had come to congratulate me on the Company's great victory, word of which he said had only reached Athens several days ago. I leaned forward as he did and gave him a very angry and disbelievingly look.

"You came here wearing your gown and mitre merely to congratulate me on our order defeating the Greek heretics? I do not believe you. You insult me, and thus the Church and the Holy Father, by thinking I am stupid enough to believe your lies. God will punish you for lying and wasting my time. And if he does not, either the Pope or I will. Now tell me the truth. Why have you come?"

The poor sod quickly changed his tune and began insisting that congratulating me was not at all the main reason he had come. The main reason, he said, was to let me know that the Duke of Athens wanted me to present myself at his castle and explain why I had started a fight with the men that were in charge of the slave market.

The idea that I might be stupid enough to put myself at risk by entering the Duke's castle was so insulting and absurd that I started to laugh.

But then an idea came out of nowhere and popped into my head. I immediately set it in motion by leaning forward and snarling at Bishop Francoise. Fear and caution, after all, cuts both ways.

"I am the commander of the army of the Latin Empress as well as the commander of The Company of Archers and my religious order. My men and I obeyed the Holy Father and supported the Empress, the Empress that *you* and your lord betrayed by not coming to her assistance when she summoned you and the Holy Father commanded you.

"If the Duke of Athens or any other cowardly traitor wishes to discuss some matter with me, he can come here and do it. But you and I both know that the Duke will not come because he is afraid that I might have been ordered to take his head—because he knows he traitorously failed to do his God-given duty to the Church and the Empress.

"Also, and making matters worse for him, and for you as his religious advisor, he will also not come because he failed to do his duty to the Church by obeying the Pope's command to never allow a Christian to be held as a slave."

Actually, of course, I neither knew nor cared whether or not the Pope had issued an order for everyone to help the Empress fight off the Greeks or about the slaves. He might have done either and that was close enough for what I had in mind.

"There is no doubt about it. The Duke is twice damned unless he repents and immediately buys sufficient indulgences from both the Pope and my order, the Order of Poor Landless Sailors. And something for the Empress as well, eh?

"If they are not paid by the time I sail tomorrow morning, I will leave some of my men here to besiege him—with orders to hang him and put his head on a spike above the city gate when he finally runs out of food and surrenders. I will do so if he does not pay for the indulgences by the time I sail two hours after the sun comes up tomorrow morning.

"And you and your fellow priests are no better," I softly hissed at him with a dismissive wave of my hand.

"You stood idle whilst the Duke disobeyed his God-given Empress and then again when Christians were being sold as slaves. You too need to buy some indulgences if you are to avoid being hung and having your head on a spike next to his."

We then discussed the price of each of the indulgences.

Chapter Nine
Another Gambit.

Our fleet sailed the next morning carrying an additional chest of coins from the Duke of Athens and a second chest with some of Bishop Francoise's hurriedly gathered coins and half a dozen fine silver plates and chalices which he had apparently looted from one of his diocese's churches. They had been delivered a few minutes earlier along with many meaningless swearings of loyalty oaths to the Empress and promises that no British slaves would ever again be allowed in Athens or elsewhere in the lands the Duke controlled.

Harold and old Jeffrey, his galley's long-time lieutenant, were standing nearby and listening as we watched the chests of coins and plate being carried to the forward castle to be stored under and adjacent to my string bed. Our apprentices were standing near us as usual. In the background we could hear the shouts of the galley's sailing sergeant ordering the mooring lines to be cast off.

I was in a particularly good mood as we began moving towards the harbour entrance and the Company galleys that were waiting just beyond it to get their sailing orders for the next leg of our voyage.

"There is a lesson here, lads," I turned around and said to the two apprentice sergeants as we began moving and watched the cart that had carried the coins clatter away—"never let a low-risk opportunity to gather coins for the Company pass *unless* you think it might somehow hurt the Company in the future."

After a moment's pause whilst Harold bellowed out some orders to his sailing sergeant, I asked the boys a question.

"That being the case, how many of the Duke's indulgence coins for allowing the English slaves to be held in the market should we actually deliver to the Pope? And how much of the coins he has gifted to the Empress to try to regain her favour should we send to her?"

The boys looked surprised, and then uncertain, probably because I rarely addressed them with a question asking about their opinions. Neither of them ventured an answer, so I answered my question for them.

"Every single one of the Empress's coins will go to her, lads, every single one. She is important to our future and sooner or later word will get back to her as to exactly how much the Duke paid in an effort to placate her. So it will build her trust in the Company when she finds out that she received everything he sent to her, as she will from his ambassador. She can require the Duke to pay more, or take his head, if she decides it is not enough.

"We will similarly deliver to the Holy Father every single one of the coins the Duke paid to buy an indulgence for allowing Christian slaves to be sold in his market *in the past* and promising that it would never happen again. He too, the Pope that is, is important to our company's future and will almost certainly learn how much the Duke paid. Keeping the Holy Father sweet for the years ahead is far more important to the Company than getting a few more coins today.

"Indeed, staying on the Holy Father's good side greatly helps the Company. It lets us claim to be acting for him when we need an excuse for doing something. It is the same with the Empress from whom the Company is now getting coins from her tolls. We want to keep her sweet and supportive of the Company in the years ahead as well so we can continue to collect and keep her tolls.

"We shall, however, keep all of the bishop's indulgence coins, every single one of them, because they were paid to *us* for *our* silence. Besides, the bishop is *not* important to our future and the Pope will never know the bishop gave them to us to buy our silence.

"The Holy Father will not know because the bishop will never mention to anyone that he paid us to not tell the Pope about his transgressions. It would embarrass him too much to admit he had disobeyed the Pope's orders or did not know about them.

"In other words, paying all the coins to the Pope and the Empress means we will continue to be known as a company that keeps its word and does not cheat or rob if we give our word or sign a contract—a reputation which is important for the Company's future relationships with them and with everyone else. On the other hand, we will keep the bishop's coins both because he paid them to us for *our* silence, and also because he is not important for the Company's future.

"And now, lads, I can see that the last of our galleys has cleared the harbour. That means your lesson is over and the time has come to call in the captains and tell them about our plans. So you two run up the mast and get ready to wave the 'all captains' flag to call them. Go."

It was a fine day and comfortable so long as one stayed out of the sun.

******

There were galleys bobbing about around us as the galleys of our fleet lowered their sails and began wallowing in the light seas as we drifted slowly back towards Piraeus as a result of the wind. All around us captains were hurrying to launch their dinghies. We were about four miles south of the harbour.

A few minutes later Harold and I stood at the deck railing and greeted each of the captains most friendly as he climbed up the rope ladder to our galley's deck.

It took a while for all the captains to reach Harold's galley and climb aboard. But they did and there were soon twenty-two visiting galley captains sitting on their arses yarning in the shade of the sail on the forward mast. It had been temporarily rigged to provide some shade instead of to catch the wind. The cook's helper helped the early arrivals pass the time by handing out bowls of recently brewed morning ale.

As soon as everyone had been assembled, greeted, and given a bowl of ale, I climbed up to the roof of the forward castle so they could all see and hear me. Harold came up with me and stood next to me. Our apprentices stood on the deck behind the captains, and so did a number of our galley's archers and sailors.

A "captains' call" to get their sailing orders immediately after a fleet left a port was a common occurrence when something important was to be announced that we did not want other people and their spies to immediately know about. As a result, everyone on Harold's deck knew something was up, and they were more than a little curious even though they were trying not to show it.

Finally, after counting heads to make sure every captain was present, I told them why they had been summoned.

"You all came aboard thinking that we were sailing together so that we would have sufficient force prevent the Venetians from taking the Empress's gold we are carrying to Rome to deliver to the Holy Father.

"That was the story you were told and you shared it with your men. It was given to everyone so the story would spread and the Venetian spies would think that we are sailing for Rome. In fact, we are *not* sailing for Rome with the Empress's coins, not yet at least. We have something else to do before we set our course for Rome"

My announcement surprised the men sitting and standing below me. Their response, as you might expect, was a great deal of murmuring and a bit of movement and shifting around as they looked at each other. They became even more attentive. "I knew it, by God," I heard someone say with a great deal of satisfaction in his voice.

I raised my hands for silence and waited for them to quiet down. Then I proceeded to tell them what we were going to do next.

"The articles of our Company's compact, on which every man here has made his mark, requires a great vengeance to fall on anyone that kills or in any way damages even a single one of us. The Venetians did exactly that when they helped the Greek army get to Constantinople so it could attack us. And then they made things even worse by directly attacking the men guarding our galleys which had been pulled ashore so their crews could fight on the city's walls.

"Many good men have been killed or wounded as a result of what the Venetians did to help the Greeks. They deserve the vengeance required by the articles of our company's compact and they are going to get it.

"Accordingly, we are all sailing directly for Ancona from here. We will base ourselves in Ancona for the next month or so under a mercenary contract from France which requires us to sail against Venice under the orders of the commander of the French galleys in the Mediterranean.

"More specifically, our galleys will become part of a *French* fleet coming from the Holy Land for the purpose of taking all the Venetian and Venetian-related transports and galleys the French can find in the Adriatic. We will be with the French because France is now at war with Venice. All the prizes we take, however, are ours to do with as we see fit.

What I said about France being involved was another gambit that I wanted to get out at our next port call. Besides, if France was not yet in a war with Venice and the supporters of the Pope over the Italian states, it should be, so there was no reason not to encourage them to get started and leave the Holy Land's refugees and Constantinople's tolls to us.

"In other words, my friends, our galleys and those of the French are going to spend the rest of the summer going after prize money from Venice's shipping in the Adriatic Sea instead of immediately sailing for Rome or returning to our regular routine of carrying passengers and cargos! We will carry the Empress's coins to Rome afterwards."

The captains were dumbfounded at the unexpected good news. Prize money from taking Venetian shipping in the Adriatic? Maybe even large amounts of prize money?

For a moment they just sat there on Harold's deck and looked at each other in disbelief. Did the Commander really just say they would be spending the rest of the summer in the Adriatic and they would be going after Venetian prizes instead of sailing to Rome and then spending what was left of the sailing season carrying passengers and cargos?

A moment later the captains jumped to their feet and everyone started shouting and cheering enthusiastically. It warmed my heart even though what I had just told them were lies to mislead and confuse our enemies. I knew they were good gambits because even Harold seemed to believe me.

Chapter Ten

We reach Ancona.

Our fleet of twenty-three Company war galleys sailed along the Greek coast until two days of heavy rain separated us as we approached the entrance to the Adriatic Sea. It was not a dangerous storm that would keep us from reaching Venice at the other end of the Adriatic, but the two days of poor visibility did cause the Company's fleet to get scattered and slow us down.

Once we separated it became every galley for itself and the fleet would rendezvous in the harbour at the port city of Ancona on the eastern coast of Italy. It was from Ancona that we would, "under command of the French who have contracted with us to help them," begin our patrols to intercept the shipping coming and going from Venice. Ancona was a good location for the "French fleet" to base itself as it was about two-thirds of the way between the entrance to the Adriatic and the city of Venice on its northern coast.

Harold's galley ran before the wind until the storm passed, and then continued north until our lookouts sighted the Italian coast. We were able to re-establish our precise position soon after sighting some villages which our sailors recognized as being on the Italian coast just south of Otranto.

We called in at the Italian port of Otranto briefly to take on water and supplies and to give the men a few hours of liberty. Then we sailed and rowed further north along the eastern coast of Italy towards the sheltered harbour in front of the walled city of Ancona. We would, the men had been told *after* they went ashore at Otranto, be based at Ancona whilst we and our French allies prowled the Adriatic in search of Venetian prizes.

A small fleet of five Company galleys, including Harold's, entered Ancona's harbour five days after we left Otranto. The other four galleys had been spotted by our eagle-eyed lookouts after the storm and joined up with us along the way. A number of other sails had also been seen before we reached Otranto but we made no effort to chase them.

There was no alarm at our entrance into Ancona's harbour as eight of our galleys had already arrived, four individually and four together in a mini-fleet that had formed up along the way just as our five had done. We would, I decided, wait for the others before we commenced operations. It would give our men time to go ashore and spread our lies.

Several of our scattered galleys had encounters with northbound transports sailing in the direction of Venice after they entered the Adriatic. I began hearing about them as soon as we entered the harbour and I had an opportunity to speak with their captains.

****** *Lieutenant Standish of Galley Forty-five*

The waters of the Adriatic were busy as usual. We sighted and ignored several southbound ships and cogs after the storm ended. It was not until the morning of the third day after the storm that our lookouts spotted a big two-master off to starboard. It was tacking north in the general direction of Venice with its sails up, just as we were doing.

It was not at all certain that the transport was bound for Venice. All we knew for sure was that it was headed in that general direction. But that was more than enough. We put our oars in the water and turned towards it just as we had been ordered to do if we sighted a sail that looked to be heading for Venice.

The cog must have had a lookout on its mast because it had already turned away and begun running before the wind in an effort to avoid us in case we were hostile. It was quite an understandable response; war galleys such as ours often had that effect on innocent transports.

I climbed the forward mast as soon our lookout, Andy Ander's son, a sailor from Hull, hoyed the deck to report the sighting. A few moments later Captain Adams came out of his cabin and followed me up. Men were running to their oars and sail tending positions as he did. They had been engaged in archery and sword practice up until then.

Our sails were soon adjusted and we began the chase, but with only, to everyone's great surprise, some of our upper tier oars in the water. About twenty minutes later, just as we were closing in, Captain Adams gave a strange order.

"Drop the mainsail fast, as if it had somehow failed, and turn hard to port. Cease rowing."

****** *Lieutenant Commander Harold Lewes.*

Three of the four captains that were the first to reach Ancona followed the very explicit orders they had been given at the captains' meeting. Before letting their crews go ashore to refresh themselves, the three captains explained to their men why our galleys were all flying the red Oriflamme pennant of France's King Phillip Augustus—because the Company had contracted to be part of a large French fleet whose galleys would be arriving "any day now" to wage war against Venice. Our galleys would, our men were told, be joining the French fleet and begin taking Venetian transports as prizes.

We captains were also told to explain to our men why Anacona's harbour had to be closed to all outgoing traffic, even fishermen—to prevent anyone from leaving to alert Venice that for the next month or so that the French fleet would be patrolling the Adriatic in search of Venetian prizes. More prizes, we were told to explain to our men, would be taken if the Venetians were surprised.

Unfortunately, the fourth captain did not explain things to his crew until two days later, after George had arrived and held another captains meeting for those that had already reached Ancona.

The fourth captain's excuse was that he had not understood what he had been told earlier. Accordingly, his galley had flown the red Oriflamme pennant of the French king as he had been ordered to do, but he thought he was supposed to keep the Company's plans a secret from his men so they would not reveal them when they went ashore. Harold promptly replaced him for not following orders.

Whether or not the Venetians would hear about our plans and keep their transports out of the Adriatic for the next month or so was not certain. But it was likely because our efforts to close Ancona's harbour were *not* rigorously enforced.

Indeed, due to a very deliberate oversight on Harold's part, the closure was not enforced after it was announced. As a result, a number of fishing boats and transports were able to slip away in the darkness to warn Venice that the French were out. It happened whilst our galleys were at anchor and their crews were ashore enjoying themselves in the local taverns.

Similarly, no effort was made to prevent horsemen from the city from riding overland to alert the Venetians as to "the plans of the French."

All in all, as a result of our "forgetting" to close Ancona's harbour and not preventing riders from leaving the city, and also failing to take a Venice-bound transport due to one of our galleys deliberately having unexpected problems with its sails for some reason, it was likely the rulers and merchants of Venice would soon learn of "the French plan to take Venetian prizes in the Adriatic." We were counting on it.

****** *George Courtenay.*

We "waited for the French" at Ancona until all of our galleys had rowed into the harbour. As a result, the crews of our early-arriving galleys enjoyed a pleasant time ashore for several days. They passed their time with archery tournaments, sword and land-fighting practices, and moors dancing contests which the sailors inevitably won—and their nights trying to drink the city's taverns dry and hoisting the skirts of the city's public women.

It did not take an alchemist to know that everyone in Ancona, and thus Venice within a day or two, knew that the French were at war with Venice and intended to take prizes from the transports going to and from Venice which was located at the far north end of the Adriatic.

Our captains, lieutenants, and sailing sergeants remained particularly busy during our extended port call. The men practiced their archery and worked on making more arrows. The captains and their lieutenants were particularly busy. They spent their days gathering supplies, putting together lists of potential prize crews, and discussing them with me and Uncle Harold; they spent their nights patrolling the city to keep their men under some sort of control.

We faced many unknowns whilst we waited for the "rest of the French fleet" to arrive. One of the biggest, of course, was that we did not know how soon the Venetians would find out that a fleet of French and "mercenary galleys" was patrolling the Adriatic in search of Venetian prizes.

It was also not known what the Venetians would do when they did finally learn that a French fleet was in the Adriatic. The devout hope of my lieutenants and me, of course, was that the Venetians would keep their transports safely in port until the French-led fleet sailed away to wherever it was the French fleet would be spending the coming winter storm season.

Complicating everything was the fact that we had absolutely no idea as to where Venice's war galleys were located. It was possible they had returned to Venice after the fighting at Constantinople, but it was more likely they had sailed to Crete, and then to Messina, in an effort to take the "treasure-carrying Company galley" that had sailed to deliver the Empress's coins to the Pope. We could not be sure.

And, if the Venetian fleet had returned to Venice to lick its wounds, would it be sent out in an attempt to drive the French-led galleys out of the waters of the Adriatic? Or would it be kept closer to home to protect the shipping that was accumulating in Venice whilst waiting for the French fleet to leave? We had no way of knowing.

We took no chances a result of not knowing where the Venetian fleet was located. Our galleys were tied all along the quay or anchored nearby. Their bales of extra arrows were open on their decks and their crews constantly working to produce even more.

In addition, the crews were restricted to visiting only the taverns closest to the harbour when they were given a few hours of liberty. That was so the men could hear the recall horns begin tooting and rush back aboard their galleys and begin fighting if the Venetians suddenly appeared.

It was, Harold and I told each other, probably too soon for the Venetian fleet to reach us even if they knew we were at Ancona and decided to confront us. But we were taking no chances. We would be ready to fight in the unlikely event Venetian war galleys showed up.

In reality, however, the Venetian galleys could be anywhere between Venice and the Holy Land. We thought it most likely that they had either sailed for Messina to intercept the coins we were carrying to the Pope or returned to Venice to lick their wounds after their recent losses at Constantinople.

The location of the Venetian fleet of war galleys and how soon Venice would respond to a French fleet entering the Adriatic did not matter to Harold and our captains. They would fight the Venetian galleys whenever they arrived. What mattered most to them and their crews was the prospect of earning prize money by taking Venetian transports. That excited them.

I, on the other hand, was excited about our captains taking Venice's transports as prizes because the transports were the life-blood of Venice's sea-oriented state. Accordingly, what I was attempting to do, even though Harold and our captains did not know it yet, was gull Venice into trying to *prevent* its transports from being taken—by keeping them moored in one of Venice's great harbours until the "French fleet" left the Adriatic and the galleys of its "English mercenaries" sailed for Rome.

****** *George Courtenay*

I told Uncle Harold first.

"Well, Uncle Harold, now you know the whole plan. What do you think? Is it too early for us to begin?"

"I like it, George, I really do. It is a good plan and it will almost certainly take the bastards by surprise, just as it certainly surprised me."

But then he added a warning.

"It may be too early to start doing what you really have in mind. So I think that starting up your plan needs to be delayed in order to give the Venetian merchants and their rulers more time to fall into your trap."

Uncle Harold looked at me with a twinkle in his eye, and suggested an alternative.

"We could explain the delay by announcing that you have been taken to your bed with a pox. Alternately, of course, there is something you ought to seriously consider—sending our galleys out into the Adriatic and actually starting to take any Venetians we come across in these waters.

"It would help accomplish what you want to do—because the non-Venetian transports we turn loose would spread the word to every Venetian that a French fleet of war galleys is truly out and looking for them. And as the word spreads, the Venetians will be even more inclined to keep their cogs and ships in Venice's harbours until we are gone."

Uncle Harold's suggestion was something I had been thinking about for several days—and should have thought about earlier. When he made it, I realized it was something I should have already ordered.

"I thought about doing that, I actually did; but obviously not enough. I hate to admit it, Uncle Harold, but you are right. It is something I should have ordered immediately.

"Alright Uncle; what do you think of this? We spend the rest of today getting ready and tomorrow morning we begin sending our galleys out to take all the Venetian shipping we can find as well as everyone else carrying cargos to or from Venice.

"One of our galleys will sortie out every hour starting as soon as the sun arrives. Each of them will each go east across the Adriatic until its crew sees the shore on the other side. When they do see it, they are to turn around and come back for a day or so of rest and resupply, and then go out again.

"If our galleys primarily use their sails and the weather is fair, it should take each of them five or six days to make the roundtrip plus whatever time they spend chasing and taking potential prizes.

"Oh yes, and one more thing: Whenever we stop a potential prize the captains are to always claim to be mercenaries in a French-led fleet so that the non-Venetian transports we catch and release because they have nothing to do with Venice will spread the word. Also, and on this I insist, whenever we catch and release a non-Venetian heading toward Messina, our captains are to strongly suggest that they shelter in Ancona temporarily because the waters south of here are too dangerous because they might be mistaken as Venetians.

Henry understood about our pretending to be French and did not stop to consider why we might want to encourage southbound non-Venetians to "shelter" in Ancona. *Hopefully, it meant no one else would figure it out either—until it was too late.*

"Well, what do you think?" I asked him.

Harold liked it.

"Putting a constantly moving picket line of galleys sailing east and west across the middle of the Adriatic? By God, it will catch some fat and juicy Venetians and Venetian cargos for sure. I like it, George, I really do. And claiming to be French whilst we take them makes it even better. Should I summon the captains?"

Chapter Eleven

We begin taking Venetian prizes.

Our galleys began moving out of Ancona's harbour every hour or so starting a little after dawn the next morning. The men were rested and ready to go except for the usual painful heads and poxed dingles the men inevitably acquire during their visits ashore. Those afflicted would just have to tough it out as there were no alternatives.

The day promised to be another scorcher with a clear sky. The captains had been ordered to use their sails whenever possible in order to save their men's arms for when they were truly needed—and to always fly the red Oriflamme banner of the French king from their masts and claim that they were mercenaries under contract to be part of the French king's fleet.

There was no need for our galleys to hurry. They would keep patrolling back and forth across the Adriatic searching for Venetian prizes until it was time to re-form our fleet and begin the next phase of the plan. And whilst they patrolled their men could practice their archery and make more arrows.

****** *Captain Geoffrey Monck of Galley Seventy-seven*

My galley was the third to sail out of Ancona's harbour. We sailed two hours after the sun came up. Michael Fiennes, my lieutenant, and I had spent a good part of the time since the previous day' captains' meeting making sure we were ready. That included the two of us and a file of our sergeants making a late night tour of the city's taverns to round up those of our crew that had not yet reported back aboard. We encountered sergeants of our sister galleys similarly engaged.

We pushed off from the quay with five men missing despite our efforts to get everyone back to the galley. The absence of one of the missing men, a capable young chosen man with real prospects by the name of Thomas Hastings, was a great surprise to both of us. Michael was concerned that Hastings may have run aground due to some skulduggery. The other four were problem drinkers and would barely be missed except for one of the men who was an exceptional archer when he was sober.

In any event, we cleared the harbour with ninety-six good men and the fifteen days of food and water on board as was required by Lieutenant Commander Lewes. That was more than enough to sustain us for a voyage across the Adriatic and back. It also gave us more than enough strong rowers to outrun anything in the slave-rowed Venetian fleet. Any prizes we took would be sent to Ancona with a prize crew.

Having enough men to be able to row away safely would be significant in the event we chanced upon so many Venetian galleys that we were too badly outnumbered to stand and fight.

If that should happen, I had already decided that we would do a "wounded bird" and pretend to flee in the hope that some or all of the Venetians would chase us—until our pursuers were strung out behind us with tired rowers, whereupon we would turn around and begin picking off their thrusters one at a time.

****** *Captain Monck*

The Adriatic was, as always, filled with shipping. We were only a few hours out of Ancona when one of our lookouts on the forward mast hoyed the deck to report our first sighting. Something, he shouted down to us, was coming over the distant horizon. What he saw, he said, was a speck coming over the horizon to the south that looked to be the top of a mast.

At the time we were tacking into the wind to sail easterly. We were not rowing in order to save our rowers arms. I hurriedly climbed up to the lookout's nest to see for myself, and then watched with increasing excitement as a northbound sail came up over the horizon and into view.

I gave the order to send my crew to their "chase" stations even before I started climbing back down to the deck. Our horn blower began tooting the call and the lads rushed to begin rowing and to re-rig our sails and rudder. They did so in record time and we quickly swung around to intercept the unknown sail.

We caught up to the northbound sail and boarded it peacefully less than an hour later. I myself climbed up one of our boarding ladders to see for myself. It looked to be a fine prize.

Unfortunately for us, it turned out to be a relatively new Italian three-masted ship heading north out of Taranto with a cargo of leather hides and wine for a Trieste merchant. Neither the ship nor its cargo had anything to do with Venice.

Our disappointed boarding party retrieved our grapples and we all reluctantly climbed back down to our galley's deck leaving it free to go. We would have seized it if the ship's elderly captain had been a Venetian or Venice had been his ship's destination instead of Trieste.

Before I climbed down the boarding ladder and let the Italian sail away, however, I called the attention of the ship's captain to the French Oriflamme banner flying on our mast and followed Commander Courtenay's orders—by gesturing towards it whilst telling him that we were part of a French fleet and it was damn fortunate for him and his ship that he was not a Venetian and his ship not bound for Venice.

The eyes of the Italian captain almost popped out of his head when I explained that France was at war with Venice and had seized control of the Adriatic. If his ship had had anything to do with Venice, I told the captain, we would have put a prize crew aboard it and taken it to Ancona where the galleys of the French fleet and its English and Dutch mercenaries would be based for the next few weeks prior to sailing out to the Holy Land to join the crusade.

I, of course, could not gobble Italian, but one of our sailors had spent years on an Italian crew and knew the language. He translated for me when I told the captain how lucky he was not to be a Venetian or carrying a cargo to or from Venice. I am sure that is what the sailor told him because of the way the ship's greatly relieved captain looked at me and enthusiastically nodded his head in agreement when he heard he was to be set free and allowed to proceed.

One thing was absolutely certain—when the Italian captain and his crew reached Trieste everyone would hear all about their ship being boarded by the crew of a French war galley, and their profound relief at being freed by the French because they were neither Venetians nor carrying a cargo bound for Venice.

****** *Captain Geoffrey Monck*

We resumed sailing eastward as we watched the Italian ship hoist its sails and continue on its way to Trieste. We were not alone as it moved towards the northern horizon. Captain Daniel Fletcher's Galley Forty-two came over the western horizon behind us just as we got underway.

I immediately ordered our sails re-lowered and the rowing stopped so it could reach us. Dan and his men had sailed out of Ancona an hour after we did and had been able to catch up with us because we stopped to board the Italian. We had not been gone long but things could change in an instant. Perhaps they had some news of the Venetian fleet.

After a few minutes of shouting across the water as our galleys moved side by side, our galleys separated and we both on again began moving eastward. As Dan and I agreed, my galley, Seventy-seven, moved out first using both our sails and having the archers row. We did so in order to put a bit of distance between my galley and Dan's. Being further apart meant that our lookouts could cover more of the Adriatic.

The Adriatic was filled with shipping. Less than an hour later a sail began to come up over the northern horizon behind us. When I climbed the mast I could see that it was just changing its course after initially heading straight towards Dan. He had already turned his galley towards it. Damn.

I was just starting down the rope ladder to return to the deck when the lookout in the archer's nest above me called out to me with a great hoy.

"A Hoy to the Captain. There be a sail to the south of us."

I immediately climbed back up the mast for a better look. As I did gave the word for my horn blower to once again begin tooting "chase stations."

There was once again a great burst of activity and shouting below me as our oars were once again hurriedly manned and the galley's sail handlers and rudder men rushed to their assigned positions. The rowing drum began beating, and the men on both tiers of rowing benches began rowing to the beat. Everyone was quite excited.

Sailors rushed to raise our sails, and the archers assigned to positions in the lookout nests and atop the masts assembled on the deck and readied themselves to climb up to their fighting positions when the order was given. The arrow bales, boarding ladders, and the galley's short swords, galley shields, and pikes were already in place on the deck as a result of our earlier chase.

The airs of a southerly wind were almost directly behind us once we swung around and got our bow pointed at our new prey. We began moving faster and faster with our rowing drum beating a rapid beat that increasingly got faster and faster. It was very exciting for everyone; I could see it on the men's faces and feel it inside me and behind my eyes.

Moments later, at my shouted command, the archers on the deck began climbing up to their assigned fighting positions in the lookout nests and atop the masts. The sailors that had been serving as lookouts and tending the sails simultaneously began climbing down to make room for them.

When the sailors reached the deck they squatted near our galley's two masts and waited. They did, waited that is, so they would be instantly available to climb back up to reset the sails or bring up additional quivers of arrows if the archers that had taken their places needed them.

We could soon see that we were chasing after the sails of a two-masted cog. More importantly, according to our sailing sergeant, it was almost certainly a Venetian from the look of its bowsprit and the set of its sails. Whatever the cog turned out to be, however, we could see it was sitting unusually low in the water. It was, the sailing sergeant muttered to no one in particular, either heavily loaded with cargo or taking on water.

A few moments after we swung around to begin our chase, the cog's sailors began to reset its sails in order to swing around to run before the wind. The cog's captain had no idea who we might be, only that a war galley had changed course and was coming after him. That was more than enough to cause him to run. He had to try even though it was a forlorn hope that he might somehow escape if a fast moving galley was after him.

When the cog turned to run we knew for sure it was a Venetian and, thus, almost certainly a prize if we took it—because a red banner with the winged lion of Saint Mark, the patron saint of Venice, was hurriedly raised and waved from the cog's main mast. It was obvious that the banner was raised in the hope that our knowing the cog was a Venetian would cause us to veer off and leave her in peace.

The sailors on our deck pointed and cheered when they saw the Venetian flag on the cog, and so did the archers on our rowing deck who could not see it—because they knew what the sailors' cheers meant without having to be told. We were now definitely in pursuit of a prize and every man was determined that we should take it, especially those with wives like mine that wanted more coins to spend. The beat of the drum increased slightly without any order being given.

It did not take long. Our galley easily caught up with fleeing cog and came along its starboard side about twenty minutes later. As we closed on it, the cog dropped its sails to signal its surrender and made no further effort to escape. Similarly, its crew made no effort to throw off the grapples we threw over its deck railing and did not try to push off the ladders of our boarding party.

Our boarders were unopposed as they climbed up on to the cog's deck using our boarding ladders. Indeed the only person in view as they reached the deck was the cog's unarmed and elderly captain. The rest of his crew had been sent below to hide in case we were out for blood. It was an altogether peaceful surrender.

Daniel Fiennes, my lieutenant, led my galley's boarders on to the cog's deck as was the Company's tradition. I jumped down from my fighting position on the roof of my galley's stern castle and followed them up on to the cog's deck as soon as Dan leaned over the cog's deck railing and yelled don to report it had been secured. I never did have to give the order for the archers in the lookout nests to engage its crew.

There were no other sails in sight as I climbed over the ship's deck railing and stepped aboard the first prize I had taken in almost two years. If there had been any unknown sails, I would have remained in my fighting position on one or another of my galley's two castle roofs until I was certain they were no threat.

Taking no chances when boarding a potential prize was a Company requirement for captains. It had been hammered into my head, along with Latin, scribing, and using a longbow, ever since I had first arrived at the Company school at Restormel Castle those many years ago.

As we came alongside of the cog, and even more so as we stood on its deck, we could see that the cog was probably neither new enough nor large enough to be bought in by the Company for its own use, but it otherwise appeared to be in reasonably good condition. It was, in essence, a fine saleable prize.

I was elated and so were the men of my crew. Of course we were pleased—there were no other Company galleys in sight when we took it; the prize money from the sale of the cog and its cargo would all be ours.

The cog was riding low in the water because, as we soon learned to our great satisfaction, it was heavily loaded with a valuable cargo—bales of flax that had been loaded in Alexandria, including many bales that had already been spun into threads so they could be used for weaving linen. There were also a number of bales of the little clumps of the white sheep's wool that grows on bushes and can be spun into threads and also used to weave linen. It was a valuable prize.

It was a pity Thomas Hastings had not returned before we sailed. Had he been available, I would have promoted him to sergeant to replace the archer sergeant who was moved over to serve as number two in the cog's prize crew. As it was, the sailing sergeant went aboard as the prize master and another chosen man was selected to replace the archer sergeant who went aboard as the prize master's number two.

Our prize master and his crew soon hoisted the cog's sails and began making for Ancona. We had no idea where our prize and its cargo would be sold. That was a decision that would be made by someone with more stripes than my four.

Chapter Twelve

Our gambit continues.

Geoffrey Monck was the first captain to send in a prize. Harold and I were sitting on the deck of his galley when we heard the happy shouts announcing the arrival of a prize in the harbour. It was the first one so a few minutes later we climbed into Harold's dinghy and a couple of our sturdy sailors rowed us out to it to see it for ourselves.

Our visit to the prize caused a great deal of excitement and curiosity amongst those of our men who were still in port, and especially among the men of the prize's prize crew. The curiosity of the prize crew was quite understandable. They were anxious to know if they would be able to stay on board with permanent promotions. They were not sufficiently sure of themselves to ask, however, and we did not tell them because we did not know. It was possible, but not likely because of the cog's size and condition.

The prize's Italian captain and the nine sailors of his crew were being kept in the cog's cargo hold. They were briefly brought out, at my request, so I could question them in French—and so they could see the red Oriflamme banner of the French king on my tunic and flying from the masts of the Company galleys that were still anchored in the harbour and tied up along the quay.

After speaking with captured captain through an interpreter, he and his crew were returned to the tiny remaining space in the cargo hold where they were being held. They did not know it yet, but they were likely to be in there for several weeks. We might well end up trying to recruit some of the sailors so I made sure they were provided with food, sleeping skins, a wooden foul bucket in which they could relieve themselves, and a similar bucket of water for drinking and to water their arses.

What neither Harold nor I yet know was when and to where our prizes would sail to be sold, and whether any captured crewmen would be on them when they did. That was a decision we would make after we knew how well our current gambit to mislead the Venetians had worked and we moved on to the next phase of our plan.

One of our galleys was rowing out of the harbour as we were being rowed back to the quay in Harold's dinghy. The men on its deck cheered us as they passed by and we waved and shouted our good wishes as they did.

In the distance, at the quay we could see another of our galleys getting ready to leave. It would cast off in exactly one turn of the hour bowl when Harold waved the "proceed" flag at it. He would do so when the fine sand in his hour bowl finished running out through the little hole in its bottom into the bowl that had been set below it.

After the hour passed and the second galley sailed, the hour-keeping bowls on Harold's galley would be turned and, after the sand ran out again to indicate another hour had passed, the next of our waiting galleys would get underway. There were only a few galleys left; the others had already sailed. They would all be gone by the time the sun finished passing overhead on its never-ending daily voyage around the world.

****** *George Courtenay*

The days that followed were often idle as our galleys came and went and their prizes periodically arrived. It soon became obvious that each of our galleys was going to take about six days to cross the Adriatic, and then turn around and return when they sighted the land on other side. And, of course, it took them longer if they chased a potential prize or the wind and weather changed.

There were many variables. So it was little wonder that our galleys returned unevenly such that sometimes several would return one right after another. And one day not a single galley returned or prize came in until late in the afternoon. Our initial sailings may have occurred every hour, but after that we soon settled into a routine of sending the returnees out at the rate of four galleys each day, six hours apart.

And, of course, we did not take every Venetian transport in the Adriatic. To the contrary; most of them almost certainly got past us in the dark of the night or by sailing unseen between the great gaps in our line of galleys that occurred because one was only sailing every six hours.

Missing some of the Venetians was to be expected. The Adriatic, after all, was quite large such that there were inevitably many miles between each of our patrolling galleys.

Our best guess was that we were stopping and boarding only one out of every five or six transports heading north towards Venice or coming south out of Venice. That was only a rough guess at best, a very rough guess. About all that was certain was that our captains thought many more northbound transports were reaching Venice than we were taking. Hopefully, they would stay in port "until the French leave."

Harold was in his element and constantly bustling about. Each prize had to be inspected to see what we might be able to do with it and its cargo. Similarly, each returning galley's crew needed to be inspected to see if it needed more men because of casualties and the need to provide crew prizes. Several times we took men from a galley and assigned them to a galley that needed them even more.

As you might well imagine, Ancona's harbour was beginning to fill up with prizes and the morale of our men was sky-high. There were also more and more southbound non-Venetian transports coming in to "wait safely until the French left the Adriatic." Ancona's taverns and public women had more and more customers.

It was about then that we began telling our men that our prizes would be taken to Rome to be sold and from there we would sail on to France to be paid by the French king. Rome, they were told, was where the prizes would be sold because we needed to go there to deliver the coins the Empress had tithed to the Pope for his prayers to God for her success in the recent war.

The men, of course, immediately began talking about what they would be doing next in every tavern—and everyone in Ancona knew within hours and so did the crews of the transports waiting in the harbour.

I did my part. In my role as the commander of the French fleet I reminded every merchant and transport captain I met that the Holy Father's prayers must still be working because God had provided so many prizes for "us and our English mercenaries" to sell in Rome.

When asked by the merchants and captains about the Empress's coins and Rome being their destination, however, I merely smiled knowingly and said something such as "You might very well think that, but I am sure you understand why I cannot confirm Rome as the coins' destination."

What concerned me, I soon began admitting confidentially to everyone in Ancona with whom I talked, was that we were taking so many prizes that our galleys were becoming under-crewed and unable to defend themselves and the Empress's as a result of providing so many prize crews. Our ability to defend ourselves was becoming weaker and weaker each day.

Roger, my apprentice, said my denials about being French and my fears about losing the coins we were carrying to Rome were so convincing that even he was beginning to think we were carrying a king's ransom in coins to Rome and might not be able to defend them.

What Harold and I hoped, of course, was that Venice's spies and supporters would get word of our intended destination to the Venetian fleet, and that our ability to defend the coins was being reduced as we took more and more prizes. If the Venetians heard that we were getting weaker and weaker, it was possible that they would continue to wait off Messina to intercept our prizes and the galley with the coins we were carrying to Pope. At least that is what we hoped they would do.

We also hoped, as you might imagine, that all the talk about us being part of a French fleet would set the French and Venetians at each other's throats.

What most of our men hoped when they heard about our prizes being taken to Rome was something quite different—that they would get a liberty and prize coins to spend when they arrived. As a result, the men that had been to Rome became quite popular and were soon being plied with questions such as where a man might find the cheapest wine and women that were not too poxed or smelled too bad.

As you might also imagine, the tavern keepers and the street women that served as Venice's spies soon became absolutely convinced that we would soon be off to Rome with *both* the Empress's coins and our prizes and our increasingly defenceless galleys. We even allowed a few on the southbound non-Venetian transports to leave so they could spread the word of our plans and the growing weakness of our galleys.

****** *Commander Courtenay*

All of our prizes were kept anchored in the harbour some distance from shore, and none of the sailors we captured were allowed to go ashore. They were, however, periodically allowed on deck to get food from the cook and use the shite nests that hung over every transport's stern. And when they did, they could not help but see the French Oriflamme banners flying from the masts of the galleys and transports in the harbour. The crews of the non-Venetian transports and the city's merchants and churchmen, of course, saw them constantly.

Moreover, each of the captured captains was subjected to a questioning that was intended to convince him that he had indeed been captured by the French. Whenever possible, the interviews were conducted on the prize's deck when the wind was blowing such that the

Oriflamme banners of the French king could be clearly seen flying from the masts of our galleys and prizes.

Harold's apprentice, John Soames, was given the job of keeping a list of the prizes and their cargos. It included a brief description of Harold's observations as to the condition of each prize and its cargo, his thoughts as to whether the Company should keep it or sell it, and also who amongst the men in its crew might be useful if they were required to serve in one of our prize crews before they were released.

Unlike Harold who was busy all the time, I was bored and spent most of my hours either playing chess with Roger, my apprentice, or prowling around in the city's market speaking French to those merchants who could understand me. I did so with a red Oriflamme banner of the French king sewed on to my tunic whilst pretending *not* to be a French commander waiting for the rest of his galleys to arrive.

"Oh no, I am not French, I am just a mercenary from England."

That is what I would say in French when the subject came up in one way or another. It usually happened when we were talking about how much longer our galleys would be buying supplies or how much longer we would be holding our prisoners. The merchants and the captured captains would stare at the Oriflamme on my tunic and know for sure that I was telling them lies when I claimed to be only an English mercenary.

It worked every time; the merchants and our prisoners were soon absolutely convinced that the commander of the galleys taking the Venetian shipping, *me*, was French. It was an altogether splendid way for me to amuse myself since it might very well set two of the Company's major competitors, the Venetians and French, at each other's throats in the years ahead. Every little bit helps, as the old saying goes.

At the same time, as you might well imagine, I had many good things to say about the honesty and reliability of the English mercenaries we French had supposedly contracted to help us reduce Venice's power by attacking its shipping. Fortunately, none of Ancona's merchants were French and would know from my accent that I really was an Englishman. At least I did not think any of them were French.

As you might expect, the merchants of Ancona saw the nearby merchants of Venice as their greatest competitors and enemies, not the distant merchants of France or England. As a result, they all seemed to be quite pleased to see me when I visited the market and pretended not to be French.

And the merchants should have been pleased—we were spending a fortune in coins to provision our ships with supplies. In addition, a constant stream of coins was pouring into the city's taverns and brothels as our galleys returned and their crews were given liberties whilst their galleys were being resupplied.

The men we never did see or hear from were the city's Italian lord and its archbishop. The lord was not sure how we would treat him, so he wisely stayed in his castle on the hill outside the city and kept his gate closed.

The city's bishop was similarly not inclined to take any chances. According to the local merchants and the harbour master, he had abandoned the city and fled to Rome with his plate and two chests of coins as soon as we arrived.

*****

On one of my visits to the market to talk about selling some of our prize cargos, one of the merchants, a Signor Verdi who sold linen and thread, showed me a strange sun dial he had invented and desperately wanted me to buy. He claimed that if I owned it I would always know the exact time of day, even in the dark of night.

What I saw was certainly very different from the sun dials and the hour bowls filled with sand that we were now using. It stood about half as high as a man and told the time of day using a little ball that ran down a stack of small downward sloping aqueducts.

In essence, as Signor Verdi explained in a great torrent of words and waving about of his hands, a man no longer needed to look at the length of the shadow cast by the sun or know how much sand was left of the amount that took exactly one hour to run out of one bowl and into another.

Signor Verdi called his invention an "orologio" which means, he told me, "hour teller" in Italian. According to Signor Verdi, his orologio could tell when the end of each hour had been reached, even at night when there was no sun, and also without having to turn two bowls of sand lashed together with a little hole in the top bowl to allow an hour's worth of sand to fall into the bowl below it.

I found the hour teller strangely enjoyable to watch. It had a little copper ball that ran down a stack of tiny aqueducts, one after another, until it came to the bottom of the stack.

It took, Signor Verdi explained as I sipped from the little bowl of wine merchants traditionally provide to important customers, exactly half a minute for the ball to reach the bottom. What was so interesting was that when the ball reached the end of the last aqueduct at the very bottom it somehow caused the last aqueduct to seesaw and take the ball back up to the top so that the ball would once again spend exactly half a minute running down to the bottom.

It was quite fascinating because each time the ball made the last aqueduct seesaw, it somehow turned a rounded wooden pulley wheel with little pegs sticking out of it—and that, in turn, caused yet another pulley wheel with little pegs to turn ever so slightly.

What made his orologio so valuable, according to Verdi, was that once the little aqueducts were properly bent, the second little wheel had a tiny arrow attached to it that always pointed to the correct hour of the day from amongst the twelve numbers, one through twelve, which had been scribed in paint on a piece of wood.

Signor Verdi claimed it was quite accurate. He said, for example, that at three hours after every sunup the tiny arrow would always point to the number "3," and a half hour after that it would point to halfway between the numbers "3" and the "4." It was, Verdi said over and over again, very precise.

According to the merchant, the ball in his time teller made the voyage down the aqueducts one hundred and twenty times in exactly one hour. This was accomplished, he explained, by the slopes of some of the aqueducts being bent so the ball rolled no faster or slower than was needed to make exactly one hundred and twenty trips down the aqueducts each hour.

What made it so valuable, Signor Verdi claimed, was that no one had to stand next to the hour teller and count the number of times the little ball rolled to the end of the stack of aqueducts. Instead, all one had to do to know the exact time was to look at where the arrow was pointing.

Signor Verdi said his orologio was useful because it kept the hour of the day from being lost at night when the sun did not shine or if someone forgot to turn the bowl when the sand ran out or if the bowl got broken or its hole got plugged up so the sand did not run out fast enough. It would be useful, he suggested, because people could look at and know how soon dawn would arrive or when they should begin their daily prayers or go off to a meeting or a chore.

I was sceptical about the value of such a strange contraption and initially quite hesitant about buying it. I was sceptical because it seemed to me that using bowls of sand which take exactly an hour to empty would be better because the priests calling people to prayers can ring bells and sailors on ships can call out each time the top bowl emptied and the bowls were turned to mark the beginning of another hour. Moreover, having to watch the bowl so as to be ready to turn it kept the priests and sailors awake which the hour teller did not.

There were two other very big problems with the orologio so far as I was concerned. One was that, as everyone knows, sunrise comes a few minutes earlier or later each day depending on the season of the year. The days of winter, for example, are well-known to be shorter than the days of summer.

As a result, if the hour teller was as precise as Signor Verdi claimed, it would become more and more inaccurate with each passing day that it kept going. Also it could not be used on a galley or transport because the twisting and turning of the hull in a rough sea might speed up or slow down the rate at which the ball travelled down the aqueducts.

In other words, the hour teller was totally useless except that someone did not have to watch the bowls of sand in order to be ready to turn them over when the sand finished running out at the end of each hour. Besides, everyone knows when dawn arrives because the church bells begin ringing in the cities and the cooks on our galleys and transports ring the wakeup and food bell the traditional twelve times to start the day.

Signor Verdi earned his family's bread and coins by selling various types of sewing needles, all kinds of fine linen threads and lines for weaving, and various types of wool for spinning into threads. He was, however, clearly much prouder of his hour teller and waved his hands about enthusiastically as he told me all about it and showed me how it worked. He was also obviously half mad for wasting his time on such a useless toy since it was so unnecessary.

Even so, I bought one of them, the only one he had available, and had the men that were with me as my guards carry it back to the forward deck castle on Harold's galley where I slept.

I did it, bought the hour teller that is, because it was so ingenious that I thought my Uncle Thomas and his students would enjoy watching the ball roll and the wheels turn. I also bought a chest full of linen thread for my wife to weave and some of the white wool clumps that grow on bushes for her and my daughters to spin into thread they could use to weave linen for clothes and such.

******

"Only two prizes have come in since Monday and there is still no sign of the Venetian fleet."

Harold made the announcement as he came into the forward castle and sat on one of the castle's two three-legged stools. It had been hastily vacated by Roger, my apprentice, as soon as Harold and his apprentice came through the door.

"And for the past three days not a single prize has come in that sailed from Venice. Every prize that has come in since Monday was headed north because its captain did not know we were here."

"Aye, you are right, Uncle Harold. We knew it was bound to happen and now it has—the Venetians know we are out and have begun keeping their transports in the harbour until we are gone. But where are their galleys?"

That was my reply as I looked up from where I was sitting on the castle's other stool looking at a chess board. I was happy to see Harold and get the latest news. Sitting around idle every day was very boring.

Harold, of course, did not know the whereabouts of the Venetian fleet any more than I did. But he had been talking to the captains of the captured prizes and did have some encouraging news about Venice.

"The men on our recent prizes all say the same thing—that there are only one or two galleys in Venice, but that the city's harbours are full of the shipping that made it north past our galleys.

"According to them, the shipping is waiting there because they are afraid of sailing in the Adriatic until we are gone. And, as you might imagine, the captured captains all say they should have listened to the warnings they were given and waited with them.

"They also say that the main Venetian fleet has not returned since it sailed earlier in the year to help the Greeks take Constantinople. The word on Venice's streets and in its taverns is that the Venetian fleet is in Messina waiting for a treasure ship bound for Rome.

"And that is not all. One of our recent northbound prizes, the cog carrying shipbuilding lumber to Venice that Charlie Caine brought in yesterday, came through the Messina Strait. Its captain says he saw several dozen Venetian galleys patrolling the strait or anchored in the nearby harbour."

I smiled and agreed with Harold that it was good news, and then shared the corroborating news I had heard that morning when I visited the market to once again pretend I was not French.

"It is rumoured in the market, several of the merchants told me again this morning, that the Venetian fleet is still waiting for us at Messina because they heard we are sailing to Rome with a fortune in prayer coins. They say the Latin Empress is sending them to the Pope because his prayers were so successful in her fight with the Greeks.

"But here is what is interesting—the merchants now seem to think we are here in an effort to lure the Venetian fleet north so the galley carrying the Empress's coins can slip through to Rome unmolested. I, of course, pretended to get very upset and asked them if they knew who amongst our men had revealed the secret. *And it certainly was a secret; even I had not known that was our plan.*

"If the merchants are correct, it means the lies we told both here and in Constantinople and Athens, are still being believed and the Venetian fleet is still waiting off Messina to intercept us and try to take the Empress's coins. What do you think?"

Harold pondered my question for a few moments, and then made a very good suggestion.

"I think we ought to share the merchant's story with our men—tell them that we have been here waiting for the Venetians to come north and leave the strait open for us to pass through with the coins for the Pope. But that we cannot wait forever and will have to sail for Rome soon with our coins and prizes.

"And the reason we cannot wait forever, we can tell them, is because our galleys are getting increasingly under-crewed and unable to defend themselves and the coins because we have been taking so many of their men for prize crews.

"With a little bit of luck, that story will reach the Venetian fleet and cause it to continue to wait even longer at Messina. If it does, it will give us time to take even more prizes and send them off to Cyprus and Constantinople."

"Aye," I agreed. I like the idea. From what I have heard from the local merchants, Venice's galley captains are mostly an arrogant bunch of nobles' sons who do not care what happens to the transports and cargos of Venice's merchants. So making them think we are trying to lure them north might well cause them to stay even longer at Messina.

"On the other hand, they might have already been ordered to sail north to chase us out of the Adriatic. Indeed, they could be only a few minutes away and about to fall on us, eh?"

Harold was not put off by my caution.

"So what if the Venetians do suddenly show up? We are going to have to fight them sooner or later, eh?

A decision was made a couple of bowls later.

******

The next day, Harold and I began passing the word to our men about our fleet running out of time in our efforts to lure the Venetians north—and started the countdown to the next phase of the Company's vengeance by preparing our galleys to sail "for Rome" with the treasure.

We began by limiting the number of days our returning galleys were allowed to go out looking for more prizes. At first they had to be back in four days, then three, and then two. In less than a week all but one of our galleys had made its last prize-seeking voyage and was safely back in the harbour.

It was obvious to our men and everyone in the city that we would soon be sailing for Rome. And we confirmed it so there would be no excuses for a captain not to have his vessel ready.

The men were told, and it soon became known throughout the city, that the four slave-rowed French galleys in our fleet would be sailing for Rome in a few days to deliver the Empress's prayer coins to the Pope. They would wait off Messina until the Venetians were gone and then stop in Rome on their way back to France. The Company's understrength galleys, however, would be sailing back to Athens and Constantinople with our prizes.

The four "slave-rowed French galleys", of course, did not exist. But with all the comings and goings, and Oriflamme pennants on every mast, none of the Company men knew that. So they merely repeated what they had been told in Ancona's taverns.

Most of the galleys now in Ancona, however, were those of the "English mercenaries." Unlike the French, the Company galleys, or so it began to be said, would be sailing to Constantinople to protect their prizes from the Venetian war fleet which was still out there somewhere. It sounded like a very reasonable thing to do since we had so many prizes and the prizes were so valuable.

What Harold and I hoped, of course, was that Venice's local supporters and spies would immediately inform Venice and the Venetian fleet of our plans. If they did, it was likely the Venetians would continue to wait for the "Empress's treasure" at the one place the French galleys would be unable to avoid if they were sailing for Rome, the waters off the entrance to the Messina Strait.

Moreover, they would be encouraged to do so because the treasure would only be guarded by a handful of slave-rowed French galleys instead of a large number of much more fearsome archer-rowed Company galleys. The captains of several of the non-Venetian transports bound for Rome were told that it was now safe enough for them to leave. Hopefully, they would encounter the Venetians at the Messina Strait and pass the word.

We certainly hoped the Venetian galleys would continue waiting off Messina—because what no one had *not* been told yet, not even our captains, was that an announcement was coming to the effect that the Empress's coins would *not* be going to Rome this season. They would, instead, be transferred to Company galleys and accompany our prizes and understrength galleys back to Athens.

The French galleys would not go to Athens with them. They would only accompany the treasure and prizes part of the way and then rendezvous with another French fleet, and together the two French fleets would sail out to the Holy Land to join the crusade.

Changing our destinations, we would explain to our men in a few days, and thus to the merchants and spies of Ancona, had become necessary because our taking of so many Venetian transports as prizes. It had caused our understrength galleys and those of the French to no longer be strong enough to fight off the Venetian galleys waiting for us at Messina. It would also be a lie, yet another gambit to confuse the Venetian fleet.

******

It was a feverish time for everyone a few days later. Our captains and their crews spent it loading water and supplies into our prizes and galleys for the long voyage they had just that morning been informed they they were about to "sail for Athens." It was, of course, a perfectly understandable decision because the Venetians were thought to be waiting at Messina and our galleys were now hopelessly understrength because we had taken so many prize.

We also announced our intention to stop taking prizes and told all the transports that had been sheltering in Ancona's harbour that it was now safe to continue south. They had been waiting for some time and left immediately. *This was significant and another gambit; with a little luck, the Venetians at Messina would hear about Piraeus in time for most of them to rush there and wait for us.*

The good news was that the taking of the prizes had not been costly in terms of the Company's butcher's bill. There had only been a couple of cases of serious resistance. As a result, we had lost only eleven men killed during the taking of our prizes and six of them had been accidents. The worst being three men in a boarding party crew that were lost because their boarding ladder fell over when the hull of their galley somehow separated from the hull of its prize and they fell into the sea.

In addition to the men who had been killed, our losses included eight men with serious wounds and poxes. Those unfortunates would be left behind in Ancona with ample supplies of flower paste and wine for their pain. More importantly, at least for them, we arranged for them to continue to get appropriate barbering and burials as their fates turned out to be and God willed. Those that were lightly wounded or poxed, on the other hand, would sail with us and be given light duties until they recovered.

As was the Company's tradition, arrangements had been made for the eight seriously wounded and poxed men to be housed and well-fed in a good tenement with several attendants and a barber on call. They would re-join the Company if they ever recovered enough to be fit for travel.

Similarly being left behind were the men, mostly sailors, who had deserted. In doing so, they forfeited their share of the huge amount of prize money that would be paid when the prizes were sold. If the past was any guide, they had either found softer berths or higher ranks amongst the local shipping, or women who would shelter them until their coins ran out. Sometimes it was both.

"Only eleven have run so far," said Harold with a satisfied sound in his voice. "That is not very many when you consider how long we have been here and remember that we arrived with a little over two thousand men. We surely would have lost many more if we had not taken so many prizes. As it is, a very substantial amount of prize coins will be paid as soon as we sell our prizes and the men know it."

And we certainly did have prizes to sell, more than fifty of them were now anchored in Ancona's crowded harbour. Our captains and men had been told that most of them would be sent to Athens, and then on to Constantinople to be sold, in one great convoy guarded by all of our galleys.

Everyone agreed that selling them in Constantinople was the sensible thing to do, particularly since it was well known that one or more of our now-understrength galleys were carrying coins destined for the Pope and also needed to be guarded. It had not taken long before everyone in Ancona and on the shipping waiting in the harbour knew our plans.

We did, of course, subsequently take a few prize coins to the Pope since he had no doubt heard about our use of his name to mislead the Venetians. But we did not bring him very many since "most of them had to go to the men as prize coins because of the great losses we suffered fighting for the Latin Empire." The Pope was quite satisfied, however, since what he received was unexpected new money for his personal purse.

In any event, eight of the prizes, the best of them, all relatively new three-masted ships, would not be sold. They would be bought in by the Company to increase the number of transports in our fleet. Initially, however, be used to carry additional water and supplies for the

Company's galleys during the voyage to Athens. At least, that was what everyone was told. It also was not true.

What was true was that the cargos of the eight prizes the Company was buying in had already been off-loaded and sold to the local merchants. Then their cargo holds were filled up with the water, firewood, and food supplies that our galley crews and prize crews were likely to need in the days ahead "on our voyage to Constantinople via Piraeus."

Although they did not know it yet, the captains, sergeants, and passengers of all of our prizes would be brought ashore and freed in Ancona early in the morning on the day we sailed. Their pilots and their rank and file sailors, however, would remain with us to help sail our prizes to wherever they were to be sold. They would be freed there.

Our missing galley, Number Forty-six, Captain Hammond, was never heard from again and neither was the missing archer, Thomas Hastings. To this day we have no idea what happened to them.

Chapter Thirteen
We leave Ancona.

Great swarms of sea birds were circling about overhead and the quay was filled with onlookers as all twenty-two of the Company galleys got ready to row out of Ancona's harbour in the mid-afternoon of August 2nd, 1219. The winds were not favourable for the use of sails in the harbour, so eight of the galleys would be towing out the Company's prizes we had bought in to add to the Company's fleet.

Every one of the galleys was sea-going with a deep hull, two masts, and two tiers of rowing benches. In other words, each of them was a deep-sea galley that would not need to run for a shore or shelter in the event of a storm. The eight three-masted ships were also in good shape. They would raise their sails as soon as they were out of the close confines of the harbour.

Only twenty of the galleys were fully crewed. The other two had been stripped of their crews to provide overseers for their original sailors who would comprise the majority of each prize crew. Those two had already been towed out of the harbour and set their sails. They would make the voyage to Constantinople using only their sails and their sailors.

It had been a busy day and the quay had been crowded with onlookers for hours. The local transports had finally been allowed to leave the harbour yesterday and most of the captured Venetian captains and their sergeants had been put ashore at daybreak. By midday our galleys had finished towing all but eight of the Company's prizes out of the harbour.

Once safely out of the harbour and into the open sea, each of our prizes raised its sails and immediately began its long voyage to its real destination—Constantinople via Piraeus. We were, it had been announced, too weak to make for Rome at this time.

According to the destination change announced several days earlier *before* the non-Venetian local transports being held in the harbour had finally been allowed to leave, each of the prizes would sail on to Constantinople to be sold *after* a rendezvous in Piraeus where the prizes would regroup and take on water and supplies.

The announcement two days earlier that our galleys and prizes would be sailing for Constantinople via Piraeus instead of Rome, and that the Empress's coins would return with them and be delivered next year, had resulted in much chortling and laughter in the taverns and amongst our crews and the city's merchants. They were quite pleased and amused when they heard how we had gulled the Venetians—whose cuckolded captains had stood idle and let us take Venetian transports in the Adriatic because they were waiting in vain at Messina for a non-existent treasure fleet to appear with prizes that could be easily recaptured.

What was significant was that the announcement that the Empress's coins and the prizes would be sailing to a rendezvous at Piraeus to take on water and supplies, and then on to Constantinople, had been done deliberately *before* the non-Venetian transports were allowed to sail.

We had deliberately announced our new destination before the non-Venetian transports were allowed to sail because we knew some of them would stop in Messina for water and supplies. And when they did, they would undoubtedly tell the chagrined and embarrassed Venetians that they had been gulled into waiting off Messina whilst we pillaged Venice's shipping.

They were also likely to tell them that our prizes and the coins had, by the time they reached Messina, already sailed with a rendezvous scheduled for Piraeus. They would also tell them that our galleys had provided so many prize crews that they and the prizes were virtually defenceless.

The commander of the Venetian fleet would not have to be an alchemist to add the days it took the newly released transports to reach Messina to the number of days it would take his galleys to reach Athens if they rowed hard. He also knew how long it would take for the Company's prizes to sail to Piraeus and how long they would likely have to wait there for the last of the stragglers to arrive.

And, of course, he also knew the Greeks were Venice's allies and that he and his men would be embarrassed and humiliated by being gulled into staying out of the Adriatic. There would be no doubt about it in his mind; if the Venetians rowed hard they might be able to make Piraeus in time to recapture the prizes and restore his honour. He would, of course, leave a couple of galleys in the strait to take the treasure in case the announcement about Piraeus was a gambit to clear the strait of his galleys so the treasure could slip through to Rome.

Was it true that we had actually succeeded in gulling the Venetian fleet into waiting off Messina whilst we took Venice's transports as prizes in the Adriatic, and that the Venetian fleet would hurry to Piraeus to try to retake them? We had no idea; but it was a good story and one of several gambits designed to confuse and mislead the Venetians.

But then, at the last minute, *after* the southbound Italian transports were finally allowed to sail off so they could inform the Venetians waiting at Messina that we were rendezvousing at

Piraeus, we announced, at the last minute, a new and different destination—we would avoid Piraeus and sail straight for Constantinople.

There would be *no* rendezvous in Piraeus we told our captains on the morning they were to sail. They were, instead, to avoid the sea lanes that led to Piraeus and make straight for Constantinople without stopping. They all had more than enough food and water on board to do so; Lieutenant Commander Lewes had seen to it.

Why was the last minute elimination of the Piraeus rendezvous significant? Because it was announced hours *after* the local transports had sailed for Rome. What we were sure was that when the local transports reached Messina one or more of their crews would tell the Venetians about the rendezvous; what we hoped was that the Venetians would then hurry to Piraeus in an effort to recapture our prizes which would be waiting at the rendezvous for the inevitable laggards to show up.

Whether the Venetian galleys were actually at Messina and would be gulled into sailing for Piraeus and once again come up empty was not at all certain. But the city and our men had another good laugh over the possibility that the Venetian fleet had once again been gulled into sailing to the wrong place and accomplishing nothing. They did not know the half of it.

******

All the prizes, except for eight, had already sailed by the time the twenty fully-crewed Company galleys left Ancona bound directly for Constantinople with all the food and firewood they could carry. Constantinople, after all, was a long way away. In addition, every galley's deck was covered by piles of recently butchered meat and loudly complaining cattle and sheep. They were complaining because their hamstrings had been cut so they would not cause trouble by moving about.

Similarly loud and unhappy were the bundles of squawking and wing-flapping chickens and geese whose legs were tied together. The noise was so loud a man could hardly think and had to shout to be heard. The meat and livestock, in turn, were covered with great swarms of flies that would, as usual, disappear as the wind blew them away and the galleys and transports sailed out from under them. It all made sense—we would need a lot of food if we were to sail straight through to Constantinople.

The last eight of our most seaworthy prizes were towed out of the harbour by our fully crewed galleys just as our other prizes and the two un-crewed galleys had been towed out earlier in the day to start their long voyages to Constantinople. They were all fully loaded with water, food, and firewood. *The two galleys were un-crewed because their men had been used to replace the men of the other galleys who had been assigned to prize crews. They would use their sails to reach Constantinople.*

All eight of the last prize departures were relatively new three-masted ships that Harold had selected for the Company to buy in to expand its fleet. Each of them had been fully loaded with water and other supplies so they and the galleys they would be supporting could remain at sea during the long voyage to Constantinople without making a port call to take on food and firewood.

It was the supplies of food and firewood that were particularly important. That was because additional water, if needed, could be drawn from the mouths of the streams and rivers that emptied into the seas in which they were sailing.

The Company's eight "bought in" transports were towed out after the other prizes had already sailed. That was because they and all of our galleys were about to be given a destination that was *quite different* from those of the prizes which had sailed south to Constantinople a few hours earlier.

Their new destination was something their captains would not learn about until they attended the "all captains" meeting that was scheduled to occur *after* the last of our galleys, Harold's with Commander Courtenay on board, cleared the harbour.

The meeting would occur at sea, or so we told our men, and thus the tavern owners, women, and spies of Ancona soon knew, so no word would get to the Venetians as to how we intended to our galleys to defend our prizes on their long voyage "to Constantinople." It all seemed quite reasonable and was widely believed.

What was important, extremely important, was that neither the captains of the eight prizes nor the captains of our galleys knew that they would *not* be sailing with the prizes and our two crewless galleys to Constantinople. They would not learn their real destination, and hear the story that had been made up to explain it, until they attended the captains' meeting that was scheduled for immediately *after* they cleared Ancona's harbour.

****** *Commander Courtenay*

The departure of our remaining galleys and prizes "for Constantinople" had begun as soon as the sun came up. It was watched by a great crowd of people on the quay, including a number of weeping women along with the usual pickpockets, jugglers, and minor merchants offering last minute bowls of wine.

Each of the remaining galleys and prizes sailed with full crews. Only seven men had run in the last few days before we sailed, and two who had disappeared more than a week earlier sheepishly reappeared at the last minute and climbed aboard their berths to have their stripes ripped off and their arses whipped.

In the end, only eleven men deserted, less than one per galley. It was a fine record and was no doubt helped by the substantial payouts of prize money that would soon be forthcoming once the prizes and their cargos were sold. Indeed, some of the payouts would be large enough to set a man up for the rest of his life. It was a lot for a man to leave behind and, in the end, very few decided to do so.

Harold's galley, with me on board, would be the very last to leave the harbour except for three prizes that had been taken in such foul condition that they were deemed to be more likely to sink than complete another long voyage. They and their cargos had long ago been sold to one or another of Ancona's merchants and money lenders.

It was early in the afternoon before Harold's sailing sergeant finally began bellowing out his orders and the wharfies on the quay cast off our galley's mooring lines. We rowed away from Ancona leaving behind an almost empty harbour and numerous distressed women and tavern owners.

We also left behind our prizes' astonished and extremely relieved captains and some of their sergeants. They had been put ashore just before dawn because we did not want anyone on our prizes who might be capable of leading a mutiny in an attempt to retake them.

By the time the midday sun was overhead and Harold's sailing sergeant began bellowing his orders, the two almost crewless galleys and all of the prizes to be sold in Constantinople, sixty-one Venetian and Venetian-related transports, had already been towed out of the harbour and raised their sails to begin their long voyage to the Latin Empire's great capital city. They would stay together as long as possible and then continue on their own.

Our men were not the only ones sailing to Constantinople. More than two hundred of Ancona's sailors and fishermen had been recruited to join the crews of our prizes. They had jumped at the opportunity when they were promised good food and two good silver coins for their services. It also helped that they would be carried back to Ancona for free if they could not find a sailor's berth acceptable to them when they reached the prize's final destination. Small prize crews of our archers and sailors would be their captains and sergeants.

Not everyone was happy. The original captains and sergeants of our prizes may have been freed in Ancona and left to fend for themselves, but their pilots and many of their ordinary sailors were not. They had been required to remain aboard one or another of our prizes to serve in its crew. They did not know it yet, but they would not be freed until they reached Constantinople.

The Venetians and Italians amongst the pilots and ordinary sailors were going to be especially unhappy when they learned they were on their way to distant Constantinople instead of to Rome as they had initially been led to believe. That was because the old Romans had built very good roads from Rome to everywhere in Italy including Venice. As a result, there was a well-travelled Roman road between Rome and Venice that could be walked in two or three weeks if the captured sailors had been released in Rome.

And not being freed in Rome was not the only thing that would distress the pilots and ordinary sailors we captured and forced into the crews of our prizes. They would also be distressed because they would not be sailing with their friends and original crewmates. That was because, in order to further reduce the risk of mutinies, Harold had made sure that no more than one captured sailor from each prize was assigned to serve in a particular prize crew.

On the other hand, the captured sailors would be released, each was told, when he reached the port where the prize on which he was forced to serve was to be sold. Many of them did not believe it, thinking that they would be either be killed or sold as slaves as was the usual practice when a sailor was captured in the waters of the civilized world. But it was true. The Company did not buy or sell slaves and serfs; it was in the articles of the Company's compact on which every man made his mark.

According to Harold, who had worked from dawn to late in the night for the last few days making up the prize crews, the captured pilots and sailors had been split up and randomly assigned to help crew one or another of our prizes. The splitting up of our prizes' crews and their reassignment was done so they would be unlikely to pose a threat to the three or four heavily armed archers that were assigned to each prize to oversee its crew and guard its prize captain.

It was the job of the handful of Company archers assigned to each prize to keep its non-Company sailors in line and make sure the prize stayed under the command of its prize captain. The one or two Company sailors assigned to each prize were also heavily armed with either a sword and shield or a pike.

The use of captured sailors in our prize crews did not particularly worry us; we had long ago learned how to safely employ captured sailors and unknown volunteers. If the past was any guide, many of them would volunteer to stay on board as crew members after the prizes were sold and some of them would apply to make their marks and join the Company.

Whether the prizes would actually make it all the way to Constantinople was another question, however. Certainly bad weather or Moorish pirates could cause some of them to be lost. The biggest potential problem, however, was that they might run into one of the galleys of the Venetian fleet that had been gulled, or so we hoped, into moving from one empty stretch of water to another in an effort to recapture our prizes and intercept the treasure everyone thought we were carrying.

Our reality was that the handful of archers and Company sailors on each of the prize crews would be in real danger if the prize they were crewing was chanced upon by a Venetian galley or Moorish pirates. On the other hand, even though the Company men on each prize might be few in number, they had gone out armed to the teeth so as to be as prepared as possible to fight off any enemies they might encounter.

Most transports immediately surrendered when a war galley came after them because their crews were neither properly armed nor trained to fight. All it usually took for most transport captains to lower their sails and surrender was a galley full of shouting men waving swords over their heads as they came alongside. That was unlikely to be the case with the Company men on our prizes. To the contrary.

What the outcome would be if one of our prizes met a Venetian or Moorish galley was uncertain. It would depend, as everyone knew, on how hard the Venetians or Moors pressed their attack. Victory was not certain for a galley trying to take a merchant transport as a prize. That was because it was not an easy thing to grapple a merchant transport and climb up a rope or wooden ladder to board it *if* even a few of the victim's crew were properly armed and willing to fight to remain free.

That a handful of archers and sailors in a prize crew would be able to hold off the attack of an enemy galley was not impossible for several reasons. The principal one being that the archers in our prize crews were well armed and well supplied with arrows. They would almost certainly fight to the bitter end rather than allow themselves to be taken and then either slaughtered or sold into slavery.

Taking a transport when even a few of its men were willing to fight was difficult for a war galley—unless the galley had archers on its masts who could pick off the transport's defenders until there was no one left who could fight back.

The attackers' basic problem was that galleys inevitably sit lower in the water than the bigger and bulkier cogs and ships that served as transports. Sitting lower in the water meant that the attacking galley had to grapple its potential prize to hold their two hulls tight together, and then some of the attackers' crew had to climb up wooden or rope boarding ladders to reach the transport's deck.

Climbing up a boarding ladder to get to a transport's deck was always something easier said than done. That was particularly the case if even a handful of the men on the transport's crew were chopping down on the climbers' heads with swords and bladed pikes whilst others were leaning over the transport's deck railing and pushing arrows into them.

A boarding was also difficult if the men on the transport's deck were able to cut the grapple lines. That was especially true if the grapple lines were cut as the galley's boarding ladders were being climbed. The hulls inevitably separated when there were no lines holding them together, and then the ladders being climbed to get from one hull to the other would dump their climbers in the water to drown. Indeed, the Company had recently lost men for just that reason.

We did our best to prevent such losses. Our galleys now used iron chain for the last few feet of their grapple lines so they could not be easily cut. It was also a Company rule that the men of our boarding parties were only to start climbing their galley's boarding ladders after the archers on our masts and castle roofs had cleared away everyone on their intended victim's deck who looked dangerous.

******

Harold's galley was the last to leave Ancona. It was early in the afternoon by the time we finally cleared the harbour. I gave the order to "wave the all captains flag" about thirty minutes later as we began reaching the galleys and the eight towed prizes that had preceded us out to sea. The quay was empty of onlookers by the time we cleared the harbour and entered the open water beyond it. It was as if we had never been there.

The galley captains and their tows had followed their orders and stopped to wait about ten miles beyond the harbour entrance. As we approached them we could see sea-poxed men hanging over their deck railings. Being ashore for a few days often has that effect on a man. I was already feeling a bit queasy myself.

"Loud talkers are to pass the word that the captains of the prizes under tow are expected to attend."

I gave the order as we came to the first of the waiting galleys. It was probably an unnecessary order since they had already been told to attend an immediate captains' call, but I gave it again anyhow since the prize captains on the supply ships were new and inexperienced.

Not all of the galley captains responded to the summons. One of them, Peter Brown of Galley Fifty-three, had been previously and secretly ordered to ignore the "all captains" flag and continue sailing south to join the fleet of prizes that had sailed earlier in the day. Peter and his men would do their best to escort the prizes to Constantinople—and then turn around and sail back to re-join the main fleet with any dispatches they might be given.

For several weeks the captains and crews of the prizes had gone to the taverns each night believing they would be sailing to Rome. It had been a bit of a shock when, only three days ago, they had been informed that Constantinople was their new destination with a rendezvous in Piraeus where they would take on water and supplies.

The crews were less surprised when they were told all of the galleys were going with them because the voyage to Rome had become too dangerous. It was all very believable.

Hopefully the revised destinations also shocked the Venetian spies and supporters in Ancona because it meant the Venetian fleet to once again move to the wrong place—by hurrying to Piraeus from waters off Messina.

Moreover, to make it likely the Venetian fleet would hurry to Piraeus, the non-Venetian shipping that had been held in the Ancona harbour had been allowed to leave. Some of them would undoubtedly reach Messina and carry the news to the waiting Venetian fleet—whose commander would realize that if his galleys hurried to Piraeus they would be able to get there in time to recapture our prizes and intercept the treasure.

Later, all of our captains and their crews had understood that my lies about Rome, and then Piraeus, being their destinations had been gambits to mislead the Venetians about our intention to sail directly to Constantinople. They had smiled and approved when they learned we were trying to mislead the Venetian fleet so it would not be able to find our prizes and try to retake them in addition to seizing the treasure.

As you might expect, the prize captains had been a lot less enthusiastic, but had nodded their understanding, when Harold told them how they were to respond if they encountered the Venetians or pirates without any of our galleys around to protect them. His orders were quite simple.

"Scatter and run, and fight like hell if they try to board you."

What the prize captains were never told was that the prize convoy would only be guarded by one of galleys. It was a secret some of them would never learn.

The prize captains had also been told that any "all captains" flag that they might see off Ancona applied only to the Company's galleys and the eight prizes that would be joining the Company's fleet. Indeed, they probably never saw the flag being waved because it did not happen until the last few of them were disappearing over the horizon.

Somewhat similarly, the captains waiting for the "all captains" meeting off Ancona still believed what they and everyone else had been told previously—that their galley and all the others would be accompanying the prizes to Constantinople to help guard them. They were, they thought, waiting for the meeting "so that each galley captain could get his orders as to his galley's place in the prize convoy's guard force."

They were wrong; they had been told another lie in order to once again gull the Venetians.

******

The captains were ready for the meeting when Harold's galley came out of the harbour and rowed up to them where they were waiting. They knew we were coming so, for the most part, their dinghies were already in the water and waiting for the captains to climb aboard them. The dinghies were soon boarded and the sailors on their oars immediately began rowing their captains towards Harold's galley.

It did not take long for the first of the nineteen remaining galley captains and eight prize captains to reach Harold's galley and climb up the rope ladder thrown over its side.

"Hoy George. Hoy Jack; it is good to see you both, yes it is," I said as the first two of the arriving galley captains came up the rope ladder one after another and climbed on to Harold's deck.

I said it as we beamed at each other with big smiles. I had known both of them for years and shook their hands most friendly as they aboard. Harold was standing right behind me and did the same. As we did, the sailors rowing the two captains' dinghies moved them away so the dinghies of the next captains to arrive could reach the rope ladder dangling over the side of Harold's galley.

"Get yourselves a bowl of ale from the cook and find some shade, my friends. The rest of the lads are right behind you."

It took a while because there were twenty-five of them, but the captains all came up the ladder to the same warm welcome. Five or six of them were old boys from Uncle Thomas's school; the rest had worked their way up stripe by stripe. They were all good men and Harold and I meant every word of our many warm welcomes.

After a quick count to make sure everyone was present, I walked up the steps to the roof of the forward castle as the assembled captains seated themselves on the deck below me and waited expectantly. Some of them may have guessed that there would be more to the meeting than convoy assignments, but they were not sure.

"You and your men were told that you would not be getting your sailing orders until *after* we left Ancona. The reason given for why you had to wait was that we did not want the Venetian galley captains to find out how we were going to deploy our galleys to protect our prizes.

"All of it sounded quite reasonable and, hopefully, the Venetians will believe it when they hear about it from their spies and merchants. In fact, lads, it was just another gambit to mislead the bastards into chasing off after yet another wild goose as to where we will be sailing in the days ahead and what we will be doing when we get there.

"It is true that we have dealt the Venetian merchants a mighty blow by taking so many of their transports and cargos. But the fact is that we have not yet taken the full measure of revenge that the articles of our Company's compact require for our recent heavy losses. You know it, I know it, and most important of all, our men know it.

"And in a few days the Venetians are going to know it. This is what we are really going to do when we sail on from here."

Chapter Fourteen

We sail north instead of south

The captains leaned forward and listened intently as George told them where they would be sailing next and some of what they would be doing when they got there. They got more and more excited as he explained his plan, and they jumped to their feet and cheered when he finished. So did the men in Harold's crew who had been quietly standing behind them to listen. It was a bold plan.

Even Harold was impressed.

"By God, George. That is bold. It truly is. I like it."

****** *Harold Lewes*

Everyone listened with growing excitement as George told the assembled captains where we would be heading when we raised our sails and what we would be doing when we got there. Our destination was not Constantinople as we had been told earlier; it was the Venice itself, the capital and only city of the so-called Venetian Republic whose king was called some strange name like "The Dog."

Or perhaps I did not hear George correctly and the Venetian king was called something else.

It did not matter. According to George, The Dog owed us for our recent losses and we were coming for his shipping and coins no matter what he named himself.

Venice, George reminded us, was nearby. And it certainly was; it was only about a day's sailing north of our present position if the winds were strong and favourable; and only two or three days if the winds were not favourable such that rowing and clawing into the wind were required.

What George told us that was surprising, and caused the men to sit up straighter when they heard it, was what he had in mind for us to do when we reached Venice. It was much more than a hit and run raid for prizes such as we sometimes put on the ports along the Moorish coast.

"We are going to fall on Venice and deal it a mighty blow by remaining there to take its shipping as prizes until they have none left. So long as we are there it will leave the city and its king and his nobles impoverished because they have no lands to tax and rely almost entirely on their shipping and their merchants and moneylenders for their coins."

As it turned out, of course, what George did *not* tell us was that he *also* had something else in mind. Instead, he once again reminded us that attacking Venice was more than just an effort to enrich ourselves, it was also part of revenge required by the Company's articles.

"*We* will never forget the men we lost at Constantinople because of the Venetians. Well, now it is Venice's turn. And we are going to strike a blow against the Venetians that *they* will never forget."

What George did not have to tell us was what I and the captains sitting on the deck in front of him already knew quite well and immediately understood—that the Company and those of us that survived would be even richer if our attack resulted in our taking additional prizes. What he also did not tell us was the rest of his plan.

Taking prizes out of Venice and occupying its harbours would not be easy, George admitted to the assembled men.

"It is inevitable that the Venetian fleet will sooner or later be summoned to try to drive us away. Unfortunately, there is no way for anyone to know how soon that would happen. Indeed, they could already be there and waiting for us."

The problem, George admitted, and we all knew and fully understood, was that we still did not know where the Venetian fleet was located or how soon its captains and commanders would learn about our attack or, for that matter, what they would do when they finally found out what we were doing.

Then George explained the situation. He did so as he leaned towards us and waved the pointy finger of his right hand in the air whilst using his left hand to grab the wooden railing that keeps men from falling off the castle roof on to the deck.

"Hopefully the Venetian fleet is on its way to meet us at Piraeus and will wait for us there in vain. But it does not matter when the Venetian fleet finds out that we are not coming or what it then does.

"That is because we will always be ready to fight the Venetian galleys on a moment's notice and because we are going stay in Venice' waters until there are no more prizes left for us to take and the Venetians are starving and ready to pay us a king's ransom to leave.

"If the Venetian fleet shows up before we are finished, we are neither going to run for home nor sit in the water unmoving so the rams on their galleys can sink us—we are going to use our longbows and the superior speed of our archer-rowed galleys and begin taking the Venetian galleys as prizes in addition to their transports."

The captains listened carefully to what George had to say, and then jumped to their feet and cheered at the prospect of revenging our dead and earning more prize coins when they did. The men of Harold's crew were equally excited and did the same.

The enthusiasm of the men was understandable. A major raid on Venice and the possibility of more prize coins was altogether exciting prospect for many of the men, particularly since a series of gambits may have the caused the Venetian fleet to sail away so that it could not interfere. I could see it in their eyes and on their faces.

On the other hand, to be fair, it was quite worrisome for some of them, particularly those who thought they had already earned enough prize coins and did not want to risk their necks again until they needed more coins.

****** *George Courtenay*

Harold took over from me after the commotion had died down. He began by passing out leather maps depicting Venice's islands and harbours. Roger Abbot and John Soames, our apprentices, had scribed them on leather parchments by copying a map of Venice I had purchased in the Athens market.

Every captain got a map. It was important because it showed the various entrances into the city's several great harbours. There was an "X" and a number on each captain's map. The "X" was where he was enter when we attacked; the numbers were the numbers of the galleys, including his, that would enter there and begin taking prizes.

We then spent several hours discussing various matters such as where and how we would launch our initial attacks, whose galley was to lead the way into each harbour entrance, and what to do with the prizes we took and the crews we found on them. The captured crews were a particular problem as it was unlikely many of them would be able to gobble French or the crusader French some people are beginning to call English.

Much of the time, as you might expect, was spent talking about how we would fight the galleys of the Venetian fleet if and when they arrived. It would change a little, but not much, if we had prizes to protect.

Harold made one order most emphatically and repeated it several times during the meeting—when fighting Venetian galleys, our galleys were to move off and use our arrows and never let them get close enough to use their rams.

"Keep moving and stay well away from them. And do not waste a single one of your men's lives trying to board a Venetian galley until your archers have swept its deck clean of everyone carrying weapons—and also do not board them if there are other Venetian galleys nearby that might be able to ram you whilst you are grappled together and unable to move."

****** *Apprentice Sergeant John Soames*

The wind was northerly and strong for the rest of the first day of our sailing along the Italian coast towards Venice. It was a favourable portent as we were under orders to use only our sails.

Our archers, despite their enthusiasm to get to Venice, neither rowed nor practiced with their weapons as we moved north. Instead they mostly sat about and yarned as they worked to turn out more arrows with the "arrow fixings" that the Commander had bought from the merchants in and around Ancona before we sailed.

There was an air of excitement on every deck, at least on Harold's galley where I was serving. The men were talking louder and working much faster and with more intensity than usual. No one sat idle. Everyone turned to the making of arrows, including the sailors when they had nothing else to do.

Even Commander Courtenay and Lieutenant Commander Lewes, and, of course, Roger and I, spent our time carving arrow shafts and attaching the required tips and goose feather fletchings. We could see the same activity occurring on our sister galleys whenever the winds caused them to sail close to us.

More arrows were needed because every archer on every galley, even the Commander himself, had been taxed for a dozen of his arrows so they could be given to our fellow archers assigned to the crews of each of the prizes sailing for Constantinople. They would be desperately needed if their prize met a Venetian galley.

Similarly, every galley had been taxed for four of its long handled bladed boarding pikes and eight sets of short swords and galley shields. I knew this because John and I assisted Commander Lewes as he supervised the distribution of the weapons to the men of our prize crews before they sailed.

Hopefully, of course, the arrows and weapons transferred to our prizes would not be needed because the Moors were concentrating their efforts on the waters off Spain and the Holy Land, and because the Venetian fleet had responded to our various gambits by sailing south to Messina to ambush our fleet, and then to Piraeus in an effort to catch us whilst we were waiting at a rendezvous.

If the Venetians had swallowed our lies and our gambits, our fleet of prizes and the galleys sailing with them would be safe. That was because our prizes departed for Constantinople *after* the local Italian transports were released to warn the Venetian fleet that our prizes were headed for Athens.

Accordingly, our prizes should have been out of the Adriatic and well on their way to Constantinople by the time the Venetians got the misleading information that they were on their way to Athens. Hopefully, they then rushed north across the mouth of Adriatic to recapture them and take the treasure one of our under-crewed galleys was thought to be carrying.

Our prizes' safety was not certain, of course, because the Venetian fleet could be anywhere and might chance upon them. And even if the Venetians were in Messina and were gulled into sailing for Piraeus, they might encounter some or all of our prizes due the uncertainties of the wind and weather.

One thing was certain, however—none of the archers begrudged the sending of some of their arrows to the handful of their fellow archers that were assigned to each prize. We all knew that they would need many more arrows than they normally carried if our gambits to mislead the Venetians were not successful.

******* *Lieutenant Commander Lewes*

The weather and winds remained favourable and we were able to stay together on our first night out of Ancona. And we even took a prize just after the sun arrived up in the morning— David Smythe's galley took a heavily loaded coastal cog that had come out of city of Comacchio at the mouth of the Rena River. It was carrying a cargo of Bolognaise wine and grain bound for Venice.

David immediately put a prize crew on the cog and then, following the orders we had been given at the previous day's meeting, immediately transferred its captain to our galley for questioning. The cog was added to our convoy because it was too small and did not have enough food and water on board to be sent off to Constantinople.

What we learnt from the cog's much aggrieved and very emotional Venetian captain was encouraging. His name was Antonio something or other and he had sailed for Venice because he had been told by the cog's "terrible liar" of an owner, a Venetian merchant, that "you French were not coming north."

Antonio had known there were French pirates in the Adriatic, he said bitterly. But he had been assured by the merchant who owned the little cog that they were much further south such that he could safely sail from Venice to nearby Comacchio to pick up a cargo of grain and wine.

More importantly, and after some additional friendly encouragement involving a bowl of morning ale and a promise "in the name God" that he would be freed when we reached Venice, Antonio began talking to the Commander. He told him Venice was packed with shipping that had gotten through our blockade off Ancona and now was sheltering in Venice's harbours because they dared not leave and risk being taken.

"There are transports anchored and tied up everywhere. More than I have ever seen. The taverns are full of their unhappy crews.

"At first no one knew you French were taking prizes off Ancona. So those who reached Venice must have sailed on past you in the night or when you did not see them because the sea is so big or your galleys were busy chasing after other prizes.

"Now, however, everyone knows you are out and does not want to risk being taken. So they are gathering in the harbour and waiting for you to leave. That is what I should have done."

Antonio was very bitter and full of self-pity to the point of having tears in his eyes.

"But where are the Venetian galleys that were supposed to protect you?" the Commander casually asked him as if they were the best of friends.

Antonio's answer was very encouraging. He told the Commander there were only a few galleys in Venice's various harbours. They were mostly new builds, he said, that had just come out of the city's galley yard and, for the most part, were still being fitted out. They were the only galleys in port, he explained, because most of the Venetian fleet was waiting off Messina for a great treasure galley full of all the Latin Empire's gold and Jewels.

The Empress's treasure galley and "you French," Antonio continued, were the talk of Venice—with the merchants, sailors, and churchmen getting increasingly angry at the city's lords about their losses. There had even been words and fighting at a tavern near one of the harbourmaster's offices. He himself had been there and seen it he said as he thumped his chest. And he had heard of other disturbances as well.

"It is understandable that the sailors and merchants are angry," Antonio said indignantly with a great waving about of the bowl of wine he was holding. "We paid our taxes; we should have been protected."

****** *Apprentice Sergeant Roger Abbot.*

Commander Courtenay and the Venetian captain talked about Venice and the state of the civilized world for quite some time. They did so with the help of one of the few men in our entire fleet that could gobble Italian. He was a grizzled two-stripe sailor from Galley Thirty-nine. He was an Italian named Antonio who had been a Moorish slave on a Tunisian galley when we took it some years ago and had ended being allowed to make his mark and join the Company.

We continued sailing north as they talked. John and I, being apprentices, kept our mouths shut and listened. Lieutenant Commander Lewes also listened. Sometimes he asked questions, but it was mainly the Commander that questioned the Venetian captain. He did so most kindly in my opinion.

The Venetian captain got more and more talkative and indignant as he stood with the Commander on the roof of the stern castle and talked whilst waving his hands all about. He said that everyone in Venice was quite upset and angry about the absence of the Venetian galleys.

"And they should be; look what has happened to me."

Venice's merchants and sailors, the captain said bitterly, as he nodded his head to agree with himself, and waved his hands about for emphasis, were angry with the city's lords.

"Because Venice's fleet, which the city's lords control and for which all the merchants and transport owners have to pay taxes, was not doing anything to protect the city's shipping.

"The city's churchmen, even the archbishop himself it is said, are also angry with the city's lords. That is because the galleys that should have been protecting Venice's most transports, the cogs such as mine that keep the city fed, have been sent south to seize a treasure that belonged to the Pope.

"The main problem of our city is our noble families, and that is the truth even though God himself caused them to be berthed as nobles. There are nine of them, noble families that is, and they are using the galley fleet to enrich themselves and increase their power whilst we honest sailors, and the merchants and everyone else, are left to suffer. It is outrageous."

After the cog's unhappy and slightly tipsy captain had been led away to join his crew in the forward cargo hold, the Commander turned said to us.

"It is an altogether encouraging state of affairs, lads, if even half of what he told us is true."

The problem, of course, as everyone now knows, was that the other half of what the Venetian captain told us turned out not to be true.

Chapter Fifteen

We sight Venice.

The outskirts of Venice began to come into sight on the distant horizon. It happened just as the sailing sergeant was in the process of having the sails re-sheeted to tack to starboard again. A grey mass of forested land soon appeared with a dark shoreline running in front of it. There was some kind of big building on an island off to the right.

"Oh my God, " exclaimed the sailing sergeant standing next to me a minute or so later. He said it softly under his breath, but we all heard it. It gave both me and my friend, Roger, quite a start such that we looked all around in surprise, but saw nothing.

A second later I realized what the sailing sergeant was looking at—it was not a forest of trees behind the hovels; it was a forest of masts in the water behind the spit shown on our maps. A few minutes later we could see that there were tenements and other buildings all along the spit. We had reached Venice.

Commander Courtenay jumped down from the castle roof and climbed about half way up the forward mast. He climbed very slowly and carefully. We watched as he put his free hand in front of his eyes and looked all about. Less than a minute later he came slowly back down, took a deep breath when he reached the deck, and shouted an order.

"Send your men to their chase stations, Lieutenant Commander Lewes, and have the attack flag waved from both masts."

"Aye, Commander. Send the men to chase stations and wave the attack flag."

The Commander's plan was going to be followed; we would go straight in on an immediate attack before the Venetians had time to get a resistance organized. It was very exciting.

****** *George Courtenay*

Men began running, sergeants began shouting and cursing, the galley's horn blower began tooting, and the rowing drum began pounding out the rapid burst of eight or nine beats that called some of the archers to their rowing benches and the rest of them to their chase positions. The cook dumped the embers from his fire over the side and the constant bailing out of water from our always-leaking hull temporarily ceased as everyone ran to his fighting position.

Within seconds the archers assigned to the lookout nests on the masts had begun climbing to their positions aloft. At the same time sailors began pulling bales of additional arrows out of the galley's cargo holds and readying them for immediate use. Even the livestock on the deck seemed to know something was happening and began making loud noises and struggling to move about.

Uncle Harold immediately climbed the forward mast to get a good look for himself. He did so after allowing a half dozen or so archers, his galley's strongest and best, to hurry up the mast ahead of him to get to their fighting positions aloft. He must have seen something of great interest, because he almost immediately hoyed the deck and shouted for John Soames to fetch his map of Venice and bring it up to him.

Our galley, or more accurately Uncle Harold's galley since he was its captain and I was but a passenger who happened to be senior in rank, looked like it had descended into total chaos with all the men running about and shouting.

But there was no chaos despite its appearance. To the contrary, responding properly to such an order was something our galley crews had been required to constantly practice ever since I could remember. It helped the men to know what they were to do under various circumstances, and it kept them busy when they were not rowing or engaged in archery and sword practice.

The waving flag and the sound of the horn and drum coming from Harold's galley instantly resulted in similar bursts of activity on the great gaggle of galleys following close behind us. I could hear their horns and the sound of their drums coming over the water as soon as the horn blower standing nearby stopped his honking and the drummer heard a shouted command and switched to a rowing beat.

A few moments earlier I had watched as Harold scampered up the main mast's rope ladder to get a better look at the shipping and harbours in front of us. He moved as fast as if he was an able-bodied young sailor. Harold's apprentice, John Soames, came up the ladder almost as fast even though he climbed with a map tucked under his arm.

Watching Harold and his lads move up the swaying ropes of the galley's mast ladders somehow brought into my head my own bad memories of clinging to a galley's mast as it fell into the sea off France.

Fortunately, my moment of fear only lasted for an instant and no one saw it on my face. Climbing a mast was something I found quite difficult and tried to avoid whenever possible.

****** *Captain Samuel Smart of Galley Ninety-two*

My galley was second in line behind the galley carrying the Company Commander. The distant sound of his galley's horn and drum as it began rolling over the water towards us was all I needed to know. I did not wait for the flags that began being energetically waved from both of its masts a few seconds later.

"Have the drum and horn sound boarding stations, Lieutenant Smith," I immediately ordered.

Roger Smith and my sailing sergeant, Thomas Oldcastle, were standing on the roof of the forward castle next to me when I gave the order. Even so, I bellowed it out as loudly as possible so my crew could hear.

My men had been waiting expectantly for the order ever since land had been sighted in the distance about thirty minutes earlier. They had known something might be about to happen because that is when I ordered the arrow bales to be brought up from the cargo and opened. They also knew what the sounds of the distant horn and drum meant. As a result, many of them had begun running to their boarding positions even before I finished giving the order. Everyone was quite excited. I certainly was.

Jeb Smith instantly repeated my command back to me. My galley's horn blower, a young son of the Company who had been waiting patiently on the deck in front of me with his horn in his hand, had already begun tooting the boarding stations call even before Jeb finished repeating it. The boy's father had been a horn blower too. He had fallen years ago and his son had been allowed to take his place as was our tradition.

A moment later our galley's rowing drum began beating as fast and loud as the drummer could manage. Seven or eight rapid beats and then a pause and another seven or eight. It merely confirmed what the men already knew.

The loud and rapidly repeated sounds calling my men to their fighting positions were so loud that I could not hear the sounds of the horns and drums coming from the galleys behind us. But I knew they were doing the same as I listened to the sound coming from mine.

"Take her more to starboard, Sailing Sergeant, and follow the Commander's galley north along the spit. Our assigned entrance is the harbour entrance on this side of the big building in the distance. Drop your sails. We will use our oars take us through it and into the harbour."

A moment later I bellowed again as our course changed we began to row abreast of what was shown on my map as a long and narrow spit with entrances to the harbour behind it at both ends.

"All archers report to their fighting positions for a chase. Boarding parties one and two report on deck with swords and shields; prize captains numbers one and two report to the roof of the forward castle. Ready your grappling lines and boarding ladders."

I could have kept the sails up and all the archers on their oars a bit longer, but I wanted to make sure we were fully prepared to fight and take prizes as soon as we passed through the harbour entrance.

As a result of our slowing, Commander Courtenay's galley pulled further ahead and the two galleys following immediately behind mine almost caught up with us before they too slowed their oars and sent their men to their battle stations.

****** *Captain Samuel Smart*

I had sailed into many a port in the years since I left the Company's school at Restormel, but never once had I been to Venice. That was probably because we had no shipping post here. *Venice, or so I had heard, discouraged foreign merchants and shipping companies, probably because it had so many of its own. They were everywhere*

Commander Courtenay and Lieutenant Commander Lewes had told us everything they were able to find out about Venice and its ruler at our "all captains" meeting off Ancona. It did not seem like much, just that Venice had a lot of shipping and not much land, which was something I already knew.

Even so, what I saw as we rowed along the southern spit towards our assigned harbour entrance absolutely astounded me—there was more shipping at anchor and along the quay than I had ever seen before in one place, more even than London and Constantinople. And there were apparently several additional large anchorages to the north behind an even larger spit of land. It was most amazing.

All I knew about Venice itself as my galley got ready to enter its row of its great harbours was that it was a city state on some very small islands that were close to the mainland of Italy in the northern waters of the Adriatic. What was instantly obvious from all the shipping and harbours was that Venice was truly wealthy even though it did not have a proper king, just some noble called the dog who ruled it.

I did not think Venice's ruler was a real dog, of course, but that is what the Commander called him. His name did not matter; prizes were prizes and revenge was revenge. The Company wanted both, and rightly so, and so did every man in it including me. I was determined that my men and I would do our part.

According to the Commander, Venice had a handful of nobles that got together every so often and proclaimed laws that the common people were required to obey but the nobles did not. In other words, Venice was very much like Britain and France except for calling its king a dog and its noble families having mostly galleys and transports to earn their coins instead of land. That was very encouraging and cheered us greatly; it meant there would be idle nobles and their useless sons leading the fight against us when the Venetian fleet arrived.

Our big problem, Commander Courtenay told us at the captains' meeting, was that we did not know if our gambits to keep the Venetian nobles and their galleys away from Venice had been successful or not. If not, they might be waiting for us and we would likely have a jolly good fight before we defeated them.

In any event, my galley followed the Commander's as it led our fleet along the seaward side of the spit on the southern end of the city. There was an even larger spit protruding into the water to the north. According to the map, both spits pointed at the little islands where many of Venice's people lived. The city's harbours and anchorages were behind the spits and around the islands. Water and little islands were everywhere.

My galley followed the Commander's until we came to the end of the spit and reached the entrance to one of Venice's main harbours. At that point the Commander's galley kept going and my galley and several others turned to enter the harbour and take whatever prizes we could find. I was fairly sure it was the harbour entrance assigned to us because, according to the map I had been given, it was the harbour entrance immediately south of the only really large building in all of Venice.

We had no trouble finding the city's one big building. It towered over the city and was visible for miles. It was almost certainly either a new castle or some kind of church or cathedral. From a distance there was no way of knowing for sure what it was because it was completely covered with scaffolding and still under construction.

As we got closer we could see men moving about on the scaffolding. Some of them appeared to be using a pulley to bring up some kind of statue to be placed on its roof. A king or noble would not piss away his coins on such a useless ornament, so it was almost certainly a church. That was very encouraging to me and my men as big churches inevitably had rich bishops with many coins and large numbers of silver cups, crosses, and dishes that could be sold or melted down.

The swishing sound of the oars from my lower tier of rowing benches slowed and softened as we turned to port and rowed into the harbour. As you might imagine, I was standing on the forward castle roof with my galley and its entire crew on high alert. In the event we were sailing into an ambush, I was ready to instantly give the order for my galley's rowers to spin us around so we could hurry back out of the harbour the way we had come.

My galley and the two galleys following along close behind me had been assigned to row through the harbour entrance next to the big building, and then begin taking all the prizes we could find. The captains and sergeants of the prizes, if they were aboard, were to be kept separate from their men to they could be sent ashore as soon as possible. Any ordinary seamen and slaves we found on board, on the other hand, were to be kept in their chains or held in our prizes' cargo holds so they could help us sail our prizes away when it came time to leave.

Immediately after passing through the harbour entrance we turned to port again and immediately came to a great gaggle of haphazardly anchored transports of all sizes and types. Two other Company galleys had also been assigned to come through this entrance with us, those captained by Fletcher Wood and Bob Penny. They were right behind us as we slowly rowed through the entrance and turned towards the anchored transports.

A couple of small single-masted cogs on the starboard side of the entrance had been the first potential prizes we saw as we rowed through the harbour entrance. I did not know what the captains of the galleys coming in behind me would do, but I ignored them because they were tied to a quay and appeared to be unloading construction materials for the big building with scaffolding around it. They were not going anywhere; we could take them later if we want them.

There were also many little dinghies moving about with men standing in their sterns using poles and rudder oars to push them. The men did not appear to be armed so I paid them no attention; my eyes were fixed on the large number of cogs and ships anchored in the water between the spit and the mainland.

Chapter Sixteen

Prizes everywhere.

Our entry into the harbour did not draw much attention, at least not initially. Everyone, it seemed, was used to the constant comings and goings of galleys in one of the world's busiest harbours. The people walking and working on the quay to our starboard barely looked up as we moved past them with the Oriflamme pennants of the French king flying from every one of our masts.

A big two-masted cog was anchored closest to us on the port side of the entrance. There were numerous other cogs and ships at anchor behind it. They stretched out almost as far as an eye could see. Very few were flying flags and pennants of any kind so it was impossible to know if they were Venetians. But they were here and that was more than enough to mark them as prizes to be taken.

A couple of the cog's sailors were leaning against its deck railing and yarning. They were looking at us as we turned and began to slowly row towards them. One of them lazily pointed towards us as we did. He did not seem excited; he had more than likely noted the red pennants we were flying as something to remark about.

"Make for the two-master, Sailing Sergeant, and bring us alongside. We will take her first."

My God, look at all the shipping. Will we have enough prize crews?

I could not help myself; I was so excited that I followed up on my order to the sailing sergeant by giving a totally unnecessary order to the men aloft.

"Everyone aloft is to look most sharp. Give a hoy and sound off if you see an enemy galley or anything else that looks either dangerous or interesting. And bows are free; push at anyone with a weapon.

Then I settled myself down and as calmly as possible gave another order.

"Lieutenant Smith, I would be obliged if you would lead the boarding party."

****** *Lieutenant Roger Smith, later Major Captain Sir Roger Smith.*

There was nothing at all surprising in the captain's order for me to lead the boarding party. To the contrary, it was a totally expected formality because the lieutenant of a Company galley traditionally leads its boarding parties.

I promptly knuckled my head, repeated the order back to Captain Smart, and jumped down on to the deck to join the men of the boarding party. They were strung out and in position all along the deck on the port side of our galley.

This was not my first boarding party. To the contrary, I had been in quite a number of boarding parties over the years, nine in all, and had already been the first man up one of the ladders four times. This was the first time, however, that I was going up first as the commander of the entire boarding party by virtue of my rank as my galley's lieutenant.

Prior to joining Captain Smart on Galley Ninety-two I had been the first man up a ladder when I was the sergeant of a file of Galley Fifty-five's archers. The last time I had done so was when we took a couple of Moorish transports off the Egyptian coast and I had gone up the ladder as the would-be prize captain of the bigger of the two.

My men and I had gotten our prize back to Cyprus and I had been rewarded with a promotion to acting lieutenant. My acting rank became permanent last year when I was selected from amongst the Company's acting lieutenants for the lieutenant's position on Captain Smart's Galley Ninety-two.

The lads in the boarding party were as excited as I was, that is to say very excited. They had their weapons in their hands and ready as we approached the Venetian cog. Similarly ready were the sailors that were standing ready among them to throw the grappling lines and pull them tight. Several of the men were mumbling something to themselves and making the sign of the cross. I myself suddenly felt a need to pee.

Our intended prize appeared to be sitting low in the water as we approached it. That was good because it cut several feet off the distance we would have to climb on our boarding ladders from our galley's deck up to the cog's deck.

Hopefully, the cog was sitting low because it was loaded with a cargo and its captain was waiting for permission to sail. It would be very discouraging to take it and find that it was sitting low in the water because its hull was leaking badly and needed to be bailed.

An extremely nervous Sergeant Alfred Snyder was standing on the deck next to me. He was shifting his weight back and forth from one foot to the other as we slowly closed the distance to the cog to the sound of a muted rowing drum. Alfred would be the cog's prize captain if we took it. He was standing with me to get any last minute orders.

Alfred and I stood next to each other without talking as the hull of the cog neared. Then, to my surprise and after looking furtively over his shoulder at the men around us and speaking softly, Sergeant Snyder told me something that was worrying him—the men in the boarding party had talked each other into believing the prizes we were about to try to take were the transports that had carried the Greek army to Constantinople, the Greek army that had killed and wounded a number of their mates earlier in the year.

According to what Sergeant Snyder whispered to me, the men assigned to the boarding party had worked themselves into such a great rage about the Venetian's crew that he was afraid they were planning to kill them all. He was worried, Sergeant Snyder said, that the men he and I were about to lead against the cog were hoping for a show of resistance so they could justify slaughtering the cog's crew.

This eleventh hour news, as you might imagine, alarmed me. But it certainly did not paralyze me, of that you can be sure. I immediately turned around and began moving amongst the men of the boarding party to loudly remind them that as many as possible of the cog's crew needed to be left alive to help the prize crew sail it off to Constantinople to be sold. They all nodded and said "aye;" a few, but not many, said it with obvious relief.

Less than a minute later we took the cog exactly as the Company had taken so many other prizes before it. Everything went well despite everyone, including me, being over-excited and anxious. The grappling lines were *not* thrown as soon our galley's hull banged up against the cog's. Instead, the throwers waited as they had been taught until the sailing sergeant gave the order.

Ninety-two's sailing sergeant was Alec Smith, a veteran sailor who had brought a galley alongside a prize many times previously. He waited to give the "throw your grapples" order until he saw that our galley's hull was properly aligned with the prize's such that they would come together side by side when the grapple lines were pulled tight. There was a high degree of expertise required for a proper boarding and the sailing sergeant had it.

As soon as our galley's hull was properly opposite the cog's hull, Alex shouted out the order to throw, the grapples were thrown by the sailors holding them. There were great cheers and hurrahs from my men as the grapples were thrown. Moments later willing hands pulled the grapple lines were pulled tighter and tighter until our galley's hull began to bang up against the hull of the cog.

It all happened in a matter of seconds. Instantly all of our galley's wooden boarding ladders, six of them, were set against the side of the cog with designated men standing on either side of each ladder to hold it firmly in place.

As soon as my ladder was in place, and because it was the Company tradition for the boarding party's highest ranking man to lead the way, I promptly stepped on to the ladder and started climbing up to the cog's deck.

The ladder was steadier than any boarding ladder I had ever previously climbed to take a prize, probably because the water in the harbour was calm whereas in the open sea the ladders moved up and down when the waves moved the hulls, sometimes quite a lot. Even so, as usual, I was more than a little worried and fearful as I began climbing.

 It was not an easy climb despite the ladder being firmly held and the ladder not moving up and down very much due to the lack of waves. That was because I had to climb with a galley shield slung over my shoulder and a short sword in one hand whilst I used my other hand to grab the ladders rungs and climb.

As I grasped the ladder, I stopped worrying about my men slaughtering the cog's crew, and began anxiously watching for someone to appear above me with a sword or axe and use it to cut me down.

Climbing up to a prize's deck on a ladder that was constantly moving as waves caused the two decks to bob up and down, even if only slightly as was the present case, was the most dangerous time for a boarder. I found myself desperately hoping that the archers on my galley's masts and castle roofs had cleared the deck of the cog in the area around where I would be coming up. I would be well and truly in deep shite if they had not.

On the other hand, things looked promising as I gritted my teeth, made the sign of the cross in case God was watching, and resolutely began climbing one-handed whilst holding the point of my sword aimed at the top of the ladder. There had been no sign of any resistance and the archers above me on the masts and castle roofs were not pushing out arrows as they certainly would be doing if anyone had been on the cog's deck carrying a weapon.

In any event, it was soon too late to turn back even if someone suddenly appeared at the top of the ladder and tried chop down on me or push the ladder over. That was because another man was already holding on to the ladder I was climbing. He was getting ready to follow me up and a third man was right behind him and getting ready to follow him. I had no choice but to continue climbing; reaching the cog's deck had become a matter of do or die so far as I was concerned.

Just before popping my head over the deck railing, I briefly paused and took a quick look around. The other ladders had been raised and men were climbing them just as I was—and the man on top of one of them already had his leg over the railing and was climbing aboard the cog waving his sword.

He was not being opposed so I popped my head up for a quick look. I was elated with what I saw—nothing. The cog's deck was completely empty and the door to the its single deck castle was closed.

I was greatly relieved as I swung my leg over the cog's deck railing and simultaneously pulled my shield off my shoulder. At that moment the door to the cog's deck castle opened and an older white-haired man stood there and gaped at me with a look of astonishment and surprise on his face. He was unarmed.

Chapter Seventeen

Pleasant problems.

Our arrival with a fleet of nineteen war galleys totally surprised the Venetian people in addition to surprising the owners and captains of the cargo transports anchored in the city's harbours and tied up along its quays. In their worst dreams they could not imagine that Venice itself would ever be the victim of a massive sea-borne attack by a "French fleet" or any other. They were, after all, the masters of the world's seas and its most important merchants and money lenders. No one would dare.

It also surprised them to learn our raid had occurred because the Doge had actively sided with the Greeks against the Latin Empress and that the Doge's noble-owned fleet of war galleys was not available to defend them.

Rumours had long ago reached the city that the Greeks had been defeated. But the extent to which Venice's Doge and the nobles from its nine great families had actively supported the Greeks and participated in the fighting had not been known. At least, that was what the captains of the captured transports claimed before they and their sergeants were released and sent ashore.

It soon became clear that we had taken the city's people and merchants totally by surprise. They came by the thousands to stand on the quays and along the shore to watch and point as everywhere our galleys and boarding parties were moving from one transport to the next and dinghies were being rowed ashore carrying fleeing crews and banished captains. There was little or no resistance.

Large crowds of people were everywhere along the shorelines of both the islands and the mainland. The people particularly gathered around the dinghies carrying the transport captains and their sergeants to shore. They did so in an effort to find out what was happening.

It seemed, if what various captured captains told us could be believed, that the rulers of Venice had gone to war against the Latin Empire and its allies without bothering to mention it to their people or the church. Kings do not have to do that, of course, tell their people when they go to war that is, but their merchants and the owners and captains of the city's huge fleet of transports might have been better prepared for our arrival if they had.

I thought it true that the Venetians did not know what had happened at Constantinople—because the Venetian captains we captured inevitably professed to be surprised when they heard our raid was motivated by revenge.

Indeed, each and every one of them claimed he had not known the Venetian galley fleet had put its men ashore to attack the lightly defended Company galleys whose men were fighting against the Greeks on Constantinople's city walls—and some of them became quite angry and bitter when they heard about it and realized that they and their fellow captains were the ones who would have to pay.

The Venetian crews, for the most part, surrendered peacefully when our boarding parties climbed up their ladders to their decks; there had only been a few feeble attempts to fight back on the part of a handful of the transport crews. Their efforts to fight back were forlorn hopes and quickly overcome.

Our biggest loss came when loose grappling lines caused a galley's hull to move away from its prize so that a boarding ladder with three archers on it tipped over and dropped them into the harbour's foul waters. The missing men were talked about but never seen again, which probably explained why fish stew was rarely available in waterfront taverns in the days that followed.

The captain of what turned out to be the only operational Venetian war galley in the city had somehow heard the news of our arrival before we reached the quay where his galley was moored. As a result, and even though most of his crew were ashore, he ordered the slaves that were chained to their rowing benches to start rowing in an effort to escape.

Fortunately for him and those of his crew that were aboard with him, when the Venetian galley captain found two of our galleys blocking the entrance, he wisely spun his galley around and had it rowed to the nearest strand. When they reached the strand, he ran the bow of his galley up on to the strand and he and his crew jumped into the surf and waded ashore to escape. It was a close run thing, but that was what he was able to do despite our two galleys being in hot pursuit.

Rapidly spinning around and rowing hard for shore worked for the Venetian captain in that he and his men escaped; it also worked for us because we did not need to fight to take it. When our men finally boarded it, they found it empty except for thirty or so galley slaves chained to the rowing benches on its incredibly foul lower rowing deck.

The Venetian captain and his crew stood on the shore and watched as our men swarmed aboard their galley and, a few minutes later, began rowing it away. They did not know it, but they were lucky for having twice escaped almost certain death—once by avoiding a fight on their galley's deck which they surely would have lost, and a second time when we ignored them as they stood within easy range of our longbows and watched their stranded galley being boarded.

It was the right thing to ignore them; it would have wasted arrows that might be needed later. This, in fact, turned out to be the case.

******

We ended up needing two full days to take the transports that had been sheltering in the supposed safety of Venice's harbours. In all, we took almost two hundred prizes ranging from very valuable three-masted ships to humble single-masted coasters of little or no value. There were even half a dozen or so Arab dhows. Strangely enough, we never did bother to take the two old single-masted coasters delivering materials and statues to the construction site. So the workers building the church never stopped working.

Even better, many of our prizes had been loaded both with outbound cargos and with food and water for their voyages whilst they waited for "the French pirates" to leave the Adriatic. Our best prize of all, however, was not a transport. It was a second galley, a new one with a protruding ram, that had just come out of the city's galley yard and was still in the process of being fitted out with oars and sails. Harold actually clapped his hands in delight when he saw it.

"The Venetians certainly know how to build sea-going galleys and this is one we will be keeping for sure. On the other hand, and as soon as possible, we should go ashore and burn the galleys that are still under construction so they can never be used against us."

Harold and I immediately began learning all we could about the prizes and their cargos.

Starting at dawn on the morning after our arrival, we had taken one of the few Italian-gobbling Company sailors we could find and began going from prize to prize to inspect them. We did so even though the boarding and taking of the transports in the harbours was still going on. Our apprentices, Roger Abbot and John Soames came with us to scribe a list of our prizes and record our comments about each prize's cargo, condition, and crew.

Our useful Italian gobbler was a veteran two-stripe sailor by the name of Giorgio Bertoli. He had been freed from a Moorish galley some years earlier, and made his mark to join the Company after a few months of working for his food at our Cyprus fortress.

Giorgio instantly became invaluable in the questioning of the captured captains about their cargos and the condition of their transports, and also in identifying which of their sergeants that should be sent ashore. He was particularly useful in explaining to the Venetian crewmen why they were being kept on board as prisoners and when they would be freed.

At least half the transports we visited had no one on board except for one or two archers who had been left behind on each of them to guard it. Their crews were missing because they had either been ashore at the time or had managed to flee before we reached them. Unfortunately, because we needed sailors for our prize crews, many of them had seen us coming and gotten away in their transport's dinghy.

Sometimes, however, we got lucky—there was often not enough room in a transport's dinghy or dinghies for everyone, and the captains and those of their crews that got away to save themselves did not always take the risk of sending their dinghies back to save those of their crewmen they had left behind. As you might imagine, being abandoned by their captains and sergeants tended to greatly upset the common sailors who had been left behind; it made them much more willing to serve peacefully under the command of one of our prize captains.

Every Company galley, except for Harold's and those ordered to block the harbour entrances to prevent escapes, continued taking prizes all the first night and well into the second day of our raid. They were able to do so because there was no opposition and the moonlight was bright enough so that our galleys never really had to stop.

Indeed, it got easier and easier to take prizes because many of the transports, particularly those we took after the sun finished passing overhead, had been abandoned when their crews got into their dinghies and rowed for shore and freedom.

Things were going so smoothly that by late afternoon of the first day, Harold and I had left his galley to continue blocking one of the harbour entrances and had ourselves rowed off in one of its dinghies to begin inspecting the prizes and deciding what to do with each of them.

We soon realized that the capturing of so many prizes had created a number of rather serious problems for us. One was that it was taking our galleys so long to board our prizes that many of their rank and file sailors were able to escape before we could press them into our prize crews.

Another problem was that we had only one translator to tell the sailors we caught what they would be required to do in order to be freed. A third, and probably the most serious and unexpected of all, however, was that it soon became clear that we would not have anywhere near enough men to fill all the prize crew positions and still have enough archers rowing on each of our galleys so that it would be faster than the Venetians.

There were many other problems, as you might imagine, but not having enough archers and sailors for prize crews was by far the biggest and most significant.

******

Every man in the Company stayed awake and remained active all night long. As a result, our second day in Venice was, if anything, even more tiring than the first. A harried and obviously exhausted Harold made several important suggestions when we finally had a chance to speak privately. We talked on his galley where we had returned at my insistence because he clearly needed a rest, some food, and a bowl of ale. *I did too, for that matter.*

The work on the making of a list of our prizes continued whilst Harold and I sat in the shade of the stern castle and talked. Our much younger and stronger apprentices did it. They were given a dinghy, Giorgio to be their translator, a big chunk of cheese and some flatbreads, and told to continue visiting the prizes and adding what they found to the list. One of Harold's sailors was assigned to row them from prize to prize.

We had no qualms about sending Roger and John out to continue the prize inspections. They were bright lads and had accompanied us all yesterday afternoon and evening, and through the morning of the second day. They knew what we wanted scribed about each prize and what should be said to the Venetian captains and their men if they were still on board. It was very satisfying to have someone else do the work.

Despite my fears for his health, Harold recovered fairly quickly after he had a couple of bowls of ale in his belly and stopped sweating and barfing as if he was sea-poxed. As he recovered, he shared his concerns based on what he had seen on our prizes.

"We are going to have a serious problem, George, a really big one. Our galleys will soon be seriously under-manned and unable to defend themselves because too many of their men are serving in prize crews. We will be in deep shite if the Venetian fleet suddenly arrives and our galleys have to fight them with not enough men to out-row the Venetians' slaves.

"Our great advantage is the strength our archers' arms. They are much stronger than the slaves pulling on some of the Venetians' oars. The difference lets us stay away from the Venetian galleys until we finish using our longbows to clear their decks and we can take them. We cannot do that if our rowing benches are so empty of rowers that our galleys cannot move fast enough.

"You are right, Uncle Harold," I answered. "I was about to say something along those lines to you this morning, but I did not want the men with us knowing that we have a serious problem on our hands. What do you think we should do?"

"Well, for starters we could temporarily reduce the size of our prize crews to a bare minimum until the Venetian fleet is defeated; perhaps just a couple archers to guard the cargo holds where the Venetian crews are being kept, and no archers at all on prizes that have no prisoners.

"We would need no more men than that until the prizes sail. But then what? I just do not know. We have never taken so many prizes or needed so many prize crews. It is a wonderful problem, eh?"

I agreed with him, but I knew that was not enough.

"Aye, you are right about that, Uncle Harold. You are also right that we will almost certainly lose some of our prizes if we send them out with only skeleton crews. But that is the price we will probably have to pay.

"But even that will not be enough. So I think we should strip all the archers out of another one or two of our galleys and try to get the empty galleys back to Constantinople or Cyprus without any rowers just as we did at Ancona. That would leave the rest of our galleys at their full fighting strength. What do you think about that?"

Harold agreed.

"You are right, George. Of course you are. And I agree—we absolutely must keep as many of our galleys as possible at full strength so we can destroy the Venetian fleet when it arrives."

"Well then, Uncle Harold, that is exactly what we will do."

And then I told him what else I had decided to order. He liked part of it.

****** *Lieutenant Commander Harold Lewes*

After George and I finished talking, I went off to my berth for a bit more rest and George began giving orders. Messengers were sent out from my galley ordering all of our prize crews on transports without prisoners to report back to their galleys as soon as possible, and for all prizes with fewer than five captured sailors to move them to galleys with more than five and also return to their galleys. The prize captain and one archer were to be left on board prizes with five or more prisoners; all the rest of each prize crew were to immediately return to their galleys.

"Be sure to tell the prize captains that we will keep their prizes safe by patrolling the harbour with full-strength galleys and their dinghies."

That was just the beginning.

A couple of hours or so later George woke me and told me he would be taking one of my galley's two dinghies back to one of the captured transports whose captain had gobbled French with us when we inspected it. The Venetian captain had not yet been put ashore because his cog's dinghy had been gone when we captured his cog.

I felt much better and went with him. George's plan was simple—we would sell some or all of our prizes and their cargos back to their owners or anyone else in Venice who was willing to pay a fair price for them. It had the great merit of reducing the number of archers and sailors that we would need for prize crews.

As you might imagine, we were particularly keen on selling the transports that had little in the way of value and those that might not be capable of making it all the way to Cyprus or Constantinople. It was about then that I noticed the weather was changing; it was getting cloudy; a storm was coming.

Sergeant Black, the prize captain of the two-masted cog whose captain and crew were still aboard, greeted us as we climbed the rope ladder from our dinghy. He immediately sent one of his men running to get the imprisoned Venetian captain out of the cargo hold where he and his men were being held.

The Venetian captain blinked his eyes and was a bit unsteady when he first climbed out of the dark hold, but it did not take him long to stop wobbling and agree when George told him, in French, what he wanted. The captain's agreement was expected; he would, after all, get his freedom and had nothing to lose.

George was pleased at the captain's willingness to help and told him as much.

"Good, I am pleased we understand each other, Captain. We French always try to be reasonable.

"Now I am going to have one of my men row you to shore so you can carry my message to the city's merchants and the owners of the cogs and ships we have taken. Tell them to come to the quay where the church is under construction to meet them. I will be there two hours after sunrise tomorrow.

"And remember—I want to meet with everyone who is interested in buying one or more of the captured transports or their cargos. Oh yes, and be sure to tell them that anyone carrying a weapon will be killed on the spot and that everyone interested in buying a transport or cargo must bring a translator who can speak to us in French."

We did not know it at the time, of course, but it turned out to be a very bad plan.

Chapter Eighteen

We try to sell some of our prizes and cargos.

Harold and I spent half the night looking at the list of prizes and coming up with a reasonable *suggested* price for each of our prizes and its cargo. Basically, we put very high prices on those we would be willing to keep for the Company's use or sell elsewhere, and very low prices on those that were in such bad shape or so small that they might not survive a voyage to somewhere where they might be profitably sold.

The suggested prices were for our own use when we met with the potential buyers. They would not be revealed to the Venetians.

******

Rain was steadily falling on the second morning after we reached Venice. It was the third day of our raid. A large crowd had already assembled on the quay by the time our horn blower tooted to announce the arrival of dawn. It continued to grow in the two turns of the sand-filled hour bowls that followed.

Harold and I were wearing hooded leather rain skins and knitted caps as we stood on the roof of his galley's forward castle. They were quite warm so it was good that the morning was much cooler than that of the previously sunny day.

We stood there in the rain as Harold's galley slowly moved to the crowded quay with the Oriflamme banners of France waving from both masts for the waiting crowd to see. We also had little Oriflammes on our tunics and so did our apprentices. The two boys were standing in their usual places immediately behind us.

I was unarmed except for my wrist knives and unarmoured except for my chain shirt. Harold was also unarmed. Our apprentices and the men around us and on the deck would be our guards. They were carrying short swords and galley shields because the rain made their bowstrings unreliable.

There was no indication of danger or confrontation, but everyone was on high alert. As we got closer, we could see that the men on the quay were unarmed.

Even though they did not know it yet, the waiting men would be invited to climb down to our deck one at a time to meet with us in the galley's stern cabin. It had been totally emptied of the beds and bedding that had been in it ever since we left Constantinople. The clothing and personal property of its occupants, Harold, his lieutenant, our apprentices, and the galley's sailing sergeant, had been placed in the wooden boxes that served as each man's sea chest and held his personal items.

The galley's stern castle was a good place for us to meet with potential buyers, especially since it was raining. That was because the castle's door and shuttered wall openings could be opened to let in light and the candle lantern hanging from the ceiling could be lit.

Harold and I could not help it; despite the size of the crowd on the quay waiting for us, our eyes were drawn to the men moving about on the scaffolding of the big church as our galley slowly slid past it. They were up there working and moving about even though it was raining. I expected to see one or more of them fall at any moment. Watching them made my bollocks tingle.

A number of archers were standing on deck holding galley swords and shields. Their eyes were also somehow drawn to the activity of the men on the scaffolding rather than to the mostly unmoving hundreds of men waiting for us on the quay.

"I did not think there would be so many," Harold said quietly after we turned and began to approach the crowded stone quay with big logs set in front of the stones to act as hull bumpers.

"You are right, Uncle Harold. This is going to take much longer than I thought."

As we got closer to the quay we could see that none of the men waiting for us appeared to be armed, at least not as far as we could tell. We could also see that some of them were holding up sticks with a little tents stuck on top of them to keep the raindrops from falling on their heads.

What the Venetians did not know was that two more of our galleys had been stripped of all their archers and had already sailed for Constantinople along with the two new Venetian galleys that we had captured. They would use their sails all the way because they had no archers on board to row them. They had been removed from the two Company galleys so they could serve on prize crews. Only the barest few of their sailors and their captains sailed in them.

The Venetians also did not know that we had a major weakness—if their fleet arrived in the next few hours our battle-ready galleys would have to row hard to keep away from them until the rain stopped and our archers' bowstrings were dry enough to push out arrows.

Worst of all, and rain or not, if the Venetian fleet showed up we would have to temporarily abandon our prizes and the prize crews that were aboard them. Our reality was that there was no way we could defend our prizes where they were anchored. We could not because our galleys would have no room to move about in order to stay away from the Venetians' rams.

And even without the rain there was no way we could win if we stayed and fought in the harbour. We had to fight on our terms or we would lose. We were, after all, down to seventeen fully crewed galleys capable of winning a one on one fight against the Venetian galleys—which were thought to be fifty-seven in number.

We did not expect all fifty-seven to show up. There had, after all, been less than fifty in the Marmara at the peak of the fighting between the Greeks and the Empress's forces. What we did reasonably expect, however, was that there would be enough of them such that we would be seriously outnumbered.

On the other hand, we would not *permanently* leave our prizes even if all the Venetian galleys arrived, we would just leave them temporarily until we defeated the Venetians. But that was only possible so long as each of our galleys had plenty sea room so it could stand off from the enemy galley or galleys it was engaging. It had to do that, stand off with sea room that is, to take advantage of the superior range of its archers' longbows and the strength of the archers' arms when they were rowing.

Our biggest problem in addition to our need for having enough sea room in which to fight, was our supply of arrows. In essence, it was virtually certain that we would temporarily abandon our prizes whilst we went out to sea in order to get room to fight—and that we would lose them permanently if we did not have enough sea room to fight our kind of battle or if we ran out of arrows before the surviving Venetian galleys fled.

As you might imagine, very specific orders were given so our galleys would stop whatever they were doing and hurry out to sea if the Venetians arrived, and the making arrows with periodic breaks to practice their archery and sword fighting was how our archers and sailors spent every available hour from dawn to dark.

****** *John Soames*

Our galley approached the crowded quay cautiously. Lieutenant Commander Lewes was clearly taking no chances. When we got close enough, the galley's mooring lines were thrown to the waiting wharfies who promptly pulled it as tight against the quay's timbers as the galley's sacks of hull bumpers would allow.

Our galley's oars were manned and a pair of sailors carrying newly sharpened wood-cutting axes stood by each line ready to cut it at the first sign of trouble. Similarly, archers carrying long-handled pikes and dinghy oars stood ready to push the galley away from the quay on a moment's notice.

Two others of the Company's galleys also came up to the quay with their archers at the same time. One was in front of us and the other behind. They did not tie up.

A number of archers were on the decks and castle roofs of the three galleys with their already strung bows covered by leather rain sheathes that could be pulled off in an instant. I was one of them. Our bowstrings would not last long in the rain, but many an arrow would fly true in the brief period before they ceased to be effective and had to be changed out—which they could be with the spare bowstrings that we all carried under our knitted caps and in the leather pouches that hung on every archer's belt.

Commander Courtenay stood in the rain on the roof of the stern castle to address the crowd on the quay. He began to do so in French as soon as the galley's mooring lines were tightened by the waiting wharfies. I was standing not ten feet away and heard every word he said.

"Greetings in the name of my king, the great Phillip Augustus of France. King Phillip and his men have taken some of your transports as lawful prizes. We did so, and will continue to do so, because Venice betrayed the Pope and ordered its galleys to attack the Latin Empire and the men of France and England who were supporting the Empire and its Empress. Venice attacked us most foul even though we are all fellow Christians and were at peace with Venice.

"You Venetians and the Greek heretics you supported were soundly defeated which was without a doubt the Will of God. Unfortunately for you, some of my men were killed and so were some of our English mercenaries.

"According to both the rules of God and the rules of war, we French and our English mercenaries are entitled to compensation for our losses. Accordingly, you will have to buy them back if you want to recover the transports and cargos we have seized.

"Those of you who are want to buy one or more of them must form a line to come aboard. We will let those of you who are unarmed on to the deck of this galley to discuss what you are willing to pay to retrieve the shipping and cargos you have lost.

"If what you are willing to pay for each of our prizes is not enough, we will sail them away from here and sell them in some other place; and if you try to bring weapons on board we will kill you immediately. There will be no warnings and no second chances."

A single boarding ladder was raised from the deck of our galley to the quay as George was speaking.

"The first prize to be sold is the two-masted cog with a cargo of ore and charcoal for the making of iron. Its captain was Joseph Valverdi and it was bound for Sicily when we took it. Anyone who wishes to buy the cog and its cargo may now climb down the ladder and come aboard. Payment must be made within the hour if you buy it."

There was a great moving about on the quay and some shouting out to us and arguing amongst the waiting men. Within a minute or two, however, seven or eight men had pushed through the waiting mob to the ladder.

One of the first arrivals had been assisted to the ladder by a number of servants and retainers, several of whom held little tents on a stick over his head and others who were carrying swords and used them to clear people out of his way. The mob and the other potential buyers had given way as he made his way to the ladder so he was apparently someone important.

"Stop. Do not come down," George shouted as he pointed to someone at the top of the ladder. "Anyone who tries to climb down that ladder carrying a weapon will be killed immediately."

George thundered his threat in French as one of the sword carriers accompanying the important man started to get on the ladder. The swordsman clearly intended to go down the ladder ahead of the important man.

Then George turned and repeated the order in English to the archers standing about him on the castle roof. They had seen the swordsmen at the top of the ladder and had already begun to pull off the leather rain covers off their bows.

The sword carrier paused for a moment and listened as the important person said something to him and motioned for him to proceed. He awkwardly shifted his sword to his other hand and began climbing down the ladder.

"Push," George shouted as pointed to the ladder climber.

The archers on Harold's galley were ready with their arrows nocked and some of them were only twenty or thirty feet away from the climber. So it was little wonder that the snap of the bowstrings hitting the archers' leather wrist protectors, the sound of their arrows as they hit the climber, and his brief cry came together as one sound.

A moment later there was a thud as the overly ambitious thruster's body hit the deck at the foot of the ladder. The fletching of four or five arrows could be seen sticking out of the body. The sailors on the deck that were holding the ladder steady had been forced to jump out of the way to avoid being hit, first by the falling body and then by the ladder as it slowly slid to one side and then fell on to the deck such that it almost hit some of the archers.

There immediately was a lot of pandemonium and shouting on the quay. It was quite noisy. Everyone seemed to step back a few paces and number of men in the crowd turned around and hurried away. The important man who had been brought to the ladder by his retainers disappeared.

The Commander held both of his hands up over his head in an effort to silence the men that remained, and waited until the noise quieted down. He resumed in French after they fell quiet.

"I said anyone who tried to come on board with weapons would be killed; I meant it and I still mean it. Now who wants to buy the cog and its cargo?"

At first there was no response to his question. But then a well-dressed older man wearing some kind of leather head covering pushed his way through the crowd, walked over to the ladder and began climbing down. He started to do so whilst trying to hold one of the little tents over his head. It did not work because he needed both hands to climb.

Our potential buyer had a determined look on his face and quickly stopped trying to stay dry. After taking one step down the ladder, he stopped, handed the little tent up to someone who leaned down from the quay to take it, and came down without it in the rain. He reached the deck at about the same time as a couple of archers turned over the swordsman who lay crumpled on the deck facedown and began using their knives to cut their arrows out of him.

A number of other men hurried to the ladder, and began following him down as soon as they saw the first man reach the deck without being shot full of arrows or attacked.

Somewhere behind me on the deck an archer was getting a terrible bollocking from his sergeant and his mates. He must have missed the man on the ladder. They were quite right to do so; it was inexcusable to miss at such a short distance.

The dead swordsman did not scream or jump about as the archers retrieved their arrows so it was likely that he was dead when he hit the galley deck. Pulling or cutting an arrow out of someone can be quite painful such that people and horses tend to make quite a bit of noise and thrash around if they are still alive.

More and more men climbed down the ladder in the rain one after another. There were soon more potential buyers standing in the rain around me than could possibly fit into the larger deck castle on our galley's stern. Some of them had somehow gotten little tents on sticks thrown down to them, but most were getting wet and so were my men and I.

The would-be buyers were all shouting and trying to get to me to talk and were being held back by sailors and archers. Tempers were fraying. It soon became total chaos with more and more men trying to climb down the ladder.

I looked over at Harold who was standing nearby to see if he had any ideas. He just shrugged his shoulders and shook his head with a rueful look on his face and water dripping down from his beard. There was no doubt about it, my idea of taking a handful of individual buyers into the stern deck castle and negotiating a price with them was not going to work. Actually, to tell the truth, it was turning into a goddamn disaster.

I climbed back up on to the stern castle roof so I could see both the men on the deck and those still waiting on the quay. I could see them because the roof of castle was as high enough above the water such that it was only a few feet below the quay. There was nothing to do but stop what we were doing and start again later.

"Calme, Calme, goddamn it." I shouted in French as I raised my hands to quiet everyone and get their attention.

"Silencio. Silencio," Harold shouted as he too raised both arms in order to quiet the bedraggled men standing below us. At least that was what I think he said.

I just kept my hands raised until the men on the deck and the crowd on the quay finally fell somewhat silent.

"This sale is temporarily delayed so we can begin it again and conduct it properly. Everyone go home. We will try again at the same time tomorrow morning if there is no rain. Only this time everyone who wants to buy will stand on the quay and shout out their offers from there. Come back the next day if it is raining in the morning.

"Here is how we will do it tomorrow—our galleys will tow each prize we are selling slowly past the quay. Those who shout out the highest price will be given one hour to bring the coins they have offered and take possession of their purchase."

Chapter Nineteen

Things change.

George and his key lieutenants were becoming increasingly worried about the impending arrival of the Venetian galleys. Every passing minute increased the chances that the Venetian galleys would be seen coming over the horizon. The Company's luck had held so far but it could not continue forever. Accordingly, the rest of the day of the aborted sale was spent refining the plans to fight the Venetian fleet when it arrived and to provision and send to Cyprus the thirty-one prizes in the harbour that Harold recommended the Company buy in for its own use.

"What else can we do to get ready?" became the question the Commander and his lieutenants constantly asked each other and everyone else. There were many good ideas and not a few bad ones that were rejected out of hand.

One thing that was done was that two additional fully crewed galleys were sent out to join the two that were already out to sea to serve on picket duty. One or more of the four picket galleys would, or so it was hoped, spot the on-coming Venetians and rush back to Venice and sound the alarm.

Another decision was that all the prizes and crewless galleys we would send out in the near future would sail for Cyprus. We did not want to send any more prizes to Constantinople for fear that there would be no buyers left.

The captains of the remaining galleys were summoned in small groups, asked about their readiness, and given the same very precise instructions that had been given earlier to the captains of the four galleys now on picket duty.

"The Venetian fleet will be here sooner or later. When it arrives we are going to whittle the Venetians down by fighting them one on one, not as a fleet in one great battle. So as soon as the alarm is sounded each of you is to head out to sea and get plenty of sea room in which to fight.

"But whatever you do, do not attempt to close with a Venetian until its deck has been cleared of defenders and its capture is certain. There are to be no great sea battles between galleys that are held together with grappling lines unless they absolutely cannot be avoided. You must be patient and use your best weapons—your superior speed and the range of your archers' longbows.

"And rams. Most of the Venetian galleys have rams as you know. So be sure *never* to let a Venetian get in position to ram you. Stay well away from them.

"Also remember that you are likely to be outnumbered so you must be sure to keep your men's arms rested as much as possible so you can outrun any additional Venetians that suddenly appear.

"And because you are likely to be outnumbered, your best move will almost certainly be to use the Company's "wounded bird" gambit to lure them into chasing you until only one of your pursuers remains.

"Only then, and only if there are no other Venetians in sight, are you to turn back on the last one chasing you and take him. But even then you are to do so only after you stand off far enough to be safe and your archers clear his deck of defenders with their long bows."

By early on the afternoon of the aborted sale the Company's galleys began towing thirty-one of the prizes out of the harbour so they could get underway to Cyprus with skeleton prize crews.

Those that needed additional supplies of food and water for such a long voyage, and some did, were supplied from the cogs that had sailed with us from Ancona. Indeed, provisioning the prizes so depleted the supplies of one of the Ancona supply ships that it too was sent to Cyprus. And, of course, each of the prize captains was given a pouch of coins so he could buy supplies and recruit sailors if he was forced to stop along the way.

The two captured Venetian galleys sailed with them. One was more likely than the other to make it because it had been taken with its slave rowers on board. The other would have to get there using only its sails. The slaves were told they would be unchained and freed when they reached Cyprus. Until then, since we did not know anything about the slaves and knew the Venetians frequently used convicts to row, it would be too dangerous for its skeleton prize crew to have them moving about freely.

Both of our prize galleys were crewed by a handful of enthusiastic Company volunteers. They had volunteered with the understanding that they would remain in their new and higher positions, with a promotion appropriate *if* they were able to get their galley to Cyprus. In essence, if their galley made it, every man in its prize crew would be sewing on another stripe, and, in several cases, two. The same was true for the prizes.

In order to minimize the chance of being taken, all of our prizes were ordered to initially *not* sail south down the middle of the Adriatic as they normally would, but rather take a longer and hopefully safer route by sailing close to the Italian coast.

What we hoped was that the Venetian war galleys would be in a hurry and take the most direct course to Venice. If so, they would sail straight up the middle of the Adriatic until they reached Venice—and in so-doing they might well miss our southbound prizes moving close in to the Italian shoreline.

And even if the Venetian lookouts did spot our southbound prizes, the Venetian galleys might not stop to check them out because they would almost certainly be in a hurry to get to Venice. Also discouraging the Venetians from stopping our prizes was that many of the prizes would be recognizable as Venetian-owned and all would be flying Venetian flags.

Sailing south along the Italian coast on the western side of the Adriatic, Harold decided, would make it less likely that our prizes would be recaptured. Even though, he admitted, sailing close to land increased the chances that they would run aground in the dark and be wrecked.

The good news was that the prizes sailing from Venice would soon be so spread out over the Adriatic and also, of course, they would be sailing some of the time in the dark of night. As a result, a good number of them would not be seen and re-taken even if the Venetians knew they were coming. We knew that from our recent experiences when we were based at Ancona.

Darkness and the great expanse of the ocean had allowed many of the transports coming and going from Venice to pass through the skirmish line of galleys we had stretched across the Adriatic a few days earlier. We hoped that our prizes and crewless galleys would be similarly difficult to find now that they were the prey and the Venetians were the hunters.

Immediately sending every prize capable of leaving was, everyone agreed, the best we could do. It was certainly better than having them wait in Venice until the Venetian fleet returned.

******

It was still raining the next morning so the sale was postponed once again to the next day. The rainy day was not entirely lost, however. I was in the forward castle talking to Harold when there was the familiar gentle bump of a galley coming alongside. We soon learned whose galley it was and why it was here.

"One of our galleys has come alongside, Commander. It is Galley Fifty-six, Captain Adams. He says he has a couple of passengers who were rowed out to his galley and are requesting a meeting with you."

"Oh? Aye, please invite Captain Adams to come aboard and bring his passengers."

A couple of minutes later there was a knock on frame of the castle's open door and Jim Adams walked in. A couple of elegantly dressed Venetians followed him into the little room. They had highly polished black shoes and feathers in their caps. And they seemed to be taken aback by the plainness and simplicity of what they saw.

There was no surprise in that. All the little castle contained were four chests along the back wall that had been pushed together end to end so visitors could sit on them, two four-legged wooden stools, and a small wooden table where I took my meals and scribed my letters and orders.

The wooden frame of the castle's string bed had been tipped up on its side against the wall and held in place by a wooden bar. There was a galley sword and shield hanging on one wall and my clothing of various types hanging from wooden pegs on the other.

Strangely enough, the simplicity of the room seemed to encourage them if the disdainful looks on our visitors' faces was any indication of their initial thoughts. Or perhaps from their point of view the simplicity was hopeful—we might not be too expensive to buy off if this was how poorly the commander of the French fleet lived.

"Greeting Monsieur Commandant," one of them said in elegant French as we bowed to each other. "I am, Monsignor Pierre Urbano, King Phillip Augustus's ambassador to the Republic of Venice. This is Monsieur Roberto Morosini, a high advisor to His Most Illustrious Excellency Pietro Ziani, the Doge of Venice."

"And how may I help you gentlemen? Other than by sailing away with my galleys and men, of course."

I said it in French as I nodded with my very best insincere smile and made another elegant bow.

"Well, yes. Um, that is what we have come to discuss; you and your men sailing away that is. But perhaps a meeting in a more suitable location would be preferable to discuss the weighty matters that are before us. His majesty, the Doge, invites you to accompany us to a meeting at His Majesty's palace, Commander? Your safety would be guaranteed, of course."

He made his offer as he waved his hand dismissively at my living quarters.

I immediately responded.

"Ah yes, someplace more elegant than my humble quarters would be more appropriate for discussions with such important people as yourselves. I am sure you are absolutely right about that. But unfortunately I must decline the Doge's kind invitation despite your guarantee. The Venetian fleet is about to arrive and I must remain here to supervise its capture and destruction."

Would I accompany you two arrogant arseholes anywhere where you might be able to seize me? You must be mad. That was what I was thinking, but tried not to convey, as I offered them an insincere smile and regretfully declined.

The two men were somewhat disappointed at my unwillingness to accompany them, but they were clearly shocked and taken aback at my excuse for why I could not do so.

"Did you say the Venetian fleet is coming, Commander?"

"Yes I did, because surely it must. It can only stay away so long, can it? And my men and I do wish it would hurry so it gets here and can be destroyed before the sailing season ends. Otherwise we will have to stay here for months and wait for it."

Then I looked at them hopefully and dropped a rock on them.

"Is there anything you can do to speed up its return so we can get things finished here and get on with sacking the city? It is always better to get disagreeable things over with is it not?"

"But," the Doge's advisor started to say something, but then he shook his head as if it had been hit by a club, or someone's fist, and he needed to clear it.

The threat that the Venetian fleet would return and fall upon on us if we did not leave had been a non-starter. Accordingly, the French ambassador stepped in to take our discussion in a different direction.

"Monsieur Commander, I am surprised to see you here and flying the Oriflamme pennants of King Philip on your masts. King Phillip is a friend of Venice. There must be a mistake."

"There is no mistake, Monsignor Urbano, none at all, and I think you either know that or have not heard from France for many weeks. We are here and at war with Venice because King Philip is a good Christian and Venice disregarded the Holy Father's prohibition against Christians attacking Christians by fighting with the Greeks against the Latin Empire.

"I myself know that to be true. So are you suggesting that Venice did not fight with the Greeks and that I am a liar?" I said with a somewhat threatening edge to my voice as I leaned forward.

"Oh no. I mean, yes it is true that Venice helped the Greeks, but .."

I did not give him a chance to finish. I interrupted him rather rudely.

"There are no "buts" Monsignor Ambassador, Venice did more than just "help" the Greeks. It defied the Holy Father and its men joined with the Greeks in attacking the Empress and her allies.

"And I know it to be true because I myself fought there and saw the Venetians come ashore and attack the Empress's forces. They were resoundingly defeated I might add, no doubt because God was with us due to the Holy Father's prayers."

Did the Venetians defy the Holy Father and did the French support the Empress? I had no idea. But it was a good story and might even be true, so I stayed with it. One could not go wrong by confusing the French and setting them at the throats of the Company's most important competitor.

"And here you are, Ambassador, defending the Venetians' disobedience and heresy. Why is that? Are you so untrustworthy that you have you foresworn your oaths of loyalty to *both* King Philip *and* the Church? Or are you one of the Church's spies the Holy Father told me were in high places in the Doge's court?"

The Frenchman appeared stunned by my words, but not nearly as much as the Doge's advisor who had turned and begun looking at the ambassador with great deal of suspicion and uncertainty. The question as to whether my men and I were French or working for them as mercenaries had been forgotten.

In fact, I had not been told that there were spies in the Doge's court by the Pope or anyone else. But there almost certainly were some and that was close enough.

Chapter Twenty

Friends fall out.

Roger and I last saw the Doge's advisor and the French ambassador standing in the rain after our galley rowed up to the quay and put them ashore. They were waving their arms about and talking to each other with a great deal of intensity.

There was little surprise in that—Commander Courtenay had gulled them into believing they were enemies and told them that the sale of the prizes would continue and the city would be sacked if a ransom was not immediately paid.

It was a splendid gambit because spies in a king's court were expected. What had excited their emotions and increased their hostility towards one another even more was the Commander's suggestion, more of a demand actually, that a significant ransom had to be paid and indulgences purchased, *before* "France's galleys" would even consider leaving without sacking the city.

The Commander had stuck it to them quite elegantly, at least Roger and I thought so.

"Prizes are prizes, and even you must admit, monsieurs, that France's prizes were taken most fair. What is more significant, and will be very much greater in value than a few dozen prizes, is the blood money that Venice owes to the families of the many Frenchmen and English mercenaries who were killed and wounded because of Venice's treachery.

"About five thousand pounds of gold coins, or their equivalent in silver, sounds about right for the men that were lost because of Venice's treachery, plus, of course, whatever are fair compensations for the losses and inconveniences Venice has caused King Philip, the Church, and the Empress.

"Two thousand pounds for each of them and another two thousand for our English mercenaries sounds about right I think.

"That sums to thirteen thousand pounds of gold coins or their equivalent in silver. Deliver it to us by tomorrow at high noon and we will leave.

"If you deliver the coins, we will spare the city. If you do not, there will be great unhappiness amongst my captains, the city will be sacked, and the price for redeeming your Doge's honour and his regaining God's favour and that of King Phillip and the Empress will be greatly increased."

The two men, as you might expect, professed to be shocked at my requirements and the "absolutely impossible" amounts.

After some haggling, I suggested that Venice could make its own arrangements with the Pope and the Empress, and that the "French fleet" would leave with its unsold prizes for eight thousand if it was brought to the quay and delivered to us tomorrow. It was a solution Venice could afford.

"What do you think the odds are that they will pay it tomorrow?" Harold asked after the two men left.

"Less than fifty percent," I replied.

****** *Roger Abbot*

The morning of the rescheduled sale was clear and warm. The rain had stopped and the sun was out. Everyone was in good spirits because three new prizes sailed in yesterday and were scooped up as easily as dipping a bowl into a barrel of ale. Their astonished captains had obviously sailed from distant ports before word that our galleys were in the Adriatic had reached them.

One of the new prizes was a particularly fine three-masted ship with a cargo of grain-filled amphorae. Commander Lewes took one look at it and recommended that the Company keep it. Accordingly, its captain and his sergeants were sent ashore and it was immediately sent off to Constantinople with a prize captain and a couple of archers to oversee its common sailors. The other two prizes were added to the list of those to be offered for possible sale in Venice.

Also sailing for Constantinople yesterday afternoon were two more of the now-empty supply ships which had accompanied us from Ancona and another of our galleys whose men had almost all been taken from it to serve on prize crews. Their supplies had been oft-loaded on to our galleys and the prizes that were, or might be, sailing for Cyprus and Constantinople.

Some of the supplies carried by the two now-empty supply ships had been used to provision the prizes that would be offered for sale in Venice. It had been done in advance so the prizes could immediately sail for Cyprus if they were not sold.

Expectations as to the imminent arrival of the Venetian fleet suddenly became very high. I do not know why because, so far as I knew, no word had been received. But something was in the air and we all somehow all sensed it—which is why it had been decided to immediately send off as many as possible of our prizes to be sold elsewhere if they did not immediately fetch buyers in Venice.

It had taken the entire previous day to finish transferring the food and other supplies that the prizes being sold would need to sustain their men until they reached a neutral port and could buy more.

Some of the prizes that the Company intended to keep had already sailed. They were already on their way to Cyprus without first being offered for sale in Venice. Each of them had been towed out of the harbour and departed as soon as its supplies finished being loaded and its prize crew had come on board.

But we did not stop when we finished putting supplies on the prizes the Company was keeping. We immediately began loading supplies into the prizes that were to be offered to the Venetians. That was done so they could immediately set their sails and get clear of the waters around Venice if the Venetians did not buy them.

The sailors and archers doing the loading were soaked by the rain and unhappy about making the transfers, even though the rain was warm, particularly since they knew the supplies would remain aboard the prizes if the Venetians bought them.

I heard all about because my friend and fellow apprentice, John Soames, had spent all day yesterday watching the transfer of the supplies for Commander Lewes. According to John, it had not taken long to load the supplies on each prize. The loading went fast because many of the prizes already had supplies on board and also because the prize crews were so small that not much more was needed except for additional weapons and arrows.

Even so, we had taken so many prizes that it had taken all the rainy day of the aborted sale, and most of the next day as well, to make sure each of them had enough supplies and weapons on board. What was significant, according to John, was that the Venetians were coming and we were now down to only sixteen Company galleys in our fleet.

John was an interesting fellow and I like him a lot. His real name, he had once told me, was John Psalms. But the Canterbury monk who wrote to Bishop Thomas recommending him for a place in the Company school, probably his father, was barely literate and misspelled Psalms as Soames. So he had gone on the Company's roll as John Soames and been John Soames ever since.

****** *Apprentice Sergeant John Soames*

The sale of the prizes began again soon after the sun arrived the next morning. The first to be sold were the rest of the ocean-going cogs and ships selected by Lieutenant Commander Lewes for the Company to either buy in or sell elsewhere if they did not fetch a high enough price. There were sixty-seven of them, and each would immediately take on a prize crew and set out along the Italian coast for Constantinople if it was not sold.

People were everywhere on the crowded quay. They had arrived early because of the sale and were still arriving. The quay was especially crowded where the sale was being held. That was where our galley was tied up against the quay so Commander Courtenay could conduct the sale from the roof of its stern castle.

Additional security was provided by the archers of two additional galleys, one positioned alongside the quay immediately in front of the Commander's galley and one immediately behind it.

I could see everything because I and more than a dozen archers from Captain Nash's Galley Eighty-two were stationed on the quay about eight hundred paces to the north. We were there to collect the coins when the successful buyers made their payments.

A number of curious on-lookers gathered around us watching and commenting as the coins were being paid and counted. But there was not nearly so many people watching the coins being counted as there were standing about farther down the quay where the sale itself was being conducted.

The auction began soon after the sun came up and went quickly as our galleys towed the prizes one after another past the potential buyers standing on the quay. Those which fetched a high enough price were towed off to a nearby anchorage to await payment; those that did not were towed straightaway out of the harbour and sent on their way to Constantinople or Cyprus. They did so after stopping briefly at the harbour entrance so they could be hurriedly boarded by a small, *too small in my opinion*, prize crew.

It was quite an anxious time for the men of the prize crews because they did not know to which prize they would be assigned. That was because some of the prizes towed past the quay were bought by the men who assembled on the quay and shouted out their offers, and some were not. All the next prize crew waiting with their weapons on a galley anchored at the entrance to the harbour knew was that they would be sailing on the next prize that the Venetians did not buy.

If the best offer was not high enough, Commander Courtenay would shout out a final price from the list I had helped Roger Abbot scribe, and say that the prize in question would immediately sail elsewhere to be sold unless someone offered to pay that price. Sometimes someone would shout back their willingness to pay it. Mostly, however, no one did. About half the prizes sold.

When a prize was sold, Commander Courtenay's apprentice, my friend Roger, would scribe its number and its price on a piece of parchment and a sailor would climb up a boarding ladder to the quay and hand it to the buyer.

I knew all about it because I was with the archers who climbed on to quay, further down from where the buyers were assembled, to collect their payments.

When a buyer showed up with his parchment receipt and paid, I weighed his payment coins and put them into an empty grain sack, scribed "paid" on the buyer's parchment receipt, and pointed to where the prize was anchored nearby and waiting for him. I sat on one empty chest from the galley and used another as a table on which to scribe.

How the buyers got out to their purchases after they paid was their problem. It was quickly solved, however, when some of the men in little dinghies who moved people along Venice's waterways and between its islands showed up and began rowing them and poling them to out to their new purchase or wherever else they wanted to go.

The area where I was crowded with onlookers as I counted the coins being delivered by the buyers and scribed "paid" on their receipts. Many people just came to stare as the payments were made. Quite a crowd of Venetians assembled around us as soon as they realized what we were doing. The archers kept them back.

Almost all of the payments were made in silver, although a few were made in their gold and copper equivalents. Several times a buyer attempted to underpay, but inevitably came up with the rest of the coins when I shook my head, pointed to number scribed on his parchment, and started to return the inadequate amount of coins he had tried to pay.

Because I was unarmed and so many coins were present, there were at least twenty heavily armed archers on the quay with me carrying swords and shields and another several dozen or so were standing with their bows strung on Eighty-two's two castle roofs.

We were taking no chances because it was well known that Venetians could not be trusted. The rest of the galley's archers and sailors were standing guard on Eighty-two's deck or engaged in passing the sacks down to the deck and stowing them.

If there had been trouble the archers on the quay and I were supposed to quickly climb down the ladder to the galley's deck and escape with the coins that had already been loaded. That, at least, was the plan.

As you might imagine, the coin sacks had to be properly stowed so their weight would not cause the galley's hull to fail in a heavy sea. Most of them, I was told and could see, were being used to replace the ballast stones that held the galley's hull down into the water. Periodically whilst I was on the quay there would be a splash as a ballast stone being replaced was carried up to the deck by a red-faced sailor, and his mates helped him hoist it over the deck railing to be dropped into the water.

Whilst I was counting the payment coins and scribing receipts I watched and listened with some amusement as Captain Nash's sailing sergeant ran around like a chicken whose head had been wrung off. He was seeing to the sacks proper placement as ballast and seemed quite anxious about it.

Until then I had not realized that a galley carried so many heavy stones to hold it down into the water. No wonder being a galley wright required special skills and they were highly paid.

****** *John Soames*

Everything went well until a couple of hours past high noon. At least I thought it did. I was wrong. I had not known at that time that the Venetians had been given until high noon to show up with a very large ransom.

The Venetians did not arrive with their ransom coins. To the contrary, what suddenly showed up on the quay and caused the crowd of buyers and onlookers to shout and scatter in all directions, was a large force of armed men carrying swords and spears. There were several hundred of them and many of them appeared to be wearing livery, at least I think they were.

I had just finished weighing some coins, and had started scribing a receipt for the purchase of a two-masted cog, when someone cried out a warning. I looked up and saw a great horde of men with weapons coming at a run around the corner of a warehouse on the quay. *Holy shite.*

"We are finished here, lads," the lieutenant in charge of the shore party shouted a moment later. "Everyone back to the galley. Hurry."

"You too sergeant," he shouted at me as he drew his sword and moved between me and the on-coming horde. "Run, damn you. Run."

I thrust the partial scribed receipt at the startled merchant standing in front of me, grabbed up the heavy grain sack into which his coins had been deposited, and began dragging it along the quay as I ran for the nearby galley. In my haste I left my two coin-weighing scales behind. Archers with drawn swords were pouring past me on their way to the galley and those who had already reached it were jumping down to its deck.

"Mind the sprat and his bag, Charlie," The lieutenant called to someone.

A moment later the sack I was dragging towards the galley was snatched out of my hands by an archer who took off running with it and a two-striper with a big red beard grabbed my arm and pulled me along into a run towards the nearby galley. Arrows from the archers on the galley began flying close over our heads as we ran.

Chapter Twenty-one

The Venetians are coming.

A sharp warning cry "danger on the quay" from one of the lookouts caused the archers to nock their arrows, Commander Courtenay to climb part way up the main mast's rope ladder in an effort to see what was happening, and the galley's mooring lines to be cut a moment later by sailors using axes and swords. Then we anxiously watched as a large number of armed men, two or three hundred of them from the look of it, appeared further down the quay.

In the distance we could see our payment-collecting galley hurrying to re-board its men and push away from the quay. Less than a minute later the on-coming attackers were about to reach the men who had been bidding on our prizes and it was time for our galley to move away from the quay.

There was a widening swath of water between all three of the galleys at the sale site and the quay as the gang of unknown men reached the place where we had been moored a few moments earlier. There were hundreds of them and, as they got closer, we could see that they were armed and many of them were wearing liveried tunics. Some of them appeared to be wearing helmets and armour. What was significant was that they were running behind a man carrying a pennant with the coat of arms of Venice's ruler, the Doge.

The crowd of potential buyers, which had been impatiently waiting to bid on our prizes only a few moments earlier, scattered and ran for their lives. There was a lot of noise and shouting as they hurried away and the attackers arrived.

"Do not push; do not push," Commander Courtenay began shouting. "Save your arrows; save your arrows."

His order was loudly repeated before the on-coming attackers reached the spot on the quay where hundreds of prosperous coin-carrying men had been waiting to bid on our prizes. By the time they reached it we had pushed off from the quay and it was virtually empty except for the sword-carrying new arrivals.

In less than a minute the new arrivals were arrayed along the edge of the quay shaking their swords at us and howling their taunts. The Commander's order not to push had arrived just in time to save them from our arrows. His order had also been heard and repeated by the captains and sergeants of the galleys on either side of us. They too had pushed off from the quay and were conserving their arrows.

A handful of Venetian merchants who, for one reason or another, had been allowed to climb down the ladder to talk to the Commander in private stood on the deck and watched the sudden burst of activity and shouting in stunned disbelief and confusion. From the looks on the merchants' faces they obviously had not a clue as to what was happening or why. Neither did we for that matter.

The only thing I knew for certain as the gap of water widened between the quay and our galley was that we would not be putting the merchants ashore until we found somewhere where it would be safe to do so.

****** *Commander Courtenay*

Except for my order for the men to conserve their arrows, not a word passed between Harold and me until we saw Captain Nash's Galley Eighty-two safely push away the quay after its shore party of coin collectors and their guards had hastily jumped on board. It had obviously been a close call for the men who had been ashore.

Unlike those of us aboard the three galleys at the prize-selling site, the archers on the payment-receiving galley, Galley Eighty-two, had not been ordered to hold their arrows.

To the contrary, and rightly so, they immediately began pouring a storm of arrows at the on-coming attackers as soon as they came in range, and they had kept it up so long as the attackers remained in range. Their response was quite understandable and effective—from where we were standing on the roof of the forward castle we could see a number of the attackers motionless on the quay or staggering around and trying to get up.

The whole scene held me in sort of a trance. Despite the distance we could see the sun flashes and shadows as the stream of arrows poured out of the coin-collecting galley. It continued until the mob of attackers passed out of their range and began to approach where the area of the quay where our buyers had been standing and I had been conducting the sale.

At some point, as I watched the mob come down the quay towards us and the gap of water between our galley and the quay widened, I turned back to Uncle Harold and asked him what he thought was happening.

"Our coin collecting party seems to have gotten safely away, and that is good news. But whoever it is over there certainly has stopped the sale of our prizes. It would also seem that the Venetians do not intend to make the ransom and indulgence payments, not today at least. What do you think it all means, Uncle Harold, and what do you think we should do about it?"

Harold thought about my questions for a few seconds before he replied.

"I think it means the Venetian king expects his fleet of war galleys to arrive in the near future, perhaps as early as today, and is waiting to see what happens when it does. So you probably should order all the prizes that remain unsold to immediately sail for Cyprus, at least those for which we have enough prize crews.

"In the meantime we should row down to Eighty-two and tell Captain Nash to wait off the quay until he can send some men ashore to retrieve his arrows. And perhaps we should row down there and wait with him to make sure the arrow collectors have enough cover in case this ragtag lot tries to go back and stop them."

I nodded my head in agreement.

"Aye Uncle, you are right about retrieving the arrows and sending away the remaining prizes, at least those that have enough captured sailors on board to crew them. The Venetians may have been trying to recapture them before they could be sold or sail away. They probably did not know that they had already taken enough food and water on board and are ready to sail."

Harold did not agree with my assessment of the situation.

"You may be wrong about the Venetians not knowing about the prizes having the supplies they need, George. Indeed, I am sure you are.

"The Venetian king, the Dog or whatever he calls himself, almost certainly knows that most of the prizes in the harbour have enough supplies on board to sail—because they were waiting in port to sail before we arrived and took them.

"Moreover, his men almost certainly saw us moving supplies onto those few of our prizes that were not ready to sail. So it is likely the decision to interrupt the sale and not pay the ransom was made by someone high up who does not care a whit about the city's merchants and whether they get their shipping back; the Dog himself would be my guess, either him or whoever is his military commander.

"But it does not matter, does it? They have stopped the sale and that is a fact. So all we can do now is move as quickly as possible to send off the rest of the prizes for which we have prize crews. We can come back and re-take the rest of them after we see off the Venetian galleys."

"And the unpaid ransoms and indulgences? Uncle Harold. What do you think we should do about them?"

Apprentice Sergeant John Soames

My nose hurt most fierce and was bloody. The big archer pulling me along when the attackers suddenly appeared had not given me a chance to climb down the ladder. He had held on to my arm and carried me right along with him when he jumped from the quay on to his galley's deck without even breaking stride.

I hesitated for an instant when we reached the edge of the quay and, as a result, became overbalanced as he pulled me with him such that we jumped off the quay together. Even so, I managed to get my hands out in front of me before I landed, but not enough to break my fall. So I pitched forward and slammed face-first on to the deck. At first my face felt numb when I somehow got to my feet, but then my nose hurt like a fire had been put to it.

Everyone ignored me. They were too busy pushing arrows into the mob on the quay. As it turned out, I was probably the only archer on the deck without a bow. I had left it and my quiver full of arrows behind on top of my bedding when I went ashore with the empty coin sacks and parchments.

It was damn embarrassing to be the only archer without a bow, so I hurried to get it. And then, to top it off, the shooting had stopped by the time I got my bow strung and was back out on the deck.

"Hey. Over here. The sergeant is wounded." *Who is wounded? Where?* Then I realized they were talking about me and blood was pouring out of my nose.

Apprentice Sergeant Roger Abbot

We were in the midst of towing one of the remaining prizes out of the harbour when the lookout on our forward mast reported two of our picket galleys rowing towards the harbour entrance at high speed, one after another. The first one came through the harbour entrance and reached us about twenty minutes later. It was frantically waving its "enemy in sight" flag from its forward mast and blowing its horn to get our attention.

It was an alert for sure and could only mean one thing—the Venetians were right behind them.

Our galley had seen them coming and suddenly gone from carefully towing a prize out of the harbour to a frenzy of activity. There was a lot of shouting and running, our horn blower began tooting, and kept it up until he was finally ordered to stop. At the same time, the rowing drum gave six or seven alarm series of rapid beats before it dropped back to a rowing beat. All the noise was really not necessary, but somehow it helped. It certainly set a fire to everyone's arse and got them going.

In the handful of minutes between the first sighting of the picket galley and its reaching us every archer had been sent to the oars and our sailors had begun bringing up the rest of the arrow bales and slitting the throats of the nobbled sheep that were on our deck. The still-bleeding sheep and the squawking stringers of live chickens were hurriedly thrown into the galley's two small cargo holds as soon as the arrow bales and some extra water scuttles were out.

I recognized the first galley as it came down the now-sparsely filled line of prizes towards us. It was number Ninety-three, one of our newest and fastest. It slowed down and spun around in a u-turn next to us so both our galley and Ninety-three were both pointing out towards the great church under construction and the harbour entrance next to it. Ninety-three's loud talker was relaying its captain's report to Commander Courtenay at the same time.

"There be a great gaggle of galleys coming this way, Commander. Venetians for sure. They be coming along the northern coast from the east. I reckon they will be here in about twenty minutes, maybe less."

"How many did you see, Peter?"

"I did not wait to count them, Commander. It was a goodly number; at least thirty I would think, and maybe more. They be Venetians almost certain."

The galley coming in behind Ninety-three was one of our older ones, Forty-six. As I recall it was a Moorish prize and was also thought to be one of our Company's fastest for some reason. Their speed was why they had been assigned to be pickets.

I never did know for sure whether the second galley was Forty-six, and it did not matter. Its captain understood and obeyed the great arm rotating and pointing signals of Commander Courtenay and Lieutenant Commander Lewes. It did so by spinning around to starboard and moving towards the city's two other major harbours to sound the alert to those of our galleys which were still in them. Ninety-three followed it.

All of our galleys except the four on picket duty and the one at the harbour entrance with the prize crews, every single one of them including ours, had been engaged in pulling prizes out of the harbour so they could set their sails and begin sailing to Constantinople on their own. According to what I had overheard earlier, the prizes still in the harbour without crews would not be going anywhere until the fighting was over. We would return and recapture them after we won.

Everyone knew what to do when the alarm was sounded and the towing drums began their series of quickly repeated booms. Even so, there was a great deal of shouting and running about, not only on our galley but also on all the others.

Most of our galleys immediately cut loose their tows. One of them, however, for some reason merely repeated the alarm, sped up slightly by rowing harder, and continued towing its prize through the harbour towards the galley at the harbour entrance where the remaining prize crews were waiting for their assignments.

Our galley headed straight for the disobedient galley. From the loud curses and muttered threats from Commander Lewes I knew its captain was in for a serious bollocking. All of sudden he changed his tune as we caught up with the tow.

"Oh damn, there are Company men on that prize; he is doing the right thing."

The galley's tow was a rather nice-looking two-master that had somehow already taken aboard its prize crew. We could see men in Company tunics on its deck. They were working frantically to get the cog's sails ready to be raised. A couple of sailors without tunics, almost certainly men from its original crew, were helping them.

"Good man, Eric, Good man. Keep it up. There is plenty of time," Lieutenant Commander Lewes shouted encouragingly to the galley's captain as we moved up alongside it and began to pass it. One of the men raised his arm in acknowledgement and then turned back to help a handful of sailors who were laying out its boarding pikes and axes.

"Eric is a good man. I should have known better," he muttered to the Commander. "I would have had his stripes and hung him if he had left those lads behind."

The Commander's response was heartening.

"Well, the captains all know what to do. They have been told often enough, eh? So now all we can do is hope they all remember their orders and do their best to carry them out."

What I remember most is that the Commander smiled rather benignly as he said it. He seemed remarkably composed.

Chapter Twenty-two

The Venetian Fleet arrives.

Harold's galley cleared the harbour and, several minutes later, we stood on the roof of the stern castle and anxiously watched as Eric's galley came out of the harbour behind us and cast off its tow. It did so as soon the cog it was towing reached open water and was able to raise its sails.

I was standing next to Harold on the roof of the forward castle. That was where a captain and his key men always stand when a galley is moving through a crowded harbour. Harold was there along with his sailing sergeant and the rudder men. I was there to be with them. It was a warm day but rather nice due to the ocean breeze that was moving us along without rowing.

Standing on the little roof with us were our apprentices and several of the galley's best archers. Another half dozen archers were in the lookouts nests and atop the galley's two masts, and almost a dozen of the galley's best were on the much larger roof of the stern castle.

All the rest of the galley's archers, more than eighty of them, were rowing. The galley's sailors were mostly on deck standing ready with long poles and pikes to push us away if we got too close to other shipping and to be ready to work the sails. A few were down below working as rudder men and pounding on the rowing drum.

We continued sailing straight out into the Adriatic for about a mile in order to get enough sea room and avoid the shoals that might strand us; then we turned hard to starboard to run west and southerly along the Italian coast. It was midday and the sun was almost directly overhead and burning hot as we started our turn. We were rowing hard and made the turn just as the masts and sails of the on-coming Venetian fleet began to come over the horizon.

Several Company galleys had cast off their empty tows and gotten out of the harbour ahead of us. Others had been deeper in the harbour when they got word of the Venetians and had hurried out behind us.

Others of our galleys, those that had been in other parts of the great harbour, had received word of the Venetians later than we did and were still coming out of a more distant harbour entrance further to our north. They appeared to be following their orders and turning to port with the intention of proceeding north by northwest along the coast as opposed to following us in the other direction. Their archers would be rowing into the wind on a hot and sunny day.

In the distance we could see them coming out of the north end of Venice's great harbour and tacking into the wind. There were periodic flashes of sun along their hulls. The flashes meant they were rowing hard and their oars were throwing up a spray as they came out of the water.

The sails of our recently towed-out prizes, on the other hand, could be seen going in every direction including a couple that appeared to be heading straight towards the on-coming Venetian fleet. They were all sailing on whatever courses their prize captains thought would provide their best chance of not being recaptured. They were also flying Venetian pennants in the hope that the Venetian galleys would be confused and leave them alone in their haste to get to Venice and confront the French fleet.

Similarly flying Venetian pennants were all of the Company galleys. It was a reasonable gambit to attempt because, at a distance, many of our galleys could pass for Venetians. Hopefully the pennants would confuse the Venetian captains and give our galleys a bit of an edge when it came to fighting or avoiding a fight.

What we all hoped, of course, was that the Venetians would sail all the way to Venice to "liberate" it. If they did, our galleys would almost certainly be able to get away into the endless tracks of open water off Venice without being damaged or taken.

Then, and only then, would our galleys be able to fight the way *we* wanted to fight—by turning back and beginning to pick apart the Venetian fleet in individual galley against galley battles. Or, as my dear father would say, acting like a wolf that found a flock of sheep and began taking them one at a time until he had killed them all.

Fighting our galleys independently was the Company's preferred way fighting. Doing so in this instance, however, would require our galleys to get clear of the Venetian fleet so they could not be grappled or rammed. Only then would we be able to begin singling out Venetian galleys and use our speed and our superior men and weapons to fight them one on one until they were all destroyed. It was a strategy that had worked for us in the past such that we were not about to try something different.

The problem, which every man understood, was that the galleys of the Venetian fleet were between us and the great expanse of the Adriatic that lay beyond them.

******

Harold and I both breathed sighs of relief when we saw Eric's galley finally raise its sails and turn to follow us. His was the last of our galleys to leave the harbour because it had been towing an already-crewed prize.

Eric had not abandoned the men on the prize. His nerve had held and he had waited to cast off his tow line until the cog his galley was towing cleared the harbour and raised its sails. Then he too turned to starboard and began following us. His oars were throwing up great mists of water as he and his men rowed as hard as possible to catch up with us and escape the on-coming Venetians.

"He is not going make it," Harold muttered as he stood by my side. "And neither are we for that matter."

The sails of our newly towed prizes were everywhere in the distance. Others of our prizes, those that had been towed out earlier in the day had already passed over the horizon and were out of sight.

We had no idea as to the fate of our prizes, but we were fairly sure about ours. I had made a great mistake—we had waited too long in Venice; we would have to fight our way through the Venetian fleet before we could reach open water and begin fighting the one on one sea battles in which our galleys excelled.

****** *Lieutenant Commander Harold Lewes.*

We turned hard to starboard as soon as we got far enough out into the open sea, and then began following the Company galleys that had come out before us and were sailing westerly along the coast. The turn to the west gave us the use of the full force of the prevailing winds, such as they were.

Much more importantly, what we were doing was moving along the coast at a right angle to the on-coming Venetians. They were coming towards the city from due south. It initially looked as if they were headed straight north for Venice.

With a little luck, the Venetians would keep sailing north to Venice to relieve the city and retake the prizes still in the harbour. If they did that, our galleys would have avoided them by coming out of Venice and immediately turning to sail either westerly or easterly along the coast. We hoped the Venetians would continue to Venice because we wanted to fight them one on one in open water where our superior speed and the range of our arrows would be decisive.

A few minutes later and it was clear that it was not going to be our lucky day. The Venetians were looking for a fight in which they could outnumber us and overwhelm us. We knew their intentions as soon as we saw a large part of the Venetian fleet alter its course to head off those of our galleys, including mine, which were initially moving west along the Italian coast.

One of our archer-rowed galleys, or so we thought, could easily take a Venetian in single combat, and perhaps even two of them. But successfully taking on more than two at a time was difficult at best and fighting four or five at the same time was virtually impossible. The problem was that all the Venetians had rams and could use them to sink our galleys whilst ours were not able to maneuver adequately because they were engaged in fighting other Venetians.

Our only hope of was to break out into the Adriatic and then turn around and come back to find Venetian galleys to fight one on one with no other Venetians close enough to come to their assistance. Only then would we be able to get close enough to use our archers' longbows without other Venetians getting into positions where they could use their rams to sink us.

"It looks as though they are ignoring our prizes and turning west to intercept those of us who are sailing west along the coast, probably because that gives them the wind."

George made his observation quietly as he shaded his eyes with one hand in order to get a better look and pointed with the other at the on-coming Venetians.

I used both of mine to see better before I replied and agreed.

"Yes, but it means our lads heading east will be getting away clean. That is good for us; it means our galleys coming out from the east harbour's entrance will be able to turn back with the wind in their sails and hit the Venetians in the side and rear."

No more than the words had gotten out of my mouth than about half of the Venetian galleys began dropping their sails and turning to the east into the wind to intercept the Company galleys rowing along the coast into the wind.

That was actually somewhat encouraging both because our eastbound archer-rowed galleys were likely to be faster than the slave-rowed Venetians and be able to get away, and also because it meant that fewer of the Venetians would be coming after those of us that were sailing west. What was worrisome was that the rapid division of the Venetian fleet suggested some forethought was involved in the Venetian attack.

George immediately understood the implications of what we were seeing.

"Well, you always said that the best way to fight the Venetian fleet was to have each of the Company galleys constantly moving about to fight on its own," George remarked quietly.

Then he smiled and wryly added a positive thought.

"It looks like about half of the Venetians have just taken themselves out of the fight by heading east to try to catch our seven fast movers heading in that direction. If the Venetians keep chasing them, we and the eight Company galleys sailing west with us will not be so badly outnumbered. If the Venetians heading northeast do not turn back soon, it will only be four to one against us instead of seven to one. Good news, eh?"

I did not reply. I was too busy giving sailing orders to my sailing sergeant to prepare for the long day of fighting that was about to begin for me and my men. *Four to one is good news, my arse.*

"Slow your rowing beat to 'ahead slow' with only the archers on the upper tier rowing, Sailing Sergeant. But keep two men on every oar and have every oar ready to be instantly rowed hard so we can surge ahead, and also warn the rowers and rudder men to be ready for rapid turns."

They knew all these things, of course, but it never hurt to remind them.

"Aye, Commander Lewes. I am to slow the rowing beat to ahead slow with only the upper tier rowing and be ready to row hard so we surge ahead, and also be ready for rapid turns."

A few moments later Commander Courtenay turned to me and asked a question.

"What do you think, Lieutenant Commander Lewes? Is it time for us we to turn and try to break through them so we will have more sea room to move about in?"

But then he answered his own question before I could open my mouth to reply.

"No. Probably not yet. We need to give them as much time as possible to wear out the arms of the slaves doing their rowing."

Uh oh. George is as nervous as I have ever seen him. Me too.

****** *George Courtenay.*

We did not have to wait long to find out how serious our troubles were about to become. The Venetians were coming fast and spreading out. And there were a lot of them; their sails seemed to be everywhere in the waters to the south and west of the city. It soon became clear that their orders were to engage with us rather than enter the harbour to re-take our un-crewed prizes.

As the Venetian galleys got closer, it appeared that several of them were on a heading to intercept our galley whilst the others looked as if they were going after the galleys spread out in a long line in front of us and behind us. We were seriously outnumbered and in for a fight; there was no half way about it.

Harold, as our galley's captain, began giving orders as he prepared to fight. He had enough time to make them quite clear to everyone.

"Stand by to go to maximum speed with a hard turn to port." … "When the order is given, portside rowers on the lower tier are to row backwards to help with the hard turn to port, and then all archers are to row as hard as they can for maximum forward speed.

"Archers assigned to the deck and masts are to push on enemy crew whenever they are in range."… "Sailors with axes and pikes are to stand by to cut grapples."

It was all I could do to restrain myself from giving orders. But it would cause confusion if I did. Besides, Harold was best sea captain in the Company. So I stood like one of the stoic Greeks I had learned about in school and contented myself with an observation.

"I certainly hope the Venetians have not employed any Genoese crossbow men."

I muttered my hope as two Venetian galleys began to close on us. My concern was very real—the Venetians were known to employ Genoese crossbow men and I was wearing a chain shirt that was not strong enough to stop an iron crossbow bolt, especially one released at the close ranges we seemed to be about to experience. My men, of course, were even more vulnerable.

"Turn hard to port all oars and drop your sails," Harold roared.

The men on the two big rudder oars instantly began rowing frantically to help change our galley's direction and all the rowers on the port side gave ten or eleven great backward strokes.

Our galley instantly heeled hard to starboard as we suddenly turned towards the two Venetians and the wind caught our sails before they came all the way down. When we levelled off we were pointed almost straight at the first of the on-coming Venetians.

"All rowers to row for maximum speed," Harold shouted needlessly because the men knew full well what was at stake. They were already pulling hard as hard as they could because our rowing drum had increased its beat to its "war emergency" maximum.

Seconds later the first Venetian was in range of the archers on the forward mast and, a moment later, it was also within the range of the archers who were standing on the roof of the forward castle. Arrows began to fly as the distance between us and the nearest Venetian began to rapidly close.

Every archer who was not on an oar, which included me and the two apprentices, was soon pushing out arrows as fast as possible. All around and above us were the familiar sounds of archers' grunts and the slap of bowstrings against leather wrist protectors.

Our sudden change of course seemed to catch the closest Venetian by surprise. Or perhaps an arrow had taken its captain. In any event, the Venetian continued rowing straight ahead on its current course such that it would likely have rammed us if we had not turned. Whatever the reason, the on-coming Venetian overshot us by holding its course after we turned.

I held my breath as we turned, and then passed the Venetian going in the other direction by at least fifty paces. As we went past I could see its oars moving rapidly, several bodies on its deck, and men crouching down behind its deck railings in an effort to hide from our arrows.

There was nobody in sight on the Venetian's deck or on the roofs of its castles. Our archers had knocked some down and driven the rest away. We never did have to ship our oars to avoid having them sheared off by brushing up against the Venetian as we passed it going in the opposite direction.

As we went flying past the Venetian, faces cautiously popped up along its deck railing where they had been sheltering from our arrows.

Suddenly there was a cry and one of the archers on the forward mast suddenly fell on to the deck with a great crash. Almost at the same time there was the familiar thud of an arrow striking home and an "oof" as one of the archers standing next to me suddenly dropped his bow and went over backwards with a crossbow quarrel in his chest and a disbelieving look on his face.

****** *George Courtenay*

Serious trouble was not long in coming. The second of the two Venetian galleys reached us less than a minute after we successfully avoided the first. It had seen our turn and was beginning to make a turn of its own as we reached it. All of the oars on its lower tier of rowers and a few of its upper tier were rowing hard and throwing up spray.

As we got nearer, we could see thirty or forty men standing on the second Venetian's deck. They looked like a combination of soldiers and sailors and most of them appeared to be carrying swords.

Our arrows did not begin falling amongst them until the gap between the two galleys began to rapidly close. That was probably because the men on its deck had been helping their slaves row and had just been called up from their rowing positions in the expectation that the fighting was about to begin. Our deck, in contrast, was still relatively empty because most of our archers, except for those on the castle roofs and on the masts, were still on the benches rowing.

"Ship oars. Ship oars." Harold shouted as the distance between us closed rapidly and a head-on collision appeared more and more likely.

Our oars came in just in time and so did some, but not all, of the Venetian's. A few seconds later there was the loud sound of oars breaking off and a great shaking as our hull scraped along the Venetian's ram and then its hull.

As we moved along the Venetian's hull I could hear the cries and screams of its rowers whose splintered oars had suddenly snapped back and hit them. There was much shouting and commotion on both galleys.

Our hull and the Venetian's banged together right after I had planted an arrow deep into the chest of a Venetian standing on the roof of his galley's forward castle with a sword in his hand. Both galleys suddenly slowed down when their hulls touched. It happened so quickly that it threw me and almost every archer around me to our knees.

The poor sod of a chosen man standing next to me was not so lucky. He went flying all the way off the roof and landed face-first on the deck still holding on to his bow.

I regained my feet and was about to push an arrow into someone leaning down to help a wounded fellow Venetian when I saw a man with a great red beard raise a crossbow and lay it on the Venetians deck railing. He was not ten feet away and it was aimed at me.

I felt something hit my side and everything seemed to happen very slowly after that and the noise faded away.

Chapter Twenty-three

Captain Jackson's Troubles.

My galley was the last one to clear the entrance at the western end of Venice's great harbour. All of the Company galleys, except mine, had cast off their tows and headed at high speed towards the nearest harbour entrance as soon as they got the word that the Venetians were coming. We could not join them because the cog we were towing had already taken its prize crew on board. There was no way I could get away with abandoning its crew or I might well have done in order to avoid being overly outnumbered and unable to fight my galley clear.

One after another our fellow galleys hurried past us in a desperate effort to avoid being trapped by the arrival of the Venetian fleet. The men on their decks waved and shouted encouragements to us as they came rushing past us with their rowing drums beating rapidly and their oars raising great splashes of water.

Shouting encouragements was all they could do. We could not cast off our tow because it would have meant abandoning the Company men in the prize we were towing.

I thought about stopping and trying to board the prize crew. But I quickly decided against it because it almost certainly would have required our dinghy to make at least two trips and, as a result, would almost certainly have taken more time than it would take to get the cog we were towing out into the Adriatic so it could begin using its sails.

Word of our dangerous and desperate predicament spread like wildfire amongst my crew. Within seconds every man understood that our lives were at risk if we did not reach open water where we could use our superior speed to stand off from an enemy and use our longbows. The archers on the rowing benches responded magnificently by putting their backs into rowing as hard and fast as they possibly could.

The archers and sailors in the prize crew of the cog we were towing also understood the danger and did everything that could be asked of them. They raised Venetian pennants on the prize's masts and began hoisting its sails even before we finished pulling the cog clear of the harbour entrance.

Whether the pennants would keep the Venetians from trying to re-take the cog or my galley, or confuse them long enough for us to get away in a storm or the dark of night remained to be seen, but it certainly could not hurt. Every prize and galley was flying at least one.

More importantly, the prize crew on the cog began raising its sails so soon that for a few moments I was worried that the wind blowing across the harbour entrance from the north would push the cog aground before we finished pulling it clear of the spit that sheltered the harbour. It was a close run thing, but our tow successfully cleared the harbour.

"Cut the tow line and raise our sails as soon as the cog is clear, Jack," I shouted to my new sailing sergeant as soon as the tow was clear. He was standing by the tow line in my galley's stern with an axe in his hand. It was all I could do to keep the sound of my desperation out of my voice.

I looked over at my new lieutenant as I shouted out the order to Jack. Acting Lieutenant Harry Johnson was standing with the sailors holding on to sail-raising lines and had heard me give it. He quickly raised his hand to acknowledge that he too had heard the order.

Harry looked as fearful and stressed as I felt. His obvious distress and anxiety were understandable under the circumstances, but they were also of some concern to me because openly displaying them would worry the men. I resolved to speak to him about it the next time I had an opportunity.

Jack and Harry were newly promoted. It occurred when their predecessors were made up to acting lieutenants and appointed to be prize captains. They were, as a result, both more than a little anxious in their new positions. In any event, my new sailing sergeant waited a few more moments whilst he looked around and tried to gage the distances, and then began chopping on the tow line. It was quickly cut. Our sails and those of the prize were being raised as he did.

We immediately heeled over from the wind as we turned hard to starboard and hurried off to follow the line of six or seven Company galleys that were moving southwestward along the coast ahead of us. Our rowing drum increased its beat even more, and we began moving ahead faster and faster as the wind caught our sails and the tow stopped holding us back.

The sails of the Venetian fleet were already well over the southern horizon by the time we turned to the west to follow the Company galleys that had come out of the harbour before we did. And when we turned to follow the line of Company galleys that were ahead of us, the closest two of the Venetians had also turned in order to intercept us.

The day was already quite warm and our sails were immediately filled by a lightly gusting wind coming from the northeast. We all knew it was going to be another scorcher in more ways than one.

One look at the positions and courses of the oncoming Venetians and our fate was clear despite our dramatically increased speed—unless something unexpected happened, at least two of the Venetians would intercept us long before we could get far enough down the coast to get ahead of them. Even worse, a third Venetian galley had altered its course and looked like it had decided to join them.

It was soon clear to me that if we held to our current course we would be sideways to the three on-coming Venetians such that one or another of them would be able to ram us. Our only hope of getting away, I decided, was to turn towards them and use our speed and agility to slip past them. It was the only thing I could think to do.

"Stand by to turn ninety points to port and re-sheet the sails, Sailing Sergeant." ... "Turn to port. Turn to port." ... "Re-sheet the sails for running south."

It was then, in the excitement of the moment, that I made a serious mistake—I kept our rowers rowing as hard as possible; I did *not* order my galley to slow down so our rowers could rest their arms. And neither my sailing sergeant nor my lieutenant reminded me to do so. They were new to their positions and thought I knew what I was doing.

****** *Captain Eric Jackson*

We turned to port and headed straight for the closest Venetian galley. Going straight at a galley with a ram was what we captains had always been told to do. It would, or so it had been claimed by Commander Lewes, cause one side or the other of our bow to slide along the ram instead being punctured by it—and, with a little luck, it would take out the would-be rammer's oars on whichever side we scraped along it. It was the only thing I could think to do under the circumstances.

As we turned towards the nearest Venetian galley, I briefly thought of our tow for some reason and turned to look for it. It was off to our north and seemed to be tacking into the wind in an effort to sail northeast along the coast. It was the only transport heading that way and far behind the Company galleys moving in that direction. *How strange. Or perhaps it was such an unexpected move as to be smart.*

The closest Venetian galley was less than a thousand paces away when I began giving our rudder men periodic orders for little tweaks in our heading so we would continue rowing straight towards its on-coming ram. The Venetian's captain must have been worried that we too had a ram because he seemed to be doing the same thing. In other words, we both had our galleys rowing for a head-on collision. The other Venetian was right behind the first and also rowing hard and coming straight at us.

Everything seemed to very clear to me and happening very slowly. I was not afraid and did not begin shaking until much later.

"Stand by to ship your oars." I shouted. And then, a moment later, I repeated an order I had already given once before.

"Archers to commence pushing whenever an enemy is in range."

A few seconds later our archers began pushing arrows into the crew of the leading Venetian galley, and I began giving new orders as it continued to come straight at us.

"Prepare to ship your oars." ... "Ship your oars." ... "Stand by to cut grapple lines."

Our galley banged into the first Venetian with a force that shook my galley and almost drove me to my knees. There was a loud scraping sound that began as we glanced off the starboard side of the Venetian's ram and then began scraping along its hull.

By the time we got clear we had almost stopped dead in the water and the Venetian' deck was covered with dead and wounded men with arrows in them. Several of our men were down as well. The Venetian had crossbow men in its crew.

We quickly resumed rowing and got past the first Venetian without losing any of our oars. The Venetian captain must have given the same order to "ship oars" as I did because I did not hear any of the splintering sounds and the screams of rowers that I had hoped to hear when the Venetian's oars were sheared off. But at least we were past it.

Two more Venetian galleys were sailing behind the one we had just scrapped. One was quite close. I immediately began giving course-changing orders to the rudder men that I hoped would get us past them as well.

All around me as I shouted my orders was the sound of archers pushing out arrows and the distant shouts and cries and screams of excited men, many of them coming from the nearest Venetian's deck in a language I could not understand. Some of our archers continued pushing arrows at the Venetians we had just passed, and others were pushing them at the galley which was bearing down on us at a high rate of speed.

A metal crossbow bolt slammed into wooden railing next to where I was standing. Where it came from I did not know. It was about then that it suddenly came to me that our rowers' arms must be getting tired. I started to say something to Jack, but then I realized he was lying face down on the castle roof in a rapidly spreading pool of blood.

Later Lieutenant Johnson swore that he had heard some of the Venetian's oars being snapped off. I certainly did not hear it, but perhaps I was too busy pushing arrows into the men on the Venetian's castle roofs and deck as we slid past them.

We had no more than finished scraping the side of the first Venetian and showering it with arrows than we were about to collide with the second.

"Hard to Starboard," I shouted. I had taken over the role of Sailing Sergeant and shouted the order as the second Venetian turned towards us. Its captain clearly intended to put his ram into the starboard side of our hull. By turning hard towards him I brought our bow around so that it would be pointing at him—and then we kept turning too far such that now our port side was becoming vulnerable.

"Oars and rudders hard turn to port," I desperately shouted in an attempt to avoid the Venetian's ram by bringing us back to the head-on course I originally intended. "Ship oars. Ship oars."

It was too late.

The Venetian hit us hard with its ram, but it was a glancing blow and we continued on past it with much hull grinding and the sound of the Venetian's oars being snapped.

Shouting, screams, and chaos were all around me as soon as we collided with the second Venetian. Just about everyone on both galleys was flung to the deck by the impact and at least one man was shaken off out forward mast and dropped on to the deck in front of me. He had screamed all the way down and then went totally silent.

"Perhaps it did not penetrate" was my initial thought as I climbed back to my feet. It appeared as though we had come back soon enough on to our intended heading that the Venetian's ram may not have penetrated.

It may have only opened some of the seams between the hull planks, was the next idea in my head as I got to my feet. But then I forgot all about it because I could see a large number of grapples being thrown from the Venetian's deck, and being pulled tight.

"Too many to cut" I said out loud even though I could see several of my men trying to do so with their short swords, including one who suddenly jumped back when someone on the Venetian's deck swung a sword at him.

Some of the soldiers and sailors crowding the Venetian's deck were already starting to climb over the hull railings to get on to our deck. They were encouraged by the fact that we had so few men on deck compared to the number still standing on theirs.

"All hands on deck to repel boarders."

I shouted the order as I plucked an arrow out of my quiver and sent it toward the belly of a man who was climbing to his feet not twenty paces away on the roof of the Venetian's forward castle. I had marked him because he had appeared to have been shouting orders just before we collided.

"What damage do we have? Are we scuttled? Go below and look."

I screamed my question at Lieutenant Johnson as I plucked another arrow from my quiver and watched my first victim sink to his knees and grab at the arrow's goose feathers sticking out of his stomach. My new lieutenant was on his hands and knees looking at me; he had somehow returned to the stern castle roof just in time to be thrown down by the collision.

"Go below and check the damage, Johnson. Hurry damn you, hurry."

******

As many as eighty shouting archers came pouring up on to the deck in response to my order to repel boarders. They arrived with their bows and quivers slung over their shoulders and each of them carrying his short sword and galley shield. It was a drill every man had periodically practiced ever since he joined the Company fleet. Some of them even remembered to pick up the bladed pikes that had been laid out and were waiting for them at the top of the fore and aft stairs that came up from the rowing decks.

The sudden arrival of so many of our fighting men changed everything. Some of surprised and suddenly outnumbered Venetians who had climbed on to the port side of our deck went down under the archers' charge whilst others frantically scrambled to get back to the relative safety of their own galley. The tide had turned.

Within a few seconds a good number of the newly arriving archers had crossed over to the Venetian's deck and were fighting there with their swords and shields. Others were pushing arrows out of their longbows as fast as possible. Everything had totally changed. Now we outnumbered the Venetians in addition to being better equipped and better trained.

It was a good thing all of our archers were on deck with their weapons because the third Venetian galley swung around to get into a ramming position and was coming straight at us on our port side. Its sailors could be seen along its deck railing getting ready to throw their grapples and a mob of men carrying swords and shields were gathered in its bow.

The new arrival also had kind of tall mast-like contraption on the front of its deck that was being held straight up into the air by sailors holding lines attached to it. It was all new to me; I had never seen anything like it and had no idea what it was.

A moment later and I knew exactly what it was. There was another great crash as the third Venetian with the strange contraption on its deck smashed its ram into the port side of our galley. It was going as fast as its galley slaves could row it when it hit us. This time, at least, and even though the shock of the collision was much greater, I managed to stay on my feet by holding on to the wooden railing that ran around the castle roof.

As I grabbed the railing to keep myself from falling, I watched as the long wooden mast-like thing sticking up in the air slowly toppled over so that some of it landed on to our deck. I did not fully understand its purpose until a few seconds later. As I steadied myself and watched, the lines holding it up were used to lower it down on to our deck.   As soon as it touched our deck, sword-waving soldiers and sailors from the mob of men assembled in the Venetian's bow began running single file across its narrow planking to get on to our deck.

Something else I did not know at the time was that the Venetian captains had been ordered to attack our galleys in twos and to move on in search of another galley of the "French Fleet" to attack if one of ours was already under attack by two or three of theirs.

It sounded reasonable because the Venetians wanted to completely destroy every galley in our fleet—and it saved us because the inexperienced noble commanding the slave-rowed Venetians had apparently not known how many fighting men we had in each our crews or how superbly they were trained and equipped.

Chapter Twenty-four

George recovers and more Venetian galleys attack.

I had instinctively jerked my aim towards the threat when I saw the crossbow being aimed at me. My arrow hit the crossbowman about a foot below his neck just as he released his bolt. It resulted in a terrible trade—for him. His bolt had hit the side of my chain shirt as if I had been hit by a man's great punch. It spun me around, and dropped me on my arse as the great force of the bolt pushed me backwards; my arrow, on the other hand, went into his chest and had almost certainly killed him, or soon would, as all arrows inevitably do that get into a man behind his ribs.

My side began to feel as if it was being burned by a flame as I scrambled to get back on my feet. All I knew was that I had just been saved because Uncle Harold had seen the crossbowman and pushed me to one side just as the Venetian shot his bolt.

Harold helped me get back on my feet, and then held me by my elbow to steady me as he pulled me back on my feet. Fighting was raging everywhere on the deck a few feet below us and on the deck of the Venetian that had grappled us.

I did not know whether I had been saved by Harold's push or by the Venetian with the crossbow taking my arrow. And it did not matter. All I knew at the moment was that I was still alive and in the middle of a sea battle with a Venetian crossbow bolt stuck in my chain shirt. I could feel it and I could see its point sticking out of my tunic.

"How bad is it" Uncle Harold asked as he helped me regain my footing and used his right hand to pull up my tunic and chain shirt so we both could look. His left hand did not let go of my arm as he did. We both looked whilst all around us was the sound of men shouting and the familiar sound of archers pushing out arrows. *It was just a bad slice; thank you Jesus.*

"It burns most painful, but it does not look too bad at all, Uncle, thanks to you,"

I winced as I thanked him once again and let my tunic and chain shirt drop to cover my side. I was cut and bleeding under the chain, but it did not look serious—the point had sliced my side as it passed through both the front and the back of the chain.

The problem was that shaft of the bolt was caught in my chain shirt and pressing against the groove its point had cut into the skin on my side. It was the rubbing of the shaft up against my wound that made it much more painful than the minor cut it otherwise would have been. I would just have to grin and bear it until the fighting ended.

"It hurts most fierce but it is just a slice. The sailmaker can sew it up later. And thank you, thank you, Uncle Harold, for shoving me out of the way when you did. You saved me for sure."

As I thanked him I looked down from the castle roof and saw a grapple thrown by another Venetian galley being quickly grabbed up and thrown over the side by one of our sailors before its line could be pulled tight. It had been thrown along with a number of others from the deck of a Venetian galley that was newly arrived next to ours.

The others were not thrown back. Harold and I jumped down from the roof and rushed to organize our defenders.

****** *George Courtenay*

The newly arrived Venetian galley had come alongside and begun to grapple us whilst I was down from the crossbow bolt. As Harold was helping me get back on my feet we had watched and felt Venetian's hull come up to us and bang up against our hull. A couple of moments later, whilst searching for a new target for my next arrow, I watched as the Venetian's sailors pulled their grapple lines tight and began climbing over the hull railings to get on to our galley to join the fight.

All I could do was push an arrow into one of the sailors and then watch as several dozen shouting and sword-waving Venetian sailors and soldiers threw their legs over the deck railings that separated our galleys and began climbing on to our deck. My next arrow stopped one of them and caused him to fall back on to the Venetian's deck. But my arrow and the handful of other arrows pushed out by our archers did not stop the great mass of his mates from climbing over the side by side deck railings and coming on to our deck.

For a few brief moments it was a relatively easy boarding for the newly arrived Venetians. That was because most of our crew were either using their swords on the deck of the initial Venetian galley to which we first became attached, or they were still looking in that direction from our masts for someone to take down with an arrow.

Except for me and the handful of archers still with me on the castle roof and a little band of our sailors at the very front of our galley, the new arrived Venetians were virtually unopposed as they began climbing on to our deck.

That changed quickly, the lack of opposition to the new arrivals that is, when Harold began shouting out orders telling our men to return and help fight them off. A moment later he and I picked up our short swords and galley shields and jumped down to lead the men who had heard his order and begun returning from the deck of the other Venetian.

"Cover us," I shouted to the two apprentices as we did.

My side hurt most terrible for a few seconds, especially when I jumped down to the deck, but then I saw the boarders continuing to come aboard from the newly arrived Venetian and forgot all about it.

Those of Harold's sailors who had been strung out along our deck to cut grappling lines and work our sails had instantly retreated as the Venetian soldiers and sailors came aboard. Some climbed into the rigging and the rest formed themselves up in a little group at the very front of our galley—and were very effectively defending themselves with bladed pikes. Harold's new lieutenant had somehow gotten there and could be seen organizing them.

His old lieutenant had been given the Venetian galley that had been captured with its slaves on it. Being Harold's lieutenant was inevitably a stepping stone to a captaincy if you were successful; and a path to forever being a lieutenant on one of the Company's transport cogs if you were not.

The two rudder men and the drummer and our galley's horn blower had come up to the upper rowing deck and were ready to hold the two stairways down to the rowing decks, also with bladed pikes. I knew they were there because I had a good enough look into the two stairwells from where I was standing to see the tips of the pikes they were holding. Except for our casualties, everyone was where he was supposed to be under the circumstances. At least it looked that way to me.

Harold was the first to recognize the situation as an opportunity.

"Get the new bastards." Harold began shouting to the archers who had initially charged up from their rowing benches and were, by then, over the hull railings and fighting on the deck of the first Venetian. Some of them had already pursued retreating runners down into the first galley's rowing benches.

"Do not let them cut the grapple lines and get away." *What? The order surprised me. But then I understood.* A moment later I was bellowing it out myself as I grabbed up a sword and shield and jumped down on to the deck.

Harold shouted his order over and over again as he pointed with his short sword at the new Venetian galley that had come alongside and at the new wave of attackers that was still in the process of climbing over the side by side deck railing to get on our deck. It was soon being loudly repeated by Harold's sergeants, as was their duty, and then taken up as a chant by our men as they turned around and rushed back to our deck to help fight off the new arrivals.

I did my part as soon as I jumped down and landed on the deck. I pushed out my shield to stop a sword-carrying Venetian who had just thrown his leg over the railing in preparation of coming aboard. And then I was able to get a solid thrust, sort of a stabbing slice, into his unprotected leg.

The would-be boarder screamed and fell back as I got my shield back up to block the next man coming across. As I did, a Company sailor with a bladed pike somehow appeared at my side. He reached over and used it to give a great chop to the head of the man I had just put down with a leg wound.

Within moments I was closely surrounded all around me by archers returning from the deck of the first Venetian that had tried to board us. Some of them were climbing on to the deck of the new arrival and others were pushing past me to get at the Venetians who had made it on to our deck further down towards our bow.

It was about then that the last few Venetian sailors waiting to board us from the new arrival changed their minds and began to retreat. Our deck was soon clear around me, except for our own archers and sailors. It was also about then that I realized I had no idea what was happening to the rest of the Company's galleys.

Were we winning or losing? It looked good for us from where I was standing, but it was time to get back to the roof of the stern castle where the visibility was better and learn what I could about our other galleys. Accordingly, I double timed back to the castle roof to see what I could see. Harold was already there along with a couple of archers and our greatly excited apprentices. They were all looking for Venetian targets and, thank God, not finding them.

It had not taken long for the newly arrived Venetians to discover that they had made a terrible mistake. They had grappled our galley and climbed on to our deck, or so they had thought, in order to help one of their sister galleys finish off what they expected would be a badly wounded stringer of French chickens—and had suddenly found themselves face to face with a raging British bull with no place to run or hide.

When I climbed the stairs and got back to the roof, I literally dropped my sword and shield and got ready to once again begin using my bow. I instantly nocked an arrow and began looking for a good shot. It helped that I was atop the castle roof and could clearly see our deck and those of the galleys on either side of ours. As I looked about for a target, I suddenly realized that my side felt like someone was holding a burning torch to me.

A Venetian trying to run away from a pike-carrying archer caught my attention and I pushed an arrow at him. My arrow hit him and down he went on to his arse with his sword in one hand and his other hand behind him to break his fall.

Actually, to my surprise, I missed low but my arrow still had the desired effect. The Venetian dropped his sword and went all the way over on to his back—and began screaming as he clutched at the shaft sticking out of his dingle and bollocks. A few seconds later he got chopped by a pike and fell silent.

To this day it is his screaming and clutching at his dingle that I remember most about the day's fighting.

****** *Captain Jackson's galley is rammed*

We were dead in the water and the third Venetian galley was moving fast when it drove its ram straight into the side of my galley. It happened just as our archers were coming off the rowing benches and pouring on to the deck in response to the order to "repel boarders."

The shock of the collision caused our galley to move in the water and knocked just about everyone, both the Venetians and us, off their feet. Our situation had suddenly become desperate. My galley was virtually certain to sink and there were Venetians fighting with my archers and sailors everywhere I looked.

It all seemed to happen at the same instant and the noise was so loud that I almost could not think. It was quite confusing. Time seemed to stand still for me and I just stood there.

There was much shouting, screaming, and the swearing of terrible oaths all around me as the last of my archers came off their rowing benches and reached the deck. Indeed, the noise around me was so loud that I could barely hear the orders Lieutenant Johnson had begun shouting to the pike-carrying sailors who had gathered in the bow. He was shouting at them to move, but why?

I had known the ramming would deal us a fatal blow as soon as I saw the angle at which the third Venetian was going to hit us. And that was what had happened—there had been a great cracking noise and my galley shook and shuddered as the ram smashed its way through the side of our hull.

There was no doubt about it. It was a fatal blow even though the ram protruding from the Venetian's bow did not go all the way into our hull such that it left a small gap of water between the Venetian's bow and the side of my galley where its ram had penetrated us.

The gap must have been expected because a moment later the Venetian's sailors were pulling on ropes to raise something on the deck of the Venetian galley into the air. It was as if they were raising a new mast—and then they let go of the ropes so that what they had raised tipped over and dropped on to our deck.

It turned out to be a narrow wooden ramp. At first I had not known what it was that the Venetian's sailors were doing. But I certainly understood by the time they let go of the ropes they were holding and it came crashing down on our deck with a great banging noise.

I could see it clearly because the end of the ramp came down on my deck not twenty feet from the edge of the castle roof on which I was standing. That was right after I got up from being knocked on to my knees by the force of my galley being rammed.

A large pack of sword waving Venetian soldiers and sailors had been gathered on the deck in the Venetian's bow waving swords when its ram crunched into us. They tumbled about, as we all did, when the ram hit. But then they got to their feet and were shouting and screaming as they came charging down the narrow ramp one after another and jumped on to our deck waving their swords.

Not all of them made it. I watched as one of the Venetian sword wavers suddenly tripped and lost his balance. He slipped off to one side and fell screaming into water after bouncing off our deck railing. There was some kind of waist-high guide line running along the boarding ramp, but he had obviously not been holding on to it when he lost his footing and fell, or perhaps he had been hit by an arrow or the man behind him had stepped on his heel and tripped him.

Things increasingly looked desperate. A steady stream of Venetian soldiers and sailors were rushing down the narrow boarding ramp and jumping on to our deck, water was pouring into our broken hull and rapidly filling it, and we were fighting the crews of two different Venetian galleys.

Within a few seconds I could feel my galley getting heavy and begin to settle. Even worse, the first Venetian galley, the one we had successfully avoided, had turned around and was coming back.

"All hands move to the deck of the starboard Venetian. Hurry lads, hurry. She is going to sink." I began shouting. I could feel my galley getting heavier and heavier under my feet.

Archers and sailors poured down from my galley's masts, and several were promptly cut down by the new arriving Venetians when they reached our deck. The Venetians who did for them did not last long. They took arrows from somewhere and went down themselves.

As the Venetians fell, I watched Lieutenant Johnson lead the little band of pike-carrying sailors in the bow as they suddenly moved in a group to the nearest point where our hull touched the starboard Venetian and began climbing over to the relative safety of its deck.

What I looked for and did not see were our two rudder men, my horn blower, and the elderly sailor who served as our drummer and oar caller.

Chapter Twenty-five

The Tides Turn.

Harold was the first to realize what was happening and to see the opportunity it presented. As a result of his orders, the grapple lines were *not* cut and the two Venetian galleys and their astonished and quickly overcome crews were *not* able to get away.

The nobles commanding the Venetian fleet had made the great mistake of thinking that we fought as they fought, crewed and rowed our galleys as they did theirs, and trained and equipped our fighting men as they trained and equipped their men. It apparently had never occurred to them that we might have more than twice as many fighting men on each of our galleys and that each of our men would be better trained and have better weapons.

"I wonder how our captains are doing?" I mused a few minutes later.

I asked my question to no one in particular as we stood on the deck of one of the Venetian galleys. Our wounded were being tended by their mates and we were watching prisoners being brought out of the rowing tiers and cargo holds where they had run in a desperate effort to escape when the tide of battle turned against them. Every one of the captured men was terrified, apparently in the belief that he was about to be treated as he and his mates would have treated us if they had won.

What prompted my question was the state of sea around us—it was totally and unexpectedly *empty* except for a cluster of distant sails off to the north. And that prompted another question.

"Where did they all go?" I asked as I stood up and looked all around after helping an archer tip a dead Venetian over the side.

Harold glanced up from where he was helping his sailmaker sew up a great slash in the leg of a severely wounded archer, and then motioned with his bloody hand towards the little group of sails that were still close together and unmoving to the north of us.

"Damned if I know, George. Hopefully it means our lads got away and they are chasing after them. But when we finish here we best be going yonder to see what is happening up there to the north."

"Aye. But what are we going to do about these two?" I asked as I nodded my head and waved my hand towards our two prizes.

Harold answered my question by starting to ask one of his own. He opened his mouth to start to respond, but then stopped as he began using both hand to hold down the archer who had started to wake up from being asleep and, a few moments later, began thrashing about with a lot of screaming and shouting.

"Hold still, Tommy, you are going to be fine. Jack is almost done sewing you up."

A moment later, after Tommy fell asleep again, Harold continued.

"Is Lieutenant Black acceptable to you for this galley's prize captain, Commander? If he is, we can take the Venetians' wounded with us, and chain the rest of the able-bodied Venetians in on the rowing benches with the slaves. Black could sail for Cyprus straightaway with a couple of my archers and sailors to sergeant the slaves and prisoners, and with my apprentice as his lieutenant.

"We could do the same with the other prize with my sailing sergeant, Michael Adams, as the prize captain and your apprentice, Roger, as his lieutenant. Adams is capable man."

"That sounds like a good plan to me, Lieutenant Commander," I said with a grim smile. *It was a good plan.* "Please proceed."

Roger and John were standing behind us and had heard the conversation. Each of their eyes was as big as a moon. They were getting promotions—and the Company was getting two more galleys whose captains would be able to send in written reports and receive written orders.

****** *George Courtenay*

It seemed to take forever before Harold got his galley underway. That was because there were so many wounded men to be moved about, and also because many of our prisoners had to be chained to each of the prizes' rowing benches to help the men who had recently been their slaves row it to Cyprus. The rest of the Venetian prisoners were jammed into Harold's cargo hold so they could not rise in revolt.

Our own wounded men were brought aboard Harold's galley and sewed up by the sailmakers as best they could. Those of them who were seriously hurt were sewed up by one of the sailmakers and then placed in Harold's stern castle with a couple of sailors to look after them with flower paste and water. The Venetian wounded were then brought aboard and lowered into its cargo hold so their captains and sergeants could barber them.

It all took time and though everyone hurried and did their best. They understood that we would need to quickly row away to get sea room if more Venetian galleys appeared.

As the minutes passed I began getting more and more anxious. But there was nothing I could do about it as the prisoners and slaves continued to be sorted out and our wounded were carried to the stern castle for barbering. Simultaneously, the Venetian wounded were moved to our galley's cargo hold. They would be held there along with the able-bodied Venetians who had not been sent to the rowing benches.

As a result having so many things to do, it was almost an hour after the fighting ended before our prizes were able to cast off their lines and begin their long voyages to Cyprus. Only then did we finally begin rowing northward.

The dead Venetians were not a problem. We threw them overboard after we got underway. The Company's dead, on the other hand, were covered with an old sail to keep the sun off them and kept on board in the hope that we could take them ashore for a proper burial and prayers before they began to swell up and smell.

I did not hold out much hope for burying our dead because it was already a scorching hot day. On the other hand, Venice and several other coastal cities were nearby and one never knows what will happen next when sea battles occur.

The same uncertainty was true about wounds. Sometimes a man recovered from a seemingly fatal wound and sometimes he died of minor wound turning black. Everything was in God's hands when it came to wounds, barbering, and where a man ended up being buried.

******

Our galley finally got underway after spending far more time to get ready than anyone expected. Clusters of sails were now visible in the distance both to the north of us and also in the west. We headed north.

Harold was taking no chances. He slowed down and rowed slowly and cautiously as we got closer and closer to what turned out to be a raft of four galleys. They were lashed together and bobbing up and down from the waves.

We moved to the roof of the forward castle to get a better view. What we saw initially looked to be four galleys lashed together, including one that was partially sunken with water covering part of its deck. It was probably still afloat because its wood was somehow holding it up and there were grappling lines attached to it from the three galleys around it. There was not a cloud in the sky and it was scorching hot.

As we got closer, we could see sword-carrying men on one of the decks and bodies on all of them. There was a great relief amongst all of us when it was clear that the men who were moving about were all wearing Company tunics. There had obviously been a great fight and they had won. We were happy for them and, even though no one said it out loud, even happier for ourselves because it meant we would not have to risk being hurt or killed in another fight.

A few of the men on the raft lifted their hands and waved to acknowledge us as we slowly came alongside. Some were standing and talking; others were tending to some of the many men lying about on the deck. Just before we bumped up against the raft, we watched as a couple of men in Company tunics carried a wounded man into the cabin of one of the galleys.

At first I did not recognize the sunken galley, but then one of our sailors did and shouted out the bad news. It was one of ours, Number Forty-one, Captain Jackson. It had been the last to leave the harbour because it was towing a prize with our prize crew already on board. The other three galleys were Venetians. The good news was that everyone who was still on his feet appeared to be wearing one of our tunics.

The survivors were all on the deck of the most northerly of the galleys in the raft. In order to be safe, however, we boarded the galley on south side of the raft because its deck was empty. There was no need to take unnecessary chances. It was, after all, always best to avoid having to fight your way into a battlefield if it could be avoided, especially when you were not sure what you were not sure what you would find when you got there.

One thing was certain even before we began climbing over the deck railings to reach the survivors—there had obviously been one hell of a bloody battle. Dead and wounded men littered the decks of every galley including several bodies floating in the water that covered Number Forty-one's stern. Some of them appeared to be wearing Company tunics.

We were taking no chances. Eight files of archers from Harold's galley boarded the raft carrying swords and shields at the ready and began moving from galley to galley towards the waiting men. Harold and I climbed on to the galley raft first and led the way, even before our sailors finished lashing our galley to one of the Venetians. Dozens of Harold's men followed us and were soon charging on ahead in front of us.

What we saw when we climbed onto empty deck of the first Venetian was staggering, but expected. The deck was covered with dead and badly wounded Venetians. Some of the wounded cried out for help and raised their arms in pleading gestures, others pretended to be dead. It was in one sense quite normal, what one would expect if he came upon a recent field of battle.

There were also dead men wearing Company tunics, but no Company wounded. They had obviously been moved out of the sun otherwise there would have been at least a few.

"Hoy, what happened here, Sergeant?" I asked the first archer I reached.

"They be ramming us, Commander, they be ramming us. We be fighting two of the bastards when it happened. A third one arrived and rammed us. Me and my lads had just stopped rowing when it happened, but we came on deck real fast to fight them when the order was given. It all seemed to happen at the same time.

"It was not our fault the bastards caught us. We were late getting out of the harbour because we were towing a prize with some of our lads on it. We could not leave them, could we?"

"No, of course not. You and your mates did the right thing. And your captain, where is he?"

"He be in his castle with some of the other wounded. We carried him there to get him out of the sun. The bastards did for him. Hurt bad he is. Jake sewed him up nice and tidy, but it looks bad."

"Come on, Harold, I want to see if Erik can talk. We need to know what happened here."

****** *Lieutenant Commander Harold Lewes*

By the light of the castle's open door we could see half a dozen men in Company tunics. They were lying on its deck with a couple of sailors barbering them with water and flower paste. Several of them were moaning and one was thrashing about and crying out in great pain. A harried-looking sailor in a Company tunic was squatting next to him and trying to get a handful of flower paste into his mouth.

"Where is Captain Jackson?"

George asked his question in an unnecessarily loud voice. *Asking questions loudly and a bit fast meant George was upset about what he was seeing. He had been that way ever since I first met him when he was a lad.*

"Over there by the wall, Commander," someone answered. "He is sleeping from the paste."

"No, I am not," a weak voice said petulantly. "I am still awake; just a bit thirsty is all. Who is asking?"

"Commander Courtenay and Lieutenant Commander Lewes," I answered.

One of the bodies on castle deck mumbled something and started to move as if to get to his feet. He was on his back and was mostly naked as were most of the others. Their tunics had been cut away so their wounds could be examined and sewed up by one of the sailors.

"No. Do not move, Captain. It might disturb your wounds. We cannot have that, can we? We need you to recover and resume your command, or an even bigger one."

George said it in a gentle voice and, a moment later, told the two sailors tending the wounded men to come to us immediately if they needed anything. Then we left as it was instantly clear that we would not get any new information from Captain Jackson.

"Three Venetian galleys at the same time and he did not abandon the men on the tow. We need to do something to recognize him and his men," I suggested to George as we walked out of the dimly lit castle into the blistering heat.

"Every man, I think," was George's quiet reply as we stepped out of the castle and went back on to the deck. "The Company has done it before under such circumstances. Do you agree?"

"Aye, I do, George. Moving every man up a stripe means doubling his pay. So Eric will get the same as before even if he cannot continue and goes on half pay. It will soften the blow for those of our men who cannot continue."

Chapter Twenty-six

The final gambit and disaster strikes.

Harold held his galley idle just off the main entrance to Venice's harbour. Returning Company galleys were warmly welcomed as they came alongside and made their reports and, all too often, off-loaded their dead and wounded. Then they were ordered to wait within hailing distance to rest their men's arms and get themselves ready to chase after the next Venetian galley that showed up.

The news got better and better as the first and second days passed and we got well into the third and then the fourth. Every so often one or two Venetian or Company galleys returned to Venice. The commanders of both fleets had apparently ordered their captains to return to Venice when they could find no one to fight. So they returned or, in the case of the Venetians, they tried to return.

Over and over again the reports of our captains were of victories in galley to galley fights and prizes that had been quickly sent on to Cyprus as all our crews had been ordered to do. Our captains' reports were uniformly good and generated great fine feelings amongst us all—until one remembered that only those of our galleys that had either been victorious or escaped being taken were able to return and report.

And it certainly was not all good news. Captured Company galleys arrived twice with Venetian prize crews on board. Both times they were escorted by one or more of the Venetian galleys that had captured them. The Venetian captains and their crews were astonished to find our galleys waiting for them instead of a triumphant welcome from their fellow citizens.

In one sad case the entire crew of one of the re-captured Company galley was missing. It did not take long to learn that the survivors had been murdered. Harold's fury was beyond reason when the Venetian galley that accompanied it fled—and was chased down and captured and brought back many hours later.

I did not say a word or lift a finger to stop Harold when he ordered the Venetian captain to be hung and had all of the captain's crew, except his wounded men, thrown into the water to drown. *Not that I tried; I was as angry as Harold.*

Only the seriously wounded Venetians were spared. They were set ashore on the quay along with all the other Venetian wounded as they arrived. It would be up to the Venetians to barber them or bury them.

Fortunately for us, it had never occurred to the commanders of the Venetian fleet that *our* galleys might return to Venice and be lying in wait for *his* galleys. As a result, the Venetians returned to the city expecting acclamations for their victories or, at least, for their safe return after helping to drive off the "French Fleet."

As you might imagine, the Venetian captains and crews were inevitably astonished when they discovered, too late, that our galleys had returned to Venice and were waiting for them.

On balance, we were pleased with what we heard and our prizes despite our ever-increasing losses.

******

Galleys, both ours and the Venetians', stopped returning by the end of the fourth day. By then, two of ours that had been taken by the Venetians had been recaptured, and at least two others were missing including Captain Jackson's Number Forty-one. We had taken several dozen of the Venetians galleys as prizes.

A routine was soon established. If Harold thought a captured galley looked as though the Company might be able to use it, we sent its captain and sergeants to its cargo hold, boarded a small prize crew of Company archers and sailors, and chained the common sailors from the Venetian crew to the rowing benches to help its slaves row.

On the other hand, if a Venetian galley was deemed unusable for one reason or another, we immediately burned it after sending its crew and slaves to the cargo hold of one of the prizes we were keeping. We would decide what to do with them later after we had a chance to sort them out. The dark smoke from one or more burning Venetian galleys just outside Venice's main harbour puffed up into the sky almost constantly starting on the third day.

What we did *not* do was send any of the Venetian galleys we wanted to keep to Cyprus. Instead, we kept them idling just off Venice's harbour. Why? Because we did not want risk having them retaken.

If that happened, the captured galleys being retaken that is, the Venetians still searching the Adriatic for the French Fleet would learn we were back in Venice waiting for them. And that would not do at all—we wanted the Venetian galleys to continue straggling back to Venice in ones and twos so we could continue to take them in single battles where our longbows and the strength of our rowers' arms would prevail.

******

The smoke of the burning galleys and the sending the seriously wounded Venetians ashore had a great impact on the city's people. They soon began to understand that their fleet was being systematically destroyed. And, of course, the news soon reached the Doge and his nobles.

Early on the fourth day, Alfred Smith, the captain of Galley Fifty-six, rowed up alongside Harold's galley after having briefly visited the quay near the big building to put ashore the Venetian wounded from a galley he had taken.

"A priest wearing a big hat and a fancy robe was on the quay when we landed the Venetian wounded. He asked to speak to you, Commander. He gobbled in French but I could understand him. I told him I would tell you."

"You did the right thing, Alfred, yes you did. Thank you. How soon will you be ready to go out again if a Venetian appears? Do you have enough rowers? Arrows and water?"

Harold listened quietly to our conversation, and then quietly made a comment with a question in his voice.

"You seem to be concerned about something, George. I can hear it in your voice. Is there a problem? We are winning and now the Dog's men want to talk. They have almost certainly decided to once again offer us a ransom to leave. What is worrying you?"

"You are right that I am worried, Uncle Harold. I can see our success here, and it is our great success and that the Venetians see it that has me worried. That and the fact that we have received no word from the lads trying to make useful ribaldis on Cyprus."

Harold was surprised.

"Eh? What is that you said about ribaldis? Do you mean the making of lightning and using it to throw stones? Why is that important?"

"It is important because the Venetians are sure to learn from being defeated so badly. It makes it unlikely they will not keep attacking us with inadequately crewed galleys in the years ahead. Sooner or later they will start training their men properly and put enough of them on each galley. Maybe they will even arm them with longbows instead of crossbows.

"When that happens we are going to need something new on our galleys to stay ahead of them. And all I can think of that might do it for us are the ribaldis—and they are obviously not ready or we would have gotten word."

"Well, there are always catapults eh?"

"Catapults? We tried them, remember? They did not work very well, as I recall." *Except for getting the man killed who was supposed to become the Company's commander instead of me.*

And then an idea that might work popped into my head behind my eyes. I did not see how it could hurt us even if it did not help.

"Take us in to the quay, Lieutenant Commander. The time has come to start talking to the Venetians again about a ransom and some indulgences."

I did not mention what I had in mind to Harold at the time, but I was actually thinking about doing much more than merely talking about a ransom at the meeting—I was thinking about launching a new gambit.

Yes, the more I thought about it, the more I was sure I needed to do something to mislead the Venetians and send them off in the wrong direction—or, at least, discourage them from going off in the right direction. But what? Hmm.

******

Our meeting started in such a way as to give a jolt of reality to my distinguished visitors and, hopefully, soften them up a bit—I had a boarding ladder raised to the quay and then waited on the deck in the shade of a slightly raised sail until they descended. They did and our meeting began.

"Greetings Commander, I am Archbishop Berthold and with me is Monsignor Alphonse Neri, the Papal Nuncio" representing His Holiness, the Pope. Also with us is Monsignor Pierre Urbano, France's ambassador to the Republic of Venice whom I believe you have already met. We are here, as I am sure you know, to try to arrange an end to the fighting.

The Archbishop spoke in Latin and made no effort to hold out his ring to be kissed. He had obviously heard of what had happened the last time I met with one of his fellow bishops in Athens. Word spreads fast amongst those in power in the church. It almost certainly meant he knew I was both the Commander of a very small Papal order and an Englishman, not a Frenchman.

My initial response did not hold out much hope for them.

"Yes, an end to the fighting would be helpful. Unfortunately, we in the French fleet have already attempted that route to peace and our efforts failed. It seems Venice not only did *not* deliver the restitution and indulgence payments it agreed to make to the Holy Father, Phillip of France, and the Latin Empress, it also attacked us once again."

Then I leaned forward and softly, and with a touch of anger and menace in my voice, added a warning.

"As you know, we have been selling our prizes in order to begin collecting the coins that are due us. Fortunately, we have been successful so there is no need to worry; your masters will be paid every coin that is due them from Venice, my men and I guarantee it. Unfortunately, of course, you will have to wait for payment until we finish sacking the city."

"But that is the problem, Commander," the French ambassador responded angrily. France is not at war with Venice. You must stop immediately."

I accepted none of his outrage.

"Are you telling me not to collect the restitution coins Venice promised to King Phillip despite Venice's insults to France and the damage to France that Venice has caused? That sounds like the words of a Venetian, not those of a loyal Frenchman. Does King Phillip know you are betraying him and trying to deny him the coins that are his due?"

The ambassador sputtered at my reply and his face turned red. I turned my attention elsewhere before he had a chance to answer.

"And you Monsignor Neri, are you here to tell me *not* to send the coins that are due to the Holy Father?"

"Oh no. Certainly not."

"And you, Archbishop?"

"Of course not. I am here to help arrange the terms of a peace."

"Well then, you are certainly welcome because we in the French fleet also want peace. But, as you know, Venice reneged on its last agreement and, since then, has caused even *more* damage to France and my men.

"Fortunately for us, God was once again on our side. As you know, a great storm blew a large fleet of French and lowland crusaders into the Adriatic. As a result, instead of the

Venetians outnumbering us as they expected, we ended up having many more war galleys than the Venetians and each and every one of them was crowded with fighting men on their way to the Holy Land.

"The Venetians fought well, I will give them that. They would have won easily if the storm had not delivered the crusaders and their galleys to help us. But God *did* intervene such that the Venetians were hopelessly outnumbered, and their fleet *has* been destroyed. *That* is Venice's reality today.

"So here we are, my Lords. And now, because Venice ignored its last agreement, my men have suffered even more losses at Venice's hands. As a result, peace and the safety of Venice is now only possible if all of the previously agreed restitution and indulgence payments are greatly increased, including those to the Holy Father, King Phillip, and the Latin Empress. And now, of course, the crusaders are also entitled to some of them."

After pausing for moment while I pretended to contemplate the matter, I gave them the Company's new requirements.

"A doubling of each of the originally agreed payments, plus three thousand for the crusaders, seems about right. And, of course, we will keep our prizes and sell them for the rest of what we are owed."

"We will wait for two days. If the required coins are not forthcoming by high noon two days hence, I would strongly advise you to leave the city as it will be sacked and burned immediately thereafter."

The three men accepted the new demand with a degree of understanding and agreed to deliver it to the Doge. It was in line with what they expected and they hoped to get their hands on some of the coins. Our negotiations ended with me issuing a warning.

"I cannot guarantee your safety if you remain in Venice and the required coins are not paid. So you must see to yourselves. My men and the crusaders, as I am sure you understand, are quite angry about their losses. Accordingly, when the city is being sacked they are unlikely to take time to make inquiries as to who you are and your loyalties."

My three visitors all nodded their heads in agreement at the reasonableness of my requirements. Indeed, I got the impression the three of them were already thinking how they might be able to get some of the coins for themselves, even the French ambassador—who was truly a fool if he thought we would give the "coins for France" to the French king instead of keeping them for ourselves.

******

The Venetians had no choice and agreed to the terms of a new and much more expensive "peace agreement." So two days later Harold's galley and three others edged up to the quay and the chests were carried aboard. *For safety's sake each of the galleys would sail separately to a different initial destination.*

Immediately after the coin chests were loaded I began going from galley to galley releasing the most important and dangerous of our prisoners, and telling them what superior fighting men they were as I did.

My story to the Venetian captains and the other prisoners being released did not vary all that much as I went from prize to prize freeing them.

"You are being released because the Doge has finally compensated everyone for the damages and pain he caused by having his soldiers help the Greeks go against the Latin Empress.

"It was only the Venetian soldiers who were defeated. You and your crews fought heroically and defeated the galleys of the French fleet you were sent out to fight.

"It is not your fault that a storm blew a great army of French and lowland crusaders into the Adriatic such that your galleys were hopelessly outnumbered and the galleys you encountered were full of fighting men on their way to the crusade instead of their normal crews of French and lowland sailors."

The eyes of the dejected Venetian captains lit up when they heard my story. They would not be disgraced; they had a usable explanation for losing their galleys—they had fought bravely and defeated the French fleet, and then been defeated themselves by the unexpected arrival of a huge fleet of war galleys carrying crusaders to the Holy Land.

"Even a brave man can only do so much when he finds himself hopelessly outnumbered, eh?" I suggested with the greatest possible respect as I shook their hands and saluted them.

God did not intervene with a storm and there were no crusaders, of course. But it was a good gambit to try to get such an excuse for Venice's defeat into everyone's heads. Hopefully the Venetians would convince themselves it was true and come to believe they lost because they were hopelessly outnumbered by the unexpected arrival of a huge army of crusaders, not because they had too few fighting men on each galley and they were not properly armed and trained.

******

Peace had broken out and we had gone from despised enemies to gracious and lucky victors in the blink of an eye. It probably helped that we had just acquired a very large number of coins and had begun spending them freely to buy supplies for our coming voyage "back to France."

Harold and I were sitting contently on the roof of his stern castle with bowls of ale when we heard the lookout's cry.

"Hoy the deck. Galley coming in."

We turned and looked, and then went back to talking about what we planned to do next. Harold had no family anywhere. He would go wherever I decided to go. But where should I go?

It was a dilemma. If I returned to England I would have to spend the winter there and then remain for the following summer in order to get back on the Company commander's regular schedule of spending his summers in England and his winters in Cyprus.

My thoughts were interrupted by a shout from the lookout that caused me to leap to my feet.

"Hoy the deck. It be Number Fifty-three what convoyed the prizes from Ancona to Constantinople."

******

The new arrival paused briefly by the galley on picket duty off the harbour entrance, probably to get directions, and then rowed straight to us. A couple of minutes later it slowly and carefully came alongside on our starboard side.

It was Fifty-three for sure and everything looked normal with the usual crew of sailors for an arriving galley on its deck and nothing else. The nobbled animals that might have once covered its deck had been long since eaten. It looked, in other words, as a galley should after it had completed a long voyage.

The only thing wrong, although I did not realize it at the time, was that its crew did not have the usual good cheer and smiles that sailors usually have when they reach a port and are thinking about its taverns and women.

Number Fifty-three's captain, a four-striper by the name of Peter Brown, was standing by deck railing and jumped on to our deck as soon as the two hulls were pulled together. He made straight for me and Harold, and then surprised us both as he stood with an impassive look on his face and knuckled his head in salute.

"Captain Brown of Fifty-three. I have an important private message for Lieutenant Commander Lewes."

Harold and I looked at each other, and then shrugged our acceptance. Reporting to the fleet commander instead of the Company commander was a bit out of the ordinary.

I watched as Captain Brown handed a leather message pouch to Harold and then began whispering in his ear. Harold's face turned white and he looked surprised. *Something was wrong.* When he finished, Captain Brown stood to attention, saluted me, and then Harold, and quickly re-boarded his galley.

Harold looked at me intently with a strange look on his face.

"There is news from Constantinople, George. Bad news. Your father and the Latin Empress are both dead. Michael Oremus thinks they were poisoned."

--The End of the Book --

Today's Friends

Chapter One
We are surprised.

We were still anchored in Venice's great harbour when word of the deaths and possible murders of his father and the Latin Empress reached George Courtenay, the Commander of the Cornwall-based Company of Archers. It so distressed him that he wept when he heard the news. It also upset and greatly angered all the rest of us who had made our marks on the Company's roll. We were, in a few simple words, seriously pissed.

The death of one of our own, and the likelihood that he had been murdered, fell on the Company's fleet like a bolt of lightning on an old tree. It hurt us badly and we could do nothing to respond. What made it even worse, if that was possible, was that an English woman our Company had contracted to defend had been killed with him. A woman? Impossible. We were immediately filled with righteous anger.

As you might imagine, the murders and what would happen next quickly became the subject of every conversation. My mates and I talked about it constantly as we sat at our places on our galley's rowing benches or gathered for a drink of water at the scuttled water butt that was set out each day next to the door to our galley's stern deck castle.

News of the deaths swept through the fleet of Company galleys and prizes in the harbour at great speed as it was shouted from one galley to the next. We immediately began mourning our former Commander with many men making fiery declarations as to what they would do to those responsible. We also told each other numerous stories and tales that we had heard about him, including some that sounded to me as if they might even have been true.

One thing was absolutely certain and totally agreed by every man—the butcher's bill would be paid in the form of a very serious revenge of some kind. Unfortunately, we did not have a clue as to what that response might be or how it would affect us. And that, as you might also imagine, resulted in a constant stream of exciting rumours involving all kinds of actions that we might be required to undertake.

****** *Lieutenant Commander Harold Lewes*

"We need to get back to Constantinople as soon as possible."

George announced his decision when he returned, red-eyed and shaken, from the roof of the smaller of our galley's two deck castles, the little one in the front where he lived as he sailed about on the Company's business. He had been sitting alone up there for more than an hour whilst he digested the terrible news and made his plans.

Of course we would go back to Constantinople. And the sooner the better so far as I was concerned. George's young brother, John, and his even younger son were there along with hundreds of our Company's men. They might be in desperate need of a rescue or, God forbid, already dead or captured.

What George was thinking as he mourned his father, but never did say or needed to say, was fully and immediately understood by every man who heard the sad tale—we were going to find out what happened and put a great and terrible revenge on everyone who was involved.

George did not need to announce his thoughts and intentions to us, or anyone else for that matter. It was not necessary. We already knew the Company would respond in a way that would be horrible beyond words for everyone who was responsible or involved.

We had, of course, not the slightest idea as to what form the Company's revenge would take or upon whom it would fall. But that did not stop everyone from speculating as to who might have done the terrible deed and making claims and predictions as to what the Company was going to do to them as a result. The men constantly talked about the various possibilities as they stood together around our galleys' water butt and sat with their mates on our galleys' rowing benches.

As you might expect, and was always the case, some of the men claimed to know what was about to happen, and what we were going to do, because they or someone else overheard somebody else, usually a captain or lieutenant, say something.

In fact, the only thing we really knew for sure was that death, or perhaps even a more terrible fate, was in store for everyone who had participated in their murders. That something horrible would happen to whoever was responsible was as certain as the arrival of the sun each morning as it made its great circle around the earth.

We knew for a certainty that a great response of some kind was coming because the Company's articles, on which every one of us had made his mark, required that great and terrible acts of vengeance be laid upon everyone responsible for the death or injury of any man on the Company's roll or under the Company's protection.

It did not matter that George's father, William, had himself once been the Company's Commander and had returned to active duty when the Company's retired archers were called back to active duty to help defend the Latin Empire. All that mattered, at least so far as my crew and the rest of men in the fleet were concerned, was that the Commander's father was an archer on the Company's roll. That was more than enough. The fact that the Empress who died with him was an important client of the Company for whom we had made a contract to protect would only make things worse for whoever did it.

For me the revenge would be personal and I would participate in it with the greatest enthusiasm. It was, after all, William himself who had promptly freed me from slavery when he bought the galley on which I was rowing. That was in the early days right after he and the handful of surviving archers stopped crusading and took enough coins off a murderous bishop to buy a couple of galleys to take them home. At the time I was a Southhampton man rowing on one of the galleys as a result of my cog being taken by Moorish pirates and being sold along with its crew to a French crusader turned pirate.

After William freed me, I immediately made my mark on the Company's roll as a sailor. During the years that followed we had sailed and fought together many times and become good friends. It was William himself who had given me the six stripes of a lieutenant commander and responsibility for all the Company of Archers' galleys and transports.

The murders of two people under the Company's protection would be more than enough to trigger a massive response even if they were not important. That was certain. What was also certain was that our revenge would be so fearsome that it would be remembered and talked about for many years, and then some.

Of course it would be most terrible. It had to be so it would be remembered forever— William Courtenay and the Empress were entitled to revenge and the Company had a reputation to protect.

In any event, instead of waving his hands about and making unnecessary announcements about what was going to happen to whomever was responsible, George quietly began giving orders. They were, at least initially, very much what everyone expected.

"Two fully crewed galleys will take a third of the chests with the ransom coins the Venetians paid us to Cyprus, and another fully crewed two will take a third of the chests to Cornwall. The rest of our galleys will sail for Constantinople with Lieutenant Commander Lewes's galley and another fully crewed galley carrying the final third.

"We will leave as soon as the fleet is ready to sail. Make it so."

We, the Commander's lieutenants, all solemnly nodded our agreement and muttered "ayes." It was the only thing we could think to do or say. Indeed, as the lieutenant commander in charge of the Company's fleet, I had so expected such a decision that I had already ordered the captains to recall their men and finish readying their galleys for an immediate sailing.

We were done with taking coins and prizes out of Venice, so leaving Venice and returning to Constantinople to find out what happened was what we would almost certainly do. Besides, I could have quietly called off or changed our preparations if the Commander had surprised me by keeping us in Venice for a few more days or ordering the fleet to sail to some other destination.

****** *Lieutenant Commander Harold Lewes*

All of our galleys rowed out of Venice's great harbour the next morning right after the sun arrived on its daily voyage around the edges of the world. George and I stood on the roof of my galley's forward deck castle in the early morning sunlight as my galley led the Company's fleet out of the harbour. My loud-talker and sailing sergeant were on the roof with us and so was my apprentice. The rowing benches were manned as fully as possible which was required by the Company's standing orders when one of our galleys was moving in a harbour. Keen-eyed lookouts were on both masts.

It looked to be the beginning of another fine late-summer day. There was not a cloud in the sky and it was already getting warm. The heat would be hard on our rowers if George decided we needed to hurry, particularly those who would be rowing on our galleys that were going out seriously under-crewed. I thought it likely we would hurry. That meant the two galleys sailing for Constantinople with full crews, one of which was mine, would leave the others behind whilst we hurried on ahead.

Not a word was spoken between George and me as we slowly rowed through the scummy waters of Venice's Grand Harbour and into the Adriatic to begin our long voyage. We just stood there together on the roof of the forward deck castle and listened to the familiar sounds of my galley's oars, the creaking of its ever-leaking hull, the voices of my sailors and archers as they went about their duties, and the periodic complaints of the live cattle and sheep on our deck with their legs cut so they could not move until we butchered them for food,

Distant voices and the sound of slowly beating rowing drums could also periodically be heard coming over the water from the other galleys in our fleet. Noisy sea birds, as usual, were circling overhead and periodically dropping poop on our decks. It was, in other words, in all ways a normal and peaceful scene despite the fact that we were leaving a port where we had recently fought a great battle and taken many prizes and ransoms.

I could not help but notice that the harbour was significantly less crowded than when we arrived about a week earlier. The almost-empty harbour was a mark of our recent great success in taking Venetian prizes. It made me want to smile, a feeling which I kept off my face and behind my eyes so George would not see it and misunderstand my thoughts. He himself was sad-faced and appeared to be deep in thought instead of being his usual keen-eyed self and constantly looking about.

An unexpectedly large number of Venetians were silently standing on the quay watching us leave, and there were empty berths and anchorages everywhere. As you well might imagine, a few of the watchers were saluting us with obscene gestures and not a one of them was waving and shouting out to wish us a good voyage.

Poor losers. That was what they were, I decided. So far as I was concerned, the bastards got what they deserved for helping the Greeks attack us at Constantinople and were lucky we did not sack the city—which, in my opinion, we should have done. I was tempted to return their obscene salutes but did not. Some of our younger archers and sailors, however, were not so restrained, and more than a few added shouted insults to their gestures.

Venice's anchorages and the mooring berths along its quays were mostly empty. That was because the only cargo transports remaining in the harbour were the prizes we had taken and sold back to the Venetians. In fact most of our prizes had already either sailed away to be sold elsewhere or were on their way to Cyprus where they would be bought in to join the Company's fleet.

Our six coin-carrying galleys, including mine, were fully crewed as we passed through one of the harbour's entrance and entered the blue-grey waters of the Adriatic. Being fully crewed was important. It meant those of us who were their captains would have the rowing and fighting strength necessary to either run or to fight to protect the coin chests we were carrying.

It was also important in a bad way—because, as a result of fully crewing the six coin carriers, all the rest our galleys were so dangerously under-manned they had barely enough men to steer and set their sails. Every one of them was significantly short of men both because of our casualties during the recent fighting and because so many men had been taken from them to serve in prize crews and on the coin carriers.

It was clear to everyone that our under-crewed galleys would have to rely on their sails to get to Constantinople. And that raised the question as to whether George would order the two fully crewed galleys bound for Constantinople to hurry there at their best speed, or would all of our galleys remain together as a war-fighting fleet that would be able to move no faster than its slowest under-crewed member?

The unspoken question was soon answered by George—my galley and the other fully crewed coin carrier would sail to Constantinople as fast as possible. It would be hard on our rowers because of the heat, but it was the decision I and everyone else had expected. Besides, the sooner we got there the sooner we go ashore and enjoy the city's many delights.

Our fleet was seriously short of men even though we sailed with every available man; not a single man had run, and none of our seriously wounded and poxed men had been left behind for barbering. We even had a number of volunteers, mostly from among the foreign seamen on the prizes we had taken. More than two hundred of them signed on to help us row and work our sails. They did so in return for the promise of a couple of silver coins and various other undertakings.

Despite our new recruits, we were so short-handed that the captains, lookouts, and cooks would have to row if the majority of our galleys, those not carrying coins, were to get enough of their oars into the water to have any effect.

Normally our severely wounded men would have been left ashore in the care of well-paid local barbers and physicians to either be buried or to recover enough to either re-join the Company or honourably retire to one the homes provided by the Company. Not this time. Even those who were badly wounded came with us. They would live in our stern castles until they either recovered or died. Whether they did or not depended on the strength of their prayers, their mates who cared for them, and the sailmakers who sewed them up.

We had to carry our wounded and poxed men with us because we had no local shipping post in Venice to watch over them and we could not trust the Venetians to barber them properly or bury them with the necessary prayers if they died. We would bury those who did not make it at sea.

It also helped, as you might imagine, that all of our able-bodied men sailed with us; no one was foolish enough or desperate enough to desert in such an unfriendly port. The unhappy Venetians would likely have cut them down or enslaved them before the last of our galleys cleared the harbour.

Perhaps an even more important explanation of why no one deserted was that any man who ran would be giving up his share of the very substantial amount of prize money that would soon be distributed. No one knew for sure how much his share would be, but our takings out of Venice and its shipping had been quite substantial. Without a doubt it would be one of the biggest pay outs of prize coins in the Company's history, more than enough to enable a man to buy himself out of his contract with the Company and set himself up for the rest of his life.

Sailing on our under-crewed galleys did not worry the Company men who were sailing on them. Our lads were a cocky lot. Besides, even the greenest of our new recruits knew we had destroyed the Venetian fleet and that there was little chance that the Moors or anyone else would be brave enough to try anything in the waters between here and Constantinople.

Whether the Venetians liked it or not, and they clearly did not, the waters of the Adriatic now belonged to the Company of Archers and would for some years. There was no doubt about it, we would control these waters until the Venetians were able to recover from the losses we had just inflicted on them or the Moors refocussed their efforts away from the fighting in Spain and in the Holy Land.

It was true, of course, that some of the Venetian galleys had escaped. They might risk trying to re-take one of our prizes, particularly if the Venetians spotted it while it was sailing alone.

But would they try to take one of the Company's under-crewed galleys if they happened to come upon it? Probably not since they were not likely to know how few archers were aboard it. Indeed, or so we told each other, it was highly unlikely that any Venetian or Moorish galley captain who came across one of our galleys would attempt to find out how much fight it might have in it. To the contrary, he would almost certainly turn around and run for his life, and count himself fortunate to have escaped.

In the real world, it would be a cold day in heaven before a slave-rowed Venetian or Moorish galley could take a Company galley with even a handful of our longbow-carrying and pike-wielding archers on board. In other words, the prospect of meeting a galley or two of Venetians or Moors whilst we were sailing for Constantinople did not worry any of us.

An enemy fleet, of course, would be a different matter if it came upon one of our short-handed galleys whilst our galley was sailing alone *and* they knew it had only a few archers on board.

What *did* worry us at that moment was our Commander, George Courtenay, and what he would have us do when we reached Constantinople. We had absolutely no idea. He obviously would want revenge for his father's death, and rightly so. We all wanted that, particularly me who had been rescued by William from being a galley slave and had sailed with him for many years.

But would George be so blinded by his need for revenge that he would do something that would end up hurting himself and the Company? I certainly hoped not. But I was worried—it is well known that the murder of someone in a man's family can affect his thinking.

Chapter Two

Constantinople.

Our voyage from Venice enjoyed relatively favourable winds and came off without a hitch or the loss of a single man. The other galley carrying coin chests, Captain Thomas Richardson's Number Seventy-three, stayed with us when we charged ahead with continuous rowing and left the rest of the fleet following along behind. Our two galleys sailed together and sighted Constantinople's huge city walls in what seemed to me to be about ten days.

The other four fully crewed galleys that had sailed with us from Venice were not with us as we approached the great capital city of the Latin Empire. They had peeled off from us as soon as we exited the Adriatic in order to begin their much longer and more hazardous voyages to deliver the coin chests they were carrying to Cornwall and Cyprus.

The only stop we made during the entire voyage had been a very brief one when we finished rowing out of the Dardanelles Strait and came alongside the Company galley collecting the Empress's tolls. It was Captain Jackson's Number Forty-Six.

"What is the state of the city now that my father and the Empress are gone? Have there been any fighting or disturbances?" George immediately asked Captain Jackson.

"No Commander, none at all. The city and its taverns have been quiet; at least they were until yesterday morning when we came out to take our turn at collecting the tolls."

"Quiet as in normal or quiet as in the lull before a storm?"

"Normal I think. But I am not sure, Commander. Everything seemed normal when I was ashore and I heard nothing from my men and the merchants with whom I dealt. There were no cautions or alerts issued by the Commandry if that is what you mean. There was much talk about your father and the Empress, of course. But that was at the tavern and….."

At that the point the poor captain's voiced trailed off. He did not know what else to say, but felt he had to say something.

"I am truly sorry about your loss, Commander. Yes I am. Your father was good man. All of the men feel the same way."

****** *Lieutenant William Smithson*

There were only a few clouds in the sky as I watched the Commander's galley bump up against the quay that ran along the little strip of land that was the Company's concession. It was next to the towering city wall that kept our concession and its quay in the shade for a good part of every day. It was a warm late summer afternoon and everything appeared normal. A large and growing number of seabirds were hovering over us in search of food scraps and pooping on our deck.

One of the Company's three-masted ships was tied up along the Company's quay. It was discharging passengers so it must have been newly arrived. I did not recognize it. Perhaps it was one of our Venetian prizes that had recently been bought in to expand the Company's fleet of transports.

Our two galleys had, as usual, been seen by the Company's lookouts on the city wall and identified long before we actually rowed up to the quay that stood in front of the narrow patch of Company land between the quay and the city wall. The quay and our men's tents and lean-tos sheltering up against the great stone city wall beyond it were familiar sights. They had been there in one form or another for as long as I could remember.

As a result of our being seen by the lookouts on the wall above our concession, both Henry Harcourt, the Lieutenant Commander who had been left to command our forces in the city, and his number two, Major Captain Michael Oremus, had been informed of our pending arrival in time to be on waiting for us on the quay. They had not been on our great raid; they had remained behind to command those of our men who had waited in the city to help guard it whilst the rest of us put the Company's revenge on Venice.

A handful of men in Company tunics, almost certainly their guards and apprentices, were standing in a loose formation near the two men. They were red-faced and out of breath as a result of hurrying to meet us, but they were relaxed and standing casually on the quay as our galleys slowly rowed up to it and as our mooring lines were thrown to the waiting wharfies who quickly secured them.

No order had been given, but the proprieties of rank were observed. As a result, our galley had hung back to allow George and Harold, the highest ranking men in the fleet, to be the first to climb up one of the galley's hastily erected boarding ladders and go ashore.

"Our lookouts saw you coming," Michael said unnecessarily as Henry saluted and then reached out and gave the Commander a great manly hug. Of course he both saluted and hugged him; he was the Commander's honorary uncle after all, and had been ever since the Commander was a young boy of three or four years.

Commander Courtenay met his lieutenants on the quay as many hundreds of eyes watched intently from the newly arrived galleys and from the Company men who were already ashore. What we watchers were hoping to see was some sign of what might be in store for us.

All we saw, however, was four men talking intently and waving their hands about, but there was no gestures to indicate that earth-shaking news was being conveyed, or of the relief that would be apparent if there was danger in the air and we had arrived in the nick of time to save the day.

After a few seconds, a fifth man, a boy from the look of his size and the way he walked, detached himself from the little group of guards and hurried over to join them. He too got a warm welcoming hug from the Commander.

"The lad be the Commander's son, his name is also George," one of the men behind me said with a touch of sadness in his voice. "It were his grandfather the bastards killed," he added unnecessarily.

Perhaps most significant of all, at least so far as we were concerned, was that the half dozen or so archers who had accompanied Henry and Michael to the quay seemed relaxed and bored rather than tense and excited. The crews on the two arriving galleys, to a man, were relieved by the peaceful scene and many of them, surprisingly, were somewhat disappointed.

What was *not* present, that would almost certainly have been present upon our arrival at almost any other port, were the merchants and street women vying for our custom and the usual idle layabouts, wharfies, and unemployed sailors in search of a berth. That was because the quay and the sliver of land between it and the city wall were part of a Company concession that had been extracted from Greeks when they ruled the city and retained when the crusaders took it. Outsiders were not admitted through the city gate that opened into the concession unless they were there on some sort of Company business.

In other words, what my men and I saw was a relatively quiet scene. The only non-archers who were present were the sailors of the three-masted Company ship that was taking on supplies further down the quay and the passengers in the process of boarding it or already on board.

Some of the ship's crew and their passengers were on the quay next to the ship and on the ship's main deck. They were standing and watching everything that was happening just as we were watching Commander Courtenay and the men who had come to greet him.

Our fleet's arrival, it seems, had surprised the ship's crew and passengers and given them something to talk about. Seeing the men on the quay and the great city behind the wall in front of us certainly did the same for us.

****** *Lieutenant Commander Harold Lewes*

George greeted the arrival of his son, Young George, with a cheerful salute, a big smile, and a great hug. Then we listened intently as Henry quickly assured us that the Commander's young brother, John, was safe and the city quiet. John would have been with them, Henry explained, except he was away in the city delivering a routine message about buying more food supplies for the Commandry and for the wounded men who had been left behind for barbering.

"I sent him off to the market buy more supplies before we heard you were arriving," Michael Oremus explained.

But then the faces of Henry and Michael got deadly serious as they stood on the quay and briefly summarized what they knew about the sudden deaths of George's father and the Empress. It was not very much. In fact, we learned nothing new except that several extensive investigations were underway, big rewards were on offer for information, and that so far nothing of importance had turned up.

The Company's investigations, Henry said, had been organized with the help of several of the merchant associations from whom we did much buying of supplies and carrying of passengers. They had added their coins to the already-large rewards for useful information. He himself, Henry said, had immediately launched the investigation and taken personal command of it.

"There are a lot of rumours about poison and murder," Henry said as he looked at George cautiously. "Or, of course, it might have been their time to pass as the Roman and Greek archbishops seemed to suggest when they presided over their funerals."

But then Henry fiercely added something with a touch of anger in his voice.

"I did not believe either of the archbishops' ox shite explanations for a minute when I heard them, and I do not believe them now; they were murdered and that is God's truth. We just do not know who did it or why. If we knew we would have already done for them."

Then Henry said something that surprised us.

"Helen be here."

"Helen? My stepmother?" George asked incredulously.

"Aye, she be arriving from Cyprus just before your father and the Empress died. Apparently your father sent for her. She is staying in the Commandry and is quite anxious to see you.

"She is well protected and safe, of course, with a half dozen of our steadiest men as her guards. And, her son John, your half-brother, is with her when he is not doing his duties as my apprentice. He and your son are with her a lot because both Michael and I are stationed at the Commandry."

"How is she holding up?" George asked.

"She was initially so distraught when your father died that I thought she might fall down and die herself. But now she is icy and angry, quite angry actually."

"So, is young Robert now the Emperor in fact as well as name? Or has a new regent been named to replace his mother?"

George asked the question of Henry as we turned to walk through the nearby gate in the wall and began walking through the city's narrow streets to the Wisdom of God Church where both William and the Empress had been temporarily buried,

"That seems to be a problem, a big one actually. Several men, including the Latin Archbishop who buried your father, have come forward claiming to be the boy's regent. So has the boy's older sister, your, uh um, good friend, Elizabeth, the Empress's daughter. She returned with the young boy who is her new husband as soon as she heard about her mother's death.

"She stole a march on the others by moving into the Empress's rooms and maintaining the Empress's court. Rumour has it that the boy's father sent them.

"And then there is the king of the Bulgarians, Otto, him what fought with us against the Greeks. He showed up a couple of days ago with quite a few of his men, a small army of them actually. Several others of the Empire's kings and princes have come to the city as well.

"You may have to sort them out and make sure the right one is on the throne and buys the Pope's approval."

"Me sort them out?" George asked incredulously as he stopped walking and turned towards me. "Why me?"

"There is no one else to do it, is there? And the Company needs someone on the throne as the boy's regent who will honour the Company's contract to collect the tolls. You, for instance."

Chapter Three

A big surprise.

Our first destination was the burial field in the sheep pasture next to the city's huge Wisdom of God Church, the one which was now known by its Latin name as the Hagia Sofia because its Greek priests and bishop had been replaced by Latins who answered to Rome. The church's burial field was, I had been told, where my father and the Empress had been temporarily buried in unmarked graves.

According to Henry, they would remain there until something more appropriate could be built for them. And they would be resting in good company as the Company's dead from recent war with the Greeks and other skirmishes and poxes were buried there including Aron who built the ribaldis and his betrothed. It was my only consolation and it was not even close to being enough.

The Hagia Sofia was thought to be the grandest and largest building in the world. Immediately next to it stood the smaller palace that was the traditional residence of the exiled Patriarch of the Orthodox Church and was now occupied by one of his underlings, the "Metropolitan" who was in charge of the Orthodox Church in Constantinople and the surrounding countryside. The even finer "Great Palace" of the emperors was just beyond the church. The large and ornate building that housed the old Roman baths was nearby and so was the City huge central market with its many lanes and stalls.

According to Company legend and the stories I heard from my father and uncles who were there, it was from the Patriarch's palace whilst the crusaders' were sacking the city that my father and his men had "rescued" the great relics of the Orthodox Church, including the gold-covered head of John the Baptist and two of his gold-covered right hands that had baptised Jesus.

Those were the priceless relics, including several additional copies of the two right hands made for my father by London goldsmiths that were some years later sold by the Company to various princes. The princes, in turn, used them to obtain the Pope's favour by donating them to the Church. In essence, the relics reached Rome in a way that had greatly enriched the Company and enhanced the worship of God.

At the moment, the Patriarch's palace was *not* occupied by the city's Pope-appointed Latin archbishop. That was because, in an effort to keep peace in the city whose residents were mostly Orthodox, the Orthodox Church's "Metropolitan," the man who led the Orthodox faithful in the city when the Patriarch was absent, was allowed to continue living in it with his personal priests and servants.

As you might imagine, the Latin Archbishop was a prime suspect in the murders. That was because he and his priests had been extremely unhappy with the Empress because she had refused to order the city's Orthodox churches, and thus the priestly employments and coins they generated, to be turned over to the Latin Church.

What would ultimately happen to my father's body, according to what Henry told me as we walked to the Hagia Sofia's burial yard, was up to me. The next emperor or his regent would decide about the Empress's.

My initial view of my father's grave moved me to tears. It was an ugly mound of raw dirt that had been dug out of a burial hole next to his and piled on top of his hole. Apparently a new empty hole was readied at the time of each burial with the dirt from digging the new hole being used to fill in the hole with the newly deposited body. Already there were a line of dirt mounds beyond my father's with a newly dug empty hole at the end of the line. The church was nothing if not efficient in such matters.

I knelt next to the little mound of raw dirt and prayed for some time. My son and brother and my lieutenants and guards knelt behind me. No one said a word and they remained kneeling until I stood. I think they were a bit embarrassed by my great heaving sobs. I was not; I had loved him dearly.

******

My eyes were still wet and puffy as we walked through the city streets back to the Commandry from the burial ground. Later I realized that the number of guards seemed to have somehow grown while I was praying beside my father's grave. Perhaps someone had sent for reinforcements for some reason. I meant to ask, but I never did.

It was an hour or so before the sun would finish passing overhead. The streets were crowded with women doing their last minute shopping, street merchants constantly calling out in an effort to sell all kinds of things off their hand carts, and with men returning home from work. Horse carts and two-wheeled carts carrying people and goods were everywhere standing in the street or moving about. There was no sense of danger so we walked with our swords sheathed and our longbows unstrung and slung over our backs.

We walked informally and carefully through the crowds without using a marching drum. Mostly we weaved our way through the crowded streets in a line that was two men across except where we had to split apart into a single file to get around a pile of shite or a stopped or slow-moving cart.

It was particularly necessary to walk carefully to avoid stepping into the piles of poop that had been dropped on to the street stones by the horses and deposited on them by the neighbourhood people and those who were walking on them. It had not rained for several days if the sizes and smells of the piles were any indication.

As usual the city's great numbers of cats were everywhere prowling about or sleeping. And also, as usual, they were above it all and totally ignored us as we passed. They were always that way according to the local people.

A few people stared at us as we passed, but most either paid us no attention or briefly looked at us out of the corner of their eyes as we walked past them. I had the feeling that some of them knew who I was. Or perhaps the looks of sympathy I saw were all in my imagination because I wanted to see them.

I was still shaken by what I had seen—a great pile of dirt with my dear father somewhere underneath it. It was still hard for me to believe.

******

We had no more than walked through the Commandry gate and entered its little bailey when the door to the Commandry opened and Helen came rushing out with a look of relief on her haggard face and her hair all wild and flying about. What struck me was that her hair had turned grey since the last time I had seen her several years earlier. She ran across the bailey to embrace me with her arms wide apart and tears running down her cheeks.

"George, thank God. I was afraid they had killed you too." She sobbed as she choked out the words and held me tightly. My lieutenants and my son instinctively moved back a couple of paces to give us a bit of privacy.

"Here now," I said as I held her and patted her gently on her back. "Please tell me all about it. What happened?"

"I got here on a galley from Cyprus and stayed with your father in his room. And the next day…"

It was about then, as I looked over her shoulder, that I saw that every man in the bailey was looking at us expectantly.

"Wait. We should talk privately. Do you have a room?"

"Just your father's," she sobbed.

As I consoled her, I wondered why he had not taken her to the Great Palace; then I remembered. It is always hard for a man to deal with two women at the same time if they are rivals for his dingle and affections.

******

The story that emerged a few minutes later was neither enlightening nor encouraging. My father, Helen said, had sent to Cyprus for her and was most happy and enthusiastic to see her when she finally arrived.

"But he seemed terribly upset about something. He was his usual self at first. But then he had trouble sleeping despite all of his .. um.. exercise. He got up in the middle of the night and paced about. It was not like him at all. I asked him what was wrong, but he would not talk about it. All he said was "something is going bad here." *Going bad?*

"Did he say what it was?"

"No, but I got the impression it had to do with the Empress."

"Well, that is not much of a surprise. Everything and everybody in Constantinople depends on the Empress and revolves around her. *And so does the Company even though we are also fetching substantial amounts of coins from elsewhere.*

"At least, everything depended on her and revolved around her until she died. Her death changes everything. Now what will happen in the city in the days ahead, including whether the Company will continue to prosper here, will depend on who takes her place as her son's regent."

We sat and talked for some time. Helen alternately laughed and cried as she told me stories about her early days together with my father and how they first met in Syria when she was a young slave and the man she thought was her father had given her to my father as a gift.

"My mother really wanted me to be with a good man, you see, and made sure her owner agreed. And, oh my but your father was a good man. And then he married me in the church and dear old Uncle Thomas bought a dispensation from the Pope so your father could have more than one wife and would never have to use a tavern woman. That is when I sent a message to my mother and suggested that she get her master, my father, to send my two sisters to him as well."

"Oh God how we loved him." And then she covered her eyes and wept and sobbed.

It was heart breaking and I laughed and cried with her as she told me stories about their early days together that I did not know.

After an hour or so my younger brother, John, came hurrying in to join us. He was Helen's son and all wide-eyed with excitement and relief at my return. I had forgotten how young he was. And, although I said not a word, I once again wondered why Uncle Thomas had ordained him so young and sent him out to join the Company as an apprentice sergeant.

Perhaps what counts with God is the quality of a priest's Latin when he gobbles his prayers and asks the faithful for their coins, not his age and experience. I will have to remember to ask Uncle Thomas. One thing is sure—neither my brother, John, nor my son, Young George, are old enough or strong enough to stand in a Company battle line and fight; they would endanger the men on either side of them and probably get themselves killed.

The sun was setting when I realized I was getting hungry. So I finally left after promising to visit Helen every day and to keep her informed. My brother stayed behind to attend to his mother.

As I left, I gave some orders to the archer who was on guard at the end of the hall.

"Tell your sergeant to make sure the lady always gets a proper meal with some meat and bread and at least one bowl of wine every morning and evening. And make sure no one bothers her."

It was probably and unnecessary order, but he nodded anyway and cheerfully repeated it back to me and agreed that he would carry it out. Then I went in search of Henry and Michael to get more information as to what had happened and who was responsible.

******

Henry and Michael were sitting at the long table in the Commandry's hall with my son, Young George, and Harold Lewes. Erik, the great hulking commander of the Empress's

Varangian Guards was sitting with them. My son, Young George who was increasingly being called "George Young," was there because he was Michael's apprentice. Harold's wide-eyed new apprentice, Archie Smith, was there also. Archie was the red-haired son of a Yorkshire smith who had somehow gotten into the Company's school. He had been in Cyprus with Yoram.

Good, I thought as I came through the door and saw Erik. He, more than anyone else, was likely to know what happened. And then another thought came into my head. *Did he and his men do it so he and the Varangians could take over, or could they have done it for someone else whom they preferred to serve?*

"Hello Erik, it has been a while," I said as he stood up and we gave each other great manly hugs and back pats as only men who have fought side by side together can properly do.

As we embraced it suddenly struck me that Erik smelled most foul—which surprised me because I knew that Erik usually changed his tunic and visited the city's old Roman baths every week or so. On the other hand, perhaps it was me; I had not been near a bath for several months. *Yes, I decided as we let go of each other and I sat down; it is me.*

"I am so sorry for your loss, George. Your father was a fine man. My men and I respected him very much. He will be missed. I came here to tell you that. And also, of course, to congratulate you on your great victory over the Venetians and to tell you what I know of the tragedy."

"Thank you, Erik. I appreciate your kind words. Might you be free to talk after we finish eating," I responded. "I have many questions as you might imagine."

After a moment of reflection while everyone at the table stared at us and listened intently while trying to appear as if they were not, I changed my mind and made a suggestion that surprised many of my listeners. *Why did I change it? So I could talk to Henry and Michael first.*

"No, perhaps even better, if you find the idea agreeable, we could go to Roman Baths and talk after we break our fasts tomorrow morning, eh? I have been aboard a galley for several months and truly need a good watering."

"Of course, George, of course. Talking about things whilst we water ourselves is a good idea. But please know that my men and I are continuing to make strenuous efforts to find out about your father's death and that of the Empress. I will certainly tell you everything we have discovered. If you are agreeable, I will come here and we will walk together to the baths. Would an hour after dawn be good for you?"

Of course my suggestion that we talk at the baths caused eyebrows of my listeners to rise and disappointed them; they wanted to know what Erik and the Empress's guards thought had happened and many of them believed that bathing weakened a man.

****** *George Courtenay*

The food in the Commandry's great hall was a wonderful change after several months of eating on a galley. There were slices and joints of sheep and goat meat piled on wooden platters as well as warm loaves of bread in the new French round style and shredded onions, olives, and turnips cooked in butter and covered with melted cheese. It went down well with dates, good red wine, and slices of apples and oranges.

No one said a single word about my father and the Empress or of anything related to their deaths. I did not mention them because I wanted to talk to Henry and Michael in private, and no one at the table was brave enough to talk about the tragedy for fear that it might upset me. As a result, we spent the entire dinner talking about Company matters such as the prices we were paying for supplies, the cargos and passengers we were carrying, and the state of the various Company men who had been wounded earlier in the spring war against the Greeks.

Harold and I ate and drank much too much and then, finally, belched our appreciation, gave a good scratch to the lice around our dingles, and walked out into the bailey with Henry and Michael to relieve ourselves and talk privately. It was a nice August night without even a touch of chill in the air along with the usual wisps of smoke from the cooking fires of the city's families in the street in front of the bailey.

"Cornwall is probably already starting to get cold and rainy," Michael observed over his shoulder as we stepped into the bailey and he pissed against the bailey wall in the designated low spot where it would run out into the street. "But at least it is peaceful according to the word that came in on one of our transports last week."

Harold agreed about Cornwall as he and I stepped up on either side of Michael.

"Aye, and the seas between Lisbon and England will be getting rough about now. I hope our galleys with the coin chests will be able to get across before the weather in the Atlantic turns too foul to sail. I would hate to think of the coins we took out Venice going down in a storm or having to spend the winter in Lisbon."

"Alright," I said to my lieutenants as I pulled out my dingle and stepped to the wall next to Michael to pee. "No one can hear us out here. Tell me everything you know about the deaths of my father and the Empress."

It was the first time George had heard the details about his father's death, and they were not pretty. Dying of being poisoned is a terrible way to go. Painful for sure. As you might imagine, Michael and I tried to be as gentle as possible when we told him what we knew.

"According to the servants who found them in the morning, they were in the Empress's sleeping chamber. She was hanging half out of the bed; your father was on the floor stretched out towards the entrance door.

"The Empress's bed was all torn up as if she, uh, had been thrashing about. Neither of them was wearing any clothes and both of them had wild looks in their eyes and some kind of frothing, like the foam on a newly dipped bowl of ale, coming out of their mouths.

"Neither had any new wounds from being hit or cut. I looked myself to make sure, and so did Michael and the Empress's Greek physician. They were almost certainly poisoned."

"How long had they been dead before they were found?" George asked.

"From the way the servants described them, it sounded as though it had been some hours. They were already getting stiff."

"And the guard at the stairs?"

"There were three that night. Two Varangians and one of ours, John Shoemaker. And they all three swear that at least two of them were always awake and alert at the foot of the stairs, and that no one passed them coming in either direction once the Empress retired. Erik believes them and so do I."

"Could someone have come from one of the other rooms in the upper hall, my father's for instance?

"The guards say not. They could see the door into the Empress's chambers from where they stand at the bottom of the stairs. They swear they neither saw nor heard anyone once the Empress retired.

"On the other hand, there is a door between the Empress's rooms and the room next to it where your father often stayed.

"What is interesting is that your father was with his wife in her room at the Commandry earlier that night. He must have walked or ridden through the city to get there. Yet no one saw him in the city. The men on guard on the staircase below the Empress's chambers all swear he did not enter."

"But he obviously did," George softly mused. "How did he do it? And why was he in her chambers if had just been with my stepmother?"

****** *George Courtenay*

My lieutenants and I drank bowls of wine and talked until late in the night. Many reports and rumours had reached their ears about the death of my father and the Empress. We talked about them all.

The list of the possible murderers of the Empress turned out to be quite extensive. It included Erik and both the city's Latin Archbishop and a man, called the Metropolitan who directed the priests serving the city's Orthodox believers.

It also included the Patriarch and the Pope himself, each of whom might have arranged it because he wanted to install one of his favourites. And then, of course, there were all of their religious followers and the members of their entourages who might have seen removing the Empress as a way to curry favour with God by supporting their superiors.

Unfortunately, there were many other names on the list such as the father of Marie's young husband who had led the Orthodox army against the Empress and the various kings and princes of the Empire's states who might have seen becoming the new emperor's regent as a step towards the throne for themselves.

The King of the Bulgarians was a particular possibility. When we were fighting together against the Greeks he had made no secret of his ambitions and his unhappiness that a woman was making the Empire's decisions.

None of the princely suspects was in the city at the time, or so my lieutenants said, but they all had palaces and retainers in the city. On the other hand, a number of them had come to the city immediately upon receiving the news, probably to protect and advance their interests.

And that was just the list for the Empress. My father's list was even longer because it included almost all of the men on the Empress's list and just about every one of the Company's major competitors as well as the French king, and any number of Moorish princes and merchants. And, of course, there was a lot of overlap. The Venetians and the recently defeated Greeks and the Orthodox Church, for example, had undoubtedly hated them both.

In the end, the list of people who might have wanted one or both of them dead was so long that it boggled my mind. Some of the people on it had names I had never heard; others I knew because I had met or knew of them because we had taken prizes or customers from them. The problem was that the names on the list included people who might well have had a reason to kill just one of them and got the other as well.

"There are so many possibilities that I cannot get my arms around them," I said when they my lieutenants finally finished telling me all the rumours and speculations they had heard and naming and telling me about everyone who might have had reason so kill my father and the Empress. It was a long list.

"Your father and the Empress were, uh, close as you know; perhaps the food or drink was intended for one and got them both when they shared it," Henry suggested.

"If it was poison, it was most likely delivered to them by the Empress's servants or someone with whom they recently met. The servants have been questioned closely by the Varangians, but have not yet been tortured.

"So has everyone who visited either of them in the days before they passed away. They all deny being involved. Moreover, no one on the list has fled the city as they might if they were guilty. To the contrary, many have hurried here in hopes of advancing themselves"

What it all boiled down to was that there was a long list of possibilities such that my lieutenants and I did not have a clue as to who had done it or why—just a lot of suspicions and many suspects.

"Alright, that is what the Varangians and the Empress's chancellor have done and discovered. What have we heard and done?

"We too have closely questioned all the servants and we have also offered a big reward for information, a huge reward as a matter of fact—a thousand gold bezants. So far there have been many false tips from people seeking the coins, but nothing that sounded useful in any way."

"We can torture the servants, of course, but then they will all confess and point to everyone they can think of in an effort to save themselves. And besides many of them came out with the Empress as her personal servants and are likely to be ruined by her death. As a group, they are not likely to have caused it. An individual, however, can always be gotten to in some way or another as you well know."

"What about the servants of the nobles and religious leaders?" Michael asked. "We could grab some of them and see if they have heard anything."

"I think that is what the Varangians are doing," Henry offered. "But, if they are, it has not yielded any useful information, at least none so far as we have been told. You will no doubt learn much more about the Varangian's efforts when you meet with Erik in the morning."

Chapter Four

The Varangians.

Erik arrived early. As usual, he arrived alone without any bodyguards. He did not need them—one look at the Erik walking along the street carrying his big battle axe was enough to scare away anyone short of a small army.

I knew him as quite an amiable fellow. Most people did not. They hurried to get out of his way when they saw him coming and, after he passed, many made the sign of the cross to thank God for keeping them safe.

It was not just the big axe Erik carried with him wherever he went, it was also his size and the scar on his heavily bearded face that gave him such a ferocious appearance. At almost six feet I was a head taller than most of my men, and Eric was at least a head taller and two stones heavier than me. As a result, he looked as ferocious and fearsome on the street as he truly was in battle. I knew that for sure because I had seen him use his axe when we fought against the Greeks.

Erik's commitment to guarding the city and whoever was on the throne was in his blood as his father and grandfather had both been Varangian guards before him. His men were reported to adore him.

On the other hand, it was possible that Erik thought he could guard the city and throne better if he himself was the Emperor who was sitting on it. One thing was certain; I could only hope that he saw me and the Company as useful allies, not as potential rivals whose galleys were no longer needed to collect the tolls and help protect the city.

Strangely enough, it was because I knew Erik that I did not fear going alone with him to the baths. He was too smart for that—if he did attack me whilst I was with him, it would be known who did it and the Company would never rest until he paid the price by being killed most horrible along with everyone who helped him.

On the other hand, if Erik was involved in an effort to seize the throne and feared I was similarly inclined, my death would be at another time and place such that the blame would fall on someone else other than Erik and his Varangians.

******

I was sitting with Michael Oremus and just finishing the breaking of my nightly fast when Erik arrived at the Commandry the next morning. He was early.

"Hoy George."

"Hoy Erik. Have you broken your nightly fast? You are welcome to join us."

"Thank you, George, but no thank you. Your offer is much appreciated, but I always get up before dawn to eat with my men who have spent the night in the city. It is one of the ways by which I keep in touch with my men and learn about the latest news and rumours."

"That sounds very wise of you, Erik, it truly does."

I said it sincerely and meant it as I pushed my plate back and got ready to stand up to go with him to the baths. Everyone around the table nodded their agreement, even my young brother and my even younger son. They were there as apprentice sergeants and nodded instinctively when their betters did.

Erik beamed at my compliment and the response of the archers. "It is something I learned from my father when he commanded the Varangians and I was just a young recruit."

A moment later I took one last swig of morning ale and swung my leg over the bench to stand up. Henry looked at me from across the table and mouthed the question "guards?" I shook my head and stood up.

My leaving alone with Erik meant they would hold him responsible if anything happened. Even Erik understood. He nodded his acceptance to Henry and gave an agreeable little shake to the axe he was holding.

******

"Your men are right to be concerned," Erik quietly offered as we made our way out of the hall. "Someone has done this thing and we still do not know who or why. My men are angry. They liked the Empress and were sworn to guard her. Her death has made all of us look weak."

A moment later he added, "and your father's death too, of course."

We continued talking as we walked down the street towards the old Roman baths. People and carts, even horse carts, tended to move out of the way if they saw us coming. Quite a few, particularly the small merchants peddling from carts, extended friendly greetings to Erik.

"The people seem to like you," I suggested.

"They like the peace we maintain and the thieves and rioters we chop; we Varangians they do like not so much."

We talked as we walked and the great columns of the Roman baths were in sight after a brisk twenty minute walk. They were standing there as they had been for almost a thousand years. That was right after man was created by God and life began.

Chapter Five

We meet again.

"Mother wanted me to be my brother's regent until he came of age. I know she did because she sent for me when she realized she was dying. I hurried as fast as possible but, unfortunately, I arrived too late. She was already gone when I got here."

Elizabeth was looking at me intently and speaking with a great sadness and hesitation in her voice. Without actually saying so she was asking me if I wanted her to continue with her tale. I nodded my agreement. We were in the Empress's chambers where my father and Elizabeth's mother had died.

From the looks of the personal possessions that were scattered about and the way the servants had hurried out when I arrived, it was clear that Elizabeth had moved in and taken over the three rooms traditionally occupied by the Empire's rulers—the outer room where the Emperors and their regents received their supplicants and conducted their Empire's business, the middle room where they slept and received their lovers, and the inner room where the Empire's treasury was kept in great coin chests. It had been that way for centuries, both under the Empire's Byzantine Greek emperors and now under the new Latin emperors.

"I first met Helen, your stepmother, the day after I arrived. We met when we went to the church at the same time to pray for their souls. The poor woman was distraught most terrible such that it is hard to believe that she could have murdered them in a fit of jealously.

"I am told that you just visited your stepmother. Is she better now, or is she still totally distraught as I have heard? So am I for that matter, distraught that is; I am still numb. The whole thing is hard to believe. I keep thinking I will wake up and find that it was a bad night dream."

"*And how would you be knowing that I just came from visiting Helen? And why are you suggesting she might be involved, eh?*"

How would Elizabeth know I had just visited Helen? That was the thought that instantly came into the space in my head behind my eyes. It left immediately, however, because Elizabeth continued to hold on to my hand and look longingly at me. It was about then that I realized she had sent her servants away and there was no one else in the room.

I promptly forgot about Helen. It was only much later that I realized that Elizabeth had very smoothly added Helen's name to the list of suspects.

As Elizabeth continued to stroke and play with my hand, I suddenly realized that I had not been with a woman since she had been in my bed several months earlier. That was just before I led my men to Venice to take our revenge and Elizabeth, already the widow of a crusader, was rushed into a peace-making marriage with the much younger boy who was the heir to the Epirus throne.

Then Elizabeth's face changed right in front of my eyes and there was fear and uncertainty in her quavering and anxious voice.

"My situation is desperate. That is why I immediately moved into my mother's rooms where the Emperor or his regent are supposed to live—so no one else would be able to move into them and claim to be the new regent or, God forbid, the new emperor."

Then she took a deep breath and continued in a quavering voice.

"I fear for my life because it is well known that my mother wanted me to take her place as my brother's regent and protect him. But many other people also want to be Robert's regent and some of them are also determined to get the throne for themselves. My mother's death has changed everything; it has given hope to all of them."

What I did not do was share what I was thinking—you may not end up being Robert's regent, but whoever does will not change the Company's agreement to collect the tolls, not if my men and I have anything to say about it.

That was what I was thinking as Elizabeth continued holding both my hands and talking softly so no one could hear us. For some reason, as she did, I my thinking suddenly changed when I realized how long it had been since Elizabeth and I had known each other—and how good it had made us both feel when we did.

As a result, my thoughts and concerns began to rapidly change as I sorrowfully nodded my head in agreement with Elizabeth's words. It had, after all, been several months since I had been alone with a woman, and that had been Elizabeth herself.

"It will be up to God who is Robert's regent, of course," Elizabeth whispered. She said it as she moved up against me to get even closer so no one could hear us. "God will tell the Pope whom he wants as Robert's regent until he comes of age. I do hope God will choose me, or you, so that Robert is not replaced and killed."

She was looking into my eyes intently as she slowly said "or you" with a great deal of emphasis. I was as stunned when she said it as I had been when Henry had suggested it earlier.

"Me?" I exploded. "Surely you jest, Elizabeth? You know I would not set aside my position in the Company just to be your brother's regent for a few years."

"Yes, I know. But someone must be the Regent and you could do it and still be the Company's Commander until Robert comes of age. If it cannot me, it must be you. One of us must hold the position if your Company is to keep collecting the tolls.

"Besides, who knows—something might happen to Robert and my husband, and then you could be the Emperor and I the Empress."

Elizabeth had looked at me intently as she said it and appeared to be relieved when I repeated my unwillingness to leave the Company. Then she pressed herself up against me and began playing with the knot that tied my tunic together around my neck.

After a few seconds, she sighed deeply and explained the problem as she saw it. *And continued rubbing her breasts up against me as she talked. It was very pleasant. She spoke so softly that I had to hold her close up against my chest in order to hear her.*

"Unfortunately there are only a few chests of coins left in the treasury, and certainly not enough to buy the necessary prayers from the Pope as my mother did with the help of your father.

"Of course, my new and dear father-in-law, the King of Epirus, could loan my husband and me enough coins to pay for the Pope' prayers for me. But I doubt that he will since he wants to be the Emperor himself. In fact, he is just as likely to buy the Pope's prayers for himself to become Robert's regent—so he will be well-placed to become the Emperor if Robert dies or is killed."

Her concern for her brother touched me. It was also something new. In the past, according to my dear father, she had not had any use for him at all. On the other hand, it was totally understandable; they were family after all.

Elizabeth paused for a moment and then continued.

"My mother only wanted the best for me. Now she is gone and I am left with only my brother to take care of me when he is old enough to become Emperor, and my husband, of course, when he grows up. *And neither is of much use or ever will be.*

"My husband, Michael, is a dear boy. He thinks he has already got me with child. I had to help him get started, of course, but he was a fast learner."

Whoa. That was fast.

Elizabeth was still holding my hand and looking at me intently. Suddenly she stepped into my arms and held her chest tight against mine. She wiggled her breasts to get even deeper into my arms and then gave a big and satisfied sigh and continued. I held her close against me; it felt deliciously good.

"Oh God I have missed you," she said softly. A moment later she brushed her hand against my now fully alert dingle and gave me an order with a strained intensity to her voice.

"Put the bars on the doors so no one can come in. I need to show you something."

Keeping everyone out of her rooms was a fine idea in view of the thoughts that had begun swirling about behind my eyes. So I quickly rushed to do as she ordered. As I did, Elizabeth added to my excitement with even more encouraging words.

"We do not have to worry about the servants or anyone walking in on us. Jeanine, my personal maid, is outside the door with orders to turn everyone away. If anyone asks, she will tell them that we are meeting to discuss improving your Company's contract to collect the tolls and protect the Regency.

"Besides, so what if someone thinks we are getting to know each other again? I have taken over as Regent and I can do whatever I want."

"And your husband?"

"No need to worry about him. He has gone off to spend the day in the city playing with his little friends. Besides, he has his own rooms on the other side of the palace."

With that she stepped once again into my arms and began rubbing up against me once again. But then she suddenly stopped.

"I want you to look at something before we .. " Her voice trailed off. And then it strengthened and she told me what exactly she wanted me to see and do.

A moment later I felt terribly let down and disappointed—because what she wanted me to look at, whatever it might be, was not anything close to what I had hoped it would be a moment earlier. It was a great wooden chest that stood on its end with its back against the wall in the corner of the room, a chest that was taller than most men.

Elizabeth opened the door to the chest and motioned for me to look at its contents. It was filled with a collection of her mother's tunics and robes. They were hanging next to one another on wooden pegs.

"Look," she said as she pulled some of the clothes aside and pointed at the back wall.

I saw nothing.

"Do you see the long crack in the wood along the side, George? And also across the top? And the heavy strip of wood that runs all along the back of the chest. I think it is a door that opens into the wall and the strip of wood is the bar that seals it from being used."

Elizabeth told me about it with the same happy and excited sound in her voice that had made me think of other things a few moments earlier.

"My mother told me there was a way for someone to get in and out of her sleeping room without anyone knowing. But she never told me where it was or how to use it. All she told me was that one of the old Byzantine emperors must have installed it in the early days when the Great Palace was being built.

"Maybe that is how your father would come to visit her when they did not want anyone to know."

She made the suggestion with a shy little smile that clearly implied we might be able to use it ourselves.

"Or maybe it is how their murderer got to them without anyone seeing," I said grimly as I pushed aside the clothes and my dingle went limp.

******

It was easy to lift and set aside the wooden bar that kept anyone from using the door to enter the Empress's room, if that is what it was. But it took quite a while to find the secret to opening the secret door so I could get though the back wall of the tall clothes chest. We finally did—when I was twisting and pulling on the pegs with clothes hanging on them.

We found out how to open the door by accident when the wooden back of the chest suddenly swung open. It happened when Elizabeth was steadying herself by touching the back of the chest whilst I was playing with one of the clothing pegs which somehow seemed to be different from the others.

The back of the clothes chest suddenly swung open like a door. Beyond it in the darkness I could make out what appeared to be a very steep and narrow stone staircase. For some reason it surprised me that it ran both up and down. The air in passage smelled musty and unused.

"Oh my God!" Elizabeth said softly. "Where does it go?"

"We will need a couple of candle lanterns for light," I said as I pushed past her and returned to the Empress' sleeping room. "We can use those that are here in the Empress's sleeping chamber."

There were five candle lanterns in the room including two that used the oil of whale fish instead of reeds filled with bees wax. There were also a large number candles in various bowls and metal candlestick holders. None of them were lit.

That there were so many lanterns and candles in the room was not surprising. It was, after all, occupied by the Emperor or his regent and was one of the biggest of the Great Palace's many rooms. And, of course, being as it was still daylight and the day was warm, none of the candles were lit.

The unlit lanterns and candles turned out to be one of several problems. The first being that the servants who lit the lanterns and candles every day did not do so until the sun began to go down. Then they lit them with a candle fetched from the kitchen.

"Go to the door and shout down to your servant that you need a candle so you can melt some wax to put a seal on a parchment," I ordered as I closed the front of the chest so the Empress's clothes and the opening into the passageway could not be seen.

"But there is no seal. I could not find it."

"It does not matter. Just do it. It is just an excuse that is believable."

It would also suggest to everyone that we were not in Elizabeth's chambers behind closed doors so I could lift her skirts and get into knowing her again in the biblical sense—which I was determined to do as soon as possible.

I looked at the lanterns as we waited for the fire to arrive. It was at that point that the second problem became apparent—the lanterns in the chamber were very ornate and heavy; it would be nigh on to impossible to carry them up and down the steep steps that through the narrow passage way.

"Shite," I muttered as I tried to lift one of the lanterns. "These will not work. They are too large and heavy. If we cannot get a regular candle lantern we will have to use candles and hope they do not blow out."

******

It seemed to take forever before a young serving girl scurried up the stairs to the Empress's room and knocked on the door. Elizabeth and I spent the time touching each other in a way that suggested it would not be long before we once again began getting to know each in the biblical sense.

I could hardly contain myself and tried to manoeuver Elizabeth towards the Empress's great bed. Elizabeth, however, was having none of it. She pushed me away and told me to wait.

Finally there was a knock on the outer door. I opened it to admit a hesitant young servant girl who very carefully went out of her way not to look at me even out of the corner of her eye as she entered.

"Light a couple of the candles so the Regent can melt wax for her seal on our new agreement," I ordered the girl.

I was pleased with myself for suggesting that Elizabeth and I had reached an agreement that needed to be sealed. It was an explanation the girl would almost certainly mention to the palace's other servants when they asked her what I was doing in Elizabeth's rooms.

A moment later I realized that I had just recognized Elizabeth as her brother's regent. Had I just been tricked into doing so? It somewhat bothered me, but not for long. There were more important things to think about.

"Light one more candle and then run back down the stairs and send someone to fetch a couple of additional candle lanterns. They must be small enough to be moved about if the Regent decides she needs more light elsewhere in her chambers."

I gave the order to the serving girl when she had finished lighting one of the candles. She still had not looked at me, not once. Someone, probably the Empress or my father, had trained her well. I spoke in the crusader French that people are starting to call English. It was the language of the palace and the Empress's court.

Elizabeth nodded her approval at my having taken charge and the orders I had given. Or perhaps she was pleased because I had acknowledged her as Robert's regent. I had no idea. But I knew that servants had ears and the word would spread that Elizabeth was in command and making decisions as her brother's regent, and that I had recognized her as the regent. It did not particularly worry me at the time.

Chapter Six

We go exploring.

An out of breath servant arrived about five minutes later with two unlit candle lanterns. She was immediately sent away and the door once again double barred. Only then did I use one of the burning candles to light both lanterns.

As soon as the lanterns were lit, I blew out the candles, picked up my unsheathed sword from where I had leaned it against the wall next to the door, and carried it and one of the lanterns to the big clothes chest. It was time for us to see what we could see. As you might imagine, I was getting more and more excited.

Elizabeth hurriedly picked up the other lantern and ran after me. We left the door to the middle room open. It did not matter. No one could get into Empress's chambers because the outer door was barred shut.

I took neither my longbow and quiver of arrows nor the galley shield I usually carried in addition to my sword when I was walking in the city's streets. They would be of little use since I would need at least one hand to carry the lantern and the other a sword. I left them in the corner of the middle room.

For a brief moment I had thought about bringing the shield and carrying it slung over my shoulder. But I instantly decided against bringing it because I only had two hands and both would be busy holding my sword and the lantern. Under my tunic, as was my practice whenever I was not with a woman or waiting for one, I was wearing my chain shirt and had a hidden knife on each wrist.

The door to passageway was still partially open because Elizabeth had suggested that we put some of the Empress's clothes on the floor of the chest so the secret door would not be able to shut behind us. It was a good idea and I nodded my appreciation at the clothes and used my foot to move them into a slightly better position. I did so as I pushed the hidden door all the way open.

****** *George Courtenay*

I entered the secret passage holding my lantern up as I high as I could get it.

"Down or up?" I asked Elizabeth as I cautiously stepped out of the chest and on to the stone floor of the staircase. I was holding the lantern up high so I could see. She was right behind me with the other lantern.

I made a decision without waiting for her response and started down.

The winding stairway was dark and the stone steps were narrow and showed signs of being worn down from years of people scuffling up and down on them. The stairs curved to the right as stairs traditionally do to make them more defendable since most men are right-handed.

The passageway seemed increasingly cool and damp as we descended even though the walls were dry when I touched them. We had to walk somewhat crouched over in order to avoid hitting our heads on the low stone ceiling, at least I did. Elizabeth being shorter was able to walk upright most of the time.

We held our lanterns in front of us and as high as possible as we went down slowly down the steps one step at a time. It was necessary to avoid hitting our heads or falling because we missed a stair step. Elizabeth stayed close was behind me. After I had gone down only three or four steps I stopped and drew my double-edged short sword.

There was no particular reason I drew my sword, but it somehow felt right to do so. I held it in my right hand and used my left hand to hold the lantern and touch the ceiling so I would not hit my head.

It was difficult to walk despite the lanterns. Every so often I scraped my knuckles from holding the lantern too high or banged my head from not holding it high enough. The ceiling was very low and the stone steps were uncommonly steep and narrow. The stairs curved tightly to the right such that one man with a sword could easily hold them against an army.

Elizabeth walked close behind me. She was almost too close so I very tersely ordered her to walk carefully and two steps further back. It was necessary in order to prevent her from bumping into me or tripping me. I had, after all, no idea how far I would tumble or where I would end up if she did.

We were going very slowly and cautiously because we did not know where we were going or what we would find along the way or when we got there. I was pleased to be wearing my chain shirt and wrist knives under my tunic. Wearing them was a family tradition.

After what seemed to be about sixty or seventy steep and winding stone steps, the passageway levelled off and became relatively flat. I was not sure, however, that it was actually flat. To the contrary, I had the impression that we were continuing to descend as Elizabeth and I slowly made our way along the passage. Our lanterns made strange shadows on the wall and ceiling as we walked.

I did not know why, but I somehow had the feeling that this part of the passageway was even more ancient than the stairs. Later, when I had time to think about it, I decided that the tunnel was probably an escape tunnel had been built at the beginnings of the city. That was probably right after God created the earth many hundreds of years ago.

The existence of an old tunnel under the Great Palace was not surprising. Every prince or noble with a somewhat reasonable mind, meaning no more than half of them according to my Uncle Thomas, had at least one such secret way to escape from wherever he was living. That was because a secret way to escape was necessary when things went totally wrong and one's prayers and indulgences failed.

Our company was no exception. We had at least one tunnel either in place or under construction for every of the Company's fortresses and shipping posts. Indeed, every one of our major holds such as our castles in England and our Cyprus fortress already had two or three secret ways to escape from it and more under construction.

Of course we had secret tunnels and other ways to escape; the world was a dangerous place and would continue to be so until Jesus returned and there was peace on earth. Hopefully, of course, that would not be for a few more years so we would have enough time to fill our coin chests before people no longer needed us to protect them or carry them away to safety.

Our immediate problem was that Great Palace was so much older and so much larger than any of our holdings and that there was no knowing how many tunnels and escaped routes it might have acquired over the years—and every one of them could have been used to secretly enter the palace and kill my father.

But where did the tunnel from the Empress's room lead and, more importantly, was it used by whoever murdered my father?

Elizabeth and I came to a side tunnel in the passageway after about three or four hundred paces of walking in the darkness holding our lanterns out in front of us. It was an even smaller tunnel that branched off to the left and it too seemed to descend and been little used. More importantly, however, and just beyond entrance to the smaller tunnel I could see an opening in the wall that turned out to be the entrance to another staircase.

We stopped in front of the smaller tunnel whilst I tried to decide which way to go. I also stopped because I suddenly felt a great urge to piss. Accordingly, I handed my lantern to Elizabeth and pissed against the tunnel wall. It was right after I finished pissing that we heard the scurrying of little feet ahead of us in the darkness.

Mice or rats for sure. Where are the city's numerous cats when you need them? And why have they not been able to get in and take these?

Barely had we resumed walking and taken more than two or three steps when suddenly, for a few moments, there were very faint and indecipherable voices somewhere in the distance. We both instinctively stopped walking and froze.

"Shh,"

I gave the order quietly and unnecessarily as we stopped and listened to the distant voices. They faded away a few seconds later. There was no way to know where the voices were coming from or how far away they might have been. As you might imagine, we stood still and waited silently for quite some time after they ended.

"Wait here," I finally whispered to Elizabeth. "I am going to see where these stairs go."

"Stay here alone? Not on your life. I am coming with you," she quietly hissed back at me in a quavering but determined voice as she returned my lantern.

"Alright then. But be damn quiet and watch where you walk," I whispered.

I did not really need to order Elizabeth to be quiet, of course, but I did; and it somehow made me feel better to know that I was in control of something even if it was only Elizabeth.

I climbed the new stone stairs very slowly, one step at a time, in an effort not to make even the slightest noise. The stairs were narrow and set in a winding stone staircase that wound tightly to the right in order to make them more defendable against anyone attempting to climb them. They were just like the stairs that came down from the Empress's sleeping room. *Of course they were; they were probably built at the same time.*

My sword was pointed up the stairs and my lantern held high as I climbed. As I did, I realized that the dusty stairs I was slowly climbing were totally empty just like all the rest of the passage. We had seen nothing on any of the stairs or in the tunnel, not even the faint smell of long ago piss or shite.

In fact, the only thing we had had seen in the tunnel so far were the tracks of people who had left a record of their passage by walking in the heavy layer of dust that covered the floor of the tunnel. I had seen many an escape tunnel, but this was the first one that was totally empty of such things as old tools and broken ladders.

The emptiness of the tunnel was strange and somehow seemed to be significant. But I had not a clue as to why that might be.

****** *An unknown scribe*

George and Elizabeth held their lanterns high and out in front of them as they worked their way very slowly up the tightly winding stairs. Suddenly, there was a small wooden door in the side of the wall even though the stairs continued upward. They stopped when they reached the door. Whatever was on the other side, if anything, was totally silent.

"Shh," George said as he held his lantern up. What he could see, and it was not much, was that the door was very much like the door to the Empress's bedroom. At least he thought it was. He could not be sure because he had not looked closely at the *back* of the door to the Empress's chamber.

In fact, he had not looked at the back of the door in the Empress's chest at all—they had used clothes from her chest to hold it open. It was a bad mistake and George realized it as soon as he saw the door in front of him. How did it open? And was it barred like the one in the Empress's clothing chest?

George very carefully and quietly put his lantern down on one of the stone steps that continued upward. Then he gently pressed his ear against the door and listened. Elizabeth held her lantern up so he could see. After a while, he shook his head. Nothing.

He was still listening more than a minute later when an impatient Elizabeth moved up next to him and began running her hand along the top of the wooden frame that held the door.

Suddenly there was a "click" and the door moved a couple of inches. They both gasped and George instinctively brought the point of his sword closer to the door. Nothing happened.

They waited silently for several minutes before George slowly pushed the door open. It opened into another clothes chest and this one's front door was open so that they could see all the way into the empty room beyond the chest. It was dimly lit by light coming in from around the edges of the shutter-covered wall openings and barred entrance door. And it looked familiar.

"I think this is my father's room," George said so softly that no one heard him.

A moment later, despite the dim light, he was able to see the bar on the room's main door. No one could get in. At that point, he decided it was safe to climb into the chest and on into the room. He was immediately struck by the room's somewhat foul smell. It was as if its bedding had gone mouldy and its piss bucket had not been emptied for some time. Probably both, he decided.

Getting off the stairs and into the room was easier said than done. The door to the passageway was too small, much smaller than its counterpart in the Empress's chest. But he managed to squeeze through the doorway and was soon all the way into the room. Elizabeth was right behind him.

"Yes, this is his room. I recognize his old tunic and his extra pair of sandals. And there are his wrist knives and his his sword and chain shirt and his longbow and quiver. He must have left them when he went to visit the Empress."

It was about then that the reality of what George was looking at struck him. His father had gone to visit the Empress and left his chain shirt and weapons behind because he did not expect danger to be waiting for him.

Moreover, the door to the outside hallway was still barred as his father had undoubtedly left it—which meant no one could have come in to use the secret passageway to get to the Empress's chambers and kill him. Another entrance must have been used.

Chapter Seven

We march to the palace.

Commander Courtenay was accompanied by his usual guard of four archers when he left the Great Palace and walked back to the Commandry that afternoon. He was, they later commented to each other whilst visiting a local tavern, lost in thought and walking fast with a look of determination on his face. Something was up and the four of them spent the rest of the evening drinking bowls of wine and speculating as to what it might be.

Something being in the wind, they all agreed, was nothing new for the Company or its Commander. Indeed, they also agreed and assured each other sagely as they sipped their wine; it was to be expected because of the Venetian raid and the recent deaths of the Commander's father and the Empress.

It was, however, what the Commander did when he reached the Commandry that ended up truly surprising everyone. He walked into the great hall where two of his lieutenant commanders, Henry and Michael, were working on the Company's accounts and records with the help of their apprentices, and began giving orders that brought both men to their feet with a flood of questions.

"I need Lieutenant Richmond and a dozen or so good swordsmen here tomorrow first thing in the morning right after they have broken their nightly fasts. They cannot be too tall or be afraid of being underground in mines and tunnels. Men who have had experience working in mines would be the best.

"And here is something important—only you two, and Harold because you will be taking some of his men, are to know about the tunnels and that it would be best if the men were miners and not overly tall. It is an important secret that they will be going into the tunnels so the three of you will have to choose the men yourselves and not tell them or anyone else why they were selected.

"Oh, and we need to send someone to the market to buy a couple of dozen easily carried candle lanterns. If anyone asks, they are to say we need more light in the Commandry at night when we are working late."

It was, and there was no doubt about it, an unexpected order with unexpected requirements. Lieutenant Richmond was thought to be one of the Company's very best swordsmen. He had, for instance, proved his fighting ability to Commander Courtenay in a battle at the Athens slave market to free some captured British sailors. But swordsmen who were "not too tall" and "all seasoned fighting men; no young ones or apprentices?" George's two lieutenants clamoured for an explanation.

"Clear the room," the Commander ordered. "And you three," he told their wide-eyed young apprentices, his son, his younger brother, and Archie as he pointed at them, "are to go to the market right now and buy two dozen candle lanterns for use here in the Commandry. Buy only small ones that a man can easily carry from one place to another with one hand.

Normally George would have sent his own apprentice to fetch them, but he still had not selected an apprentice sergeant to replace the man who had recently been promoted to be the lieutenant on one of the captured Venetian galleys.

"And one more thing—you three are never to discuss what you just heard or anything about the lanterns or tunnels, not even with each other, or even hint to anyone about them or anything about the men or how the men and lanterns might be used. It might endanger our men if word gets out."

Everyone hurried to obey. After supping with his lieutenants that evening and explaining his plan, George took one of the lanterns that had been fetched from the market and walked back to the Empress's palace to spend the night. His four guards went with him and then continued on to visit a particularly friendly tavern. They would accompany him back to the Commandry in the morning.

Sometime later, at the tavern, the most junior of the four guards commented as to where he thought George intended to spend the night. And he would have been right. Had anyone been able to get through the barred door to the room of George's father that night, he would have seen the room to be empty with only George's chain shirt and wrist knives on the bed and an open door in the upright chest where his father had hung his clothes.

****** *Lieutenant Harry Richmond*

I was having one of my black days when all I could think about was losing Anne and my old life in Grimsby. Then everything changed. A courier from the Commandry was rowed out to my galley, Number Seventy-one, on which I was serving as Captain Blacks's lieutenant. He brought a message to the captain ordering him to have me report to the Commandry first thing in the morning with my sword and a galley shield.

Captain Black did not tell me why I had been summoned. More than likely he did not know. But he knew something was up because I was supposed to bring a sword and galley shield and leave my longbow and arrows behind. He also knew I was the best swordsman in the Company and had several times been given special assignments because of it. I had spilled a lot of blood carrying them out and was a lieutenant as a result.

The captain promptly agreed to let me spend the rest of the day practicing my swordsmanship with some of the better swordsmen in our crew. We had to use practice swords, of course, but they were better than nothing.

The prospect of action! What else could it be? It excited me and totally changed everything by letting me think about something other than what I had left behind in Grimsby. I spent the rest of the day sharpening my sword and practicing against the three most useful swordsmen in my galley's crew.

Early the next morning I was among the first few men in my galley's food line. That was when I found that Captain Black had once again shown me that he is a good man. During the night he had moved our galley to the quay. I am sure he did so in order that I might get ashore quickly.

In any event, I was fully ready despite a somewhat sleepless night and was able to present myself at the Commandry gate a few minutes after dawn. I was immediately allowed to pass through the gate and enter the Commandry's bailey. To my surprise and pleasure, I found a dozen or so other men reporting in at the same time who were also carrying swords and shields.

What was most encouraging of all was that every man waiting in the bailey with me was a veteran chosen man or sergeant with a sword on his belt and multiple battle dots on his tunic. I recognized several of them as useful swordsmen and was particularly pleased to find that I had the highest rank among them. There was the usual pre-battle sense of tenseness and good fellowship in the air. It was wonderful.

Our curiosity was great and every man's spirits were high as we filed into the Commandry's great hall a couple of minutes later. They got even higher when we were each given a bowl of wine and Commander Courtenay told us what we would be doing. What we heard certainly surprised us.

"Men, you are here because each of you is an experienced fighting man who knows how to defend himself with his sword and shield if he is attacked.

"This is the situation we face: There are tunnels under the Empire's Great Palace, how many we do not know. We also do not know where the tunnels lead or who we will find at the other end of them. What we do know is that one of them comes up to the room in which the Empress and my father were killed.

"What we are going to do is search the tunnels to see what we can find. Our problem is that we may surprise innocent people when we come out of the tunnel entrances. They may think *we* are invaders or robbers and try to fight us off.

"You have each been selected because you are known to be steady men and very good with swords and shields, men who can be counted on to be steady enough to defend themselves *without* killing the innocents and friends who do not understand what is happening and think they are being attacked.

"So here is the order of the day: We are going to search the tunnels and you are to defend yourselves and your mates if we are attacked, but you are not to make any effort to kill or seriously wound anyone unless it is absolutely necessary."

****** *Lieutenant Commander Henry Harcourt.*

"I may have white hair, George, but I am still your deputy and battle advisor when the Company fights on land; so I am going with you and your swordsmen and that is the long and short of it."

Those were my indignant words after we heard the details of George's plan and I realized he did not intend to take me with him. I leaned over the table and shook my finger in his face as I said them. And as I did I thought of something and added it to my argument.

"Besides, you need me because you have already made a mistake by forgetting something *we* will need when *we* are in the tunnels." I emphasized the word "we."

"Alright, Uncle Henry, alright. It is your right; I surrender; you can come. And what, pray tell, do *we* need that I forgot?"

"*We* need to take a couple of heavy axes or large hammers with us in case we come to a door or wall that needs to be broken down, eh?"

George just looked at me for a moment whilst he thought about what I said. Then he broke into a smile and nodded.

"Damn, Uncle Henry, you are right. We are likely to need one. I should have thought of that." A moment later he began giving the first of many orders. The first was to my apprentice, his younger brother and the oldest of the three apprentices.

"John, you and Young George and Archie are to run to the market and buy a couple of big hammers or axes. They have to be heavy enough that we can use them to batter down a door. And you are not to say a word to anyone, not even to each other, about why you are buying it or who you are buying it for. Do you understand?"

"Aye Commander, not a word to anyone," John said solemnly as Young George and Archie nodded their agreement.

We watched them go. No one said a word until they cleared the hall.

"A log from the market's wood lot would probably have been better," Harold suggested.

"Your father used one in Alexandria when Moors tried to kill him years ago. Henry and I had just joined the Company when it happened. That was right after what was left of the Company's archers stopped crusading and got into the trade of carrying passengers and cargo.

"Four of us grabbed the log by the stubs of its branches and swung it against the door. It worked quite well."

And then we had to listen as Harold once again told the tale of how the door of a couple of murderous Moorish merchants had been battered down in the middle of the night with a hurriedly trimmed log. Harold had been there because he was the pilot of the galley George's father had been sailing on and could speak a bit of the Moorish gobble; I had been there as one of the fighting men William, George's father, had taken with him.

It had happened when George's father led some of our men in a night time raid against a couple of Moorish merchants. That was many years ago in the Company's early days right after its survivors had stopped crusading and had somehow acquired a couple of galleys and began using them to earn coins by carrying refugees and cargos.

William, George's father, went after the Moors because they had hired assassins who tried to kill him on Alexandria's quay. The assassins almost got him because he was foolish enough to climb on to the quay without carrying a weapon or wearing his chain shirt. I had come to his assistance and he had marked me for it. As you might imagine, going out in public unarmed was a mistake that William never ever made again.

What Harold did not mention was that Moors had good reason to be unhappy with William, George's father, and try to kill him—because he was the Commander of what was left of the Company and we had just taken a couple of their transports as prizes and brought them into Alexandria to sell.

It had to be done, the capture and subsequent tossing into the sea of the assassins and the Moors who had hired them. The Company was just getting started in the carrying of passengers and cargos; we would not have been able to attract custom if people thought the Company was so weak it could not defend its own people. Besides, the Moors deserved it and revenge was required by the Company's charter.

****** *Lieutenant Harry Richmond*

Commander Courtenay's words both inspired me and depressed me. What we were to do was certainly different from how we usually spent our days. That was good since it took my mind away from Anne and Ramsgate. What was depressing was that it did not sound like there would be much chance of the serious fighting that I constantly craved.

We filed out of the Commandry's hall and formed up two abreast in the bailey. Two of our twelve swordsmen were given great long-handled hammers to carry in addition to their swords.

Our round galley shields were slung over our backs as we set off for wherever we were being led. A small horse-cart led by a couple of apprentice sergeants followed immediately behind us. Its cargo was covered by an old sail.

Just before we got underway the Commander ordered the men with the hammers to put them on the cart and cover them with the sail. I caught a glimpse of the cart's other cargo as they did. It was candle lanterns with their candles already in them. The Commander obviously did not want the lanterns seen. But why?

We left as soon as the hammers were safely stowed away and covered. The Commander led the way.

At the Commander's request, I called the chants as we marched behind him from the Commandry to the Great Palace. We marched in a column of twos. There was no drum, but the cadence of my calls and the men's chanted answers were more than enough to let each man put his foot down at the same time as everyone else. It was a nice morning and the sun was not yet scorching hot.

Fortunately, the city's streets were not yet crowded. Even so, our passage was periodically hindered by the women along the edges of the street cooking their families' morning flatbreads and the gaggles of children gathered around them. There were also a number of carts parked along the side of the streets and moving along them.

The women and children we passed eyed us with great interest, and some of the older children began following us and trying to march with us. Great clowders of cats were everywhere either sleeping or begging for food and arguing over the scraps that were sometimes thrown to them.

People walking in the streets tended to give way and carts were often pulled aside as we approached. As you might imagine, the Commander led us down the middle of the streets in an effort to avoid the carts, the cooking fires, and the poop.

After a while, we came upon a trio of axe-carrying Varangian guards, their great battle axes in hand, standing on a corner watching the activity on the streets around them. They pulled themselves to attention and saluted as we passed. The Varangians were friends and allies so we returned the courtesy and smiled at them. I had always wondered how it would be to fight one of them.

Our line of march was entirely in the city's Latin Quarter. The people we passed seemed quite friendly, no doubt because they thought we would always fight on their side because we gobbled crusader French and made the sign of the cross correctly. Children, mostly young boys, were constantly joining us and pretending to march until they got sufficiently bored and dropped away.

After about twenty minutes we were on a fine cobble-stoned street that took us past the huge Wisdom of God Church, the big one which the local people called the "Hagía Sophía," its Latin name, even though they were not sure what it meant because only their priests spoke Latin.

Beyond the huge church, the street continued on into an open park-like area with grass and big trees. Among the trees were several small ponds and a number of statues. Beyond the park was a building with two floors that was almost certainly the barracks of the Varangian Guards. And just beyond the barracks stood the high wall that surrounded the Great Palace itself and its park-like bailey.

The gate to the Great Palace's bailey was swung open by a pair of Varangian guards as soon as we approached it. Arrangements had obviously been made and we were expected. A long line of horse carts and man carts were waiting to enter. Their drivers and pullers watched as we marched past them. A few of them smiled and nodded, but most of them just looked at us impassively.

Commander Courtenay led the way as we marched into the palace's bailey. A huge giant of a Varangian was waiting for us in the middle of the bailey. He was holding a great axe but greeted the Commander with a big smile and a great flourishing bow of welcome with wide-spread arms. The Commander smiled back and bowed similarly. It was clear to all of us that we were among friends.

The Varangian and Commander Courtenay talked briefly, and then the Commander led us to one of the more distant entrance doors on the far side of the palace. The big Varangian came with us. I had seen the palace from the city wall when we were fighting off the Greeks, but never up close. It was made of stone and it was huge with many shuttered openings in its walls that could be opened to admit day's light and then shut to keep out the dangerous night airs.

We waited again when we reached one of the doors and the Commander and the Varangian talked again, but not for very long. When they finished, the Commander walked back to us and we were given a short break and told to piss and poop near the bailey wall. To my surprise the bailey's pissing spot was not in a low spot such that it would run out. The empire was clearly not as advanced as the Company in such matters.

When we finished pissing, the two hammers were returned to the men assigned to them and every man including the Commander was handed one of the unlit candle lanterns the cart had been carrying. Then we all marched into the Great Palace itself.

I appreciated the piss break. It was something an experienced captain or commander lets his men do before he sends them into a fight. I found it quite encouraging. Perhaps it meant there might be fighting.

Chapter Eight

We are surprised several times.

Commander Courtenay and the big Varangian led us into the Empress's palace. They entered first with the lieutenant commander and one of the two hammer carriers right behind them. The swordsmen and I followed them. The two apprentices remained with the now-empty horse cart.

I had no idea what any of my fellow archers thought about the Great Palace, but it certainly impressed me. It was by far the biggest and grandest building I had ever been in. The door we entered suggested the grandeur and importance of the palace. It was not the main entrance but, even so, a man did not even have to duck his head to enter.

Stairs running upwards and two Varangian guards were immediately in front of us as soon as we came through the entrance door. The stairs were certainly not built for defence; they did not curve and were so wide that people walking up them down them could easily pass each other at the same time.

Immediately off to the right after we entered we could see into what appeared to be a hall with several groups of people sitting and talking on benches set against several wooden tables; to the left was a long corridor. The people sitting on the benches stopped talking and stared at us in surprise.

We did not stop. Our leather sandals made loud click and clacks such that we sounded like a horde of locusts as the Commander and the Varangian led us up the stairs. When we reached the top we turned left and walked a few steps down a long hallway which was lighted by the sun streaming in from a number of wall openings all along it. There was another axe-carrying Varangian standing next to a big and ornately carved door. The door could be seen by the two Varangians at the bottom of the stairs.

Somehow, without being told, we knew that we were approaching the entrance to the Empress's private rooms, the rooms where everyone says she and the Commander's father were murdered.

We entered through the door to the Empress's chambers and without slowing down walked straight through the first room to an open door on the far side of the room.

The first room, the one we initially entered and walked through, was huge. It was almost as large as our Commandry's hall. It had a chair sitting on some kind of raised deck at the far end and there were all kinds of woven sails with many colours covering the wooden floor. An exquisitely carved wooden table and a row of sitting stools with backs on them were lined up against the wall on the left.

Colourful sails of some kind and sizes were also hanging close together, one after another, on all the walls. Some of them had designs and outlines of horses and people and faces on them. My mates and I could not help ourselves; we stared at the room in open-mouthed surprise as we passed through it.

On the far side of the first room there was an open door that was the entrance to a second room. The second room was large, but nowhere near as large as the first. Even so, it was one of the biggest rooms I had ever been in. It was at least three times the size of our galley's stern castle.

The second room had a very large string bed, a finely carved table with drinking bowls and a pitcher on it, a piss pot under a stool in the far corner, three sitting stools with backs on them, and a large chest against the wall that stood as tall as a man. There was also a second small table with a sitting stool next to it and a writing quill and parchments on it.

Brightly coloured sails and fur blankets covered the bed, the floor, and most of the walls. I saw everything in the room up close and had plenty of time to do so because that was where we halted.

There was a door in the far wall of the second room and another door on the wall to the right. Both of the doors were closed. My first thought on seeing the closed doors was that breaking them open was why we had brought the big hammers.

But I was wrong; we did not begin by breaking down one or both of the closed doors. Instead, a lighted candle was produced and one after another the candle lanterns we were carrying were lit.

When the lanterns were all properly flamed, the Commander drew his sword, uttered the command "no talking and watch your heads," and, to everyone's great surprise, he entered the upright shipping chest with his sword in one hand and a candle lantern in the other. Those of us who were near him watched as he stepped through a large hole in the rear of the chest.

The Varangian moved to follow the Commander but was elbowed aside by the lieutenant commander. He, the Varangian that is, just shrugged and became the third man to walk into the upright chest. I was the fourth.

We had all drawn our swords when the Commander drew his. Our shields, however, were still slung over our backs. The Varangian was the only man without a sword or shield; he carried, instead, a great axe. And from the ease with which he had been carrying it, it was likely that it never left his hand, even when he was sleeping.

My candle lantern and those of the men in front of began making strange shadows as we too ducked our heads and moved slowly and cautiously through the upright chest and into the narrow stone passageway that lay beyond it.

It was instantly obvious in the flickering light that we had stepped on to a narrow and winding staircase that ran both up and down. The lights in front of me went down the stairs so I held my lantern as high as I could and followed them. No one said a word. It was surprisingly cool.

My thoughts as I stepped out of the chest and smelled the cool and musty air were that I was pleased to be where I was and about to do whatever it might be that I was about to do— and glad I had peed in the bailey.

We proceeded down the stairs in the flickering light. It was so quiet and we walked so carefully that I could hear my heart pounding and the sounds of the men breathing and the scuffling of their feet. No one including me was walking with big strong steps. On the other hand, there was no feeling or scent of fear in the air, just excitement and anticipation.

It did not take long before we reached the bottom of the stairs and began walking along a flat rocky surface. We were in a tunnel that was so low that we had to crouch over to avoid banging our heads and the shield slung over our backs. Even worse, it was so narrow that we could only walk in a single file with our heads leaning forward. It was the first time I had ever been in a tunnel.

Most of the tunnel seemed to be carved out of rock. But not all of it; every so often we came to a section where the sides and roof of the tunnel were made of carefully stacked stones and rocks.

After a bit of walking, and more than a little banging our heads and the top of our shields on the tunnel roof, we came to an even smaller cross tunnel.

The Commander whispered an order to me.

"Lieutenant, remain here with the men I do not take as our rear guard."

It was an understatement to say that I was disappointed.

"Aye Commander, I am to stay and command the rear guard," I whispered back. "But begging the Commander's pardon, I respectfully suggest that I am the best swordsman in the Company and should be forward with you."

And then, God bless him, the lieutenant commander walking behind me spoke up.

"Lieutenant Richmond is right George," he whispered. "He should be up front with you. Sergeant Livingston is a steady man and senior. He can walk last and command the rear."

"Oh aye, that sounds reasonable. Make it so."

Thank you Jesus and all the saints.

******

The Commander went first and led us down the side tunnel. I squeezed past the men who had been walking between us until I was right behind him—with my sword in one hand and a lantern in the other.

We walked and walked and walked. It seemed like miles, probably because I had to walk bent forward and periodically banged my lantern hand because I was trying to hold it as high as possible, and, less frequently, my head and shield. It did not take long before I had absolutely no idea how far we had come or which direction we were walking.

The tunnel seemed forever and we got thirstier and thirstier as we walked and crawled, at least I did. At times it looked as if the tunnel itself had been hacked out of solid stone; other times the earth must have been less solid because large stones had been stacked in curved arches to prevent a collapse.

We had long ago sheathed our swords so we could hold an empty hand up to feel the ceiling when it got lower. It was the only way to protect our heads and shields from constantly bumping them on the uneven ceiling. And all too often they did despite our efforts.

Suddenly the tunnel came to an abrupt end. We came upon it so unexpectedly after walking for so long that I took a couple additional steps and stepped on the Commander's heel when he stopped. I quickly apologized and begged his pardon.

And I was not the only one who hit the man who had unexpectedly stopped in front of him—behind us we could hear a string of muttered curses and quiet apologies as some of the men walking behind us bumped into each other when the man in front of them unexpectedly stopped after more than an hour of constant walking and periodic crawling when the tunnel roof was too low.

"We must have missed something," the Commander said when we while we were holding up our lanterns and examining the end of the tunnel in disbelief. There was a more than a little sound of frustration in his voice.

One of the men behind us spoke up.

"It may have been my imagination, but I think my hand touched a piece of wood aloft a while back. We went right under it. It could have been covering some sort of hole in the roof."

"How far back?" someone asked. I think it was the lieutenant commander.

"About five minutes ago" was the reply shouted from somewhere behind us. "Someone else added, "I think I felt it too."

"Everyone turn around and start walking back the way we came," the Commander ordered. "And everyone hold a hand up to touch the roof." A moment later he added, "And do not bunch up. Give the man in front of you enough room."

We moved out smartly, or at least as smartly as one can move when walking hunched over like an old crone. Sure enough, a few minutes later there was a shout from somewhere ahead of us.

"Here, by God; I think I found it. There is wood here for sure."

"Commander coming through," the Commander shouted. "Everybody hold their place and let me squeeze past. And stop your damn talking."

Chapter Nine

An interesting find.

It did not take long for George to squeeze past the men in the tunnel and reach what we hoped was the tunnel's exit. What the Commander saw and felt in the flickering light was a blackened piece of wood. It looked as though it had not been disturbed for a long time. It also looked as if it were too narrow to be hiding an exit.

"Perhaps it is a hole for letting in fresh air?" Someone suggested. "Or a deliberately small exit hole that could be dug out in an emergency."

Commander Courtenay thought for a moment, and then made what turned out to be a very bad decision—he poked at the wood with his sword.

There was a loud "crack" and, a moment or so after the sword touched the wood, it gave way. It fell apart and dropped a great mass of wood and dirt and rocks onto the men standing below it.

There was a moment of chaos and startled screams in the sudden cloud of dust and the darkness, and then a great scramble began to dig out those who had been buried. We may never have been in a tunnel before, but we knew we had to dig them out before it was too late.

Not all the men and lanterns were covered by the downfall, just the Commander and the man who had been next to him who had been directly under it. There were still lanterns and men on both sides of the downfall. Those of us who were closest began digging frantically even before the dust settled and they stopped coughing and choking.

The survivors nearest the downfall attacked the pile of debris with our bare hands and threw whatever we grabbed behind us. Those who were further away from the fall then passed it back deeper into the tunnel.

Several of the archers were on the palace side of collapse, but most were trapped on the dead-end side of the fall. They all instantly understood what was at stake and worked desperately. They used their hands like dogs using their paws to try to dig a fox out of a hole.

"Holy Shit," said one of them as he saw in dimly lit dust what he had grabbed and was about to put behind him for the next man to push even further back into the tunnel. It was a skull. He threw it behind him and kept digging with his bare hands.

****** *Lieutenant Richmond*

There was one man between me and the dirt and rocks that had fallen into the tunnel. I coughed and the dust blinded me but I set my lantern down behind me and moved up next to him. We began desperately digging into the pile of dirt and sticks with our bare hands.

 Suddenly I felt a sandaled foot. It seemed to be twitching and trying to move. I grabbed it with both hands and pulled. The sandal came off but nothing moved. I threw it behind me and kept on grabbling and throwing rocks and sticks and handfuls of dirt,

The man next to me was a sergeant by the name of Hardy from Galley Forty-five. He and I were on our knees and frantically pulling away rocks and pieces of wood from around the leg. We grabbed hold of it and pulled again. And again nothing happened. A moment later we uncovered another leg. So again we dug our hands into the debris and pulled more rocks and wood away. We pulled again. This time there was some movement.

I braced my feet as best I could, and grunted hard as I gave another great pull. Still nothing. I moved backward and knocked over my lantern as I moved to get my legs out in front of me and got my feet firmly up against some kind of rock that was sticking out from the side of the tunnel.

Sergeant Hardy, although I did not know it at the time, was doing the same thing. I pulled again with all my strength on one of the legs while Hardy did the same and pulled on the other. Somewhere along the way we had both shrugged off our shields so we could move more freely.

It worked. We both went over on our backs as the Commander's body popped out of the dirt and rocks like the plug in a foot archer's water flask. Hardy and I were both flat on our backs when the Commander's body came free and landed on top of us. He was gasping great deep breaths and coughing in the dust-filled darkness. So was I, for that matter, but nothing like the Commander.

"Help," he croaked as he took in great gasps of air and coughed each time he did. "Help." The tunnel was full of dust and it was totally dark except for some flickering light from a candle lantern somewhere behind us

There was not much we could do to help him. So we shouted at the men behind us to "pull him off of us and further back."

A moment later he was pulled off of us. Then we sat up and returned to once again desperately trying to clear away the rubble from the collapsed tunnel. I did not know until much later, but I had bloodied the back of my head when I went over backwards and hit the rocky floor of the tunnel.

It did not take long before Sergeant Hardy and I could hear someone doing the same thing on the other side of the pile of debris. We redoubled our efforts. Less than a minute later, about the time that I realized that everybody in the tunnel was shouting orders at everyone else and my hands were hurting most terrible, we broke through.

Thank you Jesus and all the saints.

****** *Lieutenant Commander Henry Harcourt*

The sudden collapse of the tunnel came as a total surprise and caused a great cloud of dust to surround us. It immediately became impossible to see what had happened because of the dust and because of the loss of some of the lanterns.

There was a moment of silence and then much swearing, coughing, and shouting. I lifted my tunic to protect my eyes. They had instantly become full of dust and grit.

"Jake and the Commander were under it when it fell," someone shouted from somewhere ahead of me. *Mother of God.*

"Stop talking and dig them out, goddamn you. Dig them out. Hurry, lads, faster, faster."

I shouted my orders as I put my lantern down and tried to push my way past the men in front of me. Everyone was coughing and shouting similar orders at everyone else.

I got past a couple of men and then, whilst still having a severe coughing fit, began being hit in the face with dirt and stones being thrown back into the tunnel by the men in front of me. They had thrown off their shields and were using their bare hands in an effort to clear away the debris, and throwing it behind them as they did.

"Stop panicking and do your duty," the man I was trying to pass snarled at me as I tried to get around him to reach George. He said it whilst pushing and throwing debris behind him at a prodigious rate. It was not an order I wanted to hear.

The man who had shouted at me and prevented me from passing him was a stocky red-bearded sergeant by the name of Sam Keene. I vowed to look him up and put him in his proper place if we survived. Of course I would remember him; he had embarrassed me in front of the men by keeping his head whilst I was losing mine.

****** *Sergeant Samuel Keene.*

We was all coughing and digging and shouting at first. The dust was still most fearsome, but it had lessened by the time we pulled Jake and the Commander free and cleared away enough of the fall to be able to see and talk to our mates on the other side. It was about then that I realized my eyes and hands hurt most fierce. And every time I took a breath my chest hurt too.

I stopped my desperate pawing at the downfall and fell backwards in exhaustion as soon as I felt the hand of someone digging on the other side of the fall. A few moments later someone pulled me further back into the tunnel and took my place.

It was about then that I screamed from the pain. My hands began to really hurt and so did my chest. The pain was worse than after the Moor stabbed me a couple of years earlier and knocked me off the boarding ladder.

In the distance I could hear someone shouting to "go get water and sleeping skins to put them on."

Sleeping skins? They must be mad. This is no time to sleep. We have got to get out of here. I started to say something, but nothing came out. And then I think I remember bumping along the floor of the tunnel.

I woke up when I was being pulled into the fancy room where we started and someone holding my head up for a drink. There were people talking and moving about but they were so blurry in my eyes that I could not see who they were.

All of a sudden someone began pouring a bucket of water on my eyes and trying to give me a drink from a bowl. That helped and for some reason I tried to sit up. What I remember most was having dirt in my mouth and spitting it out along with some of the water. Then my hands began burning like they were in a fire.

"My hands. Pour some on my hands," I managed to gasp." Someone did and then I was so tired I somehow went back to sleep. At least that's what old Peter Pewter from Galley Seventy-eight told me when my hands gave me a great pain and woke me up.

It was quiet when I woke up. And it was a different room. "Water," I croaked as started to sit up. It was about then that I realized my tunic was gone and my hands were burning and felt heavy. "Water for God's sake."

A tall man with a robe covered with all kinds of symbols sewn on it came over immediately with a bowl. He and a serving girl helped me sit up and drink from it. It was wine with a strange taste.

It was about then, when I held up my hands to help guide the bowl to my mouth, that I first realized my hands were heavy because they were wrapped in some wet and dirty rags that smelled like olive oil. I looked at them in surprise when I finished drinking. My hands hurt underneath the rags.

"Olive oil?"

"Yes, oil pressed from the olive. Your hands are wounded from digging with them. Olive oil will sooth the pain and help them heal faster. It is well known that this is true. Sacrificing a white chicken and certain prayers are also helpful.

"I am the Empress's Greek physician, Apostolos of Nicea. You and several other English men are in my care. You are in the Commander's room in the Great Palace. He is still being attended to in the Empress's rooms."

"Will he survive, the Commander?"

"Oh, I should think so. He did not stop breathing for very long—thanks to you I am told. Now lie back and let the girl pour water on you to wash off the dirt."

Chapter Ten

We get ready to return to the tunnels.

Three days later we tried again. Commander Courtenay had recovered whilst residing in the room next to the Empress's. The Regent, for that is how the Empress's daughter, Elizabeth, was now styling herself, had insisted on him remaining there so that help could be summoned available "in the event he suffers a relapse."

Elizabeth had been quite busy ever since she moved into the Empress's rooms. She was now issuing orders, making decisions, and requiring everyone in the court of the late Empress, meaning the foreign ambassadors and the courtiers who were there for the free food and gossip, to address her as "Your Majesty" if they wished to remain.

George was in surprisingly good spirits when he addressed the new and larger group of sword carrying archers Henry had brought in to accompany him. He met them in the palace's great hall in the early morning before the free-loading courtiers arrived.

It was a fully recovered Commander who met them. He had stopped coughing soon after being pulled out of the tunnel and had been taken in a horse cart later that afternoon to the city's baths to get rid of the dust that had continued to vex him until it was washed away.

It probably helped that the new Regent had been extremely solicitous of his health; she had ordered that he remain nearby in the event he suffered a relapse and she was needed to direct the efforts to revive him. Fortunately the room next to hers was available as the Regent's young husband, who had begun residing there, had been sent back to Epirus with what the Regent described as "a very important message" for his father.

****** *Lieutenant Commander Henry Harcourt*

Not all of the swordsmen in the original party of tunnel explorers were going with George on his second attempt to investigate the tunnels. Two of the original men had severely damaged their hands digging him out and another had been allowed to beg off and return to his galley. The excused man had reluctantly made the request on the grounds that the mere thought of being in another cave-in gave him the shaking and sweating pox.

More than enough new men had been added, however, such that the second party of tunnel explorers was substantially larger than the first. It was also better equipped in that every man was carrying a hastily acquired small water skin, some cheese, and a piece of chicken that had already been burnt and was ready to eat.

What no one was carrying this time was a shield slung over his shoulder. That was because we had found in our previous trip through the tunnels that the shields stuck up too high such that they would periodically scrape up against the tunnel's ceiling—and ceilings, we had also found, can collapse.

Our second tunnel search began late due to a well-intentioned idea gone wrong. George, learning from his near-fatal recent experience, had initially required that every man enter the tunnel with a long line of ships' rope tied to each of his ankles. The idea being that in the event of another cave-in, the men walking behind someone caught by in the downfall could be located and pulled free using the rope that trailed out behind him.

It was a splendid idea, except that it did not work. What we quickly learned was that the men walking behind one another in the dimly lit tunnel were constantly stepping on the ropes trailing out behind those in front of them. This, in turn, tended to trip the men whose ropes were stepped on such that they ended up being constantly inconvenienced and periodically falling to the ground.

The last man was not yet in the tunnel when the search was temporarily called off so the ropes could be removed from everyone except for the lines attached to one man, an archer by the name of David Black from Galley Thirty-two. Black had volunteered to walk well ahead of the main party carrying a lantern with ten paces of line trailing along behind him.

As you might imagine, no one, not even Henry, was brave enough to remind George that it was him walking in the middle of the tunnel searchers who had poked at the roof and caused the collapse, not the man who had been walking at the very front, who had been caught in the collapse of the tunnel's ceiling.

George later admitted to himself that he had been lost in thought as he started walking down the secret stairs to reach the tunnel. He had been the second man in the line of tunnel explorers behind the lantern-carrying volunteer. The Company's best swordsman, Lieutenant Richmond, his sword drawn, was walking immediately behind him. All three of the men were carrying lanterns as were all the other men behind them.

He had been lost in thought and not paying attention when he stepped on line and tripped the leading man. That was because of what Elizabeth had proposed when they were lying exhausted in bed the previous night was so breath-taking and unexpected, and so unwanted— that they become the Empire's Emperor and Empress.

"Robert is not up to being the emperor and everyone knows it," she had proclaimed. "All he wants to do is take his falcons hunting. He is not even interested in the servant girls, for God's sake.

"How long would he last as Emperor when he comes of age? Not long and we both know it. Then everything will be lost including the Company's contract to collect the tolls and help defend the city.

"We must act while we still have a chance."

My rejection of her offer had so angered her that I found it best to return to my room next door. Fortunately it was after we had gotten to know each other so I had a good night's sleep. And, of course, it was a mistake to reject her out of hand. I should have waited and done it more smoothly.

I tried to see Elizabeth and make peace the next morning when I woke up. I knocked softly on the door into her room and then tried to gently push it open. No luck. It was barred. I knocked and tried the door again after I finished pissing in my room's piss pot and putting on my chain shirt and wrist knives. There was still no answer so I went down to the main hall to break my fast.

Elizabeth was eating at the head of the table when I arrived. And, to my astonishment she waved most friendly to me. I, of course, acknowledged her with a smile and a bow. I did not take the empty space on the bench next to her that was usually occupied by her husband. It might have started a rumour.

When I was finished breaking my fast with morning wine and burnt bread with cheese, I went down to the bailey meet the men who would be accompanying me in the morning on my second attempt to explore the tunnels.

Elizabeth's barring of the door between our rooms would not be a problem. The day's tunnel explorers would use the main door into her chambers to reach the tunnel entrance. Indeed, very few people, mostly her long serving and loyal personal servants, were aware that I was "recovering" in the room next to hers such that we could "visit" each other when her boy husband was safely away.

Of course, I could have just as well stayed in my father's room at the other side of the palace and used the tunnel to visit her just as my father apparently had visited her mother. Staying next door had, however, made it easier for us to "know each other" in the biblical sense, something I enjoyed and hoped to continue, but only for so long as it did not permanently attach me to her.

****** *Lieutenant Richmond*

My fellow tunnel explorers and I spent what was left of the day of the tunnel collapse taking care of our injured mates and getting cleaned up. Getting cleaned up was a problem. Neither I nor any of the other men had ever been so fouled with dirt and dust. Worse, the bones and foul things that dropped on us seemed to have come from a cemetery such that most of us smelled like we were already dead.

No choice was given to us in the matter of getting the dirt and stench of death off our bodies and clothes. The Commander himself got up from the bed where he had been temporarily placed and marched us down to the city's baths. When we arrived, he led us into the water and told us to wash ourselves as he was doing.

We even had to get all the way under the water to get the dust out of our beards and hair. It was a scary ordeal even though, in the end, thank you Jesus and all the saints, it did not end up affecting us as badly as we feared it might. What we had all feared, of course, was that watering ourselves would weaken us when we were with women.

After we finished getting the dust and the smell of death off of us, we were each given new tunics and some liberty coins according to our ranks and informed that we would be staying at the Commandry until further notice. We were also told that we would likely be returning to the tunnels "probably on the day after tomorrow."

We were then given a liberty for that evening. The only requirement laid on us was that we had to stay in the Latin Quarter. That was not a burden because the quarter had numerous taverns with public women we could use to make sure that the bathing had not weakened us.

It was both a fine evening of drinking and a great relief to learn that I had still not come down with the weakness pox as a result of being watered. I came to the conclusion that I had likely dodged an arrow and escaped being weakened after spending some time with a slender young tavern slave with little breasts and strange eyes. She probably came from the land of dragons on the other side of the great desert.

Fortunately, watering ourselves seemed to have had just the opposite effect of what we feared, at least that was case if even half the stories I heard from my fellow swordsmen that evening and the next morning were true. The effects were so encouraging that several men announced they were thinking about watering themselves again sometime.

One thing was sure even though we did not think about it whilst we were out carousing—by the time we returned to the bailey everyone in the city knew we had been in the tunnels and would be going into them again.

******

Several things happened on the day after the cave-in whilst we were idling about in the bailey and trying to recover from our previous day's experiences and drinking. For one, the Commander came out to see how we were doing. He gathered us around and told us that several companies of archers had been sent out from the city that morning to try to find the graveyard that was the site of the tunnel collapse. The Commander also told us something we had already heard from Lieutenant Commander Harcourt—we would be making another search of the tunnels in the morning.

Early in the afternoon we were joined by several dozen additional sword-carrying archers from the men stationed in the city. The new men, we were all told by Lieutenant Commander Harcourt who came out to greet them, would be accompanying us on our next tunnel search.

One of the new arrivals was a lieutenant. Seeing him bothered me greatly until I remembered he was junior to me.

The new arrivals were all long-serving veterans as we were. Even so, they sat with us in the shade and were wide-eyed as they listened to the stories we told them about what we had seen and heard whilst we were in the tunnels.

Our stories were what you would expect—about strange misshapen creatures we had vaguely seen in the dim light and the screams and other noises we heard in the darkness, and how several of our men had themselves suddenly screamed and disappeared never to be seen again.

The new arrivals were all veteran fighting men like us. Even so, many of them were clearly horrified about our descriptions of what we had heard and seen in the tunnels.

Our stories got more and more farfetched as we described how the remains of dead bodies had dropped on us—and then went on to describe sounds and screams we heard that could have only come from hell, which was obviously under our feet and so close that we might breakthrough and drop into it. A couple of the new arrivals actually trembled when they heard about the snake-like scales and black mould that covered the slimy creatures we had seen, the ones that fed on the dead bodies when freshly dead bodies were not available.

Finally, of course, the wide-eyed new arrivals realized we were funning with them and began telling stories of their own.

That evening we "tunnel rats," as those of us who had been in the tunnel were now beginning to call ourselves, all went out together to drink in the courtyard of one of the local taverns. The new arrivals came with us and were allowed to pay for the wine we drank in exchange for being allowed to sit with us and hear more of our increasingly farfetched stories and speculations.

By then, of course, even the most gullible of the new arrivals had come to realize that we had been telling them tall tales and having great merriments at their expense—and all but one or two were relaxed and reassured. The wine, of course, helped immensely.

Later that evening, as we sang chanties and walked drunkenly back to the Commandry, or perhaps I should say "lurched," I realized that I had not thought about Anne and Grimsby for several days. It was a fine thing to be among men who respect you. Living in the Company amongst such fine fellows was not at all like living in Grimsby.

Chapter Eleven

Once more into the tunnels.

It was early on a fine early September morning when we once again marched from the Commandry to the Great Palace for another day of tunnel searching. It was two days after our first tunnel search. It seemed to take a few minutes longer to march there this time, perhaps because there were more people, carts, and feral cats in the streets.

On the other hand, our walk was a bit easier this time because an early morning rain had washed away most of the accumulated poop such that we did not have to walk with extraordinary care. Moreover, at least for me, the possibility we might be about to again do something dangerous made it an even finer morning despite my sore head from a second night of serious drinking and girl-poking.

****** *Lieutenant Richmond*

"You and the lads were right about this place, Lieutenant," one of the new swordsmen muttered in a barely understandable dialect from the South of England after we had arrived at the Great Palace and walked into the Empress's room. "I never see nuffink like this in my whole life."

It was a significant acknowledgement as the sergeant who made it had claimed to have been in most of England's great holds and houses because he had driven a coach for one of London's biggest moneylenders until his master ran off with someone's coins.

The door to the big upright chest with the pegs holding the Empress's skirts and tunics was closed when we entered the room. The Commander himself opened it and led the way through the door into the tunnel. That was right after each of us was given a candle lantern with its candle already lit and two lines that were each about a dozen paces long.

The purpose of the lines had been explained to us before we left the Commandry—they would be tied to our ankles and dragged along behind us on the floor of the tunnel. They would then be available to be used to pull the man free if the tunnel ceiling came down and covered him. It certainly might have saved us a lot of trouble and grief if we had been wearing them a couple of days earlier so it sounded like a good idea to me. In any event, it was the Commander's idea so we all commented on how much we appreciated them.

An ambitious sergeant from our first exploration, David Black, led the way into the tunnel with the Commander second and me third. Behind me came Lieutenant Commander Harcourt. Our ankle lines trailed out behind us as we walked.

Black claimed to have been the son of an Oxford scribe who had to run for some reason such that he had ended up being birthed in Leicester. It was a lie, of course, but the man was one of the few archers who could scribe and, or so I had been told, did so with a particularly fine hand and used more words than most men even knew.

Our problems with the ankle lines became apparent almost immediately when the Commander somehow stepped on one of Sergeant Black's ankle lines as Black was walking down the stairs with his lantern held high.

The Commander probably stepped on the line because he could not see it in the flickering light cast from his lantern, or perhaps he was not looking because he was thinking of other things. In any event, it happened just as Black was moving his foot downward towards a lower stone step. Black's foot suddenly being unable to move forward whilst in the middle of a step caused the Leicester man to stumble and fall down four or five stairs to the bottom of the stairwell.

Black fell hard and bloodied his head, and was pained enough to yelp and swear as he did. But he was not badly stunned or hurt from his mishap and quickly got to his feet and apologized to the Commander even though he was not at fault. His lantern, however, did not survive hitting the rocky tunnel floor. Its flame went out and could not be relit.

The result of the fall was a sudden stoppage of our forward progress and much shouting and commotion because no one knew what had happened or what had caused it. Finally, a lantern from one of the men at the back of the line was passed forward for Black to carry and we started walking again.

A minute or so later there was a similar mishap somewhere behind me, and then another. There was no doubt about it; lines trailing along on the tunnel floor behind a man are hard to see when the light is uncertain. And it was made more uncertain by the walkers' spending most of their time looking for rocks hanging down from the ceiling that their heads might hit.

The Commander finally gave up.

"Everyone sit down and take off your ankle lines. They are slowing us down and causing more trouble than they are worth," he said. He shouted it loudly so all the men strung out behind him could hear.

"What should we do with them?" a voice asked from somewhere in the rear.

"Put them next to the wall so no one trips over them. We will gather them up later when we come back this way."

****** *Lieutenant Commander Henry Harcourt*

We resumed our march and a few minutes later came to the entrance of the side tunnel we explored so disastrously a few days earlier. Right beyond it was a narrow staircase stone stairs. To my astonishment, we walked past the stairs and kept going.

Ignoring the stairs surprised me; surely they must lead to somewhere we needed to know about. *Later I learned that the stairs led up to what had been his father's private room in the palace and that William, George's father, and then George himself, had stayed in the room and used the tunnel to visit the Empress's sleeping room. But by then, of course, it was too late.*

The tunnel continued on past the stairs for some distance. After what seemed like thirty minutes or so of walking we came to a fork in the tunnel. After a moment's hesitation, George made a decision and we continued down the tunnel to the left. I had absolutely no idea which direction we were headed and, so far as I could tell from the comments of the men walking around me, neither did anyone else.

I found myself increasingly tired and my knees ached so badly that I would have stopped if I had been walking alone. When this is over I am going back to Cyprus and tend to my wife and garden.

We walked in the tunnel for some time until we came to three stone steps that led up to what was clearly a trap door. We stopped.

"Quiet. No talking. Everyone be quiet."

The order was whispered from man to man as those of us at the front of the little column held up our lanterns to better see it. Nothing could be heard. All of a sudden, there was a sound of someone walking on trapdoor above of us. And then we heard the faint and muffled sounds of a woman's voice and a dog barking. We could not make out the woman's words but she did not sound agitated.

We held our breath and waited. Nothing. In the dim and flickering light I saw George slowly draw his sword from is sheath. Lieutenant Richmond saw him do it and immediately put down his lantern and drew his sword. I immediately did the same. And then the men behind us began copying us even though no order had been given. The drawing of swords rippled down our little column like a wave in the sea.

Someone in the rear started to say something and was immediately drew a quiet "shush" from several of the men around him. It immediately became so silent in the lantern-lit tunnel that I could hear my own breathing and that of the men on either side of me.

****** *Lieutenant Richmond*

Commander Courtenay started to reach up to try to lift the wooden plank above the stairs. I gently stuck out my arm to block him and shook my head. He saw my arm in the flickering light of the lanterns and stopped. Then he nodded his head and stepped back. It had become totally silent above us.

I could have easily reached up and tried to push the plank up a few inches to see what I could see. But I did not immediately do so because it would have left me in a bad position to use my sword if there was an enemy above me.

What I needed was to be able to deflect any weapon that might be waiting stab or slash me. Accordingly, instead of touching the wood plank that was clearly an exit from the tunnel, the first thing I did was slowly and cautiously climb up on to the first of the three misshapen stone steps until both of my feet were firmly on the step and my sword was in position.

When I was ready I began slowly pushing the wooden plank of the trapdoor up with my empty left hand. As I did I kept the point of the sword in my right hand aimed straight at the end of the wooden plank where I intended the first opening to appear.

My thinking was simple—if someone was waiting up there to stab or slice down at me, I intended to use my sword to slip through the opening to turn away his blade, and then let it continue on to stab into him as deeply as possible. If that succeeded, I would try to hurry through the trapdoor and put a wound on anyone who was with him. Normally, of course, I would have tried to kill everyone but the Commander said we needed prisoners to question.

The problem was that I did not know on which side of the trapdoor someone might be standing and, thus, where the thrust would come at me. So I held my point only as close to the trapdoor as I could get it and still have my blade in position to turn aside a blade coming at me from where I expected the trapdoor to first rise.

When I was ready, I took a deep breath and used my left hand to slowly push up on the middle of the wooden plank in such a way as would cause it to rise at one end. Something was weighting it down. But I kept pushing. It was heavier than I expected. But I increased my pushing until there was a slight and very strange sucking sound as the plank gave way and began to rise.

Initially the wooden plank, for that is what it was, only went up enough to provide me with about an inch of opening at one end. That was all I needed to get my first look at what was outside the tunnel exit. What I saw was nothing.

There was no one in sight so I shifted my hand slowly lifted the plank higher and higher until there was an inch or two of open space all around it. Still nothing. Then, all at once, I became aware of a somewhat foul smell and then, a moment later, the familiar sound of an animal snorting. *Damn. Yuck.*

I turned my head down and whispered my news very softly.

"Pigs. It is a pig sty, Commander.

"The opening comes up in a pig shed with a low roof so only pigs can get under it. There is no one about except some pigs.

"Wait. Yes there is. I can see a woman. It must have been the woman whose voice we heard. She is walking this way to see why the pigs are excited and moving about."

"Come down. Let me look," the Commander ordered in a similar low whisper.

There was silence in the tunnel as I stepped down whilst still holding up the plank and the Commander slowly reached up to join me in holding up the plank, and quietly climbed up on to the first stair to take a look. A moment later he lowered the plank and stepped down.

"Then he held his finger up to his lips in the age-old order for silence and whispered a decision that only the men nearest to him could hear.

"Shh. Everyone be quiet. We will leave the exit undisturbed since it is not likely to have been used to get into the palace. Pass the order on to the man behind you to turn around and for everyone start pulling back."

Something George did not say out loud at the time, but later discussed with his lieutenants in some detail, was that the escape exit through the pigsty would also be a good way for the Company to secretly get men into *the city if that should ever become necessary.   They would be able to find pigsty because he had seen a useful landmark, the distinctive dome of an Orthodox village church.*

Chapter Twelve

The Big Eye and more dead archers.

We bid farewell to the pigsty and marched back the way we had come. The men who had been bringing up the rear were now leading. Our rear guard led the way until we came to where the tunnel had forked and we had turned off to the left.

Being in the tunnel had somehow gotten easier. We were getting used to walking in it and becoming more and more relaxed, at least I was. Somewhere along the way David Black had taken off the lines that had been attached to his ankles when he was walking out in front of us.

When we reached the fork in the tunnel we stopped for a few moments to put fresh candles into our lanterns and piss against the tunnel wall. I took advantage of the stop to take a swig of water and finish off my cheese and chicken.

At that point, Commander Courtenay had us squeeze past each other and return to our original marching order. A few minutes later I was once again walking in the third position immediately behind the Commander and David Black who had remained as the first man in our column.

Lieutenant Commander Harcourt was right behind me and trying not to step on my feet. This time we took the other fork, the one that branched off to the right. It was not long before the tunnel forked again.

****** *Lieutenant Richmond*

We came to another set of rough stone stairs leading upward only a few minutes after we stopped for a piss break and to restore our original marching order. The Commander stopped at the stairs and held up his lantern to look at them.

A moment later the Commander drew his sword, held his finger up to his lips to order silence, mouthed "quiet; pass it on" to me, which I did. Then he gestured for Sergeant Black to climb the stairs.

I, of course, immediately drew my sword when the Commander did and so did everyone else; the distinctive sound of swords being drawn from their sheaths rippled down the line of men behind me. No one said a word.

David Black and his lantern led the way as we began slowly and quietly climbing the winding staircase. It wound in tight circles to the right and turned out to be quite long. We had either been further below the city than we realized or it was taking us to a floor above the ground in a big building, or perhaps both. We had no idea

In the flickering light I watched as David Black's lantern suddenly stopped. He had come to a landing at the top of the stairs and could go no further. Commander Courtenay held his finger up to his lips and motioned for David to move back and for me to come forward and join him.

David and I pulled in our stomachs and eased past each other on the narrow stairs. What I saw as I got past David and reached the Commander was a low and narrow wooden door at the top of the stairs. The stairs stopped at the door and the ceiling in front of the door was low. We had to bend our heads to stand in front of the door and look at it. There was barely room for the two of us.

The top of the doorway was even lower than the ceiling and it had a very narrow width. We would have to bend our heads even more and turn sideways to get through it. It was definitely a defensible door and it was set in a stone wall. There seemed to be some sort of black mould on the wall stones around the door.

Commander Courtenay was holding up his lantern and inspecting the door as I joined him. I promptly held my lantern up and did the same. As I did I became aware of the smell of the beeswax candles drifting up from the lanterns below me.

There was silence on the other side of the door and on the stairs. The only sound I could hear was the periodic faint scuffling of our men's sandals as they moved around on the stairs below me and a choked off sneeze from someone who had gotten too much dust and candle smoke.

I watched intently as the Commander put his lantern down and motioned for me to do the same. When I finished putting it down, he began gently pushing on the door to see if it would open. My sword was ready in case someone was waiting on the other side. The door did not yield.

Suddenly, to my surprise, the Commander handed me his sword and held up his lantern to closely examine the door. I took it and then was further surprised to see that he had a knife in his sword hand and was gently moving its blade up and down in the crack between the wooden door and the door frame around it. *Where did the knife come from?*

Commander Courtenay spent quite some time exploring the gap between door and the doorframe. Sometimes he could move his knife up and down in the gap; other times he could not. At first, I did not understand what he was doing, but then I did—he was trying to learn how and where the door was barred and if it was anywhere joined to the wall in which it was set.

******

"Sergeant Perkins is to come up very quietly; pass it on."

The Commander leaned over whispered the order down the stairs. He did so as soon as he finished probing the door. His knife, I suddenly realized, had somehow disappeared. One moment it had been in his hand, the next moment it was gone.

It did not take long before I could see a sturdy-looking sergeant making his way up the stairs towards us carrying a great long-handled hammer. I knew him slightly. His name was Perkins and he had been walking not too far behind us. There was a great deal of tension in the air by the time he reached us.

More orders were whispered.

"Everyone is to move down four steps to make room at the top to for the hammer to be swung. Pass it on."

And then the Commander whispered an order that I appreciated.

"Lieutenant, you stay here with me; Sergeant Perkins you come up and stand behind the lieutenant. Wait there but be ready to step up and take the door if we step down to give you room."

The order was given so softly that I barely heard it.

"Lieutenant, Sergeant Perkins, listen closely, lads," he whispered into our ears when Perkins reached us.

"There are two bars on the door and no hinges. The lieutenant and I are going to try to lift the bars off using our knife blades. We will try the top bar first.

"If we succeed and the door falls down, Lieutenant Richmond will go in first. I will go second, and you, Perkins, will have to go third and bring your hammer in with you so none of the lads who follow us trip over it. David will come in behind us. Do you both understand?"

We both understood, at least I did, and whispered our "ayes."

"But here is the thing, Sergeant Perkins. You will have to batter the door down with your hammer if Lieutenant Richmond and I are unable to lift the bars off. If using the hammer becomes necessary, I will give you the order and the lieutenant and I will step down a couple of steps to give you enough room and hold up our lanterns. But be damn sure not to hit us or anyone else when you start swinging that thing."

****** *Lieutenant Richmond*

It seemed to take forever for the line of men below us to move down the required four steps. I held my knife in my left hand and used it to explore the door to find the whereabouts of both the bars so I would be ready. My sword was held tightly in my right. The Commander was on the left side of the door; I was on the right.

"We will try the upper bar first. If we cannot get it off, we will try the lower bar," he whispered. "Aye," I whispered back.

In the dim lantern light we inserted our knives into the crack between the door and the stone wall, and raised them until we could feel the wooden bar on the other side. Then the Commander nodded at me and we slowly began to lift the bar using our knife blades.

It was a heavy bar to lift one-handed with the end of a knife, but we got it higher and higher until it was free and fell forward. The loud noise as the bar hit the floor on the other side of the door was enough to wake the dead. Some of the men standing below us jumped and moved about.

The Commander and I did not hesitate for a second. As fast as possible we moved our knives to get them under the second bar and begin lifting it. It seemed to be heavier but, finally, it too came up.

There was another crash on the other side as the second bar hit the floor. It seemed like it took forever even though it could not have been more than three or four seconds. Both the Commander and I had felt the bar come loose and had begun pushing on the little door as soon as it did. The unhinged door tipped over into the room on the other side from where we were standing with a loud crashing sound.

I did not hesitate when the door went over in front of me. I instantly lowered my head and turned sidewise to go through the now-empty door opening with my sword and right arm leading the way—and then charged across the fallen door towards the middle of what appeared to be some kind of large hall. I was the first man into the room. The Commander, Sergeant Perkins, Lieutenant Commander Harcourt, and David Black were right behind me.

******

We instantly realized we had come into an astounding place the likes of which none of us had ever seen. The ceiling was quite high and there was a huge and unblinking great eye covering most of the wall area on the left side of the room. Just beyond the middle of the room there was a raised area with some sort of a large chair on it.

Near the chair was an upright book holder similar to what one would see in a church. It was where a priest might stand when he was gobbling at his flock about what God wanted them to do and the need for more tithes and such if their souls were to be saved. But it was clearly not a church for prayers and money-raising as there were no crosses and not a mosque because there were no rugs.

The great eye watched over the hall. There were wall openings all around the room to let in light and some sort of long painted screen, almost a wall, behind the raised area. There was a long wooden table without benches along the wall opposite the eye. Several unlit lanterns were on the table, but nothing else.

I took everything in with one glance as I moved over the fallen door and into the room. Nothing made sense so I did what any man would do under the circumstances—I shifted my sword to my left hand and made the sign of the cross with my right.

I was still making the sign of the cross when the long painted screen at the end of the room was suddenly pushed over and a great shouting as a band of armed men carrying spears and clubs charged over and around it to get at us. There were more than a dozen of them and they had been hiding behind it and waiting for us. Their loud shouting and attack was a complete surprise.

The fighting that followed did not last long. I managed to turn aside the spear of the first man to reach me and slash him in the neck with my return stroke. But the next spear got me and pushed me to the floor before I could get my sword back down to turn it aside. And then I felt several others push into me and hold me down when I tried to get back on my feet.

Strangely enough, I did not feel anything even though I could not move when I tried to get back on my feet. For a few seconds I listened to the shouting and tried to understand what was happening and what was being said. But it was all so confusing that I quit trying.

Instead I somehow began thinking of Anne and could see her quite clearly. She was alone and reaching out to me. I was very pleased. And look at that—our roof needs a visit from the thatcher.

Chapter Thirteen.

We are surprised.

Sergeant Perkins, the hammer man, was the third man into the room. He and Lieutenant Richmond had hurried in behind the Commander. Lieutenant Commander Henry Harcourt was the fourth. One or two of the men who came through the door behind them also made it into the room before the ambush began. The archers had all gone through the door ready to fight, but the surprise assault that fell upon them was too big and they were ill-prepared for the fight in that they did not have even small shields to turn away the attackers' spears.

The result was inevitable: the handful of surprised men who made it into the room were instantly overrun. Only one of them escaped, a short and very strong two-stripe chosen man by the name of Billy Bishop from Ramsgate.

Billy had been the only name Billy ever had until he ran away from home and made his mark on the Company roll. The apprentice sergeant doing the scribing to record Billy's enlistment had asked him a few questions about himself and, upon hearing that Billy had once been an altar boy for the Ramsgate church, announced that the Company already had at least one Billy Church so he had a choice between being on the Company roll as Billy Bishop or as Billy Priest.

Being ambitious and knowing the difference, Billy had chosen to be a Bishop. What he never told the apprentice sergeant or anyone was that it was the church's priest he had been running from when he went for an archer. Someday he had promised himself at the time, he would return to Ramsgate, tell the priest he was a bishop, and kill the bastard. It was a young boy's dream and long forgotten.

Billy had been the sixth man in the archers' tunnel column and was just stepping into the room when the unexpected attack began. He had somehow kept his wits about him enough to step backwards through the door when he saw the spear carriers coming at him. Even so, he had been speared in the thick part of his leg above his knee as he did. That happened because the man behind him was still trying to move forward and blocked him from getting back through the doorway soon enough.

The thrust of the spear helped push Billy back through the doorway. The spear was somehow pulled out of Billy's leg as he scrambled backwards through the door. And then the direction of the spear's push and the wound in his leg caused Billy to fall off to the side of the door as soon as he went through it.

Billy quickly dragged himself up against the wall next to the door to escape the several spears that instantly began being poked through the door opening—and became a Company legend as a result.

From where he fell bleeding against the wall next to the door, Billy had watched and listened to the leaderless shouting and chaos amongst the leaderless rank and file archers on the steps below him. He could not see them in the dim and flickering light, but he could hear enough to know exactly what was happening.

Several spears were soon being stabbed through the open doorway in an effort to clear away any of the archers who might have been front of it. One of them just missed Billy as he scrambled towards the wall next to the door in a desperate effort to avoid being stabbed again. He was seriously wounded and he knew it even though the pain had not yet started.

A second or two later, and seeing nobody immediately in front of the doorway because all the archers except Billy were on the stairs below it, one of the attackers started to come through the door.

No one will ever know if the enemy spear carrier was trying to come through the door just to look or if he really intended to attack the men on the stairs—because Billy crouched and waited until the attacker stuck his head out, and then put all the strength of his archer's strong arms into a slicing two-handed swing of his sword to the back of the man's neck.

The sight of the man's head rolling down the stairs in the dim light so distracted the archers gathered on the stairs that one of the archers stumbled and took down two others as he fell. It was, the men later agreed, as if a carved wooden ball had been bowled on the village green.

As you might imagine, the men who fell on the stairs quickly recovered and scrambled back to their feet with their swords at the ready—and Billy was thereafter known as Billy Bowles until the bolt of a Genoese crossbow took him some years later.

Billy's end came when he was a lieutenant serving on one of the Company's transports. By then his son, Andrew, had joined the Company and made his mark using the name Bowles. Andrew ended up marrying a merchant's daughter and returning to England, whereupon over the years that followed his descendants became quite well known as useful courtesans and parliamentarians.

The other thing Billy did on the day of the attack on the tunnel searchers, however, turned out to be much more important in terms of how the Company reacted to the attack in the days that followed and the Company's future—he remembered seeing the Commander go down fighting and he remembered seeing the big eye on the wall.

****** *Lieutenant Commander Henry from Harcourt*

The end of my time in the Company came when I followed close behind the hammer carrier as he went through the door behind George and Lieutenant Richmond. We went in fast as soon as the door bars were lifted and the door at the top of the steps fell into the room. The man coming up the stairs behind me was so anxious that he stepped on my foot and damn near tripped me.

It was right after I came through the door when it happened. Some sort of low wall on the far side of the room was pushed over and a great gang of men rushed over it shouting their battle cries. I barely had time to get my sword up and start to move towards the Commander when the first spear got me. And then a couple of others did as well and pinned me to the floor.

Oh dear God, they got George too... Maybe I can ... Oh no. .... My poor wife, she will have to ....

****** *Commander George Courtenay.*

The long screen running across part of the other end of the room was suddenly pushed over towards us and a great mass of attackers came running over it to get at us. They had been in place hiding behind the screen when we entered. There was no time to form any kind of defensive position before the first of them reached me. I did not have time to do more than a hurried side-step to avoid the point of the first spear coming at me before, out of the corner of my eye, I saw the shadow of something coming towards the side of my head.

It must have been a hard knock for the next thing I was aware of was that I was on the floor and there was a lot of loud shouting all around me. There was only one thing to do so I did it—I kept my eyes closed and played dead.

All I knew at first was that I was face-down on some kind of wooden floor. After a while the shouting and sound of fighting stopped and I could pick out some of the voices—they were gobbling in Greek. At least it sounded like Greek to me.

But then I heard someone standing above me say something in crusader French. From the tone of the voice, it sounded as if he was giving an order.

"Tell them that this is the valuable one. See all the stripes on his tunic." … "Yes, I am sure it is him. Get him out of here." … "Hurry before the English can launch a counter attack."

My eyes remained closed as, a few seconds later, I felt someone take my sword and begin rummaging through my coin pouch. A moment later I was literally picked up off the floor and thrown over someone's shoulders.

I was almost six feet tall, well fed, and wearing a chain shirt under my tunic that added to my weight; so my carrier must have been a very strong man. He carried me down a flight of stairs, leaned against a well to rest for a few seconds and catch his breath, and then walked a short distance before taking a deep breath and giving a great heave that dumped me into the bed of a horse-drawn wagon.

My head banged so hard when I landed that I grunted in pain and became confused for a few moments. But I was also as surprised and pleased as a man might be under such trying circumstances—because the men who captured me had been in such a hurry that neither the man who carried me nor anyone else had thought to search under my baggy-sleeved tunic.

A great jumble of fears and ideas flooded into my head. Sooner or later they would search me, and probably sooner because I was wearing a rusty old chain shirt that someone would inevitable want for himself or to sell. And when they did search me they would find my wrist knives—which meant, I quickly decided, that I needed to try to escape as soon as possible while I still had weapons to assist me.

Three or four men immediately jumped in the wagon with me. I knew they did because the wagon bed rocked as each of them climbed aboard, and several of them stepped on my legs. Someone shouted an order, and there was a reply. Almost immediately a wagon driver-sounding command was given in what sounded like Greek, a whip cracked, and we lurched forward.

The wagon must have been in an alley because it was quiet and smelled most foul. But we soon turned left and moved out on to a regular city street. I knew we were on street because I could periodically hear street noises and the clickity-clack sound of the wooden wheels as the wagon bounced over the cobblestones.

At first no one in the wagon said a word, but then they opened up and began excitedly gobbling to each other in what was almost certainly Greek, although I could not be sure because I cannot gobble it myself. What I was sure was that my head was banging up and down against the wooden wagon bed like a galley drummer rapidly beating out a command.

I did not try to open my eyes and put my head up to look about. It would have been rather difficult since someone had one of his sandals firmly planted on my neck. It was my hope, of course, that my guards thought I was badly wounded and would leave me alone until I could escape. And that, I had already decided, was something I needed to try to do sooner rather than later.

Although I could not see, the men in the wagon must have been sitting on benches on either side with me in the middle. I knew that because their Greek-gobbling voices were on both sides of me and they were all above me. Unfortunately, I could not understand a word of whatever it was that they were saying.

Finally! Whoever had his foot on my neck took it off. I decided it was time to make my move before it was too late. What I intended to do was suddenly leap to my feet and go straight over the side of the wagon—and then run like hell.

I blinked my eyes in an effort to get a quick look at where the men were sitting so I would know where to go when I made my move. What I saw was more than a little disheartening —a couple of tough-looking men were grinning at me as they leaned towards me whilst holding their knives a few inches from my throat. I was, it seemed, not much of a mummer.

Goddamn it; they were expecting me to try.

After about ten minutes, the wagon turned off the cobblestoned street and came to a stop. A couple of men dropped the tailgate of the wagon, grabbed me by the legs and pulled me out.

I narrowly avoided being dropped on my head by opening my eyes as they did and mumbling "I can stand. I can stand" and trying to slide off so that I would land on my feet

My captors did not understand what I was saying, but they did seem to understand that I was willing to walk. They promptly decided, quite rightly, that it would be easier for them if I walked so they would not have to carry me. About all I could do to help myself escape as I walked was make a few deliberate staggers and missteps to suggest that I was too weak to be a threat.

What I saw as I walked was that the wagon and I were in the small bailey of a somewhat run-down walled compound such as might be the home and work yard of a carpenter or a cart wright. I had that thought in my head because there were stacks of wood and wagon wheels piled about and several carts and wagons that looked to be under construction. There were no men at work, but several women and their children were standing together in a little group looking at us.

I made no effort to look around and deliberately stumbled because I wanted the men who brought me to think I was no threat to them because I was still woozy and unsteady on my feet. It was not difficult because, as I realized when my feet touched the ground, I really was a bit unsteady. I was also quite thirsty.

******

"You English are not so tough," said the heavyset man in broken crusader French. He said it after I was roughly pushed into a cell-like small room and he had followed me into it. The room was dark because there were no wall openings. It also smelled as if people had been sleeping in it for many years.

It was not a prison cell was my first impression, at least I did not think it was. If anything, it was more like a monk's cell in a monastery or the sleeping quarters of a couple of apprentices.

The gobbler and the two men who came in with him had their swords drawn. I could see them by the light of the open door behind them. They were obviously ready to cut me down if I gave them any trouble or tried to escape

"We killed some of your men and took you easily," the heavyset man continued with a rather arrogant tone in his voice.

"And it is lucky for you that it was so easy for us. We were supposed to kill you. But you need not worry about that, at least not for a few more days. They told us you were valuable so we are going to get a ransom for you in addition to killing you."

He said it with a great roar of laughter and satisfaction in his voice. The men with him smiled and nodded their agreement when he turned to them and told them what he had said. The dejected look on my battered face probably encouraged them.

The speaker's appearance and speech gave me no idea who he was or what he was. So far as I could tell he was a Greek. He carried a sword but his clothes were not those of a merchant or priest. My initial thought was that he might be part of a church protection gang or a successful artisan such as a carpenter or mason.

"Who paid you to kill me?" I asked. "And how did you know I would be there or that I would be in the room where you could get to me and not still in the tunnel?"

He laughed when I asked him. And then he turned to the men with him and gobbled at them for a few seconds. And they laughed too.

It was about then that what he said suddenly hit home. *"We killed some of your men."* *Who? Uncle Henry? Oh my God. What will I ever tell his wife? And who else—the lieutenant and Sergeant Perkins, the hammer carrier?*

What also hit me about then was the realization that my captors had let me see their faces. That was when I knew for sure that they were going to kill me even if a ransom was paid. They had to do so because I could identify them.

My head was spinning with despair as my laughing and soon-to-be-rich captors left the room with big smiles on their faces. A moment later I heard the distinctive sound of the door's bar being dropped into place. I was a prisoner.

******

I was not alone in the darkness for very long. Suddenly I heard the bar on the door being lifted. A moment later, light flooded into the room as the door was pulled open. I could see a ragged young boy in the doorway. A man carrying some sort of club was standing behind him.

Taking great care to avoid me, the boy slunk into the room and grabbed up some filthy bedding that had been piled in the corner. He rushed out of the room with it whilst looking fearfully over his shoulder at me.

The door was immediately closed behind him and barred once again. The only good thing about the visit was that the room began smelling better after the boy removed the bedding — and I felt like kicking myself in the arse for not trying to make a run for it while the door was open.

Chapter Fourteen

Chaotic times and the great search.

The archers on the tunnel staircase had been caught by surprise when the fighting started, and then again when the head rolled down the stairs. Some had tried to push their way forward to join the fight and a few were overcome with indecision. The latter just stood there because they did not know what to do. In so doing, they blocked the way of the would-be fighters who were trying to move forward.

It was chaos with everyone was shouting orders at everyone else both amongst the surviving archers and in some kind of foreign gobble on the other side of the door. The headless body of the attacker Andy ha chopped lay halfway through the doorway pumping blood onto the doorway floor and the stairs below.

It did not take long before a semblance of order returned. The archer closest to the door, a sergeant, loudly announced what he was going to do and the men on stairs below him, for lack of anyone else to tell them something different, went along with it.

The sergeant's name was Harry Fletcher. His mother had been a Christian refugee from Syria and had helped feed her family when they reached Cyprus by carving and fletching arrows for the Company.

"Andy is wounded. I am going stay here with him and try to hold the door. Whoever is at the arse end of the column should run back to sound the alarm and get reinforcements. The rest of you can do whatever you damn well please."

With that announcement, and staying carefully to one side so a spear being poked through the door opening would not take him, Harry Fletcher cautiously climbed up to the top of the stairs and squatted next to Andy. He had just become the archers' decision maker.

"Where did the bastards get you, Andy?"

What Sergeant Fletcher was really asking, of course, was how bad are you hurt and can you continue to help hold the door?

"In my leg, Harry. A spear. It hurts like shite and I am bleeding out. But I can hold on for a while until you can get a sailmaker to sew me up."

"Scooch over closer to the wall so I can get past you, lad. I will take over guarding the door. You do whatever you can for yourself until we can get someone up here to help you.

"Hoy to the last man on the stairs. Take two lanterns and run back for a sailmaker and his needle. Andy needs some sewing." ... "And tell them to send up some flower paste as soon as possible. ... "And tell the reinforcements to hurry."

"And you there, Jack," he said to the next man down on the steps. "Get up here careful-like and see to Andy. He needs a bit of help with his leg."

With that, Sergeant Fletcher crawled over Andy to get next to the door opening. He raised his sword high with both hands as he did—ready to bring it down hard on anyone else who was fool enough to come through the door.

Suddenly, just as Sergeant Fletcher was moving into position, there was movement on the other side of the door. The headless body of the man lying in the doorway was grabbed by the feet and pulled back into room on the other side of the door.

It did not take long before the doorway was empty except for a puddle of blood. There was a lot of what was obviously swearing and shouting as the men who had attempted to pull their fallen mate to safety saw his that his head was missing. Then some kind of loud order was given and the shouting and swearing began to die away.

Sergeant Fletcher was not a fool as he crouched in the dim light provided by remaining lanterns and the open door. He understood what the absence of the sounds of fighting and the effort to retrieve the headless body meant—that the attackers were in full control of whatever was on the other side of the door. And that meant the Commander and the archers who had gone through the door with him were either dead or captured.

He also understood that if the attackers were going to try to get through the door and have a go at the survivors on the stairs, it would happen soon.

******

It became increasingly quiet, both on the stairs and in the room where the fighting had occurred, as Sergeant Fletcher waited with his sword ready to chop down on anyone who tried to come through the door. It might have been his imagination, Fletcher thought, but it sounded as if their attackers were leaving.

After a few minutes of silence, Fletcher announced what he intended to do.

"Jack, get ready to climb over Andy and take my place as soon as I move. I think they might be gone. I am going to chance a look when you are ready." ... "and you lot down the stairs get your arses ready."

The sergeant waited a moment for Jack's "aye" and a couple of mumbled responses from the stairs below him; then he carefully and very slowly began extending his head in an effort to look through the doorway to see what he could see.

Less than a minute later he was sure. All he could see from the doorway were the bodies the attackers had left behind when they retreated. They were all wearing archer's tunics. A puddle of blood was all that remained of the headless body.

"I think they are gone. No one is here," he shouted. *No one alive that is.*

"Everyone stay where they are. I am going to go in to check it out."

And with that the sergeant very slowly and cautiously slipped into the room. He moved quickly from body to body before he said anything more. When he looked back towards the tunnel entrance he saw Jack's head peering around the edge of the doorway to watch him. He also saw the big eye painted on the wall, but was so engrossed in checking out the fallen archers that he paid it no intention.

"They are all dead. All of our lads are dead." He shouted less than a minute later, and then he added "keep the doorway clear. Stay ready; no one is to come in or block the doorway until I finish my looking."

Of course the sergeant wanted the doorway clear. In the event anyone jumped out at him, he intended to run back and dive through the doorway to safety. He would take his chances on the hard stone stairs. He had quickly decided that a possible broken head or arm was better that than getting stabbed and killed.

There were two doors out of the room. One big door was in the corner of the room. A small one was in the wall opposite the big eye. The small one had a bar on it to prevent anyone from entering; the big one did not; its bar was on the floor next to the door.

Sergeant Fletcher moved cautiously to the big door and, as he did, he decided to open it and see what was on the other side. Before he opened it he took a deep breath and double-checked to make sure he had a clear path from the door he was about to open to the doorway to the tunnel on the other side of the room.

As he later told anyone who would listen, if there had been danger waiting on the other side of the room's one regular-sized door he intended to run to the tunnel doorway as if the devil himself was snapping at his arse and dive through it.

******

Sergeant Fletcher was no fool. Before he opened the door he took off the rope around his tunic that held his sword sheath, personal knife, and purse, and tied it with a good sailor's knot to the two hooked pieces of beaten iron upon which one end of the doors' wooden bar would normally rest to keep the door from being opened. He gave the line a little slack, but not much—just enough so the line would not be pulled tight until he opened the door a couple of inches to see what he could see.

Fletcher's reasoning was simple. His tunic rope would take the place of the door's wooden bar if someone tried to push his way into the room. It would let him open the door slightly before it stretched tight, but it would prevent the door from opening any farther. What he hoped, of course, was that the line might not be broken or cut until he had time to snatch up his purse and run to the tunnel entrance and dive through it to escape.

The sight of the bodies of the dead archers in the room had affected him greatly. He had already decided that if he was chased he would dive through the door and take his chances on the stone steps on which he would land.

When he was ready, Sergeant Fletcher took a deep breath, got a good grip on his sword, made sure his purse and other possessions were where he could instantly grab them, and turned his body as much as he could towards the tunnel entrance. He wanted to get the fastest possible start towards it if there was a danger waiting.

Only when he was totally ready did he begin using his free hand to push on the door until it opened a crack.

The door opened a crack. *Nothing.* He pushed it open until his tunic rope was tight and it could open no more. *Still nothing.*

What he saw was a small and totally empty compound whose entry gate was wide open. Beyond the gate was a busy street in which he could see walkers and carts going in both directions. Best of all, he saw that no one was in the compound or even looking into it.

Fletcher immediately shut the door and put the wooden bar in place to lock it. He and the surviving "tunnel rats" would live, he realized as he breathed a great sigh of relief, to fight another day.

Chapter Fifteen

The aftermath and a search.

The first messenger ran through the tunnel with his sword sheathed and carrying a lantern in each hand to light his way. He made good time and stumbled into the Regent's room in the Great Palace to sound the alarm to the astonished Regent and her equally astonished guards. The result of his arrival would later be charitably scribed as "all hell then broke loose and there was great confusion."

A small party of archer reinforcements, every archer then at the palace, all six of them, set out immediately for the scene of the fighting with the messenger and his two lanterns leading the way. At the same time messengers sent by the now somewhat hysterical Regent galloped through the city streets to the Commandry and to the Company's concession with the news of the ambush and fighting. As you might imagine, the fighting and need for reinforcements grew to almost epic proportions as the story passed from man to man.

The initial reinforcements, all six of them, every man a veteran archer, followed the first messenger back to the scene of the fighting as fast as possible. On the way, they met the man who had been subsequently dispatched to fetch a sailmaker to sew up Andy Bishop's leg and damn near killed him before they recognized him as a fellow archer.

Erik, the Commander of the Varangian guards, had not accompanied the tunnel explorers on their second day. He was, however, nearby in his rooms at the Varangians' barracks. He was catching up on his sleep so that he would be awake all night while most of his axe-carrying men were, as they were every night, in the city's streets serving as the city's night watch and maintaining order.

The Regent's Varangian guards sounded the alarm when the first messenger arrived and one of them rushed to the Varangian barracks with the news. Erik gathered up all the available Varangians from their beds where they were sleeping after a night of patrolling the city, shouted orders that the requested barbering supplies of a needle and a roll of thread were to be fetched from the chest where the Varangians' barbering supplies were kept, and led all of his immediately available men at the double to the Regent's rooms.

When Erik and the now wide awake Varangians reached the Regent's rooms, they found the door to the tunnel open and the regent seriously distraught at the news about George and angry at being left with only a couple of Varangians to guard her when the handful of archers who had been left behind in her rooms rushed off to reinforce their mates in the tunnel.

There was an immediate problem—the Varangians who poured into the Regent's rooms did not know where to go in the tunnel. Indeed, it was the first time any of them except Erik even knew there was a tunnel. They also had no lanterns to light the way except the two the second messenger had left behind when he rushed off to fetch a sailmaker to sew up the wounded archer.

There was no question about it; the Varangians would have to wait for the messenger to return from the archers' concession with a sailmaker so he could lead them through the tunnel to the scene of the fighting.

Before the messenger returned, however, a totally out of breath Michael Oremus arrived. The major captain was soon followed by every archer who had been at the Commandry. He had brought them all.

The major captain himself was the first of the archer reinforcements to arrive. He had galloped back on the messenger's horse with his apprentice bouncing along behind him; the rest of the archers from the Commandry had to run all the way, and did so without waiting for even a second for those who fell out due to having weak legs and not being able to breath.

An equally out of breath Lieutenant Commander Lewes arrived at the palace at almost the same time along with the messenger who had been sent for a sailmaker. He brought with him his galley's entire complement of archers, about a hundred of them, along with two of his galley's sailmakers and their needles and thread.

Harold and his men had also run all the way. All an absolutely exhausted Harold knew as he and his men hurried through the palace gate was that George and some of the archers were fighting in a tunnel under the Great Palace and desperately needed reinforcements. That had been more than enough to get them moving.

It would be fair to say that the Empress's rooms and the hallway outside them were soon packed cheek to jowl with very excited sword and axe carrying men who did not know what to do or where to go.

"Quiet, Goddamn it. Quiet. Everyone is to go to the bailey and wait for orders."

****** *Erik the Varangian*

At first the only thing my men and I knew was that there was serious fighting somewhere near the Regent's room and that Elizabeth, the Emperor's Regent, was greatly distressed. My problem was simple—I did not know where the fighting was occurring and I would have no one to lead me there until the return of the messenger who had been sent to fetch a sailmaker to sew up the wounded. The messenger, it seems, had immediately gone on to the archer's concession at the harbour to fetch a sailmaker to sew up the archers' wounded.

I had no more than arrived at the palace with my men than one of Archers' major captains, a man I knew rather well, Michael Oremus, showed up with half a hundred out-of-breath archers from the Commandry. He too had heard about the fighting and also had no idea what to do or where to lead his men.

A few minutes later another hundred or so additional archers and a couple of sailmakers rushed into the palace from one of the galleys which were moored at the quay in front of the Company's concession. The messenger was with them.

The archers from the galley were led by a lieutenant commander I knew, Harold Lewes. All of them were carrying their longbows and quivers full of arrows and many of them were also carrying short swords and galley shields. My men and I had our great axes.

Almost immediately, and after more than a little confusion and shouting, the two archer commanders and I led our heavily armed men down the stone steps into the tunnel with the sailmaker's messenger carrying his original two candle lanterns and leading the way.

The two archer commanders and I were right behind the lantern carrier and had a relatively easy time of it because we could see where we were going. The men behind us, however, had to walk in the darkness. They had a hard time as they constantly stumbled in the darkness and hit their heads and equipment against the roof and sides of the tunnel.

It did not take all that long for those of us at the front of the relief column to reach a staircase and begin climbing. The rest of our force, however, was increasingly strung out far behind us and moving forward slowly, very slowly, in the tunnel's total darkness.

Our men made the best of their difficult circumstances. Each of the men behind the column's leaders walked in the total darkness using one hand to hold on to the tunic of the man ahead of him and the other held up in an effort to avoid banging his head and equipment against the rocks sticking out of the roof of the tunnel.

It was slow going in the darkness as shields, longbows, and heads constantly bounced off the low roof. The increasingly fearful men followed their orders and walked silently except for periodic mutters and curses when they stumbled or hit something.

The men walking at the front could see the lantern lights at the front of the column and moved right along; those walking in total darkness behind them, however, fell further and further behind. The column got more and more strung out. The one and only saving grace of the narrow tunnel was that it was so narrow that no one could turn off and get lost.

My place in the relief column was a good one. I was the third man walking behind the messenger carrying the lanterns. The two archer commanders walked in front of me and were immediately behind the lantern carrier.

It was difficult for me to keep up with the lantern-carrier because he was in a great hurry and I had to walk bent over because I was too tall for the tunnel. But I did. Even so, it was a great relief when we reached some stairs and began to climb them. It meant I could finally stand up straight again.

We followed the lantern-carrying messenger up the stairs, squeezed through a narrow door, and joined a number of men wearing archers' tunics in a large room at the top of the stairs—and my heart sank when I saw the tunics on the bodies and realized who they were and where I was standing.

Impossible. This cannot be. It is impossible.

****** *Commander Courtenay*

My prison cell seemed to a small room in an old and rundown daub and wattle building. I was in the home or work space of some sort of wainright or carpenter and his family and apprentices. At least that was my impression from what I saw during my short walk from the wagon to the building, and in the room when the young boy entered the room to retrieve his bedding.

Both before and after the boy arrived for his bedding I had flexed my arms and twisted my body and legs a bit to make sure I was not dizzy, in other words, to make sure I was fit enough to run if I had a chance.

I began exploring the room in earnest after the boy left with his bedding, and door was once again closed and barred. As my eyes adjusted to the dark I began to make out more and more of the bare outlines of the room by the light that leaked through the cracks and holes in the walls and its roof.

The pinpoints of light gave me hope that the walls were weak such that I might be able to escape by breaking through them or that I might be able to climb up through the thatched roof and jump down into the compound or into a street or alley.

It was not to be. I heard someone lifting the bar on the door and hurried back to slump in the corner as if I had been seriously injured and was harmless. It was, of course, a ruse; I wanted the door left open as long as possible so I could see more of the room and the roof over it.

"Are you comfortable, English?" My questioner spoke crusader French with a heavy accent and a satisfied, almost insulting, tone to his voice. He carried a sword but it was sheathed. Another man stood guard at the door. I could see him clearly because of the sun shining on him. He had a knife in his belt and was holding some kind of heavy club by his side.

"No," I replied very softly with a moan, and then told my lie as sincerely as possible. "I think something is broken inside my head. I cannot stand up without falling down." It was a believable lie because I had bled profusely from where I had been hit in the side of my head.

My plight did not impress him, but the door stayed open and he moved closer to listen. I was clearly not a threat. The man by the door was big and relaxed; the room was so small he could see my sad condition and hear everything that was said.

"Who are you? What do you want?" I asked very weakly. It was all I could do to get the words out.

He ignored my question and got straight to the point.

"I need to know the name of the man to whom we should send our ransom demands. Who should we contact?"

"Oh yes. A ransom. That would be good," I whispered even more feebly as I lifted my hand a few inches off the floor and weakly waved it to acknowledge his question. "You should go to the Company's concession and see ....."

I said it even more softly and mumbled the name as my head slumped forward a bit due to the seriousness of my injury. He asked me to say the name again. And since I was obviously not a threat, he leaned down so he could hear it. He had bad breath.

"His name is .. "

My questioner was still leaning forward and trying to hear my answer as my wrist knives came out their sheaths. He did not even have a chance to blink or make a sound as they both took him in the throat—one on the left side and one on the right.

I ripped both of my knives towards me as I leaped to my feet and, holding my knives out in front of me and ran straight for the man standing in the entrance to the room. *I had thought about screaming a battle cry to startle him, but decided against it because it might alert others in the bailey before I had a chance to get past them.*

"Hey," the man at the door said with surprise in his voice as I threw my questioner aside and ran at him with my knives outstretched.

He was a particularly big man, taller than me and he had a much bigger belly. My initial impression when I first saw him was that he was probably a gang member more used to intimidating people with his appearance than his ability to fight. I certainly hoped so since I was about to find out. I could see from the look on his face that he was more than a little surprised to see me coming straight at him with a knife in each hand.

My questioner's back had been towards the man in the door, and the light had been dim, so the big man probably had not seen my knives until he saw them coming at him. His mouth opened in surprise and he started to raise his club, but then he instinctively stepped back through the doorway and twisted away to his right in an instinctive effort to escape the on-coming knives—and partially succeeded.

Without slowing down, I went through the door and glanced off the big man as he was turning away. As I went past him, I dragged the knife in my right hand across his partially turned back, and then continued on past him and into the little courtyard where wagons were apparently being built and repaired. I did so without breaking my stride.

The compound's gate to the street was open, the man with the deeply sliced back began screaming in pain, and the sun was going down. Without slowing down, I ran right past two poorly dressed young men who were in the process of entering through the open gate, and turned right onto the street that ran along the front of the compound. They just stopped and gaped with their mouths open in astonishment as I ran past them.

I turned to the right as I came out of the gate and continued running as fast as I could even though I had no idea where I was or how to find the Great Palace or the Commandry.

Chapter Sixteen

Confusion and suspicions.

The bailey in front of the substantial stone building where the attack had occurred was alive with lanterns and filled with armed men as the sun finished passing over Constantinople and darkness fell. It was the middle of September and the nights were already starting to get a bit chilly when the wind was blowing in from the sea.

"We are not doing any good here," Michael Oremus said to Harold Lewes. There was resignation and bitterness in his voice. "I am going to take our dead and everyone except Peter Percy's men back to the Commandry."

"Aye, that is a good idea, Michael. Percy and his men can hold this place, and search it whilst Erik and his Varangians go off to spend the night in the city keeping order as they usually do.

But then Harold remembered something else.

"It seems to be the temple of some kind of religious order. We will need to find out more about it and question its members. Maybe they are a band of poisoners or hired killers like the assassins sent out by the old man in the mountains. If you remember, they tried to kill William once before in Alexandria."

"Aye, I remember," Michael said. "But I thought we made peace with them when we started buying their flower paste and selling it at our shipping posts?" It cannot be them. My God we have made them rich and us too."

Harold agreed.

"Aye, it is probably not true, Michael. Well, we will know soon enough who is using the building and have some questions for them, eh? In the meantime I am going to take the galley crews back to the concession and keep them there at a high state of readiness in case they are needed. We will moor our galleys up against the quay so their archers are instantly available as reinforcements."

"Excellent. And be sure to put a strong force on the Concession's gate so it cannot be shut to keep your men out of the city. And you best take a couple of the palace's horses and messengers with you in case you need to get word to me or Peter. I will do the same at the Commandry."

Harold Lewes smoothed his long white beard and, thought for a moment before he responded, and then said out loud what both men had been thinking.

"The city seems quiet. There is no sign that the murders and fighting that took Henry and George are part of an effort to raise the city against the Regent or weaken it for an invader. It feels more and more like the beginning of a coup by someone who wants to replace Elizabeth as the Regent. But who?"

Michael Oremus's response was what might be expected under the circumstances, and he said it with a great deal of intensity and emotion in his voice.

"Aye, Harold. It certainly does feel like a coup. I think you are right, by God. And when I find out who is behind it I am going to cut his guts out and hang his head from the city's main gate no matter who he is or his position. Prince or Patriarch it makes no difference. "

Michael continued after a pause.

"William and George were my friends, and every one of the others was an archer. We are going to see them properly revenged even if it is the last goddamn thing I ever do."

Harold grimly agreed. Even his apprentice, Archie Smith, instinctively nodded his head.

"Aye, Michael. And you can count on me being by your side and smiling when we do. But first we need to find George or whatever is left of him."

The men started to part, but then Michael spoke again.

"In the morning I am going to send a message to the merchants, churches, mosques, and Varangians asking them to announce that the Company will pay a thousand gold bezants for information about George that leads to our recovering him. Do you agree?"

"Yes, that is a princely sum and it is a good idea. But I think you should make a thousand if he if he is recovered alive, but only five hundred if he is not, eh?"

"Aye, you are right as usual. Consider it done."

****** *George Courtenay*

People walking about and cooking their evening meals on the street looked at me with a great deal of curiosity as I ran past them in the rapidly gathering darkness. But they ignored me, probably thinking I was running because I was either late for my supper or some kind of thief or robber making his getaway in the darkness.

From the voices I heard and the looks of the people's dress I could see by the light of the cooking fires in the street, I was fairly sure I was in one of the city's poorer Greek quarters. Hopefully it was one of the quarters where the Varangians kept the peace at night instead of the protection gang of the local Orthodox Church.

My problem was that I did not know how to gobble enough Greek to ask for directions. As I slowed down to a fast walk I reassured myself that my inability to talk to the Greeks should not be a problem because many of the Empire's Greek subjects also understand crusader French, the gobble that people were increasingly calling "English." The merchants almost all did and some of them were Greeks.

In other words, what I expected was that sooner or later I would come across someone who could tell me where the Hagia Sofia church was located. Once I knew the church's location, I would know how to get to everywhere else in Constantinople where I might want to go. Hopefully I would not be killed or recaptured before I knew where the church was located or step in a pile of shite before I got there.

Other things equal, I decided as I slowed down even more, the darkness was my friend and stepping in shite was an acceptable alternative to being recaptured because I did not run fast enough in the dark. My plan was simple—remain in the dark and lose myself in the city's crowded streets until I had put enough distance between myself and the wain wright's compound.

Only when I had put considerable distance from the wain wright's yard would I stop and ask for directions. And when I did I would only ask older people and women, never anyone where there was a man close by who might chase me.

So far only part of my plan was working. I had asked two women how to find the church, but both had merely shrugged and shook their heads. That was several cross streets back. It was time to make another attempt.

"Hagia Sofia? Where is it?"

I asked my question to a young woman, barely more than a child. She was holding an infant against her chest with one hand and bent over a cooking fire by the side of the street. She was poking at it with a stick that she held in her other hand. I put a questioning and friendly look on my face and waved my open hands in different directions in what I hoped was a friendly and questioning manner.

She was the third person I had stopped to ask, all women. The first two had merely shrugged, looked in surprise at my battered face when it was lit up by their cooking fires, and shook their heads in a manner that clearly indicated they wanted me to go away. After the second dismissal it struck me that my face was summoning fear rather than pity. I was a slow learner.

"Hagia Sofia?" I asked with a question in my voice and a questioning wave of my right hand. As I did, I used my left hand to cover the side of my face where it felt painful and turned it away from the flickering light of her little fire.

"Hagia Sofia?" she responded as she looked up quickly before returning to poke at her fire. The wood was clearly not fit for her purpose, but she was doing her best to get it going.

"Oui, Hagia Sofia," I said as I made the sign of the cross in the Greek manner and then held my hands together as if I was praying. *If anyone questions her, maybe she will say that the man who asked her for directions was a Frenchman.*

She looked up again at me, nodded her understanding, and pointed off to my left. "Hagia Sofia," she said. And then added some words I could not understand.

I smiled and nodded my thanks without saying a word, and made the sign of the cross to bless her. If my coin pouch had not been taken I would have given her a coin. She and her infant reminded me of the paintings of Mary and the infant Jesus that were in many of the Latin churches. She, of course, was not as beautiful as Mary and her infant periodically pooped and peed, something a God would never do.

She smiled up at me and went back to poking at her fire. I immediately began walking through the crowded street in the direction she had pointed. I could see where I was going because there was a half-moon above the city and the buildings along the street were not tall. It was light enough for me to see the outlines of people and carts in the street as I came to them, but not enough to see what was on the ground where I was stepping.

The evening was warm; the wind was not coming from the sea. If it had been I would have smelled the harbour and run towards it.

******

I had to stop and ask two more women tending their cooking fires before I finally saw the great church ahead of me in the moonlight.   I knew I was getting close when the last woman I asked responded to me in crusader French. It was a great relief; I had made it to the Latin Quarter.

A pair of Varangians came into view almost immediately after I first saw the outline of the church against the moonlit skyline. They were identifiable by the distinctive turbans they wore on their heads when they were on patrol.

"Are you Varangians?" I asked as I hurried up to them. They heard me and saw me coming—and immediately moved apart and took up defensive stances with both hands gripping their axes. It seems that the people of the city rarely rushed up to them, especially when it was dark.

I realized what they were doing and immediately slowed down with my hands held high so they could see I was not carrying a weapon. At least I hoped they could see I was not. Getting chopped by an axe would have been a terrible ending after all my efforts to escape.

"Archer," I said as I came up to them. And I probably said it much too loudly because of my great relief at finding them.

"I am an archer. Can you take me to my friend Erik, your captain?"

It was about then that I realized I was both filled with joy at reaching safety and totally exhausted and thirsty beyond belief. One of them immediately spun me around and began patting me down to search for hidden weapons whilst his mate stood ready to chop me.

I held my hands as high as possible over my head whilst he searched me. As a result, he missed my wrist knives as most people usually did. It was when I was holding my arms up in the air that I first noticed I was trembling for some reason. Even so, I felt like laughing with joy; so I did.

Chapter Seventeen

What do we do next?

It was the middle of the night before a bloody-headed and exhausted George Courtenay walked up to the Great Palace's entry gate with two smiling and very hopeful Varangians holding firmly to his arms to help keep him upright.

Of course the two Varangians were smiling and hopeful; a few hours earlier they had been told about the huge reward that was being offered for George's safe return. They had not contributed much to his return, but they hoped it would be enough to earn at least some of it.

George's return resulted in almost as much chaos and confusion as had the first news of the fighting in which he and his fellow archers had been lost. The Regent rushed to his side and urgently summoned her Greek physician and a couple of spares, a Varangian guard ran to the Varangian barracks to inform his captain, and messengers galloped off to spread the word of George's return to the archers at Company's concession and the Commandry.

Numerous things immediately began occurring. The number of men leaving the Great Palace to spread the word was soon greatly exceeded by the number of men coming to see if it was true that George had returned alive and to find out from him what had happened.

Word quickly reached the Company's rank file archers and was particularly well-received. Their celebrations started immediately in the city's taverns.

As a result, there were dramatic increases in sale of wine and ale in the city and in the rental of women in the taverns, particularly those frequented by the archers. At the same time, the city's volunteer fire fighters left their wives and mistresses to turn out en masse with their buckets because they misunderstood the ringing of the church bells ordered by the Regent.

As might also be expected, a crowd of curious citizens, pickpockets, and small merchants selling food and drink began gathering at the gates of the Great Palace to see what was happening.

George missed most of the excitement. He was promptly honoured by the Regent insisting that he be carried off to a bed in the room next to her chambers "because the dear man is clearly too hurt and exhausted to go to his room in the Commandry."

A good night's sleep, however, was not in George' future. To the contrary, all night long he was constantly being awakened by new arrivals who wanted to see for themselves that he was actually alive and ask him what had happened, and by the poking and prodding and bickering of the learned Greek physicians summoned by the Regent. To the physicians he was just another lump of flesh to which they felt they had to do something to earn their coins from the newly established Regent.

It was not until the sun was almost ready to arrive that George was finally left alone to rest and recover. That was after George had become so angry at being constantly being poked and prodded and asked to pee and swallow potions that he pulled out his wrist knives and threatened to gut the next man who touched or talked to him.

More specifically, as a result of seeing George's knives and hearing about his reputation for using them, the Regent's physicians wisely decided he had been sufficiently barbered and would recover faster if they prayed for him and sacrificed a couple of chickens instead of constantly waking him up to take more foul-tasting potions and ask him how was feeling.

******

George finally woke up at mid-day. And then only because he had to pee because he had drunk a prodigious amount of water before he had finally been left alone to sleep. He found a number of archers waiting outside his door and was told the Regent herself had been in to look at him almost every hour since the sun arrived to light his room.

Harold was sitting in the room when George woke up. Michael Oremus and Erik the Varangian were with him. One look at Harold and Michael's sad faces and George did not have to be told if his fears about the fate of Henry and the other archers were true. He had asked about them when he returned, but his visitors and the physicians bustling about him had pretended not to know.

"All of them? Henry too?" he croaked.

"Aye. Henry and the others who went in with you are gone, may God rest their souls," Harold said mournfully.

"Who did it? And why, for God's sake?"

"We do not know, George, we just do not know. It is possible the attackers were members of a religious cult whose meeting place you entered.

"Inquiries are being made both by the Company and the Varangians, and there is a great deal of confusion and uncertainty, but it appears that the hall is or used to be the meeting place of the city's master masons and builders. Some sort of cult or secret organization apparently also uses it for their meetings. It is possible they thought you were entering it to attack them and they fought back. We just do not know.

"All of the city's wagon wrights were visited as soon as the sun arrived this morning. We think we have found the room where you were being held. There was blood on the floor, but no one was there to question and no one in the neighbourhood knows where the wright and his family are now. Is there anything else you can tell us?"

"I know very little other than what I told you last night when the Varangians brought me in. But the one thing I do know for certain is that the men who attacked us were not fighting back because we unexpectedly entered their meeting hall carrying weapons—the man I killed when I escaped said they had been paid to kill me, but they had decided to see if they could also get a ransom before they did."

"I know something important," said Erik the Varangian as he moved to close the door to the hallway so no one could overhear what he had to say. He had come into the room with Michael Oremus whilst Harold and I were talking.

"The killers had nothing to do with the Meeting Hall of the Master Masons where you were found. My men found the body of its caretaker this morning. He had been clubbed to death. And I personally talked to the men who meet there. They know nothing about the attack and swear they were not involved. They are among the most honest and reliable men in the city; I believe them."

"How can you be so sure?" Michael finally demanded. He and everyone else in the room had been surprised and quieted by what Erik had just told them.

"I know it for a fact because *I* am a member of the society that is lodged in the hall belonging to the city's master masons, and *I* know every single one of the men who meets there. They are all honest and reliable men and not a one of them has any reason to want you dead."

"But they were already waiting for us for in the hall of the Masons' when we got there," George protested as he took a drink of watered wine to relieve his wake-up thirst. It was quite tasty.

"Aye, they were waiting for you. That much is obvious. So whoever had them wait there for you must be someone who knew about the secret tunnel, and also knew you and your men were almost certain to be there sooner or later yesterday. And most important of all, it had to be someone who knew far enough in advance to be able to organize the ambush and kill the hall's caretaker so he would not be able to sound the alarm or identify them afterwards."

There was a long moment of silence. Then Michael spoke.

"You knew all that, Erik," Michael said quietly and ominously. "And you begged off and did not go out with George and his men on the second day. If you had not, you would have entered with them."

"Aye, I did know they would be in the tunnel," the Varangian admitted, "but so did half the city. The men who went with us on the first tunnel search spent the rest of the day and that evening in the taverns talking about the tunnels and how they would be exploring them again in the morning.

"So it could have been anyone who knew the tunnels were being explored and also knew that sooner or later that entrance would be found. And whoever it was, also knew that you, George, because of your position as the Company's Commander, would be amongst the first of the men to enter the room. All they had to do was get there early in the morning and wait for you to sooner or later show up.

"But they may have made a big mistake in using so many men to kill you. Men inevitably talk. So sooner or later one or more of your attackers will be overhead bragging or boasting about it. All my men need is to find one of them," Erik said grimly. "Then we will soon know the names of all the others and who hired them."

******

"Do you believe him?" Harold asked George after Erik left.

"I am not sure. Uncle Harold, I am not sure. He might fancy the Regent or the regency for himself. Or he might want me dead, in addition to my father and the Empress, so the Company would be less likely to support the Regent if he or someone else tries to replace her.

"On the other hand, he also knows the Company will continue to operate here and collect the Tolls even if I am replaced, and that I will sooner or later be gone to Cyprus and England. So why would he bother to go after me if the Company's next Commander might be even harder to deal with? It just does not make sense.

Michael made a helpful suggestion.

"Well, Erik is certainly right about one thing, Commander. There were a number of men involved in the attack. All we need is to get our hands on one of them to learn who the rest of them are and why they were supposed to kill you. And once we know who they are, we are likely to be able to learn who sent them.

George nodded his agreement, thought for a while, and then added another thought.

"You are right, Michael. The man who questioned me looked and sounded like someone who belonged to a gang of robbers or one of the church's protection gangs. All we need is one of them who can be made to talk.

"So how is this for an idea? We announce an offer that will be hard for a rank and file member of the attackers to turn down—the *first* man of the attackers who comes forward will receive a full pardon and a thousand gold bezants?"

"Aye," Harold agreed with his first smile in several days. "And we will hang the heads of all the others on spikes over the city gates, and our informant's as well if any of what he tells us turns out not to be true.

****** *Michael Oremus*

The announcement that a huge reward would be paid for information about the recent fighting that occurred when some archers were attacked caused a sensation in the city. It was accepted and believed to be true because a similar reward was immediately paid to the two Varangians who had helped rescue George and brought him to the great palace.

The Varangians received their reward coins in a hastily organized ceremony in front of the palace gate a few hours after George made his decision. It had been quickly announced by the city's criers and was such a novelty that hundreds of people turned out to watch.

They stood in a great throng, and many had their pockets picked, as they watched the gold bezants being counted one by one into the hands of the two Varangian guards. The two axe-carriers had not had much to do with George's return. Even so, paying them had been an easy decision.

George and his lieutenants had quickly decided that stiffing the Varangians on the reward was a very poor way to treat their allies and friends. More importantly, they knew that promptly paying such a huge reward would encourage others to come forward with information about both the attack in the masons' hall and the murder of the Empress and George's father.

Within hours of the reward coins being paid to the two axe-carriers and the announcement that another thousand gold bezants was available for information about the attack, everybody in the city knew about the new reward.

Even more importantly, the people of the city now knew what the Regent and the city's merchants and money lenders had long known—that the Company of Archers kept its promises and that providing assistance to the archers could bring a man or woman great rewards.

We met with the would-be informants at borrowed stalls in the market and at tables brought out from Commandry and set up in the shade of its walls.

Tips and accusations about the attackers and also about the killing of the Empress and the Company's former Commander poured in. Much of what we heard was gobbled in Greek and had to be translated by the merchants we hastily enlisted from the market to help us.

As you might imagine, the merchants all smiled a lot and claimed to have been pleased to be asked to help and provide space at their stalls. And they probably were—the Company, after all, was a very important customer.

Most of what we heard seemed to be wild shots in the dark or vengeful efforts to hurt someone the informant hated such as an abusive husband. Others were almost certainly deliberate falsehoods intended to remove a competitor or a rival for someone's affection.

And, of course, many were efforts to remove someone who stood in the way of the informant's advancement as was so often the case at the newly established monasteries and seminaries at the Ox ford near London.

Several of the leads we received, however, seemed promising. And the most promising of all pointed to Otto, the king of the Bulgarians, and his supporters.

Chapter Eighteen
Who can be trusted?

We were immediately overwhelmed with informants. The lines started forming as soon as the reward of a thousand gold bezants for "information as to who was responsible for a recent attack that killed some archers" was announced. The response began within minutes of the reward being loudly cried out on various street corners by the members of the city's Criers Guild.

Everyone in the city, or so it seemed, wanted to give us information and claim the huge reward. A few of those who lined up to come forward that afternoon claimed to been there as part of a band of robbers or a religious protection gang that had been hired to attack some archers. Even more said they knew or overheard someone who had been paid to join the attack.

Unfortunately, most of them did not even know that the fighting had occurred inside a building, others did not even know when it had occurred, and very few mentioned that spears were involved.

We listened to many reward-seeking stories all the rest of the afternoon and into the evening. Some of the story tellers sounded quite convincing even though they did not know where or when the fighting occurred.

Unfortunately, not one of the very few who correct said the fighting occurred yesterday and indoors also mentioned either the great eye that covered almost an entire wall of the Masons' meeting hall or the long wooden screen that the attackers had pushed over when they began their charge.

Our most promising initial lead came the next morning, two days after the attack, from one of the city's street women. She claimed to have been in a tavern in the Greek quarter on the afternoon of the attack with a drunken client who had boasted about having coins to spend for his drinks and access to her womanly pleasures because he had been on the winning side of a great fight the previous day.

What was significant was how he had described his role in the fighting to her, and the fact that he mentioned that it happened because he and his mates had been hired to kill someone, but had decided to try to collect a ransom for him before they did. He had carried a spear, the drinker told her, even though the fighting was indoors. All in all, it sounded very much like what we had heard of the fighting in the Masons' hall as it had been described by George and Andy Bishop.

The man who drank heavily while she sipped heavily watered wine and lifted her gown in the alley next to the tavern, she said, was a Bulgarian who wanted her company while he celebrated his last day in the city. He also told her, she said, that there had been some unexpected problems and he and his mates would be leaving as soon as it got dark to return to Bulgaria.

That evening she was questioned by three different archers and then by George himself. Her story was very convincing except for one problem—she claimed to have encountered him in a tavern in the Greek Quarter. That was a problem because Bulgarians looked to the Pope to tell them what God wanted them to do and, therefore, would have done their drinking in the Latin Quarter. *Or perhaps he was staying away from his normal haunts because he was supposed to hide?*

In the end, she was sent away with a gold coin and told to come back the next day for more coins if her story checked out. By then it was late in the evening. The Bulgarians would have been gone for more than a day if her story was true.

******

George and his lieutenants supped together late that evening to go over whatever had been learned so far as a result of the reward being offered. George himself was quite tired and had to struggle to stay awake, probably because the Regent had taken it upon herself to spend the previous night making sure he could still function after his recent ordeal.

"It could have been the Bulgarians, George," Harold said.

"The tavern girl's story rings true and it is well known that Otto the Bulgarian, him what fought with us against the Greeks, wants the throne for himself and does not think a woman should be the regent. I myself heard him say it and so did others."

"Aye, Uncle Harold, it could be. It could be. It would explain why he wanted to kill the Empress and ended up killing my father because he was with her, but why would Otto then risk everything by going to the trouble and expense of trying to kill me, eh?"

"Maybe he wants to take your .. uh .. place as the Regent's .. uh …friend and get power that way. He seemed to fancy her as I recall," Harold replied.

"Or maybe he wants his men and galleys to take the place of the Company as the Empire's toll collector and protector," suggested Michael. "Or he might even hope to become the next Regent or Emperor himself—instead of you."

George, as he had so many times previously, responded angrily.

"Not me, damnit Michael, and you know it. I am getting tired of saying it; I would rather be with the Company and spend my time in England and Cyprus than have to spend all my days in Constantinople dealing with the insipid arses that attend the court and pay for their rooms and food with flattery and meaningless gossip. So you two are never to bring it up again; and that is a goddamn order.

"In any event, we may find out more about the attack tomorrow. I have invited Erik to join us in the morning when we break our fast. He and his Varangians may have learned something from their inquiries."

****** *Erik the Varangian captain*

A messenger came late in the afternoon from George, the Commander of the English Company. He invited me to come to the palace in the morning to break my fast with him and talk about the attack and the current state of affairs in the city. I was not sure how to respond.

It was a worrisome invitation because the English suspect me of being responsible for both murders of the Empress and their former Commander and the recent attempt to murder the archers' present Commander. Would they attempt to arrest me or kill me if I show up?

I merely nodded to the archer's messenger and said what he expected me to say.

"Of course I will come; I am honoured to be invited."

In fact, I was undecided as to whether or not I should attend. It would depend, I decided, on what I could learn of the archers' intentions before I was scheduled to arrive.

I immediately sent for both the captain of the palace guards and my first lieutenant to tell them what I wanted them to do.

The captain of the guards was told to watch the palace all night and, in the morning, question our spies among the servants. I wanted to know if there were any suspicious activities or preparations before I made a final decision about attending. If there were none I might show up. It was a decision I would make at the last minute.

My number two was told to stand ready to lead our men out of their barracks and launch an immediate massive assault on the palace with every available Varangian if the servants reported me taken or if I did not come out within one hour.

"The senior men of the English Company have always been trustworthy and dependable," I told my two lieutenants. "But now they suspect everyone, including me, and there is no way to know what they might do now that their Commanders have been attacked and some of them killed."

****** *Erik the Varangian*

The next morning the captain of the palace guard reported that everything seemed normal at the palace. He said he had personally questioned the guards on duty and our spies among the servants, and none of them had reported the arrival of any additional archers.

"So far as they know, the archers' Commander, Commander Courtenay, and two of his personal guards are the only ones who spent the night there.

"But the servants did say that two additional archers with many stripes on their tunics arrived separately early this morning, and that each was accompanied by a couple of guards and a young man who was some kind of an apprentice. They all said that it is quite common for the senior archers to break their overnight fasts together and talk in one of the private rooms.

"All in all, nothing has been reported that in any way suggests there might be a treachery underway. But those English are tricky devils and I cannot be sure. And even just one or two of them can be quite dangerous as you well know."

In the end, I decided to walk over and meet with Commander Courtenay. I did so with my men ready to seize both the main entry gate and two of the doors into the palace, and lead a rescue through them.

George and his two senior lieutenant commanders were already in the room and sitting at the table talking when I arrived. It was a private room, as usual, because they did not want to break their fast in the great hall where the Regent's courtiers could listen to what was being said. *George seems to be tired. Perhaps he has not yet fully recovered.*

Several of the Company's apprentices were sitting and quietly listening at the end of the table. The guards that had accompanied George's senior lieutenants to the palace were nowhere to be seen. They were probably elsewhere breaking their fasts.

"I have news that might be helpful," I announced as I nodded to everyone with a smile and sat down.

"A party of Bulgarian merchants, about a dozen of them, left the city yesterday evening. They were on horseback except for a wagon that was carrying a man in it who might have been wounded.

"Also, one of our informers says that last week the protection gang from The Church of the Holy Apostles was hired to kill someone. It could have been you they were paid to kill, George, and your father and the Empress before that.

"What makes me think that they may be the people we are looking for is that, Gregorius Samaras, the bishop assigned to that church has also disappeared. He has gone off on a pilgrimage it is said. And some of the protectors and tithe collectors of the diocese are gone as well."

"Holy Apostles is a big Orthodox Church on the east side of the city, is it not, Erik?" George asked.

"Aye, Commander, it is. It is the city's biggest church in Constantinople other than the Hagia Sofia. And the missing bishop was one of the Patriarch's strongest supporters during the recent war. It was the bishop and the Holy Apostle's priests who tried to organize the city to rise up behind us and force open the city gate so the Orthodox army could enter and restore the Patriarch and Greek rule.

"That was not successful for them so perhaps they are now trying to get what they wish with plots and assassinations."

George nodded and asked me an important question.

"Do you think the Orthodox Metropolitan, I think his name is Andreas, has changed his mind and is involved in another attempt to return the Empire to Greek rule? If he is, it could be big trouble for the Regent, and thus for both your men and mine."

"I do not know, Commander, but I do not think so. According to the last I heard, and that was just a few days ago, he still enjoys living in the Patriarch's palace and does not want to give it up by helping the Patriarch return.

What I did not tell the Commander was it was not just something "I heard." Andreas himself told me that yesterday at our temporary meeting place when we met to discuss what those of us lodged with the Masons should do until the furore died down.

We would sooner or later return to where we were permanently lodged with the Masons. Of course we would. But there was no need to hurry. The hall would always be there because it had been made of stone by the city's master masons. Indeed, it would be there forever and so would we.

Chapter Nineteen
Surprising news.

Our morning meeting on the fifth day after the attack was held in an atmosphere of general disappointment for all of us. George was there along with me, Lieutenant Commander Michael Oremus, and Harold Lewes, the lieutenant commander responsible for all aspects of the Company's sea-going operations. Erik the Varangian captain was with us. He has begun joining us every morning so we could share the latest developments. *Or the lack of them.*

We were uniformly disappointed in that, despite the size of the reward on offer and the number of would-be informants it produced, there had once again been another day that yielded no useful information. We still knew next to nothing about either the murders of William and the Empress or the fighting in the masons' hall that cost us some of our best men and almost took George.

According to Erik, the wayward Orthodox bishop, Bishop Gregorios, has still not returned although some of his priests have done so. The priests said they had gone on a retreat to pray at a shrine in the mountains and did not know anything about the whereabouts of the bishop.

So far as they knew, or so the priests claimed, Bishop Gregorios had still been in his residence when they departed for the shrine, or so they claimed, and they had no idea where he might be. Erik said that he had several a couple of his men "talking to the priests" to check out their story, and that he expected to find it was true.

The only good news coming out of the meeting belonged to me and several men who were not present. I have been given another stripe and assigned to replace poor old Henry Harcourt, may he rest in peace, as the lieutenant commander responsible for preparing the Company's men to fight on land and keeping them ready to do so. I never thought it possible. Who would have thought a tavern girl's bastard such as me could rise so high.

George also announced what we had already known—that the Company would have to grow using our Venetian prizes so that it would not become overly dependent on the tolls we are collecting. Accordingly, the Company was somewhat reorganized and there were a number of promotions as well as some reassignments.

A captain by the name of Thomas Woods has been promoted to major captain and will report to me as the number two commander of the Company's foot archers and fighting on land. George's son, Young George, or George Young as he is now increasingly known, will be Wood's apprentice and scrivener just as he was mine when I was the number two. George's younger brother, John Courtenay, traded places with Harold's apprentice and will now go to sea to get sailing experience as Harold's apprentice sergeant and scrivener.

Also, it has been decided that each of the Company's lieutenant commanders, every one of them including me, will now have a lieutenant permanently assigned to assist him in his duties. Harold already had two on his galley, an experienced sailor man by the name of Johnny White and Jack Smith who commanded his archers.

George had decided, he told us, that an experienced man with the rank of lieutenant would be assigned to assist each of the Company's lieutenant commanders who did not already have at least one. The Company's lieutenant commanders were all already stretched thin and would need the additional assistance, he explained, now that it has been decided to grow the Company using our Venetian prizes. I, of course, enthusiastically agreed.

Sergeant Samuel Keene, him what told Henry to get a hold of himself and remain steady in the tunnel, has been promoted to lieutenant. Ordering Keane's promotion was the last thing Henry did before he was killed. Keene will be my personal lieutenant. Yoram, Richard, and Bishop Thomas will select their own lieutenants and apprentices.

George still has neither an apprentice nor captain major to take my place as his assistant, but he said he had someone in mind for his captain major and he will take the next apprentice Bishop Thomas sends out from Cornwall to help him with his scribing and run his errands.

****** *Michael Oremus*

Our meeting had no more than ended and we had walked out into the huge walled bailey of the Latin Empire's Great Palace, when an exhausted courier galloped into the bailey on a badly blown horse. He was carrying, the courier loudly announced, an important message for the Regent.

We were standing in the bailey saying our goodbyes to George when the courier arrived. Erik was with us. The messenger's urgency and the fact that he had staggered from fatigue and almost fallen when he dismounted, and also that had ridden his exhausted horse almost to death, caused us to linger to see what was up.

"For the Regent's eyes only," the courier said brusquely as he dismissed Georges offer to carry it to her and brushed past his outstretched hand. He hurried into the palace. As you might well imagine, all four of us turned around and followed him back through the door we had just exited.

The courier stopped to get directions from the servant at the door, and then hurried into palace's great hall where the Regent was socializing with the do-nothings of her court. She saw him enter and after a bit a dithering while she got rid of an elegantly dressed court dandy who was trying to toady up to her, the messenger extracted a parchment from his pouch and handed it to her with an elaborate bow.

Elizabeth Courtenay, George's "dear friend," who somehow had the same family name as George and was now the self-proclaimed Regent of her much younger brother, in turn, probably because she did not know how to read, broke the seal and handed it to her ever-hovering chancellor.

Years later I learned that the Courtenay's were an old family of very minor French nobles from Normandy. George's father, William, who had been born a serf without a family name, had liked the name and adopted it for his own after he took a castle from one of English offshoots of the French Courtenays.

William's taking Courtenay for his family name had apparently occurred after he and some archers killed one of the English line of Norman Courtenays and ended up with his castle at Okehampton. It turned out to be quite a good name because one of the Courtenays from France had gone crusading and ended up as the Emperor in Constantinople after the crusaders took the great capital city of the Greeks.

Now the two totally unrelated Courtenay descendants, one a descendant of an old French family and the other the descendant of an English serf, were periodically "knowing" each other in the biblical sense and the Company was protecting the self-proclaimed new Regent and her younger brother's Latin Empire in return for the Empire's toll coins. The world is small indeed and no one can deny that God's Will is truly great.

******

Elizabeth's elderly and very feminine chancellor, a Benedictine priest who had served both her mother and her mother's crusading brother who had been the first Latin Emperor, had seen the courier arrive and knew what would be expected of him. He had hurried to her side to read the message to her. He immediately opened the parchment and began whispering what it said into her ear as he read it.

I could tell it was important because her eyes widened and she had a shocked look on her face by the time he finished reading it to her the first time. By the time he had finished reading it to her a second time she had a very angry and determined look on her face. The Regent was, in a word, furious.

She grabbed the parchment out the chancellor's hand, motioned for George and Erik to follow her, and stormed out of the court. The courtiers gaped at her in silence until she was all the way up the stairs, and then they began chattering away in great excitement.

They were like me; they had no idea what the message said. But that did not hold them back from talking about it. All around me well-dressed fops and courtesans were everywhere gathered in small groups and feverishly speculating as to what might have happened to distress the Regent.

The Regent's boy husband and her even younger brother, Robert, the boy-Emperor, were nowhere to be seen. They were off somewhere playing together.

It was one of the few times I had ever been in the court when the courtiers were present. I wondered how things would have proceeded if either her husband or the young Emperor had been there. I decided to ask Erik when I had a chance. He would know if anyone would.

****** *Commander George Courtenay*

Elizabeth's imperious summons rankled me, but not much. I was, after all, greatly curious as to the contents of the parchment message and I knew I could put her in her proper place when she crept into my bed later in the evening.

Erik and I followed the Regent up the stairs to her private chambers. We knew it was serious when she strode right through her private receiving room and into her private room beyond it where she slept and pooped, the room that connected through a door to the adjacent room where I was, with her enthusiastic nightly assistance, still "recovering from the attack that almost took you from me."

Elizabeth was beside herself with rage as Erik shut the door behind us. She shook the parchment angrily as she turned back to look at us and give us the news.

"According to our ambassador to my Bulgarian subjects, their treacherous prince, that swine, Otto, has just renounced his fealty to my brother and proclaimed himself as the Emperor of the Latin Empire." *Our ambassador; My subjects?*

As Elizabeth angrily told us about the message, she had a look on her face that said "what are we going to do about it?"

"May I see it?" I asked as I held my hand out. She instinctively handed the parchment to me without thinking.

"Yes," I said as I read it. "That is what it says, alright."

"I want you to take your men and go north immediately and kill him. March or sail, I do not care how you do it. But he cannot be allowed to do this to me." She stomped her foot as she made her demands. *Me?*

"Whoa. Wait a minute. We need to think this through." I said. Erik nodded.

"There is nothing to think about, George. He killed your father and my mother and tried to kill you. If we do not kill him first, he will almost certainly try again and keeping trying until he succeeds."

I did not immediately agree.

"There is a lot to think about. We do not know if he killed your mother and my father or if he tried to kill me. And we do not know if he has the Pope's support or the support of any other of the Empire's princely states. All we know at the moment is that he wants to replace Robert as Emperor and you as Robert's Regent. We have always known that.

"And rushing off to fight a war before you are ready and know what you are getting into is not smart, not smart at all. In fact, it is damn stupid. And besides, there may be better and easier ways to bring him down or kill him if it really needs to be done to protect your empire and my company. I need to think about it and so does Erik."

And then, as she stood there glaring at me, I added my definitive response to her order.

"So cool your heels, goddamnit."

Erik looked away as we argued. I think saw him smile.

Chapter Twenty

Who is secretly seeking advancement?

Some of the courtiers saw Erik and me coming down the stairs after our meeting with the Regent. They hurried over to get the news. We waved them away and lied by promising to tell them all about it later. No words passed between us until we were outside and alone in the palace's great bailey.

"What do you really think about Elizabeth wanting my Company to go north and fight the Bulgarians," I asked Erik after we finally got out of the palace and walked out into the bailey so we could talk privately.

"I think she is mostly fearful about losing her new powers and determined not to go back to Epirus as merely the wife of a boy whose son may not even end up being the Epirus heir. I also think we both need to be careful, very careful, before we actually do anything she orders.

"For one, you and your archers marching or sailing north to Bulgaria would leave only me and my Varangians to defend the city against both an Orthodox rising from within and another attack on the walls. My men and I might be able to do one or the other, but not both at the same time.

"For another, we still do not know who killed your father and the Empress, let alone who tried to kill you. What if it was the Patriarch and he gathers another army? He very well might do so and order the city's Orthodox to rise against the Latins whilst you and your archers are gone north to visit the Bulgarians.

"For that matter, it could be the Latin archbishop or his priests who want a new Regent or an Emperor on the throne who will give them the city's Orthodox churches and tithes. Or it could have been the Moors or someone else who hates your father. We just do not know."

"Aye, Erik, you are right about the need to move carefully and think before we do anything, you certainly are. But if it is the Greeks, cannot your friend the Metropolitan stop them from rising against Elizabeth and Robert by telling them that God does not want them to rise?"

"Not if the Patriarch says God wants the Regent and her brother, Emperor Robert, replaced by a Greek prince or someone like himself. All Andreas can do if that happens is to try to weaken the revolt inside the city by providing it with bad leadership and reasonable-sounding orders that conflict with one another just as he did last time."

We talked for quite some time, ended up deciding to do nothing except fend off the Regent's demands, and agreed to continue meeting every morning at the Commandry to break our fasts together and talk. I had much to think about before I met Elizabeth again, as I almost certainly would later in the evening.

****** *Lieutenant Commander Michael Oremus*

George seemed very distracted and thoughtful that afternoon after he returned from the Great Palace. He had summoned Harold and me to a meeting at the Commandry. It was there, over a bowl of wine, with our apprentices listening, that he told us about Otto's decision to try to get the emperorship for himself.

Then he totally astonished us by telling us what the Regent wanted the Company to do because we collected her toll coins and kept them in exchange for protecting the city—sail or march north to attack the Bulgarians, and somehow get to Otto and kill him to remove the threat from Bulgaria once and for all.

And there was more.

"There is something else muddying the waters that we also need to think about. The Regent is pregnant from that Orthodox boy she married, the Epirus heir. If the thought of having another heir in his line pleases that old despot in Epirus, he might be willing to send another Orthodox army north against Otto to help her stay as the Regent until Robert comes of age. Or he might even bring his army here and try to replace her if we take our archers north.

"On the other hand, the poxed old bastard also might try to get rid of Robert and use the fact that Elizabeth is both in his family and the last living descendant of the old emperor as way to justify taking the emperorship for his son as her husband or for the new baby if it is a boy. Either way he could claim to be the Regent, though I doubt the Pope would agree unless he had enough coins to buy an enormous amount of prayers.

"Indeed, that sly old fox, Epirus, might even agree to become a Latin to get the Pope's approval, or even to make Epirus another papal state. I certainly would if I was him and wanted to be the Emperor or the Emperor's regent.

"But will Epirus wait to see if the baby is a boy and survives, or will he act immediately? And what will the Pope do when he finds out about Otto and worries about what Epirus or the Patriarch might do?"

I was surprised at what George said, particularly about Epirus, and said as much.

"One thing is certain, the Holy Father will never accept an Orthodox emperor for the Latin Empire. Never. He will almost certainly support Otto or some other Latin, *unless* Epirus converts or Elizabeth produces a boy who is raised as a Latin."

Harold was not so sure.

"It is always possible that nothing will happen. Epirus may decide to wait to make his move until he knows if his coming grandchild is a boy and he survives being born. But even if Epirus waits, the Company's contract to collect the tolls could still be threatened if Otto or another prince is able to takes over or there is a successful Orthodox rising."

"Aye, there is that," George replied. "There are so many possible threats to our toll-collecting contract that it gives me a pain behind my eyes."

We were all a bit tipsy from the wine by the time we finally quit for the day. When we finally decided to break-up and go to our beds for some sleep, at least so far as Harold and I knew, George was still undecided as to how the Company should respond to the Regent's demands for a war against her one-time supporter and only Latin ally, Otto.

The one thing we did agree to do turned out to be very significant—the Company would make a major effort to expand its other operations using our Venetian prizes so we would not be hurt too badly when we sooner or later lost the toll revenues for one reason or another. Although we did not know it at the time, it turned out to be an important decision.

****** *George Courtenay*

My meeting with Michael and Harold went well. Afterwards I walked back to the Great Palace and scribed messages to Richard and Thomas in Cornwall and to Yoram in Cyprus. I did so in order to bring them up to date on the situation here and to order them to do whatever they could to expand our various coin-earning operations. They were also told to send messages to their captains asking for their thoughts and suggestions.

The new orders would be a change of direction for them—they had been, or so I hoped, concentrating on recruiting and training men to replace our recent losses and provide crews for our recent prizes. Now it was time to put those prizes to work carrying more passengers and goods and clearing the Mediterranean of the pirates and our competitors. We especially needed to get rid of the Moors and the Christian and Jewish merchants who had stepped into our shoes whilst we were making the treacherous and ever-dangerous Venetians pay for the damages and trouble they had caused us.

It was time to go to the Great Palace for my supper by the time I finished scribing. And by the time I did finish I once again realized that I needed an apprentice sergeant to help me with my scribing and run my errands.

I thought about taking my younger brother or my even younger son as my apprentice, but promptly put them aside as still being too young and inexperienced. So I went back and added a few words to each parchment asking for recommendations for a useful apprentice.

Perhaps, I scribed to Yoram, my apprentice should be already be a lieutenant in order to be old and strong enough to fight by my side in addition to being able to scribe. It was about then, as I was finishing, that I remembered James Howard, the young sergeant who had done so well assisting me in Rome even though he could not scribe or do sums.

I had made James' promotion to sergeant permanent and sent him to Cyprus more than a year ago with a note to Yoram asking him to find someone to spend full time teaching him to scribe and a second note to Uncle Thomas asking him what he thought about setting up a Company school for such of our men. They had both responded that it was a good idea and agreed that the school should be started on Cyprus because most of our men were in the east. I had ordered it to be done but had not heard anything since.

In any event, I retrieved my parchments from both the primary courier pouch and the backup, and added another inquiry to Yoram who, the last I heard, had set up a small scribing and summing school for Company men with potential such as James.

"How is James Howard doing?" I inquired. "Is he or one of the others capable of serving as my scrivener? If he is, please send him to me; if James is not ready, please send me the best scrivener available."

When I finished and the messages were finally on their way, I walked briskly from the Commandry to the Great Place with my guards. The time I had spent scribing and the brisk walk had cleared my head of the afternoon's wine by the time I arrived.

******

Food was already being served to the court's usual mix of freeloaders and ambitious sycophants when I entered the hall. I was immediately accosted by a harridan with a white-powdered face and several of her simpering followers. *White face was both the latest fashion at court and made women look absolutely hideous and almost dead. Even Elizabeth had adopted it.*

It was a terrible inconvenience; I had to wash the ghastly tasting white stuff from all over me every morning to keep our relationship secret.

"Hoy, Commander Courtenay. There are rumours that you are an earl and the Regent is being challenged by the Bulgarian king. What can you tell us?"

"Why, a band of mummers?" I replied when I looked up and saw them. "How delightful. Giving us a play about dead people tonight, are you?"

The harridan was taken aback and quite aggrieved.

"I am not a mummer. I am Matilda, the wife of Lord Anthony." She said it with more than a little insulted outrage in her voice.

"Oh, you are with Lord Anthony and not a mummer? How disappointing. I heard a rumour he was ill of the French pox. Well, I am sure you will be joining him shortly. Please give him my regards and my best wishes for his recovery when next you see him." *I had not a clue as to who Lord Anthony might be or why he and his wife were attending the court, but I surely would like to be a mouse on the wall when they next spoke.*

Lord Anthony's wife, whoever she was, did not know whether to be insulted or pleased, so she curtsied and hurried away with some of her companions hurrying behind like a flock of white-faced crows. I felt much better as I sat down and waved at one of the serving girls to bring me some food and a bowl of wine. Elizabeth was nowhere in sight and neither was Erik; I was hoping to talk to him.

An Earl? My God, I suppose I am since my uncle bought the title for my father from old King John to keep him from sending one of his pompous-arsed favourites to lord over Cornwall and bother us.

****** *George Courtenay*

A parchment had come in from Uncle Thomas whilst I was meeting with Michael and Harold at the Commandry. I took it out while I waited for my food and began reading. I did so in the hope that by looking busy it would discourage anyone from sitting down and trying to talk to me before Erik arrived.

It was not to be. A party of self-important dandies marched up, flounced their lace cuffs to make sure they could be seen, and sat down around me without an invitation. Three sat themselves across from me and one next to me. *I knew I should have eaten in one of the private rooms.*

I made an effort to ignore my new companions even though one of them was somebody with whom I actually wished to speak, the Bulgarian ambassador. They were hard to ignore because they were all following the latest court custom by dousing themselves with the juice of fresh flowers instead of bathing. *At least they had not whitened their faces to look dead as Elizabeth the women of the court had begun doing; I suppose that is next.*

"An important message?" one of them inquired.

"No," I replied as I pulled the parchment closer and continued reading without looking up. Actually it was important. It was a message from my Uncle Thomas describing the latest conditions and events in Cornwall and in the approaches to it on the other side of the River Tamar.

Happily, none of my family had died and all was relatively peaceful except for a couple of highway robbers who needed to be hung and some priests that had to be turned away. Otherwise the crops were adequate and the recruiting and training of would-be archers at the Company camp near Restormel Castle was proceeding as expected. Another hundred or so archers would be ready to be sent east in the near future.

The biggest news in the message was about King Edward. According to Uncle Thomas either the queen had gone foul or his lice were acting up for he had announced another effort to regain the lands in Normandy that he considered to be rightfully his.

Whatever the reason, Edward had summoned his knights and nobles to bring their levies to Dover in preparation for being carried across the channel by the portsmen of the Cinque Ports to once again help Edward fight for his lands. They either had to report and carry out whatever duties the king demanded of them or pay a scutage to be excused. And they all would do one or the other—because failure to do so would result in them being stripped of their lands and titles.

Uncle Thomas, as usual, had regretfully informed the King of my great love for him and my temporarily absence in the east, and paid the scutage for both me and the only other knight in Cornwall, Richard, the Company's deputy commander. Richard had only recently returned from our war with the Greeks and was once again stationed with our horse archers just across the river in Devon.

We had to pay the scutage because Richard and I and several others, all now gone, had been unexpectedly knighted when we successfully destroyed an army trying to invade Cornwall. Apparently it had been led barons who were opposed to the king and he was pleased to have them defeated. It was an honour we could have done without because it cost us coins every time whatever damn fool was on the throne decided to go to war.

Uncle Thomas had promptly paid the scutage because it had long ago become Company's policy to always speak highly of whoever was on the throne, and never waste our men's time and lives fighting for him unless we were both very well paid and, because kings are kings and inevitably ignore their debts, paid in advance. Instead we would proclaim our undying loyalty to him, pay the smallest possible scutage, and lament our need to be away in the east to earn our bread because Cornwall was so poor.

Paying the scutages and doing everything possible to avoid taxes for the next thousand years, or until Jesus returns from heaven or the dragons return from the east, was in the Company's compact on which every man made his mark. Jesus, of course, is with God above the clouds and would be returning soon; it is only the dragons that are in the east according to the map makers and those who have been there and seen them.

******

I was thinking of Cornwall and my wife and family at Restormel when Erik arrived and sat down beside me. He did so after glaring and making a "move over" motion with his head at the lace-encrusted courtier sitting next to me.

The fragrantly scented fob hurriedly sidled down the bench to make room for Erik to sit next to me. He knew, Erik that is, what I thought of the useless layabouts who filled the Latin Empire's court and shared my contempt of them no matter how sweet they smelled.

"A hoy to you, Erik. It is good to see you."

"A hoy to you, George. It is good to see you too. We need to talk," Erik said softly as he put his axe-head on the floor and leaned on its handle as he straddled the bench and moved his head closer to mine so I could hear him and those around us could not. "But not here, somewhere private."

"Oh it is not necessary to move. I am sure these gentlemen will give us privacy. It is what one does when one is a courtier, eh?"

I leaned forward and said it with a great deal of certainty whilst looking directly and hard into the eyes of the courtiers sitting around me. Most of them got the message and promptly got up and moved. One tarried for a few seconds, but then hastily got up when Erik scowled menacingly and leaned towards him such that the head of the axe he was holding came off the floor.

When the last of the would-be listeners was gone, Erik leaned over and whispered some interesting news.

"I have just received word that Bishop Samaras has returned to his residence at the Church of the Holy Apostles. Would you like to come with me when my Varangians and I pay him a visit?"

Chapter Twenty-one

Something must be done.

The Church of the Holy Apostles sat at one end of a rather small square surrounded on three sides by decrepit daub and wattle tenements of two or three floors. The church and the palace next to it took up the entire fourth side of the square. The palace was the residence of the bishop and the church's priests and their families.

The ground floors of the tenements around the square were lined with small shops and merchant stalls. People were standing and squatting in them and in front of them. The remains of several of the mornings' cooking fires were smouldering by the side of the street. Narrow alleys for pooping and peeing stood between some of the tenements. Everyone else used the street.

There were people and horse carts moving on the street, and a few stationary merchant carts including a couple stacked high with some kind of melons. Many of the people on the street were children playing and women talking. Cats were everywhere. It was clearly an Orthodox quarter from the look and dress of the people. We were enough of an oddity that many of the people turned and stared at us as we walked toward bishop's palace.

A palatial-shaped residence and small cemetery stood immediately next to the rather large dome-topped church at the far end of the square. Between them they took up the entire fourth side of the square. A single low wall enclosed both the residence and the cemetery, but not the church. The door to the church was open.

According to what Erik told me as we entered the square, the palatial residence had at least two floors and the entire top floor belonged to the bishop. The church's priests and their families and a small chapel were on the ground floor. The bishop, he said, had a private entrance in the rear for himself and his family, if he had one.

Three Varangians and my four guards accompanied us as Erik and I walked on the cobblestoned street towards the bishop's palace. All of five of the archers were fully armed including me. We were carrying sheathed swords and galley shields, and each of us had our longbows strung and a quiver of arrows slung over our shoulders. Our company totalled nine in number including me and Erik.

The Varangians each carried a very large long-handled axe and had a shield slung across their backs. Their shields were interesting; they had strange animals and designs painted on them and were somewhere in size between our small round galley shields and the large infantry shields carried by knights and better-armed commoners when they fought on foot.

No one except me, so far as I could see, was wearing any armour. I was wearing a chain shirt under my tunic as I always did except when I was sleeping in my own room or with a woman. *It was something I promised my father and uncle I would always do, and it saved my life more than once.*

Erik had initially planned to send a couple of the Varangians around to the back of the bishop's palace in case the bishop decided to leave without saying goodbye. But he changed his mind when he saw a large number of men lolling about inside the little palace's walled-in bailey.

There were several dozen of them standing and sitting around the entrance to the palace and many of them appeared to be armed with spears. We nocked our arrows and continued walking towards them, but we did not draw our bows.

"Do you have any thoughts as to how we should fight if it comes to that and they decide to try us?" I asked Erik.

"How do *you* suggest we form our men?" Erik asked me as we continued towards the gate in the low wall without breaking our strides.

"You and your Varangian form a shield line and kneel. My men and I will stand behind you in a second line and push our arrows into the leaders and thrusters until they reach us. When they do, my archers and I will pull our swords or stick with our longbows, whichever seems best."

"Aye. That will work," he said. A moment later he gobbled something to the three Varangians that I did not understand.

A moment later he explained.

"I also told my men we needed prisoners to question," Erik said to me as we walked up to the gate in the wall and prepared to enter. But prisoners may be hard to take if this lot closes with us; a good axe chop usually finishes a man rather quickly."

"Not to worry. Some of those who go down with an arrow will be able to talk for a while. We will wait to pull or cut our arrows out until we are finished questioning them."

Erik grunted his acceptance, and then said something over his shoulder to his men.

Over the top of the low wall as we approached the entrance gate we could see the men lounging about in the courtyard get to their feet and start to move about. They had seen us coming. There were a number of women and children with them and at least one priest.

"They look like they might be the men of the diocese's protection society," Erik said as we walked toward the closest gate in the wall. And some of them are carrying spears—just like the men who surprised you and your men in the Mason's Hall.

"I hope that is not a coincidence and these are the men that we seek. It is also very interesting that they are carrying spears—because the hard men in the church gangs rarely carry spears when they are protecting their diocese's people and collecting their tithes and donations. In fact, I have never before seen one of them who did. It must mean something, but what?"

As he spoke, one of the men in the group facing us broke away and dashed into the bishop's palace. Obviously he was going to sound the alarm even though his warning was probably not be necessary. Faces had already begun appearing in the palace's wall opening both on the ground floor and on the floor above it.

Someone must have said something when we got close to the gate into the palace's low-walled bailey because the women and children suddenly began running to get inside and the men began gathering together around a man wearing a grey tunic. He was waving his arms and pointing towards us as he spoke with them. The priest went inside with the women and children.

Unlike the others, the arm waver who appeared to be their leader was wearing a sword. The rest of the men, we could now see, were carrying spears and clubs. I would have said they looked like the toughs of a church protection and collection gang if it were not for the spears.

"Erik, have you really never seen anyone in the city's church gangs carrying spears?" I asked as I reached the gate in the low wall and pushed it open.

"Never. It is something totally new. Perhaps this lot are something else, eh?"

"Well, we will know soon enough, I think; here they come."

Actually it was only the man wearing the sword and one other man who left the larger group and began walking towards us as we walked into the bailey of the residence. I held my bow and nocked arrow by my side as I moved forward and to the side a few steps to greet them. It might have been my imagination, but somehow the two of them looked different from the men in the group that were standing together behind them and staring at us.

"This is church land," the sword-wearer announced. "Visitors are not welcome, especially those who come bearing weapons. I regret that I must ask you to leave."

He spoke in crusader French with a heavy accent. I do not know why, but somehow he struck me as neither one of the city's Greek residents nor one of its Latins. It was also my impression that he spoke too smoothly to be the leader of the band of hard men who collected the Church of the Holy Apostles' tithes and protected its believers.

I moved forward with a hand at my ear to better hear him and get him closer. I also took a few steps forward and to the side to separate myself from Erik and our men. It seemed natural and unthreatening. He, after all, had done the same by coming forward with only one man and not drawing his sword.

"Hoy," I replied as the sword wearer stopped some ten paces or so in front of me.

"We come in peace. All we want to do is talk to Bishop Samaras about a matter of importance. We are not here to arrest him and take him away."

I told my lie as sincerely as I could manage. Unfortunately it was not enough. The man did not immediately send someone to fetch him. Some people are just naturally suspicious, and that is God's Truth.

"His Eminence is not receiving visitors today; he is praying and hearing confessions. You will have to make an appointment and come back later." He said it as if he was a young priest making an excuse for one of his betters."

"Tu es sacerdos in?" Are you a priest? I asked in Latin because I did not have Greek.

He understood my question. I could see the surprise in his eyes as he started to reply, but then he caught himself and merely grunted.

"You must go away and come back later," the surprisingly well-spoken man said again in crusader French. By then we were all through the gate and the Varangians were casually standing in front of the archers.

Although the men we were facing probably did not realize it, I was the only member of our party not standing ready to instantly move into a battle formation; I was standing by myself a few feet forward of Erik and our men and a couple of steps off to their right.

Of course I was not standing directly in front of the archers and Varangians whilst talking to the priest or whoever he might be; a man could get killed standing in front a Varangian swinging an axe or between archers and their targets.

****** *George Courtenay*

I turned my head and spoke quietly to my men and Erik.

"This is the man we need to keep alive for questioning. The others are no great loss. Does everyone understand?"

Erik immediately gobbled something to his men. "My men and I understand and are ready," he said a moment later with a big smile and a nod.

"Thank you," I replied with a smile and a bowing nod of my head to acknowledge him."

The man in front of me looked a bit uncertain. He may have heard what I said so there was no time to waste.

"Kill them all except this one," I said.

And this time I did not turn my head and try to speak so I could not be overheard. Instead, I fixed my eyes on the sword carrier and, as I spoke, I raised my bow and there was the familiar sound of my bowstring slapping against my wrist protector as I pushed my first arrow straight into the sword carrier's hip to the right of his dingle.

It all happened so fast that the sword carrier had no time to move. And he was so close that I could not possibly miss. The sound of my bowstring hitting the wrist protector and the "thud" as the arrow took him in the hip ran together as one sound.

All hell instantly broke loose and everything seemed to happen at the same time. All but one of the Varangians instantly kneeled and my archers raised their bows and pushed out their first arrows—and every single one of them had selected the second man as his target.

As you might imagine, the man who had come forward with the sword carrier was killed instantly. He went over backwards without saying anything except a loud "ooff" as three of the arrows hit him in the chest at almost the same moment and the fourth took him in the side a split second later as he was going down.

Within a few seconds my archers and I had each pushed two or three more arrows into the men gathered near the palace door. At that point I shouted "forward" and began moving towards them at a rapid walk whilst continuing to launch arrows as fast as I could. My men and the Varangians followed. Everywhere there was screaming and shouting and men running.

My archers and I moved forward at a fast walk whilst pushing out our arrows and taking a deadly toll from the bishop's spear carriers. Erik and the Varangians, however, were not slowed by the need to nock arrows and push them out accurately—they ran as fast as they could straight at the spear carriers shouting their battle cries and swinging their great axes.

Our unexpected and very ferocious and deadly attack caught the suddenly leaderless men in front of us totally by surprise. There was no resistance of any kind, just confusion followed by desperate efforts to escape. Their response was similar to ours when they surprised us in the Masons' hall—non-existent.

Some got away whilst their mates were being chopped down and shot down, but many did not. And the badly wounded sword carrying priest, for that is what he was, was one of those who did not get away. He was down and unable to move enough to get up. I stayed with him while Erik led our men into the palace.

"What is your name and who are you?" I asked the priest. "Tell me everything about why you tried to kill me and my men and I will give you some flower paste for your pain and have you barbered. And if you tell me something truly important I may even decide to let you live."

"You will not get anything from me," he said through gritted teeth as he looked at the arrow sticking his hip. It was little wonder that it pained him. It had obviously gone into the bone.

I responded to his refusal to talk by grabbing the shaft of my arrow and giving it a little shake to see if I could get it out without using one of my knives. It did not come out and the man who had killed my men screamed.

"Oh yes I will," I told him as I gave it another shake.

Chapter Twenty-two

It was the Bulgarians.

My conversation with the priest, for that was what he was, was both informative and disappointing. He was the member of an order of warrior priests that had been formed to protect the Bulgarian faithful from the Saracens and from the incursions by the horsemen from the east who had no religious beliefs whatsoever. He refused to talk at first, but then began babbling like a brook when I twisted the arrow and promised to do it again every time he told a lie or refused to answer a question.

"My order's father superior sent me and a couple of my men here to help the Orthodox tithe collectors kill you," he gasped. "Their bishop did not think his men had skills and ability to do it themselves. He was right, that much I can tell you for sure.

"It must have been important because I was told to help them even though they are heretics. I do not know why my order helped them, but it surely must have been for coins and promises for the Church and the head of my order. Why else would he have ordered me to help them?"

"Did you or one of your friends kill the Empress?" It was the first time I asked him.

He immediately denied knowing anything about the death of the Empress or my father. He had heard about their deaths, of course, everybody had. But he denied being involved in any way or knowing who was responsible. To the contrary, he said their deaths were a disaster for his order because it caused King Otto to start raising coins, including a demand for all of his order's, to buy God's acceptance of his claim to be the emperor's regent.

After a bit of digging, literally with the arrow sticking out of his hip, I was finally convinced that he was telling the truth—he did not know anything about my father's death. And he had only killed my men because he had been ordered to do so by the head of his order. What was interesting was that he was sure someone had paid his order to do so, but he did not know who.

I felt sorrow for his pain and lack of a future. The poor fellow was, or so it seemed, merely an ambitious priest trying to advance himself by doing murders or whatever else the head of his order told him to do. He would have been better off in some parish chanting prayers and selling indulgences.

But did I mind putting pains on him until I found out what I needed to know? Not in the least; the bastard killed my men and tried to kill me. He owed me and the Company more than his pain, his information, and his life even though that was all we would ever be able to collect.

******

Erik and I spent several hours questioning the priest. In between his moans and screams he admitted being in the Masons' hall when Uncle Henry and the others were killed and I was captured. He said that he and his sergeant had been met when they arrived in the city on a Black Sea cargo ship a week earlier and had immediately been led to a village near the city. He had waited in its tavern for orders.

His orders arrived late one afternoon from the same man who had led them to the village. He was almost certainly a Latin priest, even though he denied it, because he spoke both crusader French and Latin. The man had brought a horse-drawn cart full of firewood that carried them through one of the city gates without any questions being asked.

They had entered the city rode through it in the dark until they reached a merchant's building where firewood was stored. That is where he and his sergeant first met the leader of other men. He was fairly sure they were members of an Orthodox Church's protection gang because only one of them spoke crusader French and he met the rest of the gang at the nearby Orthodox Church.

Two nights later the messenger had come to them all excited and led them through the back streets and alleys to the big hall. When they got there he showed them the secret entrance and told them to hide themselves and wait because the man they were to kill would be there sometime the next day.

The messenger had showed them an archer's tunic before the left firewood warehouse and explained how the number of stripes would identify the man to be killed. The man wearing seven of them was the one they wanted. They were told he would be one of the first men entering the room through the secret entrance.

It was his decision to try to get more coins for his order, the priest claimed.

"You were the one we were paid to kill, not the others. But no one ever told me who paid my order to kill you or why. The sergeant and I were selected to do it because we could gobble crusader French and the head of my order thought that might be helpful.

"And we were paid so much to do it that I knew you would fetch a big ransom before we killed you. My order needs more coins because King Otto has "borrowed" all of ours such that we are penniless. *I did not know that.*

"Why did King Otto take your order's coins?"

"His Majesty took everybody's coins with a great scutage and a one-time tax on market stalls and all the land, even the land of all the monasteries and religious orders including mine. He also gathered up all the coins he could borrow. He even took the half-payment of coins my order was paid in advance to kill you.

"Stefan Kostov, the priest who heads my order, told me the king needed all those coins, and more, for the Pope's prayers so that God would choose him to be Emperor or, failing that, the new Regent.

"And with the help of Constantinople's Roman archbishop and Bishop Samaras, King Otto has arranged to borrow more from the money lenders here, both Orthodox and Latin, and even from the Jews. The priests have already begun collecting them."

"That is very interesting. Where are the coins from Constantinople being held and how will they be taken to Otto?"

The wounded priest initially swore in the name of God that he did not know. But after a bit more digging on my part, literally in his hip using the arrow, he told us more after he stopped screaming.

"King Otto's men will be coming on this year's grain fleet to get the borrowed coins from the Bishop Samaras and the Latin Archbishop next week. They will be added to the coins the grain fleet already has on board to carry to the Holy Father for his prayers," he gasped.

"A fleet of cargo transports will be coming soon with the first of this year's grain harvest for the city, but I do not know when. It all depends on the harvest along the Danube lands. It will be soon, I think.

"What I am sure is that it will be guarded by King Otto's galleys, probably all of them since he does not have many. Then part of the fleet, some or all of the king's galleys that is, will continue on to Rome to carry the coins to the Holy Father.

"The fleet is supposed to stop here to unload the harvest and take on water and supplies for the return trip to pick up more grain. But not all of the fleet will make the return trip. One or more of the galleys, maybe all of them, will pick up the coins collected by the bishops during their visit and continue on to Rome."

"How do you know all this?" I asked him.

"Because both the Latin archbishop and Bishop Samaras, the bishop who lives in this palace, were invited to Bulgaria to visit King Otto right after the Empress was killed. Bishop Samaras came himself, but the Latin archbishop was suspicious and sent a priest by the name of Mathias to represent him.

"King Otto had them come separately because he did not want each of the churches to know what he was promising to the other. I know what was agreed because I was one of the guards during the negotiations. That is where I heard with my own ears what each of the bishops was to get if he helped King Otto acquire the coins he needed to buy the prayers required for God's approval.

"The agreements themselves were very straightforward and perfectly reasonable. Bishop Samaras is to get one in five of the coins the Orthodox faithful and money lenders of Constantinople provide to the king and the Orthodox will get to keep their churches in the city when he is the Emperor or Regent. Similarly, the Latin archbishop will get to keep one in five of the coins that the city's Latin faithful and money lenders provide and the Latins will be allowed to take over the Orthodox churches in the city."

"They were invited separately so that each church could be promised what its leaders wanted and each of its leaders would get a share. I understand that. But why did they go to Bulgaria and do you know who killed the Empress?" *I asked once again just to be sure.*

"I already told you," he gasped. "I do not know who killed the Empress and my order has lost its coins as a result, so I am truly sorry it was done. But I can tell you that the representatives of both churches went to Bulgaria in order to negotiate directly with King Otto. Of course they did–because they did not trust the promises of King Otto's ambassador's or want to share the coins with him."

"I can understand why the Latin archbishop agreed to help the king. He wants to take over the Orthodox churches and their revenues. But why did the Orthodox bishop agree? Is he sharing the coins with the Metropolitan Andreas?"

"Oh no. Bishop Samaras intends to keep all the coins for himself and use them for his own advancement. That was part of the King Otto's agreement with him. The other part was that the

Metropolitan is to be killed so Bishop Samaras can use his coins to buy the Patriarch's prayers needed take his place. That is why I was sent here—to kill you *and* him."

Samaras risking a trip to Latin Bulgaria to negotiate for his personal advancement was understandable and so was King Otto's duplicity. I immediately began thinking as to how we might turn that to the Company's advantage in addition to seizing the coins.

"Erik, I assume you will warn your friend, the Metropolitan, about Samaras?"

"Perhaps. But it may not be necessary if we take care of Samaras ourselves. Best to do it ourselves without letting Andreas know until the deed is done. He might get merciful or let the dog off the leash, eh?"

"You may be right, Erik. But might it not be better to wait until all the coins have been gathered so we can get those too?"

"Why should we wait? Bishop Samaras will know we are after him when he sees this so he is likely to run instead of sticking around to collect the Orthodox coins and pass them on to the Bulgarian fleet when it arrives."

"Not necessarily, Erik, not at all. All Bishop Samaras knows so far, and needs to believe, is that we have discovered and killed the men who tried to kill me. They fled here to the bishop's church because they were trying to reach a holy place in an effort to find refuge in a sanctuary. But they failed; we caught them before they could get inside and save themselves."

Erik smiled and nodded his agreement when I finished telling him what I thought we should do. Then he hefted his axe and went to settle Uncle Henry's account with the wounded priest and those of his followers we had captured.

The wounded priest saw Erik coming and knew what it meant. He tried to struggle to his feet and get away. He did not make it. Neither did those others of the priest's men we had taken alive. It was just as well; Samaras would be reassured that there was no one left to tell the Regent about him.

Did I feel troubled by the Varangians slaughtering them? Not in the least; it had to be done to prevent the bishop from finding out that we were on to him and knew about the coins being collected for the Pope's prayers. Besides, they deserved it and the Company's charter required that the men killed in the Mason's hall be revenged.

On the other hand, we still had not a clue as to who had murdered my father and the Empress.

******

I smiled sincerely and, with Erik translating for me, apologized profusely to the priest for soiling the ground near the good bishop's residence and his fine Holy Apostles' church. We would, of course, I assured the terrified man as I counted coins from my purse into his trembling hands, pay for the burial of the murderers we had just killed and compensate the church for any trouble they had caused.

"And they were murderers, Father," I said most sincerely to the Orthodox priest, "and Latins as well. Before he died their leader admitted to murdering some of my men in the hall of the Masons and that they came here to obtain sanctuary until they could make their escape. Fortunately, thanks no doubt to God, we were alerted to their presence by a reward seeker and were able to catch them before they were able to get inside and claim sanctuary."

"Well, what do you think?" I asked a blood-splattered Erik a few minutes later as we began walking back to the Great Palace. "Will Bishop Samaras buy my story?"

"Oh, I should think so. Giving them the coins and apologizing for causing the bishop trouble was a master stroke. It gave enough support to your lie to make it believable.

"Besides, it is likely the bishop will believe we chased the murderers here and they were killed for murdering your archers because that is what he will *want* to believe. He may not be sure, but he stands to gain so much that he is likely to convince himself that it is worth the risk for him to continue to collect the coins and turn them over to Otto's fleet when it arrives. That is particularly true because Bishop Samaras will think the men we killed were merely street scum who did not know of his agreement with King Otto."

"Aye, you are right my friend. Men like Bishop Samaras are so interested in themselves and their betters that they do not pay any attention to their servants and underlings when they are around them." *At least I hope so.*

Chapter Twenty-three

Coins are collected.

We never did see Bishop Samaras or even bother to try to find him, not that day nor in the days that followed. The recently-departed priest who had been employed to murder me said he had been told the bishop was in his palace only a few minutes before we arrived. But we never searched his palace or even inquired of his priests about him. It would have done no good. Besides, it is likely he fled our arrival either by running out the back door or by hurrying into a secret escape tunnel.

Erik's men made discrete inquiries in the days that followed and so did Harold and several of our captains who had close relations with the merchants that sold us supplies. We were able to confirm that the city's biggest money lenders and its richest merchants and families were all being approached by high-ranking churchmen from both the Latin and Orthodox churches for big gifts and loans "for the church and your future"

Every man who had been approached was promised many good things if he would temporarily part with some of his coins—big repayments in the years ahead, the Church's prayers for their health in the next plague, indulgences for their past and future sins, reduction in their tithes and protection fees, and the church's assistance in getting lower taxes. It was a long list with promises carefully tailored to fit each man who might be persuaded to part with some of his coins.

The result was inevitable—the coins rolled in and within days everyone in the city including Elizabeth knew that King Otto was raising money in the city for the Pope's prayers that God recognize him as either the Empire's emperor or as young Robert's regent. Which position he sought was not clear; probably the emperorship with a fall back to being the Regent if he could not buy enough prayers to immediately get the emperorship away from Robert.

As you might imagine, Elizabeth was beside herself with rage when she found out that the city's churchmen and Otto's representatives were already doing what she herself was just starting to do—raise money to buy enough prayers from the Pope so God would choose her to be Robert's regent. She immediately began working through her chancellor to discourage the city's money lenders and merchants from making gifts and loans to anyone except herself. She even made a list of people she thought were helping Otto despite her efforts and got quite angry with me and Erik for not immediately leading our men out to kill them.

Elizabeth was also now visibly pregnant and increasingly spent her time with her courtiers extolling her wonderful young husband as "a true son of his great father." She was probably hedging her bets in case she was not able to stay on as Regent and had to run for her life back to Epirus. She was also spending a lot of time at court dropping veiled threats as to what her confessor suggested would be the fate of those who "do not support the family chosen by God to sit on the throne."

Erik and I were met with Elizabeth almost every day. When we did, we attempted to placate her by telling her we were constantly and systematically contacting Otto's potential coin suppliers among the merchants and moneylenders and warning them not to help him. I also did what I could to calm her along the same lines at night when we slept together.

It was a lie, of course; Erik and I were doing no such thing.

We did not tell Elizabeth what we were planning, let alone why, because we *wanted* Otto's coin collecting to proceed—so we could take *all* the coins whilst they were being carried to Rome. We dared not share our plan with her because she, being the woman she was, was prone to gossiping and sharing secrets with the courtiers who pretended to be her closest and dearest friends.

Elizabeth, by Erik's count, had over a hundred people in her court with whom she regularly talked and gossiped as she whiled away her days. In other words, we had good reason to fear she might say something and inadvertently give our plans away.

I said "our plans" because the Company and I had promised Erik one coin in ten of any coins the Company ended up taking off Otto and his coin providers. As you might imagine, Erik had come around to thinking that taking Otto's coins was a splendid idea.

Our basic plan was simple—we would practice "benign neglect" by patiently waiting while the city's two traitorous churchmen collected coins for Otto. And then we would continue to wait patiently until the coins from Constantinople and Otto's lands were all together and on their way to Rome to be delivered. Only then would we seize them. And, even better, we would pretend to be pirates from various different countries when we seized them so the Pope and Otto would be uncertain as to who to blame.

More specifically, our plan was to intercept Otto's coins when they exited the narrow Dardanelles Strait on their way to Rome. After we had the coins in hand, would we return to Constantinople and, if we could, put paid to the accounts of the traitorous churchmen by quietly killing them and trying to get our hands on the coins they had held back "to cover their expenses."

So far as I was concerned, it was a good plan and the Christian thing to do since Elizabeth's family had been awarded the throne by God himself.

That we were going to try to intercept the coin carriers and seize the coins was a closely held secret known only to Harold, Michael, Erik and me. And, of course, Harold's and Michael's apprentices also knew because they had overheard us. Elizabeth did not know; she could not be trusted to keep her mouth shut.

Despite our optimism about the plan in general, my lieutenants and I understood that had a major problem—we were short of both the time and men needed to accomplish it. Since we returned from Venice we had recruited enough sailors and pilots to replenish our losses and crew our prizes.

Sailors and men who claimed to be pilots were, as always, a copper a dozen, particularly in a major port such as Constantinople. It was useful fighting men, English and Welsh archers who knew how to use longbows, where we were short-handed.

Indeed, the Company was so short of fighting men that Harold, Michael, and I seriously considered trying to borrow some of Erik's Varangians. But I decided against it because, as I told myself and later explained to Erik, his men were not used to fighting at sea and might get in the way because they used different weapons and did not fight as we did. Also they were In and might be too sea poxed to fight.

The big problem, of course, was that Erik would almost certainly demand an even bigger share if his men helped with the fighting at sea.

There was also a rumour, and I believed it likely to be true because it sounded reasonable, that the galleys delivering the prayer coins for Otto would also stop in Athens to pick up more coins. It suggested that we might be able to enrich ourselves even more if we waited to take Otto's coin carrying galleys until the Athens coins were added to the total.

After a lengthy discussion over several bowls of ale, and remembering the bible's adage that a squirrel on a spit is worth two in the trees, Harold and I decided *not* to be greedy and wait for the Athens' coins to be added to the shipment. We would attempt to take them as soon as the coins being collected in Constantinople were added to the shipment.

Besides, greed is not a good Christian thing to have. It says so somewhere in the bible. On the other hand, neither is sloth so we decided to think of other ways by which we could also get the coins being collected for Otto in Athens.

Could we send a galley to Athens pretending to be from Otto? Would we have to give a share to Erik? Would the Pope be angry if he knew the Company had taken coins raised by the moneylenders and merchants of mostly Orthodox Athens and we did not tithe some to his private purse? There were many important questions that needed to be answered before we could finalize a plan.

****** *George Courtenay*

We did our best to get ready in the days that followed. The first thing we did was send one of our faster galleys, Captain Jackson's Number Forty-six, into the Gulf of Varna in the Black Sea. It would be our spy picket and watch the grain fleet that assembled in the Gulf each year after buying up the grain that was sold off the riverbanks and out of the towns and villages along the Danube River and its tributaries.

Jackson's galley would hurry back and report when it appeared the grain fleet was ready to sail for Constantinople with the grain for this year's bread. We needed to know because it would be escorted this year by galleys carrying King Otto's prayer coins. At least that was what several of the merchants who enjoyed our customer told us—and they would know because they had each been tapped for contributions "for the church" and had it explained to them when they inquired before parting with their coins.

In other words, that the coins would be carried safely to Rome by the galleys had become an open secret, probably because so many people were involved who had big mouths and no common sense.

Otto's plan was for his galleys to arrive in Constantinople as part of the great mass of the grain fleet. Then, unnoticed in the annual hubbub that always accompanied the arrival of the grain fleet, they would pick up the coins collected in the city and proceed on to Athens and Rome instead of accompanying the grain fleet back to the Black Sea.

After consulting a map and some merchant sailors, Harold estimated that with hard rowing Jackson's picket galley would be able to reach Constantinople about two days ahead of the grain fleet depending on the weather.

Harold's lieutenant, Jack Smith, and his sailing sergeant, Johnny White, agreed with Harold—and, because they were both good men, they agreed because they really did agree with him.

Whilst we waited for the picket galley to return, Harold worked diligently to gather up every available archer including almost all those who had arrived on the skeleton crews of our Venetian prizes. He also took most of the men serving on the crews of our toll collectors and at our local shipping post. He even taxed the two Company transports that arrived that week for the half dozen or so archers each carried to protect its captain in the event of a mutiny and to fight off any pirates who tried to take it.

By the time the hastily dispatched picket galley returned and reported that the transports in the grain fleet had set their sails and were on their way to Constantinople, we had enough archers to fully crew six galleys, including the picket.

It was late on a Tuesday morning when the picket galley, its crew exhausted by two days of non-stop rowing, returned with word that the Danube grain fleet forming up in the river' Bulgarian estuary appeared to be on its way and the galleys thought to be carrying Otto's prayer coins were escorting it "to keep pirates from getting the grain" as an excuse to bring the galleys to the city.

We immediately announced a similar lie to our men and the city's merchants—that we would be sailing first thing the next morning "because we had just received word that our fortress on Cyprus was about to be attacked by the Moors."

And to make sure the word got out of our immediate departure and that we would be gone for many weeks and the coast was clear for the galleys coming to pick up King Otto's coins, we made sure every captain gave his men liberty coins that night so they could rush to the taverns and street women for one last bowl or poke.

Getting to Cyprus and fighting to defeat the Moors would take time. We would obviously be gone for months, at least so far as everyone in the city and our men knew. The traitors were suddenly free to finalize their betrayal of Elizabeth by adding the coins they had raised in and around Constantinople to those that were already aboard King Otto's galleys.

We reinforced the idea that the traitors could safely deliver their coins by spending the rest of the day hastily loading our Cyprus-bound galleys with the live cattle, sheep, and poultry that would typically be carried on a long voyage. They would go overboard if we had not finished eating them by the time King Otto's coin-carrying galleys reached us where we planned to intercept them—on the far side of the narrow Dardanelles strait.

Travelling through the strait was the only way to reach Rome from Constantinople and King Otto's lands at the mouth of the Danube without going by land through many kingdoms. Going by land would take months with so many dangers along the way that it would be total folly for King Otto's prayer coins to be carried overland. They would be robbed ten times over before they reached Rome.

There was no alternative. King Otto's prayer coins would have to be carried to Rome by sea—and that meant the galleys or transports that carried them would have to pay their tolls and pass through the extremely narrow Dardanelles strait.

****** *George Courtenay*

Elizabeth was furious at my suddenly need to hurry off to relieve Cyprus "when I am with child and need you the most." She was so angry that she threw a bowl at me and was heading for the piss pot when I ducked out the door. That last night before we sailed I moved back to the Commandry and slept alone.

Truth be told, being away from Elizabeth was a great relief since she had begun constantly barfing. It puts a man off when he is in bed with a woman who barfs, yes it does, even if she washes her mouth out with wine immediately afterwards.

Although we did not know it at the time, the grain fleet and its escort of galleys was about two days out when our six galleys and their hungover crews cast off the next morning for our long voyage to Cyprus. Numerous people, mostly lamenting women, were on the quay to see us off along with the usual fortune tellers, pickpockets, and small merchants selling last-minute bowls of wine and the religious icons needed to guarantee that a man would have a safe voyage.

We were already through the Dardanelles strait by the time the first of the grain fleet's ships and cogs began arriving in Constantinople along with King Otto's coin-carrying galleys that were ostensibly guarding them. By then five of our galleys including the picket from Varna were already tucked away out of sight in a protected anchorage near the exit from the strait.

Our sixth galley, once again Captain Jackson's Number Forty-six, was at the entrance of the strait. It would hurriedly row through the strait and sound the alert as soon as its lookouts sighted the coin carriers.

In order to avoid anyone in the constant stream of inbound transports warning off the coin carriers, Captain Jackson's galley was moored alongside old Galley Number Twenty-nine which was acting as the Empire's toll collector for the inbound traffic even though it now had no archers aboard. A galley or two waiting at the entrance to the strait to collect the tolls from inbound transports that had just finished passing through the strait was so normal that it would attract no attention or comment.

A close watch would be kept from the very top of Forty-six's mast. Any outbound galleys that they sighted coming towards them from Constantinople would almost certainly be King Otto's coin carrier or carriers. As soon as the first galley was sighted, Captain Jackson would put everyone on his oars and hurry through the strait to alert us that the coins were coming.

The rest of our little fleet of Company galleys waited just out of sight at the other end of the strait. While we waited the men practiced with their longbows and with their galley's pikes and short swords. It felt good to get the archers back to soldiering again as Marines.

While the men were practicing, the captains and lieutenants of the waiting Company galleys met with Harold and me to discuss the finer points of fighting and boarding another galley, and especially what each captain might expected to do under various circumstances. As you might imagine, there was much uncertainty because we neither knew how many galleys would be guarding the coins nor whether one carried them all or if they had been divided up to insure that as many as possible reached Rome. We tried to think of all the possibilities and what we would do to respond to each.

And whilst we practiced and talked we prepared our galleys to mislead the coin carriers when we met them—we began by flying the three-pointed oriflamme pennants of the French king on our masts and having the men turn their tunics inside out to hide the front and back stripes that would identify them as Company men.

I myself had an additional minor personal decision to make—what name to use if we took the coin carriers and I met their captains. It was an important decision for it is always better to have someone else blamed if the Company ends up with something whose ownership might be claimed by others.

After giving it some thought, I finally decided to trim my beard very short and introduce myself as a French cleric with a common French name. I would, at least initially, be Father

Maurice Lemieux from Anvers. Harold would be the fleet's commander; I would be his translator and the cleric who did his scribing and summing.

It would be easy for me to take off my archer's tunic and become a priest. There was a priestly robe and large wooden cross at the bottom of my wooden chest for me to wear when I thought it might be helpful. Indeed, Latin was the language of the Company's school and every boy passing out of it was ordained and provided with a priest's robe. It gave him something to do to earn his bread if he was not up to making his mark on the Company's roll.

Our captains were, I initially informed them, to claim that our galleys were Burgundians sailing under a contract to help protect a French fleet that had carried crusaders to the Holy Land. That would be believable because it would tie into the story we put out about our being part of a French fleet when we raided Venice earlier in the year.

But then I changed my mind about the story—I decided that I would keep my French name and priestly position as Harold's cleric and translator, but our galleys would be independent galleys of lowland pirates, Burgandians from Holland, men whose galleys had remained behind to seek their fortunes independently when the French fleet sailed back to France to pick up another cargo of crusaders.

The oriflamme pennants on our masts were quickly replaced by hurriedly sewn flags with the saw-toothed cross of Burgandy. If adding Burgandy and pirates to the list of those who might have taken the coins did not confuse and mislead everyone, I did not know what would.

Our problem, of course, was that our own men would sooner or later be in a tavern or whorehouse somewhere and let the rabbit out of the sack such that the Company would be blamed for the loss of the prayer coins. So our men and their captains had to be misled so they would tell a different story. In fact, as many different stories as possible in order to cause the greatest confusion and uncertainty.

Accordingly, I explained to the captains what they were to tell their men and how they and their men were to behave when dealing with the men and galleys we hoped to capture "for the Duke of Burgundy."

"Each of you is to tell his men that your galley will be sailing independently under a French flag as part of a fleet of Burgundian pirates searching for some enemy galleys that are reported to be carrying a treasure in coins.

"Tell them that you were given a choice, that if you did not want to help the Burgandians take the coins and get a share of the prize money, you could sail away and return to Malta to await further orders. Tell them that you want the prize money so you have decided to stay.

"As a result, for the next few days they will be sailing under the flags of France and Burgundy. They will do so as part of a fleet of galleys from many states that is under a contract with the Duke of Burgundy to help him take some enemy galleys that are reported to have several crates of coins on board. The Company of Archers is not involved.

"So the first thing you must do when you return to your galley is assemble your crew, point to the Burgandian flag on your mast, and tell your men that you have accepted a single one-time independent contract for your galley that should not last more than a few days.

"And here is something for you alone and not your crews—since the Company is not involved, Harold will be posing as the commander of the Burgandian fleet and I as his priestly clerk and translator. We will claim to be Burgundian mercenaries who had been under contract to help defend the French fleet of crusader-carrying transports, but are now pirates taking prizes for ourselves."

Spirits were high and our men were pleased at the prospect of prize coins even though no one had any idea as to how many galleys we would face or who they would face when we closed with King Otto's Rome-bound fleet. They did not fully understand the need to turn their tunics inside out or why we were flying new flags, but they were truly elated to learn that there was the possibility of prize coins and that a Moorish invasion force was no longer gathering to invade Cyprus.

Captain Jackson and his men of Galley Forty-six would be particularly pleased when they re-joined us and learned that we were going after coin carrying galleys. They had remained behind to collect the Empress's tolls and help defend the city when most of our galleys sailed to Venice and the men in their crews earned fortunes in prize coins. Jackson and his men, I was sure, would be excited by the prospect that their turn to collect significant prize coins might have finally come.

Chapter Twenty-four

My epiphany.

That night, alone at last in my cabin, I was unable to sleep for some reason. Instead, I began worrying. At first I worried that I should have left a galley other than Jackson's with the archer-less toll collector, and tried to decide which of the other galleys I should have chosen. Then, for some reason, I began reflecting on my life and the Company.

Why was it, I asked myself, that we always seemed to be competing with the Churches for people's coins? That was when it first dawned on me that the two great Churches, Latin and Orthodox, were really just companies of men very much like the Company of Archers. The only difference being that the Churches were older and bigger and providing different services to earn coins and provide advancement for their men.

Our companies were similar in many ways. For one, we all three employed men who had volunteered to made their marks on our rolls in order to earn their daily bread and get ahead in life. The Churches' men made their marks as priests and as members of the gangs that collected the tithes and sold protection in each diocese; the Company's men made their marks as archers and sailors. Indeed, those were about the only choices a man had if he wanted to better himself.

There were many other similarities as well. In all three companies the higher a man's rank the more coins he earned and the better he lived. The priests and monks worked out of churches and monasteries; the archers and sailors worked out of transports, galleys, and shipping posts; the Churches had priests and bishops and cardinals with Pope or Patriarch leading them, and we had sergeants, lieutenants, and captains with a Commander leading them.

All this, I decided, was in great contrast to the princely companies such as those of the Venetians, French, and Moors whose men stayed forever with the rank at which they were born. That was because they were all the vassals of a prince who was himself born to lead them no matter how weak and stupid he might be. As a result, good men *could not* rise and the princely companies were riddled with weak and incompetent leaders at all levels because they had been born into their positions rather than acquiring them with accomplishments.

In contrast to the princely companies, companies such as ours and the two Churches tended to be relatively well-led because good men *could* rise to leadership positions including to the very top if they had family connections or could acquire enough coins. Accordingly, it was inevitable that companies such as ours and the two Churches would end up larger and last longer than the princely-controlled companies such as those of Venice, the Moors, and the French whose incompetent leaders would sooner or later bring them down.

Once I began thinking along those lines I could not sleep. I realized there were other fundamental similarities between the men of the Churches and the men of the Company of Archers. For example, the men of all three companies wore clothes that identified their ranks. The main difference being that we identified our ranks with stripes running across the fronts and backs of our tunics and the two Churches identified their ranks with different types and colours of hats and robes.

Similarly, the two Churches took people's coins to save their souls and answer their prayers; we in the Company of Archers took people's coins to save their lives and move their cargos and money orders.

In essence, I decided as I rolled over yet again in my bed, the Holy Father and the Patriarch were the heads of companies of priests and monks just as I was the head of a company of archers and sailors. We were mostly similar because, I decided as I sat up and took a slurp from a bowl of morning ale to moisten my mouth, at the end of the day both they and I were leading coin-seeking companies filled with men trying to advance themselves in order to get better food and shelter for themselves and their families.

Where we differed, I realized, was that we provided people with different services in order to get them to give us their coins. One would think, because we provided different services, that there would be no reason for us to ever be in conflict. But that was not the case and never would be—the Churches and the Company of Archers were doomed to be forever in conflict, even after Jesus returned in a few years and peace finally arrived. I reached that sad conclusion because there were only so many coins in the world and we all three wanted them.

Being in constant conflict with the two great Churches in the years ahead until Jesus returned and everything was peaceful was not a pleasant prospect even though we were often allies when we could get ahead by assisting each other.

It helped, I realized, that the leaders of Churches did not yet appear to realize that we were competitors for the available coins, and that we only pretended to be submissive to them because it suited us not to get into an open conflict with competitors we could not yet easily defeat. Even so, and despite the future appearing to be brighter for us because of our inherent advantages, there were serious problems and potential conflicts between the men of the Company and the men of the two Churches.

The Company's basic problems at the moment, I decided, were that the men of the two Churches had God's ear, outnumbered us greatly, and its men were allowed to put some of the coins they collected directly into their pouches to enrich themselves. The men in the Company of Archers, on the other hand, had a fixed annual pay based on their ranks, the possibility of periodic prize monies and promotions, and we used weapons and specific contracts requiring our performance whereas the priests only had to use words and promises.

One great advantage the Company had over the two Churches was that it did not take as long to teach a man to push arrows out of a longbow and step down on a foot to a beat of a drum as it did to teach a man to gobble Latin or Greek and memorize the prayers and chants needed to get God's attention. That was significant; it meant we could recruit men and expand more quickly when an opportunity arose.

Another great advantage was that we had a better reputation for honouring our promises and agreements than did either of the Churches. People could count on us to do our very best without crossing our fingers behind our backs or mumbling disclaimers in Latin or Greek which people could not understand. Also, and unlike the churches and all the others, we neither held nor bought and sold slaves and serfs; instead, we freed them and many asked to join us so they too could get ahead in life.

Yet another great advantage was that we could immediately kill our enemies and send them off to purgatory and God's judgment instead of having to employ others to do it as the priests were required to do. That was because the bible said "thou shall not kill" and the churchmen had to pretend that there was a difference between killing someone and ordering it done. We, on the other hand, did not have to wait; we could get on with eliminating our enemies when it was necessary.

All in all, I decided as I shook my head to clear out some of the thoughts that were swirling behind my eyes, my priestly Uncle Thomas was probably right: the future was ours and two Churches were only larger than the Company because the churches had started providing their services to people long before the Company started doing so.

And that was certainly true—the Church, before it split into two separate companies of men, had started many years ago right after Jesus came back alive a few days after the Romans killed him. The Company, on the other hand, only really started coming into our own a few years earlier when my father and uncle used the coins they got off the murderous archbishop of Damascus to buy a boat to carry the Company's survivors back to England. That was when my father and my Uncle Thomas discovered they could also use the boat to earn coins by carrying refugees to safety.

Actually, they started out by buying three boats, a cog and two galleys, because their poxed owner would not sell just one of his boats; it was, according to my father and uncle, all or nothing—they had to agree to buy all three before their poxed owner was willing to sell his little fleet and go ashore.

According to Uncle Thomas, our Company had already passed the biggest princely-led companies, those of the Venetians, French, and Moors, in terms of our ability to recruit useful men and earn coins. And sooner or later, he said, we would catch up with the two Churches. It was hard for me to understand, but he truly thought the Company had a bigger and brighter future even though he himself was a priest who had bought a bishopric and was already doing well for himself in the Latin-gobbling Church.

We would end up bigger than the Churches, Uncle Thomas always claimed, because people would always prefer to give their coins to the Company so they could live longer and better today instead of giving them to one of the Churches because its priests promised that if they did they would sooner or later come back to life after they died just as Jesus had done.

In other words, our Company was more in tune with the realities of the modern and civilized world in which people actually lived. For example, we did not chase after young boys; our wives and the street women were more than enough. Besides, giving coins to the Company in order to live better and longer today was a better result than giving them to one of the Churches in return for its priests' promises of being resurrected in a few years, particular since no mortal man or woman had ever made it back.

In essence, I decided as I lay in my bed sleepless, the Company's future was brighter because more people desired to live better today, and continue living in the case of refugees, instead of dying today and coming back sometime later in the future. That was especially true since people were not fools. They knew that only Jesus had made it back so far. And he did not last very long when he did.

All things considered, according to my priestly Uncle Thomas who knew about such things because he had read so many books, it was inevitable that the Company would sooner or later overtake the Churches in terms of both the number of coins in our chests and in the number of men who made their marks on our respective rolls as priests and archers.

In other words, the day was coming when the Company would have more earners on its rolls and more coins in its chests than the Churches. *Would we make the priests kneel and kiss our hands and get our blessings when that day arrived? I did not think so even though I could not speak for all of our men when it came to having women on their knees in front of them; some of the men seemed to enjoy that sort of pleasure.*

It all seemed very reasonable to me as I turned over once again in my narrow bed and the galley rolled back and forth from gentle motion of the sheltered waters around it. Even with my eyes closed I could see that sooner or later in the years ahead there would likely be more archers delivering cargos and passengers than priests delivering another life after someone died.

Today, however, was another story. We were only number three and would have to try harder to stay in the running if we wanted more coins. Our being smaller and having to try harder was understandable—the companies of the Pope and the Patriarch had been around longer and were much larger than ours in addition to being more blessed by God and having someone who could talk to God to find out what he wanted people to do.

The lessons to be learnt by comparing the three companies were clear to me, or so I thought as I rolled over in my bed once again in an effort to get more comfortable—it pays for a company to be the first mover and get an early start; a Commander or Holy Father and his men have to try harder if their company is number two or three. In other words, your men need to be better trained and have better weapons and provide more valuable services if your company is to whittle down the other big companies and replace them as the biggest and most powerful.

I had never truly understood why Uncle Thomas bought his diocese and bishop's mitre until I had experienced the Church's ambitious and treacherous priests for myself and realized we were competing with them for coins and men. Now I finally understood—he bought them so he could keep priests and monks out of Cornwall. If he had not, they would have competed with us in the pursuit of coins and people to work for our company's prosperity and advancement.

On the other hand, and despite all that, was it somehow significant and right that he taught me and the other lads in his school how to gobble Latin and ordained as priests? Yes, I decided, because it gave his boys something to fall back on if he was wrong about the Company being the wave of the future. But it raised questions even so.

My thoughts were just turning to the Moors and Venetians and other free companies as possible competitors of ours for the world's coins when the next thing I knew it was morning and I could smell the pleasant smell of newly burnt bread. As I did, I was instantly aware that I desperately needed to pee and that I knew for sure who had killed my father and the Latin Empress.

Chapter Twenty-five

Chasing the coins.

"Hoy the deck," the lookout shouted from the very top of the mainmast where he was perched, "a galley be coming and coming fast."

Everyone everywhere stopped whatever he was doing and listened. A few moments later the lookout added more information.

"It be Forty-six and she be waving her enemy in sight flag."

The lookout's cry ignited a long-awaited frenzy of activity on our galley. Harold began roaring out orders. This immediately led to his archers hurrying to their rowing benches and his sailors to begin hoisting the anchor that had kept us from drifting ashore. The sounds of similar activities could be heard all around us on the four Company galleys anchored around us.

Harold and I immediately began climbing the mast to see for ourselves. Harold shouted "stay here" to his apprentice and went up first.

It was an impressive sight—Harold literally ran up the rope ladder with his long white hair streaming out behind him in the wind. I went up behind him, but moved very differently; my fears about once again being on a falling mast kicked in and I went slowly up the mast and only part of the way. *I did not have to climb it and I certainly did not want to do so, but the men expected it of me, at least, I thought they did.*

Everything began according to our plan. I looked around for a minute or two before I began climbing down whilst Harold remained aloft and gave his orders from the top of the mainmast based on what he saw.

Our galley's rowing drum was loud and beating faster and faster as we began rowing to get closer to the distant entrance to the strait. We were moving to get into a position such that we would be able to see the enemy coin carriers coming out of the strait from the very top of our mast.

The other four galleys in our little fleet were holding back, way back, also as planned. It was about then that I realized Captain Jackson would *not* know where to position his rapidly approaching galley or what to do when he joined us. That was because he had not been present when I gave my orders to the other captains.

It took me a while, but I was still on the mast ladder when I finally realized that Captain Jackson would have to be told what his galley was to do, I shouted down an order for a "form on me" signal flag to be waved at Jackson's galley. I wanted his galley to come alongside so he could be told where to position it and what its role would be after he did. When he got close enough I would use our galley's loud talker to shout my battle orders across the water to him.

My order was instantly carried out. A wide-eyed two-stripe sailor with a determined look on his face and carrying the "form on me" flag quickly came up the rope ladder and scurried on past me to the lookout's nest atop of the main mast and began waving it—and that was the moment when everything started to go wrong.

******

I resumed my slow and careful climb down the mast and returned to my position on the roof of the forward deck castle a minute or two later. Climbing down was a reasonable thing to do and would not distress the men, at least that is what I hoped. Besides, Harold could see well enough for both of us. He did not need me up there pointing things out to him.

When I finally reached the deck, I breathed a sigh of relief and looked towards the north where the four galleys that had been following us were supposed to be waiting—and my heart sank when I realized what had happened; they had seen the "form on me" flag intended for Captain Jackson. As a result, they had abandoned their assigned out-of-sight positions behind us and begun raising their sails and rowing hard in order to move forward to join us.

My carefully constructed plan to take the coin carriers was starting to collapse before it even began.

Our carefully conceived plan had been for *only* Harold's galley to be in view to north of the strait's entrance when the coin carrier or carriers came out of the strait and entered the Aegean. My thinking was that we only needed one set of eyes on the exit from the strait to know when the coin carriers were starting to enter the Aegean, and that if the enemy lookouts saw just the top of one mast off to the north, the enemy galleys carrying the coins would not be discouraged and would likely keep on coming out of the strait and into the Aegean.

Moreover, even if Harold's galley inadvertently got close enough to the enemy coin carriers such that they could identify the mast as belonging to a war galley, all they would see would be a single galley that was not using its sails to close on them. What they would *not* see, and thus would *not* be alarmed by, was the rest of our galleys. They would be staying far enough back so they too could only see the top of Harold's mast, and thus, not even the top of their masts would be seen by the more distant coin carriers.

Once Harold saw the coin carriers were out of the strait and into the Aegean Sea beyond it, he would order the attack flag waved. Then and only then would the rest of our galleys, which had heretofore been staying back so as to be unseen, raise their sails and row hard in order to come charging up and join us in engaging the enemy.

Each one of the Company's galleys was supposed to chase after one of the enemy galleys and stay with it until it was taken. Harold's galley would wait off the mouth of the strait and take the sixth coin carrier as it came out of the strait. Alternately, he and I would decide which of the potential coin carriers his galley would go after if there were more or fewer than six.

Waiting until our would-be prizes and the coins they were carrying moved out of the strait and into the Aegean's endless miles of open water before they were engaged was the most important part of the plan.

It was in the endless miles of open water in the Aegean where our archer-crewed galleys would be most effective. The open water and the strong arms of the archers doing our rowing would allow us to stand off and use the superior range of our longbows to harass and weaken the men on the enemy coin carriers. And we would continue to do so for each of them until it crew was either willing to lower their sails and surrender or were weakened enough such that we could come alongside to grapple them and fight our way aboard.

It was a good plan—and it immediately fell apart. A couple of unknown galleys came out of the strait and into the Aegean. They may have been the coin carriers we expected or, perhaps, they were scouts or an advance guard. It did not matter—whoever and whatever they were, they spun around and re-entered the narrow strait as soon as they saw our entire fleet coming over the horizon towards them.

Turning around and running was a reasonable thing for the coin carriers and their escorts to do and it was probably pre-planned. For all they knew, there were even more of our galleys behind those they could see.

The coin-carrying rabbits were out of the sack and running; there was nothing we could do but go into the long and narrow strait and chase them down before they could get away. We had lost our greatest advantage and we still did not have any idea as to how many enemy war galleys we faced or how hard they would fight.

For that matter, we did not even know if they were carrying coins. Perhaps they were decoys or just some poor dorks who had somehow ended up in the wrong place at the wrong time.

****** *Lieutenant Commander Harold Lewes*

I could see everything from where I was perched at the very top of my galley's main mast. The lookout's nest where the "form on me" flag had been waved was about ten feet below me. The lookout was long gone and it was now crowded with three of my best archers.

Several sailors were squatted down and waiting at the foot of the mast. They would carry additional arrows up to the archers whenever more were needed. There was another similar nest about ten feet below the one near the top. It also had room for three archers but was not yet manned.

Similar empty nests were on the slightly shorter stern mast. Also mostly empty were the roofs of my galley's forward and stern deck castles. The castle roofs and mast nests were good positions for archers to stand because from them the archers could push arrows down on to the decks of an enemy galley without being charged and chopped by enemy swordsmen.

As you might imagine, when the fighting began the roofs and lookout nests would be occupied by my galley's best archers. At the moment, most of our fighting positions were not manned because the men assigned to them were still rowing.

We were traveling at a dangerously high speed as we followed what we assumed were a couple of our coin-carrying prey into the narrow Dardanelles strait. It was a normal day and the weather was good, meaning that the strait was crowded with boats and barges of all types and sizes going in both directions one right after the next. Our sails were quickly lowered as soon as we entered the strait. Oars were more than enough and using them exclusively made my galley much more steerable.

Collisions constantly threatened and had to be avoided as we threaded our way through the traffic in the narrow strait in pursuit of what we hoped were the carriers of King Otto's prayer coins. As a result I lashed myself on to the very top of the forward mast so I could see what was coming and call my orders down to my lieutenant and my sailing sergeant, both of whom were standing on the roof of the forward deck castle with George.

Being able to see everything was quite useful. Everyone below me was on high alert and I was constantly calling out descriptions of impending problems and minor course changes for my lieutenant and my sailing sergeant to pass on to our rudder men and the rowing sergeant.

The slightly smaller enemy galleys were in the strait up ahead of us and desperately attempting to escape. I could see the flashes as the sun glinted off the water being thrown up by their oars as they weaved in and out of the shipping that clogged the strait—sometimes the flashes were on both sides, sometimes on only one, and sometimes on neither when they pulled in their oars to squeeze through a narrow opening.

We were doing the same as the galleys we were pursuing, but moving slightly faster, probably because our galley was in better shape and we had more and stronger rowers because we did not use slaves. There was no question about it, sooner or later our galleys would catch up to theirs unless we suffered a mishap.

About a mile ahead of the first two I could see at least two more enemy galleys, and God alone knew what or how many were beyond them. The far two must have also spun around and begun rowing to escape in response to seeing the first two spin around and start to run when they spotted us.

We still had not a clue as to whether any of the four I could see were actually being used to carry King Otto's prayer coins to Rome; but they certainly were acting as if they were carrying something of value. Otherwise, why did four war galleys immediately turn back and start running as soon as they saw us? We were all very excited and optimistic.

George was standing on the roof of the forward deck castle with Johnny White, my sailing sergeant and Jack Smith, my lieutenant, a smith's son who hailed from a village near Stratford. Standing just behind them was my newly assigned apprentice, George's younger brother John. All four of them were looking up at me and listening carefully as I constantly shouted out to describe what I was seeing ahead of us and the changes in direction that would soon be needed.

Johnny was the son of a Deal smuggler and fisherman, and Jack had made his mark on the Company's roll as Jack Smith number three, meaning he was the third smith or son of a smith to use the name Jack Smith. His predecessor had been promoted to captain on one of the two fine Venetian galleys we took. Jack had made his mark on the Company's roll as an archer and he was a good lieutenant. I had both him and Freddie in my mind as future captains.

Johnny, based on what I shouted down to him, and what he could see for himself, was constantly calling out rowing and ruddering orders as we moved back and forth to avoid colliding with the boats and barges coming towards us and to get past those that were heading in the same direction but moving slower.

George stood silently between Johnny White and Jack after having shouted an important order up to me. My apprentice, George's younger brother John, stood quietly behind him.

"Do not slow down when you reach the first two enemy galleys, Lieutenant Commander Lewes. Go right past them and past the next two as well. We will rake them with arrows when we go past them, but do not slow down. We need to know if there are any galleys beyond these four. If there are, they are probably the coin carriers."

"Aye Commander, we are to go past the first four without slowing and rake them as we do."

I repeated the order back to George so that he would know that I understood it. In so doing, of course, my entire crew would know what was happening and be prepared for whatever we were going to do. Similarly, George and I speaking formally to each other and my repeating back of his orders told my crew that things were deadly serious and that every man would be expected to look sharp and move fast when he received an order.

A few minutes later we were coming up on the first of the fleeing galleys and I shouted down an order I probably should have given earlier.

"Lieutenant Smith, I would be obliged if you would order all of your mast and roof archers to report to their arrow pushing positions for a chase."

My words, and Jack Smith instantly repeating them at the top of his voice, created what would appear to an outsider as a lot of shouting and confusion as the archer sergeants loudly repeated them and the designated men abandoned their rowing benches and ran to their new positions. In fact, it was actually quite orderly. Archers moving from their rowing positions to their various battle positions for a chase was something that was constantly practiced on every Company galley.

****** *George Courtenay*

Harold had our archers more than ready by the time we got close enough to the first galley to begin pushing arrows at it. And the range got shorter and shorter as we began slowly pulling up alongside it. Every archer pushed out arrows as we close on the first galley, including me and John.

By the time we got alongside and began moving past it there was no one left alive on the enemy deck except wounded men who were playing dead next to those who had already died. Even so, the enemy galley was under control and continuing to move through the strait. Its rudder men and rowers were obviously responding to sailing orders coming from someone sheltered on the far side of one or both of its deck castles.

In fact, our men had been pushing out arrows at the enemy galley from aloft and from the roofs of our castles long before we actually caught up to it. And, for a brief while the Bulgarians or whoever they were, had been shooting back from behind their stern railing with crossbows—something that is hard to do for very long when twenty or thirty expertly pushed arrows immediately begin being pushed at you every time you raise your head to take aim and loose a bolt.

The coin carrier, if that is what the enemy galley was, was flying no flag when we caught up with it so we were still not absolutely certain what it was or why it was running; we, on the other hand, were flying Burgundian flags on both of our masts as were the five Company galleys rowing through the strait behind us.

I think the crew of the enemy galley was quite surprised when we rowed right on past them despite the fact that it veered off to starboard as we came alongside and its bow ploughed into the side of a barge coming downstream. The barge, in turn, was driven into shallow water and when last seen was sinking rapidly from having its side stove in by the stricken galley's bow.

We continued on past the enemy galley at the highest possible speed Johnny White thought our rowers could give us under the circumstances. Whilst we were passing it the archers on our castles and masts were pushing out arrows at such close range whenever they saw someone that it was hard to believe any missed.

And obviously some of our arrows had not; there were five or six dead and wounded men clearly visible on our enemy's deck as we went past with barely ten feet of open water between our hulls. Our victim had been rowing hard and trying to escape when it hit the barge; so most of its crew were probably still safely below deck on its rowing benches.

Although the enemy crew did not know it yet, everyone who might be alive on its deck, or anywhere else where they could be seen by one of our archers, would be receiving another hail of arrows each time one of our galleys came past. It would be boarded by the last galley of ours to reach it. At least that was what was supposed to happen. Hopefully, the enemy crew would not have any fight left in them by the time it was boarded.

The enemy galley we passed was not the only one with casualties. We had several wounded men and at least one fatality. I assumed our man was dead because he had fallen out of one of the lookouts' nests and landed hard on the deck with a crossbow bolt in his chest.

It was our men up in the rigging and on the masts that were the most vulnerable because the enemy crossbowmen huddling for safety up against the side of their galley's hull could see them—and be seen in return.

******

We showered the second galley with arrows as we caught up to it and slowly moved past it. It was rowing hard and going fast, but we were going faster. And once again we took casualties from crossbowmen before the men we could see on the enemy dec either went down under a hail of arrows or took cover behind something so our archers on our galley's masts and castle roofs could not see them.

Harold was almost one of the casualties; a bolt with his name on it hit the mast behind which he had the presence of mind to hide behind when he saw someone on the deck of the second galley start to aim a crossbow at him.

"The bastards have crossbows," Harold shouted down unnecessarily as our galley suddenly turned hard to port in response to a cog that appeared to be drifting towards us. We were closing in on the two remaining enemy galleys.

"Do you see any more enemy galleys up ahead of the two in front of us, Lieutenant Commander?" I shouted.

"No Commander. None in sight."

"Keep your galley moving forward, Lieutenant Commander. Pass the two ahead of us and keep going. We are not going to take any chances on the coins being ahead of us and getting away."

It was both an order and an announcement to keep our crew informed—and it did not happen.

******

The strait was wider where we overtook and passed the third galley with a storm of arrows and crossbow bolts going over the water between us. And then it was on to the fourth.

There may have been more galleys ahead of us, but we would never know; we never got past the fourth galley. We were behind it and showering it with arrows, and taking periodic crossbow bolts in return, when it suddenly used its oars to swing around and came straight at us. Clearly its captain had given up on trying to escape by outrunning us and was now trying to either ram us or scrape off enough of our oars that it could get away. Probably the latter.

Our sailing sergeant, lieutenant Johnny White, knew what to do. He kept our bow pointed straight at the on-rushing enemy so that we would be hit head on instead turning away and being rammed in the side.

Both galleys pulled in their oars just before they collided and scraped along each other's starboard side.

"Repel boarders. Everyone on deck. Repel boarders," I shouted at almost the same moment as Harold and Johnny White.

"Throw your grapple; throw your grapples," Johnny White ordered a moment later.

There was much shouting as the archers who had been rowing poured on to our deck with their assigned weapons and our sailors threw their grapples and began pulling the hulls of the two galleys together. The enemy galley did not throw its grapples; its captain had obviously realized he could not outrun us and had been trying to get away by scraping off some our oars so we could not keep up the pursuit.

It did not happen. Our oars survived by being pulled at the last moment and our grapples held. A horn sounded and the men of the enemy galley charged up on to its deck to engage us. They met a storm of arrows and there was great confusion on the enemy deck as many of the survivors responded to the arrows by turning around and trying to get back to the relative safety of their galley's rowing benches.

I saw it all from where I was standing on the roof of our forward deck castle. At first I thought some of the enemy galley's fighting men were staying below to continue rowing. But then I realized that those who had tried to come up on deck to fight were all the fighting men that the other galley had available.

"Of course," I said out loud without thinking. Then I began bellowing "It is slave-rowed. We outnumber them, lads, we outnumber them."

The fight did not last long. The bladed pikes of our boarders and the storm of arrows coming from our masts and the castle roofs did for most of the enemy galley's men before they could even bring their swords into play.

One of the Company galleys came alongside as our men were climbing over the hull railings to board the enemy galley. I was afraid it would stop and try to assist us.

"Continue on into the Marmara," I roared at its captain as I used my bow to point up the strait towards Constantinople. "Hurry, Robert. Do not let the others get away."

The captain of the new arrival, a Yorkshire man on our roll as Robert from Towns End, saluted and began shouting orders. His rowing drum began beating even faster as I turned away. I had more immediate things to think about; we were lashed to the enemy galley and slowly drifting towards the shore without any rowers to keep us away from the strand.

Did I know that there were other enemy galleys in addition to the four? No. It turned out there were only four. Robert rowed hard towards Constantinople for several hours before he concluded as much and turned back.

******

You would have thought that Harold would be ecstatic at our taking some of King Otto's prayer coins, for that is what we had done. Not so; I had to endure a tongue whipping from him as soon as he came down off the mast. He was very irate.

"I saw you and John standing near each other on the roof. If one of you had been hit the other might have done something stupid and we would have lost both of you. Your father's ghost would never forgive me and neither would your mother's.

"John needs experience at sea, but not on the same galley with you, George. I never should have agreed. When we get back to Constantinople I am going to find another berth for him and take back Archie Smith as my apprentice."

"Yes, Uncle Harold I agree," I said. *I did not think it was the right time to mention that we would not be going back to Constantinople for quite some time and I had other plans for my brother.*

Chapter Twenty-six

What now?

It took all the rest of that day and much of the next to sort things out. The first big problem was that our prizes and the chests with the coins they were carrying were in four different locations along the strait. The second was that Harold's galley had not taken the galley carrying the prayer coin fleet's commander and his assistants; and they were the men we particularly needed to question. The third was that we had taken a lot of prisoners and freed a number of slaves, and the fourth was that there were a number of seriously wounded men at each location who needed immediate sewing and barbering.

The good news was that we soon learned that the four galleys were the entirety of King Otto's Black Sea fleet and all four were carrying a portion of the king's prayer coins. Their captains had wisely divided the weight of the coin chests so that they would not break through their hulls in heavy weather.

From questioning the captains of our prizes and King Otto's representatives, an arrogant nobleman and a couple of priests who were his clerics, we learned many important things. For one, they confirmed that Athens was to be their next and final stop prior to sailing for Rome. For another, and more importantly, they gave us what we needed most—the names of the men in Athens who had been collecting coins for King Otto.

There were three coin raisers waiting for them—a Bulgarian nobleman who was King Otto's ambassador to the Duke of Athens, the papal nuncio who was the Pope's ambassador to the Duke, and the city's Orthodox Metropolitan, the Patriarch's man in the city.

Interestingly enough, the Latin archbishop collecting tithes, selling indulgences, and running the gangs that "protected" Athens' relatively small Latin community was never mentioned. That was a little surprising since both Otto and the Duke of Athens were Latins in the sense that they looked to the Pope to tell them what God wanted them to do and were guided by Latin gobbling priests to do it.

On the other hand, perhaps it was understandable the Latin archbishop was not involved—there were very few Latins in Athens except the Duke and his men who had been forced on the Greeks when the crusaders took Constantinople and assigned the various states of the old Byzantine Empire to the crusade's captains.

******

An arrogant and self-important young nobleman was in command of the galleys we captured. His name was Tarnovo. I never did find out if that was his family name or where his lands were located. Who he was and where he came from, of course, did not matter. What did matter was that his next stop was to be the port of Piraeus to pick up the coins that had been collected in Athens for King Otto. From there he was to carry them to Rome and deliver them to King Otto's ambassador.

Lord Tarnovo and his entourage of friends and servants were on the third galley. He was apparently the second or third son of one of the king's brothers and wore a gorgeous uniform to indicate his rank. It was immaculate, probably because he and his friends hid in one of the deck castles and barred its door during the fighting.

I put on my priestly robe and wooden cross and questioned Lord Tarnovo after introducing myself as a Burgundian priest from Toulon by the name of Conrad. Why Conrad and Toulon? Because those were the names I wanted him and his friends to spread about after, or perhaps I should say if, we released them. We would use other names elsewhere.

Tarnovo was a classic insignificant prince in that he had an exaggerated sense of his own importance, an extremely fancy sword he had never used, and could neither read nor scribe nor gobble anything except Bulgarian. But he was a Latin and had brought a couple of priestly Latin clerics to assist him and translate for him. As a result, we were able to conduct our "negotiations" in Latin with his priestly clerks doing the translating.

Questioning Taranov and the priestly members of his entourage did not take long. They all three became very talkative when their choices were explained to them, especially after Tarnovo became Bulgaria's first nine-fingered nobleman. It soon became apparent that Tarnovo was a meaningless figurehead; it was the older of the two priests who was really in charge.

I made things very clear from the beginning.

"If you tell us everything and do not lie, we will take you three and the prince's friends with us to the Holy Land. When we get there, we will free you all so that you can make your way back home or join the crusade, whatever you wish.

"But if you do not truthfully answer ever question immediately, or if you lie and tell us something that differs from what we hear from one of the others when we speak to them privately, we will cut off your fingers one at a time until you tell us the truth."

One of the things I wanted to know, of course, was what arrangements had already been made with the Pope and what King Otto had been promised. We needed to know that so we would have some idea as to how much of our prize money we would have to "donate" to the Holy Father to keep him sweet.

The other important thing we needed to know was the names of the man or men in Athens who had the coins they were to pick up there. "And, by the way, have you ever seen any of them?" *Which was another way saying "would any of them recognize you if they saw you?"*

Our archers and sailors worked all the rest of that day and part of the next to move our galleys and the two usable prizes to one place, a wide section of the strait, and to redistribute their coins, slaves, and crews into the six galleys, four of ours and two prizes, that would be leaving immediately for Cyprus.

It was a happy time and our men were cheerful, and rightly so despite our casualties. They instinctively knew that we had taken an unexpectedly large amount of coins such that many a man's share might well be enough for him to buy himself out of the company and retire— twenty-one chests of gold and silver including a surprising number of gold bezants.

The surviving able-bodied and lightly wounded common sailors and soldiers of the four captured galleys took the place of their slaves and were chained to the lower rowing benches of two of the captured galleys. The two galleys were given very strong prize crews and immediately set their sails for Cyprus with some of the captured coins and a few of the slaves.

Jack Smith and Johnny White were each immediately given an additional stripe and appointed as the two captured galleys' prize captains with a couple of senior archer sergeants as their lieutenants and a couple of newly promoted sailors as their sailing sergeants. They were all quite pleased since it doubled their pay and prize shares and greatly improved their sleeping quarters.

My brother John went with Johnny White as his apprentice sergeant. I thought about promoting John to lieutenant but did not; he was still much too young and inexperienced to take over if Johnny went down, and the men would know it and be concerned.

We freed the slaves on all four of the captured galleys because they posed no threat as there were not nearly enough of them to have any chance of overcoming the archers with whom they would be sailing. They were scattered about all six galleys that would be sailing to Cyprus. Besides, they had no reason to rise against us. They would help with the rowing and be allowed to go ashore and begin making their way home as soon as they reached Cyprus. The captured galley crews would be released somewhere in the Holy Land.

Two of the enemy galleys were burned after the supplies they were carrying were removed. One because its hull was too badly damaged from colliding with a northbound barge to be quickly repaired, and the other because it was so decrepit and its hull was in such bad shape that Harold thought it would likely give way and the galley would sink if it encountered heavy seas.

All the captured coins were distributed among our four Cyprus-bound Company galleys along with all of the captured captains and sergeants to help them row. They too immediately set off for Cyprus.

The six galleys of our Cyprus-bound fleet, four of ours and the two prizes, would attempt to stay together all the way. It was a formidable force, both individually and as a fleet, such that it had more to fear from foul weather than any Moorish or Venetian pirates it might encounter. At least that is what we all thought.

Harold's galley and Captain Jackson's Number Forty-six did not sail with our Cyprus-bound fleet and did not take on any of the coins or slaves or prisoners. We would end up in Cyprus, but first we were going to Athens—to see if we could gull the Athenian supporters and financiers of King Otto into giving us the coins that were being assembled there for Lord Tarnovo and his men to carry to Rome.

Everyone in the crews of our six galleys who understood and gobble Greek was going with us to Athens, both of them. So was the nine-fingered leader of the Bulgarians and the two priests who were his clerics—they were in chains on the lower rowing bench in case we needed more information or their "assistance" when we reached Athens and had to deal with King Otto's coin collectors. In the meantime they would help with the rowing.

******

Our eight galleys were full of happy Company men as we sailed out of the strait and into the Aegean, and rightly so—we had captured a lot of coins such that there would be substantial prize money for everyone.

There was certainly more coins than I expected. That was because, according to young Lord Tarnovo, who had become extremely cooperative after our initial discussions, one of the great lords of the Eastern Rus had provided King Otto with several chests of coins in exchange for some disputed lands along the Danube. Otto had, or so his nine-fingered lordship claimed, accepted the Rus coins in order to reach the total that the Pope's nuncio, the Holy Father's ambassador to King Otto, said would result in the Holy Father's prayers being successful.

Did the nuncio actually know how much it would cost to get sufficient Papal prayers to have God decide that King Otto should be the Latin Empire's Regent or Emperor? Probably not: There had not been enough time since the Empress was murdered for the nuncio to be informed of her death, and then for a messenger to then carry an inquiry to Rome and carry the Pope's answer back to Bulgaria, and then for all the required negotiations and necessary arrangements to be made.

No, I decided. It would have been impossible for the nuncio to tell King Otto how many prayer coins would be needed and all the necessary arrangements made to get them *unless* the inquiry had been made and the negotiations started *before* the Empress died. As you might imagine, that interested me greatly even though I now knew who had killed her and my father.

On the other hand, at least so far as I was concerned, it was reasonable for the nuncio to tell King Otto a specific number of coins that would be required and for King Otto to begin raising them—it was reasonable for Otto because there was always the chance that the Pope would accept whatever Otto ended up being able to pay such that Otto's dreams would come true.

It was similarly reasonable for the nuncio to tell Otto a specific amount even though he had heard nothing from the Pope. He almost certainly been in Rome long enough to know that there was such a number and to have some idea as to what it might be.

More likely, however, was that the nuncio claimed to know the precise number to encourage Otto to obtain as many coins as possible—because he knew some of the coins would inevitably stick to his fingers even if the total ended up not being enough for the papal prayers needed to get a positive response from God.

I especially understood, or at least thought I did, why Otto had done everything possible to get enough coins to buy the necessary prayers—because even having a longshot chance of getting his hands on the entire Latin Empire was better than having a few more fields along the Danube. Besides, if he really missed his lands he could take them back by decree if he did become the Empire's Regent or Emperor, or by force if he did not.

And how much would Otto be willing to pay the Company to help him get his lands back if the Holy Father did not pray hard enough to get God to accept him? Hmm.

In any event, based on what I now knew about the Empress's death, Otto's odds of success at becoming the Empire's Regent or its Emperor were probably better than he thought even though he would almost certainly have to raise more coins and try again to get them to Rome.

That led me to begin daydreaming behind my eyes about how we might be able to get some or all of the next chests of prayer coins in addition to the current chests. It could be done, I decided. For example, we could carry them to Rome for a fee as we did for the Empress when she bought the regency. Or we could once again intercept them and take them all.

But how could we get away with them without making the Holy Father angry or risking the loss of the toll coins?

Stop thinking so far into the future, I told myself as I shook my head to clear it; we have not yet even taken all of the currently available prayer coins nor even safely reached Cyprus and Cornwall with those we have already taken.

****** *Commander Courtenay*

After we cleared the Dardanelles strait I sat alone on the roof of the forward deck castle with a bowl of wine and turned my thoughts once again to King Otto's coins—both those we had already taken that were disappearing over the horizon on their way to Cyprus and those we might be able to get our hands on when we reached Athens. What I was mostly thinking about were the coins that were thought to be waiting for Otto in Athens.

In the normal course of such events, the Holy Father's ambassador to King Otto, the papal nuncio, would get some of Otto's coins "for his services" and be able to use them to advance himself. The nuncios and ambassadors in Constantinople and Athens would similarly expect a share of whatever coins they helped to provide—and I wondered if they had already gotten them.

And that led to another thought.

Nuncios and ambassadors always expect to end up with some of the coins that pass through their hands. And "intermediaries" and "agents" almost always do. That raised the interesting question as to how they might be made to shoulder the blame for the loss of the coins.

Could it have been, for instance, that one or more of the papal nuncios or Otto's ambassadors tipped off an agent of the Moorish or Burgundian pirates, or some other pirates for that matter, as to the fact that the coins might be successfully taken when they came through the Dardanelles Strait?

I knew that was not the case, of course, since we were the ones who took them. But it could have been a nuncio or ambassador who told the Moors or the French or the Venetians or someone else about the coins in exchange for getting more of them.

And if it had been someone like that, or if everyone just *thought* that might be the case, it would certainly be helpful because one or more of them would be suspect in the coins disappearance so that less attention was paid to the Company.

It was a gambit I decided to try—nothing would be lost if providing more suspects did not work. But if it did, the list of those who might have been responsible for the coins going missing would get much larger because it would not be limited to the Burgandians or the French or, God forbid, the Company.

Suggesting that one or more of the nuncios or ambassadors tipped off one or more of the pirates who infested the Mediterranean in order to get a larger share of the coins was an interesting idea. It would, at the very least, make the disappearance of the coins even more confusing and the source of their loss even harder to pin down. The more the merrier so to speak. *Hmm? Yes, that would be a fine move to make.*

Thinking about how to get others blamed for the missing coins got me to thinking even more, which is always a good thing to do when one is trying to decide what moves to make to get his hands on more money. And then it came to me how we might be able to get the coins waiting in Athens and get someone else blamed for their loss.

We had a shipping post serving Athens, so once we cleared the strait and were underway I got to work scribing an important message for our post captain and his men. I decided to send it to Lieutenant Edward Sparrow at our Piraeus compound instead of to Robert Archer, the captain of our Athens shipping post which included Piraeus. It ordered Edward to deliver a second message which would accompany the first, a message that would already be written and sealed. It would go to the papal nuncio in Athens

I decided to use Edward as the messenger because Robert Archer was *not* the man to do what needed to be done. Edward was smarter; he was more likely to read between the lines and understand both what needed to be done and what must *not* be done.

Besides, Edward was literate and Robert was not, meaning Edward could read the first message with my instructions and Robert could not. If I sent Robert a message ordering him to secretly deliver the second parchment to the Athens nuncio, someone else, almost certainly an Athenian employed as a scribe, would have to read the delivery order and explain it to Robert.

Involving someone from outside the Company would not do. We had already suffered from one disloyal scribe in Athens; allowing his replacement to also hurt us would be unforgivable. And it would also be dangerous since it might lead them to be waiting for us with swords instead of with coins.

With that in mind, I scribed the second parchment that I wanted Edward to deliver to the nuncio in Athens. I did not suggest how Edward should accomplish the delivery of the second parchment to the nuncio, only that it be done without anyone being able to find out where it came from or who sent it. Edward was smart and knew the local situation; he would figure it out.

This is what I scribed in the message to be delivered to the nuncio. It was, of course, scribed in Latin.

"Excellency, we are here to collect King Otto's prayer coins and we are concerned because there are reports that the French and Moorish pirates and the Duke of Athens know about the coins and have spies in the households of the ambassador and the Metropolitan. The risk is too great that the coins will be intercepted. So please make the necessary arrangements to meet us without informing either of them as to when and where we collect the coins.

"We will bring one or two of our galleys to the north end of Piraeus's north quay on Wednesday evening just as the sun goes down. Please be there with the coins and as many guards as possible one hour after dark. I will try to be there, but I am in my bed with a terrible coughing pox and may not be able to come myself. If I cannot be there, our man will be one of my clerics, Father Mathias. He will accept delivery and sign for them.

I signed the parchment as if I were a cleric writing for "Lord Tarnovo" and sealed it with his lordship's ring. I felt good about the message because it was not entirely a lie—I was not Father Mathias, of course. But I was probably close enough since I was a priest and could gobble Latin. And if I had even the smallest of opportunities, I would let it be known that I was from Constantinople.

There was, I knew for sure, a Father Mathias in Constantinople—he was Elizabeth's confessor. And from what Elizabeth had told me about the various penances and indulgences he had required of her as a result of her knowing me, I knew he was a greedier and more devious priest than most, and thus a worthy scapegoat whose elimination would benefit everyone.

Indeed, the more I thought about it, the more I was sure that no one was more deserving of the Holy Father's and King Otto's anger for the loss of the prayer coins than Father Mathias. And if not Father Mathias, then the other nuncios or any of the many others whose names I intended to suggest took whatever blame and penalties resulted from the loss of the coins.

Blaming anyone except the Company was quite acceptable so far as I was concerned, especially if they were like Father Mathias and deserved it. I know he did not alert any pirates about the coins, but he probably would have done so if he thought he could profit from it and that was close enough.

After I sealed the parchments with Lord Tarnovo's ring, which he had eagerly provided when I sent for it, my thoughts turned to the fact that I spent so much of my time trying to get more coins for the Company. I wondered if the Pope and Patriarch spent as much time thinking about coins as I did.

Probably not, I decided. They had other more important things to do. Why at this very moment the Holy Father might be standing at the top of the great stairway that leads up to the church that is the Holy Father's private chapel, the newly rebuilt ones the Spanish prince donated to the Church a few years ago, welcoming Jesus back and the dead people he had brought back with him.

Surely the Holy Father would not be thinking of coins at a time like that. He would be distracted the same way I was when I was fighting with someone who was trying to kill me or poking Elizabeth.

There was no doubt about it behind my eyes—we who were the commanders and captains of the still-growing companies of coin collectors like the archers were all alike. We had to work harder than the churchmen because our companies have not yet collected enough coins to see us through the peace that would occur when Jesus returned and brought some of the good dead people back with him.

Of course, like the Pope and Patriarch, we archers also wanted Jesus to return and bring the dead people who paid their tithes back with him as the Pope promised. Hopefully, however, that would not happen not until we had enough coins in our Restormel and Cyprus strongholds to see us through lean days of peace that are sure to follow Jesus's return and continue until he decides to go back to heaven again. Only then, when Jesus leaves again, would men turn on each other once again and we could get back to earning our daily bread by carrying refugees to safety and the like.

Is it possible Jesus has been periodically returning to see how we are doing? Uncle Thomas says it is possible because there have been several brief periods of peace when there was no fighting and we could find no mercenary contracts on which to make our marks and there were no refugees to carry to safety.

But who really knows if he did, return that is. I certainly did not. In any event, I had things to do until he decided to return and bide with us for a while—there were coins to fetch and blames and revenges to shift on to others, preferably those who deserved them.

Chapter Twenty-seven

A delivery is arranged.

We raised our sails and rowed hard in order to get to Athens before the news of the fighting in the strait could reach the Greeks' great city and alarm the coin collectors. We hurried because we were afraid that news of the fighting would put the gatherers and holders of coins for King Otto on guard and hamper our efforts to get our hands on them.

Fortunately, the weather was good and the winds fair so we made good time. The men were even able to take turns practicing archery and sword fighting when they were not rowing. Captain Jackson's galley kept up with us and did the same.

Perhaps even more important, we were also able to do what we could to make our two galleys look as much as possible like the Black Sea galleys we had taken a few days earlier. We would, of course, fly King Otto's pennants from our masts, the ones we took from the galleys we burned.

But merely flying King Otto's pennants was not enough, not near enough. The problem was that Harold's galley had forty-four oars to a side and Captain Jackson's had forty. All of the Black Sea galleys, on the other hand, were slightly smaller with a unique and noticeable thirty-six oars to a side that was common to the Black Sea. Accordingly, if there were any seamen amongst those who had gathered the coins or were guarding them, they might spot the difference and sound the alarm.

We responded to the problem by keeping our galleys' carpenters and their mates busy doing whatever they could to convert both of our galleys into what Harold and I hoped would look like Black Sea thirty-sixes. They mostly did it with hull patches that covered some the holes in our galleys' hulls where their oars were poked through to row.

The covers looked false when one got close enough, but we hoped they would pass at a distance. Even so, we decided not take any chances when we reached Piraeus—we would come in just as the sun was finishing its daily voyage around the world and anchor far enough out in the harbour that the number of oar openings in our hull could barely be counted by someone standing on the nearest shore.

As you might expect, our men would *not* be given a shore leave and no supplies would be purchased. Our plan was for Harold's galley to come in alone at the very end of the day to land the message telling King Otto's men that we were there to pick up the coins the next night at the far end of the north quay, and then, as soon as the messenger returned the next morning, immediately go back out to sea to re-join Number Forty-six.

Both galleys would then return together the next day, once again at the last minute just as it was getting dark, to pick up the coins. It was a reasonable plan. It was also the only one I could come up with that had any chance of success.

****** *Commander Courtenay*

The rain squall and its sudden winds hit us as I was being rowed ashore in the galley's dinghy. Harold's galley was anchored somewhere behind us with its archers almost certainly having been called to begin rowing so that it would hold its place against the gusting wind. The fading light of the day had suddenly turned into darkness and there were waves in the usually calm and sheltered harbour. It would pass.

I was being rowed ashore by two sailors so I could deliver my parchments to Edward Sparrow personally instead of sending them via a messenger. Why I was doing it myself? I was not sure. I told Harold I was going to go ashore and deliver the messages myself because I was afraid they would fall into the wrong hands, and also that I wanted to make sure that Edward Sparrow knew exactly what I wanted him to do.

What I told Harold was not exactly true, and I think he knew it. A better explanation was probably that I suddenly had an urge to get off the galley and walk on dry land. The big problem at the moment, of course, was that the land we were approaching was anything but dry.

Whatever the reason, I seemed to have made a mistake. The quay where the Company's shipping post had its Piraeus compound was quite a distance from where our galley was anchored. That was by design in case someone was watching. But it increasingly looked like it was a bad decision not to drop me off closer to our shipping post, or so it seemed to me now that I was sopping wet and my teeth were chattering from the cold wind.

One of the two sailors rowing me ashore in the gathering darkness was Anthony Thatcher, a two-stripe chosen man from Walmer whose father was, he claimed, the best roof thatcher in all of Kent. According to Harold, Anthony understood Greek and could gobble it fluently due to having a Greek wife on Cyprus and six children. I wanted him with me in case we ran into any Greeks and needed to talk or bribe our way out of trouble.

The other rower was Edwardo. He had no second name on the Company roll, probably because he was the only Edwardo in the entire Company. Edwardo was from a little fishing village somewhere on the Spanish coast. Apparently he had somehow joined the Company years ago when my father's galley put in there whilst searching for some missing relics. He was particularly good with a dinghy and was known as the best cook in the fleet.

Edward had always been favoured by my father because he too, like my father, had a bad leg and walked with a limp. Edwardo had been a fisherman as a boy but broke his leg when he fell off a mast. It had been set badly and Edwardo had walked with a limp ever since. That is what apparently caught my father's eye and caused him to be accepted as a recruit. Or it may have been that Edwardo was a very good cook and my father liked to eat. It was probably both.

My father, of course, had limped for another reason—he had taken a sword run all the way through his leg in a fight with some Moors. I was not sure how it happened as he never talked about it.

******

Water had to be constantly bailed out of the dinghy and I was wet and shivering by the time we finally made it to the strand next to the quay used by the Company's transports and galleys. The quay was empty except for a forlorn-looking three-masted ship and a couple of cogs. I did recognize any of them. And to make things worse, a wave came in and washed over me all the way up to my knees as I climbed out to help my two rowers pull the dinghy above the water line so it would not be caught by a rogue wave and float away. The water was cold and so was I.

Pulling the dinghy high enough on to the strand turned out to relatively easy even though we had to haul it quite a distance before we reached a large number of similarly stranded dinghies and small fishing boats. Most of them were turned over so they would not fill up with rainwater. Some, however, were tilted on their sides and there were men sheltering under them from the rain. They just looked at us in the dwindling light.

A couple of men sheltering under one of the fishing boats had somehow gotten a little fire going and were warming their hands on it. They looked up and one of them said something to us as we pulled the dinghy up next to them and turned it over.

Anthony, our Greek gobbling sailor, responded with a smile and they smiled back. One of them lifted his hand in acknowledgement of whatever it was that Anthony said. No one seemed to notice that I had a messenger's leather message carrying pouch slung over my shoulder and that all three of us were wearing sheathed swords.

After we got the dinghy placed amongst all the others pulled up on to the strand, and turned it over so it would not fill with rain water, we sloshed through the rain and mud to the Company's nearby compound—and damn near walked past it because of the darkness.

The compound's gate was already closed and barred for the night because the sun had finished passing overhead and night had fallen. I was exhausted and cold even though I had not had done any of the rowing, just the bailing which had been bad enough; God only knew how Edwardo and Vincent felt.

The walking helped but my teeth were still chattering and I was shivering as I pounded on both the gate and the little door in the gate with the handle of one of my wrist knives. It seemed to take forever until there was a voice on the other side. *Finally.*

"We are closed. What do you want?" a voice on the other side asked in crusader French. He sounded quite aggrieved at being out in the rain.

"We are archers. Let us in," I shouted.

"I cannot let you in without the lieutenant's permission," was the reply. The man was clearly quite suspicious about who we might be and our intentions. It was understandable; only fools would be out and walking about at night in such foul weather. Hopefully the city's night watch believed that and was staying in their guardroom.

"Well go get Lieutenant Sparrow and get permission. And run, damn you. It is wet and cold out here."

******

A few minutes later we were in the relative comfort of the Company's unheated post and being attended to by a very surprised and concerned Edward Sparrow and his wife. His little file of four long-serving Company veterans and their wives and a couple of children gathered quietly and looked on from the room beyond the post's reception area where they lived in separate tented spaces.

Normally I would have made straight for the archers and greeted them. This time I did not. What I hoped, instead, was they would not recognize me because I was wearing a one-stripe tunic, had cut my beard almost down to my skin, and was totally bedraggled from the our trip in the rain. If they recognized me they or their wives might talk.

Edward, however, had instantly recognized me and understood that I was there incognito. He was, however, visibly concerned about my unexpected arrival and worried that I would be angry about being kept out in the rain.

"Please excuse me for not letting you in right away, Commander," he said quietly so that no one else could hear what he was saying. "Charlie is a good man and he was following my orders not to let anyone in after dark."

"I agree with you totally, Edward; I only would have been unhappy if Charlie *had* opened the gate without making sure it was safe to do so—especially today."

And then I told him why I was there in a quiet voice so that once again no one else could hear.

"There is an important message from King Otto of Bulgaria that must be delivered to the papal nuncio in Athens as earlier as possible tomorrow, and it must be done without anyone knowing it was the Company that delivered it or ever finding out that we did or that I was ever here to help deliver it."

Edward thought about what I said before he replied.

"The nuncio will almost certainly be at the Duke of Athens' hall in the morning to get a free meal. If we walk fast it will take us three hours to get there. We could start before dawn and be there whilst he and the members of the court are breaking their nightly fasts in the Duke's hall."

"Aye, that would do." … "But there is more. No one must ever know that I have been in Greece and I have to leave first thing in the morning at dawn's earliest light. So *you* will have to arrange the delivery of the message parchment to the nuncio. Can you disguise yourself and do it without anyone knowing that you did the deed, not even Robert Archer or your men or wife?"

"Aye Commander, I can do it. What should I tell my men and my wife?"

"Tell them that I am merely a messenger who brought rumours that the post might be attacked and robbed such that the men must be prepared to fight on a moment's notice and everyone must remain inside for their own safety. And starting now you are not to let anyone, not even the wives, leave the compound or talk to anyone for any reason for at least the next four or five days, not even to go to the market.

"Moreover, the Company's involvement in delivering the message must never be known and neither should it ever be known that I am the one who brought it to you. That is very important. So for the next week or so you and you alone are to do the Company's business by meeting with anyone who comes. You are to handle everything all yourself without any of the men or wives being present or allowed to talk to any visitors.

"And you are especially *not* to tell anyone, not even your wife, that you are going to Athens to deliver a message. I will also be leaving as soon as it is early light so you can tell everyone here that you will be accompanying us to the quay to bid us farewell and wish us a safe voyage.

"Now here is the thing, Edward, and mark it well. It may well be that the message you deliver to the nuncio will cause something to happen that will cast suspicion on the Company. I do not think it will if you disguise yourself properly before you deliver it, but it might despite your best efforts.

"If it does, men might come here and make inquiries. So stay on your guard and keep your gate and doors barred. Try to keep everyone out by claiming you are all down with the spotted pox. And, if you must, only let one or two visitors in at a time and make sure they have no weapons and that yours are at hand. Explain that the Company requires that no armed men be allowed to enter because the post has coins and other valuables here that must be guarded.

"Alternately, you might be summoned for questioning. If you are, plead a serious case of the pox and also that you must stay here to guard the post because of the coins and valuables. But keep up the appearance of being innocent and knowing nothing by saying you would be happy to talk to anyone who wants to visit and is willing to risk the pox.

"Can you handle all that?"

"Aye, Commander, I can handle it. You can count on me. But can you tell me what the message is about?"

"I can, but it is best that you not know so that you remain innocent if a problem ever develops. Even so, I want you to put your post on high alert. Make sure your men have their weapons at hand at all times and your emergency escape routes are ready for immediate use. Tell them that we brought word a possible robbery.

******

We spent the night at the post and returned to the dinghy as soon as the sun came up the next morning. We immediately launched it and rowed back to the galley. The weather was good and our clothes were dry because we had traded our wet tunics with three of Edward's men for their dry tunics.

Our stomachs were full as Edwardo and Anthony rowed me back. Edwardo and Edward's wife had arisen before dawn and used the kitchen in the courtyard to make what has become my favourite meal to break my nightly fast—"donkitos."

At my suggestion, Edwardo had brought a sack with the ingredients with him and enough additional food so that no one at the post would have to go to the market for three or four days. I asked him to bring the food because I knew we would have to break our fasts early and I did not want anyone going to the market and mentioning that the Company's shipping post had unexpected visitors, not until we were long gone.

Donkitos for breaking one's nightly fast are typically a combination of cheese, eggs rumpoled by being burnt on a piece of metal after being rapidly beaten with a wooden spoon, and sliced onions and peppers, and all of them then rolled up together in a soft flatbread such that nothing can fall out before it is eaten.

Edwardo had long ago told me he called it a "donkito" because it is like a little donkey that can carry a great load of many different things at the same time." He sometimes cooked other donkitos such as those with beans and slices of meat for my suppers or to carry about in my coin purse to eat during the day.

In any event, in the morning after the donkitos were properly burnt over the cooking fire, Edwardo covered them with the juice and seeds of the hot pepper juice that the Company's galley cooks sometimes put on meat when it is starting to smell. As a result, they were quite tasty and went down into my belly surprisingly well with a bowl of the post's morning ale despite the fact that I was coughing and sneezing and ached all over.

******

The early morning food was good but I had slept poorly and not enough. By the time we climbed back on to Harold's galley my face was red and I was coughing and sweating. I was poxed for sure.

Chapter Twenty-eight

The Athens coins.

Harold took one look at me as I climbed on to the deck of his galley and ordered me to go to the forward castle and get in bed. Then he began giving orders for the galley to begin rowing out of the harbour. The anchor had been hauled up as soon as the dinghy was sighted so we left immediately.

For a while I could feel the hull move each time the oars bit into the water. Then I did not remember anything until I woke up all wet from being drenched in sweat.

****** *Ten hours later*

"You look like shite. Are you sure you want to do this tonight? I can go to the quay and stand in for you if you would prefer to go back to bed."

Those were Uncle Harold's cheery words some hours later when I emerged coughing and sneezing from my berth in the galley's forward deck castle and made my way across the deck to the shite nest hanging over the galley's stern.

I was in a foul mood and very hungry. It was late in the afternoon. It was almost time to row back to Piraeus and, hopefully, pick up the coins. We were wallowing in small waves outside Piraeus's harbour with Captain Jackson's galley off to our starboard waiting with us. It would take us about an hour to reach the quay.

"No damn it, Harold. I will do it myself. I must; I am the only one other than your apprentice who has the Latin that will be needed to talk to the nuncio. And he would not be useful if something went wrong and you had to fight your way out, would he? So it must be me."

A few minutes later, and much relieved, I returned to Uncle Harold where he was waiting on the roof of the forward castle. I was still sneezing and coughing, but even hungrier. The roof of the forward castle was a captain's proper place when his galley was about to enter a harbour. His lieutenant, sailing sergeant, and apprentice had already been sent away so we could talk privately.

"Is everything ready for tonight?" I asked as one of the cook's helpers approached with a warm flatbread, a piece of beef that had been left on the fire so long that it was so over burnt and hard, and some cheese and morning ale. *I wonder how Edwardo is doing. He is obviously not doing the cooking this morning. That was the thought behind my eyes as I reached for the food.*

"Everything is as ready as it can be," was Harold's reply. Then he explained.

"We will arrive just as it gets totally dark and use our oars to hold our galley against the quay without using our mooring lines. Captain Jackson and his Number Forty-six will come in right behind us and do the same.

"As soon as we arrive you and I will climb up to the quay along with some sailors to help lower the coin chests down to our galley's deck. All the rest of our galley's men except the rowers will be armed and on the deck as a boarding party. They will be ready and waiting in case a rescue is needed.

"The boarding party will be up the ladders and on the quay in a lightning flash if everything turns to shite. The men know you and I will be carrying candle lanterns to identify us if there is fighting. So whatever you do, do not drop your lantern until you jump down to the deck."

"And the sailors will be ready to stow the chests? Do they know they will be heavy?"

"Aye. Robby Morgan, Johnny White's replacement, knows how to lower chests from a quay to a galley's deck. He has been doing it for almost twenty years. He will be on the deck sergeanting the sailors and archers who have been assigned to receive the chests and stow them.

"You and I will stay on the quay and see that the nets are loaded and lowered, and to make sure all the sailors doing the lowering get safely back on board. Jack Smith's replacement, William Castle will stay on deck with the boarding party and be instantly ready to lead the boarders up the ladders and on to the quay if a rescue is needed. I will already be there with you, of course.

"Captain Jackson will bring his galley up to the quay alongside us at the same time we get there. He and his men will also be instantly ready to join in the rescue if we need one. But he will do nothing unless William Castle leads our boarding party on to the quay."

******

There were already men waiting on the quay as we slowly approached it in the dark. We knew there were at least three because we could see the lanterns they were carrying moving about. There may have been more men and, hopefully, coin chests or carts carrying them. But if there were, it was too dark to see them as we slowly and silently rowed up to the quay and used our oars to hold our galley against it.

And it was too dark to see. The storm had passed while I slept but there were still a lot of clouds in the sky and only a partial moon.

Not a word was spoken as we approached the quay and the light of day totally disappeared. The only noise was the sound of our oars, the creaking of the hull, and the crunch of the twigs and branches in our hull bumpers as they were pushed up against the stone side of the quay. Even the harbour gulls were quiet; they had gone off to sleep away the night.

The silence was understandable—the men had been ordered to maintain total silence at all times; any man who spoke so much as a single word would lose all his stripes.

"Who are you and where did you come from?"

A voice in the darkness asked in Greek and then in Latin as the boarding ladders were put in place and Harold and I began to climb them.

I answered in Latin as I began slowly and cautiously climbing the six or seven feet from the galley's deck to the quay.

"We are King Otto's men and we have just arrived from Constantinople to collect some chests that belong to him. Is everything ready? Is there any danger?"

I gave my answer and then coughed such a great rasping cough and sneezed that I would have become overbalanced if I had not grasped the ladder tightly with my one free hand.

There was no doubt about it, I decided; climbing even a short distance on a boarding ladder set on a galley's slightly bobbing deck is not the easiest thing to do when you are carrying a lighted candle lantern in one hand and have a big wooden cross hanging from your neck and a sheathed short sword hanging down under an ankle-length priest's robe.

My rusty chain shirt and wrist knives, on the other hand, did not bother me, probably because I was so used to wearing them at all times except when I was sleeping or with a woman.

"There is no danger." ... "Where is Lord Tarnovo?" a man asked as he held his lantern up for a moment so he could get a look at my face as I swung my leg from the ladder to the quay.

"He is greatly poxed and may be dying even though he has not yet made his final confession and received his last prayers. Many of us are poxed. It is God's Will and cannot be changed. I am Father Mathias, his cleric." ... "Do you have the shipment ready?"

"Two carts with the chests are waiting nearby, Father. A man was sent to fetch them when we saw your galleys approaching. They will be here in a few minutes."

A minute or so later we could hear distant voices and the wheels of the carts as they clattered over the quay towards us. A few moments after that we could see the very dim outlines of carts and the horses pulling them.

There were two carts and they seemed to be surrounded by a large number of men on foot. We could hear them talking quietly and moving about. The men appeared to be carrying weapons but I could not make out for sure what they were carrying because of the darkness. Spears and clubs I later realized when the clouds parted for a moment. A church's protection gang for sure.

"Here they are. You can start unloading them. Best you hurry so we can get out of here before the Duke's night watch sees the lights and comes for a visit."

I waved my lantern back and forth.

Waving the lantern was the signal for the loading to begin. Silent figures immediately began climbing up the boarding ladders. They were carrying the galley's loading nets with them.

Within seconds the loading nets were being spread out along the edge of the quay. Not a word was spoken as the chests were hurriedly unloaded from the horse carts and placed in the middle of each net. The chests were heavy. It took two men to carry each of them. The guards appeared to be gathered in a great semi-circle around the carts but did not volunteer to help.

Ropes attached to the corners of the nets were then used to lower them down to the men waiting on the galley's deck a few feet below. There were dozen or so sailors and archers assigned to the task, three for each net on the quay and three more on the galley below to receive them.

It went smoothly despite the darkness, and there was no surprise in that; not only were Harold's men experienced at loading a galley, they had spent most of the previous day practicing climbing up to a quay and lowering heavy chests down to the galley's deck. They had used chests full of ballast rocks for the coin chests and the roof of the stern castle for the quay.

Then it happened. Someone held a lantern up to my face and looked at me closely.

"You are not Father Mathias from Constantinople," he said accusingly in Latin. I did not know who it was but I suspected the nuncio.

"Well you are certainly right about that," I whispered in reply with an unfriendly laugh and a cough that bent me over and sprayed him. "I am Father Mathias from Burgundy. Who are you?"

"Your men are strangely quiet," he said venomously in Latin instead of answering my question. "Why is that?"

"It is probably because they were told that any man who uttered a word would be hung," I replied in a hissed whisper. "Piraeus has an active night watch, or so we were warned in Constantinople, and we do not want to attract their attention. Is it true or not that the city has a night watch?"

"Well, yes it does. But I do not ...."

"Then kindly lower your voice and get that light out of my eyes so I can see what King Otto's sailors are doing, eh?"

I whispered my order with an arrogant snarl and pushed away the lantern. He stepped back and obeyed. I was relieved—and he would have been too if he had realized how close he had come to getting one of my wrist knives in his throat.

Chapter Twenty-nine

Another deception.

Both of our galleys remained at anchor near the quay all night and for most of the following morning. The sun was high overhead and the sky was only partly cloudy when we finally rowed out of the harbour and set our course for Cyprus. It was a brisk day in late October.

Originally we had planned to leave quietly in the night as soon as we finished loading the coin chests. That was changed after we finished loading them when Harold and his new sailing sergeant decided that leaving the harbour that night would be too dangerous because it was too crowded and visibility too poor.

"Why take a chance when it is not necessary, eh?" was how he put it.

Harold and his sailing sergeant were right, of course. There was no need to risk a collision in the dark now that we had the chests on board. And the idea that there was a fighting force in the harbour, let alone anywhere in the Aegean, that could take two fully crewed Company galleys was just plain absurd. At least that is what we thought at the time. Accordingly, when we finished loading the coin chests we merely moved about an arrow's flight away from the quay and dropped our anchors to spend the night.

And after thinking about it whilst we were hoisting a few bowls of ale to celebrate our Company's newest fortune, I decided to change our departure time again—we would, I announced to everyone's surprise, remain in the harbour and close to the quay for most of the next morning because "there are changes that have to be made."

Our galleys would continue to be on alert, of course, but they would remain anchored off the quay such that everyone on shore would be able to see them quite clearly when the sun returned on its daily trip around the world.

******

Our galleys spent the night together just off the quay, and then continued staying there throughout the next morning whilst they were implementing my new plan. It was actually quite simple.

We had used King Otto's pennants and the hull coverings over some of the oar ports to gull the coin collectors into thinking we were Black Sea galleys so they would turn the coins over to us. Now it was time to shift the blame for the theft of the coins and further increase the confusion and uncertainty as to who had taken them.

Accordingly, we did *not* sail away in the dark towards Rome as the nuncio and other collectors of King Otto's coins had undoubtedly expected us to do. To the contrary, we remained in the harbour near the quay in plain sight of everyone on the quay and aboard the nearby boats in the densely packed harbour.

About two hours after sunrise, when the quay was crowded with people going about their normal activities, I ordered the Burgundian flag with its blue and gold stripes hoisted on the masts of both galleys to replace King Otto's pennant and the fake covers removed from our oar ports.

As I expected and hoped, the changes were seen and noted as soon as they began being made. The quay soon became more and more crowded with onlookers. Most of the onlookers did not know what had happened or why, but they did know that it was significant and worth talking about when war galleys suddenly changed their flags and altered their appearances.

There was no question in my mind; it would soon be the talk of both Piraeus and Athens that a couple of galleys that initially looked as though they belonged to King Otto had suddenly changed their flags and appearances to become Burgundians.

There was no way to know if the nuncio and his fellow coin collectors actually came to the quay in time to see for themselves that they had probably turned the coins over to the wrong galleys. It did not matter; word would sooner later reach them about the galleys fighting in the Dardanelles strait, about the coins not reaching Rome, and about the strange happenings in the Piraeus harbour the morning after the coins were collected by Lord Tarnovo's galleys.

Sooner or later King Otto and his coin collectors would put things together and understand that the coins had been turned over to someone other than Lord Tarnovo and had promptly disappeared. And that raised a number of questions as to what everybody involved would then think and do. Perhaps, for example, Lord Tarnovo and his men had sailed off with them. Or perhaps it was the Moors or French or Venetians or the English archers. It was impossible to know for sure. *We hoped.*

The immediate questions, of course, were whether King Otto would blame the Burgundians or Lord Tarnovo or someone else for their loss, and what would happen to Father Mathias and those of King Otto's supporters who would be suspected of helping them or were guilty of letting them get away with the coins. I myself really did not care who was blamed or what happened to them so long as there was enough uncertainty and confusion about the loss of the coins and their whereabouts such that nothing bad happened to the Company.

A much more important question, at least so far as the Company was concerned, was how King Otto and the Holy Father would react to the loss of the coins and how their loss would affect the current and future regents and emperors of the Latin Empire. Specifically, did Otto's inability to pay for enough of the Pope's prayers mean that Elizabeth and her young brother would still be in those positions when I returned to Constantinople in the spring?

I certainly hoped they would be able to hold on to the throne and be there when I returned to Constantinople next year, and not just because I wanted the Company to continue collecting the tolls and keeping them.

Chapter Thirty

Return to Cyprus.

Our voyage to Cyprus turned out to be quite uneventful. We encountered one storm that blew us slightly off course and separated us from Captain Jackson for a day, but otherwise we had a rather pleasant time of it with plenty of archery practice and moors dancing.

We reached Cyprus and came around the island to Limassol on a fine October day. There was great happiness aboard the galley as we did. It was understandable. This was the galley's home port and some of the men had families here. And most of the rest had their favourite taverns and public women.

What really had everyone excited, however, was that Harold's crew would soon be receiving their prize coins for both Venice and for the more recent fighting in the Dardanelles. It would be a huge amount for every man and they knew it. Harold was concerned. He thought that as many as half of his crew would take their coins and retire, even the young one-stripers.

I was much less concerned about it.

"Yes, Uncle Harold, you are right. We will lose some good men. But think of what it will do for our ability to recruit good men to replace them when they return to England with their prize money and begin buying land and hovels in their home villages!

"Besides, serving in the Company is a good life compared to living in a village or the foulness of London. In the end I would wager that less than one in five of your crew will take their prize coins and leave us. The rest will either leave their prize money on the Company's books until they have even more, or they will take their coins and squander them on women and gambling—and I will wager you an amphora of good Italian wine on it."

"Less than one in five, you say. And for an amphora of wine? Done, by God, even though it is the first time I ever made a bet I wanted to lose."

We smiled at each other and laughed as we spit on our hands and bumped our fists to seal the bet.

"I know they are good men, Uncle Harold, I truly do. And I hope you are wrong about so many of them leaving. I would be as surprised and unhappy as a fish out of water, or perhaps I should say out of wine, if more than one man in five leaves.

"Now how about we get out of the wind and have one last game of chess and a bowl of ale before we go ashore and have to face Henry's widow?"

******

Yoram and a large throng of people came hurrying down to the quay to greet us as we rowed into the harbour. The six galleys from the Dardanelles strait fighting had arrived safely some days earlier so everyone had heard about the fighting in the strait, and the new additions to our fleet and coin chests that came of it; what they wanted to know now was where the galleys of Harold and Captain Jackson had gone afterwards and what they had done and who had been lost.

Harold and Captain Jackson and their sailing sergeants knew where we had been, of course, and so did their lieutenants. They had to know so they could get us to Piraeus. But it was a Company secret for obvious reasons and they had been sworn to never mention it to anyone, not even their wives.

Our men, however, were not entirely sure where we had been or what we had done. Some of them thought they had sailed to Piraeus after the fighting in the strait, because that was what a few of the sailors were claiming to be the case. But most of the sailors were not absolutely sure since they were never allowed to go ashore and everyone had originally been told that the port we would be visiting was Thessaloniki.

Even more importantly, only Harold and I knew for sure what we took aboard when we crept to the quay as the light was fading and loaded a dozen heavy chests in the dark. The men thought it might be coins because the crates were heavy and because of the great care that was taken loading them. But they were not certain because Harold and I had deliberately confused things by allowing ourselves to be overheard calling such things as "are you sure the flower paste has been stored where it will not get wet, Sailing Sergeant?"

Yoram, of course, wanted an immediate report as to what was in the chests and what losses we had suffered getting them. I put him off.

"Their contents are valuable and that is a fact. But it is a long story. Tonight at supper Harold and I will tell you all about buying the chests of flower past in Thessaloniki. But first I want to know about the men who were wounded fighting the French galleys in the Dardanelles Strait, the ones that raided the grain fleet."

I said it loud enough that the people walking around us could hear. If the past was any guide, it would be repeated in the taverns that night, known to every merchant in the Limassol market before noon tomorrow, and talked about in every port of the civilized world within the month.

That was all I told Yoram about the chests as we walked from the quay to the Company's fortress. We did so, walked to the Company's fortress that is, leading a grand procession of several hundreds of people including Yoram's wife and children and a horse-drawn wagon on which the chests had been loaded.

We passed through the familiar gates and baileys of our fortress's four curtain walls and kept walking until we reached the citadel in innermost bailey. The chests were immediately unloaded from the wagon and stowed away in one of the two rooms on the upper floor of the citadel.

The room where the chests were taken was the most secure place in the entire fortress. And rightly so because it was where Company's coins and the priceless pain-killing flower paste were stored. And the chests certainly were safe once they were in it. It was a room with no wall openings whose only entrance was a door in one of the walls of the room where Yoram and his family lived and slept.

Yoram's room, in turn, had no entrance door at all, just an opening in the floor through which a ladder poked up from the hall below, the hall where I and the Company's visiting lieutenant commanders and major captains ate and slept when we were ashore. The ladder was pulled up at night and whenever else Yoram wanted to further isolate himself and the Company's treasures.

The citadel, and thus the chests stored in it, would be extremely difficult for invaders or robbers to reach. It was in the centre of a fortress with enough water, food, and firewood to withstand a three year siege. It was also a particularly powerful fortress because it was ringed by no less than four separate tall and thick curtain walls that an attacker would have to fight through to get to them and their defenders.

Each of the walls that ringed it had only one entrance gate and enclosed a bailey where the men with certain ranks and their families lived. And each of the stone walls had periodic towers along it that were within arrow range of the towers on either side of it. Each bailey's wall was longer than the one it surrounded and housed more people.

The innermost of the four baileys and the towers of its wall were inhabited by the Company's Cyprus-based men with the rank of lieutenant or higher and their families. The next innermost bailey and its towers was home of the men and families with the rank of sergeant and higher. The third was inhabited by the Company's one and two-stripers, and the fourth by the Company's servants and workers.

A fifth wall was under construction to keep everyone busy and out of mischief. It would circle the outermost of the existing four and enclosed an area so large it would almost reach the Limassol city wall when it was complete. Passengers waiting for passages lived in the immediately adjacent city of Limassol or in cell-like rooms in the fifth wall's partially completed bailey.

Each bailey had at least one kitchen and a well. As you might imagine rank had its privileges. Accordingly, the baileys got larger and larger and the living quarters of the men and their families living in them got smaller and smaller the further out they were from the citadel where Yoram and his family safely lived in splendid isolation.

Taken all together, the Company's fortress on Cyprus was probably the strongest fortress in the world. It certainly needed to be in view of the state of the world and its location.

So how would we take it if we were on the outside instead of the inside? It was a question we constantly asked ourselves when we were drinking. Trickery or starvation or hostage taking seemed to be the only answers. And hostage taking would not work because anyone in the Company who was taken or compromised would be immediately replaced by someone being promoted into his position.

The Company, in other words, would not be going away if someone killed or captured its Commander and his heirs.

******

Harold and I visited Henry's widow as soon as the chests were safely stored away. I brought her a coin pouch full of the latest prize coins Henry had earned and assured her of what she already knew—that she and the Company's other widows would always get their husband's half pay until they remarried.

The widow's name was Jeanette and she was French. She had met Henry years ago whilst the crusaders were preparing to assault Constantinople. My father had recruited her as a spy when she was a forlorn and starving widow in the foetid crusader camp across the water from wall that circled the city. Henry had met her and gotten to know her when she came to the Company's little strip of neutral concession land next to the wall to make her periodic reports.

I told Jeanette what I knew of how Henry died even though I really did not see him go down or how it happened. And, of course, I lied and said it all happened so quickly that he probably never felt a thing. It was what we always said when someone fell.

Jeanette's eyes teared up and she wept for a while as I hugged her and patted her on her back. Then she listened carefully whilst I told her why we were in the tunnels and how I had been knocked on the head and played dead after Henry and I entered the strange room and were almost instantly attacked and overwhelmed.

"He is buried in Constantinople, George. Is there any chance my daughter and I could go there to visit and pray for him? He would like that, I think."

"Of course, Jeanette. I know he would. You just say the word when you want to go and Yoram will arrange everything.

Damn I hate it when someone weeps and sobs for a good reason. It makes me want to weep and sob too. So we all did, even crusty old Harold.

******

We talked of many things that night whilst we sat in Yoram's little hall and ate our supper of freshly burnt fish and lamb with the new-style round bread loaves with balsamic vinegar and olive oil. Yoram was absolutely delighted when we explained what had really happened at Piraeus and why we were deliberately spreading confusion such that others might be held responsible.

Yoram, in turn, told us how the Company's regular custom and shipping posts were doing and explained the numbers to us. They were very encouraging. It seems the renewed fighting between the Crusaders and the Saracens was causing more desperate passage-buying refugees and the renewal of charters for standby escape galleys at Alexandria and several of the Syrian ports.

Also up were our revenues from money transfers and general cargos. There was no doubt about it; we would have a large number of coins to send to Cornwall as soon as the winter storm season passed.

And send the coins we would. According to Yoram, a total of eleven different galleys and eight transports were already scheduled to sail for England in the spring and many more were expected to follow them. They would be carrying everything from spices and flower paste to passengers such as returning crusaders and pilgrims. And every one of them would be carrying a chest or two of coins. Some of the cargos and passengers would continue on to France and the Low Countries; the coins would not.

Another bit of news was that our relations with Cyprus's King and his regent remained cordial and were expected to continue that way just as they had for many years. That was understandable since the current king was two years old and lived on the far side of the island with his mother who was his regent.

It also helped that his mother was quite young and very much under the control of her chancellor, a minor lord and distant relative named Phillip Ibelin. According to Yoram, Ibelin was smart enough to recognize that the Company was far stronger than the kingdom. Accordingly, he was apparently afraid, and rightly so, that we would throw them out take over the entire island if they bothered us in any way.

At some point in the evening, I asked Yoram about the Company's relatively new scribing and summing school for men with potential who are already archers. I particularly wanted to know about the progress of Sergeant James Howard who had been in Constantinople as the assistant to the Company's late and greatly lamented alchemist.

James had been sent here to the new school to learn to scribe. He needed to be able to do so in order to write reports and keep records as he tried to perfect the man-made lightning and the "ribaldis" that the Company's alchemist he had been assisting in Constantinople had built— and died when he used them against the Greeks.

What really got to me and that I remember most from that evening was seeing Yoram surrounded by his loving family and suddenly realizing how much I missed my wife and children. In the spring I would definitely return to Cornwall to spend the summer.

Chapter Thirty-one

Homeward bound.

Time flew by and the beginning of spring in the year 1220 arrived before I knew it. It was time for my annual voyage back to Cornwall, the one I had missed last year because of the fighting in Constantinople and our great revenge raid on Venice. This time would be a little different in that I was adding Constantinople to the stops I would make along the way to visit our shipping posts.

Harold and Yoram were greatly fluxed by my decision. They pointed out that a visit to Constantinople would definitely involve a major detour that would add weeks to the voyage.

I had a reason for going, a very good one so far as I was concerned, but I did not share it with my lieutenants. Instead, I reminded them that the Company's biggest single regular source of coins were the tolls we collected from all the shipping that used the Bosporus and Dardanelles straits.

The tolls, of course, being the tolls the Company collected and kept in exchange for helping to protect the Latin Empire's great capital city by keeping pirates and enemy fleets out of its waters and helping to man its wall when it was attacked. The waters being the Marmara Sea and the Bosporus and Dardanelles straits at either end of it.

I expected my return to England would involve an interesting and comfortable voyage on Harold's galley. For one, James Howard, the Company's only expert on turning lead into gold would be sailing with us. He did it by using the man-made lightning that occurred when a flame was put to a proper mixture of powdered sulphur, charcoal, and bird shite.

James had just been promoted to Lieutenant to give him the rank and authority to get it done. He also played a good game of chess. I was looking forward to learning more about his progress whilst we played.

Hopefully James will sooner or later be able to make gold by focusing sufficient amounts of the man-made lightning on pieces of lead. In the meantime he has been told to concentrate on making better ribaldis for the Company, the hollowed out logs and strapped together horse watering troughs that can be used to throw stones long distances when fire is put to a mixture of the powders and causes the thunder and lightning to occur.

James was sailing with me because Uncle Thomas wanted him to make both the gold and the ribaldis in Cornwall so he, Uncle Thomas, himself can learn how to do it and be able to teach it to the boys in his school at Restormel. Accordingly, Cornwall is where I am taking James. Moreover, and even though James is only a new lieutenant, he will be accompanied by a young apprentice sergeant from Uncle Thomas's school by the name of Alfred Hayward.

Alfred was an orphan lad from a village of royal heath wardens and deer hunting guides in Sussex who was spotted by the village priest who called him to the attention of Uncle Thomas. He was successfully learnt to scribe and sum and gobble Latin in the Company school at Restormel, and came east with the early leavers from the Company school for the Greek war.

Initially Alfred was one of the lads assigned to assist Yoram as one of his clerics. Yoram, in turn, determined that Alfred was good at thinking behind his eyes and assigned him to work with James. His assignment was to assist James in the making of gold and ribaldis, and to help James improve his scribing and summing—and in the process learn and scribe all he can about the making of gold and ribaldis in case James goes down.

Having men in the Company who know how to make gold would be very useful when Jesus returns. For when he does our coins from carrying refugees and cargos will almost certainly dry up because peace will break out and everyone will have enough to eat and not have to worry about such things as invaders and pirates.

In the meantime, until Jesus does return, knowing how to make and use ribaldis would help the Company earn coins by killing invaders and pirates, particularly if we can figure out how to use them on our galleys and transports.

In other words, and despite the uncertainty surrounding Jesus's return, it would clearly be a win-win situation and guarantee the Company's future if the secret of making of both gold and man-made thunder and lightning could be perfected and known only to the Company—and that explained why the Company was putting so much effort into it.

******

It was a brisk spring morning when we threw off our mooring lines and began rowing out of Limassol's harbour to begin our long voyage to Cornwall via Rhodes and Constantinople. Gulls were circling overhead and several hundred people were on the quay to see us off and have their pockets picked.

Harold's galley was prepared for every eventuality. Our hold was full of food and water and our deck was covered with struggling birds and beasts to be killed and eaten along the way. Every man aboard was either an experienced archer or sailor. In other words, we would be virtually impossible to catch or take.

We were carrying parchment orders and offers for merchants and also parchment money orders directing our shipping posts to provide certain amounts of coins at one post as a result of larger amounts of coins deposited at another post. What we were not carrying were passengers and cargos.

As the highest ranking man on board I was living alone in the galley's forward desk castle. And I was living luxuriously with my own bed and sleeping furs that I did not have to share with anyone else. I also had two wooden stools in case I had a visitor I wanted to sit with, and a flat wooden board with raised sides fixed to the wall such that it would not slide about and could be used for scribing or playing chess or holding a bowl of ale or wine if the sea was not so rough as to cause sloshing.

An amphora of wine was lashed securely into the far corner of the little castle. I had won it in wager with Uncle Harold because fewer than one in five of the galley's crew had run. He had paid under protest because some of his crew had their prize coins with them and were likely to leave the Company as soon as they reached England.

On the other hand, there had been no problem about the collection of my winnings. I promised Uncle Harold that we would drink it up together during the voyage and that, because he might still win the wager, I would pay to have the amphora re-filled in Lisbon for our trip across to England and back.

There is never any need to wait when good wine is involved.

******

Harold's galley called in at the island of Rhodes even though we had enough water, food, and firewood supplies on board to reach Constantinople without stopping. We did so at the request of Rhode's self-proclaimed Caesar, Leo Gabalas.

A few weeks earlier his chancellor had used our little four-man shipping post to send a message to Cyprus requesting that Company have someone call in at Rhodes for a visit—someone of high rank who was "authorized to discretely negotiate a matter of mutual interest and make his mark on a contract related to it."

It was an intriguing message and I decided to follow up on it. As a result, less than an hour after we arrived in Rhodes' harbour Harold and I were being ushered into the court of the island's self-proclaimed Caesar. The ushering was done by a very officious and highly costumed courtier who tried to tell us how we were to behave when we met "Caesar." I nodded my head in agreement and told Harold to ignore him and copy me.

We were led into a great hall that was conspicuous by being empty of everyone except two men—one sitting in an elevated chair with a golden ring atop his head and the other standing next to him. Being quick witted and intelligent, I quickly deduced the "Caesar" was the man sitting in the chair and no one else was present except his advisor because he did not want anyone to know about our conversation.

I walked up to them and gave a great sweeping bow to convey great respect, even if I did not particularly mean it. What I did not do was what the flunky pointedly told me was expected and appropriate—bang my head on the stone floor as my father told me old King Guy used to require on Cyprus before his death and Elizabeth had recently begun requiring new arrivals to do when they first came to her court.

In fact, I would have banged it if I had thought it would improve my bargaining position for whatever the island's Caesar wanted, but I did not bang my head for Elizabeth and was not about to begin for this one just because he wanted everyone to think he ruled his island with a strong hand. It probably meant he felt as insecure as Elizabeth.

The Caesar of the island motioned for me to come forward, and then surprised me by gobbling to me directly in crusader French instead of using a translator.

"Thank you for coming, Commander. We asked you to visit Rhodes because the Venetians are sniffing about and *We* have heard many good things about the Company of Archers, including that it honours its mercenary contracts. We would like to negotiate such a contract with you to help protect our island against the Venetians."

Ah, so he is a "we" and a contract is what "we" wants.

"That would require many men and galleys to be available on relatively short notice, Caesar. It is possible, of course, but only if there are enough immediately available coins to pay them and buy their food and shelter."

Of course, I pretended he was a Caesar and addressed him as such; a coin is a coin no matter the name of the man who hands it to you. Besides, anything we received for keeping the Venetians out of this corner of the Aegean would be found money as we were not about to let the Venetians or anyone else bring galleys into the waters between Cyprus and Constantinople.

"Ah, there is something else, Commander. We will also require a galley to be stationed here that is instantly available carry messages in the event the Venetians or any other enemies arrive and infest our waters. We have a galley of our own, of course, but it may be away sometimes when a message needs to be sent quickly for some reason or another.

"We understand that your company has contracted to provide such messenger galleys elsewhere. Is that true?"

"It is true, Caesar. You are indeed well informed. Our Company presently is providing standby messenger galleys at Alexandria and Acre and several other ports. They are immediately available to instantly take whoever contracts for their use to wherever he wants to go."

He kept calling them messenger galleys, but they were really instantly available escape galleys. He obviously wanted one in case his people rose against him or the Venetians or the Nicean king who was his overlord or anyone else came for him. I immediately began wondering what was worrying him; just about everything from the sound of it.

"Caesar, the cost of a fully crewed and provisioned galley for a year depends on how many of our archers and sailors must be instantly available to launch it and to work its sails and do the rowing. And they must be fed and have a place to live in addition to being paid and there must be a place where the galley can be pulled ashore and quickly launched whenever it is needed."

Caesar and his chancellor, who turned out to be his brother, nodded their heads and we commenced to bargain. It is always necessary to bargain when dealing with Greeks.

******

Harold gave his men liberty coins to spend in the handful of taverns in the little island's one walled city that night. In the morning I made my mark on a two-year contract and we rowed away with another chest of coins. The chest had enough coins in it for two years of the Company of doing whatever was necessary to keep the Venetians out of the waters around Rhodes and half of the coins for the first year of a two year contract for a crewed "messenger galley."

The rest of the first year's coins were to be paid upon the arrival of a seaworthy galley with no less than twenty able-bodied archers and sailors to crew it. The Caesar of Rhodes would keep it stocked with supplies and provide the rest of necessary rowers, no doubt from his loyal servants who were running away with him.

"It is not just the Venetians he is worried about, is it?" Harold had asked as we watched the chest with the coins being stowed away.

"He is probably worried about everyone. Nicea even more than the Venetians I would wager and the Hospitallers more than the Niceans. And also, or so it sounds, he is worried about the loyalty of his galley's crew or that it might not be seaworthy. Probably both.

"What he knows most of all, I would think, is that his enemies are quite likely to go after his galley and are not likely to risk of attacking one of ours."

Harold reflected on my words for a few moments, and then nodded his head.

"Well, at least the coins are right and we have found employment for one of the Black Sea galleys we took last year. Now if we could just find another dozen or so archers to serve in its crew."

Chapter Thirty-two

The end of an affair.

We returned to the company's concession next to Constantinople's great city wall on a windy and rainy day in middle of April of the year 2020. "It is good to see our concession," I said to James Howard as we stepped ashore.

"This little strip of land between the sea and the city wall has been the Company's ever since my father and his men defeated the Byzantine Emperor's army when the Emperor was foolish enough to send it out from behind the city walls to fight them. I would hate to be known as the man who lost it."

A messenger had been sent to fetch Michael Oremus as soon as our galley was sighted as it rowed toward the quay. Michael showed up immediately and gave me a brief report of the state of things in the city. Then we started off so I could pay my respects to the Empress and gage the state of her feelings toward me and the Company.

Harold remained behind with the captain of our shipping post to deal with the inevitable minor galley matters such as arranging the delivery of new supplies and finding a barber for an archer who had broken his arm the day after we left Rhodes.

People and wagons of all types filled the streets despite the rain that was causing some people to run from one place of shelter to the next. The only things that had changed in the city in the months since the sunny day I sailed away were the absence of the city's numerous cats and the increased need to be careful where you put your sandals down, particularly in a puddle of water because you had no way of knowing how deep it was or what was in it.

Of course we did not see any of the city's many cats as we walked to the Great Palace; they were too smart to be out in the rain. We, on the other hand, were getting wet and chilled from the driving rain despite the hooded wool-covered rain jackets we were wearing over our tunics.

What we needed were some of the little leather tents on the top of poles that some of the gentry-dressed people on the street were carrying.

Michael brought me up to date on the various things that had happened whilst I was gone as we splashed our way through the streets to the Great Palace. I listened carefully even they were things I already knew about from the parchment reports he had sent to Cyprus some months earlier.

"The Regent delivered up a boy while you were away, Commander. So far as I know it is still alive and healthy. The merchants say the young lad from Epirus who is her husband is amazed and his father is ecstatic because there is another boy available if her husband should be lost. Rumour has it that her husband does not know enough about his wife or his father to be worried."

Michael looked at me out of the corner of his eye after he delivered the news. Then he continued.

"I also received your message and did what you suggested Commander—I had an audience with the Regent and reported that King Otto's efforts to buy the Pope's prayers had been totally nobbled and his prayer coins lost. As you suggested, I spoke with her privately when I told her and did *not* tell her who did it or how it was done.

"She asked, of course, but I said I did not know the facts, only that I was sure that King Otto's ability to buy the necessary prayers had been ended. She said she was pleased but I got the feeling that there was still some kind of problem."

My only response was to nod to Michael and say "thank you." I did not tell him that it would not make any difference.

******

Michael and I handed our dripping wet sheepskins to a servant as we entered the Great Palace's hall. There were courtiers everywhere and the smell of people and the rose juice they sprinkled on themselves was intense. Overlaying it all was the faint smell of wood smoke from the fireplace at the far end of the hall. It was not cold enough for a warming fire in England, but people here seemed to need them more.

A number of conversations suddenly stopped as we entered. As a result the noise level in the hall dropped noticeably and almost faded totally away. The courtiers looked at us with great interest as Michael and I walked into the hall.

I had no illusions of being important. We were of interest primarily because our arrival gave the courtiers something new to talk about instead of how many buttons or feathers someone was wearing.

My nagging fear that Elizabeth would refuse to see me, or reject me when she did, was soon put to rest. She saw me enter and immediately sent away those with whom she had been chattering so I could approach.

Michael hung back as I walked toward her and gave a great sweeping bow when I reached her.

"Your Highness," I said with a smile. "I have returned."

"I have missed you," she said very quietly as she nodded her head to agree with herself. "We have much to talk about."

"Indeed we do," I replied in a similar whisper. "But not here."

"Stay here tonight in the room next to mine and come to me after supper. And please feel free to visit the baths before you do." *The invitation was clear and reminded me that I had just come ashore after spending weeks on a galley.*

I gave another sweeping bow and withdrew. Before I did, however, I smiled and quietly, very quietly, said "Your wish is my command, Your Majesty. However, people word might get back to your husband's father if we are too blatant. I will come to you using the tunnel."

She smiled and nodded her head in agreement. I gave her another grand bow and withdrew. My head remained unbanged.

Two minutes later Michael and I were back in the rain with our little guard of archers and Elizabeth's courtiers, with nothing else to do, were no doubt feverishly gossiping about the purpose of my visit and the things that were important at the Empress's court—such as the cut of my clothes and the length of my hair.

"I am going to visit the city baths, Michael. Please send one of your guards to fetch a new tunic for me from the Commandry's slop chest. Tell him to bring it the baths and not to worry if it does not have any stripes on it."

******

Elizabeth had been waiting impatiently and opened the door to the upright clothes chest quickly when I tapped lightly on the inner door of the upright chest that served as the entrance to the tunnel. I used the rhythmic little knock on the wood that had somehow become a tradition between us. It felt like old times—except it was not.

She seemed initially to be rather tense and, for that matter, so was I. It was understandable; we had not been alone together for many months. We could see each other clearly because the room was well lit by six or seven lanterns and candles. She was certainly thinner than the last time I saw her.

"I am told you have a fine new son," I said. " Where is he?"

"No need to worry. A wet nurse has him. He will not bother us?"

"Well that is good to know. Having someone walk in on us is not at all what I have in mind." *That is the understatement of the day was my thought at the time.*

"My brother does not want me to be his regent," Elizabeth announced as I sat myself down on her bed and looked at her. She remained standing. "Some of the people in my court have been telling Robert that he is ready to rule the Empire without a regent."

"It will happen sooner or later," was my response.

"He is like my mother; he is not strong enough to rule by himself," she responded with a strange tone of anger in her voice. And then she added somewhat ominously, "and he never will."

"King Otto, on the other hand, is strong. Did you know that he is once again gathering coins? This time so the Pope would pray for God to recognize Him as the Emperor and me as the Empress? I have agreed by the way.

"Otto is the one who tried to kill you," she said. "He said he needed to kill you if we married so he could use the toll coins to hire mercenaries to replace your archers."

I looked at Elizabeth closely, and then took our conversation in a different direction instead of replying to her comments.

"I know it was you who told Otto that I would sooner or later be in the Mason's hall whilst searching the tunnels. Do you intend to kill your brother just as you did your mother and my father?

She ignored my question and answered with one of her own, and rather sternly at that.

"I know the Company's concession is important to you, George, and so is the contact to collect the tolls. But surely you know that you are not the only one who wants the toll coins and can use them to hire men to defend the city?

"So if you want to keep your concession and the tolls you will have to defend me and marry me. If you will not, then I will have to find someone else; probably Otto since he has already asked me and thinks I have agreed.

"On the other hand, if my brother is removed you could be the Emperor and I the Empress. What say you to that?"

I looked at Elizabeth a long time before I responded.

"I am sorry Elizabeth, truly I am. It is an interesting proposal but there are several reasons why I cannot agree. One is that you killed my father. The second is that I would prefer to be the Commander of my company rather than tied down here with your insipid courtiers. *I did not mention the third reason, that if I was foolish enough to give up the Company she would probably end up killing me so she could rule alone.*

"I knew you would say something like that." She said with a touch of exasperated pity in her voice.

"Besides, some things are more important than money," I said as I stretched out on the bed. And then I asked her the question that had brought me back to Constantinople instead of sailing directly to Cornwall.

"I know you killed your own mother and my father with her. But why?"

My questioned surprised her. She reacted as if the answer was obvious and I should have already known it.

"It was necessary. My mother was not strong enough to be my brother's Regent. She wrote to the Pope saying she wanted Otto to become his regent if anything happened to her. She did not want her own daughter to rise. Can you imagine how I felt?"

I shook my head and waved my hand to indicate she should continue.

"I knew I had to act when I found out about her letter to the Pope. I did not trust her to protect me. She might have sent me back to Epirus."

Then she asked me the inevitable question.

"But how did you learn that it was me who killed them?"

Elizabeth asked the question with a degree of surprise in her voice as she turned away and began unrolling a roll of linen she had been holding ever since I arrived.

"I knew last year when you told me about meeting Helen when she was at the church saying the prayers for my father. That was when I knew you had lied to me about rushing to the city as soon as you got the news of their deaths. There was no way you could have been there for the prayers unless you were already in the city.

"It is a long way from Constantinople to Epirus. It would have taken a couple of days for a galloper to reach you with the news and more than a week for you to return. There is no way you could have talked to my father's wife in church a couple of days after the murders unless you were already here in the city.

"I also knew it was you because I saw a candle lantern and the tunnel dust on your sandals when I searched the room you used before you moved into the Regent's chambers. You had already explored the tunnels.

"That was when I realized you had only pretended not to know about the tunnels and the door in the upright chest. And also that you were only pretending when you helped me discover how to open the door. You found it so quickly because you already knew.

"I know you killed my father and your mother, and probably intend to do your brother as well. But why did you and Otto try to have me killed?" I asked.

"Because Otto said he needed the tolls to hire mercenaries and to pay for the prayers so I could get divorced and marry him. I knew you would never give them up. Father Mathias said it was the only choice I had and that God would understand."

"So was it you or your confessor who told Otto's men about my exploring the tunnels and that I would sooner or later be in the Mason hall?"

She ignored my question.

"It does not have to be Otto I marry in order to become the Empress, George. Your Company has the toll coins and I have the Empire's taxes and fees. We could buy the necessary prayers for us to marry and be the Emperor and Empress."

I, in turn, ignored her suggestion.

"So there it is –you came through the tunnel and killed my father and your mother in order that you could take her place as Empress.

She stiffened at my words and began shaking her head. Finally, after a pause, she spoke.

"Silly man. I did *not* have to use the tunnel to get into her room. I talked with her in her chambers until late in the afternoon when the servant brought in the bowl of watered wine she kept by her bed in case she or your father became thirsty.

"It was easy. I just poured the poison into the bowl next to her bed when I went in to use the piss pot. They both most have drunk out of it."

Then she looked over her shoulder at me and told me more.

"It is your father's fault for being where he should not have been. So you should not blame me. That is what my confessor, Father Mathias, says."

"But I do have a surprise for you, think of it as a gift from Otto," she said as she turned to unfold the linen she was carrying and then turned back to lean over me—and pushed the blade she had unwrapped straight into my chest. Her eyes widened in surprise as she did.

There was a slight scratching and scraping sound when her blade hit my chain shirt. She had never known I wore it because I always took it off before I went to her or was waiting in bed for her to arrive.

I did not hesitate. I did what I had come to Constantinople to do—my wrist knives went into both sides of her throat without making any sound at all.

"Well, one thing is certain; your brother is either going to need a new regent or he is going to have to rule without one."

I said it rather viciously as I used the knives in her throat to pull her face towards mine and hold her there.

By the light of the rooms candle lanterns I watched Elizabeth's panic-stricken eyes as she realized what had happened, and then as they dimmed when she finished her struggling and trembling.

I left by the tunnel and was wearing a new tunic without blood on it and enjoying a bowl of wine in the Commandry by the time her servants found her.

Epilogue

Erik was very serious as he sat down across from me. I thought he was there to ask me if I knew anything about Elizabeth's mysterious murder two days earlier. I was wrong.

"George, when the war with the Greeks was over you asked your father how it was that he knew the Orthodox Metropolitan, Andreas, and why he thought the Metropolitan could be trusted. Do you remember?"

George nodded warily at the captain of the Varangians.

"Your father, and Andreas *and I* were all part of the same fraternal brotherhood that meets in the Hall of the Masons under the eye of the all-seeing God who watches over everyone no matter who we are or what our earthly religion might be.

"People think we are just another drinking and social club, because that is the part of us they can see. But we are much more than that. We are a group of men who believe in one God and are sworn to always honest with each other and to do what we can to make the world a better place for everyone.

"We would like you to take your father's place. Would you like me to tell you about us?"

The end

There are more books in *The Company of Archers Saga*.

All of the books in this exciting and action-packed medieval saga are available on Amazon as individual eBooks, and some of them are also available in print and as audio books. Many of them are available in multi-book collections. You can find them by searching for *Martin Archer Stories*. The first book in the saga is *The Archers* for those who wish to start at the beginning and read the stories in order.

A bargain-priced collection containing all of first six books of the saga is available as *The Archers' Story*. Similarly, a collection of the next four books in the saga is available as *The Archers' Story: Part II;* the three novels after that as *The Archers' Story Part III;* and the four after that as *The Archers' Story: Part IV*. There is also a *Part V* with the next three.

A chronological list of all the books in the saga, and other books by Martin Archer, can be found below along with a few sample pages from the first book in the saga.

Finally, a word from Martin:

"I sincerely hope you enjoyed reading the latest story about the hard men of Britain's first great merchant company as much as I enjoyed writing it. If so, I hope you will consider reading the other stories in the saga and leaving a favourable review on Amazon or Google with as many stars as possible in order to encourage other readers.

"And, if you could please spare a moment, I would also very much appreciate your thoughts and suggestions about this saga and its stories. Should the stories continue? What do you think? I can be reached at martinarcherV@gmail.com."

Cheers and thank you once again. /S/ Martin Archer

Books in the exciting and action-packed *The Company of Archers* saga:

The Archers

Today's Friends

The English Gambits

eBooks in Martin Archer's epic *Soldiers and Marines* saga:

Soldiers and Marines

Peace and Conflict

War Breaks Out

War in the East (A fictional tale of America's role in the next great war)

Israel's Next War (A prescient book much hated by Islamic reviewers)

Collections of Martin Archer's books on Amazon

The Archers Stories I - complete books I, II, III, IV, V, and VI

The Archers Stories II - complete books VII, VIII, IX, and X

The Archers Stories III - complete books XI, XII, and XIII

The Archers Stories IV – complete books XIV, XV, XVI, and XVII

The Archers Stories V – complete books XVIII, XIX, and XX

The Soldiers and Marines Saga - complete books I, II, and III

Other eBooks you might enjoy:

Cage's Crew by Martin Archer writing as Raymond Casey

America's Next War by Michael Cameron – an adaption of Martin Archer's *War Breaks Out* set in the immediate future when Eastern and Western Europe go to war over another wave of Islamic refugees.

And the Saga Continues. The next book is *The English Gambit.*

The readers of this book can be of good cheer about the possibility of another book about the fighting that was about to engulf the archers and threaten the future of their company. What will happen to them after that is uncertain. Oxford's taverns, however, are uncommonly enjoyable so there is every reason to hope that Martin Archer and his fellow scholars will continue the Oxford tradition of drinking and debating about what really happened in the medieval world until either someone with authority decides the story is complete, or they are forced out of their favourite Oxford pubs by a shortage of Newcastle Ale.

There have been several close calls. For example, the scholars responsible for the words in these pages almost stopped writing when Henry the Eighth had the heads chopped off several of them because they suggested that the Company had prospered in its early years as a result of its relationship with the Pope and the Church in Rome. A memorial to them can be found in the Tom Quad of Christ Church College. Inquire at the porter's lodge just inside the tower gate.

There are other books in *The Company of Archers Saga*.

The next book in the saga is *The Venetian Gambit*. All of the books in this great saga of medieval England are available as individual eBooks, and many of them are also available in print and as audio books and multi-book collections. You can find them by searching Amazon,

Google, Goodreads, and Bing for *Martin Archer books*. The first book is *The Archers* in the event you would like to start at the beginning.

A bargain-priced collection of the entire first six books of the saga is available as *The Archers' Story*. Similarly, a collection of the next four books in the saga is available as *The Archers' Story: Part II;* the three novels after that as *The Archers' Story: Part III;* the four after that as *The Archers' Story: Part IV;* the next three *as The Archers' Story: Part V.* And there are more after that.

A chronological list of all the books in the saga, and other books by Martin Archer, can be found below.

Finally, a word from Martin:

"I sincerely hope you enjoyed reading the latest story about the archers of Cornwall as much as I enjoyed writing it. If so, I would most respectfully request a favourable review with as many stars as possible in order to encourage other readers.

"And, if you could please spare a moment, I would also very much appreciate your thoughts about this saga of medieval England, and whether you would like to see it continue. I can be reached at martinarcherV@gmail.com."

Cheers and thank you once again. /S/ Martin Archer

eBooks in the exciting and action-packed *The Company of Archers* saga:

The Archers

The Archers' Castle

The Archers' Return

The Archers' War

Rescuing the Hostages

Archers and Crusaders

The Archers' Gold

The Missing Treasure

Castling the King

The Sea Warriors

The Captain's Men

Gulling the Kings

The Magna Carta Decision

The War of the Kings

The Company's Revenge

The Ransom

The New Commander

The Gold Coins

The Emperor has no Gold

Protecting the Gold: Fatal Mistakes

The Alchemist's Revenge

The Venetian Gambit

Today's Friends

The English Gambits

Tomorrow's Enemies (coming 2021 – click on Amazon's "follow the author" link to be informed when it is available)

eBooks in Martin Archer's epic *Soldiers and Marines* saga:

Soldiers and Marines

Peace and Conflict

War Breaks Out

War in the East

Israel's Next War (A prescient book much hated by Islamic reviewers)

eBook Collections on Amazon

The Archers Stories I - complete books I, II, III, IV, V, VI

The Archers Stories II - complete books VII, VIII, IX, X

The Archers Stories III - complete books XI, XII, XIII

The Archers Stories IV – complete books XIV, XV, XVI, XVII

The Archers Stories V – complete books XVIII, XIX, XX

The Archers Stories VI – complete books XXI, XXII, XXIII

The Soldiers and Marines Saga - complete books I, II, III

Other eBooks you might enjoy:

Cage's Crew by Martin Archer writing as Raymond Casey

America's Next War by Michael Cameron – an adaption of Martin Archer's *War Breaks Out* to set it in the immediate future when Eastern and Western Europe go to war over another wave of Islamic refugees.

Printed in Great Britain
by Amazon

75709265R00424